ANGELESIS

John VanOrsdell

Coppola Productions, LLC
Norfolk

ANGELESIS

Books may be ordered through booksellers or by contacting:

Coppola Productions, LLC
999 Waterside Drive
Suite 2525
Norfolk, Virginia 23510
757-777-3887
www.CoppolaProductions.net

Because of the dynamic nature of the Internet, any web addresses or links contained in this book may have changed since publication and may no longer be valid. The views expressed in this work are solely those of the author and do not necessarily reflect the views of the publisher, and the publisher hereby disclaims any responsibility for them.

ISBN: 978-0-9915676-3-8 (Trade Paperback)
ISBN: 978-0-9915676-2-1 (PDF)
ISBN: 978-0-9915676-1-4 (Kindle)
ISBN: 978-0-9915676-0-7 (e-pub)

Printed in the United States of America

Coppola Productions rev. date: 03/27/2015

ACKNOWLEDGMENTS

First and foremost, I am deeply and eternally grateful to my triune celestial teachers:

Sandy Leotta

Susan Marshall

and Delinda Drury

along with their life-long personal Spirit Guides, whom they were willing to share—for their extraordinary wisdom, generosity, understanding, and patient forbearance.

I also thank Ed Kuljian, for sixty years of deep friendship, loyalty, and high humor. And bless my mentor, Ron Klein, for decades of spiritual and geo-political insight and guidance.

And there are others: my heartfelt gratitude to Scott Adams, Reverend Peter Panagore, Bill Beasley, and Charlie Kulp, and all the others whose encouragement kept me going.

But most profoundly, and spiritually—I thank and bless Literal God-send:

Emilio Coppola

As—who, for long, frustrating decades, had devoutly prayed to be shown the Holy Pathway he was meant to follow. Then, out of the blue, ANGELESIS appeared—which he instantly recognized as being the Mission/Destiny he had long prayed for—and for which he had been so lovingly prepared.

In simple terms, were it not for Emilio, my manuscript would still be languishing in some dark and dreary corner, awaiting just the right publisher to somehow appear. And what appeared was Emilio: publisher, dedicated partner, dearly beloved spiritual Brother.

And—my life's partner
for more than sixty years,
beloved

ALYS

Selfless Service Incarnate
Living proof
of the
Power of Love

To Quietly Honor
The Gentle-Man from Maine

Congressman

STAN TUPPER

The Clarion Voice Of
Enlightened Republican Liberals

All Across the Land

In Recognition of
and to Honor

JIM BELL

For a Lifetime of Selfless Devotion to the Needs and Well-Being
of others.

The Purity of his Purpose and the Clarity of his Light

Bring Honor to the whole of his Universe

PART ONE

The MENTORS

HARBINGER

The famed Three Gorges Dam in central China was the largest construction project anywhere on earth—and upon completion, would meet the electric power needs of a billion people.

From breaking ground with mega earth-movers, to massive pours of fresh concrete, the individual with responsibility for and final authority over all operations was the brilliant Dr. Yo Hua Sing, called Dam Father by his workers, who all but worshipped him. Then one morning a freak accident took Dr. Yo's life. He was accorded a full state funeral and his Last Request honored: his body would be forever enshrined within the dam itself, buried under a fresh pour of concrete.

Last requests of the elite are taken seriously in China.

ALARMS

It was precisely 3:00 a.m. Wednesday when acoustic sensors triggered the alarms.

Two guards converged at the exhibit almost simultaneously. Since the Pioneer Communications section of the Smithsonian contained nothing a thief could readily sell, their arrivals were colored more by curiosity than concern. The midnight shift was always numbingly uneventful, and anything at all became a welcome diversion. The source of the sound was instantly apparent: Inside its glass case, the first-ever Western Union Telegraph key was clattering loudly.

The guards exchanged bemused glances. "Well, that's a first" shrugged the taller, thumbing his radio to report in. Moments later the alarms fell silent. The duty officer in Control logged the incident and returned his attention to a magazine. Seconds after the alarms shut off, the telegraph key once again became mute.

Following every shift, any Incident Report is reviewed by Security Chief Charles Hughes—who saw no security issue in the 3 a.m. odd occurrence, and referred it to Maintenance.

An hour later his phone rang.

"Better tell them guards o' yours to go pee into cups!" He heard Mort Smith laugh.

"What the Hell you talkin' about?"

"That there telegraph key couldn't have been operating; it's not wired up to anything!"

"Well it damn sure is now! Lt. Conte heard it himself-in the background when the report was being called in. So get Somebody's ass down there pronto—and find those wires! If somebody's screwing with us; and I wanna know who. Just find those damn wires!" Before Smith could respond, Hughes hung up. He took a gulp of coffee and leaned back thinking:

Who wasn't nearly as interesting as Why? An hour passed. He was about to leave for lunch when Smith called back.

"No wires, Charlie. No radio receiver. No power source. No nothing. Least of all wires!"

Hughes had given this possibility no consideration whatever. It was simply inconceivable.

"We went over that thing with every instrument we got—nothing. Zero. Zipperino."

Hughes thanked him and hung up slowly. Someone, for reasons he couldn't begin to imagine, was playing games. Maybe NSA was field-testing some new techno-toy—with the Smithsonian as the target! He buzzed for his deputy.

That evening, after the public had left, Hughes' own Tech-Sec Team moved in. By 2:00 a.m. they'd mounted sensors, digital cameras, and recorders throughout the Pioneer Communications exhibit. Any sound, any movement, any electronic emission or signal would be captured in micro-detail.

Captain Hughes knew that three of his very best guards hadn't undergone some damned shared-hallucination experience!

At precisely 3:00 a.m. he was proven correct. The venerable telegraph once again sprang to life—but this time with a difference: After fifty-two seconds of conventional dots and dashes, the ancient key suddenly burst into a frenetic dance, singing like a high-speed dental drill. As a Sony digital video camera—its long lens riveted on the tip of the flying key—devoured it all, byte by byte.

*   *   *

Charles Hughes normally logged in by 7:45 a.m. each morning, but this workday began at 3:09 a.m. with the ringing of his phone. Twenty-six minutes later he burst unshaven into the Tech Lab. His deputy was already there.

By 4:30 a.m. they'd reviewed the video and audio a dozen times. Then Hughes leaned back to think.

Finally, he turned to his deputy. "OK. First off, we find out whether there's actually some kinda message here, and if so, what code's being used. Wake Max Shapiro in Accounting, and get him down here—used to be a signalman in the Coast Guard. Maybe he can tell us what the Hell we got here." He turned back to his lab chief. "Hal, play that audio again—only this time slow it way, way down. Call it a hunch."

At 6:22 a.m. Max Shapiro phoned in his findings: "What you got here," he reported, "it's English—and good old Morse Code." He sounded nervous, shaken even; Hughes took no notice.

3

"Really? Well good. So, what's it say?"

, Shapiro hesitated, and then read from his transcript—.

"THE METHOD BY WHICH YOU RECEIVE THIS
COMMUNICATION DEMONSTRATES IT COULD
NOT BE OF TERRESTRIAL ORIGIN (STOP) THE
TEXT WHICH FOLLOWS IS TO BE DELIVERED
TO YOUR EXECUTIVE HEAD OF
GOVERNMENT FOR IMMEDIATE ACTION
(STOP) PRESERVE THE MECHANISM OF THIS
COMMUNICATION FOR POSSIBLE FUTURE USE
(STOP)"

Max Shapiro paused to clear his throat. He was starting to shake. "That was all contained in the first part of the message. Now, here's the rest—what was in that second, speeded-up part—"

POTUS

The President of the United States was not disposed to report for work before 8:30 a.m. in the morning. Atwood Samuel Bryce had no intention of letting the job turn him gray. After three years in the Oval Office, he appeared not to have aged a day. A singular accomplishment in his view.

He insisted on leisurely, private breakfasts with the First Lady. And even if the King of Jordan or some Queen of the Blues had spent the night in the Lincoln Bedroom, they'd not be included. Moreover, any staffer interrupting a Bryce breakfast better be reporting the outbreak of war somewhere.

They were in mid-omelet when his chief of staff appeared. Bryce looked up and pointedly laid down his fork. "Good Morning, Oscar. I assume—whatever this is won't keep."

"'Morning, Mr. President—Mrs. Bryce." Oscar Benton pulled up a chair, waving off coffee. "Actually, it would keep until Morning Staff— but—it's so bizarre, I figured you'd want a heads up."

Suddenly intrigued, Bryce leaned back and faced his friend of twenty years. "Okay, Pal—let's have it."

Benton cleared his throat. "The past two nights—events which—defy all explanation—transpired. He recited the happenings at the Smithsonian, and then handed the president a copy of the message's initial instructions. Bryce read, his eyes slowly widening. He passed it over to his wife. "You said, 'events which defy all explanation'—explain."

Benton shifted in his chair. "As reported, the telegraph key, was and is, wholly unconnected to anything. No wires. No magnets. Nothing. Moreover, the messages were not tapped out by any human hand; the duration of and interval between each dot and dash is identical, to the millisecond. Mr. President, the problem is, there's simply no way, by all the laws of physics, that that telegraph key—encased as it is in shatterproof glass—could be induced to move up and down by any known external force!"

Bryce scowled as he digested it, shooting a dark look at Abby. "Okay, Oscar, let's have the rest of it. What makes this of such immediate White House concern?"

Benton cleared his throat. "When—the technicians slowed down the second part of the message, the 'main text,' that is, was compressed into what's known as a burst transmission." He slowly passed it to Bryce.

"YOU HOLD IN YOUR HANDS MANIFEST PROOF THAT THERE IS INTELLIGENT LIFE IN THE UNIVERSE BEYOND YOUR OWN.

WE WILL PRESENTLY VISIT YOUR WORLD FOR THE PURPOSE OF SHARING ELEMENTS OF OUR KNOWLEDGE.

YOUR PLANET STANDS AT PERIL. EARLY ACTIONS MUST BE UNDERTAKEN TO PREVENT GREAT LOSS."

The president read more slowly, the shadow of a tremble crossing his hands.

"OUR ARRIVAL IS IMMINENT. WE WILL NOT ENTER YOUR ATMOSPHERE BUT WILL REMAIN IN LOW ORBIT.

IN FIVE DAYS TIME WE WILL PLACE OURSELVES IN PROXIMITY TO YOUR SPACE SHUTTLE AND INVITE AN ASTRONAUT TO BOARD AND INSPECT OUR CRAFT. YOU WILL BE UNABLE TO DETECT OUR PRESENCE WITH YOUR INSTRUMENTS. DESPAIR NOT. WE WILL RENDER OUR CRAFT VISIBLE TO MORTAL EYES AND CAMERAS AS THE AMERICAN SHUTTLE PASSES ABOVE YOUR SALT LAKE CITY FOLLOWING SUNRISE FRIDAY. AT THAT HOUR WE WILL MANIFEST ASTERN YOUR SHUTTLE.

WE REQUEST YOU INSPECT OUR INTERIOR SPACES AND THEN ASSEMBLE A DELEGATION OF ELDERS TO ATTEND EARLY CONVENINGS ABOARD OUR CRAFT.

FEAR NOT. WE HAVE COME BUT TO COUNSEL."

"Good God—" breathed the president.

*   *   *

The American shuttle Discovery would pass directly above Salt Lake City at 5:21 a.m. Friday, local time.

President Bryce lost no time in creating a crisis team: Chief of Staff Oscar Benton; Domestic Policy Adviser John Bozorth; Vice-President Stuart MacDougal; National Science Adviser Nathan Nevares; Secretary of Defense Ralph D'Orio; and National Security Adviser Iana Ravenscroft, who in turn brought along her top strategist, Dr. Peter Klein. She wanted him on board, and the president assented.

After brisk discussion, the group quickly concluded that the 'communications' had to be either the sickest hoax of all time—or—not a hoax at all. And that was simply too overwhelming to contemplate. Everybody assumed it could only be a hoax—with each convincing him/herself that it was all merely some warped, albeit brilliant stunt.

6

Possibly perpetrated by political enemies, out to make them look the fools. Or—more ominously—a new whole breed of techno-terrorist. But hopefully, just some demented genius from Akron out to make headlines. But until they knew more, it was decided to leave both the Bureau and Agency out of the loop. After all, they wouldn't have long to wait: If nothing appeared in the wake of the shuttle Friday, they could all get drunk. And then turn it over to the Bureau.

Shortly before Midnight local time Thursday, the chief astronomers at five western observatories, all operated by or under contract to the Federal government, received priority directives ordering them to suspend all other observations, and to realign and refocus their optical and infrared instruments to acquire and track the shuttle Discovery as it rose in the northwest sky just after sunrise. Specifically, they were ordered to observe and photograph the area "behind and proximate to" the shuttle—and look for "anything out of the ordinary."

*　　*　　*

The President had an evil feeling about this whole alien business. Sleep was impossible. He flopped back and forth, snapping left hooks into an overheated pillow. He was being haunted once again by what he called "Terminal Choices." He'd coined the term after punching out of his F-14 several premature moments before it slipped over into a death-spiral—a panic choice which had washed him out of flight training. Poor Woody, on the verge of being swept into a raging, intergalactic cataract with nothing but Terminal Choices around every blind bend!

What's more, she couldn't even reach over to comfort him; separate bedrooms had been his idea. Well then—his loss. And so, sleeping alone, Abigail Bryce didn't exactly ache for her husband. She maybe twinged.

And as POTUS thrashed and churned next door, she herself began to reflect on the crisis. Staring up into the silent darkness, it wasn't long before her mind became captured in orbit around that one overarching, ghastly possibility.

What if—if this isn't a hoax after all?

SPACESHIP

Following DOD instructions, Dr. Marcel Trigot acquired Discovery the instant it sprang from behind the Humboldt Range, then—tracking back along its path—found nothing.

As instructed, Trigot held focus on the area astern the shuttle, slowly swinging the great reflector to remain on station. Then, all of a sudden—as Discovery arced directly above Salt Lake City—Trigot beheld it:

"Oh my God! Another vessel! It's h-u-g-e! Must be—twenty times the size of the shuttle! Jesus God!"

Suddenly remembering the recorders were on, the chief astronomer caught himself and began making a record—

"The spacecraft is—a dazzling white—blindingly white—with iridescent gold!

Just—incredibly beautiful! Uh—as to how to describe its shape—It appears to be designed to fly through an atmosphere—long and sleek, with minimum drag resistance. I can see what appear to be power nacelles—four in all."

He paused for a quick sip of water without removing his eye from the viewfinder:

"There's a smaller central section—maybe one-hundred meters across—which looks to be in the shape of a—Yup, a heptagon! With an elliptical roof, or floor, above and below—"

As he continued his observations, an assistant noted that the infrared sensors were registering nothing at all.

Then, precisely three minutes after the alien craft first became visible, it vanished from sight.

*   *   *

For the next two hours, a torrent of digital recordings and photos streamed into the Situation Room. Computer enhancements portrayed a mammoth, sophisticated, totally unknown construct in orbit. Individual photographs could not begin to capture the craft's shimmering beauty, but the high-definition videos which followed filled the room with awe.

"Lord God A'mighty—" someone breathed.

Everyone's immediate concern was containment. Any hint of the presence of an alien spacecraft in our skies could easily trigger panic all agreed; absolute secrecy was imperative thus even allies would not be informed. Additionally, they'd not go on DEFCON Alert although it was time to brief the Secretary of State. Since Bryce had referred to the thing overhead as "a nightmare in orbit," the code name CHIMERA was assigned.

But what no one in the Situation Room could have known that very morning, the Zero Gravity Club of Boulder happened to be at the University Observatory to view Discovery's first pass after dawn.

*   *   *

In the privacy of the residence, the President was pacing and venting, his belly poking defiantly through his bathrobe. Abby had never seen him so agitated, and sensed that he was already feeling things starting to spin beyond his control.

"You realize," he stabbed, "when the story gets out, it'll dominate the front page of every newspaper on earth—day after day, month after month? From here on, every decision I make, every action we take, will go down in history—with me the one being held accountable by the whole God damn world!"

"Woody," she countered firmly, "we've certainly no way of knowing what that spaceship's doing up there. Therefore, we have no choice but to wait for them to tell us. However, one thing is clear—they already know a great deal about us: 'Salt Lake City'—'Friday'—'cameras'—not to mention English, Morse Code, and even the Smithsonian. So let's not go and underestimate them." He started to interrupt, but she continued. "I know we must assume their intent to be hostile until proven otherwise. But since you admit there's not a whole lot we can do anyway, why not take them at face value?" She turned and looked at him. "And consider this: they must have had excellent, sound reasons for choosing the American Government as their first contact point with Earth—and the basis to entrust us with such responsibility. Mull that one over. By the way," she squinted, "do we have any idea even what corner of the galaxy they came from?"

"None whatever. Nor the foggiest idea which direction they came from. We don't even know how long they've been here. What's more,

9

they could have hundreds of additional ships out there with them—a whole friggin' invisible armada! For all we know, this one's only a scout for their main force—here to size up our capacity, our courage, and our will to resist them!"

"Then what options are being considered?"

"Mostly we're just trying to decide whether or not to let an astronaut take a spacewalk to check them out—assuming they show up on Tuesday as promised."

"In other words, the ball's in their court."

"Not altogether. Before long we'll have to notify key allies, and seek their cooperation in mounting a united and coordinated response to whatever the aliens might choose to do next. This could—"

"Including the Russians?" She interrupted.

"Hell no. As the only other nation able to launch someone into orbit—and thereby to potentially muck things up—it's not a risk I'm prepared to take. Especially with the Kremlin's strategic rocket forces under such—uncertain command. I don't trust Gusev, especially when he's drunk."

"In the event the aliens do turn out to be hostile—what do your experts say can be done?"

He looked at her as if she was malfunctioning.

"Experts? There are no 'experts' on this! It flies in the face of everything we thought we knew! Abby, we don't have a clue what might work. Yeah, we could fire off lasers and missiles, but we've got no assurance they'd have any effect at all and might only serve to piss 'em off! Hell, Babe, you know as much as any 'expert'—what do you think we oughta do?" He checked his watch. "Hey, Cocktail Hour." He poured a scotch and offered it. She shook her head.

"You sit; I'll pace," Abby directed, rising to her feet.

"What boggles me—is that until a few hours ago, we honestly and truly thought we might be all alone in the universe. Now we find we may be surrounded by intelligent life—some of it so far beyond us we must look like Neanderthals to them! Yet, if they are that far beyond us both technologically and intellectually—then doesn't it stand to reason they may be light years ahead of us morally and socially as well?" She stopped and placed a hand on his shoulder. "They told us 'Fear not.' Well just maybe: They've evolved beyond deceit."

10

"And maybe—" He sighed after brief reflection, "Earth's but a rest stop on their trip across the cosmos. To them we may be nothing more than fast food—with an astronaut served up for a taste-test!"

*   *   *

For one with such serious White House responsibilities as Peter Klein was assigned, it was oddly comforting to know that he would find rich humor lurking somewhere within every crisis. In total contrast, his boss, Iana Ravenscroft, President Bryce's national security adviser, was utterly humorless. Even when Peter came up with some gem of high humor, she'd only stare at him, as if he thought being funny solved anything—which in turn struck Peter as particularly funny. Were he not so driven to come up with a creative, often humorous resolution for each new Crisis-of-the-Week, he was certain Iana would have replaced him with someone more like herself temperament-wise. But it would have been a pleasant surprise had he known that such a notion had never so much as crossed her mind. However, it would have blown his mind to smithereens had he known that what actually crossed her mind nearly every day was wondering whether he'd be as creative in bed as he was at his job.

Whenever his 'Drop Everything and Get your Ass in Here' emergency beeper went off, he knew there was a major crisis brewing somewhere—that rarely did the beeper go off.

After being fully briefed on everything that was known or even suspected about the Aliens in orbit, Peter knew he needed to think. His power of reason always seemed to peak at its sharpest and most insightful when he was soaking, eyelids at half-mast, in a hot tub. Disclosing the secret of his creativity to Iana one day, after she'd tasked him to come up with some fresh ideas to put an end to the ongoing border clashes between the Turks and Kurds, Peter had half seriously said they might ask the UN to create a neutral zone strictly for Turds. Iana had simply looked at him. But the next day, a brand new top of the line hot-tub was delivered in the East Wing along with a sign: "National Security Use Only"—to which only Peter and his boss seemed to have keys.

This raised more than a few eyebrows.

RUSSIANS

At 11:18 a.m. EDT Saturday, CNN's Morning Anchor broke into the weather report with a Breaking News bulletin:

"This just in: Minutes ago—at a special news conference called by the Chief Astronomer of the University of Colorado Observatory—Dr. Nilsson Svendhal announced that a mysterious, 'very large' spacecraft suddenly appeared yesterday morning a short distance behind the space shuttle Discovery. The Observatory has just released color photos, taken through their telescope, of the mysterious spacecraft we switch live to Denver."

Screens around the globe cut to Dr. Svendhal standing behind a small lectern, holding up a series of large color enlargements for a dozen stunned reporters.

"Just how big is this thing anyway?" One called out.

"Exactly six-hundred and six meters in length and one-hundred meters from top to bottom at the thickest point. As to its depth, we can only approximate. However, it appears to be something under three-hundred meters measuring front to back. In other words, quite large for any spacecraft."

"Dr. Svendhal," a female voice sang out, "are you stating to a scientific certainty that some unknown spaceship has been shadowing our space shuttle?"

"I am. At least unknown to any of us. And I don't stake my reputation lightly."

"Could that thing in the pictures possibly be some secret new NASA space vehicle?"

"You'll have to ask NASA about that. But frankly I would doubt it very much."

Seventeen-hundred miles to the east, all eyes in the Situation Room were on CNN. "Get me Chester," the president snapped, angry at being forced now to explain to America's allies why he'd deliberately kept them in the dark. We'll have to tell 'em we believed it was just an elaborate hoax, he decided.

The Secretary of State took the call on the seventeenth green. He never played the final hole.

At 12:55 p.m. the White House announced that President Bryce would respond shortly to the reported spacecraft sighting.

Twenty minutes later A. Samuel Bryce strode into a jammed East Room and began reading from a prepared statement:

"The spacecraft sighted yesterday morning by astronomers at the University of Colorado was also observed and photographed by our own Government observatories at the same time."

He paused and looked directly into the television cameras.

"Its appearance was not unexpected: Many of our telescopes and cameras were in fact pre-positioned in anticipation of its arrival."

There was an excited stirring, even among the most jaded.

The President laid out the events at the Smithsonian and then read in full the communique from the alien craft He ended by announcing that sending an astronaut over from Discovery was "an option under active consideration." His statement finished, he'd take questions. A dozen voices called out at once: NBC got the nod.

"Mr. President—how can you be sure the aliens' intent isn't hostile?" It was the question all would have asked.

"We can't," Bryce confessed, "but so far, they've given us no reason to believe they came here for any hostile purpose. In fact, all evidence is to the contrary. However, this does not mean we won't take appropriate precautions—exactly what is not open to discussion." He leaned forward on the lectern. "Let me say this: Mankind suddenly finds itself confronted by something of cosmic significance. Totally unexpected. Utterly beyond human experience. And, arguably, the single most momentous event in all of recorded history!" He paused. "And we'll be prepared to respond, whatever their intent might turn out to be."

"Have you consulted with other heads of state?" asked a French correspondent.

"We've been doing just that all morning. This is clearly a matter which affects all nations."

"Have any of the astronauts been asked to volunteer to go inspect, and perhaps even board, the alien spaceship?"

"That's of course something no astronaut would ever be ordered to do. That said, should one volunteer, it will be considered," Bryce evaded. He paused, looked into the television camera, and turned philosophical.

"What is circling above our heads at this precise minute is an unprecedented opportunity to take a quantum leap in our knowledge of the Universe which we inhabit. For centuries Man has peered up at the stars and wondered whether we whirl alone through the vast night of space. Well, we now have the answer—for the very first time. And that, I believe, is good news—certainly nothing to fill us with trepidation. Only perhaps with awe. Therefore, let us not cringe and quake before the unfamiliar, but rather let the human race stand together—tall and unafraid—before our Universe!"

*   *   *

By Sunday, as Bryce predicted, the Aliens dominated the world's media. It was as if no other news were taking place.

'Meet the Press' featured the President's national Security Advisor, Iana Ravenscroft, her gleaming black hair drawn back tightly for the occasion. She fielded a number of questions before revealing that every astronaut aboard Discovery had already volunteered to walk in space for a close-up look at the alien spaceship—assuming it reappeared as promised.

"What's more—they're all dying to take a look inside," she added.

Meanwhile, the Secretary of State appeared on Face the Nation. Tasked to be reassuring, he reported that President Bryce was in daily consultation with key allies, each of whom shared in his belief that a single craft, regardless of its intentions, could pose little threat to an entire planet.

Conversely, hewing to the view that there simply were no experts to interview, MSNBC opted instead to counter-focus with the wisdoms of 'ordinary folks'—"They're staying above our atmosphere because they plan to poison it!"—"I think they came to steal our DNA—and then take it back to their home world to create a race of human slaves!"—"They're gonna melt the polar ice caps and drown us all!" By the first commercial break even the production crew wished they'd invited the putative experts like everyone else.

On the Truman Balcony Sam and Abby Bryce watched silently. It was a magnificent early-summer morning; the kind of day precious little could spoil. But neither noticed. A phone buzzed; the President muted the TV. A heated Secretary of State was on the line—

"Mr. President, the Russians are now demanding a cosmonaut be included for any visit to the alien spaceship!"

14

"Gusev must be losing it," the president groaned.

"The Russians are actually feeling pointedly left out. And they figure that, since they're up there just like us, they're entitled to be included."

"Balls! If the damn aliens wanted to speak to the world in Russian, they'd be doing it! But they picked English. They picked the United States. They picked us. So tell Mr. Gusev he can take his complaints up with them directly—should he come by the opportunity."

"How 'bout letting me tell him we'll try to include them in any 'subsequent convenings?' A small bone, to be sure—but it might shut him up."

One caveat Mother Bryce had drilled into her son was, "Have No Truck with Fools." "Absolutely not," he replied. "When and if we have something to share—we will do so. And if that doesn't satisfy him, you might suggest he try signaling them with a big fat friggin' spotlight!"

Secretary Severinghaus, though less than pleased, knew enough to drop the matter.

*   *   *

His obese yellow cat was so glad to see Peter; he kept rubbing up against his ankle, purring as loudly as he could. Peter got the message. He sat down, patted his lap, and instantly Cheez Whizz was upon it, purring like crazy and kneading Peter's crotch. He'd never known a more affectionate animal. And this only intensified his guilt trip. He'd been trapped in the Situation Room for days, which was hardly fair to a hungry, lonely, bored cat who was stuck at home, unable to even go outside.

Peter had thought about getting another cat for Cheez Whizz to play with, but realized that that would only double the stench from the litter box which had to be emptied constantly. But he just didn't have the stomach for that. All he knew for certain was that he loved The Whizz Man dearly, who in turn loved Peter, his own fat cat—it was mutual—so wherever he went his cat would go as well.

Peter leaned back to relax and let his brain freewheel. He never tired of turning it loose to see where it might take him. He closed his eyes and soon he was on Air Force One—along with Iana. The President was in the nose, taking a nap.

Suddenly, the pilot appeared and turned to Peter. "You gotta see this, Pete—" He turned and headed back to the flight-deck, Peter in

15

tow—and guess who was at the controls: Cheez Whizz! Just then President Bryce appeared. "Iana will not be pleased," POTUS said. "No matter how good a pilot your cat may be, I'm afraid the FAA will have to be told as well."

Peter woke up chuckling and kissed the cat, who was still curled up in his lap, then kissed it again on the top of its head.

"Now that's what I'd call a world-class catnap," he mused.

His cat looked up at him and yawned.

*   *   *

Ellen Kate (27) never knew what awaited her when she unlocked the door to her apartment. But there would be something, of that she could be certain. Something evil and ingenious. Something dark and sinister poised to strike. When, she never knew, only that come it would. Maybe not the minute she walked in the door, maybe not for an hour, when her guard was apt to be down. Yet Ellen couldn't help but adore the perpetrator, and it would have amused her no end had she known that her beautiful feline friend was profoundly humiliated by the name Ellen Kate had bestowed on her the day she was born: OooYaYaBangToy (What the Hell kind of a name is that!). The cat had no idea what it meant—only that it made everyone laugh when they first heard it. By way of retaliation, the offended one, after some deep thought, had retaliated by naming her owner 'Guptslutch'—the ugliest sounding name she could conjure up.

There were two sides to her Siamese cat: one sweet and loving; the other, over-the-top creatively diabolical.

What Precocious Cat (Ellen Kate's other name for her) would do, when left to her own devices all day long, was spend a good portion of it plotting some highly entertaining comeuppance—one which could involve anything from, say, launching herself off the top of the bookcase just as Ellen Kate was walking by, expertly scattering her hair every which way upon landing, and producing a most rewarding screech—or in the alternative, might just as easily involve treating Ellen's favorite red fuzzy slippers to a day on the water—in the toilet.

CHIMERA

Peter Klein had barely been anywhere but in the Situation Room since the morning CHIMERA was created. During the supper break Sunday, he dashed home to shower, change clothes and feed Cheez Whiz.

Something kept bothering him, and he couldn't shake it. Why, why would any alien race—sophisticated and advanced enough to be able to fly halfway across the galaxy—invest vast resources and decades of travel time, all to visit one small, insignificant, backward world like Earth? And, what a cosmic conceit it was for us to think they had!

With a Ph.D in Physics from M.I.T., Peter Klein didn't suffer illogic gladly. He'd spent ten years with the CIA before joining the national security staff as a senior analyst. At first he'd been excited at being selected to join CHIMERA, but with each passing hour he found himself almost wishing he'd never left the company. Almost. Now it was the White House. With the stakes the world itself. The pressure, already excruciating, was growing by the hour. Everyone was demanding firm answers and viable options, with precious few of either to be had.

CHIMERA, in the evening session, was growing ugly.

Other than to scan, take myriad close-up photos, and send over an astronaut, no one had come up with any other substantive course of action—.assuming the aliens even showed up.

With communication totally one-sided, Bryce said that what they needed most was some means of questioning the aliens. "How, by using a blinker light?—Or holding up signs in the shuttle's windows?" Iana sniffed. The notion was quickly dismissed, if only because doing things through windows felt intolerably primitive. And appearing primitive to the aliens was the last thing anyone wanted.

"Then our astronaut'll just have to do the interrogating," Bryce said, settling the matter.

When deliberations inevitably turned to speculating on the aliens' motives, Peter summarized: Yes, someone clearly was up there. Yes, to a certainty they were not of this earth. Yes, they knew a great deal about us. And yes, their words were friendly enough. But—did they really journey all the way here just to, quote: 'Share elements of their knowledge.' W-h-y, Klein challenged, should these aliens give a fig about

17

Earth? Would not other far more advanced or kindred worlds be of far greater interest to them? "Something just doesn't compute," he warned.

But to his dismay, no one was interested in contemplating cosmic logic or illogic. Aliens had arrived; that's all that counted. So CHIMERA turned its efforts to deciding whom to send over to the alien spaceship for a look-see.

Just before midnight final agreement was reached: Anthony J. Junker—Major, USAF—would go for a spacewalk the next day providing everything appeared safe. Just how the aliens intended to have anyone "board" their craft to "inspect" it was unknown. And until this was revealed, no entry would be authorized. Permission would be granted, however, to make tactile contact with the outside of the alien craft, if and only if, the major felt it was safe to do so.

At 7:50, the President spoke directly with Junker ("A.J.") to satisfy himself that the major fully appreciated, and willingly accepted, all the risks—to the extent that they could be understood at all. Junker replied that he was eager to go. "Then your place in history is assured," Bryce decreed—although that would just as readily apply posthumously.

A significant factor in Junker's selection had been the fact that he was single.

*   *   *

Vice President MacDougal was beyond taciturn; he was verbally abstemious. As much as possible he avoided the telephone, which tended to involve dialog. And he never agreed to give a speech unless required for an occasion of State. Moreover, he never granted interviews—all of which made him the ideal vice president from a presidential point of view.

However, a personal phone call from the Boss required the fullest of response.

"Okay, Mac," Bryce began, wasting no time on pleasantries, "what's your gut tell you? You think our uninvited cosmic visitors have come to do us ill?"

MacDougal reflected briefly before answering. "Well, if that is why they're here, I can't imagine why they'd be going about it in this manner. Given the friendly overtures, maybe they've really come primarily to capture our minds 'n' hearts. Or maybe win us over by dazzling us with their technology—like we did with the Indians: 'Have we got a warp-drive for you!' Call it neocolonialism."

Bryce smiled at this. "'Cosmic Colonizers'—interesting. But what do we say if all they've brought for us is sparkly beads?" "We sparkle our gratitude. But if I was a betting man I'd wager they have no interest in our primitive technology." He took out a kitchen match and poked around inside his ear. "Could be they just have a hankering for our women."

*   *   *

"SPACE ARMADA HIDING BEHIND MOON!" Cried a leading tabloid. Not to be outdone, another announced "ALIEN ATTACK IMMINENT!" The exploitation quickly became pandemic. From Barcelona: "BLESSED VIRGIN WEEPS OVER EXTRA-TERRESTRIALS!" Osaka: "U.S. TAKES NUCLEAR AIM AT SPACESHIP!" London: "FIVE NUDE ALIENS SPOTTED OUTSIDE PUB!" Rio: "SPACE BEAST CLAW PRINTS FOUND ON THE BEACH!" And from Tehran: "DEATH TO THE INFIDEL ALIENS!"

The world over, people stood somewhere between 'Genuinely Concerned' and 'Scared to Death.' The only thing everyone could agree that they wanted done: 'Something!' Those habitually driven to protest were in deep turmoil over having no one to picket. Prayer groups prayed, students got plastered, the talking heads got portentous, and the militia got ready. However, most people just quietly panicked in private.

While in capitals around the globe, those in charge knew this was only the beginning.

SHAMPOO

Peter lived alone by choice, after divorcing Sally nearly a dozen years ago. At thirty-three, he was the youngest of the White House senior staff—usually giving President Bryce at least one good chuckle per

Cabinet meeting, which made him a welcome addition. This delighted Iana.

Peter didn't have much of a social life, and even less sex life. When a date signaled she'd like to spend the night with him, he'd take her for a short cruise on the Potomac in his small, aging Chris Craft and then repair to the cabin below for a somewhat more vigorous ride. However, his one-night-stands-only policy was less than fulfilling emotionally.

Nonetheless, his apartment in McLean remained strictly off-limits. It was a converted basement affair, with deep window wells for air and light. Somehow it was simultaneously clean and a total mess—strewn with an unholy mix of clothes and low-level classified documents from work.

On one recent occasion, his No Visitors policy been violated. Every now and then, Iana would drop him off on her own way home, usually when his '63 Stingray Vette was in the shop overnight. Such was the case one November evening, when a snowstorm out of nowhere burst upon the District. Her rear-wheel-drive Audi was slipping and sliding like crazy, and they barely made it to Peter's.

"Looks like it's One-for-the-Couch night," she proclaimed, leaving little room for him to demur.

"I'm a notorious litterbug, Iana," he said. "You're going to embarrass me—my cat has a Litter Box Account, in which he makes regular large deposits. My very own Fat Cat contributor, if you will." She shot him a look followed by a brief Mona Lisa smile.

Peter thought Iana was maybe the sexiest women alive, but he never let on. "How 'bout a shower?" she suggested.

"Did I just hear—an invitation?" Peter grinned foolishly, scarcely believing his ears, and then his eyes, as she began to undress.

A fantasy realized.

"Suit yourself." She began removing her clothes, down to a half-slip and jersey top. He hurried to catch up with her—when he was down to his shorts, they stepped into the shower as one. This then was to be the night she'd at long last find out whether Dr. Peter Klein was a creative lover.

Finding a full bottle of shampoo, she began dribbling it slowly across his chest, smearing it sensually around. Then she handed him the bottle, so he could reciprocate. He was thrilled to do so.

"You suppose we have an audience whom found himself—up there, watching?" he asked.

"The thought crossed my mind. But if they are, I seriously doubt they've come as voyeurs."

Finally, with every nook and cranny clean as never before, Peter and Iana towel-dried each other and headed eagerly for the bedroom— trailed by an intensely curious Yella Fella, who was wondering what was coming next. Not easily surprised, he was utterly shocked by the bodily combat he witnessed for the next hour.

*   *   *

As everyone at work had noted, Iana never wore a bra. Or needed to. The First Lady had told her husband that was "unseemly." But being one of Iana's many mammary admirers, he did nothing. Her unofficial Code Name was Titty-Tit-Tits—but no one within earshot ever referred to her as such. However, it fit her perfectly, particularly in light of her self-image. Even its cadence had a pleasing feeling as it rolled off the tongue, so early on it become a term in nearly universal use. She simply had to be aware of that, but wrote it off to female envy rather than derision. Men were just googly-eyed kids in a candy store. From time to time, she was tempted to whip out a proud Hooter, just to see them react. But wanting to keep her job, she resisted the urge. Bryce would never risk the risqué, especially in an election year.

*   *   *

CHIMERA convened in the Situation Room promptly at 0815 Monday. Rendezvous with the alien craft was due to take place sometime the following day.

National security adviser Ravenscroft set the agenda. "The primary decision now before us is how, and under what circumstances, do we permit Major Junker to enter the alien craft, assuming he's invited inside." She turned to Klein. "Peter, what are our operating assumptions?"

He consulted his notes— "First: the Alien craft does, in fact, show up on schedule; Second: the Aliens are able to maneuver safely alongside Discovery at a safe separation, and then hold on station for perhaps sixty minutes." He glanced at the Secretary of Defense, who merely shrugged. "Assumption number three: the Aliens still want an astronaut to 'board and inspect' their craft; Fourth: they'll have some means of communicating with Major Junker—perhaps one method while he's outside the craft, another once he's inside. And lastly: the Major finds nothing on the exterior to cause him concern, and he's Go to enter the spacecraft."

"Will we be able to speak with Major Junker only while he's outside on the tether," Bryce asked, "and not once he's inside?"

"We simply don't know whether radio communication will remain operative once he enters the spacecraft."

"Aye, there's the rub," allowed MacDougal.

"We don't even know whether they plan to use an airlock, Mr. President. We'll just have to wait and see. Anything more would be pure speculation," Klein declared.

"That's all we have here!" Bryce railed, "Everything we decide is based on nothing but God damn speculation and conjecture!" The strain was starting to show. "One thing is decided: Major Junker is Not Authorized to enter their craft if doing so would interrupt voice communications or vital telemetry." There were general murmurs of assent.

"Dare we assume that the major's life support systems would remain functional once he's entered their spacecraft?" Oscar Benton pointedly asked.

"We 'speculated' on that as well," Klein said, "concluding that for them to invite human beings aboard, providing them with a breathable, pressurized atmosphere would have to be a given. Knowing so much about us already, the fact that we're air-breathers couldn't have escaped their notice."

"Maybe they'll even have porta-potties," D'Orio smirked.

CHIMERA spent the next hour wrestling with one imponderable after another, trying to apply human logic and judgment to what was essentially beyond either.

SQUAB

The First Daughter, Ellen Kate, lived just a mile from the White House in a small walk-up studio. Having a roommate had never been an option; there simply wasn't room. But she did manage to share space with OooYaYaBangToy, a female Siamese with a dark sense of humor.

She was a slender and lithe twenty seven, with long, utterly straight hair cascading down over her chest like lemon satin shampoo. She wore quiet earth tones and invisible make-up. Yet when the occasion demanded she could slip into a silk sheath gown and dazzle any gathering.

The past three years had been an unwelcome adjustment. She longed for the days when she could walk down the street unrecognized, unescorted and not photographed. She truly hated being a public figure, being discussed and written about by strangers, and never feeling free to just be herself.

More than anything, she hated having the Secret Service hovering around her, duly noting in their records the exact time that a date arrived—and left.

On the other hand, she'd readily admit to enjoying certain of the perks: being waved smartly through White House gates; debating serious issues over haute cuisine with her parents, and always, right there: the very locus of global power—within the warm meat just behind her father's eyes. For an aspiring journalist, heady stuff.

Tonight would be the first time she'd visited with her parents since the Aliens arrived. She hoped they were okay.

The White House gates whispered open, and Ellen Kate swung her black Miata into a reserved space in the shadow of the Executive Mansion. Julio greeted her at the side entrance, smiling broadly. "Another warm evening, Miz Bryce. We've had to turn up the air conditioning!" Escorting her to the private family elevator, he announced, "Cracked Ginger Squab this evening—just the way you like it!" He stood there beaming as she stepped into the elevator.

Julio was right. The squab was perfect, and the Bryces dug in, pointedly avoiding any mention of Aliens.

"Still being wooed by Channel 33?" Abby asked, passing her daughter a pale glaze. "Here, dear, try a dab of this."

23

"They even upped the ante," Ellen Kate grinned, "offered to make me their Arts and Entertainment Correspondent." She tried the glaze. "Mmmm—hey, that is good!"

"Thought you'd like it," her mother winked.

"Question is: would they still be interested in hiring you if you refused to appear on camera?" Her father posed almost rhetorically.

"No way. That's why I'm still looking around. Listen, even if a real paper wants to hire me as a reporter, I'll make it clear: Only if I can write without a byline. Much as I want to work—I won't trade on your name."

"It's your name too, darlin'. Writing under your own name wouldn't be trading on mine," Bryce chewed.

"Of course it would—they wouldn't be hiring me in the first place if I wasn't your daughter!"

"Don't be too sure," he said, taking a sip of wine.

"Ellen Kate, I agree with your father. Should you get a decent offer, take it—and then go out and show them how talented you are. And just watch; your next job offer will be based solely on merit." She knit her lips in satisfaction.

"So then, young lady—how's your love life these days?" The President inquired, switching to something with a greater potential for amusement. Anything lighthearted would do.

"Ha! Haven't told you yet about B-l-a-i-r—" She chimed, "an orthodontically-challenged marine biologist with overly proximate eyes. Took me to Ermilio's for a stuffed lobster last week—and then proceeded to tell me all about how lobsters are 'bottom feeders' who relish feasting on human 'overboard discharge' bet that little gem wasn't in any Secret Service report!"

Sam Bryce threw his head back and laughed for the first time in days.

Shortly after taking office, Bryce asked that a billiards room be built in the White House basement. Imprinting the gold Presidential Seal on the felt so as to not interfere with the roll of the balls had been a daunting undertaking.

But eventually all was perfect, and lighted for dazzling, even distracting, effect. Watching the Seal throw off the games of first-time opponents entertained POTUS no end.

The President shot pool whenever enmeshed in a crisis. It seemed to help his game as well as the crisis. He viewed politics as being a lot like billiards: all angles and repercussions, where seeing every possibility, calculating every angle, anticipating every consequence, taking careful aim, then shooting carefully would leave one in an excellent position. As he saw it, crisis management itself came down to figuring all the angles, and then taking your best shot.

Following supper, the President summoned his chief policy wonks, Jack Bozorth and Iana Ravenscroft, to the billiards room for a "campaign working session." To Bryce they were "the two savviest political brains inside the Beltway." And as such, he decided it was time they focused on the potential political impact of the Aliens' presence.

Bryce then turned to his daughter.

"Katie, I'm heading down to the Billiards Room now—to explore our options for dealing with the Aliens. Why don't you come along—with everything off the record, of course? Jack Bozorth, Iana, and her creative brain trust, Peter Klein, will also be there. Should be pretty interesting."

She grinned broadly at this extremely rare invitation, hugged her mother, and followed her father to his elevator. The others were already there, taking practice shots. The President introduced his daughter all around, and picked up immediately on how pleased Ellen Kate and Peter seemed to be over meeting each other.

Peter racked up the balls and gestured for Ellen Kate to break, which she did—sending two balls flying into pockets by way of accidental good fortune. Peter looked at Bryce.

"I can see why you've been keeping your daughter a State Secret."

Throughout the rest of the evening the two kept stealing looks at each other. A good sign, the Cupid-playing President realized, as he carefully positioned all ten balls in the next rack. Ellen Kate again managed to sink one ball on the break, but unfortunately it was the cue ball.

"Now that's more like it!" she commented.

Her father and Peter were charmed.

Exercising executive prerogative, the President broke, but nothing found its way into a pocket. Bozorth glanced at the table, snapped off an easy shot and ran three more balls before sinking the cue. Bryce admired the swiftness of the man's play, exactly like his politics: play-by-instinct.

25

It was Iana's turn. Positioned behind her, Bryce watched her line up over her stick and take slow aim. He liked the fact that, in contrast to Bozorth, she always took considerable care before every shot, even the easy ones. She cracked off a three-way combination—and very nearly made it.

"Jack, exactly what's our exposure on all this? What the hell are people thinking out there?" The President asked, arching out over his own cue stick. "I'm thinking about next year, of course."

Bozorth waited for Bryce to take his shot before replying. "Well, people seem kinda frightened. The Unknown scares 'em. But mostly, they seem alarmed by the fact that some spaceship from another world could sneak up on the Earth completely undetected. That's what really rattles 'em."

Bryce faced him. "We could claim we've been tracking the Alien craft for weeks—who's to say otherwise?"

"That'd be worse," Iana cautioned. "Because then we'd be blasted for withholding vital information from the public."

"I concur," added Bozorth.

Bryce turned to other questions. "You guys think I look too trusting, even naïve, letting an alien craft take up station alongside Discovery?" He drew a bead on the nine ball and sank it. "Beyond that, will people think that sending Junker over for a look-see is too great a risk?"

"I wouldn't worry about the Major," Bozorth rumbled. "It's a risk that by any measure has to be taken. Remember: everyone out there is bursting with questions. Anything that promises to provide answers is going to be welcomed. People are desperate to know what the Aliens are up to—and will brook any risk to find out." The President applied chalk for his next shot. "However," Bozorth went on, "I think it best that the Aliens perceive you as the Powerful Earth Leaderabove all direct involvement. If something's going to blow up in someone's face, let it be not yours. Make no mistake: this whole business is ripe for disaster." He glanced at his watch. Being sixty-six, he liked to be in bed by nine; it was 8:05. As to being perceived as naive and trusting, some are bound to accuse us of that. So what? By tomorrow, the whole damn world will know whether or not we can believe the visitors and the issue becomes moot." He peered over his glasses and fixed his gaze on the President. "And dare I say it: Standing here now, trying to figure out the impact on next year's elections, should be the very last of our concerns."

Bryce stiffened, accepting the rebuke—that much did he respect John Bozorth. He chalked his stick one last time took aim, and missed.

An hour later, as the Bryces were getting ready for bed, the British Prime Minister phoned. It had to be urgent.

"I'm sorry to have to disturb you at this late hour, Mr. President," apologized the PM in peerage tones.

"Think nothing of it, Sir Edward—you're the one who's up at four in the morning."

"Indeed. The reason I'm calling: minutes ago I myself was awakened by my Defense Minister—with a report that one of our naval aircraft observed a most unnatural atmospheric event above the Lesser Antilles just over an hour ago. At first, it looked to be a common meteor. But then it made a U-turn before continuing its descent! Conclusion: in all likelihood, it was that alien spacecraft of yours."

This was all news to Bryce; he had no idea what to make of it. He thanked the Prime Minister for the sighting report, rang off, and immediately phoned Klein.

Peter listened closely to the report of the Prime Minister's late-night phone call, gathering himself and shaking off the last precious remnants of sleep. He stifled an insistent yawn but was sure Bryce must have caught it. There followed a long pause as Peter processed the new information he'd just listened to.

"They could either have been making a Deposit—or a Withdrawal of some kind. Let's hope it was the latter. The former is just too ominous." He yawned loudly and pointedly.

"Okay, go back to sleep. We'll pick up where we left off in the morning." The line went dead. Peter glanced at his watch: 1:08.

HOT GOLD

Spectacular sunrises greet astronauts sixteen times a day, and one could easily become jaded. But today was the promised Fifth Day, and all aboard Discovery were experiencing intense anticipation. They'd discussed at length how a rendezvous might actually take place, and finally concluded that, if the alien craft did in fact show up—given its propensity for stealth—it would most likely do so while both spacecraft were in the blackness of the Earth's shadow. Therefore, they wouldn't even be aware of its presence until sunrise, when they could actually look out and see it.

During the first sunrise of the day, and then the second, the shuttle crew held its breath. Nothing.

In the Situation Room far below, it was beginning to look as if CHIMERA might turn out to be an empty exercise.

On the Third sunrise all that changed—

Just as Discovery burst from behind the planet into dazzling sunlight—there it was:

A blinding, pure white—hot-gold spacecraft.

RENDEZVOUS

Telescopes around the world remained locked on the two spacecraft as they circled the planet the news networks tracked them through relays of live feeds around the globe while billions watched in awe.

All screens revealed the same wonder: An enormous, utterly unearthly vessel, gleaming iridescent in the sun.

Viewed from Discovery, the spaceship was an explosion of light. Lt. Col. Dwayne Traysides was Shuttle Commander; the final decision to allow Junker to go outside on tether was his. He squinted to make out detail on the alien craft—but could not. There were no panels, no apertures, no windows, no hatches, and no running lights visible anywhere. Not even any sign of texturing on its surfaces. It was as if the entire construct was a huge clear-glass ampule, encasing and admixing iridescent currents of the purest white, yellow and fire gold, a true Spacecraft of the Gods.

For forty minutes neither vessel moved relative to the other: a tableau hanging in space. Traysides imagined that from back on Earth they must look like a tiny cabin cruiser riding in the lee of a great ocean liner.

Twenty minutes passed. "Everything appears nominal," Traysides confirmed. "They're maintaining precise position just sitting there—looking right back at us, no doubt. Our move, it would appear. A.J.—what say you?"

"I'm Go!" Replied Junker without hesitation.

"You ready then to speak with the White House?"

"Sure." The com-link was established.

"Major Junker, this is Peter Klein in the Situation Room. How's everything look to you up there?"

"Everything's nominal, Sir—I'm anxious to go visiting."

"Major, you understand that you are not to enter the alien craft without direct authorization," came a familiar voice.

"Yes, Mr. President. I understand."

Nineteen minutes later A.J. Junker stepped into the vacuum of the open cargo bay and gazed over at the spaceship. Even with his visor down it was like looking into the sun.

He began releasing small thrusts of gas, maneuvering over the fifty meters separating the two craft, secure on his tether to Discovery. Drawing gradually closer, he could make out a construct permeated with myriad "speckles of sparks," as he described them in hushed wonderment. "Infinitesimal sparks, firing deep within. I can see pale blue ones—turquoise pale green—even amethyst. Absolutely gorgeous!"

"What do you estimate to be your distance at this point?" Klein interrupted.

"Perhaps twenty more yards. Holding position—just, taking it all in—Hold On: there's something happening!—No one on the com-link breathed. "The, the—blue speckles seem to be—coalescing in an area directly in front of me—to form words! Wow! It reads:

> 'WELCOME'!"

Wait—there's more:
> 'MAJOR JUNKER'

My God! They know my name!"

"Confirmed!" Broke in Traysides, "I see those words, too!"

"Hold it—" continued Junker. "Yeah: Something else's going on—right next to where the words are they're forming a, a—doorway? Yeah, a human-sized translucent portal of some kind. Through it, I can see another doorway at the far end of a—maybe a twenty foot by twenty foot compartment. Might be some kind of airlock—"

"Look for other details, anything at all," Klein radioed. "What can you observe of their propulsion or drive systems?"

"Nothing really. Those four pods that seemed from Earth to house the power drives could be just about anything. Or nothing. There are no apertures or intakes. Anywhere. Everything's curved and absolutely smooth. Wait, I do see a small half-ring affair sticking out next to the doorway, possibly to hook my tether. Okay, I'm moving in now—

"No closer than ten yards," Bryce ordered. "And, A.J. watch your Six."

"Roger that. I'm just about at ten yards now. Can't make out much. Wait—more words are forming! Smaller ones on the opposite side of the doorway. I'm reading:

'YOU WOULD HONOR US BY COMING ABOARD WHERE YOU CAN SEE US AND WE CAN SPEAK. YOU MAY LASH YOUR SAFETY CABLE BESIDE THE ENTRANCEWAY. ONCE INSIDE YOU MAY REMOVE YOUR HELMET AND BREATHE AIR WE BORROWED FROM YOUR OWN ATMOSPHERE.'"

In the Situation Room all eyes turned to the president. He alone would decide. "A.J., how do you feel about going into that thing? I want an honest answer."

"I'm not feeling alarmed at the prospect, Sir. Everything appears quiet and stable. Just wish it weren't so damn bright! Maybe once inside, it'll be easier to—oh, oh! New message:

'WITHIN OUR SHIP YOUR COMMUNICATION AND MONITORING SYSTEMS WILL REMAIN OPERATIVE. ELECTROMAGNETIC SIGNALS PASS UNIMPEDED THROUGH OUR MOLECULAR MATRICES.

WE WILL ALSO FURNISH SYNTHETIC GRAVITY.'"

Bryce shot a hard look at his National Science Adviser. "Nathan, is that business possible?"

"Mr. President, we know nothing whatever about their—'molecular matrices.'" He was feeling utterly inadequate. "And as to artificial gravity—until now, that's only been the stuff of science fiction."

Bryce muted the com-link. "So, what we've got here then is a God damn crap-shoot!" he shouted "with the life of Major Junker as table stakes!"

His authorization received, A.J. hooked his tether beside the portal and stepped inside, going from being weightless one moment—to one-hundred and eighty-five pounds the next! Several seconds after he entered, the portal behind him closed, contracting to its center from all sides and then disappearing altogether. Suddenly fresh air began filling the chamber. He continued to describe what was happening over his com-link. They'd been truthful; he was still coming through loud and clear, and the minicam on his shoulder was transmitting color images with digital clarity.

The doorway in front of him seemed to evaporate, and he found himself standing before a long, bright tunnel leading to the central section of the spaceship. He'd just begun to describe it, when all of a sudden, a commanding voice spoke—clearly audible to everyone listening on the com-link:

"Welcome aboard, Major Junker. You honor us and your nation by coming. If you remove your helmet, you will find the air refreshing. We withdrew it from one of your fragrant island rain forests. We also borrowed a quantity of your purest water from a mountain stream."

"Major Junker," radioed Peter Klein, "if you think it safe you have permission to test the air. But do not remove your helmet."

The astronaut slowly turned a small valve—and tasted fresh air! "I've just taken a whiff—and it's great! Raising faceplate now," he announced confidently.

"The passageway before you leads to the main chamber of this craft, where we hope shortly to convene small delegations chosen by your government for the purpose of discussing critical matters confronting your planet and your peoples.
Feel at liberty to address us at any time."

"Ask them when this 'convening' thing is supposed to take place?" Klein relayed, and Junker asked.

"We will rendezvous with your next shuttle flight. But delay not. Critical issues require action.
Major Junker our conference chamber awaits your inspection."

Junker proceeded down the passageway, a long square tube with rounded corners. He began a narrative: "There's no apparent light source, but it's bright all over, not glaring like outside. Temperature reads same as Discovery. I've already come approximately twenty

31

meters, which—looks to be about halfway. Walls—ceiling—floor—are all a pale yellow—with zillions of those same gold speckles!"

"Can you see outside the spaceship?" Klein asked.

"Negative. No portals, windows, anything like that. But I can see the main chamber now, just up ahead—stepping into it. Whoa! This is really something: it's like—a really intense flower garden from some other world! It's even got a waterfall down into a flowered pool! Uh—let's see: The central chamber is in fact your basic heptagon, with seven equal sides and a wide, shallow, opaque dome for a ceiling, which is dark and facing away from Earth."

"Nothing before you is a living organism. It is in fact: Art."

"Amazing! Uh, may I ask how you learned my name?" Junker queried as Klein had directed.

"We have much knowledge—with some to share."

Junker saw the chamber was furnished with four reclining contour seats set in a soft arc before a convex proscenium.

"We anticipate a series of three-hour sessions. Please advise us whether these seats provide suitable comfort for humans."

A.J. eased himself onto one seat, seemingly inspired by the shape of those aboard the shuttles. Only this one was far more comfortable, even in a spacesuit. He looked up at the dome, then around the chamber. "You said, when I was outside, I'd be able to see you. But I can't—"

"Direct your eyes to the elevated area before you."

He did, and suddenly beheld three shimmering beings, each taller than most humans—each surrounded by a pale cerulean radiance effectively diffusing and concealing their features.

ALIENS

The dazzling images coming from within the alien craft were being relayed via secure closed-circuit to the Situation Room—and not being released to the media. Everyone stood mesmerized.

"Ask them where they came from," the president directed; Klein passed it on. The reply was short:

"We are not prepared to reveal our origins."

"Then, ask them how they know so much about us," Bryce snapped. Moments later:

"We have been observing you for an exceedingly long time."

"How long?"

"Many—many years."

"Then, you've been here before," Klein inferred. "How many times?"

"To answer that would invite questions which cannot be meaningfully addressed at this time."

"Then just tell us why you're here!" Bryce demanded.

"To guide and advise you. We invite delegates to attend three Convenings. Each will focus on a particular area of planetary concern.

The First Convening will guide you on Resources. The Second on Social concerns. And the Third on matters Economic. We invite you to send four participants to discuss these issues.

Each Convening shall consist of three sessions of three hours. A month's interval between flights should afford sufficient time to prepare and train participants for the next Convening."

Bryce, along with other members of CHIMERA, was beginning to resent being told what to do by these Aliens—who only answered the questions they chose to and spoke to them all as if they were children. Bryce decided to see how they'd handle a little resistance.

"What if we decline the invitation to attend any of these 'Convenings'?" Klein had Junker ask.

"You would compel us to invite Russians instead."

There was a prolonged pause. "What if more turnaround time is required between shuttle launches?" Junker relayed.

"We will be patient. While continuity is desirable, cooperation is paramount."

"If we should agree to send delegations, whom would you suggest?" Klein radioed.

"For each Convening send three delegates who are well studied in the subjects under discussion. That makes total of nine persons. In addition, send a single newsperson to attend and report on all three Convenings for the world media.

Please release to the public the recordings you have made of this day's visit. Cameras and recorders will not be permitted at the Convenings, as they would distract and inhibit participants."

Bryce was stunned. All terms and conditions were being dictated. Their only choice was to accept their demands, or let the Russians attend instead. And that was unacceptable.

"What would you have us call you?" the president asked, buying time to think.

"You may designate us whatever pleases you. It would be appropriate to regard us as mentors."

"Mr. President," Bozorth quietly interrupted, "there's absolutely no way we could put civilian participants into spacesuits and have them go EVA!"

"What I was just thinking myself," Bryce covered, having entirely overlooked the indirect question. "Ask them about that." Klein complied.

"We have anticipated that matter. For each Convening, we will project a passageway to the shuttle's main hatch. Your delegates will not require spacesuits."

Klein instructed Junker to pan around and take pictures of the entire chamber while CHIMERA wrestled with its dilemma. They all felt utterly impotent and liked it not. National pride is a tough swallow.

It would clearly be some time before decisions were made.

"Our next shuttle flight is scheduled for early next month," Klein relayed. "Should we agree to send participants, how are we to let you know?"

"We will know."

It was the final exchange, one which the president found smug and annoying. Twenty minutes later Junker was back aboard Discovery, filing reports for CHIMERA and being debriefed.

That night Sam Bryce picked a fight with his wife. He needed the diversion.

"I think you should bag that interview on MTV. To their audience you'll just come off as an out-of-touch old fart."

Abby recognized what he was doing and decided to play along. He needed the release.

"I figured MTV would be a good place to put in a plug for legalizing pot," she said, pushing all his buttons.

"Good God, Abby, don't even joke about that!" he recoiled.

BRYCE

Arthur Frayles had been alone for a decade now, ever since Marian lost her battle with cancer. Cousin Becky had wanted to move in with him, "so's you won't be rattling around all alone in that big old drafty house!" That being the last thing he wanted, he promptly bought a townhouse.

Since being hired away from TIME to take over as Managing Editor of the Boston Globe in 1982, G. Arthur Frayles had evolved into something of a legend—exposing City Hall's trading Certificates of Occupancy for campaign contributions, forcing a popular governor to acknowledge "institutional abuse and corruption" in state mental hospitals, catching a sitting federal judge accepting casino comps, and hounding a congressman out of office for "malign neglect" in protecting the environment. In the process he'd won two Pulitzers and been honored at the White House. He'd even dined once with the Queen; her Majesty had found him "rather too blunt."

Whenever intellectually insulted, assaulted with pretense, or above all bored, Frayles was given to merciless candor and lethal wit. While this endeared him to his editorial staff as well as the reading public, it set many political teeth on edge. Arthur Frayles knew well the power of the skewer and wielded it adroitly, as numerous punctured gas bags could painfully attest.

Professionally, Art Frayles cast himself as non-political, but among friends called himself a "deflowered idealist." Over the years he'd gradually lost faith in a political system which confers power—never on the most moral and capable, but rather on those who pursued it with the most resources. Yet in Frayles' view, the very act of seeking power disqualified the seeker as being worthy of holding it.

Like everyone else around the world, he'd been following the events in orbit almost continuously, anxious for news of what was happening. But it had been two days now since Man's first direct contact with another intelligent species—and still no word. He was beginning to suspect the ominous. Out of growing concern (and rampant curiosity), he'd placed a call to his sister to find out what was going on.

But Abby Frayles Bryce had not returned his call.

*   *   *

The hours immediately following Junker's safe return to Discovery had been grueling for the eight men and women of CHIMERA. The pressure was crushing, with the entire world left hanging—desperate to learn whether Earth's first interplanetary visitors were to be feared or welcomed.

This was the seminal decision the American President had to make on behalf of all mankind. A decision which would drive all others. Yet one that must be made quickly.

CHIMERA had absolutely no evidence of hostile intent—no evidence of deception—no hint of duplicity. No promises made which were not kept. Nothing to suggest unfriendly intent. No basis for distrusting the Aliens. Yet, distrust them they did; prudence demanded it. The Aliens had, after all, been less than forthcoming as to who they were—how they came to know so much about us—and what they were doing here. Nonetheless, an invitation had been extended, and now they had to decide whether to accept. And for that, Bryce wanted the input of key allies; it was one decision for which he wanted shared responsibility.

After personal calls to key heads of state, Bryce found that, to a man, the leaders of Earth wanted to know more, and recommended a policy of Guarded Cooperation.

Bryce did not disclose the fact that video and audio recordings had been made aboard the alien spaceship, because then they'd all want to view them—and there simply wasn't time for that. If and when the president decided to release the tapes, he'd send the other leaders advance copies.

None of this sat well with Samuel Bryce. Under Guarded Cooperation and the Aliens' threat to take their business to the Kremlin, he was essentially left with no choice but to attend the Alien Ball and dance to their tune. It was not something he, nor the United States, nor the people of Earth could do without suffering a degree of humiliation.

As to Junker's videotapes, should he decide to keep their existence secret, it would be in defiance of the Aliens' wishes. To release them however, would create media bedlam. In making this decision, he'd only take advice from Bozorth, Ravenscroft and the Vice President. Plus

Abby—the unseen senior member of CHIMERA—who'd already been down to the Situation Room after hours to view and listen to the tapes.

Over dinner, that one last remaining choice was about to be taken from him.

"Woody," Abby intoned, "suppose the Aliens won't let you shoot any more video inside their spaceship, or record their voices again— then the major's tapes may be the only record we'll ever have—and that's too big a responsibility for any one person. More importantly, it's simply far too big a secret to be kept by anyone for very long. Ask yourself how many individuals already know about the recordings?"

Bryce realized she was right and flew into a rage, railing that he was being led around by the nose "by a buncha God damn condescending, smug-assed, dictatorial Aliens!" Abby let him vent all through dinner, knowing that in the end he'd reach the right decision.

He ranted on, into the kiwi cobbler. But over coffee he calmed, reason n' hope finally winning the day over anger n' pride. There remained another matter to be resolved. He patted his lips with a napkin and looked up at his wife.

"Tell me—how would you react if I asked Art to become the official press representative for all three Convenings? Think he'd be right for the job? More to the point, do you think he'd be willing to go for a ride on a rocket?"

She thought it over. "Art's one brilliant journalist, to be sure. Everyone trusts and respects him—he's a helluva writer—and yes, he'd probably jump at the chance to go for a ride in space. But, what would it look like for you to choose your own brother-in-law to cover the flat-out biggest story in history? What do Jack and Iana say?"

"They agree he'd be ideal—one advantage being, he could double as my personal representative." He blew his nose.

"That said," he continued, "I'm laying this one entirely on you because—make no mistake—there's real risk involved here. Things can go wrong. They could all be killed—or taken captive—or whisked back to some alien home world to become love slaves. In which case, there wouldn't be a damn thing we could do about it!" He sighed thoughtfully. "Abby, face it: we're all flying on blind faith here—in a very real sense placing ourselves entirely at their mercy!"

"I'm—a little surprised to hear you, a card-carrying agnostic, talk about Faith."

"Well, Oscar says that's exactly what we're doing. Even our esteemed Vice President said, 'All we can do is pray!'" He changed the subject. "Listen, give Art a call, and see how he'd feel about going for a ride in space. Use the secure phone, and if he seems receptive, put me on the line."

She reflected a few moments, and then reached for the phone. "I've been ducking his calls all afternoon. This should be interesting."

*　　*　　*

Following the last CHIMERA meeting of the day, Iana bade Peter into her office and closed the door.

"Finding any new insights in your hot-tub?" She swung her legs up onto her desk, affording him a prime up-skirt perspective. Their relationship had definitely changed since their Lather-Rama Soiree, as they now referred to it, surprisingly for the better. It had cleared the air, so to speak, of whatever sexual tension/curiosity may have existed between them—the best part being it was all so completely spontaneous thanks to a sudden snow squall. They both looked back on it with a measure of pride.

"Nothing to write home about as yet. But I'm thinking, maybe if you joined me—two heads, etc.—"

"Nothing at all?" Iana pressed. "Maybe a clue or two—such as something that just doesn't fit. We need to get into their heads."

The President stuck his own in the door, and Iana swung her legs down. "Am I interrupting?"

"Not at all. We were just trying to get into the Aliens' heads. You're welcome to join us," she invited.

"I'll just listen in, if I may." He found a chair.

"We're trying to fathom their motives," said Peter, "and this is where things begin to look harebrained. What have we conceivably got that's worth a trip halfway across the galaxy—? Not to mention how many light-years that would require."

"Our DNA perhaps?" Bryce wondered.

"How would they even learn that we have DNA? Or that it's all that superior," Iana challenged.

"Maybe we're coming at this with a whole bunch of false assumptions," Peter suddenly interjected—"Time and Distance being chief among them."

"Go on," the Chief Executive encouraged.

"Well—suppose they were actually headed for some other world—spotted us en route—and decided to make a small detour to check us out. Nothing hostile in that."

"Mmmm—I have a couple of problems with that," Iana said slowly. "They already know far too much about us and our problems to be just passing through. Not to mention their fluency in English."

"But what if they're simply extremely bright—with IQs measuring in the tens of thousands?" Bryce asked. "No one with a brain in his head has ever argued otherwise. What's more, no one's ever even suggested that there's so much a theoretical ceiling on intelligence."

"I think you may be onto something there, Mr. President," Iana jumped in, "but it would still have taken them a very long time to master a language as complex as English. See where that takes us?"

"That tells us they have to have been here for a very long time," Peter added. "This means they didn't just arrive in that fancy spaceship of theirs, as they would have us believe. If it's all just an elaborate hoax then, what in the Hell are they up to?"

"I'll tell you what it means," the President growled darkly. "Contrary to anything they may say to us, they're no longer to be trusted. They are arch deceivers. And that, I'm afraid, changes everything!"

*   *   *

Up on the Hill Senator David Onager was as partisan as the next guy, but the alien matter was about as nonpartisan as anything could get. If there were ever a time for mankind to stand united, this was surely it. Not a time for criticizing or second-guessing. The Republican commander-in-chief would have Dave Onager's fullest support—and still would even if he didn't happen to be a friend.

The senior senator from Ohio sat in his office, eyes locked on the television. Tommy Raffle, his administrative assistant, and other staffers huddled in rapt fascination. No one uttered a word—as the President described to the world what had transpired aboard the alien spaceship. Bryce ordered the lights dimmed. There followed a thirty-three minute unedited video and audio of Major Junker's entire excursion. Exterior close-ups were glaring and bright despite being shot through polarized filters. But with filters removed, the digital pictures of the interior were sharp and well illuminated. The vivid color images and soft, authoritative voices of the visitors evoked murmurs of amazement. Yet no one spoke. Without context, comment was impossible.

When the recordings ended, the President waited for everyone to resume breathing, and then opened the floor to questions.

"Mr. President," someone shouted, "are you going to send anyone up for these—'Convenings'?"

"Yes, we are. To refuse to attend would be worse than inhospitable, it would be insulting. Moreover, had they requested permission to come aboard the Shuttle to hold their Convenings, we would have likely agreed. The opportunity here is simply too—incredible for us to turn our backs."

"Whom will you be sending? Do you know yet?" CNN asked.

"As a matter of fact, we already have made one selection—one I'm sure you'll find of particular interest: Arthur Frayles, managing editor of the Boston Globe, has agreed to attend the three Convenings as the official designated journalist. As some of you are aware, Arthur also happens to be my brother-in-law, and can therefor serve in the capacity of my personal representative as well."

"Have you—any fear for his personal safety?"

"Everyone's convinced he'll be safe," the president lied.

Watching half a world away, the president of China caught the slight catch in Bryce's voice.

"And when will the first of these so called 'Convenings' take place?" came the follow-up.

"Since we already have a shuttle scheduled for launch July sixth, we can simply modify its mission plan. This gives us a little over two weeks to prepare, and get delegates trained for a trip into space. Sufficient time, we're assured."

He pointed to Reuters: "Are you only planning to invite Americans to participate, Mr. President?"

"That hasn't been decided yet."

He pointed to another.

"What if the Aliens should decide to—just take off with our delegates? Have you considered that possibility?"

"Of course we have. If we thought that was even a remote possibility, we wouldn't be sending delegates up there at all. Major Junker already faced that very risk and returned safely. Moreover, the fact that he was treated with genuine consideration and respect by our visitors leads us to accept them for what they clearly are: A race of highly superior beings—who have journeyed a very great distance to meet us—who arrive with considerable foreknowledge of our world. That, I think, carries its own imperatives."

Senator Onager clicked off when the press conference ended and the talking heads took over. He looked around at his still speechless brain-trust. His AA was first to speak.

"Everything was so clear, you could see—everything!"

"Except for the Aliens themselves," Sarah Lissy, Onager's media advisor, corrected.

"Yeah—why didn't they want us to see their faces?"

"You're assuming they've got 'faces' to begin with. But personally, I find it reassuring." Onager looked up at her expectantly. "Hey, if you catch a burglar in your bedroom, and he's wearing a mask—you can be pretty sure he doesn't want you to know what he looks like," she spelled out slowly. "He wouldn't bother with a mask if he planned to kill you."

"Exactly right," said Onager. "For some reason the Aliens just don't want us to know what they look like. But why? It makes little sense."

"Maybe they figure that knowing what they look like would distract us from the work at hand," Raffle speculated. "Or maybe they're just saving it for the right occasion."

"No, there's gotta be a better reason than that. Maybe someone should simply—ask them," Onager shrugged.

"Frayles will, count on it," Sarah snuffled. "I wonder if those Aliens realize what they've opened themselves up to. That guy can be Mr. Inquisition!"

"So, what do y'all think of the President choosing his own brother-in-law?" Onager asked. "Frayles might have been my first choice as well—despite the fact that his kid sister is married to a low life capitalist and he's a mediocre golfer."

*   *   *

Ellen Kate was one of only two people permitted to drop by the White House unannounced. The other was the First Mother. But comfortably ensconced at Boca Raton, Isabel Clothier-Bryce had no intention of ever doing so. If her son wanted to see his mother, he could "God damn well do the traveling!"

Isabel loathed Washington, and often declared she'd sooner visit Bosnia. She never minced words, and thoroughly enjoyed being abrasive. So nasty was she, one Capitol wag had called her "a bilious little hedgehog in designer suits," thereby confirming everything Isabel believed about Washington.

Dropping by after supper, Ellen Kate found her father shooting pool with Peter Klein, who was notably new to the task—he was still squinting from the Seal.

"Katie!" the President beamed, wrapping her in his arms.

"Hi, Daddy." she squeezed back.

"Am I interrupting affairs of state?" she asked, walking around the table. She could feel Peter's eyes licking her butt.

"Only thing you're interrupting is my streak," Bryce said, lining up a shot—which he missed badly. Peter and Ellen Kate exchanged quick smiles. "I caught that, you two. Peter, if you'll direct your attention to the table, you'll note that I have left you with abominable position."

"Duly noted," muttered Klein, taking his only shot and duly missing.

"I think I've jinxed you both. Perhaps I'd better leave," offered the First Daughter.

Bryce put up his cue and wiped chalk from his hands. "Nonsense. We're finished anyway, so your timing's perfect." He led them to a small private elevator which went directly to the living quarters. "Peter, come on along. It's time you got a peek at the Laird's Lair."

Minutes later they were sipping cocoa with the First Lady.

"Abby, we got any jelly crumpets around?" Bryce called out. Within seconds a smiling steward glided in bearing a Limoges tray of cellophane-wrapped Tastycake Crumpets. Klein was charmed.

"So, Peter, tell me: What is it that makes you an expert on Aliens?" Ellen Kate challenged.

"I went to M.I.T." She waited for him to elaborate; he did not. Then, realizing it would sound peculiar to just leave it at that, he appended, "I don't know any more about Aliens than you do, Ellen Kate. However, one Halloween I did dress up as one," he deadpanned.

"Had any more—baked lobster?" her father teased, angling for a non-alien turn in conversation. The Bryces exchanged a chuckle and

Peter looked away, as if overhearing a private joke was a breach of good manners. The diversion failed.

"I thought your press conference went really well, Daddy. What's been the reaction?" She could see him turn serious.

"Mostly relief, it would appear. People had been afraid the Aliens came here to deliver an ultimatum, or to enslave us, or for some other sinister purpose. It's remarkable how, almost universally, people want to imagine the worst. What does that say about us, I wonder—?"

"You're doing the only intelligent, honorable thing you can," Abby rallied. "Anyone who thinks otherwise—anyone who thinks we should simply reject their overtures and refuse to meet with them—outta just go pound sand!"

"Who says we shouldn't even meet with them?" Ellen Kate demanded-.

"Oh, some of your father's more zealous—patriots and contributors."

"Patriots And Contributors; sounds like a PAC to me," she punned. Her father took it the wrong way.

"Listen, a lot of educated people out there feel we're being humiliated by the Aliens—and that we'd be a damn sight better off letting 'em make dancing puppets out of the Russians!" he snapped. Realizing he'd overreacted, he softened his tone. "Don't mind me. It's just that I've been getting it from all sides lately. The French think I should be demanding answers in exchange for cooperation. The Post editorializes that 'Trust is the hallmark of an advanced civilization' (whatever the Hell that's supposed to mean). Then Wally Furst labels me 'dangerously naive'—and now Douglas Nash in Newsweek is telling readers the Aliens might be here to 'Herald the beginning of a New Age'!" he sighed. "So far the only one smart enough to keep his mouth shut throughout all this has been the Pope."

"On the other hand," the First Lady countered, "just look at the caliber of people who've been calling—all anxious to be chosen as delegates to the Convenings: Simon Wasserman, Eleanor Van Dank, Geoffrey Sands, Cynthia Cryer-Kubbs! Hell, Woody, you can fill that shuttle with nothing but Nobel Laureates, if you want!"

As Abby topped off everyone's hot chocolate, the President watched Peter attempt to observe Katie without being noticed. But he was less than ept; she caught him and couldn't hide her smile. It was apparent to Bryce that they were already in Mutual Attraction mode—and once

43

again found himself glad she enjoyed ardor-dampening Secret Service protection.

*   *   *

The following morning Discovery returned to earth. And two hours later Anthony Junker found himself facing a packed auditorium filled with reporters from every continent.

"Major Junker, how would you describe these alien beings—in your own words?" asked Al Knox of the Chicago Tribune.

The astronaut cleared his throat, gathering the right adjectives. "Even though they all stood behind some sort of 'energy screen,' I could see they were all about the same height—six foot-seven or-eight. And fairly lean. I also got the impression of—like, they had manes or long hair or something."

"What about their voices?" Knox added. "We all listened to the tapes, but you were there. What were they like?"

"Ah—quite pleasant actually. Clear. Firm. Soft, but strong at the same time—quietly confident, you might say. But there was a—a— certain respectfulness to their tone. A friendliness even."

"Major, did you get any sense of—personality?" UPI followed up. "Were there any differences between them? Any sense, for instance, which one was in charge?"

A.J. had been asked the same questions during his debriefing and had a ready response: "No one seemed to be in charge, as such. Each did speak at one time or another, and they all sounded pretty much alike. I did get the impression, though, that they were male—and by that I mean not female. But as to any personality differences, I can't say they seemed all that different one from another. Yet—somehow I did sense that they each possess individuality."

"GAS!"

Sam Bryce liked to put his feet up on the desk in the Oval Office, but only in the presence of close associates. He'd once tried to picture his predecessors doing the same, but only images of Democratic presidents had come to mind. He decided he could live with that.

His sultry national security adviser had her feet up as well, and Bryce was powerless to keep his eyes from seeking an under-thigh shot. This never failed to amused her. It afforded her a power over the most powerful man on earth.

"Did I tell you, the Japanese want us to select one of them as a delegate?" he asked.

"What did Chester say to them?"

"The truth: that we intend to keep this an all-American show—in accordance with our visitors' expressed wishes."

"So besides Art Frayles, who are you going to pick?"

"That's what I wanted to talk about. We've had a lot of volunteers. And I think it might be smart to include someone from the Hill for each Convening. That way, if something does go wrong they'll be in for their share of the blame."

"I agree." She re-crossed her legs; zap went the eyes. She had a sudden image of him huffing and puffing atop her. It didn't repel her; it simply didn't interest her. The intercom flashed. Bryce picked up and listened for a few moments before replying.

"Oscar, the Chamber's just going to have to find itself another speaker. Until this business is over with, I've cleared my calendar. Let 'em know I even blew off my trip to Israel next week." He listened some more. "Look—forget my calendar and concentrate on the Budget. It's time to play hardball—call in a few markers—lean on the Districts hurting for contracts—even burn a few contributors if you have to. Just do it. It's crunch time!" He hung up, returning his covert attention to Iana's undercarriage.

"Gothier's still seething over being kept in the dark, you know," Ravenscroft remarked.

"Let him seethe. CIA's got no Alien Intelligence Section: no alien informants—no agents-in-place aboard alien spacecraft—no message intercepts. So their contribution would be nil. Frankly, I'm taking some enjoyment at seeing their noses pressed up against the glass for a change."

"On the other hand, don't you think we need to be aware of what the Russians or Chinese are up to regarding the aliens?"

"Yeah," he sighed, "I suppose it's time to bring 'em on board." The phone rang again. Something told him not to take the call.

"Atwood, what in Hell's the matter with you?" his mother brayed. "This whole alien spaceship thing is a God damn hoax—as any damn fool can plainly see! Why are you even talking with them?"

"Hello, Mother, it's nice to hear your voice," he replied brightly. "How's your appetite?"

"Everything I eat gives me gas!"

"Then try fruits—melons. You love casabas—"

"Gas!"

"Well then, salads—"

"Gas!"

He could see this was going nowhere. "How's the weather down there anyway?" he ventured.

"A God damn hoax, I say! You listen to your mother: someone out there is playing you for a sucker!" With that, she hung up on him, a unique experience for a President of the United States!

*   *   *

Ellen Kate Bryce picked up instantly on her father's deep down, fear-born worry. He was showing the strain of assuming primary global responsibility for dealing with the Aliens. Suppose things began to unravel in his uncertain hands—or ratcheted up over his failure to respond wisely to some unexpected development—or to seriously misread some Alien move or pronouncement. He could find himself in deep shit in front of the entire world. Or worse. In which case, he could forget about a Second Term.

He was sitting behind a tall, sniper-proof window, gazing vaguely upon the South Lawn with unseeing eyes. He didn't hear Ellen Kate coming up behind him, and gave a startled jump as she placed her hands on his clenched shoulders and began to knead.

"Mmmm—that feels so good. You always seem to know just how to restore me, doncha—"

After a minute or so of kneading, she said, "You're all knotted up. A good, deep Puff on the old Magic Dragon's what I prescribe. They say it works wonders."

46

By way of full reply, he merely grunted. "So, tell me about Peter Klein," she switched. "I was wondering what accounted for your exceedingly welcome presence. It turns out I have Peter to thank—which I'll do the next time I see him."

"Don't you dare!" she hissed.

"Hey, to react like that you must find him pretty cute."

"Well—there is something about him—"

"Listen, all the really good stuff's on the inside. He's smart as a whip. Has a rip-snorting sense of humor. Ideas galore—most of them good. He'll make quite a catch for some young woman."

"So he is single then."

"You think I'd be blowing his horn like this if he wasn't?"

"I see that his office is right next door to Titty-Tit-Tits. What's his title?"

"He's the Deputy National Security Adviser. And he's damn good."

"If you say so. But let me tell you—he's also got one bitchin' butt!"

*   *   *

Her mother often said Ellen Kate was a Closet Empath, which she took to be a high compliment. Ellen thought the ability to truly feel what others were feeling was both a blessing and a gift. And every now and then, when her heart would suddenly leap out in shared pain for someone's suffering, especially a total stranger's, she could almost feel a soft, sweet waft of affirmation pass softly over her. A gentle, feather of cosmic far away Love, if you will—almost like a fleeting brush with the Divine.

What a thrilling, exquisite feeling!

*   *   *

Ellen Kate decided to try using her empathetic powers to feel what others are feeling, to see whether Peter would get all horny over her if she pushed the right buttons.

Every girl has an old, faded pair of jeans, some dating back as far as high school, that still fit like they were painted on—and still whipped heads around just walking down the street. Ellen thought of her jeans as Eye Magnets, and deemed them infallible.

On Friday there was to be a Retirement Party for a highly popular White House reporter, and as a good friend Peter was sure to be there. As were her jeans.

*   *   *

The First Daughter stood before her full-length mirror on the back of the bathroom door and gave herself a rare head-to-toe appraisal. Her signature liquid lemon hair—perfectly straight and long enough to nearly cover her butt—was as glorious as ever. (One wig maker offered her a record twenty-six thousand and three-hundred dollars for her hair, its owner being so prominent and admired. Ellen Kate promptly dismissed the offer).

The invisibility of her make-up finally satisfied her. It had taken her over an hour to achieve the effect she was after—even though Peter was sure to be oblivious.

Then her demanding eye drifted down to her favorite jeans. She did a slow three-hundred and sixty degree turn—"Dr. K.", if'n all this don't git to yer gonads, they oughtta be hung as useless ornaments on a White House Christmas Tree.

She took a ten-minute reflection break. This was all so unlike her. She never even flirted, let alone set out to seduce anyone. Jumping someone's bones in the Executive Mansion was beyond foolish. And looking for a husband was the farthest thing from her mind. So what was all this nonsense with Peter about? She finally realized it was his brain which turned her on. Few men could keep up with her intellectually—and none were a challenge. But Peter might prove to be the exception.

The more she thought about it, the more convinced she became that the best way into her jeans was through her mind.

Small wonder she had such an abstemious love life.

*   *   *

As expected, Peter spent over an hour at his friend's Retirement Party on Friday. Ellen Kate waited until Peter and Ted were talking alone, and wandered over to join them."

Peter, how about introducing me to your friend?" she smiled.

48

"Of course—Ted Rheeme: meet First Daughter Ellen Kate Bryce." They shook hands warmly.

"I've enjoyed your work for years," she said. "Do you really, really have to retire?"

"'Fraid so. Unless I want all-out war on the home-front. I once promised Carla an Alaskan cruise but had to cancel for an important assignment. She was so angry; I didn't get no boom-boom for a month! So this is one promise on which I dare not neg—let alone renege."

"Just think of all that perfectly good Viagra you might as well throw out," Peter chuckled.

"Or worse yet, having to go back to emptying the old lizard manually."

"That's not Erectile Dysfunction—it's Reptile Dysfunction." A loud snort escaped Ellen Kate.

Following the party, she shocked herself by asking Peter to show her his office. Already a big fan of her jeans, he was delighted to oblige. As they walked in the door, one of his phones was ringing—a call he had to take. So she decided to have a look around. The first thing to catch her eye was a framed cartoon on one wall, depicted a well-coiffed French Poodle lying on the floor of a major dog show awaiting its turn to strut. But, unnoticed by its owner, a long-haired male Dachshund had hiked its leg and was peeing all over the prize poodle. Caption:

'Getting a Leg Up on the Competition'

Peter's call over, he hung up and turned to her. "Love your cartoon," she said.

"It pretty well captures the essence of things around here," he said.

On his desk she spotted a leather-framed, very posed looking photo of him and his boss supposedly tending to, of all things, the Rose Garden.

"So tell me—what's it like, working so closely day in, day out with Titty-Tit-Tits?"

"I never let her boobs get in the way. But those jeans you're wearing could be a whole different story."

Without showing any reaction, she asked, "Do you find working in the White House enhances your love life—or just the opposite?"

"Little bit of both, I suppose. One-night-stands aboard my boat are one thing, but relationships take time, of which I have very little."

"What about you-know-who next door?"

"Not my type," he lied. Then, following a long, thoughtful silence, he looked at her and said softly, "I'd love to feel that incredible hair of yours—"

She hesitated, weighed the implications, then walked over and sat lightly on his lap. It took ten minutes of nuzzling her hair with his face, and ten more for hair-stroking to give way to the breast stroke, which in turn led to a night aboard Sea Particle—all under the watchful eye of the Secret Service, which exercised appropriate discretion by identifying her "companion" as "Bureaucrat One" in their daily log.

Peter gazed over at Ellen Kate sleeping contentedly in an old pair of his pajamas. He mused about what a remarkably accomplished lover she was for a woman with no man in her life.

A few months earlier, finding he couldn't take his eyes off her whenever they were attending the same White House function, he finally yielded to temptation and used his A-7 Clearance Access to have a look at her Secret Service logs—and discovered to his delight, that she'd gone pretty much dateless, and thus presumably celibate, ever since her father announced his candidacy, now nearly five years back. He chalked up her carnal hunger and acumen to going without so long.

But now he had a new problem. Ellen Kate was hardly dalliance material—he couldn't just blow her off, even if he wanted to—which he very much didn't. But what would her parents think? Furthermore—what would he do should Iana insist they play Nook and Cranny again? Factor in the Aliens, and he was destined to have a very challenging and peculiar year ahead.

To put it mildly.

*　　*　　*

David Onager and Sam Bryce had become friends a dozen years earlier when both served in the Senate, albeit on different sides of the aisle. They enjoyed working together, and came to admire the depth and deftness of each other's intellects when doing battle over a bill, and especially when debating principles. Best of all, each could make the other laugh. One day over lunch they'd discovered they had the same golf handicaps and began playing regularly thereafter. Making no effort to conceal their friendship and mutual esteem, they became useful to their leaderships as effective go-betweens, quietly bridging the gaps between positions, and now and then opening the door to genuine compromise.

But that was back when they were both senators. Now that one of them was president, they became a useful back channel between often opposing branches of government.

Bryce lay in his hot tub, turning his mother's parting shot over in his mind. Isabel Clothier had been unabashedly self-centered every one of her eighty-eight years—spoiled, lazy, opinionated, rancid of disposition. Born to wealth, disposed to indulgence, abusive to everyone about her, she had not one true friend—even her son came in for his share of vitriol.

Isabel's sole redeeming quality, at least in her son's eyes, was a fierce protectiveness of "the one I spawned." Atwood Samuel was her only child. And when she'd phoned to tell him he was being suckered, it was out of primal instinct to protect her cub. Problem was, her instincts had always proven pretty damned infallible.

Bryce gladly took Onager's call while being pummeled from beneath: a nightly water-jet massage was his one sacrosanct indulgence. Tonight he needed to hear a friendly voice.

"David, I was wondering when you'd call."

"Well, to all appearances, Sam, you've been a mite busy. What's that gurgling sound—your stomach?"

"No, I'm in the hot tub, getting water hosed up my ass-pretty much like what goes on at a press conference." They shared a chuckle. "So, you callin' to find out what we know that we haven't released yet?"

"And that would be?—"

Abby stuck her head in the door, and then withdrew when she saw he was on the phone.

"Not one damn thing, Dave. And that's what really galls me. From the very beginning, when the Boulder Observatory blew everything onto front pages around the world, I've had no choice but to release whatever we knew, even to the point of airing Junker's tapes, in their entirety. Yet the fact is, we're being led around by the nose—told what to do, whom to send—right out there in front of the whole world. It's like trying to operate in a God damn fishbowl!"

"Sam—you're doing exactly the right thing. In your position, I'd be just as frustrated, and feel just as compelled to cooperate."

"David, thank you for that. Everything's on fast-forward now. We'll be announcing final delegate selections tomorrow. Then, assuming they can all pass the physicals, they'll begin intensive training at the Cape: Emergency procedures—How to throw up while wearing a helmet— How to take a weight-less piss—other cool stuff."

CONVENING

"Sweet—Jesus—in—Space!" cried G. Arthur Frayles, as Atlantis roared clear of the launch tower, rolled onto her back, and blazed for the heavens.

Aboard were the four delegates selected by the president for the Resources Convening. In addition to Frayles, were Congressman Michael Obst (R-FL), Vice-Chairman of the House Subcommittee on National Resources; Elizabeth Freelander-Greene, Executive Director of the One Biosphere Institute; and Oliver Brewstier, President/CEO, Elemental Technologies.

Three weeks before, none of the four had remotely dreamed of ever going into space, much less boarding an actual alien spaceship to meet beings from another world! But when the White House phoned, all had leapt at the opportunity.

Now, hearts pounding, eardrums cavitating, triple gravity crushing down, each was in feral flight—ripped from a safe known reality, and now hurling violently into a neo-reality.

Booster cut-off and separation—Main engine cut-off—Main fuel tank jettison—Orbital maneuvering engines—Attitude stabilization—

Shuttle Commander Richard Sappio eyed his four charges.

Outside of normal Zero-G facial bloating, all appeared okay considering they'd been blasted aloft on a column of fire, everything roaring and vibrating; squashed back in their space suits—beholding their home planet falling away beneath—going from hundreds of pounds to weighing nothing at all—all in a span of minutes! Each sat utterly mind-blown. Sappio smiled dryly and informed his passengers they were now free to remove their helmets and unbuckle.

At the first muscular urging, each floated gently free of their seat and became instantly occupied with experiencing weightlessness. Then, pushing off toward the windows, their focus became external, gasping as cloud-swept continents and azure seas slipped past overhead. They watched day-become-night-become-day in less than an hour. And, for the first time, saw their moon in naked clarity, gashed by jagged mountains and scarred everywhere by countless craters. A brutal mosaic in black and white, something used by the cosmos for target-practice. Then they lifted their eyes beyond—and beheld the immensity of the universe itself: ultra-black, perforated by billions of burning suns. Stupefying magnificence.

Even Art Frayles could find no words worthy of utterance.

*　　*　　*

Then, with the seventh sunrise of the first day, the alien craft suddenly appeared, blazing white and holding steady station thirty meters off the shuttle's port beam.

Everyone aboard Atlantis watched in silent wonder as an oval structure began to emerge from the nearest surface of the spaceship and project itself toward their main hatch, exactly as promised. When the projection made contact with the shuttle's skin, no impact whatever could be felt, and no sound heard. For several tense minutes nothing seemed to happen. Then they heard the sound of a gas flooding into the connecting passageway—and moments later, a familiar voice:

"You may safely open your hatch whenever you wish. We note with pleasure that each of you has dressed for comfort. You may wish to visit your relief facilities before coming aboard. We will however furnish fresh water for any who may thirst."

Upon receiving formal authorization from the White House, Commander Sappio ordered the main hatch cracked a fraction of an inch. When no air from within the shuttle rushed out, he allowed the hatch to be opened just enough to sample the air from within the passageway. And as before, it was sweet.

Sappio then ordered the hatch opened fully, and the seal joining the passageway to the hull closely inspected. The joining, Atlantis radioed, appeared virtually organic, with a perfect mating and union of contours. The seal was airtight.

Twenty minutes later, all four delegates pushed off in the direction of the main hatch—free-floating and untethered—and then on into the gleaming oval tube awaiting them. It was high and wide enough to walk four-abreast, and once inside, they remained weightless for only the first few meters—and then began to feel weight returning, growing with every step. By the time they actually entered the alien spacecraft, full Earth gravity had been replicated.

"Welcome, Dr. Greene—Welcome, Congressman Obst—Welcome, Mr. Brewstier—and Welcome, Arthur Frayles!

Please proceed to the Convening Chamber by way of the conduit directly before you. We will await you there."

The delegates did as invited, inhaling the rich fragrances of rain forest flora as they walked—marveling at the pure beauty of the sparkling structures about them.

Looking up ahead, they recognized the 'art garden' they'd seen in the Junker video. But stepping into the massive central chamber, they found they were wholly unprepared for the exquisite magnificence which lay before them. Openmouthed they drank it in. A full minute was allowed to pass before their hosts appeared, shimmering behind their energy screens. The one in the middle spoke:

"As you can see, we have gone to considerable lengths to impress you."

Frayles managed to reply first. "May I say that it really wasn't necessary. We were already pretty impressed with the telegraph key business."

They actually heard their hosts—laugh. Another spoke:

"You appear surprised we are able to enjoy your humor. In truth, we count it high among your many virtues.

Come forward and join us, that we may discourse together. If the seating is not satisfactory, you may fault Major Junker."

The Americans walked forward and took their seats.

"Could you give us some idea of what agenda we'll be following?" asked the congressman.

"Gladly. You have many questions for us, and we can begin by responding to those which we are permitted to answer. This process will also afford the opportunity for us to learn about one another."

"May we begin then by inquiring as to whether you possess what we refer to as 'gender?'" posed Frayles. "It would be an enormous help for my reports—to know whether to write He said, or she said, or it said."

"Think of us as male, as this approximates truth."

"Why didn't you want to tell Major Junker from which world you hail?" Frayles followed up.

"Such knowledge would undermine the discussions we are about to undertake. If warranted, we will return one day and reveal ourselves at that time."

"Should we elect to return, it will only be once you have demonstrated that our counsel is valued, and allowed to bring about change."

"Are we to infer that you've come to change us somehow?"

"Mr. Frayles, we were well pleased by your selection as the one to report and indeed interpret the Convenings for all mankind. You are at liberty to interpret our words as you deem appropriate."

"How would you have us address you?" asked Brewstier.

"If you so wish, you may designate us: Alpha, Beta, and Gamma, from your left to your right. As you might surmise, these are not our names. You could not pronounce our names, and it would pain us to hear you try."

For the remainder of the first hour the questioning continued. The delegates learned, among other things, that their hosts were presently standing up—that they did not require an atmosphere in which to respirate—that there exist "many, many inhabited worlds"—and that they did not learn Major Junker's name "by electro-magnetic means."

The second hour the Aliens got down to business. Beta spoke first:

"As we have declared, this First Convening will center on the subject of Resourceswith primary attention devoted to your imminent crisis in world population.

There is a point at which the population of a planet can surpass the resource limits of that planet; a point at which its air, its water, its soil, and its plant-life become insufficient to sustain all its inhabitants.

There is an even more critical point at which these same elements, essential to human survival, can become so fouled that requisite purification cannot take place within the mortal lifespan.

TAKE WARNING THEN: Your world approaches both these points—when famine, disease, and warfare will step forward to limit populations.

These Convenings are given to help you design far less drastic ways in the time you have remaining."

WARNINGS

When the four delegates emerged from the oval passageway and floated back aboard Atlantis, the moment was captured live and fed to television broadcasters around the world. Not only were they returning safely from the first session of the Convening, but all were smiling broadly. With no small difficulty, they finally managed to pull themselves into seats and face the camera. Evan Drum of CNN was the interviewer.

"Congratulations one and all—and welcome back! Judging by your smiles, it would appear everything went very well."

"I suspect—we're mostly smiling over being weightless again," Frayles corrected. "It's like losing twenty pounds with every step you take."

Drum chuckled. "Tell us then, did all go well—Anyone?"

"What happened was, we were issued a planetary warning," rumbled Obst. "They informed us, rather bluntly, that we must very soon bring world population and pollution under control—or let war, famine, and disease do it for us!"

There ensued a detailed discussion of what happened aboard the spaceship, followed by their personal impressions.

"They seemed—very genuine to me," said the Director of One Biosphere hesitatingly. "I—I sensed honest concern, especially when they spoke of the 'unchecked destruction of our tropical rain forests.' And, yes—I do think they came here to help us."

"Then, why do you all suppose they're so secretive about where they came from?" Drum followed.

Frayles checked his notes. "When we asked, one of them pointed up at the overhead dome and said, 'Whether we come from there—or from over there, how does knowing profit you?' However—when I asked Gamma how many other worlds in peril they had visited, his answer was most interesting: 'Our focus has always been, and shall remain, on you.'"

"What does that suggest to you?" Drum pressed.

"Well, I'm not at all sure. But it's something I surely plan to question them further on. It could perhaps suggest that Earth is one of their closer planetary neighbors." He looked over at the CEO in grey flannel sweats. "Ollie, describe their reaction—when you asked them what it was that made our world of such particular concern to them?"

Brewstier cleared his throat, searching for proper words. "Well, they made sort of—pleased, humming sounds. And then Alpha complimented me on the question, and said—" He nodded over at the notebook, from which Frayles read:

That is a question worthy of your deepest reflection, as it goes to your true worth.

56

*   *   *

Breakfasts, lunches, and suppers around the globe sat untouched as transfixed millions gaped at their TV screens. Everyone had viewed the Junker tapes, aired repeatedly while the delegates were off attending the first session. And as a result, billions of humans now stood bound together by a common experiential imprint for the first time. An Alien imprint.

At Camp David that evening, the President and his golfing buddy from Ohio could be numbered among the billions. It was barely July, yet the mountain air was cool enough to warrant a fire (which the President stirred).

"You even blew off Sir Edward?" Onager whistled. It invariably amused him when the high and mighty were humbled.

"I've officially cleared my decks until all this is over. No exceptions. Not even for Budget talks. And for once, everybody accepts it, figuring we must be incredibly busy. Truth is we're mostly waiting for events to unfold."

"You see the text of Art's first story yet?"

"No, it's due in shortly."

"Sam—" Onager squinted, "have you considered sneaking some kind of camera on board anyway?"

"Of course. But if they detected it there's no telling what the consequence might be."

"Perhaps. But—what if, officially, we didn't know about it? Suppose for instance—Brewstier went ahead on his own and brought along a hidden camera?"

The President threw a cherry log on the fire and sat back down. "This goes no further, Dave—the Company came up with something that may give us another kind of picture, PISA: passive infrared sensor array, sewn inside Obst's sweater. Whenever he faces an Alien, we ought to be able to record a measurement of whatever body heat it gives off."

"You—certain they won't spot it?"

"We don't expect them to conduct strip-searches."

*   *   *

John VanOrsdell

The second session of the First Convening got off to a robust start. Gamma spoke first:

"Yesterday we identified certain critical problems threatening your planet. Today we will examine values. Tomorrow we will consider solutions. Looking first at population: Is life itself a right or a privilege? The true issue is whether everyone has a right to conceive. Or to adopt. Or is that a privilege which one must earn?"

Congressman Obst stood up. "On our world, questions like these instantly raise the issue of selective reproduction and the horrors of one nation's efforts to create the super race. Are you actually asking us to revisit the question of the selective breeding of human beings?"

Frayles saw that things could easily become heated.

"Maybe soon we'll have no choice," Liz Greene weighed in. "And maybe that's what they want us to face up to: If there's not sufficient room on this planet for an infinite number of people, does that not mandate that the number of births be significantly reduced?"

"Never by selective breeding!" Obst harrumphed.

"But, whenever you resort to contraception—abortion—sterilization—are-you-not-already breeding selectively? Think about it, Michael."

Beta spoke next:

"You are to be commended on addressing the proper questions. In order to answer them, you must first examine your societal values. Do you value the one over the many? Do the rights of one count for more than those of many? Are the natural resources of a planet owned by all its inhabitants? Or by the nation where they are discovered? Or by those who pay to extract them? And what of the air and of the waters? Who bears responsibility for their protection? Is there a collective responsibility for safeguarding your own planet? What is the true meaning of the term 'commonwealth?' Does wealth carry responsibility? Is it the responsibility of the strong to aid the weak? Is it the responsibility of wealthy nations to assist poor nations? Is good health a right or a privilege? Is proper nourishment a right or a privilege? On these issues, must you focus your efforts over the months ahead. Sound policy is founded on sound values. Flawed values beget flawed policy. And flawed policy eventuates in collapse. Know that it is your flawed values, and policies thereof, which have caused us to come just above your world to undertake these direct talks."

*   *   *

An hour into the second session, with no knowledge of what was transacting overhead, the members of CHIMERA turned their attention to Arthur Frayles' report and commentary on the first session. Their group now included presidential press secretary Reene Valek and by special presidential invitation, David Onager.

"I see where Frayles has started calling them 'Mentors'," mumbled Benton. "Not a bad name I suppose."

"Unless they turn out to be lying to us," said Bozorth.

"Or just plain dispensers of lousy advice," cracked Iana.

"Reene how's all this playing out there?" Bryce queried. "Everyone would appear to be taking it all rather calmly."

"I know, it's really amazing. By now people are talking about the Mentors as if they were just another big story that accustomed to media sensationalisms have they become."

"What still bugs me," Bryce groused, "is all this blather about values. They sound more like preachers than teachers! Any you guys consider the possibility they might be some kind of self-ordained Cosmic Crusaders—off to the boonies on a mission of spiritual enlightenment?"

An hour later the four delegates returned to Atlantis, and minutes later CHIMERA was informed that PISA had registered no body heat from the Aliens whatsoever.

There followed a thirty minute risk/benefit analysis of concealing an audio recording device on the person of one of the delegates for the third and final session.

*   *   *

Moonlight crowned each spruce with silver the full length of the mountain ridge. A single thin rope of white smoke snaked up to meet the moon—betraying the secret location beneath the boughs of a private presidential dacha.

Guards posted, staff dismissed for the night, Gregor Gusev sat alone, glaring into a dying fire. The humiliation, both national and personal, over being publicly excluded from the Convenings had summoned up angry acids to sear at his ulcer but he barely took notice. Gregor Gusev was not a man to be humiliated.

He waited until the last of the logs crumpled into hot orange mounds about the andirons, his visage darkening with the fire, its imbrued shadows digging deeper. He downed a final vodka—and reached his decision.

"BEHOLD…"

The final session of the First Convening began with several minutes of pure awe. As soon as the four Americans settled into their seats, Beta extinguished the illumination, gave time for mortal eyes to adjust, and then directed everyone's attention to the dome overhead. In an instant it changed from translucent—to invisible, revealing—

The UNIVERSE

Black beyond belief. Brilliant beyond belief. Beautiful beyond belief.

After granting a generous interval for collective primal experience, Beta raised his arm and pointed up, beginning a lesson he'd later denote as Cosmic Civics:

"Behold—your true Home—A child, born to a small hamlet in your land, becomes by birthright a national citizen. So likewise do you, born to a small world, become by birthright enfranchised Universe Citizens. Know that citizenship also confers responsibility. We manifest at this time to guide you toward assuming responsibility for your own planet. And for one another."

The audio recorder concealed between Greene's breasts failed to actuate—except, as it turned out, when the delegates themselves spoke. Non-mortal voices did not record.

Illumination returned and the dome became translucent once again. Alpha spoke next:

"It is ever wise that unwanted children remain unconceived. No woman should ever be required to bear or rear a child she does not want, nor for whom she could not properly care or provide. No child should be born a ward of the State. Proper parenting can only take place in the home. Parenting will be discussed more particularly at the Second Convening."

"Does this mean you're—suggesting that we resort to sterilization?" Liz Greene challenged.

"Coercion must never be a component in any system of population control. Moreover, full and informed consent is always essential. With that caveat, wise inducements

might well prove effective. Whatever systems nations employ, it is the moral responsibility of wealthier societies to assist poorer ones in direct proportion to their ability to grant such assistance. Congressman Obst: as a national legislator, this teaching is designed for your enlightenment in particular."

GELATT

The Domenico Gelatt rode gently at anchor, her rusting hull caressed by dull swells from the east. The coast of Surinam wilted a few miles to starboard, its torpor begetting its stillness. The scarred and battered freighter formally scrapped the previous year, wallowed high in the water, her holds manifestly empty. A tattered, sun-bleached Liberian pennant hung like a dead tongue from the stern. Not a gull circled. The sole sign of life was a shimmering of blue heat rising from a blackened funnel. The bridge was deserted, no lookout in evidence. Even the radar stood mute.

A sinking sun painted the ship molten orange, her countless rust moles rancid red. Beneath her fantail, the top of a single propeller blade rose in a blazing arc as if ignited by the fires on the waters around it.

Suddenly, a few meters above the exposed prop blade, a slew of sparks exploded from within the hull, showering down to hiss the sea. Acetylene fires began to carve out a four foot square of steel plate— which fell backward into the ship with a dull clank and once again, all was still.

Several minutes passed. Then, a dying sun momentarily flashed off binocular lenses high in the crow's nest, making a slow sweep of land and sea. Somebody was on watch.

LOVEBOAT

While the other delegates met with the press shortly after touching down at Kennedy Space Center, Art Frayles was whisked off to the White House. The First Convening over, the President wanted an immediate first-hand Oval Office briefing. That was the deal they'd struck. Writing and filing stories would come second. The world could wait.

"There have to be more of 'em!" Bryce paced. "I tell you, no society, no government, no matter how advanced, would send a two-thousand foot spacecraft trillions of miles across the galaxy with a crew of three! No way in Hell!" He sat down. "So then—we're left with the question: How many more are they hiding from us? And, my friend—Why?"

"I can only quote what they said on the matter when Obst asked, namely—" He referred to his notes and read: "'The question is without merit.' Let me tell you, being dismissed out-of-hand that way tended to put something of a damper on everyone's curiosity."

"Small wonder. Art, none of this makes any damn sense—Why are they here?—What are they up to?"

Frayles took out his pipe and began packing its bowl with dark, malevolent shreds of burley.

"Is it so unreasonable, so far-fetched, and so inconceivable, that their purpose might actually be to help us? Why is everyone so damned suspicious of altruism? Which might just be what any truly advanced culture is all about!" He struck a match and puffed vigorously. "Could be—we're the truly primitive society here, Mr. President." For the next forty minutes Bryce grilled Frayles, but in the process learned nothing to mitigate his concerns.

"So where does that leave us?" the president sighed. "Thus far, they haven't said anything unreasonable. In fact, what many of us have been saying for years about pollution and over-population. Nor have they said anything potentially destabilizing—or for that matter anything to make us even suspect deception!"

Ergo: everything would proceed as planned. Unless the Aliens got cute.

*   *   *

White House chief of staff Oscar Benton did not suffer pontificating Aliens gladly. There was a government to be run—but their overhead and overbearing visitors had driven everything else off the stage.

Congress had ground to a halt; critical negotiations over the budget had been suspended; Bryce's trip to Mexico was on hold. Even on-going trials stood in recess. And were it not summer vacation, schools would likely be closed as well. Malls, theaters, and golf courses remained largely empty.

Only business itself managed to limp along—as an entire nation, indeed all mankind, fixed its collective gaze upon television. The global calm was astonishing, considering. Only a handful of religious ultra-fundamentalists seemed outraged by the alien presence—claiming variously that they were: Direct Emissaries of Satan—an Abomination unto the Lord—the Evil Creations of Western Imperialism—an Attack on all Islam—even the Dark Heralds of Armageddon. But few were listening. Most were too busy watching the four delegates recount their every moment and impression while aboard the alien spaceship.

Among other things, the world became informed precisely what percentage of the planet's initial endowment of fossil fuels, both discovered and undiscovered, remained. It was told where famines were most likely to first occur—and when food wars would likely commence. And it received one blunt admonition: 'Cease commercial logging in all remaining stands of ancient forests forthwith!'

Primetime specials dominated the first week, with CNN and the major networks broadcasting virtually continuous updates, analysis, and opinion. For the first few days the majors dominated, but by mid-week interest had waned, and many began looking for entertainment on their cable channels.

Michael Obst became a frequent guest on Sunday morning and late evening talk shows, acting learned and sharing his view that, "Our guests above deserve our most attentive respect. They have much to teach us, and thus far have demonstrated a willingness to do so."

Oliver Brewstier was the toast of the business media. His every interview and speech spoke of "a watershed opportunity" and the possibility of being "guided to vast, undiscovered oil reserves and brand new mineral deposits."

Arthur Frayles' published reports had been virtual transcripts of the three sessions, accompanied by scrupulously objective descriptions of everything he had witnessed, with impressions and interpretations saved for sidebar pieces. In print, his every word was crafted with great care, precision, and balance.

This was after all, the biggest story ever reported.

However, when Frayles appeared on late-night TV shows, he'd often allow the hosts to elicit pithy observations, even on his fellow delegates, "some of whom seem to be replacing objectivity with credulity." Even Alpha, Beta, and Gamma were not immune: "The color of glow-worms, only brighter"—and who "at times tended to give sanctimony a bad name." Yet he could also wax sanguine, telling more than one audience that, "Our friends upstairs may constitute First Evidence of a peaceful and purposeful universe!"

But Elizabeth Freelander-Greene was the most hopeful of all, appearing primarily on morning news and daytime talk shows, and holding high the prospect of "a quantum leap in consciousness for all mankind, thanks to the timely intervention and guidance of our celestial visitors."

By mid-week the chief of staff had had enough. With everyone home safely, the Mentors invisible once again, and the Second Convening still two and one-half weeks away, it was time to turn off the TVs and get back to work. Time to resume holding cabinet and staff meetings—reset appointment schedules—get on the phones to the swing votes. In short, get everyone cracking again.

But first Benton had to jump-start the president.

By the second week, world media had swung its attention to the upcoming Convening on planetary Social problems as viewed from above. Not surprisingly, this redirected focus followed a joint press conference held by the next three delegates slated for space: the junior senator from Maine, Neal Simmons(R)—Harvard Professor of Sociology, Avery Eastman—and Jennifer Romero, Judge of the United States Third Circuit Court of Appeals.

*　　*　　*

Ellen Kate Bryce was holding her uncle to a promise. She flew to Boston, was driven by the Secret Service to Frayles' townhouse, and admitted by Alma, his housekeeper of thirty years. She found him upstairs in the living room. "Uncle Artie—!" she greeted, devouring him with a rowdy bear hug. Dragging him out onto the terrace, she chimed, "Am I glad to see you!" and flipped open her laptop.

"Katie, I can't imagine what I can tell you that I haven't already said or written—" he said.

"Just consider it a ploy to spend a little more time with you." She held up a hand. "Before you ask, No—I'm not reconsidering your latest job offer. Maybe someday though."

She referred to her notes. "So: shall we get the business part of this over with—? Let's see then—one subject I haven't heard you speak about is the Aliens' mastery of English. How could that possibly—be possible?"

He look over at his niece and winked.

"Good question, Katie, that I haven't been asked. Did think on it though. Maybe I'll just up and ask 'em at the next Convening. As to their mastery—and that's not an over-statement—someone up there must a been doing a whole bunch of eavesdropping down here! And over a considerable period of time, I should think." She made several notes.

"Were the Mentors ever condescending toward any of you?"

"Hard to say, kiddo, without the benefit of their frame of reference. I do recall wondering though, if we weren't but little piss-ants in their eyes?" He offered her some nuts. "Tell me, how's your Dad bearing up?"

"Oh, you know him: never met an extraterrestrial he didn't dislike."

"Mmmm—especially ones who talk like Liberals."

*   *   *

Senator Onager swiveled alone in a darkened office, his staff long gone. He was a night-thinker. Troubled by the Mentors' plea for what he'd begun calling 'sterilization on the incentive plan,' he struggled for a better solution. But short of forced separation of the sexes, he came up dry.

Soon he found himself wondering whether sterilization could be accomplished chemically, rather than surgically. Then, to his own shame, he caught himself thinking how much cheaper doing it that way would be.

*   *   *

Peter Klein's sole indulgence was a thirty-two foot, twin-engine, fiberglass and teak cabin cruiser, which he kept moored in a marina just below Alexandria. So far this summer he'd been on Sea Particle exactly twice: once to get her cleaned up and ready for the season, and once to replace the Fathometer.

He'd phoned Ellen Kate to invite her for a Saturday sunset cruise. And to his delight, she'd accepted. Predictably, the Secret Service became problematic—their dictum: No sailing without escort.

Following fruitless protest, they agreed to remain tied to the mooring, albeit under continuous scrutiny from shore. Ellen Kate welcomed any physical separation, if only fifty yards of water.

Peter had mastered the art of broiling honey-basted Tybo cheese balls over a hibachi, and treated Ellen Kate to some succulent mouthfuls. They nibbled off each other's skewers, sipped their wine and laughed until well after midnight—their playful compatibility more than apparent at fifty yards.

The following Saturday they climbed aboard Sea Particle once again, this time to broil Cajun-style Chesapeake soft-shell crabs and suck on slices of over-ripe mango. And over the course of the evening, their gustatory lusts yielded to more primitive varieties.

Below decks.

Where nothing was evident at fifty yards.

SOYUZ

Columbia blasted from the launch pad exactly on schedule, roaring off to a new Convening.

One-hundred and thirty-eight minutes later, the Russian shuttlecraft Soyuz ignited, flaming into the skies over Sibirskaya.

Air Force satellites had been watching for such a launch, and within two minutes CHIMERA was informed. An urgent call was then placed to President Gusev from President Bryce. It took less than a minute to connect the two leaders—since the call was not unexpected.

"Gregor, what the Hell are you trying to do, for God's sake?" Bryce fired, foregoing opening amenities.

"Samuel, Samuel—did we not implore you to secure an invitation for us? But you did not. So we are left with no recourse other than to present ourselves at their doorstep. All smiles of course!"

"And—if they choose to simply ignore you?"

There was a pause before Gusev replied. "We are prepared to, as you Americans say, 'crash the party.'"

"HOW?" Bryce was now genuinely alarmed.

"By sending a cosmonaut over to Columbia and entering through your cargo bay. Major Ivanova will then step out of her spacesuit—and proceed to board the alien spaceship via the same passageway your own delegates will be using. Easy enough, wouldn't you agree?"

"Did I hear you say 'her' spacesuit—?"

"Indeed: Ivanova is our most comely cosmonaut! What alien in his right mind could refuse to admit her?" he laughed.

Bryce glanced around the room; every head was shaking now. "Mr. President—it was very rash of you to launch Soyuz without consulting with us. And now you expect us to jeopardize everything that is underway—just so you won't feel left out? Well, that's—totally unacceptable!" He began choosing his words carefully. "Gregor—to have three spacecraft—all maneuvering in close proximity—could pose very grave dangers! Moreover, it could well cause the Mentors to not show up at all. Now hang on—I'm putting you on Hold." He turned to the others and told them what he had decided. There was no dissent and he reopened the line.

"President Gusev: I must inform you that no cosmonaut will be permitted to board our shuttle—and any attempt to do so would—force us to place that cosmonaut's life at hazard. Do you—understand what I am saying, Gregor?"

There was a long silence before Gusev spoke. "In that case, Mr. President—let us all pray that your 'Mentors' will prove more hospitable."

*   *   *

Soyuz rendezvoused smartly with Columbia—taking station a hundred yards off her starboard wing, the opposite side from the shuttle's main hatch. Radio communications were quickly established.

But the alien spacecraft was nowhere to be seen.

"Soyuz, this is Columbia—your presence creates an unacceptable hazard. We direct you to descend to a lower orbit at once."

"Columbia, this is Soyuz. You are hereby advised that we are operating under the direct order of our government—and regret we are unable to comply with your request."

A full minute passed before the American response came.

"Soyuz, be advised that no cosmonaut from your ship will be granted permission to board Columbia. Furthermore, any attempt at an EVA approach would place said cosmonaut's safety at high risk." A pause followed. "We are, however, authorized to inform you that Major Ivanova's request for admittance to the talks will be presented to the Mentors at the first session tomorrow—that is, assuming they show up at all." There was no reply.

With the tenth sunrise the alien craft appeared—taking its customary position and deploying the connecting passageway. Ten minutes later Arthur Frayles, accompanied by the three new delegates, boarded the alien craft and made their way to the central chamber.

"Welcome, Dr. Eastman—Welcome, Senator Simmons—Welcome, Judge Romero—and welcome back, Arthur Frayles! You each honor us with your presence. Before turning to this day's agenda, we would be pleased to respond to any questions you have."

Senator Simmons seized the opportunity. "Well, we thank you for inviting us and for welcoming us. I think I speak for everyone when I say; we're all very excited to be here. As to questions, I believe what we all want to ask you first is—what is your reaction to the Russian spacecraft sitting out there? May I hasten to add, the American government did not invite them—in fact, quite the opposite." It was Gamma who responded.

"Major Ivanova is not welcome unless invited by the American Government. Are there any other questions?"

Jane Romero spoke next. "What struck me in reading the accounts of the first Convening—is the fact that at no time did any of you make mention of Deity. Do you accept the concept of God?" There was a pause before Alpha responded:

"God is more than Concept. Creation is more than happenstance. And Life is more than fortuitous. Existence itself is the consequence of a Plan. And a Plan presupposes a Planner."

Her Honor was used to having responses framed a bit more directly. "Excuse me, but—I don't think you answered my question: Do you, Alpha, believe in God?"

I was not being evasive. You raise a subject which cannot be meaningfully addressed in the short time before us. Should we elect to return, we herewith pledge ourselves to a: Presentment on Deity."

Avery Eastman raised his hand. "May I ask—exactly what will determine whether or not you return?"

"As stated at the First Convening, our return is wholly predicated on your true receptivity to our guidance, as evidenced by your actions. However, if you will not listen, we will not shout."

"What will you do?" Eastman pressed, surprising the others with his confrontational tone. "Will you take some action? Will you intervene in some way? In other words will you force us to pay attention?" After a short pause, Beta responded:

"If our counsel goes unheeded, the Third Convening will be the last time that you see us. More accurately: The last time we make ourselves visible to you."

UNIVERSE VALUES

"God dammit, they've gone and dumped it right in our laps!" Bryce fumed. "Now Gusev's sure to blame me personally if we say no. Jack— Iana—Mac—help me on this."

With the first session of the Second Convening concluded, the delegates faced CNN the moment they floated back aboard Columbia. The very first question concerned Soyuz.

While in the Situation Room far below, Bryce's first concern was also what to do about the Russians.

"You said No once," Ravenscroft warned. "To change your mind now would make you appear to cave to Russian pressure. Not the best choice, from a domestic political standpoint."

"The one thing you simply cannot do is deal in empty threats," remonstrated Bozorth. "What, for instance, would be your response should they send this Ivanova on a spacewalk over to the shuttle, having been denied permission to board? Shoo her away with the crane? Send out an astronaut to do battle? Or simply ignore her, and leave her there, pounding her little fists on the hatch, until her oxygen runs out? All Live, mind you, before a worldwide television audience."

"Shit," said the president.

When the Russian leader phoned shortly thereafter, he was informed by a somber American president that, "Any additional national presence in orbit at this time would be inherently disruptive and de-stabilizing—and set an unacceptable precedent, whereby other nations might demand inclusion."

*   *   *

The following morning, an hour before the scheduled start of the second session, Captain Jamian ordered the cargo bay doors closed.

Gusev was enraged. But Major Ivanova remained on Soyuz.

And the cargo bay doors were reopened.

*   *   *

Beta was concluding his Introduction on Societal Values:

"In truth, only a freely elected representative government, enacting and abiding by laws reflecting the desires of an enfranchised majority, can be considered legitimate and adjudged sovereign. A national charter, or constitution, reflects the highest wisdoms of its framers, its worth being measured by its durability and duration—with amendment by super majority being the only valid means of maintaining its applicability over time. Most social problems take origin in flawed personal and social values—and as such do not readily submit to legislative remedy. There is not one social problem afflicting you—poverty, crime, violence, drug use, the spread of disease, family disintegration, racism, hunger, homelessness, illiteracy, mental illness, neglect of the elderly—not one, which is not rooted in your flawed values."

Beta fell silent, allowing his words to find purchase in the minds of all present. He then noticed Jane Romero was smelling the air.

"Judge Romero: You may wish to sample the water as well. And, as you take refreshment you might reflect on why we selected America as our point of action with the mortal races."

"Perhaps," replied Frayles, "because we're able to meet you in orbit—with the Russians as a poor alternative."

"I can think of another reason," offered Senator Simmons: "English is the world's second tongue."

"I—suspect it goes rather deeper than that, Senator," intoned Avery Eastman. "The government ideal which Beta just described is exactly what we have in the United States. And was in all probability requisite for our selection." He took a sip of water—and then a long drink.

"Most astute of you all. Beyond that which you have so correctly deduced, we were particularly influenced by your national ideals and character—your national morality—your leadership among the nations of the earth—your vast wealth, economic power, and global influence. And lastly, your pre-eminence in global communications and entertainment. If true change is to be wrought—if societal evolution is to be enhanced—if your world is to be redeemed—the United States of America must both light the path and lead the way!"

Arthur Frayles got the feeling celestial smoke was being blown up his earthly behind, and changed the subject. "So tell us: what do you fellas think about the decision to exclude the Russians from these talks?" Gamma replied:

"It pleases us. Russia is so beset with social and economic problems that it must be a receiver, not a giver, of assistance. There is little that Major Ivanova could have added—or that Russia could contribute. The inclusion which they sought is motivated more by national hubris than by a genuine desire to contribute to these undertakings."

*   *   *

In St. Paul, Governor Ordahl had stayed up late to catch the 'Returning Interviews,' as they were now called. As the putative frontrunner for the Democratic nomination the following year, Bill Ordahl closely tracked Bryce's every statement and action regarding the Mentors. A single major misstep and the presidency could be his! But thus far he could not fault his opponent.

Not so Gordon Fenstermacher, portly publisher of The Conservative Cleave—and the only Republican likely to challenge Bryce in the primaries. He too was watching.

"Talk about adding insult to injury!" he whooped. "First, Bryce goes and slams the cargo bay doors in Gusev's face then the Aliens go and accuse Russia of 'hubris'! This is gonna infuriate Gusev!" His wife retreated to the bathroom, but he only bellowed louder. "Sam Bryce and his glowworm pals are screwing up royally—and I say it's time to get rid of his alien-kissing ass once and for all!"

*   *   *

The third and final session of the Second Convening led off with another awe-inspiring unveiling of the firmament.

After illumination returned, Alpha began:

"At yesterday's session we spoke of the dichotomy which is America: Your great idealism—versus your rampant selfishness. Today we shall consider the social and personal implications of putting others ahead of self—rank heresy to most people living in a competition-driven society. To illustrate— in the name of individual rights, you grant far too many citizens the privilege of 'bearing arms.' Ask yourself—do you feel safer residing in armed society? Truly—if no person placed his own needs above those of others, you would require neither arms nor fences nor locks to assure protection of self and property. If however you are successful in overcoming that which threatens your planet—one day your world will indeed evolve to a high state of fraternal harmony and social comity! In all the Universe, few worlds exhibit the paradox of high technological achievement in the face of gross social retardation. Consider your very language: it contains words for acts unknown on worlds where civilization has attained the heights of social justice: Oppress—Exploit—Deceive— Swindle—Intimidate—Humiliate—Ridicule—Torment—Threaten—Bully— Persecute—Abuse—Molest—Assault—Destroy—Terrorize—Rape—Maim— Torture—Slay—Slaughter—You have thousands of odious words and concepts. Your vocabulary indicts you!"

"Then you must hold the human race in very low regard—" Avery Eastman muttered. Beta replied:

"That is not so. We admire much of your art, music, literature, and theater. You have deciphered the genetic code—conquered many diseases—extended life itself. You struggle to create a better world, and you sacrifice for your children. As Americans, you linguistically unite the world. You trade, travel, publish, entertain, and converse globally. Moreover, you strive mightily to foster peace. No people, no nation, is more charitable or more generous. So there is indeed much to admire.

Conversely, as individuals, too many of you are egocentric, greedy, cruel, lustful, hedonistic, uncaring, mean-spirited, vengeful, abusive, and violent. You injure your precious brains with alcohol—your bodies with drugs—your air and water with chemicals—your children with bias. You lie—you cheat—you steal—you break your word. But worst of all: You fail your children: You fail to appreciate them—to listen to them—to cherish them. You fail to endow them with sound values—to respect others—to show compassion, to cherish the earth and all that lives upon it—to regard

72

*all human beings as brothers and sisters. You fail them in all this because you fail
them by example.*
ATTEND CLOSELY: *No society—no person can or will change unless and
until their values change."*

*   *   *

Ever since Ellen Kate and Peter had become lovers, whenever they
found themselves attending the same meeting or White House function
each felt a certain unfamiliar awkwardness.

Ellen knew her father approved of their relationship, but wondered
whether he'd feel the same way had he known that it had already
become sexual, largely at her instigation. He knew her to be headstrong
and determined, but a lusty, calculating seductress? Never.

For his part, Peter took comfortable refuge by being Doctor Klein,
an unlikely banger of presidential daughters. But in contrast to Ellen
Kate, he was not at all sure Daddy didn't suspect they'd become
intimate. What he wondered was whether Bryce also figured he and Iana
had bumped ugly. All Peter knew was that his conduct had better be
impeccable from here on in, especially with the Secret Service taking
notes.

BEYOND BOOBERY

There was high consternation in the Oval Office. The Second
Convening was now over; the Mentors had ended it by challenging
mankind itself. While most had anticipated guidance toward solving
specific social problems, people had been told instead that solutions
would not be "bestowed freely from above"—rather that, "Mortals must
look inward, to their own personal values, for salvation."

Politically, Bryce couldn't decide whether he should express
'disappointment' over the Mentors' lecturing us on morality, which he
took as bordering on condescension, or to remain publicly 'supportive'
and express continuing hopes for the final Convening. He didn't like the
tack the Mentors had taken at the last session and was apprehensive

73

over what they might 'advise' at the Third Convening. His options were essentially reduced to two: send up a third delegation—or withdraw from further participation.

Throughout his career Sam Bryce had made it a practice to choose action over inaction, and so far it had served him well. But the more he thought about the Aliens, the wiser withdrawal seemed. Yet, he couldn't stomach tucking his tail between his legs and backing away. He began to realize there was simply no positive spin they could put on withdrawal, and that politically, he really had no choice but to press ahead.

With this realization, some of his survival synapses began firing, warning him that There Be Dragons overhead. Exactly as his mother had warned.

Gordon Fenstermacher's editorial blast only reinforced Bryce's own deepest doubts, calling him "credulous beyond boobery"—accusing him of "toadying up to the aliens" and "behaving like an aborigine before sparkly beads"—and "shamefully refusing to share the spotlight with any other nation." And the most galling epithet: "Space Puppet."

Opportunistic prick—Bryce muttered, buzzing for his National Security Adviser to join him.

"Just finished reading Frayles' accounts—" Iana panted, presumptuously heaving herself onto the crescent love-seat by the fireplace. Taking no offense, Bryce got up and took a seat opposite her. (Such legs could ameliorate any crisis.) "First thing that jumped out at me," she began, "was a change in Frayles' tone. He seems more— respectful, even a tad reverential this time around. Can that be good?"

"He says he's persuaded that the Mentors came to instruct us, as Universe Citizens, on our planetary responsibilities. And help us 'realize our planetary potential.'"

"Sounds like somebody's been breathing too much rarefied air," she sniffed.

"Let's face it: the fallout from this whole damn Mentor business is likely to determine whether or not I even get a second term! It's insane that the events of a few weeks could totally eclipse the efforts and achievements of the past four years! Now, all of a sudden, we discover Bill Ordahl isn't the one we have to worry about next year, but the God damn glow-worms! So, we'd better make damn sure the fallout blows the way we want it to." He plucked a gumdrop from a dish on the table and flipped it in her direction; she lurched and caught it in her mouth.

"Don't do that again," she chewed.

"Iana—I was going to wait a bit longer before broaching the subject, but in light of what we've just been talking about—I'd like you to think about taking over as my deputy campaign manager next year." He watched for her reaction, knowing he'd just tossed a major goodie on the table.

Several seconds passed. "In other words—give up being National Security Adviser—?" she squinted suspiciously.

"Heavens no—you'd wear both hats. You've got a capable deputy—let him run things for you here."

Iana knew this would take some thought. She looked over at the President and wondered if any part of his motivation was testes-driven. Should she agree, it meant they'd be spending a lot of time together on the campaign trail. As a mini-test, she began absently scratching a pretended itch under her thigh. She kept it up for ten seconds; his eyes never wavered from her fingers.

The phone buzzed; it was Dave Onager. Bryce took the call and pleasantries were exchanged.

"Well, Mr. President—just calling to find out whether you've picked the final three delegates?"

"Yep, I'll announce 'em tomorrow afternoon. Why?"

"I was hoping you might have selected your own chief economic adviser."

Bryce grinned. "You're another one o' them Smarter-Than You-Look types."

He listened to Onager chuckle and winked at Iana. "I'm pleased my choice will meet with your approval. Truth is, I asked Caroline weeks ago—she agreed on the spot. That's the part that worries me. I'm thinking all she really wants to do is visit The Great Planetarium in the Sky!"

"I was afraid maybe this time around you'd feel compelled to pick a Democrat from the Hill, your previous choices being Republicans—what with Space being a bipartisan district."

"No, I felt no such compulsion. My other choices are: Sid Clothier, chairman of the New York Fed, and Bert Jorgenson, chairman of IONTEC. But hey, maybe Caroline's a D."

"Outstanding choices," said Onager. "But if Caroline Whitehead is a Dem, I'm a closet terrorist."

"I see Lisa's flashing me. Dave, we'll talk again." He rang off, listened to his secretary a few moments, and turned to Iana "The Bishop's here. I promised him a one-on-one." She nodded, got up, and left, smiling at Bishop Archambault as they passed at the door. Bryce walked over, hand extended. "Good to see you, Charles! Let's sit over here, shall we? Can I get you some coffee?"

"No thank you, but I do appreciate you taking the time to see me, Mr. President. I can imagine how busy you must be," he smiled. "I promise not to stay long."

"Take whatever time you need. And call me Sam—we've been friends far too long for titles."

"Okay—Sam. Now, I assume you realize I'm not here on my own initiative—" Bryce nodded. "As you might surmise, the Church is not at all happy about certain aspects of the matters taking place overhead. All this Alien talk of morals and ethics—and us taking responsibility for one another—could simply be a cunning ruse for getting us to drop our guard. If their purposes are hostile, how better to dupe us, than to come cloaked in the raiment of morality?" He paused to dab his upper lip with a handkerchief. "In all candor—priests across the country are being asked whether the Aliens could be actual 'Emissaries of God'! There is grave confusion and misconception out there, make no mistake. Yet the Church harbors no illusions: These Aliens have nothing whatever to do with the Lord. Would His emissaries require a—spaceship for transportation? Indeed, if there was anything 'spiritual' afoot here, I'd suggest precisely the opposite: Satan is surely clever enough to know how to capture the entire world's attention!"

"Charles, I truly appreciate your concern, but you're not here to drag this office into any kind of theological debate, I certainly hope."

"No, of course not. Yet you might find an opportunity to set all these spiritual rumors to rest by affirming that the Alien spaceship is constructed of real physical matter that the hard dockings were real and physical—that all the materials inside the spaceship are real. A statement by you, as President, would be enough to dispel all notions of some spiritual, non-material intervention."

Bryce furrowed his brows and considered it. "I don't suppose that would do any real harm," he finally allowed.

*   *   *

Following the collapse of the Soviet Union, the Russian defense industry had struggled to remain viable. Military budgets had been slashed; factory orders drastically cut; troops left unpaid and unfed; unfueled fighters and bombers sat idle; warships rusted at their piers; tanks rarely conducted field exercises; unused munitions piled high—and Loss by Inventory accumulation remained one of the last sure ways to make money.

Naval commanders fought over every drop of available fuel, and refused to burn any which wasn't absolutely necessary. Accordingly, newly manufactured torpedoes were stockpiled at their assembly plants, rather than burning precious gasoline to deliver to distant submarine bases only to pile them up once again, this time in naval warehouses.

Such a policy left the director of the Zuyevka Naval Munitions Works with a problem: a warehouse bulging with unpicked up, unpaid-for torpedoes. And he had another problem, a demanding wife and five spoiled brats.

So when the offer came—one-hundred and ninety thousand dollars, U.S., in cash, for Four Mark 11-E, conventional warhead torpedoes still in their crates—he dismissed any thought of reporting the bribe. Frankly, he saw it as a Godsend.

But he'd have to move quickly: the deal demanded delivery in twenty-two days.

*   *   *

"Okay," Iana said quietly into the phone. "If you really want me to wear two hats, I guess I'm ready to become your two-headed monster."

ZUYEVKA

Her mother called him Woody; to close friends he was still Sam; the Secret Service designated him Titanium; to everyone else he was Mr. President—except Ellen Kate, for whom he would always be her Pappy.

She'd seen the changes come over him since the arrival of the Aliens, and she was boggled by the global impact these three creatures had had. It was three versus six billion—with the three calling the shots. Small wonder Pappy was so rattled. No one had any hard answers, and this pleased him not. Even Titty-Tit-Tits and her creative Tour de Force, Peter the Great, were coming up dry.

"What really stumps me," Bryce told his daughter, "is that they've mastered English to the point of outright eloquence—it, mind you, being one of our most complex and idiosyncratic tongues."

He felt blessed by having Ellen as a totally secure sounding board, one he could safely bounce truly dreadful, even dopey ideas off.

"Do you suppose they could have learned English simply by watching our TV on the long, dull voyage here?" Ellen wondered out loud. Just then, a fleeting shard of something wholly new flitted across her cortex—and she heard herself asking her father, "What if they learned English the same way we did—by being born here—?" It took a few moments to sink in. Then he called Iana to immediately convene CHIMERA to consider his daughter's daring hypothesis.

In exploring her premise, corollary concepts quickly surfaced which required evaluation. One: The Aliens are Spirit Being residents of Earth, the same as Human Beings. Two: Their number could exceed that of humans. Three: If evolutionary, they could be way beyond humans. Four: They can reveal themselves at will. Five: They can manipulate material reality, witness their spaceship.

Each new possibility only gave rise to countless more—leaving the members of CHIMERA frustrated and forced to admit that they needed answers only the Aliens could provide.

Ellen Kate listened quietly as the members of CHIMERA kicked around the mind-bending possibility that the Aliens just might not be Aliens at all—but rather life-long residents of planet Earth. Peter said it was the one explanation which fit all the pieces, and as such should be seriously considered, no matter how far fetched.

"Why not simply have Art Frayles put the question to them at the next Convening?" Ellen Kate challenged, cutting through all the colorary concepts.

"Good question." Said POTUS. And just that quickly, the First Daughter officially became a core member of CHIMERA.

*   *   *

Now that she and Peter had valid reason to meet in private, his office neatly served that purpose. Not everyone on the presidential task force was pleased by her sudden inclusion, but they wisely kept their reservations to themselves.

"Whatever made you come up with such a far-out theory?" Peter asked.

"I have no idea; it just suddenly popped into my head."

"Some head."

"If true, would that necessarily mean spirits—procreate?"

"You mean, do they Get It On?"

"I'm not sure I know what I mean. For instance, as our population grows, would the spirit population have to keep pace?"

"Good question."

'An excellent question' she thought she heard in her mind.

"You—have a strange expression on your face."

"I happen to have a strange face," she said, shrugging it off, while wondering whether some Mentor might be trying to mess with her head.

*   *   *

"I wanna make love by moonlight—right in the middle of the Rose Garden!" Ellen Kate grinned.

"In that case, I suggest you find yourself a partner with a more low-profile butt," Peter rejoined.

He was behind the wheel of her Miata, a charcoal sedan trailing behind like a pull-toy. They were headed for the marina, the only place they'd found where they could count on a little privacy. And to go even there required advance notification of and approval by the Secret Service.

What neither realized nor suspected was that her guardians closely examined Sea Particle prior to every visit—diving under to inspect her hull and the river bottom, and carefully searching the boat for explosives, listening devices, or other threats to security. Today, as usual, she was clean.

Ellen Kate and Peter arrived, rowed out, and climbed on board. Both were hungry and immediately fell to preparing the hibachi. Tonight's experimental fare would be crayfish, lightly bonded with walnut butter and dipped in honey glaze. Each harbored silent misgivings.

"You think the glaze'll drip into the fire?" Peter wondered. "Should I maybe roll 'em in breadcrumbs first?"

"Wouldn't the crumbs catch fire?"

"Not if you use treated breadcrumbs—duh!" he clowned.

"How 'bout just rolling 'em around in garlic powder?"

He snapped his fingers and went to the galley, emerging moments later with a box of Grape Nuts.

It turned out better than either had expected, and Ellen Kate popped a champagne cork in celebration.

"So, tell me—whadda you guys figure Alpha, Beta, and Gamma will do for their Grand Finale?"

He sipped twice before answering. "Classified."

"Classification is for Information, not Personal Opinion. Just give me your personal opinion," she pressed.

He reflected for a few moments and shrugged. "I imagine they'll do more of the same—only focus on economics."

He could see she was unsure what he meant. "This time around—sharing the Wealth would be my guess."

She slid closer and snuggled against him. He felt the breeze pick up and wrapped her shoulders with his arm. She looked up and kissed his chin.

"Peter—has CHIMERA looked at all the really far-out possibilities as well? Like—suppose the Aliens are actually planning to annex us—and they just want us to get the place cleaned up for them first!"

He laughed and hugged her tighter.

Meanwhile, on a cruiser moored nearby, her guardians passed the time by testing a new directional microphone and were experiencing excellent results.

"Gothier's the one tasked to come up with the far-out scenarios. His Company training, no doubt."

"And he thinks—" she prodded.

He hesitated, and then grunted. "Oh, Henry's just carrying around a lot of old Cold War baggage, that's all."

"Then—he suspects the Russians are going to try something!" she shot back.

"I suppose he wouldn't put it past 'em."

*   *   *

Having been informed that Iana Ravenscroft would soon be sporting two hats, the First lady was less than pleased. She sensed her husband's carnal interest in his National Security Adviser, and it pissed her off. She wasn't jealous; she was offended. To Abby, Ravenscroft was distinctly unattractive—all tits and overbite and sharp edges. Her face, pretty by some standards, she supposed, was hard and tense with eyes that never looked directly into hers. A black cat slinking about came to mind.

To think of such a creature as an actual rival was beyond insult—it was humiliating.

MENTORS

"Welcome, Mrs. Whitehead. Welcome, Dr. Jorgenson. Welcome, Mr. Clothier. And Welcome back, Arthur Frayles! You all do us honor by your presence."

Beta greeted the final delegation to the opening session of the Third Convening.

"It has been our custom to begin each new Convening by responding to questions. Our time together being limited, we wish to begin today with a Presentment of Beauty. BEHOLD":

The illumination faded—the dome overhead 'disappeared', revealing once again: the UNIVERSE!

Suddenly the very air surged with a kinetic symphony of earthly fragrances and aromas. Then, as mortal eyes gazed up at the grandeur of the celestial vault—and mortal nostrils became suffused with the beloved smells of their own home planet—the connection was made, instantly bridging all intervening distance.

The humans lay utterly still, awash in ambient ecstasy. Then, a new sensory enrapturement took rise as The MUSIC of the SPHERES permeated the chamber: a trillion carillons pealing forth, Cascades of choirs heralding joy; the chords of the cosmos entwined in anthem; the harmonic conjoining of the spheres; the supernal harmony of all Creation.

For the next twenty-one minutes the Presentment unfolded, awakening in each human a profound sense of personal place and worth, of purpose and universe value—and of the certainty of survival itself. Each would later look back on these twenty-one minutes as a seminal, transforming spiritual experience.

*   *   *

Gamma began the second hour with startling pronouncements:

"A primary responsibility of any national government is prevention of the disproportionate accumulation of personal wealth. In free-market, free-enterprise, non-authoritarian economies functioning under a democratic form of government, this is especially important.

While such economic systems do indeed reward the great mid-class majority, they break down at the extremes—bestowing vast wealth at one—and abject poverty at the other."

Gamma paused before continuing. He seemed somehow to be radiating a more intense energy field.

"Any nation which is home to both beggars and billionaires cries out for economic justice. When held within equitable limits, differences in personal wealth are normal and healthy in an advanced society. But wherever great wealth finds its way into the purses of the relative few while the needs of many go unmet, social harmony and progress stand at peril!"

A billionaire himself, this was hardly what the president of IONTEC wanted to hear. He was aghast. "Are you calling for— redistribution of wealth?"

"Until your human and social values evolve, nothing can or will change. You are the architects of your own evolution—both as individuals and as a society.

All you need do is think—and you will evolve."

*   *   *

"God dammit, what're they trying to do—set off class warfare down here?" The President was as angry as anyone could remember seeing him. The members of CHIMERA were viewing the return of the delegates from the first session, and Bryce was livid. "Now the Mentors

82

are becoming a threat to our social stability—and thereby to national security!"

"Perhaps not all that destabilizing—" Vice President MacDougal uncharacteristically spoke up. "According to the polls, sixty-two percent now dismiss the Aliens as posing no great threat—with forty-four percent tending to dismiss their advice as well. All I'm suggesting is we shouldn't overreact."

"Stuart," Bryce shot back, "all it takes is one ill-chosen adjective from the lips of the Fed chairman to trigger a three-hundred point selloff on Wall Street. What the Mentors are saying could result in a one-thousand point plunge! A trillion dollars would instantly—vanish! And that's something investors would not soon forget—or forgive." He kneaded his scalp. "I shouldn't have to remind you, ten million unhappy stockholders equals ten million unhappy voters."

Iana turned to Peter. "What are our options?"

"One: Continue with the delegates—Two: Cease participation altogether—or Three: Continue to attend, but on a modified basis. For instance, you could skip tomorrow's session to demonstrate your displeasure—and then send the delegates back to deliver a message of your own."

"Wait—let's focus on that one," Bryce interrupted. "What message?"

"Go Home!" Bozorth snapped, evoking chuckles all around. Except for Peter Klein, who was afraid they might just leave.

COBALT TOAD

Arthur Frayles was the sole delegate in attendance for the second session the following morning. He walked to the Convening Chamber and took a seat. Beta alone appeared. Greetings were exchanged, and Frayles spoke first. "As I previously stated, I'm also here as the personal representative of President Bryce, and it is in this capacity that I attend today. As you can see, I've brought along an audio recorder in hopes I can speak without the burden of having to take written notes. Might I have your permission?"

John VanOrsdell

"Indeed you may. We are quite saddened by your President's decision to curtail participation. But as we promised: If you do not hear us—we will not shout.
Today will mark the final session and conclusion of these Convenings.
Arthur Frayles: You have served your world well and faithfully. Your accounts and interpretations have been meritorious, and we stand in your debt. You may tell President Bryce that he, too, has been well served and stands in your debt. And now—before imparting our final words of guidance to the mortal races—Extraordinary Authorization has been granted for a single, direct 'Intervention'."

Beta pointed to a transparent container rising slowly from an area directly in front of Frayles: Inside squatted a glistening, cobalt-colored toad with large alizarin eyes.

G. Arthur Frayles and the toad stared at each other—and blinked several times.

"Shortly before your shuttle's arrival we undertook a descent to a rain forest in Paraguay to extract this specimen for delivery to your scientists: It holds the key to overcoming one of your most egregious biological defects. BUT BEWARE: There remain less than two-hundred such creatures on your world—all within a single habitat—who face early extinction at the hands of commercial loggers."

"In that case, I'd be more than pleased to deliver this little guy to our scientists." He turned back to face Beta. "Lest I forget—let me say what President Bryce asked me to convey, namely—"He read from his handwritten notes: "He is most gratified over your 'evident concerns for our planet'—and he 'sincerely appreciates your efforts to guide us in dealing with our problems'—and 'The American Government shares your concern over the growing disparity between the earth's natural resources and human population, and his administration intends to address the problem.'"

"How very reassuring."

Wondering whether he'd just heard an example of space sarcasm, Frayles continued, "However—President Bryce and his advisers are troubled that, 'In your well-intentioned efforts to help us deal with our problems, you have unwittingly sown the seeds of social unrest by espousing economic philosophies inimical to the American system.' The President therefore requests 'in the firmest terms possible,' that you agree to refrain from making 'further egalitarian pronouncements' before he'll allow 'participation in these gatherings to continue.' "He looked up at Beta, unable to suppress an embarrassed smile.

"With your president's admonitions firmly in mind, let us 'continue':

The treasures of the earth are the inheritance of all mankind—and the responsibility of their temporary owner-conservators.

The wealth of the earth is intended to sustain all of its inhabitants, generation following upon generation. Your remaining natural resources are all you will ever have—and as such, must be conserved to last for at least another million generations.

Wealth can be shared through economic aid and assistance from the richly endowed nations to those lesser endowed. Instead of ever seeking ways to reduce what you term 'foreign aid,' your political leaders would be better advised to increase assistance to those nations in greatest need. Compassion and social assistance are the hall-mark of every highly evolved civilization."

"What you're calling for would sound to an awful lot of people like out-and-out Marxism: 'From each according to his ability; to each according to his needs.' A discredited economic philosophy, I might add."

"As well as an unrealizable ideal on worlds such as yours. Where individuals and societies are motivated principally by the material, culture will languish and social evolution will stagnate.

To measure everything in terms of material worth, including persons themselves, grants primacy to the superficial—fails to value that which has eternal value—and betrays a low order of social evolution.

Return now to your President bearing the following counsel: Retire your national indebtedness. To carry it forward year after year gains the people nothing—while costing them dearly in taxes for the payment of interest. Public debt always yields a regressive transfer of wealth: From the general taxpayer into the hands of those of sufficient means to be able to loan money to the government.

A few suggestions: Enact an annual national property tax on excessive personal wealth;

Prevent the movement of wealth beyond taxation;

Tax real asset appreciation using progressive rates.

Taken in aggregate you should agree they afford sufficient political grounds for President Bryce to summarily withdraw from these proceedings."

"I'll say," chuckled Frayles, "this will sure put a twist in Republican britches!" He thought he heard Beta chuckle too.

'My friend, I will truly miss our congress.

In parting, can you assure us there will be no abridgment of this day's discourse?"

"Not to worry, no one would dare censor us at this point. There'll be all manner of criticism resulting from early termination of the Convenings. It therefore becomes doubly imperative that I report in full on all that's transpired. And, so I shall. On this you have my word." Beta nodded.

"People of the Earth: Hear now this, our Terminal Warning—that which brought us here at this most critical juncture:

BEWARE THE METASTIZATION OF FISSILE MATERIALS, TECHNOLOGY, AND WEAPONRY FROM WITHIN THE ERSTWHILE SOVIET EMPIRE!

Following the last Great War, the American victor wisely employed its wealth to enable the vanquished to recover and rebuild. Yet following the Soviet collapse you exhibited little such wisdom. As a direct consequence you now stand in mortal peril:

All that was stolen or sold must be recovered and kept from the arsenals of nations and madmen.

VERILY I SAY: The United States alone has the might and the resources to avert planetary social, political, and ecological disaster.

As in everything, we have endeavored to teach you: Salvation lies in serving the needs of others.

As we take our leave, know that we will ever be watching and know that it is our cherished hope to be able soon to return.

Arthur Frayles: We rest secure in your hands."

With those words the Epochal Convenings above Planet Earth came to an abrupt end.

A somber and subdued journalist returned to the shuttle—tenderly bearing a cobalt toad in its alien container.

When Discovery emerged from the shadow of the earth at the next dawn, its blindingly beautiful companion had vanished.

PACO GORDO

Jane Blaney met the man she would marry in the middle of a mud puddle at a three day psychedelic music festival. It was love at first glop. She was eighteen—and he was twice that. Nevertheless, she was thrilled to become Mrs. David Onager.

Their son, Justin, was born a month after the wedding and duly cherished. And seventeen years later, blissfully goalless. Penny, born two years after her brother, was equally loved and cherished—and at fifteen: the very promise of trouble.

Justin wasn't in the least impressed at having a national figure for a father. He dismissed politics with utter indifference, and was thinking vaguely about going to USC to maybe study film-making. He'd never been a problem-child. No booze, no speeding tickets, no druggie friends. Simply, no ambition. He did however have one passion: getting into places he had no business being—via the Internet.

Conversely, Penny thought having a national figure for a father was a hoot, and dressed accordingly. She hung with the colorful, the neo, and the rebellious, smoked pot, and talked about sex by cell phone. Her parents had wanted to send her off to a private girls school, but she would have none of it. All her best friends were boys.

For Penny Onager, school was a purely social activity, her academic apathy well quantified in report cards. Most vexing, her I.Q. was one-hundred and thirty seven—'high' enough, it turned out, to get caught under the gym stands smoking a joint. Summoned to his daughter's school, the Senator and his post-hippy wife had been appropriately shocked, but mindful they themselves had met in the mud, well stoned. [Jane loved telling people—careful to omit the controlled substance part—how she and David had met and her shock at discovering that the "cool dude under all the mud" was in fact a state representative!]

"Daddy, I think it's time we had a serious automotive discussion—" Penny began, drowning a stack of blueberry pancakes in syrup. "I'll have my license in less than two months—so it's not too early to begin making plans."

Her father sipped his coffee. "What kind of plans?"

"Oh—maybe a low-mileage MR-2, red, with a black interior, a kickin' sound system—"

"What's the matter with your bike? It's red."

"David—" Jane protested softly.

"I—just think I'd be a whole lot safer doing my own driving than riding as a passenger with some guy who might have had one too many beers, you know?" she said, taking her best shot.

"Nice try, Sweetheart. And don't forget 'But jeez, all the other kids have cars!' Frankly, the longer we can keep you out of any automobile, the safer you'll be," her father intoned with a solemnity well-honed on the Senate floor.

"Get her something old—large—an' really, really slow," Justin suggested. "Like a nice big-assed Packard."

"Justin, Butt Out!" Penny snapped. "Just 'cause you drive a big-assed Roadmaster!"

"You should bear in mind, Penny Bright," her mother joined in, "you'll need our written permission to even apply for a learner's permit. And—I'm sitting here thinkin' just maybe—perhaps it's just a tad premature to be raising the subject of having your own car—ya know?"

"Would you—consider a red rickshaw if it had black leather seats?" her father asked, a tiny twinkle in his eye which Penny caught in a flash.

*   *   *

Back when such things were still affordable, the Bryces had bought a three and one-half acre island in the Bahamas. This being just after the birth of Ellen Kate, they promptly christened it Katie Cay. And over the years the tiny island had become their one true family sanctuary, treasured by all. But when the Bryce family became the First Family, all manner of communications and security systems became instant additions. A dreadful price to pay, but they were given little choice.

Since childhood, Katie had always been permitted to bring along one friend, and now such invitations were most prized.

In the wake of the truncated Convenings, Katie Cay became the family's sanctuary once again. Except this time, the 'friend' Ellen Kate invited along was Peter Klein.

"I call it: 'Haute Ball Cuisine'—!" Peter crowed, busy concocting his latest 'cremation sensation' over a fire on the beach. "Don't know why we never thought before to use a lime-ginger glaze on barracuda balls."

"How about for psychological reasons?" Ellen Kate offered.

"Now, there's what I'm looking for in a campaign manager: a barracuda with balls!" Bryce said, warily eyeing a skewer with chunks of melon and pineapple flanking limed-up balls of fish. "How's the corn-on-the-cob coming, Katie?"

"Lookin' good," she assured. "Yo, Peter—what if, what if it really sucks?"

"On the other hand, what if it's Simply Succulent! No great discovery ever comes about without some element of risk," he elucidated, hanging four skewers in the flames. "Listen, all you guys are placing at risk are your palates—while for me, this constitutes a bold career move."

"You got that right," Bryce growled.

The four watched the flames work their magic—tiny incendiary spitlettes popping up and flaring off. When the moment arrived to taste 'Cuda Balls Supreme,' each took a small bite and chewed tentatively. Stumped, no one could decide whether they loved or hated it, so Jane re-christened the dish 'Ambivalence Supreme.' Yet President Bryce abhorred indecision above all else, and in the end decreed (with full concurrence) that these particular delights not be whipped up ever again.

Following an after-dinner brandy, it suddenly began to pour. Everyone grabbed their glasses and ran inside. Ellen Kate waited until they were settled, then tapped her snifter with a knife.

"I—have a small announcement." She looked at Peter. "Hey, pal— you and I are gonna be making grandparents out of POTUS 'n FLOTUS." A clap of silence filled the room. She went over and sat beside Peter, taking his hand in hers. "My love—I adore you as a friend—and yes, as a lover. But you and I are not in love, as we both know, so—marriage isn't even on the screen. But I do intend to have our baby—and everyone's just going to have to accept that." She looked squarely at her father. "Even in an election year."

*   *   *

The fallout from the aborted final Convening had not been helpful to the President. Many said he'd been too proud—too short-sighted— too thin-skinned—too demanding—too imperious. In the weeks following the collapsed Convenings, accompanied by intense media focus and debate, polls showed that most voters believed the Mentors had simply found Man to be wanting and taken their leave—never to be seen again. Surprisingly, to the profound disappointment of many.

Not one to miss an opportunity, Gordon Fenstermacher accused the President of "Alien Aiding and Abetting," and anointed him "The Prince of Pawns." He kept up a relentless attack, and mail poured in urging the feisty publisher to take on the President. He joked that any decision to run should properly come under the heading of Reader Service.

The Conservative Cleave had been running almost daily pieces highly critical of "Alien meddling and interference," decrying their "egalitarian sophistries" and declaring "good riddance" to the uninvited visitors. The response had been immediate: his readers wanted no part of any alien scheme to redistribute the wealth. Fenstermacher's readers were nothing if not affluent.

Over the Labor Day weekend he made his decision: He would challenge President Bryce in the Republican primaries.

*   *   *

The four Russian torpedoes, still in their factory crates, made their way by fishing trawler from the White Sea through the Barents and into the Norwegian Sea—there to rendezvous with an aged Moroccan tramp steamer bound for South America.

The delicate cargo transfer to the Poco Gordo took nearly an hour, but no one complained. Both captains had been well paid in dollars.

*   *   *

A new moon hung just above the horizon, still too thin to reflect off the rolling sea. Anselmo paced the bridge, watching for the Paco Gordo, now five and one-half hours overdue. The ancient diesels were overhauled and ready—the four pneumatic launch tubes were welded firmly in place at both ends of Domenico Gelatt—her skeleton crew was exhausted but anxious to set sail for martyrdom—and the five Holy Warriors under Anselmo's command were drilled, psyched and pumped. All that was missing was the torpedoes. Anselmo thought he glimpsed something on the horizon—and squinted through his binoculars—nothing.

He didn't dare try to raise the Paco Gordo—his orders called for maintaining strict radio silence. And for what he was being paid, he was following those orders. For an even more compelling reason as well: Fa Haad was the only man alive he truly feared.

*   *   *

By the time Paco Gordo arrived, nearly nine hours late, Anselmo was borderline convulsive. It was pitch dark, a storm had blown up, and Domenico Gelatt bucked roughly at anchor. Lashing the two vessels

90

together for the transfer of torpedoes was a treacherous affair, with the sea playing their hulls like cymbals. For forty minutes Anselmo screamed commands in Spanish into a whipping rain—until finally the ships were firmly roped, well bumpered, and riding as one.

It took nearly two hours of screaming to complete the transfers, with Anselmo far more concerned with the safety of the crates than his crew. When the torpedoes were secured in the hold at last, he counted up the toll: one smashed ankle—two cracked heads—a few cuts—on balance a bargain. His anger eased. He signaled the engine room to Stand By, and as soon as Paco Gordo's lights disappeared from sight, he ordered the anchor hoisted. Barely waiting for it to clear the bottom, he called out, "Course three-hundred twenty degrees—Maximum Turns!" He looked at his watch and clenched his fist, worried over how much longer their journey would take due to these seas. When they were finally managing a steady eleven knots, Anselmo turned over the bridge and went below. After a trip to the head he assembled the strike team in his cabin. He reported they were now ten hours behind schedule—time which would have to be made up by uncrating, inspecting, testing and loading the torpedoes en route in spite of the rough seas.

They spoke only practiced Spanish, using Hispanic first names. No one listening would ever suspect each was a devout follower of Islam—and headed for martyrdom at eleven knots.

BARRACUDA BALLS

Egon 'barracuda balls incarnate' Ovid was Sam Bryce's first choice to manage his re-election bid. At first Iana had balked, fearing he'd run not only the campaign but the candidate as well. Bryce had sworn that would never happen. Unconvinced, she reminded the President that Ovid had a reputation for ruthlessness and making dark deals if that's what it took. "Hey, this guy's gonna answer directly to me," Bryce had assured her—and then with a practiced hillbilly twang added, "He ain't gonna take so much as a damned pee without I give him my say-so!"

"Say it ain't so," she'd quipped—but in the end came to see her boss's perspective down the fairway: "Egon Ovid is the titanium club with which I can win the tournament."

*   *   *

The meeting took place at Camp David, with only Iana and Jack Bozorth looking on. In less than an hour Egon Ovid accepted the offer. Hands were shaken and the deal sealed.

"Now that you're officially on board," Bryce said, "I need to tell you something that's going to come out at some point: my daughter's pregnant—with no intention of marrying—or of ending the pregnancy. How do you propose we handle it?"

Ovid reflected briefly. "How would she come across in an interview?"

"Oh—Proud. Certain of herself. Candid, even blunt. Totally decent. Principled. Warm. Engaging. The kind of person who can make it all sound virtuous, I suppose. Why?"

"Then we let her say whatever she wants—and portray you as the Loving Father, unable to agree, but unwilling to be anything other than supportive—political consequences be damned! As a father you won't be blamed, and may actually come off a hero to many. My read: a net plus of four points." Ovid sat back and smiled. Then all were smiling.

*   *   *

Hurricane Gina slammed into the Carolinas September eighth. Though heavily battered, the northern Outer Banks had been spared the brunt of the storm according to reports.

David and Jane Onager drove down to assess the damage. Their hilltop cottage was well north of Corolla Light, and could only be accessed by jeep driving along the beach. At first, the damage appeared minimal. But as they drew closer, they could see that several windows were blown in—and this meant water-damage inside.

"I knew we should have had someone come and board her up," Onager groaned, taking Jane's hand in his. They walked in—and saw that hours of clean-up lay before them.

"I'll get the upstairs; you deal with down here," she assigned, producing mops. "At least we have power so I can do a laundry. Our bed must be an unholy mess—"

Six hours and four laundries later they collapsed on the porch, exhausted. The sun was just setting. Jane produced some juice. For several minutes they simply chewed, too exhausted to talk. All day long David had been hunting for a right moment. But there won't ever be a right moment, he finally concluded. He glanced over at her. In the failing light she looked eighteen again.

"I have something to ask you. And this is as good a time as any, I suppose—"She turned and peered at him, instantly apprehensive. He cleared his throat and drew a breath. "How would you feel about it—if I decided to seek the presidency as an Independent?"

Her jaw dropped, her eyes blinked. She couldn't believe her ears. "Have you decided to?"

"Not if you say no. But I have been giving thought to it. It would take real money and an entire organization—neither of which I have."

She eyed him suspiciously. "David—why on earth, all of a sudden, are you thinking about running for president? You've never even mentioned it before—"

"We—never had the Mentors before." He leaned against her, a sure sign he was serious. "What they had to say moves me, Janie. They are— right in everything that we have to do before it's too late. Someone has to take up their call. Someone has to pick up the Mentors' ball and run with it. And that may just as well be me—if no one else steps up to the plate."

"Now hold on: You can make speeches on the Senate floor— introduce bills—appear on talk-shows—you don't have to run for president, for God's sake!"

"Anything I can do as a senator pales beside what I could do as a presidential candidate. The media's all over any serious contender, even if he's a relative unknown before entering the race. Look at what Pant-Load Forbes did in '96. A national campaign is the only venue for anything national."

"But, you just said you have no money, no organization—"

He kissed her before answering. "I'm far less interested in getting elected than in getting results. If I can manage to arouse and mobilize public opinion, I can get results—legislative results."

"Dave, how on earth do you plan to run in the primaries without any money?"

"I don't have to run in the primaries. I'm talking about running as an Independent—thereby neatly by-passing the whole money-guzzling primary process, remaining free to concentrate on November from the very beginning!"

"But—for the general election you'd have to get on the ballot in all fifty states. And that means an organization. Not to mention—money."

He gazed out to sea, the surf still roiling from Gina. He reached over and took her hands in his. "I could do it as a write-in candidate," he replied slowly.

The senator's wife did not hold the Mentors in the same high esteem her husband did. And she had major qualms over any bid for the White House, be it serious or symbolic. He could see this and pressed ahead.

"During my trip last week to that fund-raiser in Boston, I met privately with Art Frayles. He too takes the Mentors' warnings very seriously. Moreover, he says these beings, whatever solar system they hail from, went to considerable effort and expense—and traveled an enormous distance just to advise us! He argues they'd never have done that unless it was vitally important that they come." He paused and smiled at her. "G. Arthur Frayles is nobody's fool—and he's convinced that the Mentors came here to warn and advise us before we do ourselves in."

The sun had just set—and Jane began to shiver.

*   *   *

Peter and Ellen Kate had laughed over enough OooYaYaBangToy and Cheez Whizz stories to be anxious for the day the two cats would meet face-to-face. With the onset of chilly nights they spent more and more time at Ellen Kate's apartment, where a small, cheerfully crackling wood stove warmed them and BangToy. While he got a fire going, she brewed a fresh pot of 'Marsh-mallow Flotsam' hot chocolate. Then they'd break out their Scrabble Humor Board and play by a set of Rules like no other. Each player begins by drawing ten Tiles—

NO fourteen letter words—four letter words with double vowels only

94

NO Biblical Body Parts—unless prepared by one who keeps a strict Kosher home

NO Proper Names—Improper names only (e.g. Titty-Tit-Tits)

NO National Holidays—Exception: Presidents' Pass Gas Day

NO Bodily Fluids—Pus is not a fluid, it's a dessert topping

Peter's job involved so much pressure and stress, he looked forward to quiet evenings sipping Flotsam,—which was not only mentally relaxing, but psychologically therapeutic. Moreover, the sillier, the more imaginative, and the more outright stupid the words became, the more beneficial.

At first Ellen Kate had been a little too stiff, even reticent, to throw herself willy-nilly into the spirit of the game—finding Peter's humor a bit much at first. But whenever she let herself go—and went for the outrageous—genuinely funny stuff began bubbling to the surface. And the evening she offered the opinion that fresh pus would make a Bavarian Gourmet Dessert Topping, Peter got to his feet and gave her a standing ovation.

TORPEDOES

As the four Russian-made torpedoes made their way slowly down the Atlantic, welders steamed under a boiling heat to finish installing bow and stern launch tubes inside the rusting hull of Domenico Gelatt—while others sweltered over her engines, readying them for one last voyage.

Meanwhile, in an air-conditioned office in the outskirts of Damascus, the terrorist known only as 'Mustafa' prepared a series of blind cutout wire transfers: Singapore to Lagos to Jakarta to Recife to Cartagena. Untraceable.

*   *   *

The cobalt toad had arrived alive and well at the National Institute of Health to undergo testing which, it was hoped, would lead to years of intense research. The day the toad was delivered, it was still sealed in its alien-matter container. And when the top was removed, the instant the toad was lifted clear, the container simply vanished—to the enormous disappointment and frustration of the dozen scientists gathered about eager to examine it.

*   *   *

Gordon Fenstermacher had an instinct for timing. And one week before President Bryce was expected to announce he'd run for re-election, the publisher called a press conference.

"I stand here today—to announce my candidacy for the Republican Nomination for President of the United States," he intoned with great gravity. "I take this step reluctantly—born of grave concern that the current leadership has failed to protect our nation from Constitutional assault from without—or take any action whatsoever in the face of rank ideological aggression! Such inaction constitutes an intolerable dereliction of duty on the part of the Commander-in-Chief. As president, I can assure the American people I'd be prepared to deal decisively with any future intrusion should the Aliens ever return and try to butt in again! Yet, I can see no evidence of any response plan being developed by this White House!" He held up both hands to signal Wait. "We can however count ourselves fortunate in one regard: All this is taking place in an Election Year—thereby affording voters an early means of making some very necessary changes." Well pleased, he returned his unused notes to his pocket.

"Mr. Fenstermacher—"a campaign plant called out, "how you gonna fit your name on a campaign button?"

"With no small difficulty," he chuckled.

"Mr. Fenstermacher," the AP correspondent asked, "you've been pretty harsh in your magazine of late, calling a fellow Republican, who just happens to also be the President, among other things: 'derelict to a fault'—'pusillanimity personified'—and then, just last week: 'more wishy-washy than a Kenmore.' So, how big a price do you think Republicans might pay next November as a result of your insurrection?"

"I think the question might be more properly put: What'll happen to the Party next November—if voters are forced to choose between a Democrat—and someone who dances to the tune of the Aliens?"

"Mr. Fenstermacher," called ABC, referring to notes, "you have previously stated that you'd—'be prepared to deal decisively with any future alien intrusion.' Could you be just a bit more specific?"

"That I cannot discuss publicly. But I will say this: when the Aliens first arrived, I would have insisted they meet us on our turf—and that they be far more forthcoming on questions put to them. I'll not amplify beyond that."

However that night on CNN he did.

"There are three questions to which I would have demanded answers: Where did you come from?—How many others came with you?—and what do we have that you want?"

"'Demanded'—how?" challenged the host.

"Look, you invite them politely to come over to the shuttle for the next scheduled session. If they refuse, you break off talks until they agree to accept the invitation. Simple. If we'd done that in the first place, things would have gone very, very differently." He looked at the host and then into the camera. "I tell you, it's a wonder they didn't make our people wipe their feet before entering!"

"But Gordon, politically, how could you, or any president for that matter, break off talks that had only barely begun? If the Aliens simply shrugged and left, there'd be hell to pay. The world's crying for answers, not one-upmanship."

"Look," the publisher bristled, "instead of standing up to them—the most powerful man on earth meekly acquiesced to their every demand—and gave them a platform to infect us with some deadly, alien strain of 'socioeconomic' virus!"

SMITHSONIAN

Behind the thick walls the only sounds to be heard were the remote hum of blowers circulating the air—the buzzing of a fluorescent tube somewhere—and the cough of a guard. At three in the morning, the Smithsonian was asleep.

Suddenly, The Western Union telegraph key began to dance.

In a secure area created to house the telegraph originally employed by the Mentors, the lights instantly came on, alarms sounded, audio recorders sprang to life, and ultra-high-speed cameras sprang into digital frenzy.

Seven minutes later, POTUS was awakened. "The—whole message—" Bryce snarled, "the entire, friggin' text reads:

'BEWARE IYERBORG DOMENICO GELATT'

—Now just what in the blue perfect Hell are we supposed to make of that?" He looked at the others: Bozorth, Benton, MacDougal, Ravenscroft, Klein, and his CIA and FBI directors—and fixed his gaze on the latter, Martin Murtaugh.

CHIMERA reconvened ninety minutes later. Both the Bureau and the Agency had been running the three names, looking for a connection. Director Murtaugh cleared his throat.

"We finally got Interpol cracking on a global search for this 'Iyerborg Domenico Gelatt'—had to call it a Suspected Terrorist to get priority. Here at home—lots of hits on the partials, but on that exact combination of names, we're coming up dry. No criminal records, no passports, no Social Security number, no driver's license, no service record—not even a credit file. Plus: no corporations, no tax filers, no copyrights, no patents. We'll keep digging." He turned to his counterpart. "Henry, your boys turn up anything yet?"

Murtaugh suspected CIA was faring no better. "No known terrorists or operatives using that name—no record of any organization or group—no published works or writings—no code names—no geographic locations—Nothing thus far."

Brows knit all around, but no one came up with any ideas. It was Klein who finally broke the silence. "I was thinking, maybe it's not the name of a person or place or business at all—maybe it's the name of a thing. Possibly a ship?"

"We'll begin checking registries at once," said Murtaugh. "Good thinking, Dr. Klein."

*   *   *

Fenstermacher was the first to declare his candidacy, with Bryce a close second—followed a week later by Democrat William C. Ordahl, the popular Governor of Rhode Island. Several lesser Democrats threw their hats in as well, but the pundits all agreed that the nomination was Ordahl's to lose.

October twelfth the national political landscape changed: Senator David Onager announced that he too would seek the presidency. The announcement was made at noon.

At 12:08 p.m. the White House phoned, catching Onager still at the studio.

"David!" the president roared, "haven't I got enough problems with Fensty and Ordahl—without you climbing into the ring behind them?"

"Sam, I tried to reach you yesterday to tell you I was getting ready to announce, but you didn't return my call."

"Well-I-guess-I've-learned-a-lesson!—Now, Dave, what the hell is this all about? I can't believe you want to be president—I know you too well."

"Actually, it's got more to do with Fenstermacher than you. Someone's got to answer his attacks on the Mentors!"

"Why?"

Onager drew a breath before answering. "Because I happen to believe the Mentors are right. And their advice, at the very least, should be the subject of extensive public debate and discussion—along with an intensive reexamination of our fundamental human and national values.

"The actual process of rethinking everything we value, Sam, can produce only good. Either we end up reaffirming our present body of values, in whole or in part—or—we replace them with new, more enlightened values. And thus, the very process is a win-win! But in my own view, there's only one way to be certain of getting the requisite forum—and that is to have a major presidential candidate making Values the central issue of his campaign. Now, as you know, I have no wish to be president. So, old friend—if you can think of a better way, let's have it." He waited a few moments for an answer, but got none. "Well, hell!—I can think of one: make Values—and following the Mentors' advice, the focus of your campaign! You do that, Sam, and I'll withdraw in a heartbeat."

"You know I couldn't even if I wanted to. It would drive my base and the whole damn business community straight into the arms of Fenstermacher. No, my best stance on the Aliens is one of respectful tolerance—neither embracing nor condemning," he sighed. "So, tell me: who you got in mind for a campaign manager?"

"Don't know yet. But, Sam—I am thinking about asking that brother-in-law of yours to become one of my campaign chairs. Would you have a problem with that?"

"What? Of course I'd have a problem with that! How'd it look, for God's sake?"

"He may well turn me down anyway. But Art Frayles has spent more time with the Mentors than anyone else alive, and he believes we ought to be paying damn close attention to what they advised. And so do I. Look—run it by Abby, and see what she thinks of the Art idea."

"Dave, this is all nuts. You don't want my job—you don't have a campaign organization—you don't have $50 mil in the kitty—what the hell are you thinking anyway?"

"Guess I'm just persuaded there are a lot of people out there who want to believe in the Mentors—and want to see them return. It's a cause in search of a leader, Sam."

"And—so that becomes your calling?"

"It could be you, Mr. President. It-could-be-you."

"It would be political suicide," Bryce dismissed. "But I'll speak with Abby. Now listen, we can't let any of this crap get in the way of our game. I'd still rather Birdie you than anyone else I know!"

*　　　*　　　*

Testosterone and alcohol competing for dominance, Egon Ovid began Halloween Eve by weaving into Iana Ravenscroft's inner office, unzipping, and saying "Trick or Treat!" Fatal error. Bryce was no neo-Clinton, and the next day Ovid found himself updating his resume.

He didn't have to job-search very long.

*　　　*　　　*

Following his morning shower, David Onager stood naked before a full-length mirror—and shook his head. You look like a three day floater, he winced. Nonetheless, he'd have no truck with exercise. His credo: Precious Little Warrants Physical Effort—but Nothing is Worth Exertion.

He'd expected his candidacy declaration to be greeted with polite respect. Instead the media was in a swarm, pressing him over his support for the Mentors and their aims. As the first political figure to embrace "Universe Values"—and the only presidential candidate to do so—Onager became an instant lodestone for all who shared his beliefs—which, all the polls agreed, was a growing number of people.

Onager had entered the race simply to make people pay attention to what the Mentors had declared, planning only to wage a symbolic write-in campaign. But with contributions suddenly flooding in, he realized he could actually mount a serious challenge. It would mean entering the primaries—building an entire campaign organization from scratch—raising millions—being on the road all the time—working twenty hours a day—making speeches until he was hoarse—shaking hands until his own swelled. Yet the one truly daunting question remained: did he want to run the risk of actually being elected?

The mirror was unforgiving. His whole life Onager had scrupulously eschewed athletics or any physical exertion of the non-carnal variety, and knew that what he saw sagging before him could scarcely be called muscle. No—there'd be no photos of this candidate jogging. Or even in shorts.

Corporal insults aside, he knew a decision had to be made, and quickly. He'd first consulted Art Frayles, then Tommy Raffle. But in the end it was Janie who would decide. He put on his robe and walked into the bedroom. Jane was stretched out on the bed, reading letters from voters. He slipped in beside her and gently put his hand over whatever she was reading.

"I need you to help me make the call, Darlin'—Do I wage an all-out battle for the White House, with an intent to win—or, do we just go through the motions?"

"Hell, that's easy—Do you want the job?"

"It's not what I want. It's a matter of what's best for the country."

"Bullshit."

"HOT DAMN!"

Computerized records of ship registries only went back forty years. Anything prior to that meant a visit to the archives. It took Peter more than five hours to find it.

"Hot Damn!—there she is: IYERBORG—Merchantman, nine-thousand and four-hundred tons. Launched Rotterdam, 1933. Liberian Registry. Re-Christened—DOMENICO GELATT, 1947—home port: Valparaiso! Yee Haa! Call the Director!"

GLOBAL ALERT

Army Colonel Leigh Hipple commanded the American half of the Panama Canal Joint Security Force, established on the first day of the new Millennium. She was the first of her gender to hold the post.

Her prime directive was to protect the Canal against any and all threats, whether from within or without. First and foremost, this meant protecting the upper lock gates at Gatun on the Caribbean, and Pedro Miguel above the Pacific—the massive structures which held back the waters of Gatun Lake, which constituted the canal and operated its system of locks.

The ancient seven foot thick hollow steel gates are the Canal's Achilles heel: Destroy them and the lake level drops forty feet in a few hours, stranding all Canal traffic—tankers, cargo, and cruise ships alike settling helplessly into the mud. The damaged gates could be quickly replaced, but not the water: It would take over two years for tropical rains to refill Gatun Lake, and before ships could again cross the Isthmus again.

Hipple's counterpart was Col. Manuel Rodriguez, and she couldn't stand him. Not because he was a patronizing, vainglorious libertine (which she could handle), but because he didn't take his job nearly seriously enough. With the Cold War over, the Americans essentially gone, and Panama at peace with her neighbors, Rodriguez regarded the military defense of the Canal as being largely ceremonial.

Accordingly, he was content to let "our paranoid friends" do the security grunt-work, inspect and maintain defenses, patrol, dive, and run practice drills.

The only thing the colonel took seriously was the annual Joint Forces Military Exercises: i.e., making sure there'd be comprehensive coverage, with television cameras pre-positioned at all the best vantage points. Not surprisingly, Rodriguez always ordered that Panamanian and U.S. Forces would Pass in Review at the conclusion of the Exercises. He loved a parade.

At the monthly staff meetings his attitude was generally dismissive, waving his hand vaguely to signal bemused assent to the latest Pentagon threat assessment update. But he was always careful to treat Col. Hipple with the respect protocol demanded. However, he often amused himself by pointedly staring at her bosom whenever she spoke of imagined dangers.

Sometimes she almost wished there would be an attack.

*   *   *

The four Russian high-speed torpedoes had been inspected, systems checked and rechecked, and the pneumatic launch tubes successfully test-fired. 'Angel' knew his job. The seas had finally calmed and the engine room was managing a steady twelve knots. 'Lius' knew his job, too.

On the bridge Anselmo checked his watch against the plot board. "We should be able to make Cristobal by dawn," he calculated.

"And then how long?" enthused 'Lorenzo,' his olive-skinned second-in-command.

"It depends how many other ships are in line ahead of us. We'll have a few hours to wait, but at the latest we should be entering the Canal by evening." He licked at the tips of his mustache, his sole concession to tension. "Assemble the men. I want one more run-through."

Anselmo made a detailed entry in the log before leaving the bridge. The Canal Pilot was bound to examine it at some point, and he wanted it looking authentic.

There must be nothing to arouse his suspicions.

"But what if they want to inspect the hold—what then?" worried Lorenzo.

"They won't. We carry no cargo to inspect. We're just a load of scrap efficiently delivering itself to the salvage yard. What could be of less interest?"

Anselmo's orders called for Gelatt to enter Limon Bay, drop anchor alongside the other vessels awaiting their turns, radio for clearance, and stand by until Canal officials boarded, examined the ship's papers, and collected their toll.

His orders also provided for one critical contingency: CIA had learned of their mission and was waiting for them. The orders read, "If approached by any boat carrying more than four persons, you are to assume that mission cover has been blown. Open fire, cast loose-the gangway, drop hull plates fore and aft, make slow turns on the prop and swing at anchor to bring either bow or stern tubes to bear. Primary target: any low-riding Panamax tanker. Secondary target: a heavily burdened Panamax container ship.'

Andelmo allowed a small, fatalistic smile. *Whatever happens, the Great Satan will discover exactly how close the Panama Canal came to total destruction!*

*   *   *

Dr. Henry Gothier, Director of Central Intelligence, had already received two calls that morning from Dr. Ravenscroft pressing for a report on the location of the Domenico Gelatt. Yet all the Agency had learned thus far was that, after being sold for salvage in 1995 to a company in Caracas, the ship had been "purchased for parts" four months later by a now-defunct trading company in Mauritania. Delivery was in March of 1996—at which point Domenico Gelatt simply disappeared without a trace. But to Gothier a dead-end was unacceptable, and the search continued. Specialists pored over satellite photos and field teams asked questions in a hundred ports, while computers searched the globe for firms that had done business with the defunct trading company—and who its owners were.

At the White House the main fear was that this officially scrapped ship was, at this very moment, tied to a dock in some doomed seaport—a nuclear device ticking in her hold.

All this, Gothier said was because of "the President's belief that the Mentors aren't shitting him."

ASSAULT!

The sun rose like a molten dome from the sea, silhouetting Domenico Gelatt as she lined up to enter the breakwater protecting Limon Bay. Forty minutes later she dropped anchor—a fat PANAMAX tanker square in her sights.

Anselmo radioed his request for clearance, and at 0750 ordered his men to take cover, Uzis at the ready. Minutes later he picked up the approaching launch in his binoculars. To his relief, there were only two men aboard—one being lobster red with silver hair. They tied up and climbed the gangway to the main deck, where Anselmo stood waiting.

"Welcome aboard," he smiled, returning their salutes. "I am the Master, Anselmo Patos." They shook hands. "The bridge is this way, if you would follow me—"

"We notice you're riding very high, Captain—" the ruddy one said, "no cargo this trip?"

"The ship is the cargo," he laughed, "headed for the scrap pile—with only a skeleton crew to mark her final voyage."

Anselmo was relieved they hadn't noticed the torpedo cutout plates, which had been carefully reset into the hull and their seams painted over.

The red faced one examined the manifest and the expertly forged Temporary Registration, took a perfunctory look at the log and, based on capacity, calculated their toll at seventeen-thousand four-hundred and fifty dollars. Anselmo went to the ship's safe, extracted a pile of hundred-dollar bills, and paid in cash. He was handed a receipt and told to expect a wait of twelve to fourteen hours. Their pilot would board shortly before departure time, accompanied by a Canal deck-crew to handle the hawsers and towing cables.

His adrenaline spurting, Captain Patos promised to have coffee ready. Martyrdom was but hours away.

*   *   *

Col. Hipple made it a practice to periodically check both North and South transit schedules, updated in real-time on her monitor. When she noticed that one Domenico Gelatt was bound for a Pacific salvage yard, it struck her as odd that anyone would pay a seventeen-thousand and four-hundred fifty dollar toll to deliver a pile of scrap. But then her phone rang, and she forgot the matter.

*   *   *

At 2145 a Canal launch drew alongside the rust-bucket of a freighter; two pilots and a deck-crew of six climbed her gangway.

The compressed air tanks fore and aft were fully charged, the torpedo hull plates poised to drop to the water with a single yank on their holding pins—the Old Lady of the Sea stood at General Quarters, terrorist-style.

Domenico Gelatt would enter the lower chamber of Gatun Locks within the hour.

*   *   *

It was a hot, moonless night. A faint odor of bunker fuel mixed with the sweet tropical air. Arc lights blazed down on Gatun Locks, bathing the complex in a cool, ersatz daylight—machinery hummed softly—a faltering breeze rolled down from the mountains. And all scent of the sea was gone.

A tug nudged Domenico Gelatt alongside the approach pier, and cables were hooked to special electric locomotives which would tow her into and on through the triple set of locks.

As the pilot nudged Gelatt toward the lower chamber—its massive gates towering overhead—Anselmo glanced astern—and discovered to his dismay that another small freighter was being towed into the lock chamber directly behind them—effectively blocking their stern tubes.

Anselmo swallowed grimly and shifted his mind to the Alternate target: the upper chamber at Pedro Miguel, where vessels en route to the Pacific were lowered thirty-one feet in a single step from Gatun Lake.

Another ship blocking the stern tubes was nevertheless a possibility for which they had made allowance. The Alternate mission plan was starkly simple:

Upon entering the Upper Chamber, sequentially fire torpedoes at both the primary and secondary pairs of gates before you.

Once in line, ships remain in the same position all across the Isthmus, meaning the small freighter would follow them to Pedro Miguel. But Anselmo would allow nothing to prevent him from destroying the target. Just as ordered, Domenico Gelatt would sequentially fire her bow tubes while entering the lock through its open upper gates—destroying the first pair, and then the second pair of gates at the far end of the chamber. Gatun Lake would become an instant Niagara, the lock—a raging cataract one-hundred-ten foot wide—flushing Domenico Gelatt forward to its doom. Any attempt at that point to close the still-open upper gates would be a disaster, since the deluge would instantly rip the eight-hundred ton monster leaves from their hinges, which would only compound the devastation downstream.

Of the two targets, Anselmo preferred Pedro Miguel because its destruction would bring along all the other ships caught up in the torrent pouring through the narrow approach known as the Gaillard Cut—and thereby become part of the trillion-gallon rampage smashing down on Panama City itself!

The Greater the Death Toll, the Greater the Glory.

*   *   *

It was just after Eleven when Domenico Gelatt cleared the locks and set out upon Gatun Lake. As the tall arc lamps faded behind them, a heavy rain began to fall. Both pilots came into the wheelhouse from the bridge wing.

"Whew! By Maria, you'd never know the dry season was upon us!" bellowed the heavyset one, shaking off his cap.

For the next ten minutes the pilot spoke by radio with Marine Traffic Control along with his colleagues directly ahead and astern, maintaining the proper intervals.

They were advised the squall would pass quickly.

*   *   *

The satellite photos were useless without a clear overhead shot of the actual Domenico Gelatt for comparison purposes. Over a thousand small freighters were plying the seven seas.

Gothier was frustrated; worried valuable time was being lost. It was nearly midnight when he finally phoned the President with the recommendation they issue a global alert for the vessel—which meant asking every harbormaster and port director in the world for help. In all likelihood it also meant the search would hit the news. And this was what made Bryce so reluctant, because they were in no position to offer explanations. Gothier suggested a Suspected Terrorist Alert designation, using DOD as the initiating agency. Despite serious political misgivings, Bryce finally agreed.

At 0010 the Alert went out.

GATUN

Eduardo Salazar was the midnight shift Director General, and tonight he was reporting for work a little sleepy from over-eating. Maybe a few more burps and he'd feel better.

He'd just begun reviewing the previous shift's Passage Reports, when he was handed the Alert from Washington. In an instant he was wide awake: Domenico Gelatt was at this very moment southbound on Gatun Lake! Salazar sprang into action:

"Find Colonel Rodriguez!—Notify Colonel Hipple! Open a direct line to Pentagon Emergency Ops Center—Call the Ministry," Salazar barked "Radio the—No don't!—if we've got a vessel full of terrorists out there, we can't risk trying to alert the pilot!"

* * *

"All right, Major, just what are we faced with here?" Bryce demanded, hastily dressed in bathrobe and slippers, as he swept into the Situation Room. Fresh coffee steamed in one corner, ignored by everyone except the Vice President, who'd fallen asleep at his desk when the call came in: Some kind of crisis in the Panama Canal. He'd arrived in the Sit Room just ahead of the President.

Major Ted Espenshade, US Army, had grabbed his maps and photographs and sped to the White House, arriving at 12:33. Using a laser pointer, he began the briefing with a satellite photo of the Isthmus. "This is the land bridge connecting the two Americas at its narrowest point, the Isthmus. The Continental Divide is here. Now, as you can see, the Panama Canal is not a canal most of the way—rather, it's a lake. Gatun Lake: world's largest man-made body of water, created when the canal builders threw a dam across the Chagres River here just before it

108

empties into the Atlantic. The dam's hydroelectric plant powers Panama City on the Pacific. And right next door, here, the triple locks at Gatun—"

"So it's the lake that provides the water to operate the locks," Bryce deduced.

"YES SIR. YOU SEE, EARLY EFFORTS TO DIG A SEA LEVEL CANAL FAILED MISERABLY: FAR TOO MUCH EARTH TO BE REMOVED FROM WHAT IS NOW CALLED 'THE GAILLARD CUT'—HERE, AT THE DIVIDE. THE WATER LEVEL IN THE CUT AND GATUN LAKE IS EIGHTY-FIVE FOOT ABOVE SEA LEVEL. AND, BUT FOR THE VAST MOUNTAIN RAIN-FORESTS AND THE ONE-HUNDRED PLUS INCHES OF RAINFALL THEY PRODUCE EACH YEAR, THAT RIVER OF RUN-OFF WOULDN'T EXIST. THERE WOULDN'T BE ANY LAKE— AND THERE WOULDN'T BE ANY PANAMA CANAL."

"Major," Ravenscroft interrupted, "you're saying that the Chagres River depends upon rain in the mountains for its waters—and if anything took out the dam, and all the water in the lake drained out, the Panama Canal would be totally out of business? Until the dam was rebuilt, and tropical rains refilled the lake?"

"That's it—precisely correct."

"Dear God—"breathed Bryce, "and just how long would that take?"

Espenshade hesitated before answering, knowing it was the one fact no one wanted to hear. "Assuming normal rainfall, about two years, Mr. President." Stunned, each struggled to grasp the full implications. Only defense secretary D'Orio was not shocked; he'd been fully briefed en route.

"And what about the gates on the locks—wouldn't losing them be the equivalent of losing the dam?" Bryce challenged.

"Yes sir. Trillions of gallons would drain out in a matter of hours. However, if the gates of an upper chamber were lost they could be replaced with spares in a matter of days. But rebuilding the dam would take months, if not years."

109

"And exactly how vulnerable are those gates, Major?"

"The upper chambers, meaning the vital ones, are protected by a double set of gates at both ends: should anything breech the first pair, the back-up pair would still contain the lake. In addition, safety cables are strung across in front of each entrance a few feet below the surface of the water—kept in the raised position at all times, and lowered only when the gates are actually opening. These cables prevent a ship from crashing into the gates either by accident or by design."

"Is that it?" Bryce asked. "You mean, if the gates were somehow blown up we could do nothing to shut off the flow of water before the whole damned lake drained out?"

"Well, originally there were emergency dams which could be swung out into the flow—skeletal frameworks, into which steel plates could be lowered, one by one, to gradually cut off the water. During World War II, they were replaced by large, submerged, hydraulically raised caissons. But when the war ended, they too were removed—and never replaced."

The President swore and turned to D'Orio. "Ralph, we've got to know whether there's a nuke aboard that ship! Don't we have some kind of detectors we can over-fly it with?"

"The only ones equipped for that are the Nuclear Emergency Search Teams, Mr. President."

"Christ!—and how long will it take to get a NEST team down there?"

"Out of Kirtland AFB, approximately four hours. They've already been placed on Alert and are ready to go."

"Issue the order immediately—Iana, get Hector Rojas." He turned to Klein, "Peter, where's that ship right now?"

He checked his watch. "Almost halfway across Gatun Lake—with just over two hours before they enter the Gaillard Cut and then another hour to the locks at Pedro Miguel."

The President rubbed his temples. "We have to know if there's anything aboard that ship before taking any actiona nuclear explosion anywhere in the Canal would be a total disaster. We need options—and fast!"

"President Rojas on Two—" Ravenscroft interrupted.

*   *   *

110

It was 1:10 p.m. when the briefing began. Eduardo Salazar had received instructions from Government House to "investigate immediately, taking whatever action is necessary to safeguard the Canal and its traffic." He'd summoned Colonels Rodriguez and Hipple to determine the best course of action, with the first priority the protection of the Canal itself and its traffic second.

"The American NEST team is airborne—ETA 0245," Salazar reported. "Until their arrival we do nothing which could alert the suspected terrorists we're onto them. The vessel will reach Gamboa in one hour, so we must decide quickly whether to let it enter the Gaillard Cut uninspected. Bear in mind, we have no hard evidence that this ship is anything other than what she claims—only Washington's suspicions."

"And upon what are their suspicions based?" demanded Col. Rodriguez.

"They claim having a 'confidential informant'—one they apparently consider 'reliable' enough to warrant waking El Presidente in the middle of the night." Salazar looked at Rodriguez; it was Panama that now bore ultimate responsibility for the Canal. "Colonel, what can we do before that ship reaches Gamboa—without arousing their suspicions?"

He gazed up at the central monitor: a live color image portrayed Domenico Gelatt, night-vision intensified, moving slowly across Gatun Lake.

Rodriguez, arms akimbo, puffed the cigar clenched in his teeth, his eyes fixed on Hipple. "Yankee paranoia aside, Traffic Control could simply radio the pilot that a tug will be taking them through the Cut—with our men hidden inside the tug, ready to board and seize control of the ship before they know what hit them! Then, should we find no explosives or atom bombs—" he sneered, "we'll thank them politely and send them on their way!"

Hipple struggled to contain her fury. "Colonel, that very possibility is why we must move with such extreme caution! What if your men were to be spotted before they'd even drawn alongside—and the tug comes under fire! You'll get your own men killed—the two Canal pilots for sure—set off the terrorists—and put at hazard the entire Canal system!"

"Well then, Colonel Hipple—what safe, cozy course of inaction would you recommend?" he bristled.

"You might invent some 'emergency' to bring all Canal traffic to a halt—and then wait for the NEST team!"

Salazar gave this some thought. "We—do have in place an Emergency Procedure for stopping all Canal traffic in the event of, for instance, an oil spill—"

* * *

Anselmo walked out on the port wing and gazed astern. There was no moon, but he could easily make out the small freighter a thousand yards behind them—followed at the same interval by a PANAMAX tanker and behind the tanker a large container ship. Beyond that he had no interest.

He came back into the wheelhouse, Lorenzo at the helm. The two pilots stood together on the starboard wing, one speaking with someone over the radio.

"You think they suspect anything?" Lorenzo whispered.

"You worry to the point of worrying me! Relax, my brother—lest they begin to wonder why you are looking so jumpy!" He consulted the chart, lining up the beacons on shore to estimate their position. "In less than twenty minutes, we enter the Cut—our pathway to glory!" Lorenzo flashed a smile.

One of the pilots stepped into the wheelhouse.

"Captain, we'll be picking up a tug to nurse us through the Cut. There's two way traffic tonight." He checked his watch and headed back to the wing. "In about twelve minutes."

* * *

Suspicious by nature and cautious by instinct, Anselmo watched the approaching tug off the port bow—his men well hidden, positioned to open fire on his command. He fine-focused the night-vision binoculars that he'd insisted on. The tug was now less than fifty meters away, slowing down and turning to come alongside. He squinted, trying to see inside the deckhouse—suddenly he caught a glint of gun barrels!

His screams into the radio were answered with an eruption of automatic rifle fire from the superstructure. The tug's deckhands dove for cover or overboard as the fusillade rained down. Panamanian Marines ran out on deck, taking cover, attempting to return fire. One shoulder-fired rocket managed to destroy a paint locker before the tug turned and churned frantically away. The Canal Pilots lay where Lorenzo had shot them. Gamboa lay just ahead: "Flank Speed!" Anselmo shouted into his radio, aiming straight for the Cut.

Iyerborg Domenico Gelatt had gone to war.

*   *   *

Leigh Hipple raced for the helicopter, adrenaline firing. She'd been powerless to stop Col. Rodriguez from giving the order to board and search the suspect ship—but the instant gunfire erupted she ordered the troops on Alert at Fort Clayton to move on Pedro Miguel, and ordered the Canal's U.S. Rangers airborne for a possible assault in Gaillard Cut.

First she had to see the tactical situation for herself; she climbed aboard and buckled up. The chopper leaped into the air and streaked for the Cut. Marine Traffic Control reported thirteen southbound ships presently in the Cut, plus three small pleasure craft They also reported Domenico Gelatt was already three miles into the Cut, passing all other vessels and making for Pedro Miguel—which lay but twenty-two minutes ahead at the speed the old ship was managing.

Marine Traffic Control had ordered all pilots in the Cut to reduce speed and intervals, with just enough headway to maintain steerage. The intent was to have no vessel within five miles of Pedro Miguel by the time the outlaw ship arrived. All lock gates were ordered closed, and all other traffic was halted at Balboa.

Hipple knew they must find open water fast for an airborne assault—there could be no tankers nearby. The Panamanian President had specifically forbidden any action which risked sinking a vessel in the Canal. She had to find an area safe for the Rangers to operate—

*   *   *

Pilots aboard the other ships in the Cut could scarcely believe their eyes as the kamikaze merchantman thrashed heavily by barely fifty feet off their port beams, her wash scooping out large chunks of dirt from the banks. The Gelatt crossed the Continental Divide; ten minutes to go—"Helicopters!" screamed Lius, stabbing at the sky aft.

"I see them!" Anselmo yelled. "Fire the Stingers!"

Moments later three shoulder-fired, American-made missiles streaked for the choppers—which fired off decoy flares, leaping aside a split instant before the warheads detonated. Obeying orders, the Rangers reluctantly broke off and took up station just beyond Stinger range.

Hipple saw the Rangers taking fire ahead, and the chopper banked sharply away to avoid becoming a target itself.

"The tie-up station at Pedro Miguel!" she shouted at the pilot. "Tell'em I want two tugs ready to move on my order! And I want two SLLAM teams at the end of the approach pier!"

*　　*　　*

"Domenico Gelatt just passed the last vessel in the Cut and is now approaching the dogleg before Pedro Miguel—ETA four and one half minutes," Ops Center radioed the Situation Room.

"Meaning: if they're carrying a nuke, it's already too late," groaned Bryce. "We should have blown that tub to pieces back in the lake while there was still time—Rojas be damned!"

"Mr. President—I seriously doubt they're carrying a nuclear device," Iana Ravenscroft demurred, her voice in its very lowest register. "Otherwise—they'd have used it at Gatun, when they had the chance. To be honest, I'd decided the Mentors were just jerking our chains until the fire-fight on the lake. But at this point, odds are the ship's carrying conventional explosives, if any at all. And, let's not overlook the possibility they're simply running drugs—since that could easily explain why they opened fire on the launch."

"But we have to act under the assumption that the ship is a nuclear bomb—headed for the God damn lock complex at twelve knots!" D'Orio bristled. "Colonel Hipple has the tactical situation well in hand; that ship'll never get close to those lock gates!"

*　　*　　*

All four double sets of gates were closed, safety chains raised in front of them. In addition, Hipple had ordered a Canal tug anchored fore and aft in front of each chain. She also had two SLLAM teams(Shoulder-Launched Laser-Aimed Missile) positioned at the tip of the central access pier, which jutted two-thousand feet into the Cut from between the side-by-side locks. Hipple herself was now ashore at the tie-up station, with a commanding view of the northern approaches to

Pedro Miguel. She'd been met there by Lt. Col. Lyle Yokum, her second-in-command.

"Lyle, tell Alpha SLLAM to wait 'til they have a full three-second paint of the wheelhouse—I don't want any misses! Beta SLLAM's to take out her rudder if she's still moving!"

Domenico Gelatt emerged from the dogleg: Pedro Miguel lay before them bathed in light.

"Hold Steady—" Anselmo ordered, scanning the complex through binoculars. "Shit! They've got tug boats blocking each chamber! Drop Plates! Drop Plates!" he screamed into the radio. "We're going for the starboard gates, the starboard gates . . . !" There were four loud splashes, as bow and stern hull plates hit the water.

"But, the tug—the torpedoes will be wasted on it!" yelled Lorenzo.

"No they won't! They're set for a running depth of four meters—they'll go right under the tug and hit the gates!"

"Bow torpedoes Ready to Fire!" squawked his walkie-talkie.

"Come Right twenty degrees!" Anselmo called out, the last rudder command the old ship would ever obey.

"S-t-e-a-d-y— Bow Tubes: FIRE ONE!" He counted off two-seconds—and heard the first torpedo hit the water. He counted off three more. "FIRE TWO!"

Leigh Hipple had seen the splashes just behind the prow, but missed the twin splashes astern. She was trying to figure them out—when she saw a torpedo leap from the bow!

Suddenly, it was all too clear: "Torpedo!" she shrieked. Then a second torpedo hit the water. "Torpedo!"

She watched the tug—in her mind's eye seeing it erupt into a fireball. Instead, there was a deafening blast just beyond it as the first pair of gates exploded, capsizing the tug and creating a swell which nearly swept the SLLAM teams from the approach pier. Suddenly, sixty feet behind where the first gates had been the second pair erupted violently, showering torn metal and water everywhere, eviscerating Pedro Miguel and leaving a gaping, open wound. All that now stood between Panama City and a billion tons of water—were four very old, hollow gates.

A cry of triumph went up from the bridge as the terrorists saw the second pair of gates disintegrate. They were now but two-hundred meters from the approach pier.

"Victory is ours, my brothers! The Gates of Heaven stand open before us! We now make the ship itself the Hand of God to smash through the final sets of gates—to sever the Great Satan's femoral artery!"

Death-gripping the helm, Lorenzo glanced down to the end of the rapidly approaching pier—and shrieked with pain as a ruby beam cauterized his retina. An instant later, a blinding ball of white fire replaced the wheelhouse, vaporizing one Yorin Mussadeh, alias Anselmo Patos.

But the old ship was not to be denied. She plowed on past the pier, smashing aside the hapless tug. Her holds empty, her bow high, Domenico Gelatt rode up and over the submerged safety chain as if it wasn't there.

At that moment Hipple spotted the two torpedo cutouts in the stern. "Beta SLLAM: Target one of those square holes in the stern, just above the waterline!"

Funnel belching, wheelhouse completely gone, with rudder amidships the ancient vessel drove on blindly, smashing through the wreckage of the first four leaves—and taking dead aim on the other four, now less than a thousand feet ahead! It was the War of the Relics.

At that moment Beta Team's SLLAM warhead streaked in, scoring a direct hit on the unlaunched after torpedoes. Two enormous secondary explosions thundered, amputating the entire stern of the ship, tearing away prop and rudder.

Though sinking fast, her stern blown away, raw momentum kept her going—shattering the closed double gates of the water-filled upper chamber, screeching and banking along its concrete walls. And at the far end of the chamber, the last-ditch pair of safety gates braced for impact—a Canal first.

In her death throes, broken, never to float again, the Domenico Gelatt nonetheless clawed on, massive inertia her one remaining weapon. Mortally wounded, she smashed aside the first lower gates of the upper lock, her speed now bleeding off quickly. Then, a last, valiant twist and lurch to starboard.

She groaned to a dead-in-the-water halt. A scorched, smoldering carcass, she ended up oddly cleaved to the final emergency gate—looking for all the world as if she were begging to be let in.

Moments later, from the other side of the gate, a urine-like stream of murky lake water arched out and down. A fitting, symbolic ship's end, and far cry from her band-playing birth long ago, when a bottle of champagne sent her sliding down well-greased ways—all anxious to haul cargo and evade U-Boats.

Today—the far older, yet far stronger gates of the venerable Panama Canal—held. For a few moments—all was still, until a single siren broke the silence, triggering an exuberant cacophony of horns, ships' whistles, and wildly revving engines.

NEOSQUIRE

Justin Onager preferred his own company to that of just about anyone. Not out of social or intellectual snobbery, he simply found his own brain totally entertaining. He was his own personal, high-performance fun machine. His chosen realm: cyberspace He was a self-made, world-class hacker. He would be known only as NEOSQUIRE. And no one, absolutely no one, on the web would recognize NEOSQUIRE as being the son of a United States senator.

His parents were away on a campaign swing, Penny was at Holly's, and Justin remained at home with only his brain-toy for company. His kind of day.

To be an UH (Unapprehend Hacker) required extraordinary finesse at concealing one's electronic tracks—and Justin had invested the better part of two years mastering 'cipher castration,' as he dubbed it. It all came naturally to him. After a few serious practice runs and a dozen high-security break-ins, he'd anointed himself Cyber Master. And best of all, he was a full UUUH (Unsuspected Unidentified UH)! And as such, he now felt free go about his business with no fear of being identified through retro-trace.

Unhappily for others, his business was monkey-business.

*   *   *

The final Domenico Gelatt tally was steep: eight Canal employees, three Rangers and nine terrorists killed; one noncombatant and five noncombatants wounded; six gate leaves destroyed; one tug capsized;

one launch damaged; and one merchantman sunk in an upper lock chamber.

Cutting up and removing Domenico Gelatt's hulk, plus lock repairs would cost millions and take months. Hundreds would be hired to process claims—lawsuits and appeals would go on for years. Only the rolling of heads was performed with dispatch—beginning with that of Colonel Manuel Rodriguez.

A senior Canal official in Washington issued a statement: "The incident at Pedro Miguel was a tragic and costly demonstration of the vulnerability of the Panama Canal—and of the urgent need to upgrade its designation from that of Very Important—to that of Vital national interest."

Congress was in full uproar, with Senator Hagopian (D-NY) accusing the commander-in-chief of "sleeping on watch!"

Republicans were literally howling for blood, calling for DNA forensics to point the finger of racial responsibility.

One member of the House Armed Services Committee demanded that the Canal's old emergency dams be restored, while another called for the return of the torpedo nets used inside the locks in World War II. Months of damaging, finger-pointing hearings lay ahead. Yet all agreed: It could have been far worse. One estimate put the worldwide cost of losing the use of the Canal for two years at three-hundred and ten-billion.

It was also a time of humiliation for the United States, with few nations holding Panama primarily responsible. World anger was focused on Washington, and the press was in full piranha mode. A particularly galling cartoon showed Bryce perched atop mangled lock gates looking befuddled and forlorn, with the caption: 'Small wonder the Mentors gave up on us!'

Not all however suffered ridicule; CIA was unofficially credited with uncovering and thwarting the terrorist plot in the nick of time. With a smug twinkle in his eyes, an Agency spokesman would neither confirm nor deny.

The FBI had launched a major case full-bore investigation, with early suspicion centering on radical groups funded by Saudi and Iranian sources. There was a possible Pakistani link. Libya was suspect, along with Iraq, Syria, and Yemen. Only North Korea was genetically cleared.

It was nearly Thanksgiving, and the President's plate was already piled high with problems. While Abby and Ellen Kate were off to New York for the weekend to Christmas shop and catch the hot new musical IZHAL—Iana and he had gone to Camp David to work. A roaring fire greeted them. Bryce poured snifters of cognac. It had begun to snow.

"Fenstermacher's merciless," he groaned, slumping back, his slippered feet stretched toward the fire. "First the Aliens—now the Canal. And people are starting to listen—our people. He's gaining in both Iowa and New Hampshire. We can't afford to let him nibble away at our base! We've got to counter-punch with something, Iana—and we have 'til tomorrow to come up with it!"

She held up her own feet for warming. "Putting any kind of positive spin on the Aliens or the Canal is risky, if not impossible. I also think it's time we stop pretending his challenge isn't real. Take off the gloves and go after him! He's a wing nut—and that still scares most Republicans."

Bryce frowned. "Ovid knows Katie's having a baby out of wedlock—we start playing hardball and he might use it. I won't have her dragged into the campaign—or allow it to degenerate into some damned debate over family values!"

"Bear in mind," Iana drawled, "historically, whenever a sitting President's been challenged in the primaries, he's always won the nomination—but then gone on to lose in November. I don't like the odds. I still say we need something to blow his ass outta the water before New Hampshire!" She sipped her cognac and stared into the flames—an idea gathering. "What—if we were to turn the tables on him—and give the Mentors full credit for alerting us in time! Thereby demonstrating that they are: One; Still around—Two; Able and willing to provide emergency assistance—and Three; Communicating their help directly an exclusively to us."

Bryce considered it briefly and shook his head. "No way. Most Republicans find the Aliens' brand of social economics odious. The last thing we want to do is pass on credit to our celestial friends. What's more, we don't want to say anything to confirm they're still up there—watching. To do so would only serve to keep the focus on them—something which would play directly into Dave Onager's hands."

Painful experience had taught Iana to avoid the razor-wire options—Suddenly she felt a palm on her thigh—and promptly removed it. "Think of my leg as a third rail, Mr. President. Albeit one with zero current flowing through it." She knew by his expression he had no idea what she meant.

She stretched, tongues of flame licking at her eyeballs. "So then, we're left with nothing else to do but exalt form over substance. In other words, spend a bundle running lots of really slick, high-minded thirty-second paeans to you. You sure you can live with that?"

He shut his eyes and sighed. "May not have much choice."

*   *   *

Senator Onager made no public comment on the incident at Pedro Miguel, and would not. He was not one to pile on when an opponent was down, especially when that opponent was a friend.

It was Saturday and he invited his AA, Tommy Raffle, to lunch. It would give them a private opportunity to discuss campaign strategy—and to hit Tommy with his plan for redistributing the wealth. He was considering making Raffle his chief policy wonk, and this would be the acid test.

Jane's grilled salmon was sublime, but her apricot pie with crème de cacao and raisins was a major disappointment.

Onager and Raffle retired to the library to talk politics. "Tommy, what do you think constitutes the biggest waste of taxpayer money of all?" Onager asked.

"Waste, Fraud 'n Abuse, I suppose."

"Wrong. It's the billions we piss down the drain every year servicing the National Debt. Money which buys us nothing—we have nothing to show for it!" Just getting wound up, he began to pace. "The country is once again trillions of dollars in debt—and essentially in perpetuity! It's like owing a loan-shark: you kill yourself paying the interest—and never touch the principle!" He walked to the window in time to see the wind insolently whip about the leaves he'd raked into a neat pile just an hour ago.

"Eventually," Onager continued, "voters are gonna rebel—and demand that something be done. Of course, should annual deficits take off again, with the attendant rise in interest rates—the debt keeps climbing—with the likely choice in the end being to either monetize the debt—meaning devaluate the dollar—or—default, which clobbers all the bondholders—and drives the economy into recession!"

He directed a silent curse at the wind and turned.

"Therefore, I say the only sane course of action, the only one that's both fiscally responsible and socially ethical is to pay off the National Debt in its entirety!" There was fire in his eyes. "For years all we heard was the flap of gums over 'reducing the deficit' and 'balancing the budget.' Well sir, the National Debt is perpetual debt—and it took the Mentors to wake us up, for God's sake!"

Raffle knew to shut up when the boss was this torqued.

"Hell, Tommy, it's like a ship at sea taking on water: the first thing you do is plug the leak! (meaning, stop taking on more debt) —and then start the bilge pumps! (meaning, pay down the principle!) And how do we do this, you ask—?

One; take debt Service off-budget —thereby creating huge instant surpluses;

Two; establish an Office of National Debt Service—an office, not an entire bureaucracy;

Three; enact a one-time Federal Property Tax on all assets here and abroad—levied on the top three percent of corporations."

"You want all the millionaires out there throwing Molotov cocktails at your motorcade?" Raffle blanched.

Onager's face darkened a shade or two. Raffle knew this meant magma was shifting below. Something was coming.

"Tommy, do you know that the personal wealth of the top three percent is enough to pay off the National Debt many times over, nearly twenty-five trillion!" He turned and smiled. "So, while the top three percent pick up the tab for all the interest, the rest of us can begin paying down the principle—beginning with automatically applying all budget surpluses and asset sales directly to the debt! And lastly, sell off all unused or under-used federal non military assets."

"You don't exactly deal with small ideas, do you?" Raffle breathed, struggling to assemble all the fiscal and economic implications, domestic and foreign, of actually paying off the whole damn thing.

"Now, Tommy, get this: With only the wealthy paying the interest, if they're heavily invested in T-Bills, most of it goes right back to them anyway! For them all it amounts to is a redistribution of the wealth among the wealthy!"

That notion produced a moment of political delight. "By the way," Onager went on, "as the principle is paid down by all of us the property tax rates on the superrich would be reduced accordingly by the Office of

Debt Service, which would set the rates each year. Now Tommy—imagine the long-term effect on new investment—when Debt Service no longer sucks up hundreds of billions in capital every year!" He grinned. "Know what the real irony is? Paying off the debt is the soundest way to protect bondholders from possible one-day devaluation or default! Hell, the rich should get down on their damn knees to thank us!" he roared.

"Are we to assume then that this proposal will become the centerpiece of your presidential campaign?"

"I'm certainly giving it some quality thought." He eyed his AA. "Tommy—if you can buy into this whole concept, I'd like to name you as deputy manager of my campaign."

"You realize—"Raffle squinted, "you pull this off, and the Mentors will return for sure."

"There now, you see?—Here I thought I was being so clever, and you see right through me." He said it with such cheer, for a moment Raffle thought the senator was serious.

*   *   *

In the aftermath of Pedro Miguel the media were clamoring for a news conference, and Bryce allowed press secretary to talk him into holding one. It was a decision he'd rue.

The very first question was discomfiting. "Mr. President, how did you first learn of the threat to the Panama Canal?"

"We, uh, received a tip. From a confidential source."

"'We' meaning the CIA or the FBI?"

"I—suppose one could say that."

From there it only went downhill.

In Baltimore a security technician at the Smithsonian was home watching the news conference. He'd been on duty the night the Iyerborg-Gelatt message arrived. Now, as he heard the President LIE to the world, he was suddenly glad he'd thought to make a surreptitious copy of the tape. He could smell money—or at the very least, his fifteen minutes of fame. He wondered how much the tabloids would pay, then closed his eyes and imagined himself on the Tonight Show.

*   *   *

Peter Klein sat at his desk trying to figure ways to cut four-hundred fifty-thousand dollars from next year's NSO budget. Already short-staffed, there were times when he wished he worked for a Democrat.

The CHIMERA file was now closed, and would so remain unless the Mentors staged a return. Frankly Peter was glad; the pressure had been gut-wrenching. Thank God Ellen Kate had been there! And in fact still was. She was now in her fifth month, and it wouldn't be much longer before the White House had to put out a statement. Every time they were in the same room, her father would level looks at him. The message clear: If you love her, do the right thing! When Karyn buzzed to tell him he was wanted in the Oval Office, he gave an involuntary shudder—this could not be good.

He was ushered directly in. Another bad sign.

The President looked up from his desk, Iana Ravenscroft seated to one side also gazing up at him. Both wore serious expressions.

"You sent for me, Sir?" Peter asked tentatively, stopping about half way to the desk.

As if on silent cue, Bryce and Iana suddenly stood and broke into broad smiles. The President walked over and shook his hand. "Had you going for a minute there, didn't we?" he chuckled. "Come sit over here—Iana—Good. Peter, I asked you here to undo a slight—in the credit department." Peter began to relax. "At my press conference I implied that the credit for saving the Canal could go to CIA or FBI and their confidential informants. To have done otherwise would have only opened up one God-awful can of worms!"

Bryce leaned closer. "I want to personally acknowledge the debt we all owe you, Peter. If you hadn't seen in the nick of time that the name could be the name of a ship, right now Gatun Lake would be a mosquito-infested mud hole—and I'd be standing up to my neck in shit!"

"Peter," Iana smiled, "we can't give you a medal or a raise, but we want you to remain in charge of CHIMERA."

"I thought we'd closed it down."

"Officially we did. But since we now know the Mentors are still up there, watching, we must develop a strong position, with the appropriate responses in the event the Mentors stage a return. But it seems we may have some time. They spoke of a possible return in 'a year.' So try to think of all the possibilities: what we can foresee, we can deal with.

Peter, how many individuals actually know about the message, including everyone at the Smithsonian?"

"I'll compile a list—less than a dozen, I imagine."

"Get right on it. We've gotta keep a lid on this, Peter. I shudder to think what Festerschmucker might do with it." He brightened and slapped Peter on the knee. "You free for supper? Katie's coming over. We're having 'Squall'—quail stuffed with squid."

Peter couldn't tell whether Bryce was messing with him again. He was beginning to like the man.

Iana motioned Peter to follow her back to her office.

"Don't let all that go to your head," she snapped, closing the door behind her and pointing to a chair. He sat. "I need to know all about you and Ellen Kate."

"And why is that?" he countered.

"Frankly, the idea of you boinking the First Daughter and breaking bread with the First Family sets my teeth on edge." She lit a rare cigarette. "There's but one national security adviser around here: Dr. Klein; and I won't have some senior staffer dispensing opinions on policy matters."

"I've never discussed policy with the President. He's never asked for an opinion and I've never offered one."

She decided to accept this at face value. "Should he ever seek your opinion on anything other than squall—and you should be so rash as to come up with one—and I find out, I may have to fire you on security grounds."

"What the hell are you talking about, Iana?"

"I'm talking about certain disclosures you made to Ellen Kate aboard your little Sea Particle—when you were below decks—and thought no one could overhear you."

*　　*　　*

NEOSQUIRE was up to no good. Cracking the final cyber security gate erected by the National Rifle Association to safeguard its data, Justin rubbed his hands in anticipation.

He punched up his list of pornographic vendors hawking everything from crotchless panties and anal lip gloss to mink ball warmers and inflatable love objects. He giggled aloud and entered the E-mail command which would give every N.R.A. member's name and address to all fifty-five vendors.

"OHHHH-SHIT!"

"I say it's time we introduced them," Peter declared with arch confidence. It was their third phone conversation of the day.

"And I say it would be loathe-at-first-sight," Ellen Kate countered with matching conviction.

"You have to understand, my love—Cheez Whiz is a very stately, very dignified gentleman. I haven't seen him bare a claw since the Bush Administration. By design, he remains utterly above any fray. He's pure Zen. A good name for him would be Mellow Yellow."

"Fine. So maybe OooYaYaBangToy won't actually jump the old boy's bones—she'll just send him screeching up the nearest tree! She'd do it for the entertainment value alone—which for her would be considerable. She'd deem it high comedy." He snorted in appreciation.

Saturday was the day of the fateful meeting. As promised by the 'meaty urologists' (as Ellen Kate called all weather-persons), it was bright and crisp, with winds out of the South. Autumn color lingered here and there—a few fields were still green—and a killing frost was due.

Peter had picked them up just before noon. Ellen Kate wore faded jeans and looked more like someone bearing a large breakfast than a small person. They placed the cat carriers on the back seat—open ends facing so the beasts within could begin getting acquainted. The hissing started at once, and continued sporadically into the foothills.

Peter knew a place called Clyde's Landing where one could rent a canoe and paddle down still waters for seven languid miles. The Secret Service had approved the outing, and would guard them from astern in the "chase canoe." A half-dozen more agents, if needed, would be only minutes away.

It would be another half-hour to the river. Peter wondered whether the cats would make it.

"Okay—"Ellen Kate groaned in rank skepticism, "let's review The Plan: We load both carriers into the canoe and then, when we're well away from shore, open the cages. This—is your idea of a Plan?"

"Right—there'll be no place for either to go, so, they'll have no choice but to get along! They'll find themselves in the same boat, as it were." She held up two fingers, scoring the pun 'two Pukes.'

"How much longer?"

"Thirty minutes, give or take. They still having hissy-fits back there?"

As promised, they were soon picking out canoes. Ellen Kate said she wanted the black one, "to match the mood of the cats." The agents selected a large brown one.

The concessionaire, a bloat of a man with a mean porcine face, toted the black canoe down to the dock, plopped it into the water and waddled off.

With assistance, Ellen Kate stepped gingerly into the canoe and quickly sat. Peter then passed her each cat carrier, which she carefully placed in the bottom facing forward. He handed down the paddles, and suggested she stand so he could pass down the large red cooler.

"I have to stand up?" she asked, becoming apprehensive.

"Hey, if you prefer, I can ask your bodyguards to lend you a hand," he teased. She hesitated, and then stood up, planting her feet as widely as possible. She wobbled tentatively for a few moments, and then steadied. "Good, you got it. Now here—take it by the handle—that's it—"

"No, wait!—I—can't.—Oh, SHIT!" she screamed as the canoe tipped over, depositing her and both cats in frigid water. She leapt instantly to her feet, waist-deep in the stream, and grabbed the cat carriers which were beginning to fill—wide eyes blazing accusingly from within. Suddenly, with commendable dispatch, an agent ran down the dock and jumped in beside her, snatched the draining cages, flung them into shallow water, and grasped his wet charge by both hands. Peter looked down at the two in the water and began to laugh. Reaching down, he hauled the First Daughter up onto the dock, struggling to muzzle his mirth.

The outing aborted, they headed back to the city. By now the cats had been removed from their cages and thoroughly dried—yet were hardly mollified. The animals sat quietly on the rear seat in a comradeship born of shared ordeal.

This was not quite the case with their owners—one of whom, after all, had remained completely dry.

They were halfway back to Washington when Peter's beeper went off: The Post had just broken the story that it had been the Mentors who in fact alerted the White House to the danger of "Iyerborg Domenico Gelatt."

John VanOrsdell

BILLIARD'S BALL

The balloon was up and Gordon Fenstermacher, appearing on NIGHTLINE, lost no time capitalizing on the opportunity.

"It's a sorry spectacle—the commander-in-chief ordering military action based on a cryptic tip from some celestial snitch—and then trying to cover it up by claiming it was a CIA or FBI informant," he railed. "Small wonder. When Nancy Reagan consulted an astrologer, everyone in politics had a fit! Well by comparison, this makes her astrological dalliance look like a minuscule political peccadillo!"

When asked by a reporter later in the day whether he'd care to respond, Bryce was quick to counter that "This so-called 'celestial snitch' in fact enabled us to save the Panama Canal from being put out of business for two years! As an alleged Republican, he should understand the implications of that. Moreover, I'd remind him that the Mentors entrusted us with this warning—and we were able to act in time."

Unfortunately, the President had just opened a whole new can of worms: Why hadn't the United States known beforehand of an impending terrorist attack? Bryce had all but conceded that without Mentor intervention the Canal would have been lost. They'd be finessing that one for some time.

Then there was the other question: Were the Mentors still up there—watching—even listening somehow? They had certainly known exactly what the terrorists were up to. The very notion of celestial eavesdropping made everybody extremely uncomfortable—with the exceptions of Dave Onager and Art Frayles, who found it reassuring.

*　　*　　*

Liu Biao Teng was arguably Taiwan's most demagogic and destabilizing political figure. As leader of the fast-rising National Sovereignty Action Party (NSAP), he openly and fervently called for total independence from China, and for full international recognition as the Republic of Taiwan.

"I too advocate a One China policy," Liu quipped in a televised debate: "One China—One Taiwan—One United States." It was promptly dubbed the 'One-One-One Policy.'

On December fifteen Liu Biao Teng announced his candidacy for president, and overnight thousands of 'one+one+one = Liu' campaign buttons bloomed on the streets of Taipei.

Nationalism had become the chant of the crowd.

Beijing was enraged, and thundered its determination to keep the "renegade Province of Taiwan forever part of the People's Republic of China."

Washington viewed all this with growing alarm. A military defense of Taiwan and a confrontation with China was the very last thing the United States wanted. But should Liu and his fellow NSAP candidates take power, Beijing could well resort to force to crush what they'd already branded "an intolerable insurrection." In the event of hostilities, Taiwan would of course mount a savage and valiant defense, but ultimately the United States would be forced to step, in lest Taiwan fall. Congress and the American people would demand nothing less—exactly what Liu was counting on. Over the weekend he all but "guaranteed" the Seventh Fleet would come to the defense of Taiwan—at once emboldening his countrymen, infuriating those who ruled his ancestral homeland, and forcing Sam Bryce to straddle a very pointy fence.

Pressed for comment on Liu's statement, White House press secretary Reene Vallek reaffirmed America's One China policy, adding a pointed caveat: "It would be a grave miscalculation for any potential aggressor to ever assume the United States would stand idly by in the event one of its friends came under military attack."

*   *   *

The First Family tried to make the most of the holidays, but no one was feeling especially merry.

The President was worried about how the exposure of his working relationship with the Mentors (whom he'd stopped referring to as 'Aliens') would play with voters. At least in the wake of Pedro Miguel, one could no longer criticize the Mentors for 'meddling in terrestrial affairs.' As to the presidential race, the fact that a warning was given at all primarily benefited Onager by demonstrating that the Mentors were truly here to help us—and the wisdom of paying them heed even, one might easily extrapolate, when being given environmental, social, and economic advice.

For her part, the First Lady's Christmas was completely clouded over by her husband's recent, all too transparent carnal interest in Iana Ravenscroft. Abby thought that his concupiscent proclivities had gone the way of his libido but apparently only when it came to conjugal relations. So when he'd tried to give her fanny a Xmas pat, she brushed his hand away—suspecting where it might last have been.

He would have been wise to notice.

Ellen Kate's Xmas wasn't much better. Well past mid-term, she was beginning to show. And draw looks. It had been decided that the Big Announcement would come in January.

Looking ahead, she didn't know how long she could not work and still maintain her apartment—maybe four months. The idea of going to work each day and depositing her baby in some day care center was abhorrent—she wanted to be with her baby, not off covering the dumb Washington social scene. Peter of course wanted to set up housekeeping, cohabiting cats and all. But Ellen Kate had always intuited that there was a path she must walk alone. A destiny, if you will. Worst case scenario: She might have to let her parents help out.

All agreed the Bryce Family Christmas "sucked," as Abby put it. Gift-opening had been pro forma and listless. As usual, Art Frayles had joined them for Christmas dinner, but the tension over his new alliance with Dave Onager had spread a grey glaze over the turkey. Adding to their discomfort, on no fewer than five holiday occasions Bryce and his wife were forced to gaze down upon babes in crèches—instant reminder that a spate of baby showers and paparazzi lay ahead. Not to mention afternoon talk shows focusing on 'Women who Choose to Have Babies Without Husbands' and 'Single Mothers who Reject Live-in Fathers.' The President could hardly wait.

New Year's Eve at the Residence was a small, quiet affair. The Vice President and his wife dropped by to toast the New Year, as did the Bentons, the Severinghauses, the Bozorths, and Ms. Ravenscroft, but Katie and Peter were no-shows.

Everyone had been en route to one party or another and had departed well before midnight with the exception of Iana, who hated parties in general and New Year's Eve blowouts in particular. Drunken tongues celebrating inside her mouth was not her idea of fun.

"Well—you two can stay up all night talking campaign strategy if you want," Abby yawned around 11:30 p.m. "Me, I'm going to bed. Happy New Year, everybody—" She stifled another yawn, waved, and departed.

"Happy New Year, Dear—" Bryce called after her, then turned and faced Iana. "How 'bout a little game of pool?"

They descended to the Billiards Room, where the national security adviser kicked off her heels while the president removed his smoking jacket and poured them drinks.

"If you think getting me soused is going to give you the edge you need to beat me, think again," she smiled.

Iana took her glass and downed it—then whirled on the table and broke with a smash. Balls flew to every cushion; two sank. Then, having left herself with poor position, she walked around the table in search of a shot. Seeing nothing promising, she tried a tricky combination and missed.

"You always go for the tough ones," Bryce observed, lining up a combination of his own—as the thirteen ball dropped from sight. "Pretend that was Fenstermacher," he said, circling for his next shot. He sank two more, and then missed an easy one. "Shit."

Iana took the first game. They refilled glasses and chalked sticks. She suddenly remembered to check the time: "Hey, Happy three minutes after New Year's!" He grinned, walked over, took her in his arms, and bestowed a deep, open-mouth kiss. "Happy New Year yourself," he purred, arching his back and pressing his groin into hers.

She pulled her head back. "I know what you're up to—you're just trying to distract me. It won't work, buddy." She pulled away, and turned to the table. "President or not I'm gonna clean yer clock!"

From that moment on, Sam Bryce played for position.

On any shot he knew he was likely to miss, he'd merely try leave the cue ball close to the center of the table, his ploy being to force her to lean way out—one foot on the floor, the other leg up and stretched way back—in order to line up a shot. It was the reason he'd imposed a No Bridge rule. Stationing himself directly behind her during such shots, he wondered whether she'd picked up on his little trick.

For New Year's Iana had worn a beige silk blouse, tucked into a short, tight bronze skirt that rode well up her thigh every time she had to stretch out long for a shot, which tonight seemed to be frequently the case. Damn right she knew what he was up to.

131

They celebrated with another drink, the President looking pointedly down at her chest as they sipped. She ignored his gaze and turned to deal with another cue ball he'd managed to leave smack in the middle of the Seal. She pushed her hair back, and arched out over the stick.

Bryce licked the contours beneath her skirt with his eyes—then unbuckled, unzipped, and climbed up on her. Spotting his pants on the floor, she suddenly knew this was no overture. Fight him off? Create a crisis? Is it worth it? Oh hell, I've submitted before. One more time won't kill me.

The act of sex didn't repel her—it simply bored her. "I thought—" she breathed, feeling his hand grope for her panties, "you were saving this for Gordon." He chuckled, managed to bare her bottom, and mounted her.

They were well into mid-hump-frenzy when the First Lady appeared in the doorway. For several moments she stood frozen—watching—glaring—and unnoticed. When at last she spoke, her tone was arctic.

"The Mentors must be enjoying this about as much as I am."

ULTIMATUM

"Either the bitch's resignation's on your desk by tomorrow or divorce papers will be the next day!" Abby stood up, her breakfast untouched. "Take your pick, Woody."

She was playing hardball. They both knew it could cost him the election were she to file on grounds of adultery. He pictured that press conference—and shuddered.

Iana might actually have to go.

*   *   *

The host leaned back and eyed his guest. "Gordon, w-h-y are you so wound up over the Aliens? Some people accuse you of using them as an excuse to enter the campaign. How do you respond?"

"It should come as no surprise to you, my friend, to learn that I have a lot more on my mind than interference on the part of Aliens. The GOP has always fought to lower taxes, and if you'll recall, President Bryce pledged to do just that. Well, I don't have to tell you: in the last three years he's not only failed to propose one single tax cut, he's actually called for raising taxes on large businesses! So there are many, many reasons why I'm in this race."

"How about making some news then—by announcing tonight what the theme of your campaign is going to be."

"Well, since you asked—"he smiled, "someone came up with 'Standing Tall for Us All.' Kinda got a nice ring to it, don'cha think?"

*   *   *

Peter Klein had a lot more on his mind than a pregnant girlfriend. The President had been stung by Fenstermacher's attack, and the polls reflected it. Accordingly, Bryce had tasked Peter to devise a 'sound, pro-active Action Plan' for dealing with the Aliens (as he now called them, having dropped "Mentors" altogether), should they return. "Something that gets a standing ovation," he had stipulated.

Pay-back time for knocking up his angel, Peter decided.

He'd considered trying to buck responsibility up to Iana, but knew better than to try. So he scheduled a National Security brainstorming session for 1:50 p.m. He was damned if he was going to try to design a Bryce Pleaser all on his own. At 1:51 p.m. the meeting began.

"Shaky Assumption Number One:" Klein led off, "The Aliens have left. Actually all we know for certain is that we can't see them anymore. But, what if they're still up there—watching—?"

"Or worse: watching and listening," contributed Reba, team cynic. "Suppose right now—they're up there listening to this very conversation!"

"Talk about a worst-case-scenario—that would have to be it," moaned Nick Rheme, ex-Navy Seal, grandmaster tactician, and lethal poker player.

"You're right," conceded Iana. "Because anything we might come up with would instantly be known to them. We'd be better off doing nothing at all under those circumstances."

Klein leaned forward. "Are we not therefore compelled to accept as Shaky Assumption number two that the Aliens are not listening—mankind being immobilized in the alternative?"

Following extended discussion ranging from psychics to metaphysics, Shaky Assumption number two was finally adopted.

*   *   *

"Senator Onager, believe me, I've racked my brain trying to find a plausible alternative—without success," Arthur Frayles confessed.

"In other words—you're convinced, mind and heart, that the Mentors are benign. That they're here purely out of High Purpose. Truthful, if not forthcoming, but above all: benign—posing no threat other than ideological. Am I correct?" Onager pressed.

"In a word, Yes. But tell me, since we're off the record, do you plan to make the Mentors the central issue of your campaign?"

"And how the President dropped the ball? Hardly. But on the record, their advice will be the heart my campaign."

ORIGINS

Arthur Frayles sat at his desk and mulled over the single question people most wanted answered: Where did the Mentors come from? He pulled out his transcript from the First Convening and searched it yet one more time for any possible clue he had overlooked. Nothing. He turned to the transcript of the Second Convening—and reread the Mentors' sole pronouncement on the subject. It had come in response to Avery Eastman's frustrated query, "Can you at least confirm that we all call the same galaxy Home?"

"That would be an accurate statement," Beta had allowed.

Not much, but something at least.

The Mentors' role in saving the Panama Canal was the subject of endless analysis, discussion, and debate, dominating the global media day after day, week after week. The public's appetite was insatiable.

In America, public perception and reaction were beginning to emerge. In rounded numbers, of those having already formed an opinion:

Nine in ten believed something was going on;

Eight in ten believed the Mentors were real;

Seven in ten believed they were from a nearby planet;

Six in ten believed they would soon return;

Five in ten believed they were still here, watching;

Four in ten believed them to be truthful and trustworthy;

Three in ten believed we should heed their advice;

Two in ten believed the government wasn't telling all;

One in ten believed the Mentors posed a genuine threat

—and should be dealt with accordingly.

Not surprisingly, every presidential candidate was being pressured to take a clear stand on the Mentors, every other issue being in total eclipse. Of all the hopefuls, this posed the least problem for David Onager, who had already publicly sided with the thirty percent who believed the world should be heeding the Mentors' advice. The challenge would be translating their guidance into concrete legislative proposals.

Just as firm in his position, and unimpressed by the Mentors' Panamanian intelligence tip, Gordon Fenstermacher remained adamant that the Aliens constituted a mortal threat to the American System. And his strategy quickly became one of making Republicans fear for their very economic survival.

Bill Ordahl was somewhere in the middle. Having closely studied the polls, he strove to formulate a popular political position. He didn't see this as merely telling people what they wanted to hear, but as being "appropriately responsive" to the will of the people.

The lesser Democrats lurched about, conspicuously unsure of what exactly to say. Only one, Rep. Valen of Texas, took a clear stand: he declared that the Aliens journeyed here to study us and to test our resolve. Beyond that, he declined to elaborate.

But of all the aspirants, President Bryce had the biggest problem taking a position. He could easily forfeit his conservative base through further cooperation with the Mentors, although his responsibility as President might demand it.

Monday evening the President called his National Security Adviser into his private office and closed the door.

"Iana," he began, "we have something of a problem on our hands." She settled into a leather armchair and crossed her legs. His eyes flickered down before he could stop them; reflex, he dismissed. "I'm afraid the First Lady is still pretty pissed over—Well, she's hit me with an ultimatum: Either you go—or she files for divorce. And I don't have to tell you what that would do to my chances in November."

Iana narrowed her eyes at him. "And so—you want to fire me? Is that what you're trying to say?"

"No, I—what I want is for you to be my new ambassador to Switzerland. The Alps are—"

"You know where you can stick the Matterhorn!" she spat. She'd anticipated something like this. "In that case, Mr. President, permit me to respond in kind: You fire me—and I'll call a news conference and reveal exactly why in lurid detail—and charge you with sexual harassment! Lawsuit to follow." She stood and strode from the room.

*   *   *

Senator Onager had tasked his staff to compile figures on U.S. wealth distribution since 1980.

When the numbers were crunched, the picture which emerged was potential social and political dynamite.

By early January Onager's campaign wonks reached agreement on his basic economic theme:

Wealth distribution in America had gone haywire;

Republicans cut taxes for the wealthy and exploded the National Debt;

It's time for the wealth distribution pendulum to swing the other way.

Plus, agreement on one central proposal:

Let the wealthiest three percent pay the interest on the National Debt, while the rest of us pay off the principal. Let the Federal Property Tax paid be a deduction towards their personal Income Tax calculation.

That was something everybody should be able to understand.

It was decided to unveil the Onager Plan on January tenth—three-hundred seventy-five days short of Inauguration Day.

*   *   *

136

"Sexual Harassment?" Abby sneered. "I should let her do it! You deserve no less. But then—you wouldn't be Mr. President any more, would you!"

The First Lady was pacing in her nightgown, smoking a unfiltered cigarette. Bryce watched her in the mirror as he tied his tie. The cigarette was not a good sign.

Finally she wheeled on him. "All right, here it is—the bitch can stay, with one proviso: From this moment on you have a Co-President! Meaning—and now I want you to pay real close attention to this, Woody—I have de facto veto power over any executive decision you might be planning to make! So get used to the idea of running everything by me whenever you think you've reached a decision. Otherwise—I still file for divorce. And then, Cupcake: Neither of us'll be president!"

That night Abby got her first good night's sleep of the new year.

And dreamed of becoming a grandmother.

PART TWO

ABYTOR

ABYTOR

Sandovar Abydos was half visionary genius and half feral capitalist. He was at once an arch jingoist, a bold gambler, a darkly handsome billionaire and, not surprisingly, irresistible to women.

Having a grandfather from Athens and a mother from Milan, Abydos claimed to be Greco-Roman in spite of being born in Newark and growing up in lower Manhattan—fewer than a dozen blocks, it turned out, from where he'd make his millions as a stock trader and hedge fund manager, and his billions as a currency speculator. He had reached sixty-four without marrying, but had nonetheless taken care to make sure his genes were spread liberally throughout the female population. Only one male offspring did he ever acknowledge as his progeny, adopt at birth, and rear in his own image: Epizutus Marcellus Abydos.

In 1991, Sandovar Abydos scooped up his winnings and left the money game to devote full time, energy and resources to what he called his "crowning achievement."

'Zooti' Abydos, though fully as cunning and calculating as his father, had inherited not a rung on the helix of his dad's visionary DNA. Not at the outer reaches of his prosaic imagination could Epizutus have ever conceived the wondrous creation his father had wrought—ABYTOR.

The most exclusive, expensive, and highest corporate conference center and retreat on earth, lavishly constructed on top of an eleven-thousand six-hundred foot summit in northeastern Utah. A massive three-story, five-hundred and sixty foot diameter, glittering discus of glass and stainless steel—hanging out over space as if skewered in flight, forever impaled between earth and sky.

Finding the right peak had been problematic, since Abydos' dual stipulations were severely limiting: one: The Mountain must be isolated, and two: It must rise steeply to its summit on all sides. A small task force had spent weeks poring over topographical maps, satellite and aerial photos, and invested long hours in helicopters circling a handful of candidate peaks in five states. With Indian Reservations and National

Parks eliminated up front, the search ultimately narrowed to a single mountain in Utah. It then took some fat bribes in high places to finally secure federal approvals and a ninety-nine year lease.

On the positive side, by being located inside a National Forest there were no abutters to oppose, no neighbors to complain, and no preservation groups to march in protest.

Design and engineering had been accomplished in a mere seventeen months. Abydos had raided several of the top architectural firms in Europe and assembled a gifted creative team headed by Holland's foremost designer of cantilever bridges. They eventually came up with a concept which genuinely excited Abydos, structural engineering could finally commence.

From the outset fresh ground would be broken every step of the way. First, a stunning all-weather, outside, cog-elevator system, involving a four minute, four-thousand nine-hundred-thirty foot ascent—at a heart-stopping seventy-nine degrees angle of inclination! The twin elevators would gently whisk tons of steel, concrete, and glass to the peak—and later tons of food, furniture, and guests. All this would be accomplished by a pair of thirty -by -thirty -by -thirty foot glass 'Vista Cubes' with belted seating for the faint of heart.

There would be three-hundred-eighty opulent Grand Staterooms, twenty-eight Executive Suites, and five Owners' Suites for VIP guests and dignitaries. A central three-hundred-sixty degrees dining room-auditorium would serve five-hundred, with breakout rooms for smaller meetings. The elegant Celestial Cocktail Lounge—with its sixteen inch reflecting telescope for gazing upon the heavens—beckoned all drinkers. And for the physically adventurous, a plunge into Thor's Grotto—said to be bottomless, its underwater side lamps swallowed up by the deep as the eye descends.

The permitting process had been a nightmare—from scores of costly environmental impact studies, to locating proposed access roads, to assuring emergency ingress and egress, to waste treatment and snow removal. Although the Center was to be built on federal property, a local planning board, and not the Interior Department, retained jurisdiction. The Town of Rushing Gorge predated the national forest by a century.

The five-member, flannel-shirt board, which had never before dealt with anything more complicated than reviewing a permit for a filling station, suddenly found itself facing cadres of lawyers, engineers, environmentalists, and technocrats from a dozen bureaucracies—all this exacerbated by vocal groups of local residents who wanted no part of "any damned large-scale corporate development" in their town. Hearings dragged on for weeks.

As set forth in the application, water and fuel would be pumped to storage tanks concealed on top of the mountain; there would be zoned automatic sprinklers throughout; redundant emergency generators could provide power for six weeks if necessary; and sufficient food would be stockpiled for a month. With blizzards in mind, the board asked for a well-equipped and staffed medical infirmary, plus an emergency helicopter landing pad. The applicant promptly agreed.

The issue which fostered the most debate was the proposed indoor atmospheric system—designed to pressurize and oxygenate the rarefied outside air to equal that found at five-thousand feet of elevation. One board member wanted to know what would happen "should the pressure blow out a whole section of window?" This quickly broadened into protracted discussion of security measures and systems. Ever since Pedro Miguel, potential terrorist attacks loomed in the minds of many. One board member urged as a condition of approval a requirement that all guests and staff be screened and searched before stepping into a Vista Cube, "As if they were about to board El Al!" The project manager hastened to assure the board that, "a large number of high-tech, very sophisticated methodologies, which cannot be discussed in public, will be employed. I can assure you, Sir, Mr. Abydos believes in protecting his investments."

Yet in the end, it was fear of fire that most troubled the board. It concluded that smoke could be readily vented, but getting people out was a problem inherent in the site. "By the time firefighters arrive and get to the top, everyone could be dead," warned the chair. The sheriff jumped in: "How do you evacuate a thousand people in two elevators?" The fire chief shrugged. "Until you can get 'em all out, you just gotta keep 'em soaked." This made eminent sense to the board.

Thus, engineers agreed to pipe water from the fifty-four foot deep "swimming crevasse" into the sprinkler system, which had a "high-douse capacity"—and final approval was granted.

ABYTOR opened for business in late 1998 and had been booked to capacity ever since.

Sandovar Abydos alone decided which corporations and which groups would become invited guests. To no one's surprise, he favored ultraconservatives over conservatives, conservatives over moderates, fundamentalists over environmentalists, rich over poor, management over labor, Republicans over Democrats.

Progressives and Libertarians were promptly referred to the Greenbrier—while "flaming liberals, tree-huggers, and gun-bashers" were directed to Hell.

Politically and economically, 'Sandi' Abydos' views were extreme. He believed men convicted of sex crimes should be given a choice: "twenty years behind bars—or twenty minutes on the operating table being relieved of their genitalia. How's that for instant rehabilitation!"

He even had a solution for students rioting after a game: "Fly over'em in choppers and spray'em with puking gas!"

He was even less forgiving of drunk drivers: "Summary curbside execution!" But his real salvos were saved for "the tax-ocrats who want to take away everything we have—and their God damn fellow-travelers overhead!"

It had been of particular interest to Sandovar Abydos to learn that Gordon Fenstermacher had named Egon Ovid to run his Campaign: Egon and Zooti had been Wharton School classmates and fraternity brothers. And they had remained close friends ever since.

*   *   *

AXE-TAX-PAC was the personal creation of Sandovar Abydos. Its Mission Statement was short and blunt: "To support the election of candidates who oppose progressive taxation."

Under January's full moon, ABYTOR became the setting for a three-day "Fenstermacher for President Fund-raiser and Hell-raiser"—featuring "two-hundred Lovelies in Waiting."

Invitations were much sought-after, but the guest list was limited to "hard-core, hard-on supporters." Demand was so high that one less-than-horny software CEO reportedly used his invitation to leverage a buy-out.

While everyone else was busy fund-raising—Zooti, Egon, and two Lovelies played Bobbing for Boobies in Thor's Grotto.

By the time four-hundred bleary-eyed, poorer, but sated fat cats glided down to the valley floor Monday morning, the Fenstermacher campaign had raised two-million one-hundred thousand dollars—and

AXE-TAX-PAC had pledges totaling another six-million eight-hundred thousand dollars.

*   *   *

That afternoon Justin Onager struck again—allowing the CBS Evening News to close with a bit of humor:

"Today a cyber-hacker known only as 'NEOSQUIRE' broke into the Florida Department of Corrections computers and posted a notice entitled 'INMATE PULL-TOY REGULATIONS' on its web-page. Among its requirements: 'No inmate may own more than one pull-toy'—'Pull-toys must be left outside the dining hall in the assigned parking area'—'Pull-toys may not be equipped with loud quackers'—'Pull-toys may not be used after 8:00 p.m.' and 'Any inmate who kicks, damages or urinates on another's toy will face severe Disciplinary Action.' (pause) The Department of Corrections was singularly unamused and refused all comment."

FA HAAD

The week that began with such corporate largess on behalf of the Fenstermacher presidential bid became progressively worse for Sam Bryce with each passing day.

On Tuesday, Abby deftly executed an act of sweet revenge by telling her husband that she had informed his mother of her son's tawdry coupling on the pool table.

On Wednesday as promised, David Onager unveiled his plan to pay off the National Debt within a generation. Media coverage had been massive, with CNN running day-long special programming on the issues the senator had raised, and the solutions he proposed. Every network invited Onager to appear on its shows—a bonanza of exposure his campaign could never have afforded.

To cap off his week, Friday afternoon Bryce was in the Oval Office greeting and congratulating members of the Super Bowl Champion Redskins, when suddenly everyone could hear a muffled commotion out in the antechamber. Oscar Benton swore under his breath and strode quickly to the door. The instant it parted, the President heard a familiar staccato of shrill expletives,—the First Mother had come to lecture her son and would brook no delay. When it came to berating, Isabel was formidable. "Nincompoop" was her kindest pejorative.

Truly the Week from Hell. Yet Sam Bryce would soon look back on it as one of his better ones.

*   *   *

Of all Soviet 'loose nukes,' the gravest danger was posed by SADMs: Special Atomic Demolition Munitions—designed for and delivered to the erstwhile KGB two decades earlier. One-hundred thirty-two portable, one point one kiloton atomic bombs—disguised as suitcases. Of which eighty-four were missing and unaccounted for.

The Mentors knew whereof they spoke.

Fa Haad had been enraged when his carefully orchestrated assault on the Panama Canal had failed so completely—mere inches from success. After a brutally objective postmortem, he concluded his plan had been too elaborate, too costly, and above all, involved too many people. These were mistakes he'd not repeat on the next attempt.

He'd never find another target with the Canal's power to injure and humiliate the United States; he'd have to settle for second best. Next time he'd strike inside the country.

His Islamic sponsors had been less than pleased with their return on investment, yet were still disposed to underwrite a second destructive venture. It was after all Fa Haad—and he was the best in the business.

Fa Haad had purchased Russian weapons before, but always through the military, using a chain of double-blind cutouts. But to get his hands on a functional SADM, he had no choice but to deal directly with the Russian Mafia—natural home to scores of former KGB senior officers.

Arkady Budayev, former KGB Second Directorate colonel and present millionaire gangster, had sold four SADMs to date—each expertly modified so that a single individual could arm, enable, initiate, and detonate. The fifth suitcase bomb was now ready for delivery, its plutonium pit radiating malevolently, its timing and firing circuits tested, checked, and rechecked by the very engineer who'd designed the lock-code circuitry which for decades had prevented the unauthorized launch

144

of a Soviet nuclear missile at sea. His extraordinary care with the current device was understandable: he had been bluntly informed that any malfunction in the field would occasion "the Wrath of Allah." The threat had been taken fully to heart, exactly as intended.

Thus it was with high confidence that Fa Haad awaited delivery of his 'luggage,' his plan all but finalized. And this time success would attend his efforts because he would personally be the delivery vehicle. It was a matter of professional pride and reputation—ideology and money coming second.

He relished the symbolism of his new target. As with the Canal, its elimination would be both strategic and economic—and even more enraging to the Americans.

One of the most-wanted terrorists on earth, Fa Haad had been the most bedeviling to law enforcement agencies. He'd suddenly appear, and then vanish the next instant. No one knew his true identity, nor even his nationality. Essentially he was known by his crimes—and by his operational signature: brilliant originality and brazen execution. It was this hallmark which quickly pointed to Fa Haad as the brain behind the outrageous attack on the Panama Canal. Reputation was a two-edged sword.

Fa Haad had never been identified, much less caught, for one primary reason: he was able to travel freely to any place on earth using an Austrian diplomatic passport. And he wasn't even Austrian.

*   *   *

Following the peaceful and successful re-assimilation of Hong Kong under a policy of 'One China—Two Systems'—and the subsequent quiet repatriation of Macao, the old men in Beijing had turned their attention to Taiwan. They'd tried using honey for nearly a decade, but all that their friendly overtures had produced was suspicion and a hardening of the island's will to achieve self-determination. And now with Liu Biao Teng effectively fomenting secession, it was time to apply a little vinegar.

Liu, gaining steadily in the polls, had boldly called for a national plebiscite. The government in Taipei, theretofore reluctant to offend China, had held a wet finger to the wind and decided that twenty-five million Chinese couldn't be wrong. So the cabinet debated a national plebiscite at length, the foreign minister arguing vigorously against one—characterizing any vote on sovereignty as "a sharp finger in Beijing's eye." Since everyone already knew which way the vote would go, he warned it would be viewed as a calculated provocation.

"Those behind the vermilion walls will not tolerate any deliberate provocation. They will surely resort to force!" the foreign minister heatedly warned.

Thirty-three nations already thumbed noses at Beijing by recognizing Taiwan as an sovereign state. America, unfortunately for the Taiwanese, was not among them. To Taipei, China and the U.S. were already so economically bound together. There was only the prospect of continuing growth in trade, and thus interdependence, between the two giants. Although Taiwan was the world's seventh largest economy, its leaders knew they weren't worth a full-blown war in the Pacific to either superpower.

Liu was compelled to agree, viewed logically. But he also knew freedom was an emotional issue for Americans—and that if one of their friends stood in mortal peril, they'd come to the defense of that friend.

The cabinet debate in Taipei churned on without reaching consensus. Playing it safe, the president ultimately opted to let the legislature decide whether to hold a plebiscite. It was a decision taken without consultation with Washington.

*   *   *

Egon Ovid had never before been sued for sexual harassment. But he'd attempted to play Pudenda Piñata with one lady lobbyist too many—and now had to sweat out Iana Ravenscroft coming forward to testify on the plaintiff's behalf.

He had thought lobbyists, if anyone, were still fair game. After all, how could anyone trying hard to sell you something then turn around and accuse you of exerting pressure on them?

Viewed in that light, who was the Harasser—and who was the Harassed?

Iana could be a major problem. She'd be bound to have high credibility with any jury. He had to find some means, anything, that would keep her mouth shut about gropings past. He decided to call Merle Starn at the White House. Having brought Starn on board shortly before being fired himself, he knew how to call in a chit when one was needed.

*　　*　　*

Senator Onager decided to forego the Iowa Caucus in order to concentrate on the impending primary in New Hampshire. He arrived in Manchester to a hail of cameras and waved, smiled and promised he wouldn't set foot outside the state until after Primary Day.

Though still stumping in Iowa, Governor Ordahl began heavy media buys in New England, shamelessly flattering the Granite State as "The Tax-Anathema State"—a slogan which cracked proud smiles across even the most geologic of faces. Ordahl was gaining slowly in the polls, but most troubling to his campaign—only in New Hampshire. Iowa was still soft.

The lesser Democratic hopefuls, having read the same polls, knew it was rapidly narrowing to a two-man race—as they began losing the power to attract donations. It wasn't long before drafts of eloquent withdrawal statements began coming together on a number of laptop screens.

NBC would host the first Democratic Debate in Concord, with the audience expected to be huge. Interest had quickly focused on David Onager. When Ordahl managed to win the Iowa Caucus, people barely noticed. It was the guy with the Mentors looking over his shoulder who everyone was watching. Some even told pollsters they intended to vote for Onager in hopes that doing so would bring back the Mentors.

The Fenstermacher camp was beginning to feel the heat of Mentor fever. In response they came up with an ad campaign of cartoon glow-worms in orbit preaching: "Lo, the rich shall be made poor—and the poor shall be enriched."

It was an already a presidential campaign like no other.

*　　*　　*

Merle Starn and Egon Ovid met for drinks at Bovina's.

"Well, I can tell you this much—" Starn whispered, leaning closer, "something happened down in the Billiards Room New Year's Eve. Don't know where the rumor started—a housekeeper, a steward, the Secret Service—but someone sure saw or heard something!"

147

"Like, what?" Ovid pressed, his juices suddenly surging.

Starn glanced around to make sure no one could hear, and then leaned even closer. "Scuttlebutt is—Bryce was banging Ravenscroft in the middle of his friggin' pool table when Dear Abby walks in and catches 'em in the act!"

"You're shitting me—!" Ovid breathed, his mind wildly spooling up the potential political impact. "And just how reliable is all this, Merle?"

"Well—everyone's noted an icy chill in the air whenever the Bryce's have to appear together.

"At last week's reception for the Canadian prime minister," he continued, "I caught her glaring at him when he asked her to dance. Then later on I saw her snarl something in his ear. All is definitely not well at sixteen-hundred."

POT PLANT OP

Penny Onager traveled to join her father in Concord for a weekend of campaigning. He was always delighted to have her at his side, since teenagers considered her 'really cool.' Penny was so open and spontaneous, so quick and funny, it was impossible not to like her. Reporters loved to interview her, and she thought being on local TV was a blast. More than once that weekend did the senator beam with pride.

To the genuine discomfort of Onager, his daughter stood in embarrassing contrast with fat, sullen, and zit-ridden sixteen year old Gloria Ordahl. The governor had scheduled a family appearance at a church supper in Nashua, not knowing Penny Onager was coming to town, and had to endure the inevitable whispered comparisons that followed.

It snowed overnight, and Sunday morning found all the candidates out tossing snowballs for the cameras: Penny Onager scored a bull's-eye on the back of her father's neck.

He whirled around, bending into a foolish dance to shake off the snow running down his collar. She came rushing over and started brushing it back in, thereby creating the photo-op of the day. Onager knew Penny knew exactly what she was doing, and decided she'd make a Hell of a candidate one day. Or stunt pilot. Or tattoo artist. It was still a little early to say.

That afternoon father and daughter Onager went for a sleigh ride outside Wolfeboro, trailed by camera trucks and running teenagers. Out of nowhere, someone ran up and thrust a fat marijuana joint into Penny's hand. She glanced down, instantly recognized what she was holding, and flashed a quick smile. No less than three cameras captured the moment.

When Egon Ovid saw the incident on the news, a small smile found its way onto his lips as well.

*   *   *

Sandovar Abydos had sized up the presidential races and already concluded that in November it would be Bryce vs. Onager. Moreover, he now accepted that his efforts on behalf of Fenstermacher would ultimately prove insufficient to deny Bryce the nomination.

Of course he'd continue to back the Republican spoiler, because in that way he could still go after the Aliens and everything they espoused. But following the convention he'd switch his support to Bryce, and bring his big-buck guns to bear on the real enemy: David Onager.

The arrival of the Mentors had shaken the very foundation under everything Abydos believed in and cherished. Suddenly the whole international system of economic order was undergoing profound reevaluation—as people began to question the material ethic itself. This was intolerable.

Shortly after the collapse of the Convenings, Abydos had created KAPPA UNO: a deep cover action group, chartered to "Devise ways and carry out means to permanently rid the planet of all Alien influence." There were eight members, all male: one reactionary astrophysicist—one fired aerospace engineer—two former intelligence field operatives—one militia colonel—one black belt computer geek—one explosives expert—and a forced-retirement police chief. The eight were hired as 'marketing consultants' by ABYTOR and paid a hundred-thousand dollars apiece. No additional personnel or subcontractors would be employed. And KAPPA UNO would have an unlimited operating budget.

Sandovar Abydos was far from alone in his hatred of the Mentors. The rich and powerful around the world, most particularly in the United States, felt threatened and endangered. Not all were willing to simply stand by and watch things fall apart. Some were disposed to act, and some were prepared to fight. It was from this latter group that Abydos had recruited the members of KAPPA UNO. He was its CEO—and his son remained wholly unaware of its existence.

The afternoon before the New Hampshire primary, ABYTOR hosted the fifth formal meeting of KAPPA UNO. A detailed mission plan was ready for review; today would be the final troubleshoot. If found solid, Abydos would green-light the operation. Time was becoming critical.

*   *   *

The next day David Onager won the New Hampshire Democratic Primary with forty-one percent of the vote; Ordahl managed only thirty-two percent.

Sixty-six percent of Republicans voted to re-elect President Bryce; Gordon Fenstermacher received twenty-six percent. But this was not good news for the White House; a serious insurrection was afoot and gaining momentum.

THE EMPEROR'S CAROM

It was the third time Ovid had tried to reach her. Iana sighed and decided to take the call.

"Well, Egon," she answered coolly, "I'm surprised to be hearing from you—what's the matter—your fish die?"

150

He ignored the insult. "Iana, I only called to find out whether you anticipate being called as a witness against me. I assume you know to what I'm referring."

"Should I decide to take the stand, Egon—you'll be the last to know." There followed a long pause.

"In that event—I think you should be aware that under cross-examination you'll be asked exactly how you and the First Phallus celebrated New Year's Eve—" There was a loud silence. Followed by a click. Ovid took this as mute, but nonetheless absolute confirmation.

She was horrified, knowing that her shocked, reflexive hanging up could spell trouble. Dare she tell Bryce? Did Ovid get her on tape just now? If he did—what had only been rumor before could now be transmuted into sworn testimony. And the sexual harassment lawsuit against Ovid was set for trial in September—in time to impact the election.

Iana could now see clearly that an out-of-court settlement was very much in the presidential interest. The White House itself could never approach the plaintiffs—which left Ovid holding aces. By refusing to settle, she reasoned, he'd be in a position to squeeze Bryce and Co. into paying him enough to settle the suit—plus generous compensation for having been so summarily sacked!

On the other hand, she reasoned, could Ovid simply be out to destroy the Bryce candidacy? One simple, not-for-attribution leak of the midnight billiards 'ball'—and the Hounds of Hell would be baying at the White House gates. Bryce might not even make it to Super Tuesday, she realized. And—Gordon. Fenstermacher could one day sit in the Oval Office—with Egon Ovid at his side—!

For twenty minutes she mentally kneaded it, taking no calls. Then she buzzed the boss and reported Ovid's call. Bryce was livid. "If the son of a bitch is planning to blow me out of the water, he'll have do it damn soon—otherwise I'll have the necessary delegates locked up. And to wait and spring it just before the convention would be too late to deny me the nomination. Worse, it would help Democrats and piss off Republicans! I seriously doubt even Ovid would want that. On the other hand—I don't see how he can afford to wait."

"You're right—he has to make his move soon. But, if that's what he's up to, why show us his hand? Maybe he's just trying to scare you into dropping out to spare yourself any humiliation. I have heard a few snickers."

Bryce began fume-pacing, his BP already up thirty points. "In other words, just by learning that he's heard some, some God damn rumor—I'm supposed to start shaking in my boots and withdraw? In a pig's pitootie!"

Ten minutes later Iana had Ovid on the phone, with the President listening on an extension.

"Egon, know this: Should I ever pick up a newspaper and read anything, anything at all about being 'taken' at a game of pool—I shall assume it came directly from you—in which case they won't have to subpoena me to testify at your trial: I'll be outside waiting when the doors open! And forget about cross-examination—we'll argue materiality and admissibility. Better settle, Blinky!" She hung up.

At the other end, Egon Ovid smiled broadly—they'd gone for the bait! Fenstermacher had given him carte blanche to bring down Sam Bryce, along with whatever it would take to settle his suit. Now it was time to set the hook.

*   *   *

The interview had been scheduled for two weeks, and Isabel Bryce was greatly looking forward to it. Her own 'white house' overlooking Biscayne Bay was a matter of great pride, and she was flattered that Peregrinations wanted it for a feature pictorial in the Spring issue. Shamelessly upscale, the magazine traveled the globe, peeking in on 'The Private Retreats of the World's Gentry' to interview their owners. Isabel Clothier-Bryce had long considered herself among the gentry, and it was going to be nice to see it in print.

What she didn't realize was that Peregrinations was a wholly owned subsidiary of Fenstermacher Publications—or that this photo shoot was the brainchild of one Egon Ovid.

The camera crew arrived and Isabel donned on her sweetest disposition, which was about an inch north of bitter almond.

"Now, just look out there—!" she crackled, pointing vehemently at a small armada of watercraft. "Too many people with too many boats! Means nothing anymore! Look there; that one's going much too fast! And—and half those girls aren't wearing any tops at all!" she spittled. Amanda Stack-House checked and made sure her recorder was catching it all.

"One way to avoid tan lines, I suppose," she smiled. "Tell me, Mrs. Bryce, how often do you get to see your son?"

"Him? He can stay right where he is, for all I care! Last time I saw my son, he didn't come here—I had to go there! Hate Washington in the winter! Hate it!" Suddenly she smiled. "Did I show you the Ming figurine—?"

Pay Dirt? "It must have been something pretty important then—for you to go all that way in the dead of winter—"

Isabel had not anticipated this turn. She hesitated, and then took refuge in the truth, as was her custom when cornered.

She gave Stackhouse a stern look. "Anytime a responsible mother learns that her child has behaved badly it is her maternal duty to reprimand that child—and just as quickly after the, the misbehavior as possible. Oh, now don't give me that! You know how men, especially presidents, can be. All that pressure and everything. And he certainly isn't the first, I can tell you that!" she clucked. "Look it there," she finger-stabbed fiercely, "another God damn boat going too God damn fast!"

*   *   *

While the Democrats were busy debating one another, the Republican race was one-sided—with the usurper spending millions to attack the head of his own party—while the President ignored his tormentor's very existence. There'd be no debate among Republican candidates. The Campaign to re-elect was more than content to run ads lauding the historic accomplishments of the Bryce Administration. It came as something of a surprise then, when Fenstermacher phoned the president to request a private one-on-one, "away from prying ears." After a brief hesitation, Bryce invited his rival to Camp David on Sunday to talk. Fenstermacher quickly agreed.

It was late afternoon when the two men sat down before a snapping fir fire, in private, as agreed. An ill-mannered north wind buffeted the lodge and banged against the sash as if to remind the mortals within how truly mere they were. After a sip of wine, the publisher cleared his throat.

"Mr. President, as you know, our campaign has the support of mainstream Republicans from coast to coast—plus a number of major religious organizations as well. And the more your friend Onager sings the praises of Alien economics, the more alarmed people become—and the stronger we grow."

"And you've come here to ask me to start going after the Mentors for the good of the Party," Bryce said facetiously.

Fenstermacher paused, and then leveled his gaze. "No, Mr. President—I've come up here today to urge you to withdraw from the race for the good of the Party."

Bryce's jaw dropped. "You can't be serious," he said.

"It's no longer felt you're a man who can lead the nation in a fight against the Aliens. Your support is crumbling by the day. But if that's not enough to convince you, history teaches that damaged incumbents may win re-nomination, but never re-election. And you, Sir, are a damaged incumbent."

He bent down and removed a micro-cassette player from his briefcase. "Seems those rumors about who was spread-eagled on your pool table besides the American Eagle have been confirmed. I believe you'll recognize the voice—"He switched on the tape player and handed headphones to Bryce.

He hesitated, and then donned them—instantly, rage seized the President's face as he heard the familiar gouge of his mother's voice. He listened on, his color darkening. Then he slipped off the headphones and stared into the fire.

After a while, without looking up, he gave his answer: "I'll not submit to blackmail. Period."

*   *   *

The following day the White House announced that Ellen Kate Bryce was expecting her first baby.

*   *   *

The North Korean Minister of Intelligence, Kim Buk Chu, sat at his desk in Pyongyang watching CNN. The upcoming plebiscite was certain to provoke a showdown with Beijing, the polls showing most Taiwanese planned to vote to end any further claim to being the legitimate government of China—to sever all ties with the mainland—and to become the independent Republic of Taiwan.

154

The question was, what would Beijing do about it?

A small tingle began to skitter up and down Kim's spine: This could be the very opportunity we've been seeking! The dam stands nearly complete, holding back a virtual ocean of water—He clenched his brow in deep thought—And then it hit him: The Emperor's Carom!

THREE GORGES DAM

In the Great Leader's revered words, "One well-placed bullet can win a war."

The men who ruled North Korea were not stupid. They fully appreciated that they could never hope to win an all-out war with the South as long as it was defended by the Americans. Not unless—the North was backed by the full weight and might of the People's Republic of China—at present a wholly unrealistic prospect. All that was lacking was a way of forcing China to back their play—one well-aimed, very powerful bullet.

(And just such a bullet lay deep within Three Gorges Dam.)

* * *

Beijing had no intention of waiting to be humiliated in the upcoming plebiscite. On March tenth a new policy was announced: Effective April's onset, any ship, under any flag, en route to any Chinese seaport would be required to possess a validated Permit of Disembarkation prior to entering Chinese territorial waters.

And by definition, Taiwan was a Province of China.

Washington was quick to react, announcing that American warships would escort merchant vessels safely into Taiwanese ports. But the door remained open to a diplomatic resolution—which, the State Department took pains to communicate, was exactly what the White House wanted and urged.

Yet Beijing had brazenly drawn a line—declaring as non-negotiable the issue of Taiwan's secession. Short of using military force, trade was the best leverage Washington had.

Of late the Bryces had dined largely in silence. So it came as a surprise when Abby raised the subject of foreign affairs. "Katie said something today which I think makes a lot of sense." She had the President's full attention. "She suggested that, rather than risk war with China, why not simply p-u-r-c-h-a-s-e Taiwan—the same way we bought Alaska from the Russians! And that way everyone saves face. We could offer China—say Four Trillion Dollars—then turn around and sell it to Taiwan! We front the money; they pay us back. Smart kid we got there, Woody. I'd only change one thing; instead of paying Beijing in cash, pay them in trade credits. Essentially it would only be a matter of settling on a price. Of course—if the Taiwanese don't want their independence badly enough to pay for it—well, screw 'em! At least you will have made the offer."

"You mean—simply chuck our whole One-China policy?" Bryce said incredulously. "Tell Katie it's a dopey idea and to leave such matters to the professionals. Thank her, and tell her to just concentrate on having a healthy baby."

"You condescending son of a bitch—"

"It's naive, Abby. We'd be laughed off the world stage!"

She lowered her voice and glared at him. "Just-do-it, Buster! Consider it my first Executive Order."

Bryce glared at his wife—and suddenly the whole notion of not running for a second term bulked large in his mind. By withdrawing from the race, he'd simultaneously de-fang Abby, rid himself of Iana, silence Fenstermacher, and be able to retire with dignity.

There were worse things, he decided, than being an ex-president. He could kick back and enjoy being a grandfather, travel around the world and collect big bucks for making speeches, play a lot more golf—maybe write a book—and even get himself an Audi S4 Avant! That he could handle!

*   *   *

The private yacht Iscarat, on loan from a friendly sultan, sailed under cover of darkness with but a single passenger: Taiwan's deputy minister for state security, Ho Wing Gao. His government was undertaking the most bizarre, potentially critical diplomatic mission in its history. In a recent back-channel communication, the People's Republic of Korea hinted that they might be in a position to "compel" China to grant Taiwan its independence! They also hinted that they were prepared to do so in exchange for a generous bilateral trade agreement. Taipei concluded they'd better find out quick what Pyongyang was up to, and dispatched Minister Ho. Until they knew more, Washington would not be advised.

The rendezvous took place three days later in the Sea of Japan, thirty kilometers off the North Korean coast, under a moonless sky. Kim Buk Chu himself attended.

Ho and Kim exchanged formal greetings and took their seats, the sea quieting in gentle respect.

"What I am now showing you has been seen by no other eyes—" Kim began, spreading out several eleven by fourteen inch color photographs on the table.

"Three Gorges Dam—" said Ho, recognizing it immediately.

Kim ceremoniously then placed a single photograph in front of the deputy minister. It was a color enlargement of a Soviet nuclear device. "four-hundred fifty kilotons," he said simply.

Ho looked up at him, stupefied.

"This very bomb now lies deep within the base of the dam—ready to be detonated with a coded radio command." He paused to watch Ho struggle to grasp the implications. "At the proper time, we intend to reveal its existence to Beijing—knowing there is absolutely nothing they can do about it!" He took a slow sip of tea." It can never be removed from the dam—it can never be deactivated—and the new lake it impounds already holds far too much water to be drained."

"What proof of its existence do you have to offer them? This photograph by itself proves nothing."

"They will be instructed to send divers down one-hundred eight-eight meters from the exact mid-point—where they will find affixed to the wall—" he placed another photograph before Ho, "the original manufacturer's identification plate—complete with serial and lot numbers, service designation, weapon series and design yield." He then smiled coldly.

"Should the dam be destroyed," he intoned, "millions would die in the flooding alone. The mighty Yangtze would race through a white-hot radioactive crater, and carry irradiated water through the very heart of China—and on to the sea!"

"But—what if Beijing decides to vaporize you instead?" Ho managed, still reeling from the revelation.

"Should they dare to attack us a signal will instantly be generated and the bomb detonated. It is—automatic!"

Ho was scrambling to figure out ways it could all come undone. "But—how do you keep the detonator energized year after year? Even the strongest batteries eventually die."

Kim allowed a small smile. "Aha! That's the ingenious part: contained within the device is a small plutonium generator, of the type used to power space vehicles when they are great distances from the Sun. It generates sufficient power to receive a radio signal through two-hundred meters of concrete—and then deliver sixty Amperes of power to fire the Detonator. Of course," he shrugged, "eventually even this generator will exhaust its energy supply—we may have but a thousand years left!" He emitted a rasping cackle, revealing a slightly askew gold tooth beneath his left nostril.

Ho was stunned. "So—what exactly are your demands?"

"We have two: The signing of a Sino-Korean Mutual Defense Treaty—and Beijing's formal relinquishment of all claims to the province of Taiwan."

"And—from us?"

"A bilateral free-trade agreement." He held up two fat fingers. "Additionally: two-hundred billion dollars in economic assistance. Surely Taiwan is worth that much to you."

*   *   *

Sam Bryce strode into his wife's bath, caught her in the tub reading Winning Poker, and marveled at his timing.

"I thought you'd be interested to learn, Madame President—" he sneered, "In the words of a celebrated gigolo, I'm going to withdraw!"

And he did, having just pulled the pin of a mind-grenade.

That afternoon President Samuel Bryce called a press conference to announce "a very difficult decision."

"I'll not be seeking a second term as your President," he intoned, citing "family reasons" and "imminent grand parental responsibilities." He expressed "great pride in the many accomplishments of our Administration"—and confidence that the party's new standard-bearer

158

would do "just fine" in the Fall. He then turned and left without taking questions.

Despite Bryce's withdrawal, Republicans in states with primaries still had a choice: Gordon Fenstermacher vs. Stuart MacDougal—ballot petitions having been filed in the name of the Bryce-MacDougal ticket. It was already too late for any other Republicans, though, to jump into the race.

Nevertheless, votes were cast—and after Super Tuesday, Gordon Fenstermacher had nearly twice as many committed delegates as Vice President MacDougal.

The following day the Dow Industrials shot up one-hundred and forty-six points.

SUITCASE NUKE

Dr. Karl Scheuer, putative attaché with the Austrian Mission to the United Nations, cleared JFK Customs using a diplomatic passport. The heavy suitcase he bore passed through unscreened and un-inspected.

Fa Haad had arrived in the land of the Great Satan minus the elaborate beard he always wore when in the Middle East. Except when he was there as the bespectacled Dr. Scheuer.

The wheeled suitcase he pulled through the terminal behind him was indeed heavy—it contained one point one kilotons.

It marked the first time in history that a hostile nuclear weapon had been introduced onto American soil.

And neither the Pentagon, DIA, CIA, NSA, Customs, or the Justice Department's own Nuclear Interdiction Team (NIT) had any hint of what just transpired at JFK.

TAIWAN

The NSC concurred with the president: Beijing's recent demand for written authorization to enter Taiwanese waters was completely unacceptable. If imposed, it would constitute a naval blockade—by definition an Act of War, and a clear violation of international law.

Suddenly freed of all concern over re-election, Samuel Bryce could now base his decisions on moral and ethical grounds. He had a legacy to think about—not to mention the Mentors, should they be watching.

"I say we inform Beijing that—should push come to shove—the United States will immediately confer full diplomatic recognition on the sovereign state of Taiwan, formally vacate our One-China policy, and come to the military defense of Taiwan. Of course, we do that, and the Asian balloon is up." He glanced around the table. "Chester, what would be their likely response to such a threat?"

The Secretary of State shifted in his chair. He despised speculation. "That's not at all clear, Mr. President. That said, my best guess is some kind of military counter-initiative. I don't see them simply backing down. Remember, Taiwan's the main course; Hong Kong was just the appetizer."

The President turned to his CIA director. "Henry—?"

"I'd have to agree. They will resort to military action if necessary to keep Taiwan."

Bryce looked at his secretary of defense. "Ralph—?"

"It's a question of how far they'd go. They've got too many assets at stake to risk a full military confrontation with the United States. They know the Seventh Fleet could eat them for lunch."

The President leaned back and laced his fingers behind his head. "Chester—I think it's time we let Beijing know just how much we value Taiwan."

*   *   *

The American Ambassador to the People's Republic of China arrived in the foreign minister's office precisely at noon. He was kept waiting for eleven minutes; it was a show of displeasure. When he was finally ushered into the foreign minister's office, bows were exchanged and seats taken; tea was offered and declined. This being a meeting held at the "most urgent" request of the U.S. Ambassador, he spoke first.

"Mr. Foreign Minister—my government has instructed me to inform you that the U.S. Navy is prepared to defend the right of free passage anywhere in the South China Sea including the waters around Taiwan." He paused and lowered his voice. "In the event your forces attempt to deny passage to any commercial vessel in said waters, the United States will cease to recognize your claim to sovereignty over Taiwan—grant formal diplomatic recognition to the new Republic of Taiwan—and come to its immediate defense." The minister stiffened visibly. "President Bryce wants you to know—exactly what is at stake."

* * *

"So you finally proved you're not as dumb as you pretend!"

"Why, Hello, Mother—it's always nice to hear from you. And just how 'dumb' is that?"

"These days?" she sneered, "Pretty damn stupid, if you ask me—getting caught with your tallywacker where it didn't belong! And caught by your wife, for God's sake!"

The President gave a long sigh. "Mother, I haven't got time for this now."

She softened her tone. "Fact is, I phoned to tell you that I'm proud of you for dropping out! It was the smart thing to do. To spare yourself and your family humiliation!"

"Well, I do appreciate that. Sometimes—I actually count myself fortunate to have you for a mother," he said.

She considered it. "Oh—Balls." The line went dead.

* * *

Using a Pennsylvania driver's license and titanium Visa card, Conrad Magnusson, a.k.a. Fa Haad, rented a Camry and headed west on Interstate Eighty. In the trunk lay a warm token of his esteem for America.

The spring thaw had yet to begin in the mountains, but the roads were already clear and dry. In Ohio, I-80 became I-76 then I-71. He did admire the American Interstate system. He'd give them that. Fa Haad was now heading southwest and glad when he could lower the windows. The moment he crossed the Kentucky State line it felt even warmer. He reasoned it to be a simple auto-sanguinary target-proximity response.

*   *   *

Two weeks earlier—

The lights burned all night inside the Forbidden City, and just before dawn the People's latest deep-penetration x-ray equipment was airlifted to Three Gorges Dam.

Upon viewing color photographs of a Soviet nuclear device, with close-ups of its manufacturer's identification plate and explosive yield, the Central Committee had moved quickly.

The first diver to descend from the center of the dam made it down nearly one-hundred and fifty meters before running into the fresh silt which had already accumulated against the base. Shortly thereafter, a barge arrived to begin dredging. With the silt removed it took only two dives to locate and retrieve the target: a Soviet ID plate affixed to the face of the dam.

The second day workmen had begun erecting scaffolding along the exposed face of the dam. Then, when the large x-ray machines arrived, rumors began flying that there was official fear over the dam's structural integrity.

The government had moved quickly to quash the rumors, assuring the local populace that the dam was completely safe.

However, all the scaffolding and all the activity spoke volumes, and villagers below Three Gorges began evacuating as alarm spread downriver as far as Nanjing and Shanghai.

Official claims that the inspections were "standard safety protocols" fell on deaf ears, and within forty-eight hours the rumors had surfaced in the foreign press.

For the first time in their careers, the old men ruling in Beijing experienced what being powerless felt like. Out of the blue, the North Koreans had presented them with an unthinkable ultimatum. And after three weeks, they still didn't know whether or not an atomic bomb hummed somewhere deep within the dam. They were effectively helpless.

The North Korean ambassador arrived to an icy reception.

"Do you see any nuclear bombs in here?" screamed Minister Yao, stabbing at a light wall covered with x-rays. Most dam negatives revealed only a dense network of steel reinforcing bars, while a few revealed certain objects as well: shovels, hard hats, wheelbarrows, sections of concrete chute, even an entire vibrator—the detritus of progress. Also visible, the corpses of four careless construction workers, two dogs, and a steel coffin.

The ambassador peered at the concrete-encased objects with both interest and disdain. "Messy—very messy," he hissed. Suddenly he found what he was looking for and brightened. He pointed to a white rectangle on the x-ray. "Aaah! This must be the casket of Yo Hua Sing—entombed the tenth February 1997—along with a four-hundred fifty kiloton remembrance gift!" He smiled and held up a finger. "Permit me a small word of caution: Any electronic bombardment—or any attempt to neutralize the weapon would have—the most unfortunate of consequences."

*   *   *

With Sam Bryce out of the race, Fenstermacher could turn his full attention to David Onager and his Alien pals. With a clear path now to his party's nomination, he decided to leapfrog ahead to the Fall campaign—by challenging Onager to a one-on-one televised debate. It was the brainchild of Egon Ovid—a move sure to be perceived as imaginative and bold while at the same time a display of strength. But most of all, he relished being able to put Onager on the spot so dramatically. And he'd have to accept the challenge. The press would hound him until he did.

(And following the debate, he'd have five whole months in which to practice acting and looking presidential.)

Senator Onager leapt at the challenge. Polls showed voters were anxious to hear the issues debated—Mentor-nomics and wealth redistribution in particular. Thus, Dave Onager saw he was about to don the cloak of cosmic responsibility.

*   *   *

As the Ministry saw it, there were but two possibilities: either there was an atomic bomb within Three Gorges Dam—or there wasn't.

Evidence for a bomb's existence was obvious: they had a manufacturer's identification plate authenticated by experts. Moreover, the North Koreans knew about the buried casket, as well as who was inside—all information which could have been bought. However, the mortician who prepared and sealed the casket had vanished shortly after entombment. And that—sent chills.

To know for certain whether there were an actual bomb would require removing the casket and examining it. And for this, its position could not be worse; it lay one-hundred seventy-one meters above the very base of the dam—eight-hundred six meters in from the southern base-terminus—and eighty-eight and one half meters in from the exposed face. Drilling an access tunnel became the preferred option; their top engineers had assured them it could be done without compromising the dam's structural integrity.

The closest inspection tunnel passed ninety-six meters above the casket. Cutting and burning through that much-reinforced concrete could take months. It would, of course, be far easier to go straight in from the exposed face of the dam-but to do so would be unacceptably conspicuous: Should the Koreans observe tunneling activity anywhere near the coffin, they might panic—and transmit the firing codes.

After all, the Great Leader was considered to be nuts.

A final decision was made: they would tunnel internally in order to be able to drill unobserved.

*   *   *

'Marion Dixon' sat on the floor of his room at the Holiday Inn—and slowly lifted the suitcase lid. By now he knew the device better than his own hand: its bright ganglia of colored circuitry—its polished timer switches—the crimson digital read-outs, already on-line and glowing darkly—the yellow detonator harness. Beneath it, gleaming unseen within the grey, shaped-charges that surrounded it, a shining, finely-milled, plutonium pit. The Power of the Universe—lying at his feet. Every time he looked at it he experienced an almost religious bloom of awe.

It was 4:11 a.m. Fa Haad ran his checklist of circuit tests, performing each with infinite care, and rendered his SADM ready to accept a manual firing command. The Russian had done his job of circumventing all the safeguards well. The fusing device would be timed to the second. He closed his eyes and saw the target Before—and After.

THE UNITED STATES BULLION DEPOSITORY, known to the world as Fort Knox, lay thirty-five miles southwest of Louisville. It was a single, squat, two-story, bomb-proof, stone-faced concrete structure surrounded by fences, walls and gun towers, and guarded around the clock by the Department of the Treasury. Inside, behind a thirty ton vault door, lay fifty-six billion dollars in neatly stacked gold bars—the strongbox of a superpower. Tangible wealth to back the U.S. dollar. Bedrock of international currency. Gleaming symbol of American economic might. And enough to service the National Debt for all of nine weeks.

Fa Haad drew in and held a deep breath—and released all but the final two safety switches. He armed all three firing circuits and readied the detonation timer at plus or minus six minutes.

Then he faced east, touched the carpet with his forehead, and prayed for Glory.

At 4:35 a.m. he checked out, placed his 'suitcase' in the trunk of the Camry, and drove the eight miles to Perkins Field—where he'd rented a Cessna the previous evening, producing an Ohio pilot's license and Gold Card in the name of Bryant Chandor.

Being an accomplished pilot as well as a timing fanatic, Fa Haad was wheels-up at precisely 5:00 a.m.. He climbed to an altitude of three-hundred feet, and then took a northwesterly heading. The open suitcase, with a drogue chute now attached, lay beside him on the copilot's seat. Fa Haad flew on for another two and one half minutes—looking up ahead, he easily picked out the all-night Texaco station which served as his Approach Point. Passing over it, he turned on a final heading of two-hundred eighty degrees.

He reached over—disengaged the two remaining safeties—praised Allah—noted the exact time—and pressed hard on the INITIATE button, holding it down for a full three seconds. He closed and double-latched the suitcase—extinguished his running lights—cranked on twenty degrees of flaps—and began his descent.

He could see a bright, blue-green glow of lights directly ahead. He was now in Restricted Airspace, counting on being taken for some dummy who didn't know any better. Simplicity. The best plans were always the simplest ones.

He reached across and pushed out the copilot's door—saw the outer fence of the Depository flash beneath his wing—and shoved the suitcase out the door. He banked up and away, catching a parting glimpse of the little drogue chute.

What Fa Haad could not see was that his drop had been exceedingly well-timed: the suitcase had settled directly on the flat rooftop surrounding the central vault structure. The moment it impacted, lights blazed and klaxons blared. Sensors instantly located the intruder as being on the lower roof, Section E-32. Guards on top of the corner towers instantly swung their glasses—and spotted a dark suitcase lying on the roof with a small parachute attached!

That could only mean something intentionally delivered. Both FBI and Army bomb squads were immediately notified, and an urgent call placed to the FAA to request assistance in locating and tracking the suspect aircraft.

But by this time Fa Haad was already rolling to a stop back at Perkins Field. He switched off the engine and glanced at his watch: fifty-three seconds to go. He climbed out, sprinted for the Camry, and sped off in a fury of gravel.

Back on the highway, he mentally counted down—On the Depository rooftop—the timer digitally flashed off the seconds:—five—four—three—two—one—zero.

The next Nanosecond a bolt of Soviet lightning leapt for the Detonator—But it failed to arrive.

It had been intercepted and re-vectored up—into the heavens.

Fa Haad braced for the blast and shockwave—

N-O-T-H-I-N-G !

He couldn't believe it—the SADM had been guaranteed to survive a fall of fifty meters and still detonate—even without a drogue chute! This was one guarantee he'd collect on personally.

*　　*　　*

By the time FBI agents managed to trace things back from 'Bryant Chandor' to 'Marion Dixon' to 'Conrad Magnusson,' all three were snoring softly thirty-thousand feet above the North Atlantic.

FORT KNOX

Sandovar Abydos, AX-TAX-PAC, and the massive fund-raising team for Fenstermacher combined to persuade Arthur Frayles it was time The Globe did an in-depth series on Mr. Abydos and his mountaintop activities. Investigative reports by their very nature were best undertaken when subjects could be observed over time without their knowledge. Frayles had an idea.

He placed a call to Karyn DeLeo and invited her for lunch at Peabody's. Karyn was working as a tape editor for UPN Channel Thirty-eight, but she desperately wanted to be a Globe reporter and had made sure its managing editor was keenly aware of her continuing interest.

They'd met only once, at her roommate's wedding reception two years earlier. Upon learning that The Arthur Frayles was among the guests, Karyn had simply walked up and introduced herself, and they wound up talking for the better part of an hour. At first it had been difficult to get past her looks, that striking was she. Eurasian, her mother was a celebrated Hong Kong artist, her father an Italian writer. Her mind impressed Frayles, but it was her spirit which enchanted him. As dedicated as she was to becoming "a serious journalist," she didn't take herself seriously at all. Frayles had been charmed and always took or returned her calls. One day he'd find a spot for her.

That day was finally at hand. Unfortunately, it was her exotic looks which Frayles knew would get her into ABYTOR. Physical attributes were a prime hiring consideration: Zooti Abydos was nothing if not a connoisseur of body parts.

And Karyn DeLeo came with a world-class parts department.

*　　*　　*

The Russian Ambassador was summoned by the Secretary of State to the White House, ushered into the Oval Office, and told to sit. President Bryce raised the lid of the suitcase on the table—and glared pointedly at the startled Russian.

"I trust what you see before you is not wholly unfamiliar: it's a God damn Russian nuclear bomb—something you people call a 'SADM'!" There was controlled anger in his voice. "Relax, the pit's been removed.

Night before last it was dropped on the roof of the U.S. Gold Depository in Kentucky! But as you see—it never detonated. It should have—but it didn't." He cranked on a few decibels. "What does the Russian government have to say about this?"

The ambassador was visibly trembling. It was no act.

"I—I know absolutely nothing of this—thing! I've—never even seen one of these before. And I can guarantee you one-hundred percent that this—abominable act was carried out without any knowledge whatever on the part of my government." He waved a frightened finger at the device. "This—this is insane—Only a madman could do such a thing!"

Secretary of State Severinghaus replied. "The United States is not accusing your government of complicity, only of unconscionable carelessness in allowing a nuclear weapon to fall into the hands of a terrorist!"

"Have you captured the criminal responsible? Do—you have any idea who is behind this?"

"We do not. The trail appears to have gone cold."

"Do you—suppose it could be connected in any way with the attack on the Panama Canal?"

"We're looking into that possibility," Bryce answered crisply. "In the meantime, I want a detailed history of this bomb. If it can be traced back to whoever sold it or stole it, along with any others that may be out there like it, we may be able to prevent another SADM crisis in the future."

"I—believe you can depend on our fullest cooperation," the ambassador mumbled, still staring numbly at the device.

"Needless to say," continued the President, lowering his voice for emphasis, "Should any word of this incident leak we could have widespread panic on our hands."

"I can assure you of our total and absolute discretion."

*   *   *

Fenstermacher's challenge accepted, final arrangements were made. The Great Debate, as it was being hyped, was set for May twenty-third in Baltimore. Though the television audiences would be enormous, both the Republican and Democratic parties were less than enthused. Debates by presumptive nominees in the spring of an election year would make the conventions pointless. It was already dawning on both parties that national political conventions were the anachronisms of the future.

For his part, Gordon Fenstermacher viewed the Great Debate as a prime venue for an ideological showdown between economic populism and free enterprise. And he'd attack Onager only on his views and proposals, never personally. The senator was much too highly regarded for any of that.

He reminded himself that Dave Onager was quick on his feet and a very potent speaker. Under normal circumstances he'd never take him on directly—but this was a battle which had to be joined. Mentornomics was so horrendous, so antithetic to American economic values, so grave a threat to social stability—it had to be exposed for the economic sophistry and political twaddle it was!

David Onager looked forward to the debate as well. He too saw it primarily as a confrontation between economic, human, and societal values—on which he and Fenstermacher stood poles apart. One of them was extremely wealthy, driven to protect everything he had—and to accumulate more. This didn't make him an economic psychopath, Onager decided, just another greedy member of a greedy society. Of course, in the debate he wouldn't disparage wealth per se, only its grotesque accumulation at the very top. And addressing that problem was long overdue. David Onager regarded the distribution of wealth in America as an obscenity. And a matter of economic and social morality.

Onager saw Gordon Fenstermacher's zeal to protect wealth from taxation as fatally flawed, since it flew in the face of the most fundamental American value of all: Fairness. And excessive wealth was inherently unfair.

*   *   *

Creating tunnels and passageways within the walls of a dam while it's under construction is a relatively simple matter. Creating them after-the-fact is all but impossible.

Cutting and drilling through reinforced concrete deep inside a dam—with no effective way to vent the dust—had become a long, worsening-by-the-day nightmare for Chinese work crews. Massive dust collectors were struggling to stay operational, with workers in breathing gear able to endure only an hour of drilling before having to be relieved. Only the urgency of the mission kept the crews working.

After being kept waiting, the North Korean Ambassador was granted an audience with the Chinese foreign minister.

"I am compelled to offer an apology for having neglected to furnish you with certain information regarding the Soviet device—" the ambassador began. The foreign minister stiffened perceptibly. "You see, its designers took the precaution of equipping it with a very sensitive, gimbal-mounted trembler switch—activated several hours after entombment."

"Therefore," he gurgled, "any attempt at all to move it will result in a detonation." He paused to let this sink in. "Perhaps Buddha will guard your dam against earthquake."

SPIDER'S LAIR

Zooti Abydos lived in one of the owner's suites at ABYTOR, and whenever he felt like having a little fun, which was at least once a week, he'd pop down to Vegas. His current watering-hole-of-choice was Arachnid's—offering on-line dating via Charlotte's Web Site www.arachnidmeet.com.

The Globe's research department had done its work well: Zooti and Karyn arrived at Arachnid's entrance at the same moment. He smiled broadly and held the door for her.

"Why, thank you, sir. Hey, you—you're—Zooti Abydos, aren't you?" DeLeo chimed, her eyes gleaming. Sheathed in fluid black velvet, she walked slowly past, affording him a choice gluteal prospective.

"Ya got me," he grinned, "and you are—?"

"Karyn DeLeo." She offered her hand and they shook. "I read in TIME, I think, about—Oh, you know—"

"ABYTOR."

"Yes, that's it!" She allowed him to take her arm and escort her into the bar. "And just how can one get a look at it without having to attend some convention or something?"

"Not easy, I'm afraid. One has to be an Invited Guest." They ordered drinks and headed for the hors d'oeuvres line. "Here, try these—if you like spicy, that is—" She smiled and helped herself to six Cajun crawdads.

Over drinks she told him of her "boring" job at a Boston cable station and of her passion to find "something new and exciting"—before "getting down to making babies." She mentioned having a week of vacation left, and by their third round the Abydos heir had invited her up to ABYTOR for a personal tour.

"You never know, we—might be able to find a place for you there," he trolled.

She widened her eyes. "Seriously?" She paused. "Listen, you're a, a very good looking guy, Zooti. So I need to tell you, my interest is in finding a great job—not a lover. Just as long as you understand—You OK with that?"

Nonetheless, he felt himself stiffen—wonderfully.

APRIL FOOLS BLOCKADE

With tunneling now halted following disclosure of the trembler trigger, the bomb had taken on all the aspects of an inoperable tumor. Sooner or later it would kill.

On March twenty-ninth the North Koreans made Beijing an offer they couldn't refuse: A Way Out. There existed a deactivation device—which could be placed against the face of the dam at the nearest point and transmit a coded command to the bomb—which would in turn trigger a De-Activation Executed signal from the bomb itself.

The Chinese were given photographs and wiring diagrams of the device and assured that once deactivated, it could never be reactivated. It was an assurance offered without proof.

The following day, engineers confirmed that the circuitry, components, and design of the purported deactivation device were consistent with the operational description given by the North Koreans.

In light of the crisis at Three Gorges, it was agreed this was no time to provoke a military confrontation with the U.S. The decision was taken to "postpone" the planned interdictions at sea near Taiwan without explanation, leaving the Seventh Fleet to steam around in confused circles—and them free to concentrate their efforts on the bomb in the dam.

April first—the date announced by the People's Republic of China requiring advance authorization for ships entering Chinese waters— came and went without incident, as Chinese naval forces remained on standard patrol. No one in Washington had a ready explanation.

It quickly became known as the April Fool Blockade.

The Chinese president had demanded a list of options, with accompanying risk-assessments. It proved to be a short list. The one seemingly viable proposal, put forward by the Ministry of Science, was to bore a small hole through the concrete directly to the casket itself, and then slowly cut through its five-eighths—inch steel wall—in order to be able insert probes and take radiation readings without disturbing the casket. The bomb might yet turn out to be a monstrous hoax, the last desperate act of a desperate regime. The president intended to find out; He authorized boring to commence.

*   *   *

Penny and Justin were often mistaken for a cute couple, not brother and sister. This tended to amuse them, and they'd occasionally jerk around those within earshot by saying outrageous things in malls and elevators. They had always been close, in spite of having very different interests, lifestyles and friends—largely because they found humor in the same things, and could always make each other laugh. And that made spending time together a mutual priority.

It also led to the sharing of confidences. And pot. In fact, Penny was the only one who knew Justin Onager smoked.

Being older by two years, he felt a certain protective responsibility for his high-school sophomore kid sister, especially when it came to the guys she dated. And he was beginning to have his doubts about Gaithers

Roby, her latest boy toy. A senior at nearby Brynwood Academy, Roby seemed too cool by half. But he had great weed, he'd give him that.

"This shit is excellent—!" Justin managed without exhaling, passing her the bowl. "Where's it come from?"

"Gaith called it—mmm—'Crater Green, I think. Whatever that means. Oregon maybe? Says it's really cheap too."

"How cheap?"

"Like—one-thousand five-hundred and fifty dollars a pound." She eyed him. "Wanna—split one? He said I could buy."

Justin thought it over. That price was just a bit too good. "How much you actually know about this dude any way; ever meet his parents? Ever been inside his house? Do you have any mutual friends?"

She didn't like the edge in his voice. "Yes, Yes, and No. Why?"

"That price is way too low. I smell a set-up."

"A bust? You gotta be kidding!"

He took another hit. "No, but I'm thinking, maybe someone's trying to get at Dad. You get popped holding weight, it could seriously hurt him, ya know?" He struck another match and toked. "Remember the stink over that photo of you smiling down at that joint up in New Hampshire?"

"What're you saying—I should break up with him?" Resentment flared in her eyes.

"N-o-t necessarily—" he smiled, popping a grape into his mouth. "I was just thinking—what if we could come up with a way to, you know: One Good Sting Deserves Another—if in fact it is a set-up!"

"Like how?" She wasn't sure how she felt about this.

"Well—that's what we have to give some real creative thought to. Step One: Define the Objective."

As he refilled the pipe, they reflected quietly. Suddenly he had a thought so amusing he choked.

"What—?"

He blew his nose and smiled. "Okay: Urinary Largess equals?"

She realized he'd suddenly switched to playing Stoned Definitions. This was within the rules. She knit her brow in Search Mode—and finally shrugged in resignation.

"Philanthro-Pee-Pee!" he trumpeted. She flung herself back on the futon and roared. "You're right, man—this is dynamite shit!"

*   *   *

After only an hour's interviews, Karyn DeLeo was offered a position as Assistant to the Director of Special Events (one Epizutus Abydos)—at an attractive salary. She accepted at once.

Upon returning to Boston she "quit" her supposed job—sub-let her apartment—went clothes-buying (authorized by her true employer)—packed what she'd need—and flew off to Salt Lake City. She was met at the airport and driven to ABYTOR, where all full-time staff were housed.

It was dark by the time they arrived at the base station. Gazing up at the dazzling discus straddling the high summit, Karyn experienced a—tiny ephemeral echo of some forgotten spiritual alter-reality. A peculiar shiver of 'recognition' flittered through her—as she intuited that this place was exactly where she was meant to be.

*   *   *

Penny Onager was more than a little conflicted. Gaithers Roby was a hunk and a half. Smart—cool—funny—exciting to be around—the kind of guy lowly sophomores never got to date. Yet, here they were, in a pseudo-relationship—with Justin saying he might be using her to get at their father!

And the thing that kept gnawing at her was—how that would explain his interest in her. Not at all flattering.

She had to find out. Being to the manor born, as her dad often said, was not synonymous with quality. If this was a set-up—then who was most likely behind it? Who'd benefit the most politically? And if it were all political, why would Gaithers Roby ever get involved? It just made no sense at all. But she had to know whether it was all just a set-up-which unfortunately meant going along with her brother and letting him put her boyfriend to the test.

On their date last night, Penny recalled, Gaithers had mentioned again that he'd be happy to sell her some weed—"just for your own head and a few friends." She had claimed she was paranoid about "having any weight around, you know the campaign and all." He'd nodded and dropped the subject.

Meanwhile, Justin had come up with a plan.

*   *   *

Vice President MacDougal was at best a vapid campaigner, on his best day no match for Gordon Fenstermacher. Abby had once called him "Mr. Grand-bland."

As to the Democrats, Ordahl's oratory had stirred precious few minds and hearts. As for the others, money dried up with each ensuing primary, resulting in yet another candidate folding his tent. Before the primary season was half over it had become clear to all that Gordon Fenstermacher would be facing David Onager in November.

It was already shaping up as a watershed race, with many voters expressing a willingness to cross party lines, hewing to the issues and beliefs of the candidates themselves.

*   *   *

Sandovar Abydos had directed his son to serve as his cash conduit to the Fenstermacher camp. In that capacity Zooti met regularly with Egon Ovid, but was not made privy to everything requiring "special funding." Accordingly, it was Zooti who unknowingly provided the untraceable buy-money for springing young Gaithers Roby's trap for the Onager kid. The entire Roby family was known to be arch-conservative, and it had taken only small ideological persuasion (along with not small compensation) to bring young Roby fully on board—all without his parents' knowledge or consent of course.

*   *   *

Zooti traveled about half the time, leaving Karyn DeLeo with little to do, beyond coming up with lists of ideas for 'Special Events.' It was an assignment she found enjoyable, but reminded herself that Zooti's number one goal was still getting into her pants. Nonetheless, her 'job' afforded her an ideal basis for nosing around and talking with people. Mr. Frayles would be most pleased.

Sandovar Abydos was seldom seen by staff. It wasn't even known to most when he was actually present at ABYTOR; his comings and goings never disclosed. It was a bit of a jolt when Karyn looked up and saw him approaching her desk.

"Mr. Abydos! It's—a pleasure to meet you. I'm Karyn DeLeo," she said, rising and thrusting out her hand, which he took lightly and shook once.

"How do you do." He sat, and after a moment, she did as well. "I thought it time I met my son's latest acquisition. You being an Assistant with ill-defined responsibilities, it would be helpful for you to have some orientation—so that you'll understand exactly what is expected of you." His tone was gentle, but his words came cloaked with pure menace. She realized she was looking into the eyes of near absolute power and gave an involuntary shudder. Which he caught.

"May I—offer you some juice? Or perhaps some tea?" His head gave a single shake.

She could smell his aftershave: strong—expensive imported burning rubber. Or possibly incense. Calculated intimidation, she decided.

His eyes bored in. "Ms. DeLeo, it is important that you appreciate the confidential nature of all that transpires here. Our guests must feel free to speak openly, often of highly confidential matters. From time to time, you may be required to submit to a drug test, blood test, or polygraph. Standard practice for all employees. In addition, you will be required to sign a performance bond in the amount of one year's salary, and to execute a Confidentiality Agreement which carries severe sanctions in its breach. Meaning, in the event you divulge confidential information, you will be immediately dismissed for cause. In addition, you will be effectively barred from employment in any position requiring a last-employer reference. Finally, legal action will seek to recover the full amount of your performance bond. Now, all this may sound a bit drastic. But let me assure you: it is as nothing—unless of course you should activate its provisions through disclosure." He eyed her. "Now, have I managed to scare you off the mountaintop?"

"Is that your intention, Mr. Abydos?"

"Only if you think there's a possibility you might violate our confidences."

"That, I assure you will never be an issue," she lied. "But—why wasn't I told any of this before I quit my job and moved all the way out here?" She made her face flush with anger.

"Pure corporate self-interest: we'd scare too many people off before they ever even started. Besides, we want to give any new employee a little time to psychologically recast their life in accordance with their new salary. By doing business this way, the only ones we lose—are those who know they might not to be able keep their mouths shut."

She was conflicted, wanting to tell this smug bastard where to get off. But she also desperately wanted to do the story. "Okay, putting that aside, I guess maybe what's bothering me is being treated like some—some vassal!" This raised a slight smile at the corners of his lips.

"In that case, you'd be well-advised to give most careful consideration to all such aspects before signing."

He rose to leave. "My son will have everything ready for your signature upon his return Monday. That will afford you the weekend to think things over." He nodded once and left.

Karyn decided it was time to have a talk with Art Frayles.

PHONE TRAP

Egon Ovid, feet propped up on his desk, studied the latest polls. The Likely Voter numbers were impressive: eighty-two percent planned to watch the Great Debate—seventy-one percent considered the races for both party nominations to be Already Decided—and ninety-three percent regarded the Protection of Property as Important or Very Important. The disturbing number, however, was that only twenty-eight percent viewed the present distribution of wealth to be Equitable. And therein lies danger—

His phone rang. "Yes?"

"Mr. Ovid, there's someone insisting on speaking with you, someone named 'Gaithers'—?"

Ovid blanched, hesitated, and then decided he'd best take the call. "Yes—?" he answered cautiously.

"Mr. Ovid, this is Gaithers Roby—I think you know who I am. I'm calling 'cause there's something I need to hear directly from you before I go ahead. An' that is—if this whole thing goes south, and she names me as her dope connection—I want your personal guarantee I'll be well defended, and generously compensated."

Ovid was livid; this kid was shaking him down! And over an open line! But the damage was already done. "You have it. And don't ever contact me again!" He hung up angrily, a Nixonesque glistening visible above his upper lip.

His perspiration would have become copious; had it occurred to him that the young man on the other end of the line was not in fact Gaithers Roby.

*   *   *

North Korea was the cat, the People's Republic of China the mouse. Only after nineteen days of round-the-clock drilling toward the casket was Beijing informed by the government of North Korea that there had been "a regrettable oversight." The casket had also been configured with an acoustic trigger, and its wiring diagram was submitted as proof.

The following day drilling abruptly ceased.

The old mice were being tormented—and yearned to vaporize the cat.

*   *   *

KAPPA UNO convened at ABYTOR for a final vote. With no debate at all the decision was unanimous:

Should the Aliens return, they would be destroyed!

CANDIDATE DEBATE

Dwyer Auditorium was packed. Media hype for the Great Debate had been borderline manic. Demand for press passes was unprecedented, and eight-hundred general admission tickets were awarded by drawing. Organizers anticipated one-hundred forty to one-hundred fifty-million viewers world-wide.

Both candidates arrived about twenty minutes before air time and went to their dressing rooms. By Executive Order, both had been awarded Secret Service protection. Fenstermacher was first to come on stage and take his seat. Onager walked on seconds later and the two shook hands briefly.

The moderator was Aaron Diamond of MSNBC. He greeted both candidates and waved to the audience. The director began a finger-countdown—and the camera's ON light glowed red.

"Good Evening, ladies, and gentlemen. I'm Aaron Diamond. We're coming to you Live—from jam-packed Dwyer Auditorium in downtown Baltimore with The First Presidential Debate! The primary season is drawing to a close, with the eventual nominees of both parties already foregone conclusions. Tonight we bring you their very first face-to-face debate on the issues—between Democratic candidate Senator David Onager of Ohio and Republican candidate, New York Publisher Gordon Fenstermacher. Welcome to you both."

"As agreed by both candidates, all questions this evening have been selected by representatives of the leading news organizations. In order to get to as many of them as possible, please limit your answers to sixty-seconds. Each candidate has chosen to make a closing statement rather than an opening statement, so we'll get right to question number one—" Beginning with you, Mr. Fenstermacher: What do you regard as being the overriding issue of this campaign?"

"Taxation!" he roared. "Pure and simple. My opponent wants to tax success—by going after the most successful among us. These are Americans who've worked very, very hard for everything they have. Well, Sir, we don't intend to let you do it!" There was a quick explosion of applause.

Turning to the audience, Diamond interrupted. "Ladies and Gentlemen—I know these are matters many of you have strong feelings about. But according to the agreed to ground-rules: There will be no displays of support for either candidate. Mr. Fenstermacher, you still have forty-five seconds remaining—"

"This is a very dangerous notion" the candidate continued, "singling out the most successful among us, and taxing them for their success! Tax away the incentive to invest—and you destroy the very thing that makes America great!"

"Most people don't know this," he went on, "but in the original draft of the Declaration of Independence, Thomas Jefferson wrote

179

'Life—Liberty—and the 'Protection of Property'! The Founding Fathers held property rights sacred—knowing the grave threat posed by a government empowered to take possession of citizens' property through taxation!"

Diamond fired a warning look at the audience, and turned to the Democrat. "And for you, Senator Onager—what is the overriding issue of this campaign?"

"I'm afraid it's not a single issue, Aaron, it goes much deeper—to the very values by which we live. We're that 'shining city on the hill'—the oldest existing democracy on earth—the place where one can live in absolute freedom, with the right and the opportunity to work hard and get as rich as he or she is able. America's the best there is, the world's paradigm of peace and prosperity. That's not to say we're perfect. Far from it. Consider our divorce rate—drug use by kids—our bulging prisons—our pollution our over-consumption and waste."

"But then match that against our generosity and compassion, our abiding faith—our willingness to spill our blood in defense of another." He looked directly at his opponent.

"No, it goes far deeper than taxes—way beyond economic fairness. It goes to taking responsibility—on a global scale. It goes to cleansing the environment and sharing the world's resources. It goes to the proper parenting of our children—to serving and helping and uplifting and teaching and protecting. And when we do all that, we do learn how to live up to our true potential—and how to utilize our strength and power. And when we master all that, there's nothing we can't set right!" Stifled applause could be clearly heard.

"Senator Onager—" Fenstermacher challenged, as allowed under the rules, "you sound as if you're preaching that we should increase foreign aid on a massive scale! Does that fall within your definition of fiscal responsibility?"

"Perhaps that's what it all comes down to for you, Gordon—Fiscal versus Social responsibility. But I assure you, they are not mutually exclusive."

"Turning to our next question—" the moderator decided, "How do you each feel about taking advice from the Mentors?" There was a stir from the crowd. "Senator?"

"Wise advice self-validates. And I find much of their advice to be profoundly wise, rooted in responsible values."

The camera caught Fenstermacher's grimace—"Senator, not only do you swallow the 'advice' of these Aliens—you want them to come back and dispense more! Especially, no doubt, should you be sitting in the Oval Office!" He knew this was Onager's point of greatest vulnerability. "Tell us that as president—you wouldn't be taking their advice—!"

Onager had seen this one coming. "A president is always surrounded by advisors, all kinds of advisors. That's how he comes to his decisions—by listening to and evaluating all the advice, and then acting. Now, in the event the Mentors should return—yes, Gordon, I would indeed listen closely to anything they had to say. I'd be derelict if I didn't."

"And Mr. Fenstermacher," Diamond switched, "as president, would you listen to the Mentors?" There was an audible ripple of chuckles.

"Hey, why not? I might even create a new Cabinet post: Secretary of the Exterior!" he sneered, evoking a short burst of quickly suppressed laughter. "But let me say this: In the unfortunate event these Aliens should decide to return to the scene of the crime, I'd invite them to meet with us at a time and place of our choosing! And if they can't breathe our air, they can always don little alien-world spacesuits!"

More laughter; a tart look from Diamond; another question.

Atop ABYTOR, Sandovar and Zooti Abydos watched the debate, well pleased with Fenstermacher's performance thus far.

At the Residence the President rooted for his golfing buddy and friend—his very pregnant daughter's head resting gently on his shoulder.

Also watching were various premiers, presidents and prime ministers; brokers, bankers and CEOs; senators, generals and judges—along with assorted millions of 'ordinary' folks.

Onager counter attacked. "The top three percent is worth at least sixty trillion dollars! They could pay off the entire national debt by themselves—three times over! That much wealth, in so few hands, is beyond all justification. Almost beyond comprehension as well: Try to imagine just how much twenty-trillion dollars is—If, for example, it were divided equally among the other ninety-seven percent of the population—every last person in the country would receive nearly eighty-thousand dollars! Gordon, you can't defend the indefensible—it's time the wealth-distribution pendulum began to swing the other way!"

"That's rank social engineering!" snapped Fenstermacher.

"Look," Onager shot back, "when one finds gross distortion at both economic extremes, it doesn't take a rocket scientist to recognize that

181

something is dangerously out of whack! The net worth of the top two percent shot from three point two to six point one trillion dollars between 1982 and 1986—the very years when Reagan cut taxes in half for the rich, while borrowing hundreds of billions on new defense spending. And the result? The national debt exploded—and we've been paying for it ever since! Now here's the ugly truth: while the country plunged ever deeper into debt—the top two percent increased their net holdings by an even greater amount! In other words, every cent we borrowed went directly to the rich! Do the math."

"Mr. Onager, that kind of talk flirts with, with—class warfare!" Fenstermacher harrumphed.

"Well, should it ever come to that," he smiled, "I'm glad. I'll be fighting on the side of the ninety-seven percentage!" More laughter.

Diamond moved on. "Next question: Senator, do you agree with the Mentors' astounding assertion that government has a primary responsibility to, quote: 'Prevent the disproportionate accumulation of personal wealth'—?'"

Onager looked into the camera. "Let me answer this way—any grossly disproportionate accumulation of personal wealth is at once socially undesirable and economically counter-productive. As to whether it's the responsibility of government to redress gross inequity, I say Yes—since it was government tax laws which enabled the obscene enrichment to occur in the first place! That coupled with inheritance laws designed to perpetuate family fortunes."

Fenstermacher looked mortified. "Good God! Next thing you'll say, we should tax unearned income and corporate profits—and nothing else!" he roared in pious outrage.

"Don't put words in my mouth. It may surprise you to learn that I think a very good case is to be made for the total elimination of corporate taxes—letting competition pass the savings on to consumers and making American products that much more competitive in the global marketplace."

This was something Fenstermacher had never anticipated. He looked like a deer caught in headlights. "So—if that's the case—how would you make up for the lost revenues?"

Onager was waiting for this.

"Why, Gordon, the very same way you would. Let me quote you from a speech you gave to the American Association of Manufacturers last year: 'Eliminating federal taxes on corporate earnings would increase after-tax profits, which would then be passed on to shareholders and customers thereby stimulating higher spending, economic growth, and the consequent increase in federal tax revenues.' I agree with you, a tax on corporate profits is in fact a pass-along tax, doing nothing but making us less competitive. All this while other countries are subsidizing their industries!"

Fingers flew across keyboards the world over—crafting the headlines that had just been made.

Had Gordon Fenstermacher's cage not been rattled so badly, he might have had the presence of mind to ask Onager whether he were actually proposing the elimination of corporate taxes? He was not. He was merely stating an agreement in principle—and giving people something to think about. His primary objective of course was winning the debate.

The next morning Wall Street went into spasm, as markets porpoised up and down in confused frenzy. By the time the final bell rang, the Dow closed down one-hundred and twenty-three points.

The next day Ellen Katherine Bryce gave birth to a seven pound boy, whom she named Josiah Peter Bryce. The new father, overcome with feelings of pride and parental responsibility, begged her to name him Josiah Bryce Klein. Then, kneeling down beside her hospital bed, he proposed. Ellen Kate told Peter she'd always love him dearly, and that Josh would always be his son—but marriage? Not even a 'maybe someday.' She very much doubted she would ever marry.

*   *   *

Upon listening to Justin's tape of his phone call to Ovid, Penny experienced the shock and outrage of betrayal—and the insult of being used. Now she felt only a cold hunger for revenge. *How dare the bastard try to set me up! How dare he use me to injure my father?*

"The main question," Justin explained, "now that we know who Roby's working for, becomes: How's he planning to expose you—have some camera crew hiding in the bushes when you score the pound? Have cops waiting to bust you? Have the press on hand to capture it all?" He shook his head. "No, if you were busted, he's gotta figure you'd turn around and give him up. Since you're only fifteen they'd cut you a deal. It—just doesn't compute."

"Maybe he'd simply tape the deal going down—and then use it to blackmail Dad—!"

"Possible. That's why we have to pick the time and place. Someplace indoors—and private—where we can tape him," he grinned. "He'd never suspect that in a thousand years."

"But," she worried, "what if Ovid did say something to Gaithers—and now they know it wasn't him on the phone?"

"Then they'd never be going forward with the deal—not if they knew we were onto them! I'm betting Ovid and Roby have never spoken. Whoever it was that contacted Roby in the first place with this scheme, you can lay money it wasn't Egon Ovid—he lets others do his dirty work for him."

Penny was less than reassured.

"Don't you see?" he explained. "Even if he did manage to pull it off somehow—and it hits the news, we immediately turn around and expose it all as an Egon Ovid dirty trick! What a low-life thing to do—use a young girl to get at her father. Dig it: we play the tape of my phone call to Ovid plus the video of the buy going down—and that'll be all she wrote! Fenstermacher and Co. will have self-destructed!"

Penny mulled it over—how she would be the one making the news—how the kids at school would react—how her parents would react—and how it was sure to follow her around forever—assuming Gaithers Roby did manage to pull it off. "I still say we oughta tell Dad."

"You gotta be kidding—he'd spank us and send us to our rooms for even thinking about copping a pound of weed! An' even if he did think exposing 'em was a cool idea, he could never know about it in advance. No way we tell him!"

But Penny was sure something would go wrong.

"Sis, it's always been me that never took chances—while you were the one who always made the waves. This is no time to switch. Trust me: if we can nail Ovid for setting up a drug deal—we can hand Dad the presidency!"

Penny allowed herself to entertain the fantasy—and then cracked up. "Imagine the world of shit the Secret Service'll be in—if we pull this off right under their noses!"

'Their noses' already knew Onager's kids smoked pot. But it was not viewed as a threat to the candidate's physical safety—and ratting them out was not one of their duties.

POTPLOT

For thousands of years the rulers of China had been beset by enemies, both within and without. Yet until now, none had ever managed to all but paralyze them.

The leadership in Beijing was finally persuaded that a four-hundred and fifty kiloton nuclear device was entombed within Three Gorges Dam—and could presumably be detonated by radio command. Worse, they could not remove it. This was intolerable.

While surrendering Taiwan was anathema.

Finally, on the fifth of June, desperate decisions were taken. June ninth, Pyonyang would be informed that:

One; Should the bomb detonate for any reason whatsoever, North Korea would cease to exist;

Two; Economic aid for North Korea would be exchanged for deactivation of the bomb;

Three; Negotiations on a bilateral defense treaty could commence once the bomb were deactivated;

Four; And on June twenty-ninth, it would be announced that nations could trade with China or Taiwan—but not both.

*　　*　　*

The government of Taiwan had belatedly apprised Washington of their secret meeting with the North Koreans, and of Pyongyang's atomic stratagem to extort both protection from China and money from Taiwan. CIA had known only that someone met with the North Koreans aboard an Arab yacht out of Taipei, thanks to satellite reconnaissance. Now they knew Who and Why.

State had action plans for every conceivable crisis—but was caught without even a policy, let alone a strategy, for dealing with something like this. Pyongyang sneaks a Soviet nuke inside the biggest dam on earth—then warns Beijing they'll detonate it? On but one thing there was immediate agreement: The nuclear threat to China must be kept absolutely secret. Were it leaked, chaos could erupt.

185

No one at the White House could imagine China submitting to blackmail by anyone. Moreover, it was clear that North Korea had made a threat, it would be suicide to carry out; rendering it ultimately empty.

Short of pushing the unpushable button, the White House had no notion what the demented leader in Pyongyang might do next to up the ante. And that was the frightening part.

It was therefore concluded that time was on the side of Beijing. Chinese patience being legendary; Bryce and his advisors could see nothing which could ever force China to acquiesce to Pyongyang's demands.

Had the members of the NSC been aware of the trembler trigger, coupled with the risk of an earthquake, they would not necessarily have seen time as being on China's side.

For each of the old men in Beijing, it was like being told by a doctor that he could suffer a crippling stroke at any moment.

*   *   *

Some mothers are mortified at the prospect of becoming grandmothers. Not so Abby Frayles-Bryce. Little Josh had pushed all the right buttons, and by his third visit to the White House, Granny Bryce was reduced to a state of abject devotion. She had turned a small bedroom into a nursery, with staff hovering about to Oooh and Aaah at every baby grimace/smile. For the first time in years mother and daughter felt truly close. Abby loved to watch Katie nurse Josh—a precious bonding opportunity she herself had chosen to forgo. A decision she'd regret forever.

"He's doing it again—" Abby cooed, watching him suckle, "—batting his eyes at me."

"Yeah, he sure knows how to—ouch!"

"What's the matter?"

"He thinks my nipple's a teething ring."

"And that's only using his imaginary teeth. Just wait'll he's got the real thing to bite with!"

At that moment the president walked in, with Peter in tow. "I see somebody got the jump on lunch," Gramps observed.

Peter bent over, kissed his son, then Ellen Kate. "You leave some for later, buddy!"

Ellen Kate looked up and smiled. "He doesn't realize yet there's no such thing as a free lunch."

Sensing all the attention, Josiah ramped up his sucking.

"Hey, easy man—" his father laughed, "remember, you got another full one to go after that!"

They sat down to a quiet lunch of truffles in aspic over couscous—a First Daughter request. Bryce took a fork and poked suspiciously at the concoction. "Looks like some cretaceous sea critter squatting on top of a mound of albino roe—We got any ketchup around this place?"

"Oh, hey," his daughter rejoined. "Clearly you missed your calling; you'd make an awesome food critic! Try it with a bite of garlic toast, why don't you?"

He did—and liked the result. Bryce was grateful Katie hadn't found out he'd boffed his national security adviser. Katie was liberated, but there was a limit. He had Abby and his mother to thank for their discretion.

"Peter—" Bryce said, in an effort to redirect his thoughts, "I hear you think Bush forty-one dropped the ball after Iraq invaded Kuwait. How so?"

"Simple," he shrugged. "If Kuwait had offered say, fifty-million dollars in gold for the head of Saddam Hussein—how long do you think it would have been before it arrived C.O.D.?"

The President gave a derisive snort. "Peter—somehow I don't see you becoming a career diplomat."

*   *   *

Justin and Penny debated at length the ideal setting for their sting. A suitable location was vital—essentially a place which met the hidden requirements of both parties. He argued they had one major thing going for them: Roby would never suspect they were setting him up. Moreover, Justin was fully convinced that nothing would happen to his sister at the buy itself, or even shortly thereafter. Ovid's game had to be to catch her with the pot at some later time. An idea hit him: "Or, maybe it's something else altogether—like hitting Dad with just the threat of exposure!" This he liked—it made more sense. He shared his new insight with Penny.

"But, to do that, wouldn't they still need something to expose—some kind of evidence?"

"Yup. The weed's the evidence. They could wait a week, then catch you holding in school—or maybe search your locker—or hey, this is a good one: Get some chick in Geometry to try to cop a dime or a Z from you, saying she heard you had some really good shit. Or, possibly even burn one of your smoking buddies—and then squeeze 'em to give you up. Could be most anything—if the price were right."

"But, we get to pick the place, right? And the time?"

"Right. He's never gonna risk arousing your suspicions by making you do the deal on his turf. You just tell him where you want to do the deal, and he'll go along. You'll see."

FIRST CONTACT

For Ellen Kate, one real benefit to living alone was being able to sleep with Josh right next to her. Whenever he got hungry in the night, all she had to do was roll on her side and whip out a late supper. This way they could both half-sleep right through it and wake up rested.

It was just past five, Sunday morning. Summer Solstice. The sun was barely above the rooftop next door, streaming through her bedroom window, ruffling the curtains. At least that was how she liked to think of it: it was the sun that was blowing the curtains, not the wind. She could still smell the lilacs outside, by now well into their dotage. She lay on her back, eyes closed, half awake and half asleep—adrift on a gentle sea of June fragrances—Suddenly, there appeared in her mind a silent 'statement'—just hanging there—

You are loved—as you love your own.

Ellen Kate puzzled vaguely over what would ever make that thought pop into her head—

You are a devoted mother—and I am well pleased.

Another unspoken 'statement'—just—hanging there. A wild thought flashed across her mind—and instantly she was wide awake, alarm bells clanging. She opened her eyes to run a reality check: there, yes, Josh was still asleep—a golden sun was still pouring in—and

OooYaYa was staring at her from on top of the dresser. Wow, was that ever weird—she decided, slowly closing her eyes again—

Fear not, your psyche is sound. The Voice you hear is real.

She sat bolt upright: T-h-e M-e-n-t-o-r-s!

No. They are here for the world. I am here only for you.

A warm chill suddenly suffused her—as a soft dawning broke bright within—

Yes, Dear One—you do know who I am.

"Oh—My—God!" she wailed aloud, her voice quavering. For a long moment she sat stunned, not daring to breathe.

I have been with you since you were very young. We have been through much together, you and I when you thought you were alone, but you never were—

And from this moment you will never again feel alone—. For I AM within you.

And to a certainty beyond anything she'd ever before experienced, Ellen Kate Bryce—KNEW—!

But—but, how can you—be inside my head just talking to me? she silently asked. There was a pause.

Never Underestimate Omnipotence!

Hearing that, she laughed aloud. She'd always been drawn to the concept of a 'God Within'—but had never dreamed that God came equipped with a sense of humor! And this sudden realization produced a rush of—pure elation!

We will become fast friends—you and I—forever inseparable.

Know that I am not of you—nor am I you.

Just know that one day—you and I will become One!

GROTTO

Sandovar Abydos had no sooner acquired a permit to construct his conference center, than he made the mountain bow before its new master. He ordered the top of its peak lopped off—instantly rendering every Utah map which showed the heights of mountains inaccurate by eleven feet. He was for all intents and purposes the only man in history to actually lower one of the Rocky Mountains.

With its granite tip blasted away, the remaining base had been chiseled, rasped, sanded, leveled, and polished to a high luster—leaving a massive, elevated stone stage at the center of the eight-hundred seat dining auditorium. It was initially envisioned as a dramatic platform for guest speakers—when Zooti came up with the first original idea of his life, saying it would also make a "bitchin" stage for performers. Aghast, his father hastened to decree that there would be no singers, musicians, smoke generators, music fountains, multimedia displays, or descending movie screens. However, Zooti was so crushed by the summary dismissal of his first Big Idea that Abydos Sr. relented a bit, deciding that perhaps the stage could serve as more than merely a speaker's platform. He then invested eight-hundred eighty-eight thousand dollars to light his geological masterpiece with high-intensity micro-footlights, overhead spots, strobes, argon and krypton lasers, lenses of every color, shape and motion—and the megabytes to drive it all.

The great stone stage was shaped like the sliced-off stump of a giant redwood, but was, effectively a gleaming black mirror—capable of reflecting a dazzling, high-tech light show up onto the parabolic dome high overhead. And though it was the personal toy of Abydos, it became a prime ABYTOR attraction.

As required by the FAA, a red beacon pulsed on top of the dome. Yet any pilot within a hundred miles would recognize the dazzling fire-ring of light as ABYTOR, without even noticing its bright warning beacon.

Karyn DeLeo had fallen for ABYTOR big time, thrilled she'd signed the employment contract. To her the place represented a thing of spectacular beauty wrought by Man—set amidst a spectacular beauty wrought by Mother Earth herself.

She took advantage of everything the Center had to offer: eating at the very top of creation surrounded by breathtaking grandeur—taking awesome Vista Cube rides—diving for the bottom of Thor's Grotto—and sleeping with nothing but tempered glass between her and the valley so far below—

Karyn especially loved walking through an air-lock and out onto the great circumferential balcony, where the thin, icy air slapped at your face and the beauty was—infinite.

Out on the balcony one could blister from the sun in the time it took to walk around it once. But it was being out on the balcony at night that—transported Karyn. She found it almost spiritual—standing so utterly alone out among the blazing stars and frozen peaks.

She'd occasionally let Zooti join her for a swim, despite her discomfort at feeling his eyes on her butt every time she climbed out of the water, her suede bikini clinging like a second skin. During such optical caressing his cell phone almost invariably went unanswered. But not today. Climbing out of the water, she heard him shout, "Hey, don't gimme that shit, Eddie. There's something going on, and I wanna know what! Start with those four clowns from L.A. who checked in yesterday." He punched off angrily. Karyn strolled over and dripped next to him, memorizing everything she'd just overheard. A secret being kept from Zooti? Only his father would dare do that. [She happened to know Eddie was head of security.] The first actual evidence of something secret afoot? Frayles will want confirmation, she thought—

"Listen," she apologized, "I've got the makings of a killer headache—I'm gotta go lie down for a while." She gave him a pained half-smile. "Catch you in the morning."

In her office early the next morning, Karyn called up on her screen all the guest arrivals for the previous week and was startled to discover that the names of the "four clowns from L.A." did not appear anywhere. On a hunch, she checked the owner's suites—and found them all listed as being Occupied. Names—she needed names—

11:45. Zooti had been in some hush-hush meeting in the Eagle's Roost all morning, and Karyn suspected he was finally being included in whatever it was that had been kept from him. Her suspicion was reinforced when he returned to his office fully energized over something. She brought him his midday cup of hot chocolate—with precisely ten mini-marshmallows floating on top as stipulated.

"About time. Where've you been all morning?" she greeted.

"Busy. Had a meeting," was all he'd say. She stole a glance at the omnipresent doodling pad which accompanied him everywhere—and noticed, among all the various lines and shapes; a bold arrow aimed up at an elongated ellipse bearing a stylized 'M'! "Wow, that could be the Mentors' ship," she thought to herself. She snapped a mental photo and headed for the door. "Don't forget, when you have a few minutes we need to talk about the Young Republicans dinner."

Wednesday was Karyn's day off, when she'd go to Provo to shop, run her errands, and call Frayles. But it was only Monday, so she had plenty of time to dig around before then.

191

*   *   *

Ellen Kate and her Voice had been busy, conversing silently mind-to-mind when she was alone.

That time when you fell through the ice—it was no coincidence someone was there to throw you a rope.

You did that?

No. You have your Seraphim to thank.

Were there—any other times they came to my rescue?

On one occasion Direct Intervention became necessary.

To do what—?

To momentarily suspend physical law.

That—can be done?

Only in an emergency—to spare an essential life.

Just—when did all this happen?

A boy was showing off his new sports car for you. You were approaching an unseen stone wall at high speed. Forward momentum had to be transformed into rotation.

Oh—that summer in Revere! We just sat there, spinning around and around—!

Three and a half revolutions to be precise.

So, are you saying that—if I hadn't been in the car that boy would have been killed?

Intervention would not have occurred.

Why—why—me?

Because you are essential to the spiritual economy of this world—and because you volunteered.

Yet even now—you are free to withdraw.

Withdraw from—what?

From bringing Light unto your brothers and sisters from supernal service in My name.

Are there others like me who're serving too? Or am I the only one hearing your Voice?

Others are indeed serving—for I AM within all.

Yet precious few are able to hear my words.

It is not that I can speak to you—it is that you are able to hear me.

This is possible because you are truly pure of heart.

But—I don't even go to church—

That matters not—only your abiding desire to serve
For when you serve all my children—you serve Me

I—I don't know—this is getting really heavy all of a sudden. Exactly what did I "volunteer" to do?

To speak on behalf of others.

That's it? Just—"speak on behalf of others?"

Do not worry—you'll find it most challenging.

It was all her Voice would reveal. Her brain felt utterly drained. She needed time to sleep. And to think.

Ellen Kate could truly feel a great Love Within—and instinctively loved back. She somehow knew on her deepest level that she could absolutely trust her Voice—and that God would never ask anything of her that was not in her own best interest. This she—knew.

She gazed down at Josh—sucking away for all he was worth—and wondered if it were symbolic of things to come.

KAPPA UNO

KAPPA UNO was meticulous. At considerable expense, a full set of engineering drawings for all four space shuttles had been obtained showing every structure, assembly, thru-section, and detail. Concomitantly, in-depth investigations had been undertaken for every Vehicle Assembly Building employee at the Cape, with special focus on any who'd recently filed grievances, any seeing therapists, any with troubled marriages, and any with financial problems.

Far more costly had been mounting a covert field operation to obtain eighty pounds of FOMEX, a new generation micro-foam high-explosive (MFHE), developed by Cyndyx Industries of Chula Vista under a CIA black program of the late Nineties—and well known to one member of KAPPA UNO. Not even the Pentagon was aware of its existence. The toughest part had been figuring out how to steal eight aerosol canisters of FOMEX without Cyndyx even realizing a theft had taken place. An expedient fire was briefly considered, then ruled out. Their breakthrough came upon learning that the canister casings were manufactured by a subcontractor under very lax security. It was decided that an empty (possibly a reject) canister would be obtained, reverse-engineered, and replicated eight times. Filled with common window putty, the eight dummy units would then be quietly substituted for eight genuine canisters in Cyndyx's warehouse.

An elaborate penetration and recovery operation was carried out on the Fourth of July—on the whim of Sandovar Abydos.

By the time the canister switch was discovered, and a secret CIA investigation undertaken, the Mentors would be long dead—should they be so foolish as to return to Earth.

*   *   *

Valuing profits over politics, corporations the world over were being forced into contracts to conduct their business only with China. And as a result, Taiwan found itself, for all intents and purposes, on its own.

By contrast, any president's bottom line is profoundly, selfishly, and perpetually Political. Sam Bryce was no exception. In the fourth and final year of his presidency, he was suddenly free to rise above both political and economic self-interest. But he was still a captive of his imprinting and it would take Abby to shake him free.

"Woody, you can't just leave Taiwan hanging there, withering in the wind. The Taiwanese are an endangered species. For once listen to the Mentors: We're meant to use our economic power to protect, help, and assure the survival of others!"

"You talking about that hare-brained notion of Katie's to buy Taiwan from China?"

"Consider the alternatives: do nothing, and see Taiwan get swallowed up—or go to war. I say buy it—it's the one way Beijing can save face! You know they'll fight to keep Taiwan a part of China. And, once the bombs start falling on Taipei, how long could we afford to stand by and do nothing?"

"You're talking about—a trillion dollars, at minimum!"

"Well, I'm sure back then seven point two million dollars for Alaska must have also seemed like a fortune. But this time we'd be buying it on behalf of another. Essentially it would be a long-term loan, in the form of trade credits repayable by the people of Taiwan. In the meantime it becomes U.S. Territory, and like Puerto Rico, immune to attack. In return for this, Taiwan would merely up its national debt by another trillion or so. And we can certainly show 'em how that's done!"

"You're beginning to sound like Onager," he growled.

"Woody, it's a peaceful solution. And it doesn't get any better than that—as even your dumb twat national security adviser will tell you."

He started to say something, and then stopped—for the first time giving the idea actual consideration and running its permutations. "It would be pretty damn humiliating to make Beijing such an offer—only to have 'em spit on it!"

"Woody—no one spits on a trillion dollars."

"I—get your point."

*   *   *

Penny and her mother were sitting in the breakfast nook sipping hot lemon tea while awaiting Jane Onager's latest batch of Authentic Philadelphia Cinnamon Buns.

"Mom—tell me what you think of my latest idea: a book called, 'Opening Lines I Never Got Beyond.'"

"Good title. What was your inspiration?"

"Oh, I forget. But I wouldn't get 'em out of actual books—I'd just make 'em up!

"Wouldn't that be like—cheating?"

"Oh, I'd say right on the jacket that they're all made up," Penny shrugged. "Lemme think of an example—Okay, here's one: 'Tammy made him feel like a hairball, frozen in the compote of time.'"

For a few moments Jane did not react. Then she asked for another example. Penny closed her eyes to get it just right. "Yeah, here's one: 'Fetid lay her dreams of insouciance.'"

At this her mother nearly spilled her tea—then cracked up. "Where'd you ever pick up a word like that?"

"Means 'carefree—not a worry in the world.' I heard Dad use it to describe Justin."

DIGITAL TRAP

On their date Friday, Gaithers Roby told Penny that "the really good shit just arrived." She acted excited—and it was no act. The Sting Was On! Following Justin's instructions, she invited Roby over for a swim the next afternoon, suggesting he could bring the pot with him then.

"Dad's off with Mom campaigning in L.A., so no one'll be around," she had assured. "Total privacy."

Roby arrived shortly after lunch, the Secret Service agent at the front gate waving him in. Ten minutes later he and Penny were sitting in the Onager sunroom—a green mound of homegrown buds piled high on the glass-top table between them Penny pressed her face to the fragrant pile and toked—as Gaithers Roby snapped digital photos with a tiny camera disguised as a wristwatch. More than satisfied, Penny pulled out a wad of fifties and passed it over; Roby pocketed them without counting. She cocked her head, puzzled. "Hey—I trust you," he shrugged.

Little did Roby suspect the entire transaction was being videotaped by Justin through a knot hole in the pine paneling behind the wet bar, or that in a nearby planter a tiny microphone lay hidden amid the lobelia.

* * *

Arthur Frayles was troubled. The more he reflected on the various pieces of information provided by Karyn DeLeo, the more convinced he became that something foul was afoot at ABYTOR. Something well-funded and highly clandestine. It was also now evident that both Sandovar Abydos and his son were directly involved.

What Karyn had established was that there was some kind of covert group, possibly designated 'K-1'—four unregistered guests from L.A.— secret comings and goings—plus Zooti's very pointed doodle. But most telling of all, K-1's membership: former intelligence operatives, radicals, and felons.

However, the sole evidence to suggest that the Mentors were K-1's target was Zooti's doodle of an arrow aimed up at an oval bearing the letter 'M'—with a line drawn below it which Karyn thought might depict the curvature of the earth. It was of course still something of a leap. Yet the longer Frayles thought about it, given Abydos' outspoken antipathy for the Mentors, the more convinced he grew. But what to do? Where to go with his suspicions? They had nothing conclusive to pass on to the FBI. After a while, he reached for the phone—

Whoa, if the Mentors are the target, they probably know about it already—and therefore might not return at all.

"Good afternoon, the White House."

"Dr. Klein's office, please."

*　　*　　*

Peter Klein had spent nearly every waking hour of the past month trying to devise some way, any way, for the Chinese to safely extract an atomic bomb from inside Three Gorges Dam. He was obsessed. But Arthur Frayles' call that afternoon had driven the dam problem clean out of his mind.

Now he lay in bed, staring into the dark. If Frayles is right—which remains to be seen—the Mentors could be in danger, should they return. So the real question becomes: How does one go about attacking a spaceship? Missiles? Ground-based excimer laser?—attack by another spacecraft? an armed assault from the shuttle itself—? Each one massively difficult, if not outright impossible.

Destroying a spacecraft in low earth orbit, he reasoned, would pose insurmountable technological problems for anyone but a nation with advanced weaponry and billions to spend. This effectively eliminates missiles, spacecraft, and lasers. This leaves only the shuttle. So, what's their plan? Armed assault from the shuttle? If so—by whom? Possibly they were going to try to capture a Mentor—and bring him back alive— Or, simply open fire on the spaceship as soon as it came within range! In that case, they dare not let it get too close to the shuttle—

At that instant, a thought came crashing into his mind, losing a jolt of adrenalin. Could the plan be to blow up both the alien spaceship and the shuttle while they were moored together! Sacrifice the lives of the astronauts in order to destroy the Mentors! His spine froze. Sabotage: Simple, Effective, Cheap. His gut pounded—it was a very real possibility! Peter looked at his watch: 2:19.

He reached for the phone and punched up the White House switchboard: If you want to get someone's attention, have the White House call them in the middle of the night—

A minute later, he was patched through to Henry Salk, Kennedy Space Center Director of Operations.

"Dr. Salk, this is Peter Klein, NSC staff. I apologize for having to call at this hour, but I'm afraid we have a problem. Information has just arrived which suggests an attempt may be made to sabotage one of the shuttles while it is in orbit." He paused a moment to let this sink in. "I'm therefore directing you to undertake an immediate all-areas inspection of the four shuttles. You'll be looking for explosives."

"Including the boosters and launch tower?"

"Our analysis indicates that an explosion would only take place in orbit, so you can ignore the boosters and main fuel tanks. But pay special attention to all voids and unused spaces, no matter how small. Dr. Salk—you are looking for high-explosives which are extremely well concealed."

"Are you certain of this, Mr. Klein?"

"No. And that's why I'm not ready to call in the Bureau. If you do find something, that'll be time enough to bring them in. I figure the last thing you want is a bunch of cement-heads running around, prying off panels, and tearing into everything."

Salk drew a mental picture. "Ten-Four."

"Do you have explosives detection equipment on hand?"

"Somewhere—Yes. We'll get onto it immediately. Do I reach you at the White House?"

"Affirmative. Any hour. The switchboard will find me. Again, sorry to have to wake you."

Salk rang off, with visions of cement-heads running amok.

*   *   *

Reduced to expensive ratification pageants, both national conventions were pretty much a yawn. The night David Onager made his acceptance speech and named as his running mate, the Independent governor of Maine, the Democrats managed only a six point two percent audience share—while Fox's Conjugal Congregation held onto the top slot.

The Republicans fared only marginally better, thanks to a massive ad campaign hawking: "Gordon—Defender of the American Way—Fenstermacher." To many it sounded like a prize-fight introduction.

The polls showed, however, that the fall campaign would be anything but a yawn. The Oval Office was still anyone's to win or lose: Fenstermacher thirty-eight percent; Onager forty-one percent; Undecided twenty-one percent.

SIX SADMS

Iana Ravenscroft delivered the bad news: "After weeks of intensive investigation, the Russians report that, in 1993 a total of Six suitcase SADMs had been sold on the black market by a former KGB general named Yuri Ivanovich Rodorenko—who was 'killed in 1996 in an automobile accident in the Urals.'"

"By now the Russians say the trail is long cold, but they 'most firmly assure' us their investigation will continue." The sarcasm in her voice was ill-concealed.

"I expected as much," Bryce snarled. "If they do know where those nukes are now, we're probably the last ones they'd tell. So we'd better get every agency cracking—I have to have answers!"

*   *   *

August eleventh was a day the Onager family could have lived without: Crisp color photographs of Penny, grinning from behind a green mound of primo sativa, adorned every newsstand.

Jane had just started breakfast when a breathless Tommy Raffle appeared at the door, tabloids clutched in both hands. The senator let him in, then physically recoiled as he saw the papers—and grasped what he was looking at.

At that moment Penny shuffled in, sleepily tying her bathrobe.

"Are these pictures genuine?" her father demanded, thrusting the papers out at her.

Penny was shocked awake in an instant. "Justin—!" she screamed in the direction of the second floor. She turned to face her father, rage now blazing in his eyes. "Daddy, now I know it looks bad. But you gotta wait 'til—Justin—!"

"My God, Penny—what could you have been thinking?" Onager stammered. At that moment Justin burst in—saw the papers—flashed a smile—and put up both hands.

"Whoa. Don't be jumping to any conclusions—" Pausing to throw his sister a tender look, he turned to his father. "We got a couple of tapes for you to see and listen to—"

* * *

"Dr. Klein, Hank Salk here. I'm afraid you were right—we discovered four powerful bombs hidden inside all the shuttles' They're disarmed, but it'll take some time to remove them."

"Where were the bombs found? Were they hidden on the port side?" The hair stood erect all the way down Peter's spine.

"Yes. How did you know?" There was astonishment in the director's voice.

"Exactly how much explosive was found?"

"Enough to bust open your average size warship!"

Iana Ravenscroft had not been pleased when Klein took it upon himself to call the Cape and declare a Security Alert, but in the end agreed that bringing in the Bureau at that point would only 'compound our problems.' But with Salk's confirmation call, all that was about to change.

FOMEX

Special Agent Hy Depkawitz was a minority of One at the FBI: a Jewish Vegetarian Buddhist. He was also one of the Bureau's best and brightest.

When Klein informed the FBI that bombs had been found aboard all four shuttles, Depkawitz had been quickly pulled off the Gold Depository case [Fa Haad remained the prime suspect], and reassigned to head a Major Case investigation into the shuttle sabotages. As Special Agent-in-Charge, he was advised he'd have the full resources of the Bureau at his command—along with an open budget. Apprehending the perps was all that mattered.

The investigation would center on three areas: Explosives—Radio Detonators—and Personnel.

Hidden above Sub-frame Section C-146 in each shuttle, the bombs had been found and immediately disarmed. The explosive turned out to be a high-density, aerosol-applied micro-foam—and this was the first time the Bureau had encountered it.

It was ingenious. Explosive foam had been sprayed against the inside of the outer shuttle wall in a non-maintenance space densely packed with pipes and conduits—but with sufficient void area to accommodate twenty pounds of FOMEX. A single three-eighths inch hole was drilled into each inner wall—the foam sprayed in—an explosive bolt inserted to plug the hole with a small wire running to a sophisticated radio receiver-detonator tapped in to the shuttle's own electrical system for its power. Thus, anytime a shuttle was powered up, its bomb was armed and ready.

As source for this unique explosive, Depkawitz suspected either DOD or the Company, with his money on the latter. It took but one call to Klein to find out—and within an hour he had received the fullest assurances of CIA cooperation.

This had damn well better not be lip-service.

Sole-source-supplier Cyndyx Industries was contacted. A hasty inventory of finished stock revealed that eight canisters of FOMEX were indeed missing and presumed stolen. Nothing had been left behind but the replacement canisters. The trail now cold, it was effectively a dead-end. They didn't even have a time frame for the theft. Other than using the precision machine-tooling marks left on the canisters for possible future comparison, the replacements yielded nothing that would help identify either their source or their maker. However one thing was already evident: they were dealing with highly skilled professionals. Moreover, Hy Depkawitz knew something else about FOMEX—the fact that few individuals even knew of its existence. And every one who did—worked for either CIA or Cyndyx. It would be a good place to start. He assigned thirty agents.

As to the receiver-detonators—other than the fact that they were the product of ingenious design, precision manufacture, and micro-tolerance installation—each component was assembled using top quality parts—available over-the-counter from any good electronics house. Depkawitz now knew these guys would leave no crumb trails.

That left Personnel.

Between the shuttle maintenance crews, transport crews, vehicle assembly teams, contractor representatives and staff, more than six-hundred individuals had physical access to shuttlecraft in one way or another—all of whom having been extensively vetted and cleared. Kennedy Space Center security was rated Impenetrable: no vendor, no visitor, no delivery truck, and no one without authorization, retinal scan, and a full-body search could possibly gain access. Ergo, it had to be an inside job. Moreover, it had to be someone with intimate knowledge of both shuttle design and construction. This narrowed the field considerably.

This was one case Hyman Depkawitz was determined to solve. Going after the space shuttles was beyond treason; it bordered on sacrilege. Despite Klein's suspicion that Abydos was behind the sabotage, Hyman wondered if they could be dealing with terrorists. But, it didn't feel like a terrorist thing; they typically employed cruder, more direct, less costly and less sophisticated methods. He just hoped it wasn't al Qaeda.

*　　*　　*

Senator Onager called a news conference in the Senate press gallery. A large monitor stood to one side. The room was jammed to overflowing with reporters and cameras.

With Jane, Justin, and Penny standing at his side, Onager read from a prepared statement—

"I've asked you here today in order to respond to the recent publication of photographs of my daughter, Penny, next to a pile of marijuana."

The only sounds were the scratching of pens and the staccato tick of keyboards. "As you are about to see, the alleged drug transaction was in reality an attempt by the political opposition to embarrass my family and myself. But fortunately, my daughter and my son Justin were suspicious from the outset. They smelled a set-up—and set out to confirm their suspicions.

"First off, my son Justin made a recording of a telephone call he placed to Egon Ovid at Fenstermacher for President headquarters, pretending to be a young man named Gaithers Roby, whom my daughter happened to be dating."

"As it turns out, this particular young man was conspiring with certain of Mr. Ovid's people to photograph my daughter supposedly purchasing a pound of pot—and then turning around and peddling the pictures to the tabloids." His face was a study in disgust.

"But they greatly underestimated the intelligence, and the very real courage, of my children who, out of a misdirected but loving loyalty, turned the tables on young Mr. Roby by videotaping him with a hidden camera and recording him with a hidden microphone as he supposedly sold his drugs."

"The first I knew of any of this was when Roby's pictures appeared in the tabloids. I needn't tell you, I was furious with both my children. I would never have condoned what they did, no matter how well-intentioned. But—unfortunately for all—it happened. And now each of them will have to face the legal consequences."

"The first thing you're going to hear is that recording my son made while on the telephone with Egon Ovid. Following that, you'll see videotape of the bogus drug transaction."

Raffle began playing the tape of the phone call to Ovid. Following that, he dimmed the lights, switched on the large television monitor, and played the drug sale videotape.

Later that afternoon Egon Ovid was fired for the second time in six months.

John VanOrsdell

SABOTAGE

Ellen Kate was nursing Josh—her favorite time for communing with her Voice.

Everyone you know is likewise host to Me the concept of the God Within is Truth. While few are able to hear the whisper of the Divine Voice—that does not mean there is no communication.

Then—how come so many people are—off doing such horrible things?

Because they are at once Ignorant and Sovereign.

One is responsible only for what one knows. Your laws hold that Ignorance is no Excuse.

But on the Universe Level—it is the only excuse.

Every mortal is sovereign over the exercise of Free Will

An institutionalized person is denied free will—

A soldier may surrender it willingly—

However in the eyes of the Universe—it is inviolate

Even unto Me.

Yet know that each of you is dearly—dearly loved—regardless of your choices.

Are you saying—even Hitler got Unconditional Love?

The farther a man strays from the path of Righteousness

The greater the Love needed to bring him back

Whosoever would return—shall be forgiven.

Ellen Kate lapsed into profound, virginal contemplation. Within hours she came to the belief that human existence is a profoundly spiritual affair. Then she heard a Voice whisper:

Amen to that.

*   *   *

Hyman Depkawitz was grateful that news of the attempted sabotage of the space shuttles had not been leaked. But he knew it was only a matter of time.

His team had already narrowed the suspect list of Kennedy Center employees to one who conspicuously stood out:

204

Robert Edwin Veschera, forty-six and the manager of the Stores Shuttle Bay Two. He was divorced on February eighteenth and the mother was awarded custody of the children. July twenty-fifth there was a wire transfer in the amount of four-hundred and fifty-thousand dollars into a numbered Cayman Island account.

Veschera apparently failed to realize that the wire transfer itself, prior to deposit, was a matter of public record.

When agents arrived at his home to question him, they discovered he'd be answering no questions. Ever. Forensics soon confirmed Hy's strong suspicion: the fatal fall in the tub had in fact been a highly professional execution.

Veschera had in all probability worked alone, having been paid handsomely for his treachery. Thus the Personnel trail was likely another dead end. They'd dig further, but Hy doubted they'd find involvement by anyone else at the Cape.

Abydos, or whoever, was making certain all tracks were obliterated.

ONE-HUNDRED EIGHTYDEGREE CHANGE

"It may not be the best answer," the President asserted, "but it may be the only peaceful—permanent solution."

Iana couldn't believe her ears. Only a few weeks before, he'd joked about his daughter's "Magic Taiwan Solution." And now, here he was doing a one-hundred and eighty degree course change! "So tell me, what's Chester gonna think of this 'magical' solution?" she mocked, knowing full well the Secretary of State's East Asian views.

"It's not him I'm worried about," Bryce murmured. "Hell, I can't even get a hundred million out of Congress for the Ukrainians!" He eyed her directly. "Objectively now—what do you think of the idea?"

"I think—you think money can be a cure-all. God, you sound more like a closet liberal with every passing day!" She saw this stung and took pleasure. "That said, there is a slim chance Beijing might actually go for it—for the money, not the face-saving." She rose and began to pace. "First, you'd have to open back-channel talks: Sell Beijing on your proposition—agree on a price—agree on terms—execute a Letter of Understanding—and manage to do it all in the utmost secrecy. Then, at some point you'd have to go public—to propose we buy Taiwan! This you'd have to sell to the American people, after having kept them in the dark. This tends to piss people off. Of course ultimately you'd have to sell it to Congress—not to mention Tokyo and Seoul. Do I think you can pull all this off?"

"You once said I could sell condoms in a convent—" he squinted.

"I was being rash."

She shifted in her chair, and he eyed her thigh. She caught it and tucked her skirt under. "Cool it."

*   *   *

Karyn DeLeo's report on Sandovar Abydos was coming along nicely. In a stunning discovery, she'd learned there was a secret Electronic Monitoring Center concealed on Lower level One, quite apart from Security Control on Level Two. It took getting Zooti drunk to learn its true function: Eavesdropping on guests.

Twice each month ABYTOR hosted a corporate retreat for the CEOs and wives of a particular industry: 'A sky-top weekend get-away—where you can relax, drink, dine, and visit with your peers in luxurious comfort and the utmost privacy.'

However, before ABYTOR welcomed its first guest, Sandovar Abydos had brazenly concealed eighty-six microphones to tape the private conversations of the business world's prime movers.

By this simple betrayal, he picked up hints of mergers, buy-outs, break-throughs, spikes and dips in earnings, stock splits—pure gold to any major player in the market.

Gleaning golden flecks of inside information, Sandovar Abydos watched the value of his stock portfolio rise one-hundred twenty-eight percent over the past twelve months.

Frayles was pushing Karyn for more on Abydos himself. But apart from the one time he appeared in her office, she'd not laid eyes on the man. His son, unhappily, was another matter. Lately the guy had been in Full Rut Mode, pawing the dirt before her at every opportunity. Unfortunately for him, she was operating in Full Paws Off. But every time she tried to convey this, it only aroused him more—which in turn brought about even stronger rebuffs. A sorry cycle. She finally explained that she was only capable of making love, and not just having sex.

Zooti regarded this as a minor genetic defect—one he was confident he could treat.

Karyn prayed her assignment would be finished before he tried to force the issue.

*   *   *

Arthur Frayles was in his study banging out an editorial, when his computer stopped in mid-sentence. The screen went blank, and he thought there'd been a momentary power failure; he'd lost copy that way before. Suddenly—the keypad before him began a wild, three-second dance! He recoiled in disbelief as a message lashed line by line onto his screen:

ARTHUR FRAYLES: FONDEST GREETINGS!

IN OUR NAME, KINDLY INVITE THE BRYCE FAMILY AND THE ONAGER FAMILY TO JOIN US AT ABYTOR FOR THE IMPENDING BANKERS RETREAT WEEKEND.

DO THIS IN PERSON AND TELL NO ONE. AS BEFORE, YOU ALONE MAY ATTEND TO REPRESENT THE MEDIA.

WE TRUST YOU ARE PLEASED WE ARE SO SOON TO RETURN. REST ASSURED, THE WORLD WILL NOT BE DISAPPOINTED.

BETA

John VanOrsdell

MASLAS

Just before dawn a spanking new White House 757, bearing but one passenger, landed unobserved at a Chinese military base north of Beijing. On hand to greet President Bryce's national security adviser was deputy foreign minister Zhu. Twenty minutes later their motorcade slipped quietly behind the walls of the Forbidden City.

"The United States stands prepared to help," Iana reported slowly, looking from one old man to the next. "We believe that there is a way to cut a corridor through the concrete and steel reinforcing bar—do it silently, and without any vibration." She now had their rapt attention. "Our National Science Laboratory has developed a deep-penetration masonry laser, called MASLAS, which can accomplish the task. When the casket is reached, this same laser can silently bore out a small hole, through which the Soviet device can be safely observed—and then rendered harmless."

The Chinese president spoke through a translator. "If you have such a laser—and it can do as you say—China would be in your debt." He glanced around for the affirmation of the others—which came automatically.

Iana waited for the president to continue.

"We do not wish to be at the mercy of plate tectonics," he said, pausing to fix her with his gaze. "This offer could have easily been made through our ambassador. Could there be some other matter which brings you here in such secrecy?"

Iana smiled and brushed her hair aside. "You are most perceptive." She let a few moments pass to heighten their anticipation. "President Bryce sent me here in person—to place before you a most lucrative proposition—"

*   *   *

Ever since the exposure, disgrace, and firing of Egon Ovid, Gordon Fenstermacher had kept a low profile. Fortunately, it had all come to light during the quiet interlude between the conventions and the official Labor Day kickoff of the presidential campaign—a time-out, when candidates traditionally rested up and girded themselves for a race to the finish.

Neither Onager nor Fenstermacher was willing to appear on the Sunday morning interview shows. The 'Pot-Plot-Counter-Plot' (as it was dubbed by the Post) had everyone begging to have them as guests. This amounted to Free Airtime, but was rejected by both candidates—a likely first in American politics.

The polls showed the public to be more entertained than offended by what people perceived to be teenage antics, with many amused at the idea of a political pro being brought low by a couple of kids. The 'Kiddy Coup' was of no help at all to Fenstermacher, while Dave Onager enjoyed a kind of parental sympathy. But by November it would all be ancient history.

*   *   *

After satisfying himself that the communication he'd just received was authentic (having been primarily persuaded by the manner in which it arrived, seemingly the same application of force used on the telegraph key at the Smithsonian), Art Frayles phoned his sister to request an immediate meeting with the President, telling Abby only that it had to do with a new message from the Mentors.

A White House executive jet was immediately dispatched—and two hours later Art Frayles was in the air, eating halibut.

He was delivered to the White House and promptly escorted to the family quarters. After some hasty greetings, Frayles handed his brother-in-law a printout of Beta's message. The President read it slowly—and then passed it to Abby.

"They—are coming back—" Bryce sagged.

"So it would appear," Frayles nodded. "Only this time not in orbit. I went back and double-checked my notes: they had said they chose not to enter our atmosphere—not that they couldn't."

"What do you suppose they mean by 'family'?" Abby asked.

"You—me—Katie—Josh—" Bryce shrugged.

"What about your mother?"

"Oh, God, no," he winced.

Abby laughed. "Hey—at least she'd keep 'em honest!"

"I don't think we should inflict that particular grief on the Mentors—"

209

"You don't think they could handle her?"

"I'm don't think it would be very friendly to make them have to! Art, whadda you think?"

"If the Mentors can handle those Onager kids, they can probably manage your mother. What about Josh's father? What about other staffers?"

"Only a few Secret Service agents would have to be there," Bryce figured, given the isolation. "So when's this bankers' retreat anyway?"

"Last weekend in August, ten days from now," Frayles said.

"You have to go," Abby stressed. "Personally, I can't wait. Imagine—speaking with a Mentor face to face—"

The president read Beta's message one more time—and gave a helpless shrug. "Well, I guess I'd better have Oscar make the necessary arrangements. You don't suppose Abydos'll tell us they're all booked up—?"

"He would if he knew the Mentors were coming, too," Frayles snorted. "The way he despises them, he'd cancel the whole retreat and kick the bankers out before he'd allow any Mentors atop his mountain!" Everyone chuckled.

"Now, getting back to Mother—" Bryce groaned.

*   *   *

"BINGO!" crowed Depkawitz. "There's the link: PLOSS, Avery Tindal, fifty-six—retired, 1996—last posting, assistant to the deputy director of operations, Central Intelligence Agency—architect of a top secret justification for a black ops program to develop an aerosol foam high-explosive, and a frequent unregistered guest at ABYTOR!"

"It's still only circumstantial. You'll need a lot more than that before you can slap bracelets on Sandovar Abydos," cautioned his ASAC.

"I know. But I've established our first direct link. Unfortunately, it also indicates Abydos is supremely confident there's no evidence lying around or anyone out there to incriminate him." He looked up from his desk and winked. "Yet there is one piece of hard evidence out there."

"There is—?"

"The device needed to transmit the coded firing sequences—And I'd lay money it's kept close to Sandovar Abydos himself. Far too critical to delegate. We locate that transmitter and the whole 'K-1' gang gets to play Intravenous Bye-Bye!"

*   *   *

Depkawitz would have won his wager.

Abydos' private inner office was windowless, constructed against the granite core of the mountain itself. Set behind the rock face was a small, virtually impregnable vault. Its door was five inch case-hardened carbide steel, expertly concealed behind a natural facing of granite—diamond-cut along the natural lines of the surrounding rock, and all but invisible once closed. The vault's very existence was known to Abydos alone, the technician who installed it having expired.

Within the vault rested two identical radio transmitters the only ones ever manufactured. Each was a back-up for the other, capable of performing but one task: Broadcast a preset, five-integer, triple-cypher signal in a restricted military ultra-high frequency bandwidth. The transmitters were hardwired to activate four identical radio receiver-detonators, each hidden aboard one of the four space shuttles.

Should the Aliens dare to return, Abydos could simply walk out on the grand balcony, flip a switch, and dispatch them himself. He actually hoped he'd have the opportunity.

He was in his formal office, with its achingly beautiful view of the High Uintas, when his secretary buzzed. "Mr. Abydos—Oscar Benton, White House chief of staff, on Line Two," she purred.

"Mr. Benton," Abydos answered, "an unexpected pleasure—how can I help you?"

"How would you like to play host to the First Family?" Benton asked, wasting no time on pleasantries.

"Now what good Republican wouldn't! And when would the President like to pay us a visit?"

"The First Family would like to have one last weekend together before the campaign begins in earnest. But their only possibility is next weekend—when, I believe you're hosting a retreat for bankers, with their wives and kids?"

"That's correct. You—don't suppose the President might find the time to address them, do you?"

211

"Certainly a possibility—I'll ask him. Incidentally, when I said the First Family, I was including the First Lady, the President's daughter, mother, and brother-in-law."

"That would present no problem for us. But—didn't the President recently become a grandfather? I only ask because we've never allowed an infant up here before."

"Not to worry—little Josh isn't a screamer. Also no need for heating up bottles or anything like that—he breast-feeds. And his diapers are disposable."

"Then I see no problem at all. What about Secret Service protection?"

"Given your physical isolation, only five agents will have to accompany the First Family. An advance team will review your security systems." Benton caught himself—" Oh, I nearly forgot, the Onagers will be accompanying the Bryce's: four more guests, plus three additional Secret Service. Can do?"

"Of—course." Abydos' mind was already spooling up—Invite Gordon as well, and we've got the whole presidential race-card weekending at ABYTOR! A magnitude-one coup! But no need to mention him now.

"We have several VIP suites we can make available. Are there any other special requirements—dietary or anything? Is there anything else we can do? Any special requests?"

"Yes, just one thing: Absolutely no press. No word must leak out that the President is coming—we read one word about it in the papers, and the visit's off. Understood?"

Abydos still saw an after-the-fact promotional bonanza. "You have my word: No press. Simply our own photographer.

"We'd have no problem with that. You should expect the advance team on Monday."

"Just—one question: what made the Bryce's choose ABYTOR for their getaway?"

"The President greatly admires what you've done up there, and would like to see it first-hand. But an official visit would be disruptive for you and preclude any privacy for the Bryce's. I trust you can appreciate that."

*　　*　　*

Ellen Kate still maintained her studio apartment, but was virtually living at the White House these days. The room her mother had converted into a nursery was more than she could resist. Abby had tried to draw the line at OooYaYaBangToy, but Ellen Kate would have none of it. "It's a package deal."

For the first few days the cat had tiptoed through the living quarters, sniffing out every possible place where something alive could be living. In the end she had decided the place was satisfactory, even interesting.

Josh was having his bath. "Your father and I are going to spend next weekend up at ABYTOR, and we'd like you and Josh to come along. It's supposed to be a pretty amazing place," Abby rinsed. "What's more, it could be your last opportunity to ride in Air Force One."

Ellen Kate considered it briefly. "I think we'll pass. The stress of traveling and all."

"Your uncle's going to be there too. And the Onagers-along with their infamous kids."

"And everyone gets to get stoned?" she teased. "No, we'll be better off here. You know how I detest socializing."

Abby knew her daughter; her decision was made. So, there was no choice; she'd have to be told. "There's—another reason, Katie—and you'd better sit down." She drew in a deep breath. "Art received a direct communication from the Mentors—and the invitation comes from them."

"What?"

"You heard me. But that's not all—the Mentors will be there, too."

"Down here—on earth?" Ellen Kate's mind was racing. "Oh, God—I have a thousand questions—First: How did they communicate with Uncle Art?"

"On his computer screen." She handed her daughter a copy of the message. "As you see, you're specifically invited. Incidentally, I persuaded your father to apply a broad definition of Family—one which includes your grandmother." Abby knew this would get her.

"The Mentors—and the Duchess? Boy, I wouldn't miss that for the world!"

*   *   *

213

"Gordon, Sandi Abydos." He'd phoned on Fenstermacher's private line. "I'm calling to invite you to attend a Fenstermacher for President Golden Opportunity—"

*   *   *

Ellen Kate couldn't wait for dinner to be over so she could retire and ask her Voice about the Mentors. She'd attempted to discuss them once before, but had been told: 'Later.' And then, just after sitting down to eat, her father had left to take a call and she'd put the question up again—this time hearing: 'Tonight, I promise.' She glanced at the time.

"The fact that they specifically included Dave Onager," her father was saying, "along with the timing and location of their promised appearance, suggests to me it's all being done to influence the election. And that can't be good."

"Why not?" challenged Ellen Kate, "If that's what it takes to get us to vote for candidates who can turn things around!"

"You sound like some leftover hippy," Bryce said. "Let me tell you, outside interference in domestic politics is by definition improper. Pass the sauce, please—"

"Oh, yes, above all—we must remain proper!" she fired back, her anger rising. "If God himself came down to earth and commanded us to Save the Whales, you'd probably consider it divine interference!"

Abby wisely turned the conversation back to Sandovar Abydos, arch anti-Mentorist—and the thought of him seeing his personal creation picked as the very site of an extraterrestrial visitation! Everyone enjoyed the irony.

After an hour Ellen Kate was able to bid her good nights, offering Josh to each grandparent for a kiss like a waitress passing a platter. Five minutes later they were nursing.

OK, we're alone now—so tell me, what's with the Mentors?

Good Evening, Beloved. I am flattered you see no need for formalities. It means you already regard me as a friend.

Well—I do. And I'm glad you're so flattered—now t-e-l-l me! First: Where did the Mentors come from? Second: Why did they come? Third: Can we trust them?

As they revealed—they abide in your own small corner of the Universe.

And they have already stated their purpose in coming.

As to trust—that is for them to earn—and for you to confer.

Do you—approve of their being here?

My sole concern is with you, dear one. When those you call Mentors entreat your service it will be your decision alone.

Know that whatever course you choose. I will be ever with you.

How do you know they want me for this 'service'—?

There was a pause.

You forget who I AM.

*   *   *

The President of the United States was in a situation unlike anything ever faced by any of his predecessors. Nothing even close.

He wondered what Ike, his favorite President, would have done.

At ABYTOR he'd soon come face to face with—what? A Creature from Outer Space? A Thing with more Eyes than Teeth? A Monstrosity that would terrify children?

And what of himself? Did he bear responsibility for personifying the whole human race? Would they take back to their home-world impressions of mankind as being well-meaning, unsure of themselves—and potbellied?

And what would they ever make of the Duchess? She could be loud, imperious, irascible, insulting, and pretty much all around obnoxious. On the other hand, there was a remote possibility she might decide to be as charming as beloved royalty. It all depended on her mood.

*   *   *

The President was on the encrypted phone with his national security advisor aboard Air Force One parked in a well-guarded area of the airport the Chinese reserved for foreign diplomatic aircraft—

"On balance, I'd say things went pretty well. The offer of money caught them totally off-guard. I expect them to tiptoe cautiously for a while. You agree?"

"Yep. By not rejecting it out of respect for us, they've found a basis for actually keeping the offer on the table. And I take that to be a positive. So, let's get that atom bomb the hell out of the dam—very, very, very carefully. How soon could we get a MASLAS unit over there?"

215

"Crews and equipment—seventy-two hours after Beijing clears it. But they're balking over sending a Marine security escort."

"That's their problem. Keep everyone on standby."

"Furthermore—" she read, "they 'most firmly insist' that the entire operation be kept 'Top Secret.'" (Oh, the shame of needing American help to deal with a troublesome ally!)

"More leverage, Iana, more leverage. Remind me to send Pyongyang a thank-you note someday," he smirked.

"Since you're going to be at ABYTOR this weekend, you might keep an eye peeled—" Iana said, "Peter-the-Klein's has been informed by the Bureau that the only hard evidence to connect Abydos with the sabotage sits atop that mountain."

"In that case maybe we ought to bring him along as the official peeled-eye," Bryce dismissed.

"Incidentally, did you know Fenstermacher's going to be there too? He's already notified his T-boys."

"Not surprised. Abydos'd never let him pass up a chance like this. So, how many agents does that make?"

"Three for Onager, Two for Fensty, Five for the Bryces. That's ten up at the top with twenty more on the ground ready to chopper up in ninety-seconds if necessary."

"The ones up top have to be armed?" Bryce asked.

"You betcha—Mentors notwithstanding."

"I—wonder whether that could jeopardize anything?"

"Doubt it. They must already know all about your bodyguards. And hey, those energy shields gotta be Uzi-proof!"

*   *   *

It took a call from Ellen Kate to persuade her grandmother to join the family for a weekend high in the Rockies. But to seal the deal—the promise of a White House jet to pick her up in Miami. The flight west was enjoyed by all. Justin and Penny snooped the 747 from flight-deck to "the ass-end press section"—after all, by this time next year it might be the Onagers' personal RV. But crushingly, their pleas to phone friends on the ground were to no avail. The trip was wholly unannounced—and the President decreed there were to be no leaks.

In the large forward Presidential Suite Bryce huddled with Onager and Frayles, speculating on what the Mentors might say and do and the appropriate White House responses. In the senior staff lounge Abby and Jane discussed spousal strategies for dealing with a presidential campaign—mostly how to avoid being quoted. As Abby put it, "How to remain opinion -less without appearing mindless." Meanwhile, in the empty press section Ellen Kate nursed Josh, with Isabel supervising—and for the first time with anyone, Katie shared the discovery of her newfound Friend within.

"You do believe in God, don't you, Grams?"

"God damn right I do!"

BETA PARTY

The Vista Cube whispered to a stop and the presidential party alighted. Word of the President's visit had not leaked out, and the bankers reacted with surprise and great delight: Sam Bryce—Dave Onager—Art Frayles—Gor Fenstermacher! High drama filled the air.

Sandovar Abydos greeted his guests as peers. "Welcome to ABYTOR—your home on top of the world!" he waved, declining to offer his hand. "Permit me to show you to your suites—I believe you'll find the views to be quite extraordinary."

Penny spotted an arrow leading down to 'Thor's Grotto'—and brought it to her brother's attention with an elbow to the ribs. He saw it—and they exchanged winks.

Isabel unfortunately had not enjoyed the ride up, claiming such heights made her feel "all wibbly." She fixed Abydos with a glare. "Too high! You built this thing too damn high up!" She took her grinning granddaughter by the arm. "You just stay close to me, Kate—you'll be just fine."

The presidential party consisted of nine and one-half (including Josh). Over lunch the Democratic candidate and Republican president sat next to each other, with Abydos and Fenstermacher just two tables away surrounded by bankers, CEO's, CFO's, and board chairmen.

Everyone in the dining room tried to steal looks without being obvious. Abydos was thrilled, and wondered whom he had to thank for such a fortuitous conclave.

Following lunch, active mingling was the order of the day. Fenstermacher made a point of coming over to greet the Bryce family as soon as Onager drifted off. In the wake of the Egon Ovid fiasco he was giving the senator a wide berth.

"Mr. President," he smiled, "I've not had the pleasure of meeting your family, for the first time except for your lovely wife, of course."

The President made the introductions. Knowing full well who the man was, Isabel seized the occasion to deliver an insult. Playing the crotchety old dowager was always fun.

"'Fenstermacher'—now what sort of name is that? Wasn't there some—Nazi general—?"

Nearby, David Onager was having some fun of his own with a group of investment bankers. "The fact is," he shrugged, "when it comes to taxes, Congress only looks in two places: what you earn (income taxes)—or—what you spend (sales taxes or a VAT tax). But there's a third alternative: what you own—namely property taxes!" To a man, they blanched.

Sandovar Abydos had planted himself beside the President, making introductions and participating in discussions—while his security cameras recorded everything and missing nothing.

Justin and Penny had excused themselves and repaired to Thor's Grotto for a swim, trailed by a Secret Service agent in tie and jacket feeling conspicuously out of place.

Penny looked him over and winced. "Haven't you got a pair of trunks or something—with maybe a waterproof gun pouch?"

Meanwhile, Art Frayles had spotted Karyn DeLeo, but gave no hint of recognition. He also saw Zooti Abydos, and considered just walking up and introducing himself. But he decided to wait for the right opportunity.

Of the ninety-one, only seven went through the airlock to brave the sunny gale whipping the grand balcony. Isabel wanted no part of it, and Ellen Kate didn't want to expose Josh to the wind, though she very much wanted to experience the grand balcony for herself. "later." she heard her Voice whisper.

The late August sun was still warm, the winds not yet icy, even at this altitude. Jane pointed out early flashes of autumn color far below; Penny and Justin leaned out to see who could spit the farthest.

Abby stood mesmerized by the dazzling snow-capped peaks about them; and leaning on the railing the President and the First Lady fell silent—simply drinking it all in.

* * *

Shortly before dinner, Abydos approached the President to invite him to say a few words over dessert—fully expecting that he would so honor them.

"No—this is merely a private getaway," Bryce drawled, "and I wouldn't want to turn it into anything else. But it's most gracious of you to ask."

Abydos looked betrayed. "I, I thought Mr. Benton—"

"No, and if Oscar implied otherwise, I do apologize. It's your show, Mr. Abydos, and I'm not here to upstage anyone." He turned to shake an outstretched hand; discussion closed. A sullen darkness overtook Abydos' eyes.

At that moment Abby and Jane arrived, looking striking in nearly matching black cocktail dresses. Abydos found this display of bipartisan "dress-a-likes" mildly nauseating.

"Good evening, Mr. Abydos," the First Lady smiled, holding out her hand.

"'Sandi' to my friends. Please, let us not be so formal," he said, bowing to shake her hand, the incongruity lost on him. He waved Zooti over. "I'd like to present my son."

* * *

Dinner consisted of six masterpiece courses, and lasted nearly three hours. On this particular evening, guests dined by candlelight, the lighting intentionally subdued—as a full moon painted a wintery panorama of sparkling peaks as far as the eye could see. And on top of the great stone stage at the center of the room, a string quartet played softly.

With coffee and dessert finally over, everyone stayed put in anticipation of the celebrated ABYTOR laser light show. But before it could begin, Isabel announced she had to "piddle." Others shared her problem, and for the next twenty minutes the Secret Service performed ladies room escort duty.

At last it was 9:30 p.m. Showtime. The lights dimmed. Art Frayles shifted excitedly in his seat, sensing the Mentors were already close at hand—

Suddenly: A synthesized sea of sound washed down from every quadrant of the ceiling. Bright blobs of electro-plasma bombarded the great stone stage, breaking apart on impact into myriad micro-blobs, rebounding wildly upwards.

Shards of colored light sliced the darkness, dismembering the very ether above the audience in perfect synchrony with the synthesizers.

With each new burst of light and sound, Ooohs and Aaahs could be heard everywhere. Abydos all but glowed in the dark with pride.

All of a sudden, everything went black and silent. Then slowly—the area directly above the stone stage became redolent with frenzied pinpoints of light.

This was not part of the program—!

Abydos whipped around to glare at the light show operator—only to see him backing away from his console as if it was dangerously malfunctioning.

After a few moments, the dancing pinpoints of light began to coalesce into something long and bright—

Frayles froze in recognition: A dazzling ten-foot replica of the Mentor spaceship hovered several meters above the stage! And it was no hologram!

Secret Service agents reached reflexively for their guns—then stopped, remembering the President's firm admonition to expect something "possibly supernatural" but to do nothing.

Candle flames everywhere shrank simultaneously—and then a familiar voice spoke from the center of the chamber:
Salutations, Children of the Earth. We greet you and we salute you!"

Before their eyes, the spaceship slowly transmuted into three separate columns of light, ones Frayles had beheld before. A living being could be seen standing within each column. The one in the center was the one speaking.
"I am Beta—this is Alpha—and this is Gamma.

Arthur Frayles: Hearty Greetings! We are gratified by your success in assembling those whom we requested.

"President Bryce: It is our great pleasure to finally meet you and your family. You do us honor by accepting our invitation.

David Onager: Were it not for your efforts and your abiding commitment—we would not have returned at all."

Occasional gasps could be heard; no one spoke or moved.

"Our purpose in being here is to urge the United States to apply its great financial wealth to the preservation and protection of the planet and all of its inhabitants."

"A hostile nuclear weapon was recently visited upon a well-known government facility. Stand advised: Detonation would have surely followed—had we not Intervened. Do not expect us to do so again."

"As the twin originators of such weapons, you and the Russian government must now partner to affect their total containment and one-day complete elimination. The power of the atomic nucleus must never again be loosed against the human races. It is within our power to Intervene in a time of planetary emergency. The Portrayal now before you constitutes such Emergency Intervention in a rare but not unprecedented expression.

The question paramount in most mortal minds is
Where did we come from?
And here is your answer:
Your home world is our home world!"

Footlights gradually brightened as the visible energy fields screening the Mentors slowly disintegrated, revealing three very human-like males standing on the stone stage. Each was tall, with grey-green eyes and matching sea-foam locks. All appeared mature, of indeterminate age, lean, and fluid of movement. Each wore blue sandals and what Penny later described as "cool silver jammies." Moreover, each was smiling broadly. Everyone sat stunned, struck mute.

"We have always shared the same world. Thus, our deep and abiding concern over its present and long-term well-being. Know that you coexist with Spirit life every day, and that your Spirit population exceeds your human population—and that your world is lovingly and faithfully administered by hosts of Spirit Beings.

Know finally that our shared world is held safe from all planetary disaster. We appear quite human to you at this moment—and indeed you see us in our true form. We are semi-material beings, only one step removed from humans. We are ever beside you—which explains why we understand so much of your affairs. We exist just beyond the range of human vision—but for this night's Portrayal we have shifted our ultraviolet frequencies in order that you might behold us in our actual bodies. Nonetheless, though we are semi-material, you will not be able to physically touch us.

John VanOrsdell

This evening and tomorrow we shall pass among you answering questions—sharing our knowledge, developing trust and becoming acquainted as individuals—even becoming friends. This however is more than we three can accomplish without others of our order—BEHOLD: Suddenly, there flashed into sight one-hundred additional Mentors, half appearing to be male, half appearing to be female, arrayed about the perimeter of the chamber. Tomorrow evening there will transact—A Presentment."

Then Alpha, Beta, and Gamma descended from the stage and walked directly to the presidential table while the other Mentors began intermingling with bankers and their families. And while everyone else was abuzz with wonder and excitement—Ellen Kate and Karyn DeLeo were both resonating in sudden, profound recognition.

HOME WORLD

Sandovar Abydos was in an apoplectic rage. Not only had the damnable Mentors returned, they'd co-opted ABYTOR for their own purposes! It was the final insult. They were all over the place like a cockroach infestation.

The previous evening all one-hundred and three Mentors had circulated and socialized widely, permitting themselves to be videotaped by those who'd fortuitously brought along camcorders to capture the mountaintop grandeur. Then, at the stroke of eleven each Mentor had bid goodnight—and simply blinked out of sight.

Abydos later determined that, upon their arrival his uninvited guests had summarily deactivated all telephones, FAX lines, and Internet access, along with both Vista Cubes. Clearly, he concluded, the Aliens didn't want any outside communication going on—But why?

Launching a direct assault on the Mentors was no longer an option, Abydos realized. Instead of real Alien beings from some other world, he had interfering spirits from his own planet to worry about! Thus, he reasoned, it becomes more important than ever to discredit them—and everything they stand for!

He glanced at his watch: 4:35 a.m. Time to wake Zooti.

*   *   *

Ellen Kate lay in half-darkness, fully alert, the sun just beginning to tint the eastern horizon. She'd spent most of the night conversing with her Voice; Josh being fast asleep.

But, if the Mentors were from Earth all along—why'd they have to trick us into thinking they traveled here in a spaceship?

If they first appeared as they did tonight they in all probability would have been dismissed as—hallucinations or as part of the supernatural.

But it was dishonest to do it the way they did.

Those you call Mentors are not Revelators bound to Truth. They are simply about their work in the manner they deem most effective.

However, they are not infallible.

Nevertheless you approve of their methods?

You forget; My only concern is with your spiritual growth.

Others will guide their endeavors.

Yet, in spite of all this you say we can trust them.

Trust is not transferable—they must earn your trust.

If we do share the same world, how can we be sure their interests and ours are even compatible?

Because your best interest is their only interest.

Whoa! What about other kinds of spirits—should we trust them too—?

You may ever trust in your seraphic guardians. As to other orders, judge them by their fruits. Not all spirits nor all spirit enterprises are righteous.

And yet, such 'unrighteous' spirits are still allowed to mess with people's heads?

Their exercise of free will is as sacred as your own. Forget not: I AM come to indwell all the mortal races. Those who abide in Me need not fear.

*   *   *

The Onager family was joined for breakfast by a female Mentor, who explained she was "unable to partake of human nourishment." She also revealed that like all Mentors, she bore an alphanumeric designation.

"You should try using real names," Justin submitted. "Or are you all alike—you know, clones?"

223

"No, Justin, we are each as distinct as you."

"Then, how 'bout we call you "Sarah'—?" Penny chirped.

"Short for Seratonin?" Justin clowned.

"I like it, Penny—'Sarah' it is!"

"Tell us, Sarah—" Onager asked, "why would members of a spiritual order such as your own be so concerned over our material and financial affairs?"

"Our entire concern is with you. Our purpose is to foster higher values. Nothing more."

"But," he pressed, "if as Beta said, you have the power to intervene in material matters—why not simply intervene—and save the rain forests yourselves?"

"Such would be beyond our powers. We can but strive to influence and persuade you. The act must be yours. Should we fail to influence your choices and actions, this whole enterprise will be for naught."

"And you will have failed. Is that correct?" Onager said.

"In truth—we are not confident of success. We may well be asking too much of you."

*   *   *

It was Zooti who figured out a way: the pneumatic dispatch tube running beneath the Vista Cube rails. Depressurize it by opening a single valve—and simply drop a message down! "Unless the Aliens have repealed gravity—!" Zooti smirked, jumping up and down to prove otherwise.

"Son, you might have something there," his father praised. "But what should we say to the people down below? What you can't Exterminate, you can always Evict!" his father thundered, as they began drafting a communication meant to be a bombshell. Twenty-five minutes later it was ready:

> For Immediate Release:
>
> ABYTOR has been appropriated by the   Mentors, who have severed all communications.
>
> More than one-hundred Mentors are present.
>
> President Bryce and his family are in attendance.

"That oughtta do it!" Abydos crowed. "This place'll be swarming with news helicopters within the hour!" He slapped his son on the back. "It's called 'Mentoris Interruptus.'"

*   *   *

The radio frequency used by the Secret Service had not been interrupted, and word of the Mentors' return had already been flashed to Washington. But pandemonium broke out at the base station when the dispatch dropped down the tube arrived. Everyone suddenly realized the balloon was up—and that the world's news media would soon be in an uproar.

"Mr. President," Agent Lulu Kurtis said softly, "In light of the leak to the press, we think it would be advisable for you and your family to depart before this place is besieged. We have your chopper standing by."

"Forget it, Lu. The Mentors returned for a reason, and we're part of that reason. I intend to find out what they have in mind. We stay put."

The Service immediately flew up the twenty agents on Ready Alert below, leaving their helicopter on the pad to block any other landings. Meanwhile, forty-five additional agents were flown in from Salt Lake City and Denver.

Security remained tight at ABYTOR, the only possible approach being by air. Notwithstanding that airspace over the mountain had been declared Restricted, agents were now stationed beside all six airlocks, ready to dash outside and apprehend anyone unauthorized attempting a parachute landing on the great circumferential balcony.

At Secret Service direction, the Utah highway patrol placed barriers across the only access roadway—just in time, it turned out, to block the first satellite uplink trucks.

*　　*　　*

Art Frayles had been busy interviewing the new Mentors, taping people's reactions and comments, and posing for pictures with his old friends Alpha, Beta, and Gamma. At one point Isabel caught his sleeve—and declared she very much wanted an introduction to Beta. Frayles figured this could prove interesting and took Isabel's hand, "Come on—" Beta saw them coming and smiled.

"It is truly a pleasure, Mrs. Bryce, to meet you at last. We have always enjoyed you."

"What's that supposed to mean?" she shot back, instantly wary. Beta smiled warmly.

"Your capacity for unbridled candor, without regard to station, is a virtue rare among mortals."

Isabel was far from mollified. "It sounds to me like you Mentors must spend a lot of time spying on people!"

Beta looked at Art Frayles—and winked.

"We seldom look in upon individuals—rather it is the collective affairs of all the mortal races which concern us.

However, certain individuals and those around them are instrumental in the movement of human affairs. It is in this context that we observe the Bryce family."

Well, at least that seemed—reasonable, she supposed. She glanced at Frayles' recorder, not about to let Beta have the last word. 'And what about this eavesdropping you do—can you listen in on what people are thinking as well?"

"A most astute question. There is a means by which we know what is being thought, at the time it is being thought."

Art Frayles had to jump in. "Does that mean there's no such thing as a private thought?"

"Essentially that is correct."

Meanwhile, standing in front of a balcony window, Gordon Fenstermacher was arguing with a female Mentor.

"I'll tell you why, because what you're doing constitutes de facto interference with a federal election! Down here, young lady, that's considered a felony!"

"If you believe our views hold popular appeal, you might do well to consider embracing them. Bear in mind—poor advice never finds lasting purchase—whereas sound advice self-validates upon careful reflection."

"You needn't be condescending," the publisher accused.

"Such is not my intent. The fact is—we regard you as a powerful exponent of a flawed philosophy and fully recognize your ability to influence and lead others. Condescension is inappropriate."

"Then what would you call what you're trying to do?"

"One might denominate it—Values Lobbying."

"There you go, being condescending again." Several camcorders were running, and Fenstermacher was already considering using excerpts for his next spate of commercials.

"Now then, let me put a question to you: What's so wrong with achieving great personal wealth as reward for providing something of value to a great many people?"

"Nothing whatever. Prosperity is desirable in any society. Yet property rights must ever be subject to limits—otherwise you would still own slaves. The problem is not wealth—but the value which you place upon it. The enlightened dedicate their wealth to the betterment of others. Sadly most employ it simply to garner ever greater wealth. Such is unworthy of an advanced civilization."

Nearby, a distraught bank president and her husband were huddled quietly with a Mentor.

"Your anguish is misplaced, dear Margaret. Your son's brief life upon this world was merely the beginning for him—with all experiential deficits being compensated on the next world."

"Like—what?" she snuffled.

"Jimmy never experienced having and raising a child—the joy it brings—and all that it teaches. Learning successful parenting is required of all. You are given but one life as flesh and bone. Jimmy could procreate only while he was here. Yet he will experience parenting on the next world."

Over in another corner a female Mentor was about to answer a question she knew would be highly controversial—

"Life begins—at the onset of consciousness."

*   *   *

Sandovar Abydos sat in his windowless inner office trying to figure ways to turn the Mentor invasion to Fenstermacher's advantage.

Suddenly, he heard a feminine voice speaking. He looked up and saw three Mentors standing before him.

"Sandovar Abydos: Hear well our words! Your ignominious scheme to destroy our spacecraft along with your own space shuttle is fully known to us. Your FBI is unlikely to uncover evidence to connect you directly to this treachery. Yet the evidence they seek exists—locked within the vault behind you. Know this: the vault door has been fused at the molecular level to the frame surrounding it. The twin radio transmitters contained therein will there remain—unless we decide to un-fuse the door in the presence of your authorities."

Abydos' throat was devoid of moisture; swallow he could not. He looked wildly from one Mentor to another, enraged at being threatened. Exploding to his feet he bellowed, "I want every damn one of you sideshow freaks off my mountain!"

"BE SILENT! ABYTOR is destined to become the most coveted gathering site on earth. For many it will be as a shrine—for others a place of inspiration. Thousands will come to behold it—and to pray. In consequence, even greater will become your wealth. For this you have us to thank. You might reflect on the irony. PAY HEED: Henceforth ABYTOR is to be used solely to further the preservation, protection, and health of the planet and all of its inhabitants. It is not to be employed for commercial, financial, or political purposes.
IGNORE THIS INJUNCTION AT YOUR PERIL!"

MANY MENTORS

CNN had broken into regular programming at 10:18 a.m. with news of the reported return of the Mentors. Thereafter their coverage had been virtually continuous.

Every major news organization on earth leaped into action; special editions were rushed into print; journalists by the hundreds sped to Utah; motel rooms within a fifty-mile radius were block-booked; lists of attending bankers were produced; broadcast schedules were revamped by the hour; private planes and news helicopters filled the mountain skies—as attention the world over became fixated on ABYTOR.

Karyn DeLeo sat at the very epicenter, a position any true journalist would have given a year's pay to be in. Yet being ABYTOR staff, she hesitated to speak with a Mentor herself. But not for long. She spotted one just taking leave of a young, upwardly mobile looking family—and headed over.

"Excuse me—may I have a word?" The lady Mentor turned and smiled broadly.

"It would be a pleasure. Shall we talk over here?"

"My name is Karyn—"

"—DeLeo. We know you well. Had you not come over just now—I would have sought you out before leaving. Call me 'Sigma.' I sense there is a question you would put to me—"

"I have hundreds—first off: How do you know me?"

"Let me answer your question with a question: Do you intuit that you were somehow—guided to be here at this momentous time?"

Karyn recoiled. "Yes—but how did you know?"

"We have been preparing you for many years."

"'Preparing' how? Preparing me for what?"

"Preparing you for supernal service: Seeing to your education—presenting you with key opportunities—vectoring useful people to you—helping you meet with success sufficient for the development of self-confidence.

Much may be asked of you, Karyn—but nothing beyond your capabilities."

"But—that still doesn't explain why I was chosen for this…whatever."

"You were chosen in answer to your own appeal. You have a profound desire to serve others and therefore will be given the opportunity. Exceedingly few mortals so volunteer—and great will be your reward."

"Sigma, just exactly what is it you want me to do?"

"You will be invited to serve—but the invitation will not come from us."

"From who then?"

"From one you have not yet met."

*   *   *

On the valley floor, satellite up-link dishes bloomed like toadstools beside the road, with scores of television cameras trained on the great glass discus high above. Vehicles of every description choked the roads for miles.

229

Local and network news helicopters swarmed about the mountaintop, their long lenses locked on ABYTOR. One enterprising cable network had even airlifted a camera crew, generators, and uplink dish onto a nearby snow-covered peak, where they set up shop and began providing live feed for everyone else—at sky-high rates.

*　　*　　*

The two candidates stood together in the Celestial Lounge, with Art Frayles, four Mentors, Zooti Abydos, and a score of others gathered close (Abydos Sr. was nowhere to be seen). To everyone's delight, the senator and the publisher had fallen into heated debate almost at once— surrounded by a dozen camcorders.

"Senator, you're just like any other liberal—all you can think about is soaking the rich to pay for all your money-down-the-drain social programs!"

"The National Debt is no social program," Onager shot back,"— simply the mother of all the entitlement programs for the rich! Tell me, why is it every time we manage to produce a surplus you Republicans want to instantly turn it into a tax cut instead of applying it to the debt? Hey, if deficits require automatic borrowing—then surpluses should require automatic repayment. Isn't it you Republicans who supposedly stand for fiscal responsibility!"

If Fenstermacher had learned anything about running for office, it was how to sidestep a difficult question: counter with an even more provocative one. "Let's just cut through all the rhetoric, Senator— exactly what would be your idea of an appropriate National Property Tax Rate anyway—?"

"In a perfect world," Onager trumped, "one-hundred percent—with the first twenty-million exempt." It was a sound bite he knew would make every newscast And follow him everywhere.

Fenstermacher was aghast, groping for a salient comeback. Meanwhile, Onager's tactic had worked: the idea of actually placing a theoretical upper limit on personal wealth was now out there—though his intent was only to shake people free from conventional thinking, and set them to considering higher economic philosophies.

It was more than one banker could stomach. "In that case, Senator Onager, tell us what you think of the Mentors' view that 'a primary responsibility of government is to prevent the disproportionate accumulation of personal wealth?'"

Onager saw this one coming. "Any policy which uses taxes to accomplish socioeconomic ends, rather than raise only what's needed to run the government, goes well beyond—in my view." He too could finesse an answer.

Fenstermacher jumped back in. "Does that mean you're now dissociating yourself from Mentor economic advice?"

"Not from the spirit of what they're saying—only the methodology they suggest," Onager affirmed, wondering how this would play. He glanced at Frayles and met his eyes.

It was time for damage control, if indeed any had taken place. Frayles held his recorder up. "As an occasional Republican myself, I have to ask: Are you advocating that upper limits be placed on personal wealth?"

"No, not at all, Art. I only said it to start people thinking about how much is enough? Let me put it to you, Gordon: Does anyone need a billion dollars to be happy—?"

"Probably not." He looked into a camcorder. "But I'd sure trust a man with a Billion Dollars to spend it more wisely than the government—because any billionaire has to be a damn sight smarter than a whole roomful of bureaucrats!"

Onager turned to the closest Mentor. "I'm sure everyone would much rather hear what you have to say about all this, than us—" She smiled and shook her head.

"It is one of you who will next lead the nation. We offered the extent of our advice during the Convenings. We would merely remind you—it remains primarily a matter of Values. It is your societal Values which people need to reexamine—the ways and means will unfold thereafter."

Was that a gentle celestial admonishment? Onager wondered.

Fenstermacher turned to a different Mentor. "I imagine most of us would like to know just what it was that made you decide now was the time for you to Intervene—not when gunpowder was invented—or famines washed over China—or when the atom was split—or some future day when Earth is on collision course with some giant asteroid—"

"Beyond your environmental, population, and resource emergencies—that which brought us is the peril posed by the exfiltration of fissile materials, technology, and weaponry from the erstwhile Soviet Empire. All these matters relate to the Physical

realm—while paradoxically our counsel on the utilization of wealth relates essentially to the Spiritual."

Everyone paused to digest this. "Yet—" Onager pursued, "that fails to explain why, having already dispensed your advice, you still found it appropriate to return."

"It was important you learn that we are native to your world—and that you are not alone. There is another reason as well—but that must await this evening's—Presentment."

*   *   *

Sandovar Abydos was not the sort to knuckle under. If the Mentors thought otherwise, they were in for an ugly surprise. He sat in his inner office glaring at a bank of closed-circuit monitors, keeping close watch on Mentors and guests engaged in scores of conversations. On the huge center screen CNN showed ABYTOR as seen from on top of the neighboring peak—zoomed in tight on the outside balcony where several guests were in animated conversation with a pair of Mentors. The anchorman reported it as the eighteenth and nineteenth confirmed Mentor sightings. Abydos looked up as Zooti walked in.

"Sit down," his father snarled, sweeping a hand at the monitors. "You see this shit? Mentors all over the place telling everyone we oughtta increase foreign aid and love each other! Dopey bankers taking it all in and dopey banker wives having epiphanies over lunch! Half our own God damn staff is in a state of rapture—I even caught that broad you been hitting on for a penile implant off in one corner talking intensely with some Mentor chick!"

"You see those crowds down below?" Zooti deftly switched. "There's gonna be a friggin' feeding frenzy when the bankers go down in the morning!"

"That's why I called you in. There's no time to lose. When the media swarms all over us, we have to be ready with our version of events."

*   *   *

"So where's your spaceship now?" a preteen boy asked.

"Its purpose over, it has been discorporated."

232

"An' what about that little one we saw here last night—where is it now?" he pressed.

"The craft which you beheld last evening was the very one which orbited your world— only reduced to miniature scale."

"Awesome—!"

Nearby, Alpha was seated with a silver-haired couple next to a planter of Christmas cactus in forced early bloom, a security camera peering down.

Later that evening, when Zooti played the tapes he spotted it at once—by simply editing out certain key words he could completely reverse Alpha's meaning!

"We are aware our visitations may have political impact. Our purpose is [not] to support [either candidate.] Senator Onager (implied period) [and] Mr. Fenstermacher must [each] make his own case."

*   *   *

Frayles was finally able to pull Bryce aside and question him about the Mentors' claim that a nuclear device had been delivered to a certain government building. The President glanced around to make sure no one could overhear.

"It's true—and it happened to be one of our buildings, Art. You ready for this: Fort Knox!" He went on to give the details, including the Russian role and response. He also revealed that the prime suspect was the same terrorist who tried to blow up the Panama Canal. But now that the Mentors have gone public with it, I'm confirming it for the record." He clasped a hand on his friend's shoulder. "We would have preferred it not come out, of course—creating public fear and alarm, impeding the investigation, worsening relations with the Kremlin, etc. Maybe we shouldn't try to protect the people from the truth. We're probably underestimating 'em again. Just use good judgment in writing your exclusive." Spotting Gamma, he excused himself.

Gamma and another Mentor had been chatting with several of the dining room staff, but seeing the President coming his way, Gamma left the others to meet him. Bryce looked around for a quiet corner, but there was none.

"I think we'll find more privacy in my quarters."

Minutes later the two were standing in the soon to be renamed 'Presidential Suite,' gazing out through its massive Vista Wall, the sun backlighting the sweep of mountains to the West.

"Gamma, I need to ask you about something I suspect you already know all about: Is there a nuclear bomb inside Three Gorges Dam in China?"

"There is indeed—armed and ready to detonate."

"So how come you haven't disarmed it already, like the one dropped on Fort Knox? The one in the dam surely endangers far more people!"

"Unlike the device we nullified—this bomb can serve a higher purpose. It can become a catalyst among nations. Know that the bomb can be disarmed but only through the exercise of great caution. Be advised: A major earthquake will devastate the region in approximately seventeen months."

The President squinted up at the sun. "Does this 'higher purpose' you mentioned go beyond merely fostering better Sino-American relations?"

"Considerably beyond. China is the next superpower. It's equally important they use their wealth to ease the deprivation of others—as well as for crisis resolution."

"Whose 'deprivation'?"

"The ones who authored the crisis."

Karyn DeLeo hadn't eaten anything since breakfast, and went into the kitchen to look for a little melon. She found some sliced honeydew left over from breakfast and helped herself. Suddenly she discovered Sigma standing beside her.

"Hey, Sigma—what brings you in here?" she smiled.

"Is there a place where we can talk privately?"

"Sure. I think there's—a quiet spot just around the corner. Would that be okay?"

Sigma placed a gentle hand on Karyn's forearm as they walked. Karyn looked down and marveled that there was no physical sensation whatever. They found a bench and sat.

"Karyn—I have received special authorization to inform you that your mother's health is gravely threatened."

She put a hand to her mouth and gasped. She and her mother were still very close, talking on the phone at least once a week. Her mother had remained in Hong Kong where Karyn had grown up, unaffected by the exit of the British.

But in 1995 Karyn had moved to California to attend UCLA. Sadly, her father had suffered a coronary and died while she was still a sophomore. After graduating she went on to earn a Master's degree in journalism—and was granted resident alien status when she landed a job reading the All China News for a small FM station with an Asian-American audience. Two years later, a torrid romance gone bad brought her to Boston, where she found work at UPN Thirty-Eight.

"What do you mean 'gravely threatened'?" she demanded, fear clutching at her voice.

"Your mother is loath to undergo an examination for colon cancer; she requires one without delay."

Karyn choked back tears and headed directly for her room, hoping she could phone her mother with privacy. She decided to tell her she'd had a Vision Dream—something she knew her mother would take seriously. It was the middle of the night in Hong Kong; being awakened would lend added urgency.

*   *   *

Isabel was feeling confrontational. She had a male Mentor backed up against a planter. "And just whom do you get your orders from—God?"

"Our superiors are local. Direct contact with the mortal races is a high privilege. You have little appreciation of how wondrous you are."

"Ohhh—Hooey!" she dismissed; she'd wanted to say Balls. "Only wondrous thing about us—is how stupid we can be!"

*   *   *

Ellen Kate went to her room to change for dinner. All day she'd looked for an opportunity to sit down with a Mentor to discuss her Voice. But already the sun was setting, dinner and the promised 'Presentment' were to follow, and then the Mentors could be gone! Finding a chance to sit down with one for a quiet one-on-one was beginning to look remote.

Meanwhile, out on the great circumferential balcony, Zooti had engaged a lady Mentor in a discussion of personal values. "Just what's so wrong about Looking Out for Number One?"

"The great challenge of life is learning the art of self-forgetfulness. Self-gratification is a hollow pursuit. If you wish to be truly happy, learn to forget about yourself and

focus instead on needs of others. Great will be your joy. And great will become your spiritual stature."

Suddenly someone shouted, pointing up at the sky. The Secret Service had already spotted them: fifteen skydivers—all vectoring in for landings on the great balcony.

Each touched down safely—and was immediately placed under arrest. The Mentor who had been talking with Zooti walked over and addressed the agent in charge:

"I know I speak for all my associates when I ask that you release our new arrivals that we might set a place for them at our table."

There was a tense radio exchange—and then the new arrivals were escorted inside.

"These people will be searched, identified, and released according to your wishes," the agent explained, "as soon as we're satisfied they pose no security threat."

*   *   *

Justin Onager had been one of those wise enough to bring along a camera, and he was busy posing an accommodating lady Mentor against a backdrop of now fuchsia mountaintops. "Hey, this is great! How'd you feel about letting me post it on the Internet?" he ventured.

"You would exploit my image?—Neosquire!"

"Shhh!" He glanced nervously around. "Even better: A picture of you holding a new perfume called 'Heaven Scent'!"

"Know that I have Absolute Power Over Emulsion."

Justin laughed appreciatively. "That's a good one listen, could you, uh—maybe cross your legs for me?"

She laughed, pushed back her sea-foam hair—and obliged.

He began shooting frame after frame. "I betcha—when everyone sees this—chicks everywhere'll be dying their hair green—"

*   *   *

There was a tap at Ellen Kate's door. She picked up Josh, walked over and opened it—and to her shock, found Alpha, Beta, and Gamma standing there smiling and her Secret Service escort to one side looking on awkwardly. She reeled back, stammering, "Oh! Uhhh—Come, come in—please—"

The three entered and the door closed behind them.

"We have come, Ellen Kate Bryce, to honor you and to issue the Call to Supernal Service, if to Serve still remains your deepest desire. You have been chosen to be our sole channel of communication with the mortal races following our departure later this evening. Should you decline, we will find another. But it is you whom we earnestly want."

His words locked onto a deep spiritual receptor in her soul, as she experienced a warm surge of affirmation followed by a welling certainty. Suddenly she experienced a wave of pure Love washing over her from within.

"I do wish to Serve," she declared in a soft clear voice.

SUPERNAL GATHERING

The First Family, the Onagers, and Art Frayles dined with their non-dining friends Alpha, Beta, and Gamma. The sun had already set, but the western sky remained a striated magenta behind the lofty peaks. The string quartet played quietly, the Columbia Salmondine was delicious, and all was peaceful. The remaining hundred Mentors, seated among the other guests, conversed in soft, warm tones.

The First Table had been taken aback when Ellen Kate, Josh, and Isabel arrived escorted by Alpha, Beta, and Gamma. But the President quickly recovered, quipping, "Mother, have you been bothering the Mentors again?" Over Scallop-Leek Bisque, the President turned serious and looked at Beta. "Let's suppose in the end Congress does go along with billions in new foreign aid—and the United States can by no means go it alone. Other nations will have to be on board." Frayles had placed his recorder on the table, reminding everyone they were speaking for the record. Beta smiled.

John VanOrsdell

"America will lead by example—others will follow. We appreciate that you would have us go and speak with other governments as we have with you. Verily, to do such would only invite failure. Through all here gathered—we speak to the world. Once we have departed, yet will we be with you. Should ever the need arise, we will speak to you once more through our chosen spokesperson. But know that your problems are yours alone to solve."

Dave Onager pressed for a fuller glimpse into the future. "But can you assure us that one day we will somehow manage to solve our problems?"

It was Gamma who responded.

"Know that one distant day your world will attain that level of societal evolution where violence and deceit and greed and vanity are but entries in the historic record. You will become a highly advanced culture and civilization—embracing enlightened Values—living in prosperity and in social harmony. This is not prophesy—this is Truth."

Everyone sensed his answer was unfinished.

Ellen Kate leaned down to Josh and kissed him lightly on top of his head.

"Know that human and social Values will evolve ever higher, and spiritual values will one day supplant material Values. Know that common interest will triumph over self-interest—that conflict will be replaced by comity. Aggression will end, crime will cease, and fear will vanish. There will be universal abundance, with deprivation for none.

All this WILL come to pass. It will require many generations—how many depends on mankind itself. Your responsibility is far more immediate; You must make certain the planet you bequeath will be clean, beautiful, and healthy for all forms of life and for all living creatures.

Yours is the critical generation. The decisions taken now will repercuss far, far into the future. Were that not so—and were you not prioritized elsewhere—our appearance at this juncture would not have become necessary. In the short term we are powerless to save the material world. All we can do is Awaken—Stimulate—and Quicken. We can neither compel you to heed our warning, nor respect our advice. YOU ALONE can preserve your planet—for all the generations to come."

Everyone fell silent. Then Jane Onager managed to speak. "Gamma, your economic advice essentially amounts to taking from some while giving to others—and that's a sure-fired formula for trouble." She looked at her husband. "And if this dear, decent man follows your advice and does somehow manage to become our next President—he's bound to end up in some lunatic's cross-hairs!" Her voice broke. "The Secret Service has failed before!" Alpha replied:

"As Beta stated, future communications from us will be infrequent. However we will remain on guard and should we ever perceive imminent danger to your husband, you may rest assured we will act. Additionally—whenever his government protection comes to an end—ours will not. Know, Dear One, that he's already under our continuous watch-care."

Though he feared he already knew the answer, Bryce posed a question. "Beta, who's to be this 'chosen spokesperson' you spoke of?"

By way of response, all three Mentors turned and looked directly at Ellen Kate.

PRESENTMENT

Dessert was over and the final set played. The musicians gathered up their instruments and quietly descended from the stone stage. The Mentors bade their new friends farewell and took positions around the perimeter of the chamber. Alpha, Beta, and Gamma rose from the Bryce table, walked over, and ascended the stage. Beta looked slowly from one human to the next—then spoke:

"We are soon to take our leave—not to be seen again during the lifetime of any here gathered."

There was sudden stirring and murmuring. Beta waited a few moments before continuing.

"Do not think that because you can no longer see us we are gone. We will ever be watching over you—standing close—and listening. Know that should the need arise for us to speak, we will. Yet to one alone shall we speak, and that one alone is empowered to speak for us. We vest this Authority in our beloved Ellen Kate Bryce."

Every head spun to look at the President's daughter. After a few moments she rose to her feet, turned to face Beta and bowed her head in simple accedence.

"We were granted most extraordinary authorization to spend these precious and joyous hours among you. We enabled ourselves to be seen and heard—and even to be recorded that others not present might also come to know us. Freely share your feelings and all you have learned. Portray us faithfully. Trust yourselves to recognize that

which is true. Speak gladly and speak often. You are truly our only mortal Witnesses. As such, you bear profound responsibility.

We know each of you well—and deem ourselves to be in most capable hands. We are deeply grateful for the warmth of your welcome and your willingness to share so openly with us. You honor us. The time is now at hand for your Presentment"

The lights dimmed and a palpable wave of excitement swept over the room. With all lights extinguished, the Mentors self-illuminated. Alpha spoke next:

"That to which you are about to bear Witness, constitutes a Revelation. Your world is about to receive a Universe Revelator.—Not himself a Divine Being—but One who is a true Reflector of the Divine."

With that, Alpha, Beta, and Gamma descended from the stage and joined the other Mentors. All became utterly silent. No one so much as stirred. All of a sudden a great golden light suffused the chamber, radiating outward. Embracing the mountaintop gilding the valley and all it touched. A glorious profusion of dazzling motes of gold creating, not reflecting the light.

From the ground far below came gasps of awe—as every eye and camera turned to the spectacle unfolding high above.

Then the very heavens pealed with the Music of the Spheres, hosts of Angels filled the golden cloud of light, their voices raised in anthem. And then, from high among the stars a brilliant shaft of pure azure light blazed down and parted the golden radiance.

And above the great stone stage, there quickly manifested a dazzling locus of pure white light quickly expanding to reveal a resplendent Being—adorned in raiment one of those present would later describe as "being woven of burning magnesium." Immediately upon His appearance, the heavenly hosts fell silent.

A Universe Revelator hovered a meter above the stage, soft teal and turquoise energy emanations feathering outward. He then spoke in tones suffused with a gentle love—his words seeming to flow in from all directions at once—

"SALUTATIONS

Mortals and Spirits of the world you call Earth. Under High Universe Mandate I am come to bear witness to the GRAND UNIVERSE. Vast beyond your astronomers' dreams. Older than your physicists can conceive. Within this far flung star-strewn Creation, Mortal worlds like your own ABOUND. You are far from alone. Though you dwell on but a small planet at the fringe of Creation, You are

240

administered, protected, and cherished as though you were the greatest of God's worlds. Of record you are designated a Cardinal World.

The Universe we share is an intelligent and a purposeful Creation.

Competent

Benign

Friendly

Birthed

Nurtured

Administered

and Upheld by the Love of its Creator.

This Grand Creation—the material manifestation of Love Incarnate—resides secure and safe in the embrace of its Creator.

In the annals of Creation, No world has ever been lost.

NOT ONE!

From far beyond your galaxy I have journeyed to formally Welcome you into the Family of Mortal Worlds and to Confer upon each of you Universe Citizenship.

I further Affirm that the Divine Spirit resides within each of you.

The God of all Creation, Giver and Upholder of all Life, whose very Spirit Indwells you, will one momentous day conjoin with each of you as you become ONE.

On that sacred day you will become IMMORTAL.

and GOD will become YOU.

In parting—know that your world is soon to be honored and blessed with a Divine Incarnation by The Daughter of the Creative Spirit."

With those words the Angelic Hosts burst forth in song, joyous, glorious, jubilant, exalting, valley-filling anthems of celebration. The golden radiance cradling ABYTOR grew even brighter, the music and rejoicing ever fuller.

Suddenly, every Mentor transubstantiated into a dazzling energy field of silver and began slowly to withdraw outward into the golden realm beyond the balcony.

The Universe Revelator rotated slowly, stretching out his hand in parting blessing. A moment later the brilliant azure shaft reappeared— and in a blue-white flash of light the extra-galactic sojourner departed, streaking upward in a blinding brilliance into the heavens, vanishing amid the stars. Moments later the Angelic Hosts followed.

And all became still.

* * *

With the departure of the Mentors, full communications were restored and the Vista Cubes returned to service. The Bryces, the Onagers, and Arthur Frayles choppered out shortly thereafter. Later, aboard Air Force One, Frayles filed his story. Largely finished in advance, it had awaited only an ending—and the Visitation provided a corker. Meanwhile, Karyn DeLeo would remain at ABYTOR a little longer—Frayles knew the story there was not yet over.

Several dozen guests left ABYTOR that evening by corporate helicopter, while most opted to stay on for another night to share the experience with others and linger a bit in the spiritual afterglow. However, a number of others stayed over primarily to forestall running the press gauntlet awaiting them below. To their relief, no reporters were being allowed to come up in the Vista Cubes.

Secluded in his office, Sandovar Abydos was in a state of post-traumatic shock—being "celestially black-mailed," as he put it, into transmogrifying ABYTOR into some "left-wing, wussy-liberal, theme park in the sky!" The greatest affront was being ordered to henceforth open his doors only to the very groups he most despised—lest the FBI be invited to come witness a little "Vault Un-fusing" demonstration! Before he'd let that happen he'd blow ABYTOR to kingdom come!

*   *   *

Arriving back at Andrews at 4:30 a.m., Isabel immediately took off for Florida. Ellen Kate yearned to sleep in her own bed as well—there being so much she needed to discuss with her Voice. But her mother would hear none of it; as the official Mentor spokesperson, she'd be better off at the White House than at home imprisoned by camped-out camera crews and reporters. It proved a winning argument.

The sun was already up and bright by the time Marine One touched down on the South Lawn, and Ellen Kate headed right for her room. She felt swollen and knew Josh must be hungry. Once settled in her rocker, with Josh gulping loudly, she was finally able to call upon her Voice—

Are you there?

"Of course. Good Morning, Dear One."

'Morning. Listen, I've been dying to ask you how will the Mentori contact me?

"With your consent—the same way as I. Their voices will be easily distinguishable."

You mean silently? Do I have to speak out loud? Or can they read my thoughts?

"Either way you prefer."

But—how soon? I mean, do you have any idea when they might come? Or who?

"Gamma is present as we speak—would you prefer that he come back later?"

He's here? Now? Uh, sure, I guess. "Hi, Gamma."

All of a sudden, a new 'silent' voice spoke within her mind. She recognized it as that of a male Mentor.

"Good morning, Ellen Kate—I am honored you are willing to receive me. But since you are tired and in need of sleep—let me return when you are refreshed and ready for dialog.

Although we will speak through you but infrequently—we will at all times be pleased to speak with you in private. At such times only your Divine Spirit and you yourself will hear our words.

However, if in an emergency we need to speak through you, we might arrive unannounced.

Otherwise we will come only upon your invitation. In other words, it is always your turn to call. Now sleep. May your dreams be bright with joy."

She was indeed sleepy—yawned—and quietly nodded off.

*   *   *

MENTORS REVEALED AS SPIRIT BEINGS—Washington Post

CELESTIAL REVELATOR PROCLAIMS GOD WITHIN—London Times

LADY DEITY SOON TO INCARNATE HERE—Philadelpiha Inquirer

PLANET SHARED WITH UNSEEN BILLIONS—Der Spiegel

GOD TO MAN: HELP ONE ANOTHER—Boston Globe

The world's media virtually ignored every other story in order to report and analyze the epochal events at ABYTOR.

Every member of the elite 'direct witnesses'—i.e., every chambermaid, bartender, banker, and family member—became an instant celebrity. Avidly pursued by talk shows—endlessly interviewed by the press—their perceptions, opinions, and views were quickly elevated to authority status. While a few managed to disappear into seclusion, many proved eager to don robes of sagacity. As the sole witnesses, they became instant sources of cosmic wisdom, interpreters of truth, and conveyors of Values—and basked in their newfound stature. Some sold their Mentor videotapes and photos to the highest bidders; several obtained agents; a dozen signed book deals; MSNBC hired a certain banker's wife to become its official 'Cosmic Commentator'—and one erstwhile ABYTOR waitress was paid six-figures for a nude centerfold based upon her "heavenly attributes."

By the end of the first week, Mentor posters were already in stores—'Angelic Voices' CDs were rushed into release—'Revelation Videos' were edited and mixed—and the 'First Utah Church of the Visitation' was incorporated in Delaware.

Back in his office Arthur Frayles looked out on all this and figured the Mentors must be wincing.

MENTOR JUNKIES

Justin and Penny Onager had become virtual Mentor junkies, devouring everything being aired and written about their new celestial friends. Justin had shown everyone he knew his photos of the lady Mentor with the long legs. And Penny told all her friends how "way cool" the Mentors were—and how she dared to ask Alpha whether he ever had a bad hair day.

Meanwhile, their parents had some new concerns, knowing how inexorably tied to their campaign the Mentors now were. They culled every tape and transcript, searching for anything which might get them in trouble. But they found nothing—other than the one Mentor's assertion that Life begins at the onset of consciousness. Neither was sure how that would play with either the pro-life or the pro-choice crowds.

But one thing David Onager knew to a certitude: Mentors are Good.

Meanwhile, Sandovar Abydos and Son had hired an expert to doctor, edit, and mix their own Mentor tapes, having promised the

Fenstermacher campaign "some real ammunition" for going after Onager. The presidential race was now in full swing—yet, frustratingly, no one was paying much attention.

That was something Abydos intended to change.

Ellen Kate invited Peter up to the Residence for a quiet lunch the day after their return from Utah, but it had not gone well. He'd been horrified at her willingness to accept a role as a "celestial flack." And she only compounded his horror when she tried to validate everything by revealing that she had a Divine Voice inside her head who had assured her that the Mentors were trustworthy. He looked at her as if she were demented.

"So now—you're hearing still more voices?"

She was about to reply when she heard her Voice offer a response, which she relayed verbatim:

"Ellen Kate possesses nothing which you do not. You too could hear My voice—were you to truly listen."

Dementia confirmed, Peter wanted to weep.

"Look in the palm of your right hand at the base of what is commonly called the Lifeline—There is a faded dark spot beneath the skin—A pencil point was stabbed into your hand by a classmate."

He instantly recalled the incident—though by now the small graphite spot had almost completely faded. He hadn't shown it to anyone since—childhood?—and certainly not to Ellen Kate. He was suddenly shaken, shaken to his very core. Could all this—be true—? All the more reason he didn't want his son in the middle of it.

They argued back and forth over what was in Josh's best interest and what was not. Ellen Kate's Voice stayed out of the debate until challenged by Peter: "Why would the Mentors choose Ellen Kate?" he demanded aloud.

"The mother of Josiah is mighty among mortals—Her Spirit vessel is great enough to contain Truth.

She is possessed of a fine mind and a sound psyche. Her Spirit luminosity is pure and bright—Her faith is absolute—And her desire to Serve is heartfelt."

Peter had no answer for this, indeed for any of this. He rose quickly. "I'll—be in touch." He tossed his napkin on the table and was gone.

Ellen Kate repaired to the Truman Balcony, her favorite place to nurse when it wasn't too cool or windy. Her morning had been mostly spent not taking phone calls. The media were bad enough, but now it seemed every friend she ever had was calling as well. Sitting out on the Balcony, she finally was able to summon Gamma—for whom she had many questions.

Gamma? You there? I'm awake and refreshed now.

"I am pleased to hear it. In response to your first question: No, you need not work alone. Before long you will require a working staff, but not until after the January Inauguration. Until that time, there is one in the employ of your uncle who awaits only her Call to Service. Her name is Karyn DeLeo—and you will like her."

I'll phone her. In what capacity is she to serve?

"As your designated spokesperson. It is most important that you be insulated from the press and from the public—that you may enjoy your son and your cat—free to pursue your work in peace."

This was getting heavy. She wanted to know so much more. She suddenly wanted to know everything.

How many of you Mentors are there anyway? More than one-hundred and three, I assume. And, are there little baby Mentori?

"We are several thousand, and our number is fixed."

She slumped into the rocker, thinking of something else.

"You are troubled. We selected an unmarried mother for our spokesperson—and the message which that might send.

"A child requires both a mother and a father—wed or not. Some fathers—like Peter—very much want to assume parental responsibility. You must permit and encourage him to do so."

An hour later she phoned her uncle, only to have him tell her that Karyn DeLeo was "on assignment and unavailable." He then asked where she'd gotten DeLeo's name, and she told him.

For the next thirty-five minutes they discussed her Voice—its first appearance—and its ongoing presence and involvement.

*   *   *

Fully convinced the hard evidence he needed was hidden at ABYTOR, Special Agent Depkawitz had followed the astonishing events atop the mountain from a very different perspective. He'd discussed the case in depth with the Assistant Director, and in the end they agreed that hauling in Abydos or members of 'K-one' for interrogation would likely get them nowhere. Worse, it would alert Abydos and his lawyers that he was the target of a federal investigation—which in turn carried the even greater risk the whole shuttle sabotage story would get out. They also realized Abydos might leak it himself, to embarrass the Administration with yet another near-disaster which it tried to conceal—the first being the atomic bomb dropped on the roof of Fort Knox.

It was finally decided to penetrate Abydos's organization, and try to make their case from the inside.

Meanwhile, Zooti Abydos was busy overseeing the final mix and edit of selected taped excerpts of Mentor conversations with guests and staffers—transforming them into potent, albeit ersatz, pronouncements. Abydos senior had ordered that the tapes be ready by the following morning for delivery to Fenstermacher for President.

*   *   *

The Vatican had previously ducked taking a formal position on the Convenings, claiming they were not a spiritual matter. But ABYTOR clearly was—and now the Church found itself almost literally between a rock and a hard place, with only one of three stances it could logically take: Associate, Dissociate, or Repudiate.

The first involved affirming and validating something that the Holy See had only witnessed on television along with the rest of the world. Moreover, to associate would require making certain awkward 'doctrinal accommodations.' Worst of all, it could serve to undermine Rome's spiritual authority—the very bedrock of its power, and its reason for being.

The second option was hardly more appealing: To stand apart in theological detachment, neither affirming nor denying, would only make the Church appear weak and confused, afraid even to speak out—and an impotent, pusillanimous Papacy was inimical to Roman Catholicism.

Yet the third choice was fraught with peril. To begin with, most people took the events on top of the mountain at face value: They were spiritual—and something people very much wanted to accept and believe in. To many, it was a true epiphany.

For the Church to attack the very thing so many of the faithful were embracing, would amount to institutional lunacy—especially with no evidence anywhere to disprove a thing.

There was even debate over whether or not the Pope should receive Ellen Kate Bryce, should she ever seek an audience.

In the end it was decided to dispatch special Vatican Emissaries to Utah to undertake a long and thorough investigation, just as they always did when formally petitioned to authenticate a supposedly miraculous event.

The investigation would take many months, if not years.

*   *   *

Ten days after the Mentors departed ABYTOR, Karyn DeLeo followed suit, resigning without notice and returning to Boston—her investigation at last finished. Best of all, she made it home without having to endure a Zooti implant.

Waiting on her desk was a note from the Managing Editor: he wanted to see her. "Karyn," he beamed, "welcome back! Have a seat. Here, let me fetch you some coffee—" He was actually fussing over her, she realized.

He poured two cups. "Cream—sugar? Listen, your Abydos series is first-rate. I'm not suggesting there's a Pulitzer just around the corner, but you can be very proud of it. The exposure of Abydos' secret taping system is going to totally discredit him and likely trigger hundreds of lawsuits. It'll be a first: a class-action lawsuit brought by millionaires!"

Karyn then shared something not included in her series: Sigma's warning, her frantic call to her mother in Hong Kong, and now the news that her mother had undergone surgery—and afterwards been finally pronounced cancer-free! Frayles was awed.

"You must have—very special standing with our Celestial Friends for Sigma to deliver such a warning. Speaking of which—did you have a chance to meet my niece at ABYTOR?"

"The—President's daughter? No, I'm sorry—I didn't."

"Well, I hope you're free this evening. When I learned you were back I called her, and she's flying in this evening for the express purpose of speaking with you." He knew he couldn't just leave it at that. "I think she may have an interesting—'assignment' to offer you. From the sound of it—something celestial."

248

THE DAM

A rising sun turned the massive face of Three Gorges Dam vanilla-peach, the dark Yangtze Reservoir snaking away behind it and growing a few centimeters deeper with each passing day.

Michael Xiang stood outside the director general's office perched high on the side of the gorge, and gazed out upon the colossal structure before him, now only a few years from full completion. The dam was awesome: sixty-eight football fields long and the height of a sixty-story building, it was a twenty-six million ton concrete behemoth—the waters impounded behind it creating a man-made lake three-hundred seventy-five miles long and, after full, five-hundred seventy-five feet in depth. The center spillway and flood control section stood ninety-nine percent complete; the eighty-four billion kilowatts per year hydroelectric power plants were being wired; and construction of the double series of locks along the northeast canyon wall was ahead of schedule. There had been only one serious delay: an engineering error on the huge, first-of-its-kind, indoor Mechanical Ship-lift.

Dr. Xiang, Livermore physicist and nuclear weapons expert, had been chosen by the National Security Council to serve as civilian head of Operation Harmless. The fact that he was a Chinese-American fluent in Mandarin had been a factor in his selection. Xiang's orders were explicit: 'Neutralize the nuclear threat to Three Gorges Dam.' He had now been in-country for thirty-nine days.

The MASLAS unit was already on-station, setting up its equipment. Prior to the team's arrival, a four-hundred and ninety foot tall cofferdam, site-fabricated out of eleven-sixteenths inch plate steel, had been lowered into the water—positioned against the dam, pumped dry, sealed, and ventilated. A three-ton electric hoist was then erected within the cofferdam, extending up to the top of the dam itself. Lastly, night lights were rigged to enable around-the-clock operations—all under the watchful orbiting eye of the U.S. National Reconnaissance Office.

The early morning air sluicing down the gorge bore the sweet fragrance of mountain rain forests commingled with jasmine blossoms. Michael Xiang inhaled long and deep, savoring, then preserving, the experience on his olfactory hard-drive. After a few last indulgent breaths, he turned his attention back to the work at hand.

Today involved mounting the masonry laser on its operating platform, slowly lowering it into position, and then affixing it to the face of the dam—five-hundred and sixteen feet down from the top of the spillway, and two-thousand, seven-hundred, and four feet in from the southwest upper terminus.

From the airport arrival of the Operation Harmless team and equipment, Chinese observers were always close by, watching, recording, and reporting everything they saw and heard.

All thirty-eight Americans had been designated Foreign Operatives, and as such were placed under twenty-four hour surveillance. Beijing was not at all pleased at the prospect of having Americans using Pentagon devices burning holes into their national pride—the largest engineering project on earth. Thanks to a drunk lunatic in Pyongyang, The Great People's Achievement would stand forever desecrated.

Xiang had some lingering concerns over the huge electrical trunks running down to MASLAS 4, and set off for the cofferdam. Opting for the most direct route, he fast-stepped down the long switchback stairway—his omnipresent tail huffing and puffing to keep up with him.

After consuming the entire morning, MASLAS 4 was finally secured to its positioning platform, hooked up, and powered up, with all systems checked and rechecked. Everything reported Normal, which meant the actual lowering could commence right after the midday break.

MASLAS 4 received final authorization to commence boring—but had been instructed by Washington to stop one meter short of the coffin, take final positioning x-rays, and await further orders.

Xiang wondered how the diplomatic side was coming, having been fully briefed before leaving Washington. He knew there would be no final order to Execute until 'everything else' was nailed down; i.e., Taiwan. And permission from Beijing to Execute had still not been received. This was understandable, considering what still lay ahead: "Tickling the Dragon's Tail." as it was called.

The plan finally settled upon by the NSC, the Pentagon, and the President had been largely Peter Klein's. Having learned of FOMEX during the shuttle investigation, he immediately thought of using it in paste form to solve the problem of the Bomb in the Dam. Peter had consulted with weapons experts and been assured that the odds were excellent, though not one-hundred percent. There remained a one percent possibility nuclear detonation would occur—a risk Beijing would be forced to run if they wanted to render the bomb harmless. It was therefore out of percentile recognition that Peter had facetiously suggested renaming their quest 'Operation Almost Harmless.'

*   *   *

Peter truly enjoyed giving his son rubber duck baths, while still artfully avoiding all dealings with diapers. Another favorite form of father-baby communication was to lie on the floor and let Josh abuse him.

Not only did Daddy turn into a neat, kissy-snuggly, over-and-under obstacle course—but also a ticklish one! It was a significant vulnerability Josh had discovered early on, and he now gleefully exploited at every horizontal opportunity.

Tonight added a new element. Rolling about on the floor, Josh happened upon Daddy's incipient bald spot. He became utterly mesmerized and examined it at length—to his mother's utter delight. These are the quality periods, she realized, and thanked her Voice for pressing her to create more Daddy Time.

Before long, Josh was pooped and getting drowsy. His parents tucked him in with many kisses and repaired to the couch. They exchanged smiles and fell into quiet reflection.

"If I'm not mistaken—" Peter presently declared, "you an' me have never actually bumped ugly on 'gov'ment prop'ity'—." He gave her a long, seductive look, unfortunately she found the expression on his face highly comical.

She snorted and broke into muffled giggles, "I'm—so sorry—it's just that you were—trying so hard to look alluring—" she managed, and then erupted in a new burst of laughter, "but mostly you reminded me of some dude posing for a Personals video!"

With this, they fell together laughing—their merriment quickly evolving into foreplay—which eventuated in Unauthorized Conjugal Activity on Federal Property.

*   *   *

MASLAS 4 was precisely positioned against the face of Three Gorges, inside the cofferdam, some four-hundred feet below the outside water level. With its hyper-excitation carbon dioxide laser, the machine

251

could generate a kilo-joule pulse disruption beam, its arc-like intensity exciting molecules within each stone and grain of sand—violently disrupting and dislodging them. The boring operation would produce a dense cloud of pulverized mineral dust which would require continuous evacuation, lest the laser beam become diffused. During boring, when steel rebar was encountered, a higher intensity would automatically kick in for a few hot moments, transforming a borer into a burner.

At last, everything stood ready. The laser unit was programmed to sculpt a precision hole the diameter of a nickel—through one-hundred forty-one feet of cured concrete and rebar to a two-meter coffin fabricated out of five-eighths inch steel.

Simple enough.

8:20 a.m. Thursday: rain. At the cofferdam base, Xiang was next to MASLAS 4 performing a final x-ray alignment check, a Chinese official at his side. They both wore headphones, in constant communication with those above—and with their respective governments. Finally, the moment was at hand. Everyone donned safety glasses—

"Okay, Carlo—Commence Sequencing," Xiang ordered, repeating the command in Mandarin.

There was a sharp hiss of air—the snap of a powerful arc—a loud electrical hum—and a brilliant pop of hot colorless light—searing into Great Gorges' enamel like the mother of all dental drills.

*   *   *

Meanwhile, seven-hundred miles northeast of Operation Harmless, Iana Ravenscroft was meeting privately with the Chinese president.

"Mr. President—" she confided, leaning in a bit closer, "President Bryce has no doubt whatever that the people of North Korea would be far better off living as a Chinese Protectorate—rather than under the cruel conditions and deprivation of the current regime."

She watched his face as he listened to the translation and saw major activity ignite behind his hooded eyes. She waited for it to subside—It didn't, so she continued.

"Should the People's Republic of China decide that massive shipments of food, fuel, clothing, and medicine were urgently needed to avert disaster—the United States could publicly support the introduction of such assistance—providing the matter of Taiwan independence had already been satisfactorily resolved." The key word was 'introduction'—a diplomatic euphemism for the insertion and deployment of military forces.

With this implied American acquiescence, she unleashed a new whirlwind behind the President's eyes—having sweetened the pot by hinting at a territorial quid pro quo.

*   *   *

The laser beam bored and burned ever closer to the coffin without regard to the rising and setting of the sun. The longer the work took, the greater the risk Pyongyang would get word that something was going on. By the morning of the third day, the beam had reached a point exactly one meter short of the coffin, where it halted. Xiang promptly notified Washington; his counterpart reported it to Beijing.

The President of China fully understood the inherent risks of Operation Harmless, and was deeply apprehensive. American experts had pegged the risk of a nuclear detonation at "less than one in one-hundred." Although the rest of the world was disposed to believe in all Mentor pronouncements, the President was far less credulous. Yet, on the off-chance that the Mentors' seismic predictions were accurate, he appreciated that taking no action at all was tantamount to inviting catastrophe.

Operation Harmless had the advantage of offering a total solution, and was impressive in its simplicity. One: Silently laser-bore a hole through the steel wall of the coffin; Two: Insert an optical fiber to light, examine, and map the coffin's interior; Three: Identify and locate the trembler trigger, the Detonator, the Initiator, the plutonium power generator, and the nuclear core; Four: Using extreme caution—silently and gently inject a paste-like explosive around the Detonator; Five: Destroy the Detonator—rendering the bomb harmless.

Operation Harmless was predicated on three assumptions: First, the bomb was a viable, pure, fission device not employing tritium. Second, the Russians had been truthful when assuring Washington that the lens-shaped explosives surrounding the atomic core could not initiate a chain-reaction as the result of a proximate non-nuclear explosion.

Third, any firing signal the detonator managed to generate in the last Nano-second of its existence would be successfully intercepted and obliterated in the very next Nano-second—prior to its arriving at the Initiator.

Less than one in one-hundred worried the Chinese President, but—he then had tacit American support for punishing North Korea!

The decision to proceed had already been taken—the one percent risk deemed acceptable. At least if it failed he had one consolation: Pyongyang would pay dearly for its treachery!

Final approval was given—word flashed to Washington and immediately relayed to Three Gorges—along with the admonition to "Exercise the utmost caution."

Little did Xiang suspect this last caveat came directly from a Mentor called Gamma delivered to Ellen Kate Bryce during a rubber duck bath and passed on to her father.

Unfortunately, there existed one risk which had not been contemplated: Any impurities in the steel used to fabricate the coffin could vaporize under the impact of the laser beam, and in so doing, make a sound loud enough to set off the acoustic trigger.

The North Koreans had set the acoustic trigger to fire at one decibel—the rough equivalent of a rumbling stomach.

*   *   *

It was past midnight when an encrypted radio dispatch was received in the North Korean capital: AMERICANS DRILLING FOR PAST SEVENTY HOURS AT BASE OF DAM ON RESERVOIR SIDE. STANDING BY FOR ORDERS.—(Unsigned)

THE DEVICE

An enemy determined to commit suicide must be permitted to proceed unhindered. —Korean proverb

It was not a proverb with which Huang, being Vietnamese, was familiar. He waited nervously, repeatedly checking the time. Through his night binoculars he could tell that the technicians were still at work, betrayed by the dull, moth-ridden beacon shining up from the top of the cofferdam along with all the work-lights and the thirty men on top of the dam. The lift would periodically operate, and someone would appear now and then from below. He continued to observe—

Suddenly, the hairs on his back stood erect: Something's different—. Then he realized what it was—not something which was taking place, but something which was not: The dull beacon shining up from below was clear of dust—the drilling had stopped. Which could mean that the Americans might have already reached the bomb—and could accidentally set it off at any moment!

Panic set in—what to do? Encode, Report, and Wait? Or run like the wind? If the latter, should he activate the transmitter timer before leaving—on the assumption that a Firing Order would soon be arriving?

5:19. He looked through the binoculars again—and still saw no drill dust emanating from the shaft. In fact more cars were arriving! He'd seen a photograph of the trembler switch resting beside the deceased's skull—with an acoustic trigger alongside the other ear.

With that sudden mental image, panic overtook him. Heart pounding, Huang raced for his car—fleeing before the blinding light he expected to bloom behind him at any moment in that searing instant just prior to death.

And suddenly, primal fear mercifully drove from his mind all thought of activating the transmitter timer.

*   *   *

The laser remained on stand-by as a slender magnetometer was fed slowly into the borehole. Through careful measuring, Xiang brought the instrument to a halt a quarter-inch from the end of the bore.

Readings were then taken ahead and to both sides. Xiang's laptop confirmed that they were dead on target; the laser beam would engage the coffin eleven point one-seven-six centimeters down from its top and forty-eight point five-one-four centimeters in from the left end.

"Bingo!" Xiang rang out. "'Bing—Go' in Chinese," he translated merrily. The magnetometer was withdrawn, the laser activated, and the final foot begun—

Within the steel coffin, a celestially induced pressure front materialized just above the skull and moved slowly down the corpse until all the interior air was compressed against the foot panel—leaving behind a perfect vacuum.

Moments after this transacted, half a world away, Ellen Kate Bryce was communing with her friend Gamma, who suddenly reported that a near-fatal oversight by Peter's team has just been contained.

The beam had reached the coffin and, having again encountered steel, automatically switched to a higher pulse rate, the compressed air still turned off. Xiang immediately ordered the intensity lowered to slow the burn rate. Their orders called for melting their way through the steel slowly, gently, and quietly. Their lives, after all, depended on letting the dragon sleep on undisturbed.

Exactly fifty-six seconds after beginning its burn—

The laser beam encountered an unforeseen pocket of metallurgic impurity—instantly vaporizing the moisture trapped within its mass in a silent eruption of energy.

In that atmospheric void the acoustic trigger was deaf. Moments later the pressure front withdrew—restoring a medium able to support combustion.

Suddenly, Mike Xiang knew they'd made it through safely—simply because they were all still alive!

The heavy lifting could now begin in earnest.

First, a one-hundred twelve foot long 'steerable colonoscope' was inserted and delicately snaked into the borehole—its bright beam illuminating the long passageway ahead. Xiang watched over the shoulder of 'Proctological Technician' Cheryl Merrill until she'd successfully maneuvered the optical tip up to the fresh hole in the coffin. She then eased the lighted tip ever so cautiously through it. And stopped—so that the very first person to peer inside could be Dr. Xiang.

Taking up the remote steering device, he performed a slow optical pan of the coffin's interior—

The desiccated remains of Yo Hua Sing—a red Omni-directional, mercury-switch motion trigger sitting to one side of his skull—a generic Soviet acoustic trigger at the other.

Moving on down the corpse—a small plutonium power generator beside the left waist—at the other, a Korean-made radio receiver—a small red light signaling that it was on-line, awaiting but a single coded command. And sitting right there between the spread knees of the deceased as if just birthed: the spherical Nuclear Core.

Four-hundred and fifty kilotons of fissile fury, surrounded by forty-five kilos of Semtex sealed within a polished satin-finish casing—and clutched in the light brown tentacles of the firing harness spreading ominously out from the Initiator to distribute a six-hundred Volt bolt of electricity to each shaped charge at precisely the same micro-instant.

But where was the Detonator, the bomb's operational brain center? Then Mike spotted it, underneath the Initiator, just below the man's groin: A small green box: four cables running in; one running out—straight to the Initiator.

They'd expected more separation. Now the question became, Dare they blow the Detonator and the Initiator simultaneously—? Xiang could see no other way.

Speaking in pointlessly hushed tones, he described into a recorder everything he saw just as it lay. He then turned and invited his Chinese counterpart to confirm for himself. Operations were suspended for the balance of the day while each side reported the situation and awaited further orders.

* * *

Peter Klein had gathered all five of his nuclear experts in the Situation Room in case they were needed. To his surprise, none was unduly alarmed upon learning the Initiator sat virtually on top of the Detonator. All agreed that, given sufficient explosive force, both components should disintegrate before being able to execute their missions. However, there was now concern over the integrity of the nuclear core itself. Blowing it to smithereens would create a plutonium-filled, highly radioactive pocket near the base of the dam—which, as was the case inside the Chernobyl sarcophagus, over time would seriously degrade the surrounding concrete, thereby creating potentially grave structural problems.

This concern was promptly reported to Beijing, accompanied by the recommendation 'Operation Harmless—proceed as planned.'

* * *

Weeks earlier, Klein had placed an urgent call to Cyndyx Industries to find out whether they could produce a variation of FOMEX in either paste or gel form—and was excited to learn they already had such a product in development—and could deliver a small quantity at once.

Of all the materials and equipment the Americans had flown in, the two kilos of fast-setting GELEX attracted the most official interest and technical curiosity. The notion of creating a high-explosive in gelatin form, like something squeezed out of a toothpaste tube, thrilled the Chinese mind. As the inventors of gun powder, they seemed almost ashamed at not having thought of it themselves. Had they known about FOMEX, their distress would have been complete.

Beijing gave permission to proceed—and thirty minutes later Xiang loaded GELEX in his 'proctoscope.' The plan called for easing the tube into the casket—manipulating it to just above the Detonator—downloading the gel—inserting the fuse—sealing the borehole—and allowing the gel to set.

"Okay, everyone—here—we—go—"

Xiang braced himself—and ever-so-delicately eased the tube into the casket. He first bent it downward, toward the deceased's crotch. The fiber-optic beam was bright though narrowly focused, forcing him to pause frequently and shine it about to double-check his position.

One bump—one sound—would mean instant oblivion.

At last the tip was poised mere centimeters above the Detonator, the Initiator hard by one side. The critical moment had arrived. Another deep breath, this one held longer. Lightly pressurizing the long tube, he waited for what seemed an eternity until a gleaming ribbon of lavender gel gradually oozed from its tip, coiling down like soft ice cream onto a sugar cone Detonator. He measured precisely, shutting off the air pressure just before the last of the gel was due to make its appearance. Any sudden jet of escaping air could easily set off either or both triggers.

Then Xiang withdrew his nuclear colonoscope and slumped back, physically and emotionally drained. Cheryl carefully withdrew the tube, squeezed out the remaining gel, and in its place inserted a tiny state-of-the-art radio-igniter.

"Just—one more time—" Xiang announced, feeding the tube back into the borehole.

The Situation Room was informed that Operation Harmless was Armed and Ready at the same time Beijing was told. With fingers tightly crossed on both sides of the Pacific, the Authorization to Execute was issued from both capitals.

Brief consideration had been given to evacuating civilian populations for fifty kilometers in every direction, but Beijing had no stomach for that option. The residents would thus remain, something Xiang had assumed from the outset. At one-hundred to one, he still liked the odds. Ergo:

The moment had arrived to Tickle the Dragon's Tail—

Beijing had insisted that the actual command to FIRE come from the Director General of Three Gorges himself. Standing atop the dam looking down at the MASLAS team, the man who had personally overseen his nation's greatest ever investment of resources gave the final order. Michael Seward Xiang, Doctor of Nuclear Science, acknowledged the order—mouthed a silent prayer—and keyed the firing switch—

Plutonium 239 is not a natural earth element; it is the proud creation of the human cortex—and is the most deadly substance on earth.

While but a few pounds were required to vaporize an entire city, hundreds of tons had been manufactured over the years by the United States and the Soviet Union.

Within a plutonium core, molecular overcrowding is a Design Criterion—whereby any sudden, violent crushing together of the atomic nuclei sets off an instantaneous chain-reaction.

And at this moment, waiting malevolently inside the coffin:

A heavy metal, grapefruit-size, silver-toned, warm-to-the-touch plutonium core, encircled by SEMTEX shaped-charges, sat poised to detonate.

SUDDENLY, on the outer surface of its harness,

A blinding molecular concussion

—and instant obliteration.

THE DRAGON'S TAIL

The Chinese planned the operation down to the minute. To achieve total tactical surprise, timing was everything.

5:30: Long convoys of covered trucks under military escort, preceded by armored sound trucks blaring Communist martial anthems, swept simultaneously cross the Yalu River into North Korea across eleven major bridges. The vehicles bore large signs in Korean proclaiming:

FOOD—CLOTHING—FUEL—MEDICINE. Against the music, shrill female voices cried out in Korean: "FEAST ON FRATERNAL GIFTS FROM THE PEOPLE OF CHINA!"—"WELCOME THE ASSISTANCE OF YOUR BROTHERS IN SOCIALISM!". "THE LONG NIGHT OF HUNGER IS ENDED!"

All the vehicles were enclosed and covered, with one in three concealing heavily armed soldiers.

Loudspeakers blaring, the convoys smashed through border gates without slowing. Stunned and confused, the Korean guards fell back and then raced for telephones and radios.

5:35: one-hundred twenty-six missile-armed Shenyang J-9 fighters, two-hundred ninety assault helicopters, and eight radar surveillance aircraft flew across the border—and achieved total control of North Korean airspace in thirteen minutes flat.

Two convoy columns raced to the Sea of Japan, effectively bisecting the country. Three headed for regional capitals, while the main force hurled down the coast highway for Pyongyang.

5:38 Beijing's ambassador arrived at the Great Hall of the People, demanding an immediate audience with the Great Leader.

5:40 Radio Beijing announces that "The greatest emergency humanitarian relief and assistance effort in all history has been undertaken by the People's Republic of China on behalf of its socialist brothers in the People's Republic of Korea." Powerful transmitters simultaneously beamed the announcement in Korean throughout the peninsula.

The Great Leader had been up late molesting a teenager, and was awakened after only a few hours' sleep. He had a stabbing headache and was in no condition or mood to think. His defense minister was shouting something about Chinese military convoys smashing across the border at eleven points—heading directly for the Capital!

He was also saying something about the Chinese ambassador having just arrived and urgently requesting an audience. But above all, and before anything else, Dear Leader had to pee.

When he received the ambassador twenty-five minutes later, he had been briefed—and had read a transcript of the formal announcement on Radio Beijing. He was informed that no tanks or artillery had entered the country—and that the Chinese thus far had not fired a round (except to destroy a lone APC outside Chongju which had rashly opened fire on the convoy). Dear Leader was understandably reluctant to issue an order to attack the invaders, since to do so would be tantamount to declaring war on a superpower! He needed time to think—

The Chinese ambassador greeted the Great Leader coldly. "Be advised: The nuclear device you placed within the Three Gorges Dam has been destroyed. You are most fortunate that our efforts met with success. We are in Korea now to make certain that nothing like that is ever again attempted." He paused to steeple his fingers. "It is our judgment that only conditions of extreme shortage and economic hardship could give rise to such a reckless and doomed act of desperation. Recognizing this, we have come not for revenge, but to address the root causes of the crisis. Our humanitarian aid will continue, and our management experts will remain in place until our assistance is no longer necessary. This aid will be in the form of long-term loans, and as such, will not call for early repayment." He looked Dear-hung-over-Leader square in the eye.

"In consequence of your craven attempt at extortion, you will surrender all remaining Soviet nuclear devices. In conclusion, know this: Any armed resistance will bring about your immediate replacement as head of state."

*   *   *

Michael Xiang was ushered into the Oval Office by Peter Klein. The President immediately rose.

"Dr. Xiang, it's indeed good to see you—considering the alternative!" he beamed, shaking the smaller man's hand. "Come, have a seat. Would you like coffee? Hell, champagne would be more appropriate!" he chuckled, taking a seat across from the modest young physicist. "Tell me, Mike—what was it like—the moment you actually pushed that button?"

Xiang shrugged. "Just a—sort of, dull Whump!—from deep inside. The people standing up top didn't feel or hear anything. Some of them assumed there'd been a misfire."

"Well, thank God it all ended as it did! You risked personal vaporization, and I want you to know your country—and millions of Chinese—stand in everlasting debt!"

He rose and walked over; Xiang, quickly stood. Bryce clapped him on the back and smiled. "Listen, with everyone else off running for president, Mrs. Bryce and I are planning a quiet weekend at Camp David, and we'd be so very pleased if you and Mrs. Xiang would join us. And that'll give me a chance to tell you what else you accomplished—without even knowing it."

*   *   *

Jane Onager made it a practice to swing by campaign headquarters each week to pick up tabulated summaries of letters and e-mail from likely voters, along with a representative sampling. David was campaigning in California and would be back Monday; she'd have her digest and comments on last week's write-ins waiting for him.

With Justin off to Cornell for a football weekend with a girlfriend, and Penny sleeping over at Cassie's in Falls Church, it was a perfect opportunity to catch up on the mail. She curled up on the sofa and scanned the summaries. The Motivating Issues sheet was always first: Taxes—education health care—the Middle East—and once in a while, a topic which fit no other category. Just such an item caught her eye—the issue named was: "Loneliness."

She sorted through the letters until she found it—a single page of notebook paper, written in pencil by a clearly shaky hand—

Dear Senator Onager,

I'm old and alone with nothing to do and with nothing to look forward to but dying and maybe not being found for days.

I know you won't take the time to answer this but I had to write anyway—to ask what can you do for someone like me?

You seem like a very caring person.

Very truly yours,

Todman Wesel (Cleveland).

Jane held the letter a long time, and then began to pen a personal response. With several false starts, it took nearly an hour. But it came from the heart, and she wanted to get it just right. Of course, she knew Mr. Wesel would probably reply—and that by writing to him, she'd be taking on a long-term, life-remaining responsibility. I'll simply have to make the time; she shrugged, licking the envelope.

Jane was surprised the next morning when Penny stormed in before breakfast, announcing that she and Cassie had had a "really major fight." She had walked out, and the Secret Service had driven her home.

"Pancakes okay?" her mother asked, not overly concerned.

"Yeah—sure."

"So, what was this fight about anyway?"

"Oh—it all started with Big Biz'm—some stupid new alternative rock group. Well, Cassie, she thinks they're way hot—an' I go 'They're a buncha techno-dorks!' Next thing, she's calling Crazy Ivan, my favorite group—! Now that really pissed me, so I go, 'Well at least—"

"I—get the idea," Jane cut off, holding up her hand. She poured batter on the griddle and brought her daughter a glass of juice. "Now—let me tell you about a really amazing dream I had last night—" she began excitedly.

*　　*　　*

The sun was at high meridian and blindingly bright as Air Force One touched down at Taipei Airport. It taxied slowly to a designated reception area where bands played, crowds cheered, and flags snapped nastily in the wind. Soldiers stood frozen at parade dress, tunics gleaming, eyes fixed on the horizon, chilled dignitaries smiled bravely and huddled, unsmiling flower-girls shivered on the tarmac—as the world's television covered the welcoming ceremonies live.

Shining resplendently, Air Force One turned smartly on its mark, parked, and shut down engines. A spotless boarding ramp was wheeled up and locked in place, and a dazzling red carpet rolled out. A brass-button band erupted in stirring frenzy, their efforts totally swallowed by the wind. Dignitaries, formed up in descending order of rank, turned their eyes to the forward portal of the great aircraft just now opening—

The President of the United States and the President of the People's Republic of China emerged and stood side-by-side waving, well aware the historic moment was being witnessed live by millions. Bugles trumpeted in the wind, and on cue a frantic sea of flashing pennants flailed in the stands. It was a dazzling tri-national explosion of color, the happy and proud commingling of the symbols of sovereignty—the flag of the Republic of Taiwan snapping proudly between the others.

Smiling, the two leaders descended the ramp, followed by the American secretary of state, Bryce's national security adviser, and various deputies. The President of the Republic of Taiwan stood at the foot of the ramp, bowing deeply in welcome for his honored guests. The three presidents passed down the receiving line, reviewed the troops, and saluted as their respective national anthems were played. Next, each walked to a waiting bank of microphones to express high hopes for "The new dawn of peace and prosperity about to break upon Asian shores," as Sam Bryce characterized it.

That afternoon, standing before Government House under a symbolically bright sun, President Bryce announced, and all three leaders ceremoniously set hand and seal to, 'The Triune Pacific Accord'—effecting the formal transfer of title for the Province of Taiwan from the People's Republic of China to the United States of America. The consideration set forth in the accord was four-trillion three-hundred and sixty-billion dollars—payable in annual trade credits over twenty years. It was not a treaty, but a Contract of Sale—one which the outgoing President would now have to go home and sell to both Congress and the American people. The simultaneously executed Loan Agreement between the United States and the Republic of Taiwan for the repurchase of the island, he was confident, would make the Triune Accord a far easier sell.

However, in an after-dinner speech that evening, President Bryce did make a down payment on his deal with Beijing: a public statement of support for China's efforts to "bring an early end to the suffering of the people of North Korea," and to assist the North in getting the economy back on its feet. The Chinese president nodded his approval.

Air Force One was wheels up at 9:47, headed for Beijing to drop off its president. En route the two leaders toasted each other with scotch, exhausted but well pleased with the day's events. Each fell into quiet reflection. Presently the President of China, who spoke more than passable English, sighed deeply. "North Korea's one sorry shit-hole."

"World-class," Bryce smiled. "Taiwan's nice, though."

BRYCE TAG

Bryce's statesmanlike initiative was promptly hailed the world over. Le Monde punned, 'THE BRYCE OF PEACE: FOUR POINT THREE-SIX TRILLION!' At home his regular mainstream detractors were caught by surprise and scrambled to formulate rationales of opposition. But conservatives were having no such problem, decrying the bilateral purchase agreement as "The most outrageous foreign aid scam in American history!"

With the first of the presidential debates now only weeks away, Gordon Fenstermacher had stopped talking about the Mentors altogether, mindful of their popularity. Instead he concentrated his fire on Onager's "neo-populist attempts at social re-engineering."

Senator Onager and his running mate simply ignored their Republican opponents, focusing instead on the fact that the top two percent owns more than the bottom ninety percent!

Polls showed the candidates were locked in a dead heat, with a genuine polarization of the electorate taking place. This had everyone worried.

*   *   *

The shuttle sabotage investigation had taken on new life. The FBI learned that a former CIA operative—now an active member of KAPPA UNO—had once mistakenly killed the wrong guy in a Miami arms deal shootout. The deceased was an undercover DEA agent, and the foul-up had been covered up. There being no statute of limitations on murder, Agent Hyman Depkawitz finally had some major leverage. Smiling, he held up a color photograph of Sandovar Abydos—took aim. Cocked his finger—and fired.

*   *   *

Peter Klein was a head-person, though fundamentally ruled by his heart. He'd accommodated this paradox all his life by giving his mind dominion over his emotions—and telling no one, except for the handful of women with whom he'd actually been intimate. It had been two long, celibate years (his recent kinky shower with his boss not withstanding) he fell in love with Ellen Kate Bryce. "At least you knew enough to wait for a good one to come along," she'd joked upon learning of his extended dry spell.

Now here he was, one year later, living out the emotional worst-case scenario and ultimate irony: being hopelessly in love with someone who's not reciprocating. Being loved as a friend and appreciated as a lover didn't help. It was just too painful. *Or is that just my ego hurting?* he worried.

It was Saturday, and Peter was showing off his new Saab 'ragtop' by taking Katie (with Josh strapped securely in his safety seat) for a top-down fall foliage tour through the Blue Ridge foothills—an ever-watchful beige sedan not far behind. It was a spectacular day, the air warm, tinged with the sweetness of burning leaves. He looked over at the sun-dappled pair beside him—and experienced a deep upwelling of love.

"Do I gotta knock you up again—to get you to say Yes?"

Ellen Kate was flabbergasted. She had imagined him asking that very question during her morning shower, the realization of which loosed skittles of electricity all across her skin. Peter's love was palpable! Then:

a seminal decision—but one made primarily on behalf of Peter and Josiah.

"Uhhh—very possibly." Pause. "Ask me when it happens."

Was that a Yes? A foolish squeal escaped his throat—instantly followed by a honk of laughter from hers.

THE DREAM

Later that night, as she slept—She was standing erect—moving not a muscle yet did she glide effortlessly over the landscape skimming along, barely a foot above the ground.

Then she was winging over the highlands—gazing down upon rolling meadows—verdant forests—sparkling lakes interconnected by a system of gleaming canals of manifestly intelligent design.

She adroitly descended to the surface, where the air was rain-forest fresh—a symphony of aromas.

Magnificent plants and blossoms glistened all about her—soft-eyed creatures tip-toed out for a closer peer and a cautious sniff—

Then she lifted her gaze—and though it was daytime, beheld the Heavenly Vault alive with gleaming, dazzling worlds!

She rotated for a look behind her—and saw a stupendous celestial body surrounded by seven shining spheres in common orbit.

It took her breath away.

Ellen Kate awoke, the dream still bright before her mind. She held her eyes closed, hoping to sustain the vision a little longer. But in vain—Josh was up and hungry.

She gave no further thought to her cosmic dream, now forever vivid within her memory, until breakfast when she tried to describe it for her mother—whose eyes widened in amazement the more she listened.

"Oh My God: I had that identical dream myself, just a couple of nights ago!" she gasped.

An hour later Ellen Kate confronted her Voice.

How could we both possibly have the same dream?

'Many have had the Dream and others yet will. It is a Divine Gift—a foretaste of that which is to come. It would also be appropriate to view the Dream as a reward

occasioned by a wholly selfless choice made on behalf of another. The very thing those who you call Mentors have been trying to teach you."

Seeking amplification, Ellen Kate summoned Gamma—

"We played no role in this portrayal—yet we all anticipated something of the Divine would attend the supernal events transacting over the past year. People everywhere are discovering the universality of the Dream and speculating as to its meaning. You may offer this explanation: The Dream portrays certain of the Ascension Worlds as mortals will one day experience them. The Dream is a Gift, a personal demonstration of the Truth for those who live lives of Loving Service—Cherished do they become and Eternal will be their reward."

*   *   *

Sam Bryce felt there were still a few loose ends worth discussing in the wake of all the truly amazing celestial revelations they had witnessed at ABYTOR. To explore some of these loose ends, he gathered for a quiet weekend at Camp David the members of his spiritual family: Abby, her brother Art, Karyn, Ellen Kate, Peter, and the baby. It was the first time since coming off the mountain they had all gotten together. Their excitement ran high, especially when they turned their attention to the promised ANGELESIS. They asked Ellen Kate how they might be of help to Gamma and the other Mentors in preparing the way for the Holy Daughter.

She put the question up, and Gamma responded at once:

"First, let me greet and welcome each of you. It gives me powerful pleasure to anticipate working with each of you over the continuously busy months which lie before us. To answer your question directly—Yes, there is much you can do, far better than we ourselves could manage."

President Bryce had a question, the same one each would have asked: "Will we all get to actually—meet Her?"

Ellen Kate thought she heard Gamma laugh! She had no idea.

"Did you think we have no capacity to appreciate humor?"

"Y—yes." There followed a bemused pause and then they both burst.

Everyone could tell something was going on inside Ellen Kate's head, and they awaited her explanation. But she offered none. 'A private Mentor moment' is all she would say.

So Karyn jumped in. "Gamma, you just said we're going to be really busy."

"Really, really busy—particularly you and Ellen and Peter."

"How exactly?" It was several seconds before Gamma replied.

"When God drops by for a visit, you might want to vacuum first."

*   *   *

Suddenly—the entire room took on a soft golden glow, unnoticed by the agents stationed outside, but most apparent to all those inside.

There followed a stirring in the air, not of wind but of energy. And before their eyes appeared the ephemeral shapes of Seven Mighty Seraphim—each positioned above one of the mortals in the room. After a few moments the Angel over Ellen Kate spoke to all, in tones tender and loving, yet rich with authority. She looked at each of the seven mortals and let her gaze linger on Baby Josh.

"Those whom you now behold above you are your Protectors—personal Guardian Seraphim—our visualization being sanctioned by the Chief of our Order. Know that each of you has been assigned a pair of Seraphim for your continuous watch-care—with one of us always beside you."

"Each of you will play a signal role in the great cosmic drama now unfolding upon your world. Among the Angels and other Orders you are already exalted as 'The Seven.'"

"Great will be your challenges—but true will each of you be in meeting them."

Everyone sat frozen in awe, not daring to move or speak.

"We cherish you—one and all. You have struggled long and nobly—and your glory is foreordained. For all that you have striven to achieve—we salute you. Your struggles are vindicated—and your future status is assured. The Universe itself hails you—and it is an honor to be assigned to assure your protection. We will not appear before you again until the ANGELESIS is at hand. Until that Sacred Day we bid you Fare Well."

A palpable wave of affirmation suddenly spilled over the room. A glorious cleansing. Total immersion in Divine Love. Overpowering. All-forgiving. All-healing.

All save Josh felt tears of joy welling—and then let them flow. Even the President of the United States wept openly.

John VanOrsdell

FINELLA

Sandovar Abydos was at his desk when his secretary buzzed him to report that, "Someone—is here to see you, Sir—She—says to tell you that she 'bears the sole antidote—to—'Mentor Toxin'—?"

Abydos was taken aback, a rare occurrence. Was this some kind of joke? "Describe this person to me," he snapped.

"Well, Sir—she's—fiftyish—oddly attired—but seems very sure of herself. Wait—she says to tell you she brings greetings from—'Granny Slap'?"

This rocked Abydos; Granny Slap was his secret childhood nickname for his paternal grandmother, who believed that good behavior began with a good slap. He hadn't thought of her in years. He had to know more. "Send her in."

The woman flowed into the room with a fluid grace, flower-print folds of sheer organdy wafting out behind her. She smelled of gardenias and clearly believed in lipstick and eyeliner. Gliding up to Abydos' desk, she held forth her hand. "I am Finella Bright!" she breathily proclaimed, brushing back a long spill of salt and pepper curls.

"Do sit—and tell me what you know of Granny Slap."

"Means nothing whatever to me, Mr. Abydos. You know, and that's all that matters. It was simply my Spirit Partner's way of establishing his bona fides with you. He says that he's known you since childhood."

*   *   *

Then—everyone woke up one morning to the realization that Election Day was at last upon them. The polls had detected a last-minute swell in support for David Onager as many of the Undecideds decided. When all the votes were in, counted, and tallied—it was Official: Onager fifty-two percent and Fenstermacher forty-eight percent in the Popular vote—and fifty-nine percent to forty-one percent in the Electoral vote. Not surprisingly, even with momentous issues to decide, the results mostly reflected the candidate's popularity—and the electorate couldn't warm to Fenstermacher's abrasiveness—which apparently set too many people's teeth on edge.

The Democrats increased their hold on the Senate by five seats, and now stood but half a dozen short of taking control of the House and electing a new third-in-line Speaker.

President-Elect Onager was well pleased, regardless of why people cast their ballots the way they did, and looked forward to a productive cooperation with the Hill.

*   *   *

Then, though in the middle of the hurricane season, the First Family, accompanied by Peter, Art Frayles, and Karyn DeLeo, flew down to Katie Cay. There was a lot of air which needed clearing. During the flight only small talk was exchanged, but all that changed as soon as they entered the beach house. Ellen Kate alone knew that Gamma had just joined them.

"Karyn," Bryce opened, "my daughter has never given me a satisfactory explanation of her willingness to be at the beck and call of our celestial friends—can you?"

Everyone sat down, realizing that the time for a serious exchange had just arrived.

*   *   *

Still skeptical, Abydos decided nonetheless to play along. "So then, what's all this—'Mentor Toxin' about?"

"I gather that you and the Mentors are not exactly—on the best of terms. And my Partner says he is no friend of theirs either. So, if you'd be interested in leveling the playing field, he's in a position to help."

"How?" Abydos squinted, suddenly intrigued.

She took out a long, slender cigarette holder and carefully inserted a long, slender cigarette in one end. Leaning forward, she all but compelled Abydos to light it. She took a long, thoughtful drag. "My Partner is pleased to offer you your own private CIA: Celestial Intelligence Agency. Its motto is, 'To be able to see the hand of an enemy—gives one the upper hand!'" She then crossed a long, self-satisfied leg and exhaled theatrically.

*   *   *

The following evening Ellen Kate Bryce appeared on CNN for an hour-long interview. It would be her first and last media appearance. She was accompanied by Karyn DeLeo.

"Can you explain to viewers around the world exactly what it's like to 'hear' directly from the Mentors?" asked host Al Fitch.

"I anticipated this question," Ellen Kate smiled. "Let me give it a try. It's like a 'silent voice'—but one that's distinctly Mentor-like. And it just—'speaks' quietly inside my mind. Sometimes it's soft. Other times, it seems somehow louder. It's—really difficult to try to explain to anyone who's never experienced it for themselves."

"But you say it 'sounds' like the voice of Gamma, as you remember him from ABYTOR?"

"Oh, yes, very much. We talk often—about all manner of things. He's become a genuine friend and companion."

"Truly, a remarkable phenomenon," Fitch said with ill-concealed skepticism. "Now—you say you talk often. Does he just come to you, say, in the middle of the night?"

"He never comes at all unless I invite him. As he says, 'It's always my turn to call.'" She paused. "And I can call on him at any time. Actually, though, it seems we talk mostly when I'm nursing my son."

The host turned this over in his mind—and decided an opportunity may have just presented itself. "Is this 'Gamma' perhaps with us now?"

"As a matter of fact, I asked him to come along tonight in case I needed help with an answer," Ellen Kate smiled.

"Excellent!" Fitch leaned in, sensing he might be about to make news. "One thing many have been wondering is—Why is it that the Mentors appear so human-like?"

Ellen Kate listened for a few seconds and then responded. "The explanation is simple: Going a long way back—many, many millennia—we shared a common ancestry.'"

This struck Fitch as patently absurd, so he decided to drop it. "Another question: Are the Mentors essentially the advance team for this so-called Divine Visitation—?"

"No. We are permanent citizens of this world. But we will be called upon to participate in the preparations."

"Is it, perhaps what's referred to as the ANGELESIS?"

"Yes—but I can say nothing further on the subject."

There followed an awkward moment. Then Fitch turned to Karyn DeLeo and interviewed her for a few minutes. Finally he faced Ellen Kate again. "We're given to understand that tonight will mark your only media appearance, Ellen Kate. Is that accurate?" He already knew the answer.

"Yes. I wanted to come before the cameras just this one time, to introduce Karyn—and to personally deliver the Mentors' Loving Service message."

"In plain language, Ms. Bryce—what is it that the Mentors want most from us?"

Ellen Kate appeared distracted for a moment, before realizing it was her own Voice who wished to respond—

Remember that you are Holy Children of God.
Treat one another with Respect and Fairness,
If Love is asking too much.

John VanOrsdell

HARDPAN

It was the first dawn of the twelfth month. A molten sun broke over the crest of the Granite Range, quickly searing all that lay before it. Medrick 'Hardpan' Dotson knew it would be another hundred degree day, but he didn't mind: just before sunset yesterday he'd spotted some promising "flash." "By Jeezley, today's the Big Pay Day!" he cackled, just as he'd done a hundred times before. Hardpan didn't discourage.

After downing his mandatory two cups of chicory, brewed strong to save water, he was down on his knees chipping away at a showing of what he called 'Agazite'—"Silver's little tattletale." No geologist he, Hardpan was a self-certified Field Prospector. He'd given half a century, and the vast majority of his teeth, 'hard-picking' the foothills of the California desert without hitting the mother lode—But being a shrewd one, he figured the longer he searched the better his odds became.

Hardpan's technique was to use his thirty-two pound pickaxe to hack off a chunk of stratum. He hated the effort it took to swing the large axe, so he'd become skilled at making every blow count. He could nail a penny to a table with a single smash—and had won many a beer proving it.

He reared back—took aim—and struck mightily—

The exact instant his pick fell upon the stone, he felt a great booming crack deep beneath his feet. The very ground felt like it had busted. itself! He dropped his pick and braced to steady himself. Jeezley God! what have I done?

Medrick Dotson didn't know it, but he was standing almost directly above the great Garlock Fault. Beginning beneath the Tejon Pass north of Los Angeles, the fault ran east one-hundred and fifty miles, terminating in the Mojave Desert just south of Death Valley. The Garlock was second only to the San Andreas in length, and was the state's only major east-west fissure. But what set it apart was the fact that the Garlock hadn't produced an earthquake in all of recorded history. Yet, as every geologist knew, if the great Garlock ever awakened from its long tectonic sleep, the results would be catastrophic.

Fortunately, today's movement was minor. To even feel the tremor at all, one would have had to be standing nearly on top of the epicenter.

274

It had, however, been felt elsewhere; ultra-sensitive instruments in nearby Bakersfield instantly recorded the tremor. Measuring a scant two point one on the Richter Scale, the implications were nonetheless devastating. The Garlock had stirred—and to any seismologist that was a Big One. From now on they'd be watching around the clock for any further sign of mounting geologic strain.

What no scientist could know—or remotely imagine—was that the Garlock's movement resulted from acts of Master Molecular Manipulators, dispatched to the planet Earth by mandate of the Provincial Universe Rulers.

*   *   *

Sandovar Abydos was the billionaire owner of ABYTOR, the lavish corporate retreat and conference center built atop a high peak in Utah—world famous as the site of the Mentors' earthly appearance and a Visitation by a Universe Revelator.

Ensconced atop his mountain, Abydos bent the world to his will, by force if necessary. Sandovar Abydos was not one to be denied, or even thwarted. Except by the detested Mentors—those unwelcome quasi-material spirit beings given to messing in human affairs—especially his.

Thanks to the Mentors, Abydos could feel the hot breath of the Feds. But he'd blow the place to Hell before he'd let the FBI get the only hard evidence that could tie him to his failed attempt to destroy the Mentors. The fact that a space shuttle and its crew would've been forfeit in the attempt was to Abydos a matter of utter indifference.

The FBI had called it treason—with Abydos the prime perpetrator. But without any solid evidence, the Bureau was stymied, knowing none of his co-conspirators would ever cut a deal. Each feared Abydos more than the Bureau.

The evidence the FBI sought consisted of two identical hand-held radio transmitters—each able to send a complex, encrypted firing command to a detonator concealed aboard an orbiting shuttle. The FBI had located and removed all four detonators—and could easily match them to the radio transmitters if they could manage to get their hands on one.

When ABYTOR was first constructed, Abydos had ordered that an 'invisible' vault in his inner office be built into the granite core of the mountain itself—a vault which could never be breeched or removed—a vault which now contained the very evidence the FBI was looking for.

Unfortunately for Abydos, he could not simply open the vault to remove and destroy the transmitters—because the Mentors had fused the vault door shut at the molecular level and threatened to un-fuse it in the presence of the Feds!

Reluctantly Abydos concluded that if the vault could one day be opened, then it had to be destroyed—and soon.

But all this changed the day Sandovar Abydos acquired a potent new ally. Shortly after the astonishing spiritual events at ABYTOR, a most peculiar woman named Finella Bright had presented herself at his office, demanding to see him.

Only after relaying to Abydos a long-forgotten childhood nickname of his, had she been admitted—only to proclaim she was there at the bidding of a certain "spirit being" of long personal association— someone who wanted to help him do battle with the Mentors! Ms. Bright claimed her spirit partner could furnish "inside information" on the Mentors, including their ultimate intentions. It was an intelligence windfall he could never have imagined.

*   *   *

Each morning when David Onager awoke, there came that surreal moment when he suddenly remembered he'd been elected President of the United States! Today was no exception.

And with the next breath, his mind invariably leaped ahead to January twentieth—when I take the Oath of Office—and everyone learns we've just handed the reins of power over to someone with allegiance to another power!

But all that was still nearly two months away; it was only the week after Thanksgiving.

The President-elect had moved into a small suite directly above his Transition Office in trendy Knickerbocker Towers. With a commanding view of the Washington Monument, it was to Onager the perfect place for gaining political perspective.

Following his election, he'd seen all too little of Jane and the kids, being trapped at the Transition Office trying to decide on his Cabinet and key advisers.

A single individual would be far more difficult to persuade: the President-elect wanted President Bryce himself to become his ambassador to China. No former president had ever deigned to accept such a demotion. But it was Sam Bryce who'd forged a bond of trust with Beijing following America's purchase of Taiwan—and the saving of the Three Gorges Dam.

Sam Bryce had invited the President-elect to Camp David for one last weekend with his old friend and golfing buddy. Little did he suspect what Dave Onager was about to propose.

*   *   *

Ellen Kate Bryce and Peter Klein had yet to set a date for their wedding. Each wanted to wait until after President Bryce passed the torch, because the daughter of a mere former president could marry without the full glare of the media.

Preparations for the work of The Seven—as designated by the Mentors—had begun. Karyn DeLeo had moved down from Boston and become a frequent visitor to the Klein townhouse in order that she and Ellen Kate could come to better know each other. They'd quickly discovered that they enjoyed being together, though neither was yet completely confident of the other's spiritual staying power.

Following the events at ABYTOR, the two women had been summarily paired by the Mentors, and informed that henceforth they would remain forever joined in spiritual partnership. After the Mentors designated Ellen Kate as their exclusive channel for celestial contact, she'd gone into seclusion. Karyn, her official spokesperson to the outside world, would deal with the media, while she herself attended to the needs of her infant son Josiah.

Peter had been working sixteen-hour days at the Transition Office and never made it home much before eleven, so Ellen Kate often invited Karyn for supper. This Monday evening, while the nation's Capital struggled to dig out from under a crippling four-inch snowfall, Karyn simply hopped in her Subaru (purchased to deal with Boston winters) and zipped over to Peter's. The two women hugged warmly at the door.

"How's the driving?" Ellen Kate asked, taking Karyn's coat and scarf.

"Oh, some moron in a skidding SUV damn near broadsided me! I don't know what stopped it—"

At that moment Ellen Kate's divine partner whispered to her mind. "My Voice just said you can thank your Seraphim."

They walked into the kitchen, where a rich barley soup simmered aromatically. "O Lord, whatever that is, I want a bucketful!" Karyn salivated.

Over soup, they talked about soup, about how Josh never wanted to go to bed, and about how all he had to do was lay his head on his father's shoulder and it was Instant Sandman. Anything but shop talk; the celestial stuff would come later.

The Seven now consisted of Ellen Kate, her parents, Peter, Art Frayles, Karyn DeLeo, and "another yet to come." They'd been tasked with preparing the way for the impending Incarnation of the Daughter of the Creative Spirit.

"Why on earth would the Mentors pick me of all people to be one of The Seven?" Karyn worried, gazing into a snapping oak fire. They'd repaired to the den and were lying on their stomachs with Josh, the fireplace toasting all their brows.

"Maybe the Holy Daughter picked you," she shrugged.

"How about—asking your Voice?" Karyn implored.

"It's—been my experience that our celestial friends respond only to questions they choose to."

Karyn fell silent. When at last she spoke there was a catch in her throat. "It seems that's—my problem. I can't help feeling that I'm—simply unworthy!" She looked over at Ellen Kate, her eyes filling. "I can't imagine what the Mentors see in me—"

"Now that's a pure conceit!" Ellen Kate shot back. Karyn's jaw dropped. "You can't imagine what they see in you. That's like saying, 'I can't forgive myself. Of course God will forgive me—but by my standards, being so much higher than God's, I cannot.' What a conceit!"

Karyn was stunned. This was the harshest rebuke she'd ever received from Ellen Kate. So she paused to seriously consider it—. Well, the Mentors obviously must consider me worthy—but, am I not better qualified to judge? Or do they know me even better than I know myself? Actually, it would be reassuring if they did—No—then they'd really know how unworthy I am—

"Ask anyway. I need to hear—something."

"You 'need to hear' their reasons for including you—?"

"No, I—I just need to be told I'm worthy," she moaned.

An appeal by one of The Seven. She had no choice but to put the question up. It was the Mentor Sigma who responded.

"Each member of The Seven was chosen with very great care. We not only know you as you are now, Karyn DeLeo, we know you as you were and as the person you will become.

A glorious journey lies before you—yet only you can walk your destiny pathway. Know that if ye seek, ye shall find."

DIVINE TUTORIAL

Deity is existentially replete and complete, yet, as is any Universe Being, experientially incomplete.

Having never personally experienced the planet calling itself Earth, the Daughter of the Creative Spirit could only be prepared for Her Sojourn in the Flesh by one fully versed in the affairs of that world. 'Accordingly, Her assigned tutor was an Archangel of long service in the governance and over-care of this remote, imperiled little world.

The tutorials were conducted at the Daughter's personal dwelling place on the Universe headquarter's Divine Sphere—in a domicile so exquisitely expressive of Creative Beauty, even the visiting Archangel was awed. She was speaking—

—a world held in thrall by its own technology, its races given to using military force to settle national disputes. Several of its larger states have gained the technology to transform matter into energy—yet without the requisite wisdom to contain it.

I note that the nation chosen for Your Incarnation is the very nation state possessing the planet's greatest arsenal of fission and fusion weapons.

The Daughter nodded in acknowledgement, then inquired:

For how many generations have humans had such means?

Three. The first used two in anger immediately after their development—again by the nation of Your Incarnation.

Does its citizenry support the use of such weapons?

The dismantling of arsenals would only be acceptable if such were planet-wide. Sadly, in their atomic war planning, the policy of the putative combatants has been expressed as, 'Use them, or Lose them.'

How securely are they contained?

279

John VanOrsdell

Following the economic failure of one great power, a portion of its atomic arsenal was stolen and sold for personal gain. We have twice had to intervene to neutralize imminent perils. Seraphic protection will remain in full readiness throughout Your mission.

In all the Provincial Universe, on no other mortal world has technology so grossly surpassed the evolution of morality.

Upon Your arrival, be not disheartened by the grievous immaturity and selfishness which you will find. While the mortal races while many—many humans are capable of transcendent love, compassion, mercy, and sacrifice.

They are but as babes—born unto a world rife with pain and peril. My Ministry shall be to help them rise above their origins.

Holy Daughter—I urge you to remain ever mindful that this is the one and same world where the last Divine Incarnation terminated in a display of such bestial horror—it yet reverberates within the souls of all who beheld it.

Though I would do naught to stay my own slaying—I would not hesitate to call upon the agencies of Heaven in the accomplishment of My Mission. I affirm before all: This tortured little world shall not be lost. As every other, it is and will ever remain—dearly, dearly loved and cherished.

THE GARLOCK

"Let me make sure I heard you right—you want me to be your new ambassador to China?" the President intoned slowly. "Ambassador to China—" He drew his knees up and gazed hard into the fire. The offer took him utterly by surprise—but in light of its source, warranted careful consideration.

A heavy snow whispered down on the Catoctin Mountains. And as every American president had come to appreciate, there was simply no cozier a place to be on a snowy night than curled up before a cherry wood fire at Camp David.

After letting his offer settle in a bit, Onager began to make his case.

"Tell me, Sam—who better? You've dealt with their top leadership—you presented them with a viable, profitable solution to the whole Taiwan problem—you saved their damn dam, for God's sake!

There is simply no American alive for whom they have greater trust and respect—or with whom they could work as effectively."

President Bryce weighed all this, then cut to what was for him the core issue. "Then tell me, Dave—what exactly would your fundamental policy toward China be?"

Onager knew that his next words would likely decide the issue. Choosing them carefully, he engaged the president elect's eyes before speaking.

"Over the next twenty years China may well surpass the United States as the world's greatest economic power. For me, that single seminal fact dictates that over the coming decade, Sino-American friendship must veritably bloom! We must become full business partners and full strategic allies, with shared perspectives, shared international values, and shared global aspirations. Yet none of this can be accomplished unless there's a basis for mutual trust." Onager leveled a look at Bryce. "And that's where you come in."

The President-elect watched his friend digest everything he'd just argued. After a while Bryce gave a long sigh.

"Well now—I suppose in some circles that'd have to be considered a fair beginning."

Dave Onager realized he'd just received the answer he was praying for—and broke into a very broad smile.

Their accord was witnessed with profound satisfaction by more than a score of on-looking celestial beings.

The Angelesis was off to a promising start.

*   *   *

For now, The Seven would function as The Four—with neither of the senior Bryces available until after the twentieth of January. Until then, Art Frayles and Karyn DeLeo would join Peter and Ellen Kate for breakfast at their townhouse the first and third Sunday of each month.

The Christmas tree was already up, and decorations and sparkling strings of lights were everywhere. Josh's parents were determined he'd remember his first Christmas. For lunch Ellen Kate had made her usual: Cheese, mushroom, onion, and green pepper omelets(cooked just so)—with homemade garlic toast grilled to a golden perfection. Everyone so loved it, they wouldn't even entertain the heresy of waffles or grits.

After tummies were well filled, they got down to cases. Ellen Kate led off. "I'm told it's time to begin assembling a staff to serve the Daughter at her Headquarters."

"Are we talking about maids and personal attendants here," Frayles asked, "or things more administrative in nature?"

"We're talking about aides, not maids. For Herself, a chief of security—a personal physician—and a personal aide. And for Her work, an executive assistant—a research director—a director of public communications—and yes, we'll even need a finance chairman. Bills will need paying. But my dad says direct government payments are out—on the grounds of Church and State."

"And how're we supposed to go about finding such people?" Peter challenged. "Run ads?"

"That's one of the things we need to decide," Karyn said, already aware this was the case from what Ellen Kate had told her earlier.

"Another is, where do we find the money? Somehow I don't think fund-raiser dinners are the answer," Ellen Kate smiled.

"Hey, how 'bout a Holy Water bottling plant?" Art Frayles offered facetiously. "Or, as alternatives, we might consider turning to foundations—or perhaps a handful of carefully selected, deep-pocket corporate donors."

His suggestion produced a profound silence, with each weighing the implications.

"What kind of a message would having corporate backers send?" Peter finally asked in skeptical tones.

"You might ask Beta if they all think that'd be appropriate," Frayles suggested. Ellen Kate hesitated, then put the question up. Moments later she got a reply.

"Beta says that there is nothing inherently evil about a corporation, and that each must be judged on its own merits."

"That smells a lot like a Yes," said Peter.

"It might even send a positive message," Ellen Kate said.

"Rember 'Tiz easier to pass a camel through the eye of a needle than to find a virtuous corporation.' " Peter smiled.

Everyone chuckled—and then began to discuss "an unholy variety" of candidates; as Frayles put it, for the Holy Daughter's staff.

"Should we exclude atheists and agnostics?" Karyn asked.

"Might be a good idea," Ellen Kate mumbled.

DAGNAB IDJITS

Hardpan Dotson had never seen the likes of it: all manner of damn fools tearing about in jeeps, raising clouds of dust, stopping here and there to place instruments of some kind on the ground—then, jes' driven' off! Wanting no truck with the likes of crazy people, Hardpan had moved to higher ground, taking refuge in the mouth of a large cave with a few million bats hanging out behind him. From his new vantage point he could look south and behold the great valley spread before him, the sun burnished mountains of the Avawatz range to his right, Kingston Peak rising magenta in the East.

Gazing at the scene below, his mind suddenly made a stunning connection: he was looking down on the very spot where he'd felt the ground tremble under the power of his axe! So that's what made all them dagnab idjits come! He slapped his leg, cackling loudly, astounded once again by his formidable powers of deduction.

*   *   *

Furious over the menace the FBI now posed, Sandovar Abydos ordered that every last thing be removed from his inner office and the floor covered with tarps.

A large air compressor had been hauled to the top of the mountain in one of the Vista Cubes and placed on the great circumferential balcony outside. Long air-hoses snaked into the now empty office, where the Mentor-fused vault peered out from the granite. The only other way to remove it would have been to blast, but being directly below the main dining room, that was out of the question. Jackhammers would have to do.

ABYTOR was closed for the Christmas Holidays and its staff sent home, not scheduled to reopen until January tenth. Only the security force remained on duty. Today, however, Abydos himself was there to observe a contractor with jackhammers.

It was exactly 8:13 a.m when the compressor fired up.

Abydos waited in his outer office and covered his ears. Suddenly a deafening staccato pounded in fury. But after less than a minute all abruptly ceased—and the foreman walked up to Abydos, pulling off his goggles.

"What the Hell kinda rock is that anyway?—we can't make a friggin dent in it!"

THE HALLOWING

Another Archangel tutorial was in progress:

"*...where immediate gratification is ever the rule.*"

"*Humans were making no effort to preserve their planet's finite reserves of fossil fuel—and they have only recently begun to take concern over the gases released into their atmosphere by the burning of such fuels. Protecting their rain forests from destruction has yet to begin in earnest. Some of this world's great rivers and waterways have been cleansed, but many still carry filth and poisons to the sea. Humans exhibit little concern over contaminating their physical bodies—they ingest killing chemicals in a ceaseless quest to perceive pleasure. Large portions of human energy and resources are spent in the pursuit of emotional and physical gratification. Humans willingly place their very lives at risk—so overpowering are their appetites and desires.*

So primitive this world—yet so filled with promise."

*   *   *

Back on Earth a 'miracle' was about to transact.

Dawn spilled dank and humid over an impoverished tribal village in southeast Thailand. A young wife slept fitfully, her drunken husband having been rough on her during the night. The fact that she was ovulating was of less than no concern; having many babies proved a man's virility.

What she could not yet know was that a conception had occurred, and cell division was already well underway. Nor could she know that she would produce conjoined twins.

As she slept—a precise "micro-cision" was performed in utero by a celestial spirit surgical team.

Her sons would be born unto the world separate and healthy.

The Hallowing had begun.

DEAD END

Hy Depkawitz was SAC (special-agent-in-charge) of the shuttle sabotage investigation. He thought they had the break they needed when one of the prime conspirators implicated himself with a careless comment over a cellphone under NSA surveillance. And just like that, the conspirator became vulnerable. Depkawitz hoped he could persuade the Attorney General to offer full immunity, in exchange for the testimony to put Sandovar Abydos in a federal supermax for life.

But the Bureau's opportunity was short-lived; the guy with the answers had somehow managed to topple over the railing of his thirtieth-story Wilshire Blvd. condo—rendering the government's prime witness essentially two-dimensional.

This put everyone back to square one. There was now but one evidentiary avenue left to pursue: Somewhere there had to be a one-of-a-kind radio transmitter, built to send a coded firing command to a detonator aboard an orbiting shuttle.

Now, if old Abydos has any smarts, he'll have already destroyed the incriminating transmitter, Depkawitz reasoned. But then he has one major flaw: he considers himself far too slick to ever get caught—and thus might not feel any necessity to take precautions.

It was the best shot the Bureau had left. And now the questions before them were: One: Where was the transmitter most likely to be hidden?—Two: How could they get their hands on it legally?—and Three: How could they act without tipping off Abydos and giving him time to dispose of the evidence?

Half the office staff and most of the brass had punched out early to get in some last-minute Christmas shopping, but Hy remained at his desk, trying to plumb the warped mind of Sandovar Abydos. His private line rang.

"Depkawitz," he answered.

"Hy, it's Peter Klein at NSC. How you guys coming on the shuttle case?"

285

"Not well. We're back to looking for physical evidence."

"I sure hope something turns up soon—the President very much wants to see some arrests before he leaves office."

"I can understand that, Dr. Klein—but I can't make any promises."

*   *   *

UNITED Flight 1210 was on final approach—gear down and locked—strobe lights below pointing the way to runway twenty-nine—the bright sweep of the airport beacon—taxiways where navigation lights winked patiently. Awesome. To any pilot, the ultimate video game. And now, for a perfect glide—

Everything was textbook smooth. Strictly routine. No hint that disaster was but moments away.

Rolly Scorcone had been drinking since just before sunset. He was sleepy and anxious to get home; the flight home would take twenty-five minutes. He idled impatiently at the end of runway twenty-nine, next in line for takeoff.

His mind was savoring his afternoon of tennis—it wasn't often he beat Carlo by two sets! And the seven-hundred and fifty dollars he'd won off of him?—well, that was sweet.

Using his call sign, he heard the tower say something but too quickly for his clouded mind to catch. Assuming it was his clearance, he mashed the throttles and swung onto twenty-nine.

The UNITED pilot looked ahead in horror—as the twin Beech roared directly into his path. There was no time—

At that moment—a great seraphic hand gently eased the 727 up and over the Beechcraft—at the same time slowing the smaller aircraft with an ultra-dense assemblage of air molecules.

Both planes came to safe stops. While the United pilot was to receive universal praise for his quick actions, the second pilot faced big trouble: Rolly's blood alcohol tested at one point three—his ticket punched before any investigation began.

His freewill choice inside the cockpit had been inviolate, the Hallowing notwithstanding.

*   *   *

The cabinet post which most concerned the President-elect was that of Attorney General. He wanted an innovator. A results-oriented butt-kicker. Someone with the guts to go after any violator of federal law, be it a corporation—a politician—or a connected billionaire.

One candidate caught Onager's attention early on: Luther Kane, Professor of Criminal Law, University of Pennsylvania School of Law. An African-American of high academic stature. Someone the religious right would abhor on sight.

Professor Kane had leveled a controversial broadside at the penal establishment in his book 'The Corrections Misnomer.'

In it he cited the endemic high rates of recidivism, blaming the corrections industry itself for failing to adequately prepare prisoners for reentry into society upon release.

His remedy: education; aptitude-testing; job-training counseling; skilled supervision, and community involvement and assistance; Kane argued that since most prisoners will one day he released; the money spent to prepare them for successful reentry pales against the costs to society and to taxpayers of recidivating criminals.

Despite a PTO forma uproar from Republicans aghast ever the idea of greater federal government spending on criminals, Dave Onager liked what he read and invited Professor Kane to his suite at the Knickerbocker for a private meeting and an exchange of views. The President-elect had given no hint why he wanted the one-on-one.

"Professor, what'll you have? Scotch, Brandy—?" Onager offered.

"No, thank you," Kane smiled, "I'm afraid I don't drink."

"A man after my own heart. I've even given up wine with dinner. Join me in a lime and tonic then?"

"That would be excellent. Incidentally, what do I call you, Sir—'Mr. President-Elect'?"

"How 'bout we make it David and Luther?" Both smiled and nodded. "Luther—I invited you down this afternoon to talk about your becoming our nation's next Attorney General." He watched closely for a reaction.

Kane had figured that perhaps something in the Justice Department might be in the offing—or at the very most a presidential advisership—but never a cabinet post!

"I'm—frankly stunned, Sir. I—never even suspected that—"He composed himself. "It—would of course be a very great honor. But, if I may inquire—why me?"

287

"If I read you right—and your book accurately reflects your beliefs—then I'll be frank to tell you that you're my first choice. And at this point there is no second choice." Onager paused to take a sip. "Tell me, Luther, how do you feel about chemical castration?"

Kane was taken aback. But it was not a new question. "The problem with chemicals is that in order to be effective, the sex-offender requires an on-going series of injections."

"Would you opt then for a—more permanent solution?"

"If a court still had the option of offering surgical castration in lieu of incarceration—as both ultimate sanction and instant rehabilitation— the deterrent value could not be overestimated: most young men would give up their lives before their manhood!"

Onager smiled. "Another hypothetical—if you were anointed the National Gun Czar—what would you do?"

Kane had kept his views on gun ownership private; he was already controversial enough, and saw no gain in compounding things. But then, the next president had asked him directly.

"Well okay—since 'anointed Gun Czar' would presumably not be an elective office, I'll respond apolitically." He paused for a sip of tonic. "First off, I'd outlaw every damn assault weapon! Designed for the military, their entire purpose is to kill wholesale. Then I'd go after handguns: the Bill of Rights never gave individuals a right to own guns—only 'a well-regulated Militia.'"

David Onager hadn't expected so forthright an answer, nor anything so bold. Apolitical was right!

They next turned to the subject of juvenile justice, and talked crime and punishment for the next two hours. By dusk the President-elect knew he wanted Kane to head up Justice.

The professor said he needed to discuss the offer with his wife, and would call with his answer within forty-eight hours. "That'll be plenty soon enough," Onager smiled.

In parting they shook warmly. "I confess—the idea of becoming America's second Afican-American Attorney General does have a certain—historic appeal." Kane chuckled and left.

*   *   *

Finella Bright lived in a sunbaked development on the outskirts of Salt Lake City. She'd bought a small, mustard colored ranch house in 1980, and kept the books at the same law firm for twenty-five years. She'd never married, and there were those at work who claimed she was still a virgin. They were nearly right; only at the age of thirty-nine had she made her sole foray between the sheets. It had been a painful, degrading, and thoroughly distasteful experience. One she never repeated.

From the outside, her little house was distinguished from its neighbors only by the neatness and chromatic vigor of its flowerbeds, all color-coordinated for mustard. Conversely, inside it more resembled a Greenwich Village head-shop than a cottage in the suburbs.

Finella never entertained guests and was thus free to be as bizarre as she liked in her decors. Spending forty hours a week in the black and white world of ledgers, she longed for color. So she had vibrant psychedelic hangings—bright origami beasts—explosions of lurid plastic—festive bursts of day-glow geometric spikes—and multiple tiers of well-dripped candles. Her taste was bordello plush, rendered chromatically vulgar by an ultraviolet lighting scheme.

But to Finella it simply amounted to a beautiful expression of who she really was. Had anyone ever told her that her home looked like a bad-acid hippy crash-pad of the sixties, she'd have been horrified. Not only did she not do drugs, imbibe, curse, or fornicate, she greatly admired the Mormons.

However, she did permit herself one small vice: a secret friend from the spirit world—a personal spirit guide who'd been with her for a dozen years. She called him her Prince of the Night, and fashioned a handsome mental image of him.

The very first time her Prince appeared, she was soaking in her tub, eyes closed and barely awake.

How truly beautiful you are—

She tended to agree—then suddenly realized that the assessment was delivered in a male voice! Her eyes had flown open—but she was alone. Then she heard it again, speaking silently within her mind—!

I'm not just referring to physical aspects.

Am I losing my mind? Am I hallucinating? Finella was truly terrified for the first time in her life.

John VanOrsdell

There's nothing wrong with your mind, my dear. I am a person distinct from you—a spirit being, external to you. Be not afraid; I am come to be your Guide and your Friend.

She snatched up her towel and covered herself hurriedly. "Who are you? What do you want?" she cried aloud.

All your life you've wanted to know the unknowable—well, from now on you'll have me as your access to that great cosmic library, where All is of record.

"Then—tell me something I would want to know," Finella sniffed skeptically, lying back in her tub.

You need to have a mammogram.

One week later a tiny lesion was discovered and promptly excised. In this way, with but a single declaration, the spirit being established his bona fides with Finella Bright.

Over the years a quasi-working relationship developed between the two. Early on, he had tasked her to perform only minor, benign errands—such as firing off impassioned letters to editors demanding civil rights for frozen human embryos, decrying "the Big Brother numbering of newborns," or "allowing the uninformed to vote willy-nilly." Few of her missives were ever published, but this mattered not to her spirit master; it was merely part of her obedience training.

Very few people had Sandovar Abydos' private number. But he'd given it to Finella Bright—to use whenever her spirit associate had Mentor insights for him. It was nearly midnight. Abydos lay in bed watching a NASCAR race when his direct line flashed. He figured it was a wrong number, hit the mute button, snatched up the phone, and snarled "Yes."

"It's Finella, Darling. Hope I'm not calling too late," she breezed, "but I have a Message for you!"

He stiffened excitedly. "I'm listening—"

"Well, it seems that your spirit adversaries have designs on ABYTOR. They apparently want it for their own use!"

"What?" Abydos exploded. "Well, they can't have it!"

"Don't be so sure. I'm told the Mentors can be—highly resourceful. What's more, they seem to be in something of a rush—with a need to take possession by February."

Abydos was flabbergasted. "Like Hell they will! I'll blow it clean off this mountain before I ever let them get their damn paws on it!"

"My goodness. Then perhaps it's time we came up with a plan to foil them, Darling," Finella breathed. She was in the lotus position, facing west, naked but for jewelry—an arrangement of jimson weed smoldering on a tray before her. "I'm afraid that's all I have for you at this time, my dear," she sighed—and hung up softly.

*   *   *

The Mentors weren't the only ones interested in ABYTOR. The elusive international terrorist Fa Haad—who'd already attacked Fort Knox and nearly put the Panama Canal out of business—was now taking aim at ABYTOR; that gleaming discus of stainless steel and glass impaled on a mountain peak.

To Fa Haad, the thousand person, two mile high conference center—and site of the Mentors' only earthly appearance—was the mother of all symbolic targets.

He had but one Soviet-era suitcase bomb left. In nuclear terms, it would produce only the smallest of blasts, but more than enough to obliterate the top of a mountain.

Ironically, his plan to vaporize ABYTOR would also close out his own earthly existence. But with martyrdom and seventy-two virgins as his reward, the ultimate price was a bargain.

The Saturday before Christmas, President and Mrs. Bryce hosted the traditional private dinner and personal tour of the White House Living Quarters for their successors-to-be.

Ellen Kate had purposely not been included. Her parents had no intention of letting their evening with the Onagers devolve into a Mentor Question and Answer soiree.

The dinner would mark the first time the Onager children had been inside the Executive Mansion, and Justin and Penny were duly excited— their teenage friends already angling for sleep-over invites once the Onagers took over.

Dinner was Christmas Goose Newfoundland-style, seasoned to perfection. Stewards whispered in and out also offering platters of equally perfect vegetables. Justin and his sister were thrilled; they couldn't wait to move in.

Sam Bryce and Dave Onager—erstwhile Senate colleagues and lasting personal friends—meant that tonight would bear none of the tensions customary whenever the White House was being turned over to the opposition. Just the opposite; everyone felt very merry and laughed often and loud.

Over dessert Penny had a question for the First Lady. "In the course of a year—how many times you figure you're forced to eat dinner with someone you simply cannot stand?"

The President was clearly entertained by the question.

Amused herself, Abby took a few moments to compose a worthy response. She liked Penny already.

"Six and a half; one was only married to an asshole."

Everyone cracked up, Penny beamed, and a steward serving huckleberry compote broke into a very unprofessional grin.

Later, following their tour, everyone settled in the Puce Parlor, as Bryce had dubbed it. Rum Toddies for the adults, hot cider for the kids.

"Mr. President—" Justin ventured, "how do you feel about your daughter being named by the Mentors as their Official Spokesperson?" It was the dreaded subject.

The Onagers knew nothing of The Seven, let alone that both their hosts were members. Bryce responded guardedly. "I'm—very proud. Katie has taken on a great personal burden and responsibility. But she did so willingly, with her eyes open. Her mother and I are both very proud." It was all he would say and changed the topic. "So tell me, Justin—just what do you plan as your major in college?" From the expressions on several Onager faces, Bryce knew he too had raised another best-to-be-avoided subject.

"I've—been thinking about taking a government job—instead of wasting time in college."

Bryce was taken aback. "What kind of government job?" His own expression now matched that of the Onagers.

"Actually—I'm told there are several agencies looking for what they call Super-Hackers. I'm told I qualify."

"Most impressive, I suppose." Bryce turned to Onager. "So, Dave—what's your position on all this?"

Onager smiled and sipped his rum. "I suppose—I too should feel like a proud parent: excellent starting pay-grade, job security—great bennies—" He looked directly at Justin. "What I'm really saying is, I'd have no moral right to block his hiring—though I'd far prefer he went to college. Those agencies will still be hiring in four years—"

"I know, Dad—but that's four years I'd have to spend with my nose stuck in books, memorizing meaningless facts."

Bryce jumped in. "Justin, may I make a suggestion? How 'bout I ask Ellen Kate to run it by one of the Mentors? She might get some very high level advice for you. Interested?"

He pondered this a bit, then shrugged. "Sure. Long as I'm free to ignore it."

*   *   *

Art Frayles had been given the responsibility of finding and recruiting the Holy Daughter's top staff. Filling most positions should pose no great problem, but finding the right chief of security was another matter.

Frayles knew what he wanted—he just had no idea where to look for it. It was Karyn DeLeo who came up with the best suggestion: "Find someone who's handled security for some big theme park." And he'd proceeded to do just that.

The candidate he liked best was Tony Silvagio, a retired Philadelphia police captain currently safeguarding the Isle of Atlantis theme park outside Atlanta. They'd be meeting in a suite at Washington's posh Hotel Condor. Capt. Silvagio turned out to be very swarthy, with hooded, miss-nothing eyes. The two exchanged a single handshake.

"Coffee?" Frayles offered.

"No, thank you." His voice resonated like a bass drum.

"I want you to know I appreciate your coming, Tony. And as I indicated on the phone—it's related to the Mentors."

"That's the main reason I'm here. That, and the first-class plane ticket, which told me you're serious."

"Serious as a radiation leak." Frayles packed a fresh bowl into his pipe. "You believe in God, Mr. Silvagio?" His guest gave a small shrug. "Let me put it another way: Do you believe you'll survive physical death—in some form?"

This one he liked better. "Yeah. Probably. Why?"

"We're looking for someone to take responsibility for the security and personal safety of the Daughter of the Creative Spirit while she's with us here on earth." He watched the hoods widen—and widen. Now for the tough part it has to be accomplished without weapons of any kind."

"You're shittin' me."

"I shit you not. Are you interested in discussing it further?"

"Where's She gonna be—in one place, or on the road?"

"We don't know yet. Or even how soon the Holy Daughter will arrive—or how long She'll remain among us. We were only told, 'Her hour draws near.'"

"How big a place we talkin' about? Or haven't they told you that either?"

"Based on what we do know, it will be an isolated site, somewhere in the United States." He lit his pipe. "Job pays eleven grand a month, benefits and full expenses."

"Is that an offer?"

"Only if you can show us how you'd go about assuring Her safety without using weapons—in principle that is, even without knowing what the precise physical environment will be. Feel like taking a whack at that one, Mr. Silvagio?"

Tony weighed the challenge. "How long have I got?" he finally asked. "I'd need some time."

"How much exactly?"

"Gimme a week—if I can't figure out something by then, you got the wrong guy."

"One week then."

Silvagio eased his frame out the door—appearing to Frayles like a linebacker wearing a sport coat over his shoulder pads.

He had a good feeling about this guy.

*   *   *

NEO-NAZI MARCH BESIEGED BY FLIES! Stuttgart—A downtown march by two-hundred Neo-Nazi demonstrators ended abruptly today as swarms of flies descended on the marchers, delighting onlookers. Swatting and cursing, the marchers broke ranks and ran off in disarray.

None suspected that the strange aroma which had attracted the flies was part of the Hallowing.

MEGA-VIRUS

Felix Hyle-Rothmann Bleuss IV was the two-hundred and sixty-second richest man on earth—he and the two-hundred and sixty-one men ahead of him having more combined wealth than the poorest two billion people of the world.

Bleuss Pharmaceutical of Zurich was world-renowned in the field of viral research and development, manufacturing and marketing worldwide a line of highly profitable vaccines for humans. Founded in 1944 by the late Felix H-R Bleuss III, Nobel Laureate microbiologist, the firm prospered greatly during the years of the rebuilding of Europe. But, while the firm's founder was driven by the desire to heal, his son and heir was driven solely by a passion for wealth and power.

Over the second half of the twentieth century, the races of the earth slowly degraded their own disease-fighting immune systems through the overuse of antibiotics and prolonged exposure to a toxic and biologically hostile environment—thereby becoming increasingly vulnerable to attack by newly evolving super-viruses—against which Man has no defense.

Bleuss Pharmaceutical was a wholly family-owned business, with a shared abhorrence of outside scrutiny. Accordingly, while its products were subject to government regulation, its stock was not, as it was traded on no exchange.

That was soon to change—providing the surviving and controlling heir was able to pull off his scheme to spin off a newly created subsidiary and make the first public offering of its stock. Meaning that, shortly after that momentous trading day Felix IV would become a far bigger billionaire.

In 1998 he had hand-picked an elite research task force, charged with designing a super-virus—against which early vaccination would be the only possible defense. Being funded as 'Basic Research,' its members could look upon themselves as true scientific pioneers. Every task force member was required to sign a Confidentiality Agreement, entailing such severe sanctions for disclosure that no signer would dare confide anything to anyone, even a spouse. Code-named Upsilon Epsilon, the project was assigned an open budget.

In April of 2002 they triumphed: Mega∞ Virus was born.

IT WAS AIRBORNE, BUT COULD SURVIVE
IN THE OPEN AIR JUST UNDER FOUR
MINUTES; IT COULD SURVIVE IN A FROZEN
STATE FOR DECADES; IT WAS
UNIVERSALLY COMMUNICABLE; AND
FOLLOWING EXPOSURE, IT WAS ONE-
HUNDRED PERCENT LETHAL.

Upsilon Epsilon stood for Universal Epidemic.

*   *   *

Sandovar Abydos lived in the grander of the two owners' suites at ABYTOR. His son Epizutus (Zooti) occupied the smaller one.

It was Christmas Eve and the two men celebrated alone. They had the Sky Lounge to themselves, save for a lonely bartender and waiter, both on triple-time. Swirls of driving snow lashed at the large canted windows, and Abydos ordered the great circumferential curtain drawn. Inside, everything became still—The Pines of Rome played softly. An unopened magnum of champagne rested in melting ice.

"They got me ass-up over a barrel" the old man hissed, careful the bartender did not overhear." Those God damn Mentors told me to my face—they'd un-fuse the vault should the FBI ever come looking for those transmitters! They're blackmailing me: their price for not ratting me out could be turning this whole place over to them! So what the Hell do I do?"

His son had been giving the problem some thought. "You remember that blowhard hotel turd from New York—the one who came to the Exponential Growth Symposium last spring? He told me, should we ever decide to sell—to call him first."

"Nichols."

"Yeah, that's him. You know—we could walk away with a bundle! Don't forget, the Mentors chose ABYTOR as the party they wanted to crash—and now the whole damn world wants to come for a visit! Running it as a hotel, Nichols could clean up—he's smart enough to know it. Might even go five billion! But the best part is—you sell it, and then the Mentors would have to deal with him!"

"That'd be nine times what it cost—" Sandovar calculated.

"Hey, the bigger the ticket, the higher the markup," his son grinned. Zooti could see he had his father's attention. "But, we gotta move fast."

* * *

Jean-Piet was the rogue of the Bleuss clan. Being Swiss, and possessing a keen appetite for intrigue, he'd served as a well paid informant for governments on both sides of the Iron Curtain. He'd even participated directly in several covert adventures—one time actually being arrested and photographed in handcuffs. Over the years he maintained his best contacts—and to this day was always up for a good caper.

Jean-Piet was a chronic concern and occasional embarrassment to the House of Bleuss—and seldom invited to family gatherings. Yet it was to his rogue cousin that Felix turned when he needed someone he could rely on to undertake and prosecute his scheme. The lure of adventure aside, the cash payment would be substantial, even by Bleuss standards—and Felix happened to learn that there was a certain executive jet that Jean-Piet craved, but could not afford.

They met secretly aboard one of Felix's lesser yachts, riding at anchor off the Cote d'Azur. Their meeting lasted six hours, and when Jean-Piet left just after sunset, his mind had already settled on precisely the operative he needed—a certain Serb sociopath who viewed killing as an art form.

* * *

Hardpan Dotson sneaked down from his cave after all the scientific types had left, to have a look-see at all their fancy instruments—which he'd already figured out must be for detecting and recording earthquakes. Hardpan decided to have a little fun.

He tip-toed up to the nearest seismograph—and began a wild gum boot dance on the ground around it.

* * *

Ellen Kate lay in bed next to Peter. He was in a deep sleep, while her eyes remained open and fixed on the ceiling. She was in mental dialog with Beta.

John VanOrsdell
I'm starting to worry about Karyn—should I?
No. She was chosen most carefully. Her courage and her commitment are unquestioned. She is profoundly Good.

She's afraid she won't be up to whatever might be asked of her.
That's ironic—because it is she who has been chosen to sit at the right hand of the Holy Daughter.

Ellen Kate was stunned. When—is she to be told?
The Holy Daughter Herself will announce the Investiture.

*　　*　　*

Sgt. Frank Logan thumbed through the Monday morning tabulations of Pittsburgh's weekend arrest reports. Something was very wrong—!

DOMESTIC ABUSE—DOWN FIFTY-SIX PERCENT

ASSAULT—DOWN FORTY-ONE PERCENT

RAPE—DOWN FORTY-THREE PERCENT

HOMICIDE—DOWN FORTY-EIGHT PERCENT

ROAD RAGE—DOWN EIGHTY-THREE PERCENT

Something was definitely haywire.

CELESTIA

Geoffrey Greaver had been appointed to the federal bench by President Carter, and consequently had prolonged exposure to government shenanigans. He fingered the search warrant before him,

298

well aware of its explosive potential. Yet he'd known Hy Depkawitz for many years, and had come to trust him.

Agent Depkawitz sat before him, legs crossed, waiting patiently. A late afternoon sun peered through the drapes, doing little to dispel the opaque gloom of Judge Greaver's chambers. He looked up from the warrant and peered over his glasses, the smoke from his cigarette snaking up around him.

"You firmly believe Sandovar Abydos is the prime mover behind the shuttle sabotage scheme—and now you want to tear ABYTOR apart looking for the evidence to prove it—"

"No, Judge—Only his living quarters and office."

"And what exactly do you have that convinces you such evidence exists?"

Depkawitz uncrossed his legs. "We—have a Reliable Source, Your Honor."

"Not good enough. Not this time." Greaver leaned closer and fixed Depkawitz with his gaze. "Who precisely is your informant?"

Hy had suspected it would come to this, and shifted in his chair. "Yesterday I received a call from Peter Klein, a high level NSC staffer at the White House, informing me Ellen Kate Bryce had received a communication from the Mentors—" he referred to his notes—"The exact words were: 'In the furtherance of justice, know that the physical evidence you seek does exist, and remains proximate to its owner.'"

"Your Reliable Source is—a Mentor?" He pushed back in his chair and scowled darkly at the warrant on his desk, trying to imagine how an appellate review might go. Finally be picked up his pen and signed with a flourish. "Well, if a Mentor can't be regarded as 'reliable' in the eyes of the law then who the Hell can?"

*   *   *

On January second President-Elect Onager held a press conference to announce his cabinet selections and present the nominees. All were regarded as excellent choices, but two of the nominees generated considerable interest and comment:

Luther Kane, nominated to become the nation's second Afro-American Attorney General—and soon-to-be Former President Samuel Bryce, nominated to be the next Ambassador to China.

Confirmation hearings would begin at once. The Chairman of the Judiciary Committee, a true Son of the South, pledged piously that "racial considerations will in no way be a part of the process." He then added, "However, I can't imagine that the confirmation of a sitting President wouldn't sail right through!"

*   *   *

At 7:00 a.m. the morning of January third, the FBI descended (more accurately ascended) upon ABYTOR, search warrants in hand. Abydos was horrified, suddenly afraid that the Mentors now wanted to see him in jail—and would unseal the vault! How that would help them acquire ABYTOR he couldn't imagine; the Feds would be offering DO deals.

Zooti too was horrified—because he alone knew what was locked inside his own compartment within the vault. He'd never even informed his father. And that was whom he feared now—far more than the FBI.

Seeing agents heading for his father's suite and offices, Zooti realized he'd better get the Hell out of there. He slipped into an elevator, pushed G, and began to descend. Moments later he stepped into Thor's Grotto—ABYTOR's famous 'bottomless swimming crevasse,' whose underwater side-lights became swallowed up by the depths.

What no employee knew, and no blueprint showed, was that when the crevasse was originally closed off, a small drainable compartment with doors like a diving lock was built into the base of the dam—to afford one last means of escape in the event of a disaster. The outside door opened into the crevasse itself, which in turn offered another way down the mountain by a series of knotted ropes.

Careful to leave behind no sign of his departure, Zooti dove into the water—clothes, shoes, credit cards and all—and swam for the bottom.

Meanwhile FBI agents discovered the secret vault built into the mountain's core in Abydos' inner office. "Open it," Depkawitz ordered. Abydos hesitated. Depkawitz sighed. "Or be declared in contempt of court and placed under arrest," he added, reaching for the handcuffs on his belt.

Abydos had no idea whether or not the vault door would remain fused. If it were, he knew the Feds wouldn't be able to get into it any more than he had been. It was a fearsome gamble. Sweat beading his brow, he reached for the combination dial. After three failed attempts,

300

there was a click. He swung the door open—revealing two locked interior compartments.

"Open them," Depkawitz directed.

"One—belongs to my son. I don't have the key."

"Then just open yours—we can break into his."

Visibly shaking, Abydos complied—and exposed the two radio transmitters. Eyes dancing, Depkawitz donned gloves and carefully removed them, depositing each in an evidence bag which he sealed and marked. He looked over at Abydos, slumped on the floor. "Gee, I wonder what these could be?"

But it wasn't until the door to Zooti's compartment was breeched that Abydos began to shake; inside, agents found two tightly taped kilos of pure uncut crystal cocaine! Depkawitz instantly realized that legally, they could now confiscate the whole damn place—*and ABYTOR itself would become the property of the United States Government!'*

"Find his son," Depkawitz ordered. "And call in the Marshals." At 8:51 a.m. both DEA and the U.S. Marshal Service were notified.

Agents immediately fanned out, spending the next two hours searching every nook and cranny for Epizutus Abydos. But Zooti had made good his escape—and at 10:40 a.m. was declared a federal fugitive.

*   *   *

The following afternoon Sandovar Abydos was arraigned before Judge Greaver and charged with Treason (four counts), Murder (three counts), Attempted Murder, Sabotage, and Conspiracy.

"Waive the reading, Your Honor," defense counsel Irying Weiss intoned mechanically, "and enter a plea of Not Guilty." His client, still reeling at the loss of ABYTOR, sat numb.

"Your Honor, the Government asks that the defendant be remanded," Assistant U.S. Attorney Robert McBrierty declared forcefully. "Mr. Abydos is charged with multiple capital offenses. He has virtually unlimited resources at his disposal and is considered an extremely high flight risk."

"My client has no criminal record—strong ties to the community—and an outstanding international reputation. And I should add—absolutely no involvement whatever in the criminal enterprise with which he is charged."

"The Court stands greatly reassured," growled Greaver. "However, the extreme seriousness of the crimes with which he's charged could provide your client with ample motivation for flight to escape prosecution—"

"Your Honor, Mr. Abydos will gladly surrender his passport. Furthermore—"

"And have a false one in twenty-four hours!" exclaimed McBrierty.

Judge Greaver held up a hand to silence both sides. He removed his glasses and slowly kneaded the sides of his nose. His thick white hair was the brightest thing in the court. "The defendant will be held without bail. Additionally, Mr. Abydos is ordered to undergo full psychiatric examination by court-appointed physicians. This Court intends to make certain that everyone knows exactly what we're dealing with. Lastly, I'm imposing an all-parties Gag Order—there being serious national security matters at issue, according to the indictment." He put his glasses back on and scowled down.

"Furthermore—the media's going to be all over this one once word gets out—and I don't want anyone peeing in the jury pool!"

The court stenographer, her hair drawn back in a tight bun, gave a cluck of disapproval.

*   *   *

It was cold with a light snow falling, as the Ames school bus drove slowly down River Road, twenty-nine merry children happy to be headed home. The sun was already low and traffic was light. Paul Turndorf had been driving this route for nearly thirty years and knew every pothole and rut. He squinted ahead, the wipers sweeping the snow aside before it could freeze to the glass.

Suddenly a white-tailed buck bolted from the woods, saw the bus bearing down, and froze in the middle of the road. Turndorf knew hitting the brakes could throw the bus into a skid—so his reflex was to steer around the deer. But there was not quite enough room. The right front tire dropped off the lip of the blacktop and bit into the snow, spinning the bus to the right.

Turndorf tried desperately to get back onto the pavement, but they were already sliding farther off the road, heading down a slope toward the slowly moving river. The children began to scream and panic. He tried to brake—but all the wheels locked up and the slow slide continued. He stared at the water ahead—It looked mighty deep—

Then—a miracle: With a great boom of crystallization, the river before them instantly froze solid. The bus slid out onto the ice—and came to a stop.

Several children would later swear that they had heard the singing of angels.

GSA

This was one message Ellen Kate felt obliged to deliver to her father in person. She was shown into the Oval Office.

"Hi, Kid." They hugged warmly. "Now, what's so urgent? It's not that I'm not always grateful for whatever brings you. Your Mom and I don't get to see nearly enough of you, or our grandson, these days. My fault entirely—but in two weeks I'll be outta here. Then we're gonna take a short vacation before leaving for Beijing—part of which we hope to spend with you and Josh."

"And Peter."

"And Peter," he amended. They sat on the couch. "So, what's up? You said on the phone it was Seven business."

Ellen Kate drew a deep breath, then began: "Beta informs me that ABYTOR has been selected as the site of the Holy Daughter's dwelling place while here on earth. It'll also be Her operational headquarters, and house Her staff."

"I can see why. It's not only large, comfortable, and fully equipped—it's inherently safe, perched atop a mountain Only problem is—it now belongs to the DEA."

He thought some more and brightened. "I'll have the Attorney General direct that it be turned over to the General Services Administration as an asset, pending disposal. There will be a stink, but I'll make it my final Executive Order—and they can take up any complaints with my successor." He reflected a bit further. "And, while the GSA is assessing it and trying to decide what to do with it, the Mentors will be free to use it. I'll make that the last part of my Order."

"Beta also feels it would be best if The Seven—minus you and Mom—moved up there too. I'm not exactly thrilled at the prospect, but I guess we can manage it. Peter'll join us on weekends. Any problem with that?"

"You might check with Dave, but if it's what the Mentors want— When do they want you all to take possession?"

"Sooner the better. There's a lot of preparation work ahead of us. And are you ready for this?—among a host of other things, we have to pick out an entire wardrobe for the Holy Daughter! I don't know where to begin."

"L.L. Bean—?"

She suddenly laughed. "Peter suggested the exact same thing—and says Bean's got some 'divine hiking boots'!" They shared a chuckle. "Hey, with all the excitement. I forgot to tell ya: Peter and I have set a date: March twentieth, first day of Spring. But if you can't postpone your departure for Beijing until after then, we'll just move it up."

Bryce beamed "Hey—even if we're already in China, we'll fly back for the wedding—we sure can't miss our only daughter's big day!"

"Mom upstairs?" Ellen Kate grinned.

"I think so. Go on up and tell her yourself. And ask how she feels about you and Josh living at ABYTOR."

* * *

Dave Onager was working late on his Inaugural Address. It was well past midnight and Jane was long asleep.

It was his fifth draft, and not going well. He was struggling to be both inspirational and challenging without sounding preachy and judgmental. However, his real problem was with content—Just how much can people accept?

How hard can I hit them? Dare I reveal how far I'm prepared to go? Cold Turkey farms for addicts!—Outlaw most guns! —Cash incentives for sterilization!—No drivers under eighteen. No vehicles over three-thousand pounds!—Triple our aid to the third world!—Protect the rain forests at all costs! Hell, I go saying all that, I'll wind up—expunged!

GOD SPEED

The tutorials were now complete, and the Holy Daughter was about to receive her formal Incarnation Precepts from a High Magisterial Archon:

Upon Your departure, You will vest Your Authority in the hands of Your Spiritual Vicegerent—not to be resumed until Your one day return. While in the likeness of mortal flesh You will retain all of Your divine powers—and are free to use them as You Will. All that You Will, Will Be.

As You have chosen—You will Incarnate as an adult female embracing the combined genetic heritage of all the mortal races.

You are enjoined from any physical liaison with a member of the mortal races—any act of procreation being proscribed.

The duration of Your Visitation is for You alone to determine. Physical death can take place only if such is Your wish.

Know that the entire Seraphic Government of this planet stands at Your Service. Your deeds will be set to record—while an on-looking Universe bends close in adoration.

All the Universe salutes You. Your Divine Family embraces you—and will bear watch over Your affairs until Your return.

May success crown Your holy undertakings!

May joyous be Your way!

ANGELESIS

Karyn DeLeo had been designated treasurer of The Seven, and opened a modest office in Alexandria. A few well-placed calls had brought in sufficient donations to enable The Seven to hire a secretary and begin operations.

The phones rang continuously, the FAX never stopped printing, and the e-mail poured in—as everyone from the clergy, artists, and journalists—to academics, contributors, volunteers, and well-wishers, sought to communicate.

Karyn took the important calls, but gave no interviews. She disclosed nothing concerning The Seven nor the Angelesis, instead limiting comment to the celestial happenings at ABYTOR and their significance for the planet. She confirmed that Ellen Kate Bryce had frequent dialog with the Mentors, and reported that nothing had as yet been given to her to pass along to the world.

One visitor she received would change her life.

Carl 'Rusty' Steele was a noted documentary filmmaker acclaimed for his Emmy-winning PBS special, The Corporate Counterculture, and documentaries on the population bomb. Karyn agreed to meet to discuss a film of the Incarnation.

She was unprepared for the sensual surge she experienced as he walked through her door—and would later describe it to Ellen Kate as "a near-compulsion to peel and pounce."

"Hi, Karyn, Rusty Steele." He thrust out his hand and she took it. For a moment the two just stood there.

"It's—a pleasure to meet you, Rusty. I'm a great admirer of your work. Have a seat. Care for some juice?"

"Only if it's nonfat," he smiled.

She shot him a look, then poured the juice. "You said on the phone you think it's historically important that we film an 'appropriately reverential' record of the Holy Daughter's sojourn among us." She handed him the juice and sat down. "We agree. But of course you're not the first to propose making a documentary of Her Incarnation.

Can you elaborate on what you mean by 'appropriately reverential?'"

"Simply this: If She is Divine, then I think it highly appropriate to be reverential. I damn sure will be!" He sipped his juice, fixing her with his eyes.

She studied him a bit before replying. "Yeah. Me too."

"Do you know yet where the Incarnation will take place?"

"All I'm permitted to say is 'somewhere in the United States.' And that She might remain with us for 'many months.' Would you be prepared to forsake everything else—for the entire time She's here?"

"To be in the actual presence of a Deity, whether a Him or a Her? Hey, as long as out-of-pocket filming costs are covered, it's a no-brainer: Of course I would. Gladly."

"And, would you insist on an exclusive?"

"I would insist only that all net proceeds from my film be signed over to an appropriate foundation."

"Clearly, if you're the one we select, it'd mean you'd be required to live at Her headquarters. But just you and your film crew. In other words, no family. Are you married?" She'd tried to make it sound business-like, but knew by the tiny smile on his lips that she'd failed.

"Nope."

*   *   *

The President-elect needed to spend time with his wife. He hastily cleared his Must Call list and invited her up to his suite at the Knickerbocker for a private dinner—and hopefully the entire night. He'd been working flat-out since Christmas, and was stressed, exhausted, and dying for a quiet evening alone with Jane.

Yet it would prove anything but relaxing. What he needed most was someone to whom he could vent his deepest political-spiritual feelings., and that was Jane—the one person he could depend on to let him know when he was over-the-top, and to veto those things he should never say in public.

Before they'd made it through the veal, he started in. She instantly switched to Sounding Board mode.

"Damn it all, Jane—a way needs to be found to compel corporations to put the public interest ahead of shareholder interest. Now that's rank free-enterprise heresy, I know. Nonetheless, it's the way it ought to be. And I see it as our solemn spiritual duty to do everything we can to bring about that one fundamental change."

He looked at her, hungry for a reaction, and sensed she wasn't buying in.

"You go attacking the corporate power structure in this country, and you can count on a savage counter attack! These CEO types play rough. They can destroy you, your presidency, and your place in history, should they decide you pose a real and present danger. What's more, they could sabotage every piece of legislation you want. And you should know it."

"But what if the Mentors were to urge passage of certain bills? That's one lobby they'd have to listen to!"

She put down her fork, picked up a hard roll, and bounced it off his forehead. "What makes you think the Mentors would become lobbyists

307

for you? And if they didn't support you, you'd be left twisting in the wind all by yourself! Is that a risk you're prepared to take?"

"Of course not. Before proposing any bill, I'd need assurances that the Mentors would back my play." He sliced off a wedge of veal, bathed it in juice, and chewed thoughtfully. "The larger issue, of course, is the attenuation of power-from the top all the way down."

"Money is power. You're talking about redistributing the wealth again, aren't you?"

"No—more like 'Resource Reapportionment.'"

"If that's supposed to be a battle cry, it sucks."

He sighed. "I don't know why I have to be insulted by the only person to get in tonight to see the President-Erect." He watched to see if she caught it; she did.

"Hey, that's no big deal—take it from me."

He acknowledged her pun with a smile. Then he turned serious. "Look—when the Holy Daughter arrives, it's going to have an incalculable impact. And as head of the host government, I can't simply go on as if it's business as usual; I have to either actively support Her efforts—or completely ignore Her presence. There's no middle ground. And were I to support Her on some issues while opposing Her on others, the critics would say I consider my judgment superior to that of a Deity!"

"Then—you plan to support Her, no matter what?"

"More of a parallel thing—a political manifestation of spiritual values, if you will. In essence a re-prioritization of government itself. Something along the lines of a Nonsectarian Theocracy."

*   *   *

That evening the Flyers beat the Bruins four to three. But many fans felt cheated; there was not one fight the entire match. A hockey first.

*   *   *

On January eighteenth President Bryce notified The Seven that ABYTOR was officially theirs. U.S. Marshals would remain in place only until a new security force arrived to take over.

Apart from records, documents, and evidence relating to the pending criminal charges, nothing had been removed from ABYTOR. Even the freezers remained well stocked.

The hand-over of ABYTOR was the closing act of the Bryce Administration—one which gave the outgoing chief executive enormous personal satisfaction.

Their final night in the White House, the First Family gathered to dine one last time. To mark the occasion the President had ordered fresh-caught two-pound hard-shell lobsters flown down from Maine. The butter-dripping crustacean was a new taste experience for Josh—one he found close to gross.

"Congratulations on your swift confirmation, Daddy. When do you guys plan to leave for China?"

"Shortly after the wedding," Abby said. "That'll leave us time to attend a couple of your Seven meetings. But we'll most likely be back for a visit in June or maybe July."

"Depending how we like the food there," Bryce cracked.

"Incidentally—"Ellen Kate grunted, wrestling with a crusher claw, "We've been told when the Holy Daughter will arrive: February twenty-first—somewhere just west of ABYTOR."

"Meaning Utah?"

"Who knows?" she chewed. "Some place without lobster."

"By the way, I was informed that you've discontinued your Secret Service protection. You think that's wise?"

"I won't need them where we will be. My seraphim will do just fine."

PART THREE

CELESTIA

INAUGURATIONDAY

Inauguration Day broke bright, clear, and cold. There'd been hope for a fresh snow, but Washington still awaited its first flakes of winter. The newly constructed Inaugural stand blazed white under the sun—flags snapping smartly in the wind—and an overflow crowd stamped in to warm its feet.

Dov Bakar had created special lemon and peach outfits for Jane Onager and her fifteen-year old daughter dubbed "smashing" by the press. They sat beaming in the second row alongside Justin, who was wearing the same suit he'd worn to the White House dinner with the Bryces. But he'd shaved. Twice.

The President, Mrs. Bryce, and Ellen Kate sat across the aisle, Peter and Josh next to them. The President and the President-elect wore traditional mourning clothes.

The cameras of an entire world witnessed the Taking of the Oath—administered by the Chief Justice and repeated in a firm voice by David Esmond Onager, who with a few short words became the most powerful leader on earth.

When the cheering finally subsided and the waving ended, President David Onager took to the podium and delivered his Inaugural Address:

"People of Earth: Great Works lie before us—and only by keeping God's light burning bright within our hearts can we prevail." The Address took thirty-three minutes, and ended with a demand: "Every citizen of this precious, exquisite, imperiled world must now place planetary gain ahead of personal gain." He glared at the crowd. "It's been revealed that a Universe Deity on an emergency mission is soon to arrive. She comes to save us from ourselves! How far from the paths of righteousness must we have strayed!

The crowd was stunned. Early on, it had interrupted with repeated applause. But as President Onager continued to speak, it had quieted and turned reflective.

It wasn't an Inaugural Address—it was an Invocation.

By the time the new First Family made the rounds of all seven Inaugural Balls, opinion of Onager's Address ranged from Inspirational

311

and Uplifting to Sanctimonious and Humiliating. ABC called it "a clarion summons for the best in all of us," CNN ran its clip of the new President calling on mankind to "Make manifest a world worthy of a Divine Visitation," while CNBC disparaged it as mawkish and inappropriate.

And Onager said he'd spoken from the head and the heart.

* * *

The Bryce family moved out of the Executive Mansion the morning of the nineteenth. In choreography worthy of the Bolshoi, the next day the last closet was filled with Onager family clothing just as the new tenant was being sworn in. Even Justin's computer station was set up and on-line.

Penny bounced into her new bedroom, took one look around, and squealed in delight. Her bedclothes were laid out, and a hot tub burbled merrily in her bath chamber. There was a soft tap at the door—and a pretty young woman wearing a pale almond uniform walked in, smiling shyly.

"Good Evening, Miss Onager—my name is Danielle."

"Hi, I'm Penny—"She thrust out her hand and they shook awkwardly.

"I took the liberty of laying out some clothes for you, and drawing you a tub. I thought you might want to soak for a while after such a tiring day."

Penny flung herself onto the bed and stretched herself out, luxuriating. "Awesome! Think I'm gonna like it here!"

* * *

President Onager spent his first day in meetings, all of which seemed to run long. It was nearly 7:30 p.m. when the new First Family finally sat down to supper.

Penny was in especially bright spirits. "Hey there, Mr. President— how 'bout passing them biscuits?" she giggled.

"They're closer to the First Lady—ask her," he winked.

312

"Hey, Dad—long as you're planning to shake everything up for the better," Justin interrupted, "I got a really big idea for you: A National Dress Code!"

Everyone guffawed. If anyone could be counted on to keep things in perspective, it was Super-Hacker.

Justin had rejected parental pleas to transfer to a very secure, private prep school for the remainder of his senior year, and it had become something of an issue. Jane said she understood her son's desire to "graduate with his friends." But then Penny had reminded everyone that her brother was essentially a loner, "so that argument is bogus." Still, Justin was adamant: No prep school.

"So how'd it go today, Dear—you look bushed," Jane observed.

Her husband lit up at the question. "The first meeting of the new Cabinet was—amazing. The vice president wants me to begin putting into practice the very principles I laid out in my Inaugural. Admiral Gitt actually suggested using the military as the paradigm for a merit-based society—where no one does what they do for money alone, but for the good of all. I have to admit, I was pretty blown away."

There followed an admiring silence. Then Penny broke the spell. "The Veep's a Heap," she declared.

"Now what the Hell's that supposed to mean?" her father challenged.

"In an interview in Teen, he said teenagers are far more interested in 'zits and hickies' than world problems. Well, y-e-a-h—!" she gestured, throwing her arms up.

The President forced back a smile. "He said that? I'll have to speak with him about offending the pre-voters."

Justin snorted appreciatively.

"Penny Dear, when did you want to have that sleep-over for your friends?" Jane switched.

"Whoa! Soon as possible!"

"What about my techno-geek buddies?" Justin shot back.

*   *   *

Tony Silvagio had come up with a hi-tech, imaginative solution for the problem of providing security without guns. Expanding on the principle of the Theremin, he proposed installing passive sonic energy fields in every passageway, so any disturbance would instantly pinpoint an intruder. "A full-time sonic display of the whole place!" he'd crowed.

"And—if someone is detected?" Frayles had queried.

"Then my hand-picked black-belt 'Ushers' close on said intruder(s)—an' take 'em down!"

Being so inherently nonintrusive, the concept greatly appealed to Frayles, who promptly queried the President's new science advisor, who informed him the following day that the concept "might be do-able. But no guarantees."

Frayles brought the matter to The Seven, who were about to take up residence at ABYTOR. Everyone liked Silvagio's idea, and voted to hire him, along with a contractor to put his concept to the test. Meanwhile, they'd go ahead and install a network of laser beams—backed by Tony's squad of the black-belts—to safeguard the sacred mountaintop.

No one needed to be reminded they had less than a month to prepare for the Holy Daughter's arrival.

*   *   *

The Seven's temporary office in Alexandria was closed as of January thirty-first. Except for the Bryces, the other members of The Seven moved into ABYTOR the following week—along with Rusty Steele, Tony Silvagio and his Ushers, plus assorted employees from chefs to chambermaids. Those hired to serve on the Holy Daughter's personal staff would not arrive until the eighteenth.

Fortunately, ABYTOR had been maintained in first-class condition. Plants had been watered daily and everything continuously cleaned, polished, and vacuumed. Crisp sheets covered every bed, the larder was well stocked, and logs stacked by every fireplace. Only alcohol was absent.

The single member of The Seven who had not attended the supernal happenings at ABYTOR was Peter Klein—who now stood on the great circumferential balcony, awed by the sheer grandeur of the place exponentially enhanced by the majesty of snowcapped peaks in every direction.

The evening of the day everyone moved in, Ellen Kate convened The Seven—and announced that their first order of business would be to re-name ABYTOR itself.

"The floor's open for suggestions—" she invited, glancing around the table. As yet, no one had anything to offer.

"Okay then—we'll table that for now. Next: Security. How are we coming on the sonic fields? Has that problem with the humming sound been resolved?"

"Largely. But we're also thinking about piping in soft music to cover it," Frayles reported.

"Good. Uncle Art," Ellen Kate continued, "I forgot to mention, the Mentors are 'well pleased' with your choices for the Holy Daughter's staff. Especially her personal physician, Dr. Tina Marsh—which suggests to me that She will in fact be vulnerable to illness or injury, just like any of the rest of us."

"Wonder if She'll have a sense of humor?" Karyn mused.

"I asked Beta about that a while back. He said, if I can recall, 'Deity is ever the keen appreciator of true humor.'"

"Now there's a sobering thought," Karyn mumbled. Peter overheard and snorted appreciatively.

"Karyn, tell us why you feel it's important to give Rusty Steele the run of the place so early on," Peter asked.

"I believe it's called location scouting. And he's making a film of the Incarnation. I need to spend time with him, to discuss how he'll handle being in the presence of Deity, how he'll remain objective, etc."

"I suspect you'll enjoy taking him through all that," Ellen Kate grinned. Karyn instantly blushed, and everyone laughed. Then she smiled.

"I gotta admit he's not hard to look at."

"You wish," Peter leered. More laughter.

"Ellen Kate, please instruct your lout that we're all charged with keeping clean minds and spirits," Karyn parried.

Frayles was rapidly becoming bored with all this and changed the subject. "Does the Holy Daughter plan to be doing much traveling while She's here? And if so, how?"

"I—don't know," Ellen Kate said. "Good question. Let me put it to Beta—She listened for a moment—then spoke what she heard, as she heard it: 'The Holy Daughter will travel extensively about the planet, utilizing the most secure modes of transit available.'"

"Oh, oh," Frayles grunted, "Then I'd better ask Onager if She'll be offered the use of government aircraft and crews."

"And what about a passport—does—Deity need one?" Peter asked. "If so—maybe a U.N. diplomatic passport?"

With a whole Universe for Her portfolio, Karyn thought.

"Got it!" Frayles suddenly sang out, slapping his leg". The name for this place: C E L E S T I A!"

*　　*　　*

Seismologists had positioned lasers and targets on both sides of the great Garlock Fault to detect even the slightest movement which would indicate a build-up of tectonic stress. But all their targets remained absolutely stationary.

The scientists had no instrumentation capable of detecting the work of the Master Molecular Manipulators—engaged in the lengthy process of parting a massive barrier of sedimentary strata one molecule at a time.

*　　*　　*

Jean-Piet Bleuss and the Serbian operative, code name Voyla, met at a secluded cafe on the outskirts of Vienna, a venue where neither was known. They shared a dimly lit booth and a nasty bottle of schnapps.

"Let me think," pondered Voyla. "The last time we met was in—yes: Interlaken in 1999—the Hauptfleisch File."

"You insisted we meet offshore for the exchange."

"Yes, and on a moonless night," the Serb chuckled. "One can't be too paranoid, you know."

Jean-Piet lit a very thin cigar, peering over the match at Voyla. He lowered his voice. "Would you be willing to put your life at risk for, say—ten-million, American?"

The Serb's eyes widened just a hair. "Ah, so—and just exactly where do you wish to bring about, a regime change?"

"No assassinations. This will be far more demanding. Would you like me to continue?"

"You said, 'risk my life'—how exactly?"

"By having me put out a contract on you, should you ever face imprisonment for something even unrelated." He crushed out the cigar. "Please understand, my friend, I could never risk having you cut a deal."

"Why not simply have me whacked, to eliminate all risk?"

"Because, I intend to pay you most handsomely to maintain your silence: Two million dollars additional, every year for as long as I remain suspicion-free!" He leaned back and closed one eye. "No need whatever to eliminate you; just make certain your ass never lands in prison!"

Voyla fell silent, weighing risk against reward—He could live with the terms of the deal, providing he figured he could pull it off safely. It was time to hear the details of the operation—every last one.

*   *   *

Justin Onager looked over at his sister. They were lying on the floor of her White House bedroom. "All right, then—I think I'll try: Undertakers and Underwear for two-hundred dollars!"

Penny choked back a laugh, toked, and replied, "A famous undertaker-to-the-stars—revealed that this popular singer of the Fifties wore a thong!"

"Who was—Ethel Merman?"

"So sorry. the correct answer is: Who was Mario Lanza?"

They cracked up. They'd gone to Penny's room to smoke some weed, because she'd decided Danielle was cool. Their parents were another matter altogether. They'd been firmly admonished that there was to be no marijuana whatever in the White House—not ever. And each had dutifully promised.

Tonight was their tenth in the Executive Mansion, and they marked it by getting high. They weren't too worried. "What're they gonna do—bust us?" Justin had scoffed, "I don't think so!"

"Hey," he said, leaning in closer, "dig it: I figured out how to hack into the White House mainframe and leave no footprints!" He took a quick hit. "Alarm systems—routing, codes—everybody's pay grade—the works!"

"Wow!"

"Wanna know how much Danielle or anyone else is paid or who uses the shredders—when, and for how long? Or what this place spends each month on booze? Or who trades stock on-line from their office? It's all there!" he whooped.

"Double Wow!"

There was a soft knock at the door, and Danielle entered. She smelled the pot at once and visibly recoiled.

317

"Danielle—" Penny waved her in. "Listen, I—told my brother we could trust you. You are cool, aren't you?"

The young woman was clearly conflicted. "I could lose my job over this," she sagged.

"On the other hand, if you keep our little secret—we would both owe you big time," Justin assured hopefully.

Rattled, Danielle turned to leave. "I—didn't see anything," she sighed, closing the door behind her.

The Onager siblings exchanged High Fives.

*　　*　　*

A light, dry snow had fallen overnight, and the peaks surrounding CELESTIA were afire in the morning sun.

"You actually expect the Holy Daughter to consent to be interviewed?" Karyn asked, her eyes wide. She and Rusty were just finishing breakfast. She sat with her back to the windows to avoid the glare, foregoing winter's extravaganza playing outside. He gazed across the table at her, backlit by the sun—her long, jet-black hair glowing and radiating—making her look like some kind of sexy, Sicilian icon.

"My underlying assumption," he replied, "is that She will want to get Her message out—and that requires taking full advantage of the range of available media." He flashed a smile. "I'm not suggesting I'd ask Her what She sleeps in."

"It's just that I find the idea of asking a Deity to look and speak into a camera—just a tad spiritually offensive. So, if left up to me, I'd say No. Of course, the Holy Daughter might feel differently. In which case—"

He put his elbows on the table and rested his chin on his hands. "Sitting there, like that—you look like some kind of goddess yourself! Maybe it's you I should be interviewing."

Karyn flushed, and smiled awkwardly. "Hardly."

"So—what do you think She'll be like—Demanding? Imperious? Judgmental? Preachy? Unapproachable?—Or warm, sweet, sympathetic, and very approachable?"

Karyn eyed him, tempted to pun—and gave in. "Oh—I imagine She'll be pretty down-to-earth." He chuckled, still awed at the beauty of her particular Eurasian synthesis.

"Okay—what do you suppose She'll look like?" he posed.

"We asked, and were told simply, 'tall and spare.'"

He pondered. "What if She looks like—Michael Bolton?"

Karyn choked, and her coffee sloshed.

"No, seriously." He grew serious. "Maybe, Don Imus?"

By now their senses of humor were busy commingling. It was obvious to each they were thoroughly enjoying each other—and that physical attraction was already in play. Rusty reached over and lay his hand over hers. After a few seconds—to avoid giving offense—she pulled free and stood up.

"Let's go see how the cocktail bar redo is coming along," she invited. "I've never seen a walk-thru terrarium before."

*   *   *

There was no moon, but Voyla had blackened his face. He scanned along the tall cyclone fence with his night-vision binoculars—Nothing. As promised, there was no patrol or so much as a night watchman in evidence—only a single armed guard at the main gate. And he was dozing.

Bleuss Pharmaceutical sat within a sprawling corporate complex. Without a plot plan, Voyla would never have been able to find Building D-15--home of Mega∞ Virus.

Using a small can of metal embrittlement spray, allegedly liberated from a CIA field operative in Germany, he sprayed and removed a small section of fencing, making not a sound.

The next morning the break-in and theft were discovered, to the convincing horror of Felix Bleuss—who lost no time before calling in the authorities.

The Zurich police were on scene in minutes.

"Let me make certain I fully understand you—" Inspector Jimirro began, "this—'Mega-Virus,' as you call it—was genetically developed by your firm as part of basic research into emerging mutational strains of deadly viruses against which Man as yet has no defense." He glared at the chairman of the board. "And now you inform us that someone has stolen point forty-five liters of this 'universally communicable, universally lethal' virus! Is that pretty much it, Dr. Bleuss?"

"Not entirely," he replied. "Although there is no defense against Mega-Virus itself, there does exist a means of prevention: We've derived from it a safe, effective, dead-virus vaccine for humans—which we could put into immediate production should the need arise. What—ever could be the motive behind such a crime, Inspector—"

Jimirro stuffed his hands into his pockets and shrugged. "Two possibilities: Terrorists or Extortionists. If it's the latter, they'll contact you to arrange for a buy-back." He began to pace. "You say they only stole one-quarter of your total supply—why do you suppose they left so much behind?"

"Inspector, it would require but a few drops to unleash a worldwide epidemic. They stole more than enough to bring an end to civilization as we know it."

*   *   *

Ellen Kate was taking her morning shower. Josh was sound asleep, and his father was still in Washington. She just loved long showers. It was where she did some of her best thinking.

She felt a sudden urge to speak with Beta, and wondered whether he'd just summoned her. She turned off the water, wrapped herself in a terry robe, and sat down in front of the mirror. Beta, is there something you want to say to me?

Good Morning, Ellen Kate. I'm sorry for interrupting you, but there is something which we are authorizing you to have Karyn announce.

Do I need to get paper?

No. Simply announce the underground coal-mine fire burning for decades beneath the abandoned village of Centralia, Pennsylvania, has been extinguished in order to preserve fossil fuel.

Is this—part of the Hallowing?

Yes. But reveal that to no one outside The Seven.

*   *   *

Peter was phoning from his West Wing office; that meant it had to be something official.

"Hey there," Ellen Kate greeted, "and how's our national security doin' this morning?"

"Well, you know—Some days you bite the Boss—some days the Boss bites you."

"You sound boss-bit."

320

"Oh, he's just a little pissed about not getting a heads-up on the Centralia announcement, to give him time to frame a response. Asked me to call you and convey his distress."

"That so? Well convey this: 'Mentors do not give mortals political briefings.' Use just those words, Gummy Bear. Your boss seems to have been getting a bit uppity of late. And tell him, next time, call me himself. I don't appreciate him using you as a go-between."

"Now who's getting uppity?" he chuckled.

Ellen Kate thought it over and realized Peter was right. "Okay, leave out the 'Call me yourself' part."

"Josh awake yet?" he switched.

"No. It's only six here, you know."

"I know, but I figured you'd be up. I miss you."

"Me too. You still coming Friday?"

"Count on it."

*　　*　　*

Finella Bright had a vacation coming, and her spirit buddy suggested she rent a camper for a trip into the desert. She had balked, having no wish to pee behind boulders or into a holding tank someone would have to empty later. But her spirit had told her that she should do as he asked, "If you wish to bear witness to a cosmic event."

So she rented a camper, packed it full of organic food and drink, and headed south on Interstate 15.

*　　*　　*

That evening, following an hour of star-gazing from CELESTIA's great circumferential balcony—huddled together against an icy wind—and then huddled together in front of a warming fire, Karyn and Rusty finally made love.

*　　*　　*

Zooti Abydos had taken refuge in Cuba, where he owned a hidden interest in a Havana computer service company. With Cuba still technologically stuck in the 1950s, and struggling to catch up, Computer Service was a business in boom. Having made all the right pay-offs over the years, Zooti was now a welcome resident. And he was content. He lived well, had all the women he wanted—and full government protection against arrest by the FBI or the DEA. Life was good.

Meanwhile, his father had lost both ABYTOR and his freedom. What's more, both were permanent conditions.

Zooti tried not to think about it.

*   *   *

The Assistant U.S. Attorney assigned to prosecute the KAPPA ONE defendants wanted badly to nail Sandovar Abydos.

Marcus 'Mark' Polan would be going up against a dozen of the sharpest defense lawyers money could buy—yet he fully expected to be the only one standing when the dust cleared.

The evidence—physical, testimonial, and circumstantial—was more than persuasive, and Polan felt confident of convictions across the board unless there'd been some major screw-up by the Bureau waiting for the defense to uncover and ride to a dismissal. Or worse, to acquittals all around.

Polan had summoned Hy Depkawitz so they could go over every detail of the searches—chains of custody—evidence contamination—anything at all which could undo their case.

"Have a seat, Hy," he greeted. "The usual?" Depkawitz nodded and coffee was poured. It was late afternoon, and after a long day both could use the caffeine.

"I want to go through this guy VanZanten's grand jury testimony with a fine tooth comb," Polan began, peering at the transcript. "He said he observed activity 'in what was an odd place for anyone to be working.' Now, as Shift Supervisor he'd be in a position to spot something like that. Yet he failed to walk over to the worker, to question him, identify him, or take any action whatsoever.

"This could be portrayed as DOJ dereliction by the defense-and undermine his credibility. If we aren't able to directly connect the deceased with the placing of a detonator and the FOMEX explosive, we'll never make our murder case. So, when he was first questioned, what else did VanZanten say about this guy he claimed he saw? I need you to search your raw notes for any tiny detail which we could use to reinforce the link. Hy, I'm convinced this is our one and only soft spot."

"You got it. But I don't think we missed anything."

Secure in the knowledge that Abydos' fingerprints (lifted from the incriminating radio transmitters) would ultimately seal his fate, they turned their attention to the cases against the lesser defendants.

*   *   *

Finella Bright had been guided by her spirit associate to a spot not far from Interstate 15. She parked her camper, unfurled an awning, peered about, and positioned her chair.

It was an uninhabited area of dry lake beds strewn amid rusted mountains, with breathtaking vistas in all directions. The map said she was near an area called Devil's Playground.

Finella decided it was a very spiritual place.

From the mouth of his cave, Hardpan Dotson had observed the camper's arrival, noted that the driver was a woman—and that she was alone! He squinted for a better look—By Jeezley, not all that bad! Think I'll jes spruce up a bit, mosey on down, and greet the little lady!

Finella regarded cleanliness as the highest virtue, and when she spotted the grizzled old fart bearing down on her, her nostrils puckered. He looked as if neither he nor his clothes had ever submitted to suds.

Though totally repelled, Finella sat secure in her chair and watched—having been assured by her spirit friend that "the old one is harmless." Still, she eyed him closely, glad he was downwind. Suddenly he lurched an arm skyward and began to swing it about—Is he waving at me? Is he baring his teeth? Or is that a smile? His beard's simply disgusting—Oh, God—Oh, God—his crotch is damp!

"Hallo there, young lady—Welcome to nowheres!" he hailed merrily, in a voice like wood splitting.

"That will be close enough, I think," Finella commanded, rising to her feet.

"Don't worry yerse'f, I'm not gonna rob ya or nothin'—"

"What do you want?" Finella asked irritably as the man continued to approach. He walked stooped forward, rocking as if he had a bad hip. She estimated him to be in his sixties.

"Need a little company. When ya live out here all by yerself, ya miss havin' someone to talk to. You do talk doncha?" He came to a stop a few feet away, removed his hat, and mopped his brow with a once-plaid sleeve. "It may be winter, but in the daytime ya fry! Got anything to drink?"

She hesitated, reluctant to give him even water. "Stay right there. I'll bring you some water." She stepped into the camper, and when she returned with water she found him standing under the awning—a blatant infringement of her space—but then it was the only shade around. She handed him the glass.

He gulped the contents loudly and started to hand the glass back. But when Finella reached for it, he grabbed her hand instead and shook it vigorously.

"Howdy—everyone 'round these parts calls me Hardpan. My Christian name is Medrick, but yew kin call me Rick."

"I am—Ms. Bright, from Salt Lake," she said, pulling her hand free. They stood awkwardly for a few moments.

"Sit, sit—I'll jes set m'self here on the sand—Pertend we're at the beach!" he clacked, tickled by his wit.

The old man plopped himself down and Finella had herself a guest, like it or not. Reluctantly she sat in her chair.

"Why do you live out here by yourself?" she asked, not sure she wanted to know.

"I mine God's Good Earth for its bounty," he proclaimed. "I make camp in the mouth o' that big cave over yonder—" he thumbed. "Got me a few million bats for company! But none o' thems kin talk to me—so that leaves yew!" Coll Dang, I'm sharp today!

"You mean you're a—prospector." A clear pejorative. She looked down at the man—only to discover his eyes were eagerly traveling up her thighs. She quickly under her dress tucked and welded her knees. Is the wet spot growing?

"Take off them there sunglasses—so's I kin see whacha look like!" he beamed through teeth like a few submerged logs.

"The sun is too bright," she dismissed.

"Then, jes keep yer eyes closed."

"I'll do nothing of the kind."

"So—what brings you ails the way out here to the middle of—nothin'?"

"I—came here to be Alone," she emphasized.

"Boyfriend troubles?" He saw this rattled her. "Don't see no weddin' ring in there among all them baubles on yer fingers—remember, I'm a professional at spotting gold!"

This was becoming intolerable. Finella felt trapped. She was exactly where her Prince wanted her—but this old leech was here, and wouldn't take his damn eyes off her legs!

"Want me to show ya how ta build a fire?—it gets cold after the sun goes down. Unless o' course—you want me ta stay an' keep ya warm!" Ain't been this slick in years!

"That will hardly be necessary," she bristled, rising to her feet. "Perhaps you'd care for some more water before you leave."

He showed no sign of being ready to leave.

"Mr. Dotson, I don't wish to appear rude—but I came out here to be alone. So, if you wouldn't mind—I must ask you to leave now." He stirred reluctantly. "Perhaps another time—"

"Waall, how long ya plannin' to stay?" Hardpan inquired.

"Not that long," she replied firmly, to pointedly send the message that their conversation was over.

Hardpan drew himself to his feet, squinted up at the sun and shuffled off. "Tha's one horse that needs to be rode hard and put up wet!" he muttered just loud enough to be heard, as was his intent.

THE POPE

Ever since the celestial happenings at ABYTOR, the world's media speculated endlessly over when and where the promised Divine Visitation by the Daughter of the Creative Spirit would take place. For all such questions Karyn DeLeo had a standard answer: "In the near future, somewhere in the United States." And that was all she'd reveal.

Phone calls to The Seven's Alexandria office were now automatically forwarded to CELESTIA, with callers unaware the phone was actually ringing on a mountaintop in Utah.

Today it was the Vatican calling—requesting to speak directly with Ellen Kate Bryce. The call was put through.

"Good Morning, Ms. Bryce—this is Monsignor Florini in Rome. First, let me say how much I appreciate your taking my call—I know that you speak personally with very few."

"I'm always available to the Vatican, Monsignor. How may I help you?"

"You are very kind. Let me begin by reporting that His Holiness is 'faith led' to accept both the 'validity and the righteousness' of the spiritual events at ABYTOR."

"That—is most gratifying," Ellen Kate said softly.

"What occasions this call in particular is the Pontiff's desire to know whether the Holy Daughter is planning to carry Her ministry about the world—in which case the Pope would very much like Her to visit the Vatican. If this is not possible, in the alternative would She be willing to receive His Holiness at some appropriate time and place?"

"We—have been given no information I can share with you, Monsignor Florini, but I will certainly be pleased to present the question to the Holy Daughter. Perhaps a formal written invitation would afford me the best opportunity"

"An excellent suggestion. I'll see to it at once. I confess that what we were most hoping for was an invitation to invite—and you just furnished that."

"May I pose a question in return?" Ellen Kate asked, and then went on: "Will the Church be prepared to acknowledge the Divine Authority of the Holy Daughter?"

There was a pause. "On that matter, I'm afraid I am not at liberty to comment, except to say that a personal meeting with His Holiness could prove most useful in that regard."

*   *   *

Carmelita Ruiz peered down the road ahead, clouds of dust boiling up behind her battered pick-up. She had come at the beckoning of her 'Little Voice'—a small voice in her mind which she believed to be that of Jesus Christ.

The road was all but unrecognizable as such, being nothing more than sandy dirt amid dirty sand. She squinted ahead. Some kinda camper was parked up there—in the very area she had been directed to—ringed by magenta mountains and sacred tribal lands.

A most spiritual place, she acknowledged.

She could now make out a woman sitting outside the camper under an awning—and headed for her.

Finella noticed the approaching dust cloud and liked it not. The last visitor had been quite enough, thank you.

The pick-up drew to a stop. Carmelita turned off the engine and climbed down. The two women faced each other and were a bit stunned to discover that their hair, both in color and style, matched identically. It was an odd moment.

"Buenas Dias. My name is Carmelita," she greeted with a cheerful wave. "I noticed you sitting here, and, well—I wondered what brought you all the way out here?"

This struck Finella as a peculiar question for someone to ask. "I'm—Finella. I'm sorry I don't have another chair—I wasn't anticipating company."

"Hey, no problem—I have a folding chair—"She produced one from the back of her truck.

Finella brought out two glasses of cranberry juice, and the two women sat down under the awning, eyeing each other closely. They were about the same age too; but there all the resemblance ended. Carmelita looked like what she was—a potter in well-clayed overalls. She wore no jewelry or makeup, and looked as if she could use a cool shower.

"Where are you headed?" Finella asked.

"Right about here, I believe—" Carmelita glanced about. "Yes," she said with finality, "this is the place."

"What place?"

"The place where a miracle is going to occur."

Finella was stunned. Was this woman guided here as well?

"What—kind of miracle?"

"I was told to come and bear witness to 'the Miracle of Birth.'"

"'Told'—? By whom?"

Carmelita hesitated before answering. "By Jesus."

They locked eyes, and quickly fell into a deep discussion about their respective messages of guidance—which in turn led to speculation as to what might lie ahead. And before long, Carmelita was invited to set up her tent and stay.

What neither recognized was that one had been summoned by a Spirit of Light—and the other by a Spirt of Darkness.

327

*   *   *

The morning of the eighteenth, those selected to serve as the Holy Daughter's personal staff arrived at CELESTIA.

While Arthur Frayles showed the new arrivals around and introduced them to everybody, Ellen Kate and Karyn assembled a hopefully suitable wardrobe for the Daughter and readied Her accommodations. This was the most difficult part. Would a Deity want pictures on the walls?—flowers in vases? music?—things to read? There were just no answers for such questions; all the women could do was their best. In the end, they chose laser-print photos of earth's natural wonders, gloxinias and gardenias in bloom—New Age harmonies—and the National Geographic and TIME.

They struggled most over the choice of music, ultimately rejecting the Moody Blues, Mozart, and Toby Keith, this after more easily ruling out Jesus Christ Superstar and the Beatles.

Books were another matter. Having been informed that the Holy Daughter could both read and appreciate English, they decided to provide her with a wide range of reading choices—everything from the major newspapers, to the classics, to Carl Sagan and James Herriot. They also included the Holy Bible, fearing it would be conspicuous in its absence.

They'd transformed the room adjoining the 'Sacred Suite,' as they now referred to it, into a global media room, featuring a bank of HDTV monitors and a sixty-inch plasma TV.

After prolonged discussion, however, they decided not to include a library of feature films. With so few G-rated pictures being made, drugs, sex, and raw language seemed unavoidable. Yet to censor anything could give affront and appear impertinent. But what they feared most was being judged themselves by the movies they opted to include. After all, what lowly human could presume to know the tastes and quality standards of a Deity?

Transportation was another matter. They now knew where the Holy Daughter's earthly arrival would take place, and it was several hours away by car. This being a safety issue, Ellen Kate put it up to Beta—who informed her that, "You need not fear—She will be well guarded while en route to CELESTIA." Then he added, "Be sure to keep your attention on the driving, difficult as that may be." And a parting sexist insult: "Perhaps you should allow Arthur to drive!"

*   *   *

Finella, Carmelita, and some distance away, Hardpan in his cave, were all fast asleep.

But Master Molecular Manipulators do not sleep.

Suddenly: a loud cracking sound—not far beneath—jolted all three awake.

"Jeezley!" shrieked Hardpan.

Moments later seismic alarms sounded in a dozen locations. Yet the laser monitoring instruments detected no tectonic movement along the Garlock, none whatsoever.

*   *   *

As instructed, Ellen Kate, Karyn, and Art Frayles loaded one of CELESTIA's Outback wagons with water and food, along with clothing for the Holy Daughter. And at the stroke of midnight they set off for the Southern California desert.

It was February twenty-first.

PART FOUR

ANGELESIS

STARK NEKKED

The night had been clear and chilly, and with the first hint of light in the east the stars were beginning to fade. There was a sweetness in the air. After a night on the hunt, bats by the millions were vectoring back to their cave.

Finella and Carmelita were still asleep, unaware that a station wagon had pulled up and parked nearby. After a night on the road Ellen Kate, Karyn, and Art Frayles were tired and hungry, and broke out the coffee and doughnuts they'd brought along. Ellen Kate wondered whether the camper and the pickup parked a hundred yards away were there by coincidence.

In the mouth of his cave Hardpan snored peacefully—

Suddenly, around a bend farther back in the cave, a blinding White Light erupted, causing a great fluttering of wings. Bats by the thousands, having just born witness to the Light, themselves turned the purest of white. Swirling out the mouth of the cave, they encountered their returning black brethren—who, upon beholding the strange white bats, sped away from the cave in primal terror.

The sudden flurry of bats exiting the cave awakened Hardpan, who opened his eyes, beheld thousands of white bats swirling about overhead, and figured he was in the middle of a very weird dream.

Then he noticed the Light radiating from the rear of the cave—and decided this was one jeezley corker of a dream! Shaking his head to clear it, he got up to investigate—

And then, peering around the bend of the cave, Medrick Dotson became the first human being to behold the Daughter of the Creative Spirit!

She was a tall, striking woman—not white, not yellow, not black, but a magnificent amalgamation of all three, with long wavy brown hair. Bathed in the purest White Light, what stunned Hardpan most of all— she was stark nekked!

Meanwhile, the Holy Daughter was feeling the sensations of materiality for the first time. She looked down at her hands and moved her fingers one at a time—She wiggled her toes, flexed her limbs, and tried out her facial muscles next. She discovered her breasts and hefted them, examining the nipples—then, suddenly noticing the tug of gravity, She jumped up off the ground to test its pull. And smiled.

Hardpan couldn't believe his eyes—or his good fortune: a beautiful nekked woman was jumping up and down in the back of his cave! He watched open-mouthed—then suddenly pulled back, feeling like a Peeping Tom for staring at her body.

Who the devil was she anyway—and what was she doing here at the crack of dawn? And why in Hell did she take off all her clothes? Drugs? Or just plain crazy?

It was cold in the cave, and she could catch her death. He grabbed one last peek, and then ran back to where he kept his gear. Reaching into his backpack, he took out a soft, hand-woven Indian blanket, which its maker—an aging squaw—had insisted he accept. Her Spirit Guide had told her it was meant as a sacred gift for the grizzled old prospector. This was only a few days ago, and it was so beautiful he was saving it for a Special Occasion. He decided his jumping lady was 'pretty dang special.'

Hardpan returned from around the bend and walked hesitatingly toward the Holy Daughter, holding the blanket like a screen in front of him. "Beg pardon, Ma'am—but I figure you might could use this here."

Making no attempt to conceal her nakedness, the Holy Daughter flashed a dazzling smile and graciously accepted his gift. She let Hardpan wrap it around Her, then reached up and touched his cheek, producing a bright golden glow where She'd touched. "That tooth won't hurt you anymore."

And indeed the pain was instantly gone. "Who are you, anyway?" Hardpan asked.

"I AM the Daughter of the Creative Spirit—come to quicken the imaginative resources of your world, and to pour out my Spirit upon all mankind beginning with you, Medrick, the first mortal of the realm with whom I have spoken. Long will your name be remembered."

Like a proper gentleman escorting his lady to the Opera, Hardpan graciously offered his elbow—which the Holy Daughter took to steady Herself, having no prior experience involving physical balance. She next discovered that picking Her way across loose gravel, barefoot, was at once more than a little challenging—and deliciously stimulating.

"Watch-it there, Lady—" Hardpan cautioned. "Aintcha got no shoes?"

"Not yet—I've only just arrived," She murmured, concentrating on not falling down. "Gravity is utterly uncompromising," She thought, and glanced at Hardpan.

"Do you make your home here?"

"You betcha—this here's where the gold hides!" He clicked his teeth in snappy confirmation, giving Her a conspiratorial wink as if to hint at some slick scheme he had to make himself rich.

The Holy Daughter, charmed by his eccentric personality, wondered whether all the Earth's inhabitants were just as colorful—and as malodorous.

They came to a slight rise—and just beyond, five people about to have breakfast. Unaware of the approaching strangers, the one called Carmelita remarked, "Feels like another scorcher already."

At that moment, something made Finella glance up—in time to see the annoying, smelly old prospector from yesterday, coming over a rise—holding hands with a stunningly beautiful, barefoot young woman wrapped in an Indian blanket and apparently little else.

"What the deuce—?"

Everyone turned to see what Finella was looking at with such astonishment.

"It's—the Daughter—!" Ellen Kate gasped, instantly overcome.

The Holy Daughter broke into a wide smile by way of confirmation. Hardpan squinted at the five—and wrinkled his nose.

"I know one of 'em—the one in the big dumb hat," he whispered to the Daughter. "Miss High and Mighty herself!"

The Daughter knew that three of the five had come to greet Her, and smiled warmly as She kissed each upon the cheek.

"Dear Ellen Kate, I've been looking forward to this moment for so very long."—"Arthur, dear Arthur, you are exactly as I pictured you."—"And my beloved Karyn, you and I are destined to grow joyously close," Then She acknowledged the other two: "Carmelita, you honor Me by your presence. And Finella, you too are welcome."

The Daughter sniffed the air curiously.

"Holy Daughter, is this what you smell?" Ellen Kate asked—"We call it 'coffee'—"

The Daughter accepted the cup with a smile, and held it up for a closer sniff. It was about to become Her first taste of mortal nourishment.

"Watch out—it's hot," Ellen Kate cautioned, as the Daughter took a sip—and grimaced. "Try this instead—" she said, giving Her apple juice, which the Deity gulped down eagerly. Then Arthur remembered the silk gown, panties, and soft sandals, which he handed Her.

"Why, thank you. It's just beautiful! I know Mr. Dotson will be ever so grateful for the return of this magnificent example of tribal artwork."

While Ellen Kate held the new silk robe as a privacy screen, the Daughter carefully folded the Indian blanket and presented it to Hardpan.

"My healing powers I leave within this cloth. Use them wisely to restore good health to others."

She reached out to Arthur for the panties. Bemused and charmed by his embarrassment, when fully garbed She came over and ran Her fingers through Arthur's hair to straighten it—and She then bid him do the same for Her. After a few clumsy false starts, he succeed—and earned a small round of applause.

"This desert wind is no respecter of Deity," the Divine One mused. *"I might as well be a singing platypus!"*

She cocked Her head to one side, eyed Arthur mischievously, and sounded a single, loud, pure, exquisite musical note which echoed majestically across the valley—whereupon they all shared their first real laugh together.

With everyone completely relaxed by now, Arthur made a small humor contribution of his own: "This might be an appropriate occasion to point out that if you were to change but a single letter in Holy Daughter—you'd get Holy Laughter." After a moment of mental spelling, they cracked up. Then they all sat down to share a light breakfast, after which the Daughter rose slowly to Her feet—and began to glow, surrounded by an aura of bright gold.

"BEHOLD—"

At that moment, as the Master Molecular Manipulators cleaved the remaining rock-face, and a loud crack and deep, rumbling sound transacted beneath their feet.

A few seconds later, thousands more pure white bats came spoiling out of the cave—fleeing in panic before a great onrush of water—it flushed all before it, including everything in the world which Hardpan could call his own.

Then was heard the ringing of a hundred grand celestial carillons, with a thousand voices of angels pealing forth an anthem of exultation, crowning with glory the now Holy valley below and blessing the presence of God Herself.

The nascent river snaked south, in search of an ancient riverbed. No longer trapped in dense blackness beneath the surface and running wastefully to the sea, a great underground river had been birthed and artfully vectored to slip the bonds of granite, burst forth into blinding sunlight, nourish an arid desert, and foster new life.

The Daughter looked over at Hardpan, who stood forlornly on the new riverbank, watching his meager belongings sweep past. She addressed him softly:

That which you have lost is of little value. I bid you search diligently beneath that far escarpment—where you can see six large white boulders—and you'll find treasures beyond your richest dreams.

His tongue gave an automatic click of delight.

Meanwhile, a short distance away, Carmelita stood transfixed before the clear sparkling waters rushing joyfully past. She uttered "Dios Mia!"—finally understanding what her Jesus had meant about 'bearing witness to a miracle birth.' But what she could not possibly have known, was that years before, Universe Headquarters had settled on this precise location of the Holy Daughter's arrival and incarnation on this world as the Divine Bringer of Life. It had taken years of study by Provincial Universe Geologists to locate a powerful, unsuspected underground river yearning to break free.

But She gave no hint the unique role Carmelita herself was destined to play. Still standing by the miraculous new river, awed by its power and beauty, she crossed herself repeatedly—Suddenly, seemingly out of nowhere, the perfect name flashed across her mind:

EL RIO DE DIAS.

A freelance reporter just arriving on the scene overheard her call out its name. And with publication of his story—the first by an on-scene journalist—he called the river by this name, one certain to live on forever on countless roadmaps, tourist brochures, weather maps, and official FAA charts.

*   *   *

Well before noon, people began pouring into the valley from every direction. The sudden eruption of a powerful new river in the American desert made headlines the world over. Helicopters swarmed dangerously close overhead, broadcasting Live. It was quickly decided to get the Daughter to safely at once. After hasty good byes, Arthur bade the Daughter lie on the floor beneath a cover. He climbed in, ordered seatbelts buckled, and sped off, dodging heavy traffic and heading north, carving new roadways across the sands—all without looking back once or stopping for anything.

Her Guardian Seraphim were well pleased with Arthur's driving under pressure.

REQUIEM

On the ride north to CELESTIA , the Holy Daughter sat in front beside Ellen Kate, who was now driving and at a relaxed pace. Absorbed by all the controls, She enjoyed the power windows and the air conditioning. But Her favorite was the satellite navigation system, complete with a computer-generated artificial voice giving the driver every turn to make, miles to the nearest gas, and so forth.

It was lunch time, but they had no intention of stopping anywhere. Although the Daughter was curious as to what a Big Mac involved, it seemed out of the question—no one dared put the Divine digestive track to such a test. But the Daughter appeared so crestfallen, Ellen Kate relented and decided they could risk a medium Mocha Frappe—which She devoured and absolutely loved!

Back on the Interstate, Karyn pointed to the CD player and said, "Push that button—" The Daughter did as suggested—and was immediately blasted by the Philadelphia Orchestra's loudest and angriest rendition of the 'Dies Irae' from Verdi's Requiem.

Horrified, Ellen Kate reached over and quickly mashed the Reject button—and mercifully a golden silence reigned once again. Then all of a sudden the Holy Daughter burst out laughing—and could not stop. Then Karyn—then Ellen Kate—and finally Arthur too began to howl. By the time they entered the foothills, they were already fast friends.

Soon they entered the mountains proper. Half an hour later, rounding a slow curve, Ellen Kate pointed ahead and up—giving the Holy Daughter Her first glimpse of the gleaming architectural triumph that was to be Her new home—CELESTIA.

As they drew closer, Ellen Kate slowed down, not liking what she saw up ahead.

"Oh, oh—looks like we have company—"

"Nothing the news media likes more than a juicy rumor," Arthur, former Editor-In-Chief of the Boston Globe, explained to the Daughter. "I'd say what we need is a platoon of Ushers; I'll let Tony know we're here." He reached for his cell phone.

Having anticipated the possible need for a ruse one day—but certainly not this soon—Tony had hidden in the new garage a disguise for the Holy Daughter to wear to deceive the press should the occasion ever arise. Good Thinking, Tony! —Ellen Kate told herself.

Using a service road, she quietly pulled into the back of the garage. A couple of mechanics glanced up, recognized her behind the wheel, and went back to work. When the garage was built a few months earlier, the contractor had puzzled over the Ladies Dressing Room shown on the plans. Though regarding it as most peculiar, he went ahead and built it anyway.

Screened by Karyn and Ellen Kate, the Holy Daughter walked briskly to the changing room. Once safely inside, Karyn produced a chamber maid uniform and hairnet for the Daughter, plus one for herself and another for Ellen Kate. Forewarned, the ushers made sure they all had clear passage to the Vista Cubes.

Observing all this from above, the celestial audience could scarcely believe its eyes. From racing across the desert with the Holy Daughter hidden in back under a blanket—to being musically assaulted by a bombastic symphony orchestra—to entering CELESTIA disguised as a housemaid!

Thinking about all those watching from above—and how shocked they must be—the Daughter couldn't help being amused.

What an auspicious beginning, She smiled.

*   *   *

It was late afternoon by the time the group had arrived at CELESTIA, where everything was in readiness.

The long Vista Cube ascent fascinated the Daughter—who all but pressed Her nose against its glass sides. Gazing out upon the snowy, sun-dappled peaks rising all about them, She offered a silent prayer for the planet.

Gliding up into the underside of the great structure, the Cube whispered to a stop. The Daughter alighted and found the entire staff assembled in greeting. Introductions were made, and then She was ushered to the Sacred Suite to rest and refresh Herself. This must have been a tiring day even for a God, Ellen Kate thought.

Inside Her suite the Daughter took her first real nourishment: a golden-sweet mango and a glass of mountain spring water. An hour later, She went for an extensive tour of CELESTIA-and pronounced Herself "well pleased" at its conclusion.

The Holy Daughter retired early. Shortly thereafter, while lying on top of the bed, She sensed an unfamiliar pressure within the lower torso—and realized it must signal a need to empty the bladder.

She went into the bath—and gazed down at the commode. My day of natal experience continues to unfold—She was bemused by the indignities Her mission entailed.

Meanwhile, The Seven repaired to the small conference room to rewrite tomorrow's planned announcement of the arrival of the Daughter of the Creative Spirit—now to be coupled with a second heralding the miraculous birth of El Rio de Dias.

There'd be no unimportant mention of bats turning white.

El Rio de Dias, now flowing full and crystal clear, had first been spotted washing through an arroyo running under Interstate 15, creating great excitement and massive traffic jams. News helicopters circled overhead; others traced the new river back to its source. Their live feed of pictures to every network attracted an unprecedented worldwide audience, as the peoples of Earth bent in awe.

Geologists proclaimed the new river a stupendous event in the physical evolution of the planet. Those who'd witnessed its birth were not alone; all the world hailed the sudden emergence of this life-giving river as a Divine Miracle.

*   *   *

Only an hour after the others had departed, Hardpan looked up and saw the first helicopter boring in. Gathering up his belongings, he immediately headed east—toward the distant escarpment to which the Holy Daughter had pointed.

Visions of riches danced in his head: Gold. Platinum. Emeralds. He suddenly heard the sound of many vehicles and looked back over his shoulder; a ragtag convoy was barreling across the desert toward him and the new river. He picked up the pace, muttering darkly.

Hardpan made camp at the base of the escarpment, below the designated six white rocks now clearly visible. He ate a pitabread sandwich for lunch and washed it down with warm apple juice. Then he grabbed his smallest pick and headed up the slope. It was steeper than he would have liked—but visions of gleaming veins of gold kept him climbing.

Forty minutes later he dropped to the ground alongside the white rocks, wheezing and gasping. *By Jeezley, after all this I'd better find somethin'!*

He gazed down at the growing commotion along the banks of the new river and shook his head. *Dag-Nab Idjits!*

After catching his breath, Hardpan snatched up his small pick and crawled down several feet, as directed. He peered at the rock strata before him—*Nothin'—no dang flash—anywheres!* He brushed at the crumble with his fingers—*Nothing.* He moved a few feet to his left and peered even closer—*Nothing.* Then he tried a few feet to the other side—*Nothing. Sheee-it!*

He climbed down a few feet more and repeated the entire process. This went on for the better part of an hour before Hardpan slumped down in bitter disappointment—"What the Hell does She know anyway—?"

He felt something sharp stick him in his rear end. He lifted a cheek to remove the offending item, *there she is!* He wiggled it free and held it up. *Looks like an animal fang 'O some kind—a dang big one!* He got to his knees and brushed some dirt away—but couldn't see anything more.

Then he took his pick, and gently began to dislodge bits of overburden—and quickly discovered that it wasn't a fang at all: It was a claw—one of four!

His mind was spinning—

What was his discovery worth?

How could he lay legal claim to it?

339

How could his find be safeguarded from others?

And how could he ever thank that nice nekked lady?

*   *   *

The world's press exploded:

DEITY WALKS AMONG US!

HOLY DAUGHTER CREATES NEW RIVER

DEITY PILGRIMS FLOCK TO UTAH

WORLD AWAITS DIVINE WORD

The Holy Daughter was not yet ready to speak to mankind. She divided her time between studying human behavior in the Media Center and getting to better know her new friends and associates at CELESTIA, beginning with The Seven—now nearly complete with the arrival of Ellen Kate's parents.

The small conference room seemed far too formal and sterile, so they began gathering each day in the erstwhile Sky Lounge—now known as simply as the Sunroom.

On Her third day in the likeness of mortal flesh, the Holy Daughter experienced a gustatory epiphany: Natural Vanilla ice cream, to everyone's delight. She explained by saying, I am not the Daughter of Man such as Jesus was the Son of Man. I am the Divine made into Flesh directly—i.e., a God with the full sensory capacity of the human body.

The Daughter's next joyous discovery was Mocha Chip.

She cleaned Her bowl and smiled at the others.

"I have been told of how pleasurable physical sensation could be—and I now know how greatly experience can surpass description!"

"Wait'll you try Maple Walnut," Karyn laughed, already beginning to like the Holy Daughter enormously.

She turned to the Bryces.

"When you present your credentials in Beijing, please tell President Wu that I send My Peace—and urge that he work diligently with you in the quest for brotherhood between nations."

Arthur Frayles looked uncomfortable, debating whether to ask for a clarification. He didn't want to correct Deity on Her use of grammar, but he felt compelled—

"Forgive me, Holy Daughter—but did You perhaps mean brotherhood 'among' nations? It's a small distinction—"

"In truth—I was speaking bi-laterally. Peace is My Mission. It is why you are here. Know this, Arthur: If My Will is your Will your mission will be crowned with success."

Everyone present made a mental note to never question Her use of grammar again.

"I would speak now with Mr. Steele."

Rusty, who had been introduced to the Holy Daughter upon her arrival at CELESTIA, was summoned. A few minutes later he joined the others in the sunroom.

"I have been informed that your purpose here is to make a record of My Incarnation. This is wholly appropriate—but I would have you perform yet another service. When in the days to come I wish to speak to humanity—I wish to do so by making use of your video-graphic recording devices. With that technology the words I say can be faithfully conveyed to the world's newsmedia."

Rusty nodded in assent, saying that this could be easily accomplished, and that he was honored to be able to serve in such a capacity.

"Holy Daughter," he went on, "would you—ever consent to a personal interview on camera?"

"I am come as a Revelation of the Living God. What you suggest is consistent with that purpose."

"Whenever you wish to so speak, I will be ready. When do you anticipate first addressing the world media?"

"Quite soon—But you may pose your questions as soon as you like."

"Great! How 'bout later today?"

She smiled and suggested they meet after supper.

*   *   *

Hardpan Dotson realized that only a "jeezley scientist" could properly identify and evaluate his find.

But not the seismologists and geologists who now swarmed the valley—I need one o' them there archeologists—

Hardpan had packed up the fossilized claw and hitchhiked his way to Los Angeles. After considerable difficulty, he found the UCLA campus and the office of Dr. Wyatt Robbins, Chairman of the Department of Paleontology. He carefully unwrapped the claw and showed it to the secretary, a woman in her sixties with an aversion to anyone with green teeth.

"What—is this?" she asked warily.

"Tha's what I come to find out!"

After a moment's hesitation, she picked up the phone and spoke briefly with Dr. Robbins. It wouldn't be the first time someone had shown up bearing a "major discovery"—but then there was always that chance—Hardpan was ushered in.

"I'm—Robbins," he greeted. "Have a seat, and show me what you've found."

Hardpan produced the fossilized claw—which Robbins recognized instantly as being just that—but from what? He peered at it through a magnifying glass.

"Exactly where did you find this, Mr. Dotson?"

"Out in the desert—nears where that there new river jes' bust out. Whatcha think it is? An' what's it worth?"

"Did you see anything else in the ground nearby?"

"Yep—it come from a foot with three other claws jes' like this here one. But I'll tell ya one thing: ain't no bear paw—I seen them before."

"What—did it look like?" His excitement was apparent.

"It come from a long—boney foot o' some kind."

*   *   *

The Holy Daughter was seated across from Rusty in the Sunroom. They were alone save for one of Silvagio's ushers keeping a wary watch just out of earshot. A camcorder on a tripod framed the shot and recorded the interview.

It was several moments before Rusty collected himself, overwhelmed by the nature of the company in which he found himself.
You may relax, Rusty—I will not chew.

He chuckled. "I believe 'I won't bite' is the expression you want." This caused Her to laugh merrily. "I see you are able to laugh at yourself," he beamed. "It—never occurred to me that that was an attribute of Deity!"

"Just as it never occurred to Me that ice cream is a treat for the tongue. My sojourn in the flesh will be a learning experience for all."

"What has been your greatest surprise thus far, if that's the appropriate term?"

342

"I was not prepared for the extent of human savagery I have witnessed on your television. It grieves Me deeply—and I see that there is much to be overcome."

"And—how do You plan to accomplish Your Mission?"

"Through the ministry of Love. There is no other way."

TO HOLD A PUPPY

That evening Karyn was summoned to the Sacred Chamber—It was the first time anyone had been invited there. Timidly she took a seat.

"Beloved Karyn—you have been worried that I might find you unworthy. Quite the opposite, for it is you I wish to have at My side."

Karyn was suddenly overcome with emotions on the verge of tears. The Daughter reached out and cupped her face.

"Dear One—Abide in Me, and be My friend.

I feel need of a companion—one with whom I can share feelings and trust to always speak truth. When contemplating a course of action, I will need someone who can accurately gauge how people will react. Your journalistic experience will serve Us well. It will be made of Universe record that you are become My Personal Counselor.

There may be other occasions when I merely need a friend—a sympathetic and loyal friend—one who will remain so throughout all eternity."

Karyn suddenly lost it—breaking into deep, racking sobs. The Daughter immediately leaned over and took her in Her arms, holding her close. It was the first time She had physically embraced a mortal.

For some time, neither moved nor spoke. Finally Karyn looked up—and beheld the face of God. She shivered and wept once again. But this time the Daughter laughed gently, and kissed Karyn lightly on each cheek.

"Will you be My friend—my Beloved Friend?

And accept that you are far more than 'worthy'?"

Karyn was staggered. But she felt the Purity and Power of Divine Love—and instantly realized the Love was mutual.

"I would be—so very proud—"

The Holy Daughter brought Her palms together and smiled at Her new friend.

"May I presume upon Our friendship with a small but heartfelt request? I—yearn to hold a puppy."

It was after ten when Karyn finally returned to her room dazed, awed, humbled, and absolutely overjoyed. She knew her life would never be the same. Not ever.

She was surprised to find Rusty waiting beside her door.

They both entered. "We need to talk," she said quietly. There ensued a heated argument after Karyn announced that their physical relationship had to end—offering no reason other than to say, "Sex is simply inappropriate."

Angry and confused, he left.

*   *   *

The next morning The Seven met to discuss the crowds that had begun to gather in the valley below. A media invasion had been anticipated, but the thousands of pilgrims had not.

Tony Silvagio assured everyone that CELESTIA was secure. With both Vista Cubes held up top, no visitor could gain entrance. While his unarmed ushers kept close guard on the base station, the state police, sheriff's deputies, and the Secret Service kept the crowds well back from the base station itself.

The only other way to approach CELESTIA was by helicopter. President Onager had ordered that one belonging to the GSA be repainted white and placed at the Daughter's disposal. It was also cleared for use by Peter Klein and the Bryces—and when not in service it was left parked on the rooftop helipad to prevent a landing by an uninvited visitor.

A formal press room had been set up inside the Base Station, but no further statements had been released after the announcement of the Holy Daughter's arrival on Earth, and the attendant birth of El Rio de Dias.

A Vista Cube would descend once each morning to pick up mail. In anticipation of high volume, the Postal Service had assigned CELESTIA its own zip code.

CELESTIA had created its own website—already recording thousands of hits a day from all around the world. Based on available manpower, The Seven decided that only the most compelling e-mail communications would command an individual response, with all others receiving a standard acknowledgement. They debated the wisdom of sending out an official photograph of the Holy Daughter, in the end deciding that only letters from children would be so honored.

A basic letterhead for CELESTIA had been selected by The Seven, with only its zip code for an address. Since all phone lines had unlisted numbers, the letterhead was the essence of tasteful simplicity. However, a second letterhead, showing CELESTIA's FAX number and e-mail address, had been printed up as well. There were no business cards.

The Holy Daughter began each day with a brisk walk around the circumferential balcony, now swept clear of any overnight snow and carefully salted at the insistence of Tina Marsh, Her personal physician. The crowds and journalists below had come to anticipate Her morning walks, and trained their long lenses accordingly. As a result, fresh Deity photos were able to be published each day the world over.

Her sixth day on earth the Daughter asked Ellen Kate and Peter to join Her in the Sunroom—while Karyn, who was unabashedly dotty over Josh, played with him in his nursery. They sat down to tangerines and honey, a Divine favorite.

"You are to wed in but three weeks—and I thought it appropriate We discuss your plans.

Where do you wish the ceremony to take place?"

"We were hoping we might hold it here, Holy Daughter—and that you might approve," Ellen Kate appealed. "We would of course invite only immediate family. But we truly want to be married—the eyes of God—"

Peter jumped in, "The Bryce family's long-time minister could perform—"

"Would you prefer to be married not only 'in the sight of' but 'By the Hand of' God?"

Ellen Kate looked up—tears streaming down her cheeks.

No words were necessary.

*   *   *

Late that afternoon Karyn tapped lightly on the door of the Sacred Suite. In her arms was a seven-week female Dalmatian puppy named Zoe. Her spots were only just beginning to show.

Upon seeing it, the Holy Daughter swung the door wide—wearing the widest smile Ellen Kate had ever seen.

FOSSIL FIND

A small team of paleontologists knelt beside the Dotson Dig, as it had come to be called. Dr. Robbins himself led the expedition, that intrigued was he. This was a virgin area for fossils—and that hollow claw was like none other he'd ever seen: too light to be a ground predator, too large to be a bird.

Hardpan stood to one side, watching anxiously as Robbins used a dental pick to dislodge small bits of rock from under the clawed foot.

"Whatcha think we got here?" the grizzled old fooster gurgled. "Some kinda giant lizard?" He got no reply.

A second group was busy probing the surrounding stratum for other bone fragments. Suddenly one of them held up something and let out a whoop.

It was a fossilized human tooth!

*   *   *

President Onager was more than a little annoyed at being snubbed by the Holy Daughter.

After being given long-term occupancy of ABYTOR at no cost, She won't agree to meet with me, or even take my calls! Onager thought. Peter reported that She wasn't receiving any visitors—but that, when the time came, the President of the United States could count on a personal invitation. Guess I won't be photographed shaking hands with a Divine Being anytime soon, he mentally murmured.

"God save us from Lady Deities!" he wailed into the phone, evoking a tight look from Peter.

"Well, tell me—what's She like?" Onager probed.

"Oh, you know—You see one God—you've seen 'em all."

"Very funny—now answer my question."

"She's—well, wonderful. Beautiful. Loving. Wise. In short, Perfect. Smart too. She can glance at an isobar chart and predict the exact temperature, humidity, and barometric pressure for any given location days in advance! A whole bank of Crays couldn't do that. Says it's got nothing to do with omniscience—one need only do the math."

"So what else can She do?"

347

"You mean, besides turn bats white and spawn rivers? Well, let's see—She can cure a toothache, glow in the dark, sip through a straw, point out buried treasure, and—no doubt—whistle divinely, if She has a mind to."

"Why are you taking that smart-ass tone?"

"Frankly, it was your crack about 'saving us from Lady Deities', I found it offensive." He softened. "Mr. President, the Holy Daughter came under Emergency Mandate to help and to serve our world—meaning, if anyone, She'll be the one doing the saving! I only pray She's successful."

"Pray? You gettin' religion there, Peter?"

"I am now."

That afternoon President Onager met privately with his chief political adviser, Tom Raffle.

"Tommy, there'll never be a better opportunity. If I don't take advantage of the Daughter's presence on earth to push my spiritual agenda, I'd be a damn fool. And Congress, with so many freshmen, is just bustin' to pass something major! Meanwhile, my honeymoon period is about up."

"With your highest priority still being to pass your National Debt Retirement Act, right?"

"Yes; and in case the Republicans are thinking about yet another tax cut, you tell 'em flat-out, I'll sign no bill which cuts taxes for the rich. Ever."

"Now you're looking for trouble! That's like pissing on their Holy Grail—you ready for all-out war?"

"Oh, what the Hell—then don't forewarn them. It'll be more fun that way."

*　　*　　*

The Holy Daughter had retired to Her suite early to be with Her new puppy. She took Zoe onto Her lap and caressed her softly. The pup looked up—into the eyes of a Divine Being. Zoe stretched her neck up as far as she could—and began to enthusiastically lick the Divine chin.

When the Daughter went to bed that evening, She brought Zoe along and slipped her under the sheets with Her, so the exquisite little pup could sleep secure in Divine Embrace.

And an on-looking Universe, bent in adoration, was astonished to witness such extraordinary bonding between Deity and beast.

*   *   *

Fa Haad was shocked by the news that the Daughter of the Creative Spirit was in residence at ABYTOR, or whatever they called it now. Suddenly everything had to be rethought.

ABYTOR was no longer merely the ultimate expression of godless capitalism—to a Muslim it now housed the ultimate blasphemy: a female masquerading as God!

The real question was, Should ABYTOR remain his primary target? And if so, could he find a way up to the top of the mountain—and then get inside undetected? Could he defeat whatever state-of-the-art security system they had in place?

And: Should his primary target be the Divine pretender?

If so, would she be under active Mentor protection? In which case—could she be killed at all?

Fa Haad had a great deal to ponder.

*   *   *

Ellen Kate hadn't forgotten her father's idea of asking a Mentor for some career guidance for Justin. So she'd put the question up—and was shocked when the reply came back in Biblical argot—

"Regard ye not the lusts of thy brethren,—rather tend ye to thine own fields. Speak unto thyself and thou shalt find thyself. Go forth on thine own path—seek and ye shall find. Stand ye among all men—and thou shalt know thy Destiny. Knowest thyself first—then findeth all thy brethren."

She read it to Justin verbatim. He blinked several times and cocked his head. For once, he had no snappy reply. That night Ellen Kate was told that it had arrived "cloaked in Biblical argot, because that's the way he wanted to hear it."

*   *   *

The President needed to learn more than Peter had told him, so he called Art Frayles at CELESTIA by direct line.

"Arthur, good to hear your voice," Onager opened, his tone implying being that it had been too long.

"Mr. President. Sorry I've had to spend so much of my time out here, but—"

"No problem, Arthur, I understand completely. I'd only ask that you find a few minutes every day or so to call and give me a run-down. Not asking too much is it?"

"No, Sir, of course not. Incidentally, I did mention to the Holy Daughter how anxious you remain to meet with Her, and She promised to receive you officially at an early date. May I make a suggestion? Perhaps the two of you could meet informally during Peter and Kate's wedding reception on the twentieth. I know they'd be honored if you and Mrs. Onager were to attend."

"Not a bad idea, Art. Okay, let 'em know that we'd be delighted to come and help them celebrate their union. Who's going to conduct the service, a minister or a rabbi?"

"The Holy Daughter Herself as agreed to join them together."

"Wow—that sure oughtta make it divorce-proof!"

*   *   *

To begin the seventh day of Her sojourn on earth, the Holy Daughter descended in a Vista Cube to greet the throngs gathered in the valley below. It would be Her first public appearance. Rusty noted the scores of camcorders on hand.

Tony Silvagio had been caught off-guard and hastily assembled his ushers to form a protective screen around the Daughter. Her Seraphic Guardians were not taken by surprise.

Emerging from the base station in dark blue velvet robes (concealing Her L.L. Bean no-leather slippers), the Holy Daughter radiated the same bright golden aura first seen at the birthing of Her river. She raised Her arms in Blessing, which dropped the assemblage as one onto its collective knees. Several cameras could be heard cycling. Otherwise, all was silent.

"My Peace be upon you. I am come unto your world in the name of the Creative Spirit—to stimulate the creative resources of the planet, and set to healing its most grievous wounds. Know that all which afflicts you can be wholly remedied—provided mankind is willing to make the requisite sacrifices. My Ministry will take Me to

those nation states which are bound up in religious intolerance, which is an affront to all mankind—and to the Universe itself. Know that your strife-torn world is ever held within the protective embrace of its Creator. I leave you now with your Creator's Love."

The Daughter then slowly passed Her hand above the crowd—pouring out upon it Her Joy and Her Love. She smiled one last time, turned, and walked slowly back to the waiting Vista Cube.

CNN, with its cameras in place and standing by, had broken into regular programming to carry Live the surprise Inaugural Appearance of the Holy Daughter. Millions were able to see Her and hear Her speak—and within hours Her announced Mission dominated front pages the world over.

*   *   *

Finella Bright had been frustrated when her spirit associate wouldn't let her go before the media with a first-hand account of the miraculous events in the desert. She figured her story would bring thousands of dollars, but her Prince was insistent that she had more important things to do.

Back home in Salt Lake City she watched the Daughter on CNN, resentful she herself was still a media unknown. Then she heard her spirit voice instructing her to phone a certain number. When Zooti Abydos answered in Cuba, she recognized his voice at once. Remembering her from ABYTOR, he demanded to know how she got his cellphone number.

"You will recall, I have a highly knowledgeable spirit confidant," she patiently explained. "One who thinks you should know that your father is soon to be transferred to a more secure facility."

Zooti's mind began to reel. It had been his cache of cocaine that had cost his father ABYTOR. He now fully realized that his careless betrayal had created its own imperatives: He had to help his father escape.

*   *   *

Dr. Robbins' hands began to tremble as he brushed away the few remaining bits of rock, suddenly recognizing what he was looking at—

It was a skull.

The skull of a bird.

The largest bird that had ever flown.

He couldn't believe his eyes. It was the discovery of a lifetime. He was about to make history, and about to become an international celebrity in the world of paleontology.

He might even make the cover of TIME.

Yet not for one moment did he suspect that the greatest find of all remained yet to be uncovered.

Hardpan leaned in for a close, halitosis-bearing look—"Now, what in Hell is that dang thing?"

AGUILAR STAR

Felix Bleuss sat at his desk, thinking through the implications of having a Divine Being around when the viral attacks began. Would She even take notice? Would She give a damn? Would She do anything to prevent them? Would She know who was behind them? And if so, would She expose him?

This posed a serious complication. Perhaps even a grave personal threat. He decided to put everything on Hold until he had time to sort it all out. He was able to reach Jean-Piet in Rome, and they spoke using pre-arranged terminology.

"I think we should postpone the conference indefinitely," Felix said ominously. There was a long pause.

"I'm not certain I can reach the chairman." There followed a still longer silence.

"Just—reach him."

*   *   *

Five days out of Barcelona, the bulk carrier Aguilar Star was bound for St. John's to on-load Grand Banks sweet crude.

The tanker was a sturdy affair, having been 'Built with Pride by Swedes.' Launched in 1993 and owned by a Spanish petroleum conglomerate, she'd spent her entire career plying the Atlantic with oil. She boasted a perfect safety record.

They were steaming due west, making a steady fifteen knots. The night was cold and clear, the sea calm. Light westerlies freshened the air. No other ships were in sight, the wing lookout reported.

Sitting warm and snug inside the bridge with his other officers, Captain Santos eyed his surprise gift: a box of Cuban cigars, as yet unopened. It had arrived with an unsigned note reading simply: To Help You Celebrate Your Tenth Anniversary of Command! Apparently someone remembered. He wondered who.

Well, tonight's the night—might as well fire one up!

He broke the seal by running his fingernail around the rim, and eased up the lid. Suddenly he heard a loud Snap!—followed by the light tinkle of glass shattering within the box.

He peered inside: No cigars at all—only a mousetrap and some kind of shattered glass vial!

What the hell?

MegaVirus claimed its first victims. Within seconds the encephalic killer entered every bloodstream on the bridge, sped to every brain—and within sixty seconds brought all neural activity to an end. In rapid succession, each crew member crumpled to the deck and expired.

Aguilar Star plowed on, due west, her heading locked in by computer. The upcoming course change for St. John's had yet to be entered; the captain had wanted to wait until they crossed into the Gulf Stream. Warmer on the bridge that way.

*　　*　　*

HOLY BIRD ONE, the helicopter's official FAA call-sign, was also speeding due west—crossing the Great Salt Lake Desert and on into Nevada. It was the Holy Daughter's first experience with mechanical flight, and She appeared to be fascinated and enjoying it thoroughly.

It was night, and the stars of winter were breathtaking.

Tony Silvagio and the full contingent of ushers followed behind in CHASE ONE. Tony knew where they were all going and anticipated real trouble.

*　　*　　*

353

John VanOrsdell

Yeoman First Class Arlo Hines began to suspect something was amiss. Bent over his display screen at Atlantic Coastal Defense Command in Norfolk, he'd watched Aguilar Star cross the twelve-mile limit and continue west at fifteen knots without any sign of a course change. Why would they be heading straight for New Jersey? He decided to raise them on the radio.

After several failed attempts, even trying on an international Emergency Frequency, Hines alerted the Coast Guard.

SKINHEADS

The helicopter pilot could make out a clearing behind the stage and began to hover. He could also see men below pointing up at them. And he could see their rifles and side arms.

CHASE ONE landed first and quickly off-loaded its unarmed contingent. Silvagio's men immediately formed a protective phalanx, and awaited the touchdown of HOLY BIRD ONE.

Confused and mildly alarmed, the hundred or so men on the ground quietly surrounded their unexpected and uninvited visitors—weapons at the ready.

The Daughter of the Creative Spirit had just crashed a torchlight gathering of skinheads!

The jet engine whined down and the rotors ground to a stop. For several long moments the immaculate, unmarked white helicopter sat silent and still. Soon murmuring and whispering could be heard. Yet no one made a move.

Then: soft Angelic voices pealed forth in an Anthem of Consecration—filling the clear night air with aural beauty.

The skinheads recoiled, looking about in alarm. All of a sudden the cabin door slid open—the ushers moved in, and the Holy Daughter alighted. She was adorned in robes of white and silver—a bright golden aura radiating about Her. She held up a hand, and spoke in a clear, strong voice:

354

"My Peace I bring unto you. Tonight marks the beginning of My Ministry on earth. Among you stand the first of My Acolytes."

Recognizing Her from TV, the skinheads were stupefied. Several let their guns drop to the ground and began to pray.

"I have chosen to come because you are at once a great resource—and a great waste.

There are those among you of powerful mind and spirit; seven who might become mighty among mortals. I say unto you: Mighty is he who serves all his brethren in name!

I invite those who would to go forth unto the world as Ministers of the Creative Spirit, to present yourselves at CELESTIA for Service—and turn a life based on revilement into one based on Love.

Hearty will be your welcome—and great will you become in the eyes of the Universe. Your Destiny is yours alone to cast."

With that, the Daughter walked slowly back to Her helicopter. Angels began to sing—and turbines began to whine.

*   *   *

The Aguilar Star plowed on, now less than twenty minutes from impacting the Jersey shore. On her present heading she'd run hard aground on Long Beach Island—which mercifully still lay deserted, having barely pulled free from winter's grip.

A Coast Guard helicopter drew alongside the Star, its copilot scanning the bridge with night-vision binoculars.

"Everyone's either unconscious or dead!" he hollered.

"Then we gotta get someone aboard," the pilot called back—"and fast!" He turned and barked at one member of his crew. "Nevares: buckle up—you're goin' down!"

Four minutes later Hector Nevares was lowered by harness onto the deck of Aguilar Star. It took him another minute to unbuckle, make his way aft, and scramble up the ladder to the wheelhouse.

The tanker was now six minutes from impact.

Nevares stepped cautiously inside, pistol in hand. No telling whether some crazed crew-member awaited with a weapon of his own. He looked about—all was still. He was alone except for five corpses. He radioed the situation.

"Grab the wheel, and bring her about," the pilot ordered.

Nevares walked over—moved the collapsed helmsman aside—and took hold of the wheel. It would not budge.

"The helm's frozen—!" he radioed.

"Let me think—Nevares, you're going to have to enter an AutoNav Disengage command into the computer."

"I'll—give it a try—"

At that moment a crewman from Engineering walked onto the bridge, having been drawn up from below decks by the sound of the helicopter. He glanced around, saw bodies lying about, saw Nevares and his gun, turned, and fled.

Nevares punched helplessly at the keypad. Even if he managed to disengage the AutoNav, it was already too late to bring the ship about. Desperate, he grabbed the engine room repeater and rang up Full Astern. Five decks below, the chief engineer complied—as steam slammed both main shafts into full reverse. It was too little—and it was too late.

SPRUNG

For its own security, the Marshals Service relies on one-hundred percent secrecy in transporting inmates for the Bureau of Prisons.

As Aguilar Star plowed toward disaster, a single unmarked sedan was moving Sandovar Abydos in the dead of night to the brand new Tulare Corrections Facility to await a trial still at least a year away. Abydos sat alone in back, shackled waist and ankles, with two marshals in front.

They were on a long dark stretch of road, with few other vehicles in sight. The marshal driving was telling a fishing story, not noticing the large U-Haul closing from behind.

The U-Haul drew alongside as if to pass—then suddenly swerved sharply to the right, forcing the sedan off the shoulder and into a ditch. It collided with a large boulder and rolled onto its roof.

The U-Haul skidded to a stop, and four men with gas masks and automatic rifles jumped out and ran back to the sedan. One fired a gas grenade through the shattered windshield. Forcing open a rear door, they dragged free the lone prisoner, who was choking and barely conscious. They carried him to the truck, put him in the back, and sped off.

Six minutes later they arrived at an abandoned airstrip, where a plane was waiting, its engines running. Abandoning the U-Haul, they all piled aboard—and two minutes later were winging their way to Mexico.

What the Marshals Service could not know was that the time, exact route, and details of the Abydos transfer were fully known to a close spirit associate of one Finella Bright.

*   *   *

Hector Nevares gazed in horror: a long line of street lights lay dead ahead. He'd already radioed the helicopter that he intended to remain aboard. He located the ship's horn, and began blasting the air furiously—

On shore, the New Jersey State Police had been notified by the Coast Guard that a large tanker was bearing down on North Beach just north of Surf City—and to evacuate anyone in its path. Impact was imminent.

All eleven Aguilar Star crewmen below decks heard the ship's horn—felt the ship shudder violently as she tried to backwater—and braced for whatever calamity lay in her path.

Nevares could now make out surf breaking on the beach and the flashing lights of a dozen police cruisers. The Fathometer showed almost no water remaining under the keel. Good thing we're riding empty! Hector thought, flattening himself against a bulkhead.

Trooper Ryan couldn't believe his eyes—. Bathed in the floodlights of two Coast Guard helicopters, a massive black tanker loomed high above the sea—running lights ablaze—her horn rending the night air—the sea a raging boil beneath her stern as her great props thrashed savagely at the sea. Ryan braced himself for impact.

Her tanks empty and riding high in the water, Aguilar Star's prow bit hungrily into the sand. Then, pitching up gently by the bow, her keel rode the beach ashore—cutting several feet into the sand but plowing relentlessly ahead.

Loose sand was no match for twenty-two thousand tons of mass—plus coherent motion, with thirteen knots of momentum.

It was a deserted stretch of barrier island which the tanker struck. With an eerie near-silence the ship slid on, an empty motel and a clam shack vanishing beneath her keel.

Aguilar Star came to rest straddling and effectively bisecting the island itself—her bow in the bay to the west, her huge props excavating the beach to the east. This as police, Coast Guard, and news helicopters gathered in an angry swarm above—with emergency vehicles of every denomination scurrying about on shore, lights flashing pointlessly.

Hector Nevares and the crew men on board suffered nothing worse than banged shins and bumped heads. Except of course for the five who'd been murdered.

The tanker could have fared far worse—her hull lay un-breeched. The Swedes build strong ships.

Photographs of the six-hundred and thirty-six foot tanker, perched with the island under her amidships, led every newscast.

But the main story was the biological weapon which had killed everyone on the bridge—and the cryptic note found taped inside the lid of an ersatz box of cigars:

THIS IS BUT A TASTE OF THAT WHICH IS
TO COME—THE FRONT FOR VIRAL
CLEANSING.

IDEA BUBBLES

Thus far, the only guests invited to CELESTIA were skinheads. Not the President of the United States, not the Pope, not a single journalist—just skinheads.

The first arrived on March eleventh, presenting himself at the base station. Tony Silvagio had been highly skeptical that any skinheads would take the Holy Daughter up on Her invitation to become Ministers of the Creative Spirit. So when Richie Quinn appeared—tattoos, earrings, sweaty biceps, missing teeth, and all—Tony was astonished.

"Try anything cute and I'll personally clean yer clock," Silvagio snarled. Quinn only chuckled.

The two-hundred and sixty pound skinhead was searched thoroughly, escorted to the top of the mountain in a Vista Cube, and delivered to Art Frayles—who in turn showed him to an immaculate room which would be his, and then pointedly showed him the shower.

An hour later Richie Quinn emerged to join the others, including the Holy Daughter, for lunch. His first repast involved meatless couscous with flan for dessert—causing him to briefly reconsider his decision to enlist.

"In recognition of being the first to answer My Call to Service, Richie, you will become First among My Ministers.

But before rejoicing—you should know that the position entails considerable paperwork."

There was stunned silence around the table. Quinn turned ashen. Suddenly Karyn laughed out loud, the first to realize that a Divine Being had just made a joke!

And then everyone laughed, including the Holy Daughter.

Zoe'd been given the run of the Sacred Suite, and was feeling very much at home. The bright-eyed ball of energy had already endeared herself to her mistress by waiting until She sat down, then racing in wide circles to build up speed—and hurling herself full tilt into the Divine bosoms.

After a long day of meeting and administrating, the Holy Daughter looked forward to returning to the Suite for an intimate roll on the floor with Zoe. Seeing how amazed Karyn was the first time she witnessed their game, the Daughter immediately invited her to get down and join the tussle.

*   *   *

Things were moving quickly: Financial support was being received from around the world—correspondence was getting answered—researchers were compiling data—trips abroad were being arranged—the Bryce-Klein wedding invitations were mailed—and nine more skinheads reported for training.

The pressure of the news media was relentless—and the Holy Daughter knew the hour was at hand to address the world. Rusty Steele was tasked with finding an appropriate backdrop and setting everything up. He was thrilled.

On March sixteenth the Daughter of the Creative Spirit addressed Mankind for the second time. Standing before snow-crowned peaks, backlit by the sun, and adorned in white robes, still Her aura of gold radiated bright and resplendent.

The Daughter was truly a Being of exquisite, universal beauty, when she spoke, Her voice was clear and soft, suffused with Love, and cloaked with authority.

A billion mortal souls were anxiously tuned in—the largest broadcast audience in history, holding its breath in anticipation—

"I am the Daughter of the Creative Spirit of our Provincial Universe—now at residence in the American Republic.

I have come unto your world as a Minister of Creative Light—for your planet stands dark in imminent and mortal peril.

"Know that you are surrounded by other inhabited worlds—most considerably more evolved than your own. You live in a highly ordered, safe, and secure, lovingly administered Universe. Know further that you are cherished by your sibling worlds— who had of late become greatly alarmed by your irresponsible ways.

"Yet there are no perils which you cannot meet. It will be My Mission to labor among you—help you perceive—evaluate—and creatively overcome these perils one by one. Together We shall engage the problems. And creatively We shall fashion their solutions.

This is My Mission."

The Holy Daughter then raised both arms and swept them in a broad arc.

"I HEREBY POUR FORTH MY SPIRIT UPON ALL FLESH TO STIMULATE AND QUICKEN THE CREATIVE ENERGY WITHIN EVERY MORTAL MIND!"

"As a lasting symbol of the Power of Creation I have birthed a new and powerful river in the California desert to nourish the land to refresh the spirit and to foster new life. Over the coming months I will journey to many lands, gather together the finest mortal minds, and address the most urgent problems of each region. When I move on—I will leave in place Ministers to sustain and carry on Our efforts. To the extent that governments wish to assist in these creative enterprise, they are invited to do so.

Moreover—know that those faithful souls whom you call 'Mentors' will be available as resources in all these sacred undertakings."

*　　*　　*

Nearly two-thousand miles away, in a mountainside villa overlooking Havana, Sandovar and Zooti Abydos watched the broadcast, seeing with their own eyes the Holy Usurper occupying their own personal creation—even their own beds! The very bitch who'd cost them ABYTOR—and whose celestial cohorts had forced them both to flee the law to Cuba!

They seethed as one.

Sandovar didn't blame Zooti for the loss of ABYTOR; he blamed the Mentors. Though he himself had not known about the cocaine his son had placed in his vault, he reasoned that the Mentors did—and that fixed the blame on them.

Zooti snapped off the television and snarled, "I hope all her damn toilets back up!"

"This is not a done deal," Sandovar mumbled.

"Whaddya mean?"

"Nobody steals from me and gets away with it."

*　　*　　*

Little Misha was on the floor playing with his blocks. He was attempting to build a bridge, but the span kept collapsing. He turned the problem over in his four-year-old mind, and knew there had to be a way. After all, he'd seen bridges.

He tried shortening the span—and realized that having any joints within the span invariably led to collapse. Then he squinted at the blocks before him—first from one angle, then another. Suddenly he saw it: a joint could hold—providing the portion of a block forming the span was shorter than the supported remainder!

Misha had just reinvented the cantilever principle with the creative powers of a four-year-old's brain.

*　　*　　*

Marty was an Assistant Offensive Coordinator—for an erstwhile championship team which wound up six and ten on the season, failing to capture so much as a wild card slot. Defense had played well, but the passing game had "sucked" all season long: blown timing—bobbled passes—even colliding receivers. Marty could still hear the boos.

He'd been warned that his job, along with that of others, was on the line. The front office was demanding major fixes.

Marty began wrestling with the timing problem. Toward the end of the regular season, they'd designed some trick pass plays, using imaginative cuts, stops, and crosses. But they just couldn't seem to get the timing down. The quarterbacks were frustrated, and the receivers had finally resorted to step-counting. Yet nothing had worked.

If only we had some kind of secret audio cue—

Then an idea: A musical cue, coming from the stands!

It was no burst of creative genius—but it was a bona fide idea.

*   *   *

Effie Whelan loved nothing so much as blowing the judges' minds with her gustatory creations. Her most recent Blue Ribbon had been for her Ricotta-Portobello Crepe, in a light chive and chervil cream sauce. But that was two years ago. Two long years. It was time for another winner.

She lay in bed unable to sleep, running various taste and texture combos on her mental seafood processor—Prawns sautéed in garlic butter, walnuts and sweet peppers—[Nope]

Oysters and artichoke hearts, baked in a leek and gruyere crumb casserole—[Bland] Honey-mustard soft-shell crabs—

Eventually she fell asleep—only to find herself having a dream about building a better mouth trap—

Long, fresh-steamed strands of King Crab meat, rolled in roasted sesame seeds and flash-fried in pure butter.

It was an idea she'd remember upon awakening—and one which would eventually earn Effie Whelan another Blue Ribbon.

*   *   *

Zooti Abydos had lived his entire life without exhibiting even a flake of creativity. His father had teased him about it more than once, repeatedly challenging him to try to win a game of chess without having any ideas. But Zooti would have none of it: "Chess is stupid," he invariably dismissed.

Of late his father had been pacing their villa at night, struggling to come up with a scheme to overcome security and destroy ABYTOR. But all his ideas fell short, and the only one he could turn to for creative help was his non-creative son.

Greatly flattered, Zooti had no trouble rising to the challenge; blowing things up was one of his favorite things.

* * *

The world over, people began experiencing bits and pieces of new ideas bubbling to the surface of their minds. Shards of ideation. Emerging insights. New connections.

It was all great fun as well. The human intellect enjoys nothing so much as procreating an exciting idea.

And on occasion, a truly brilliant idea would emerge.

* * *

Bart Carlisle was the salvage contractor hired by the owners of the Aguilar Star to remove their stranded tanker currently bisecting Long Beach Island, New Jersey.

The FBI had finally finished examining the crime scene, removing every last speck of evidence from the bridge. It had taken them a full week, keeping the entire northern half of the island cut off and isolated. Property owners were howling for the wreck be cut up and hauled away. And the local media had a bonafide Big Story to feed the world.

Carlisle stood on the remains of the blacktop roadway, scrutinizing both ends of the ship. It was dead-low tide, and both bow and stern were high and dry. She was canted fourteen degrees to port, lying atop crushed utility lines and pipes.

He knew he faced a formidable undertaking: pumping every tank on board bone dry—cutting the vessel up—loading all the pieces onto trucks and barges. It would require ten weeks at minimum, and the summer season was looming. Other problems too: the Government of

Spain—Lloyds of London—the State of New Jersey—local permitting boards—the Department of Environmental Protection—the Army Corps of Engineers. It would be a nightmare. Worse, it was a job he had to carry out under the glare of a watching world.

So Bart Carlisle began to speculate on other less costly and complicated ways to accomplish his task. For instance might it somehow be possible to slice the tanker into large, floatable sections—which could then be simply towed away?

And then it hit him: Re-float the whole damn ship!

He began to literally tremble with excitement, caught up in the throes of a massive creative eruption—

Excavate—? Hell no! Just suck the sand out from under the hull and wait for high tide to right and float her! Then tow her ass out to sea, pump the sand back in, and repave the road!

It would save millions, and at least two months, as well as return Aguilar Star to her owners slightly bent, badly scraped, but otherwise fully serviceable. A vast grin overtook his face—Between salvage fees 'n time bonuses—I oughta clear close to Six Mil!

Between the terrorist attack and beaching of Aguilar Star, to the Daughter of the Creative Spirit's address to Mankind, the world talked of little else. An airliner crashes in Chechnya—farmers riot in Paris—an enraged engineer slaughters a dozen co-workers in Akron—but the news-media barely took notice. There were only two stories.

*   *   *

The dozen skinheads who had answered the Daughter's call assembled at CELESTIA for the first time. They were changed already—speaking in soft, respectful tones—walking about quietly—stepping aside for others—shaving daily—using deodorants. Silvagio couldn't believe it.

The designated convening place was the new Seminarium, whose great vaulted windows looked down the length of the magnificent valley below. It was the first time the tattooed Acolytes had been in the room, and they were visibly awed. Still attired in studded leathers and earrings, they stood in self-conscious contrast to the grandeur before them.

They helped themselves to fresh blueberry muffins and coffee from a serving cart, then settled into the soft recliners facing the windows, munching their muffins and making hushed observations. Suddenly a door opened, and the Holy Daughter strode in. She was alone—and to everyone's astonishment, wore faded jeans and a sweatshirt. Her hair was pulled back in a ponytail; She was not radiating an aura. Several men started to rise, but She gestured them to sit.

"Good Morning, Gentlemen," She smiled, taking a seat in front of the windows and crossing Her legs. She looked up, saw nothing but open mouths,and flashed a glorious smile. "We're going to be spending considerable time together in the weeks ahead, so I think everyone should dress comfortably." She saw the men were still stunned. "You may be pleased to learn that as Holy Ministers of the Creative Spirit, you will be free to dress as you like." She paused. "Appropriately, this morning We will begin with a discussion of Free Will—"

As the Holy Daughter spoke, stunning even in faded jeans, all twelve of the men wondered what She'd be like in bed—only to be instantly overcome with devastating guilt.

HEALING AURA

Ellen Katherine Bryce and Peter Stuart Klein were joined in Holy Wedlock on the First day of Spring by the Daughter of the Creative Spirit in CELESTIA's chapel—before nearly a hundred human and over a thousand celestial witnesses. And for all those present, the phrase 'Those whom God hath joined together' took on new significance.

It was at the formal reception following the service that the President of the United States and Mrs. Onager were presented to the Holy Daughter by the bride herself.

"David—Jane—I am so very pleased to meet you both," She smiled, thrusting Her hand out in greeting. They shook hands warmly. "I want to express My personal appreciation for your generosity in making CELESTIA available for Our use. You are truly About the Creator's Business."

"Thank you, Holy Daughter," Onager said quietly, for once beset with shyness. "I—never thought I'd—stand in the presence of Deity— at least not for a very long time."

She leaned over and kissed him lightly on the cheek. "You must be an early-achiever then." She smiled and nodded toward a sofa. "How would you like to sit down with Deity?"

Ellen Kate took the cue and invited Jane for a grand tour of CELESTIA while the President and the Daughter settled onto the sofa. One of the wedding photographers happened by and captured the moment, later captioning it the Meeting of Heaven and Earth.

"David, I want you to know I'm gratified by your efforts on behalf of fostering higher human and societal values. Yet evolution requires time, and it's important you appreciate that any effort to expedite the process through legislation is bound to encounter resistance. People never want change forced upon them."

"But the people elected me to bring about change—how can I now fail to press for more enlightened laws?"

"Go before the people first and get them behind you. Their elected representatives will quickly understand the message. Do not merely Govern. Lead—and the whole world will follow."

*   *   *

Justin and Penny Onager had been on top of the mountain once before, when it was ABYTOR, and were thrilled to be back.

On their last visit they'd been among the privileged few to witness the appearance of the Mentors—the Angelic Hosts—and the arrival of a Universe Revelator. While they both admitted to being "totally blown away" by the experience, they were otherwise, to all outward appearances, unchanged.

Being the only teenagers among the invited guests, Justin and Penny hung together—at this moment helping themselves to more shrimp and cocktail sauce.

"Hi, guys," greeted Karyn, appearing beside them. "How's it feel to be back on top of the mountain again?"

"Cool" said Justin.

"Very cool," said Penny.

"I'm glad. It's really good to see you both again." She lowered her voice. "Listen, I come bearing a Divine invitation: the Holy Daughter would like you to join Her in the Sacred Suite this evening at seven. You should know that, outside of myself (and the chambermaids), no other

366

human has set foot inside the Sacred Suite. So it is quite an honor! Moreover, you'll be the first of your generation that She'll have had the opportunity to speak with in private."

At the stroke of seven the young Onagers arrived, greeted at the door by Karyn and Zoe—who repeatedly bounced up and down a foot or more in happy excitement.

"Guys—this is Zoe, the only creature in all Creation who gets to lick the face of Deity!" Penny squatted down and instantly received many very sloppy puppy kisses. When the Holy Daughter walked in, She'd changed from Her ceremonial raiment to jeans and a sweater.

"Hi. Thank you for accepting My invitation. Shall We sit over here—" She indicated a pillowed area on the floor, where sitting was primarily a horizontal affair. They all sat down, with Zoe pouncing merrily on her new friends. Moments later she stopped, looking pointedly at her Mistress.

"What's she want?" Penny giggled.

"She wants to chase sunspots. And if I don't accommodate her, she'll begin to mutter darkly and fidget."

"Sunspots—?" said Justin.

The Holy Daughter pointed Her index finger at the wall—as it suddenly projected a bright beam of golden sunlight!

Zoe leapt to her feet and started chasing the bright spot on the wall with frenzied excitement. When it moved up onto to the ceiling Zoe went nuts, barking furiously at it. Sunspot chasing was the one and only thing that would make her bark, Karyn explained. Penny thought that was wonderful.

"It's Zoe's primary exercise program. If humans could find such a happy counterpart, few would remain overweight. In connection with weight, I imagine you're all feeling most full from the wedding feast. If you're uncomfortable, may I suggest you suck the juice of these pomegranate seeds—"

"How'd you learn such excellent English?" Justin queried.

"It is one of the benefits of being all-knowing."

"Whoa, I guess that does come in handy!" Everyone laughed. Then Zoe suddenly sprang up onto Justin's chest and began licking his face with great enthusiasm.

"You're the first male she's tasted," said the Daughter.

"It's an acquired taste," Karyn snorted.

"Must be some cocktail sauce on his chin," Penny chimed.

Tiring of Justin, Zoe suddenly bounded onto his sister, and began frantically licking her face. Thrilled, Penny kissed back—but then recoiled: "Eeuw! she just stuck her tongue up my nostril!" she squealed, turning her face to one side. The pup happily switched to tongue-in-ear—tickling Penny's toes into an instant curl. More squealing.

The Holy Daughter looked on—experiencing pure joy as She watched the unbridled merriment before Her.

"Do dogs get to go to Heaven?" Penny asked.

"Their Life Energy returns to the Whole—while they themselves live forever in the hearts of those who cherished them."

"Don't think I'd like a place where there are no pets."

"Do not assume there are no such companions on the higher worlds. Indeed, a most pleasant surprise awaits you."

"What about cars? Or jet skis—something to get around in?" Justin jumped in.

"For short excursions you will be able to self-propel—for longer journeys there is Seraphic transport."

"Where do people live on these 'higher worlds'?" Penny wanted to know.

"In private domiciles—replete with Beauty. Rest secure in the knowledge that great efforts are made to reflect their dwellers' tastes and desires. All living quarters on the Ascension Worlds are in truth perfect reflections of their occupants' personalities."

Justin and Penny were quickly warming to the idea of Divine Revelation—as a direct line to all knowledge.

"What about entertainment—whaddya do for fun?" Justin inquired.

"We have Presentments of Truth, Beauty, and Goodness."

"An'—that's what you call Fun?" he winced.

"The residents of every world assemble in enormous amphitheaters to enjoy regular Universe Broadcasts of notable events transacting upon other worlds—just as your own news media regularly report notable events in transaction on your world."

"'Every world'?" Penny squinted.

"With the exception of those few isolated by spiritual quarantine, your world being among them, All worlds, even the billion mortal worlds, attend the Broadcasts. It is a Universal Right. It is the way Universe Citizens throughout all Creation learn of events on other worlds."

"Sounds kinda boring, if you ask me," Justin opined.

"Verily My Son—as a form of entertainment it far surpasses 'computer hacking'."

He was shocked that She knew of his on-line escapades.

"I know Everything—it's part of My job description. Never underestimate omniscience—it's almost as much fun as omnipresence."

"You know Everything?" Penny asked skeptically.

"I wouldn't be much of a Deity if I didn't—would I?"

*   *   *

Bleuss and Son were elated. On the heels of the Aguilar Star disaster, orders for the MegaVirus vaccine were pouring in from around the globe. Business was more than good—it was fantastic! Perhaps another demonstration of the virus's potency was no longer necessary.

The vaccine was already badly oversold. Even operating three shifts, seven days a week, it would take many months for production to catch up. It was sheer Bleuss.

The Holy Daughter was fully aware of the treachery afoot in Zurich. In Her first act of Divine Intervention, She mandated the immediate annihilation of MegaVirus.

MIRACLE

Slowly Hardpan made his way up to the Dotson Dig, now ringed and ablaze with lights. He shielded his eyes and peered at the six newly arrived mobile science-labs and eleven deluxe motor homes. In addition, there was now a mobile kitchen on site, and tantalizing aromas began snaking their way through the maze of hairs in his nostrils. "Jeezley Gawd, wha's all this? Then: Dang, don't that smell good!"

An armed security guard stepped in front of Hardpan, blocking his way. Then he saw it was the site's namesake.

"Sorry, Mr. Dotson—didn't recognize you in the dark. But my orders were to let no one pass," he apologized.

"Now what in Hell you talkin' about, young fella? I'm the one discovered this here place—ain't nobody got a better right to be here than me—ya hear?" he shouted.

Dr. Calvin Fandor of Yale, newly hired and placed in overall charge of the dig, heard the ruckus and walked over.

"You must be Medrick Dotson," he greeted, thrusting out his hand. "I was told you could reappear at any time—" They shook awkwardly; Hardpan wasn't used to introductions.

"Let me have Cook throw another steak on the fire—you look like a man with an appetite."

Nostrils atwitter, Hardpan let himself be led to a nearby picnic table. They sat, and a wine-bearing waiter promptly materialized and poured two goblets. With an approving click of some teeth, Hardpan downed his wine in two loud slurps.

"Why all them guards—yew fin' silver?" he accused.

"No, Hardpan—but we did find something of extra-ordinary value—" He waited for Dotson to ask what—and then went on, "You already know that we found the bones of the largest bird to ever soar the skies of this planet. And, you also will recall that a human skull was later unearthed. The natural assumption, of course, was that the bird had had the man for lunch—"He paused to see if Hardpan caught the double meaning; he hadn't. "Actually, it now appears that it might have been the other way around—.

The man literally took the bird to lunch riding upon its back as a passenger! Meaning, air transportation was invented long before the twentieth century—!

We have convincing proof that man first took flight before the dawn of time—back when inventing the wheel was still thousands of generations off—!

Hardpan was alarmed. "Ya mean all's it's good fer is sitting in some Jeezley museum?" He spat in the general direction of Fandor's tasseled loafers. "Sheee-it!"

*   *   *

Hardpan was so disappointed over the financial worth of his discovery, he left the dig and made his way along the banks of El Rio de Dias to do a little deep thinking.

As he walked, a familiar stench suddenly curled his nose: skunk! He spotted it lying in the sand up ahead, having apparently drowned in the unfamiliar waters. And not that long ago, by the look of it. Then he detected a slight movement and moved closer to investigate. On an impulse he could not explain, he took his prized Indian blanket, the one

370

that 'nice nekked lady' had returned to him, and spread it over the skunk. Now, why in Hell did I do that? He wondered whether he'd ever be able to get the stink out.

Suddenly—a golden aura appeared around the blanket. And moments later the skunk got to its feet and scuttled away.

Hardpan blinked in disbelief—What in the Blue Perfect Hell—? Then he bent down to retrieve his blanket—and found that it smelled like, like some kinda sweet flower! "I'll be damned—" he said out loud. Nothing could have been farther from the truth.

PAPAL SERVICE

Several more skinheads presented themselves at CELESTIA to sign on. Richie Quinn met them at the Vista Cube, and hugs were exchanged all around.

The Holy Daughter then appeared to personally welcome her newest Acolytes.

"You have answered My Call—I salute the Spirit Within for His success in gaining the balance of your minds."

With that, She passed among them and kissed each lightly on the cheek.

"Richie—invite your new Brothers for a tour of CELESTIA—that they may become at ease in their new home."

The Holy Daughter then returned to Her suite and placed a call to the unlisted number of the Papal Residence at the Vatican. It was late evening in Rome.

"Monsignor Baldacci speaking—" a voice purred.

"This is the Daughter of the Creative Spirit. I wish to speak with His Eminence." She spoke in perfect Italian.

There followed a stunned silence—then, "But how can I be certain you are who you say you are?" he managed.

"Dear Ruggerio—Can you not discern the Divine Voice?"

There followed another silence—She could hear muffled discourse taking place.

"This—this is not—proof," he stammered. "Can you forgive me—if indeed you are the Holy Daughter?"

"My Son—you were in such haste this morning that you neglected to take your simvastatin," She authenticated.

There was a brief pause. "Holy Daughter—" he gasped, "let me—put you through at once to the Holy Father—"

After a few moments, a firm, elderly voice, speaking in Latin, came on the line. "This is—Father John Peter."

"Antonio My Son—My Peace be upon you. As a Faithful Son you have served your Lord with true devotion. Know that your Love for Him is returned a thousand fold. I call this day to beseech you to join Me in Supernal Service—to bring Light and Life unto a dark and suffering world. Mankind must learn the Arts of Peace—and set aside the acts of war. In this Salvation Quest I am come bearing the Creative Spirit—that Mankind may set its house in order. Will you join with Me in Supernal Service?"

"I—I would be most honored to serve at Your side, Holy Daughter," the Pope said in a voice choked with emotion.

"I will dispatch the First of My Acolytes that We may set about the work before Us."

*　　*　　*

Fa Haad reached his decision—the Infidel Impostor had to die. It was God's Will.

*　　*　　*

Peter Klein succeeded in persuading President Onager that the only safe way for the Holy Daughter to travel abroad was to be aboard Air Force One, under U.S. military protection at all times, anywhere on Earth.

Though not a member of The Seven, the President had been made fully aware that, as long as the Holy Daughter were of flesh and blood, her human body could indeed be injured or destroyed. And since it was the stated Will of the Daughter of the Creative Spirit that no emergency celestial actions be taken to assure Her survival, ultimate responsibility for Her personal safety lay in the hands of Her mortal associates.

It was what had been keeping Dave Onager awake at night.

MIRACLE TWO

President Wu had been "most astonished" to learn that the Daughter of the Creative Spirit wanted to visit China on Her first journey outside the United States—clearly a very great honor. Her Mission, She had already announced, was the launching of a World Brotherhood Movement—with "President Wu Sen of China as My Co-Chairman."

At that, Wu was more than astonished; he was flabbergasted. Watching the events at ABYTOR unfold, he'd come to accept the reality of the Mentors—and that spirit beings come and go about the Universe. But a very beautiful woman proclaiming to be a God? That was not so easy to accept.

Perhaps She will make for me a miracle—he mused.

*   *   *

One question kept tugging at Ellen Kate's mind: Who was to be the final member of The Seven?

The first six were already known: her parents—Karyn DeLeo—Art Frayles—Peter and herself. But as yet no number seven. Later that afternoon, after the Daughter had finished Her daily tutorial with the Acolytes (now numbering twenty-one), Ellen Kate put the question to the Holy Daughter directly.

"All of you are understandably curious—I will only reveal that his arrival is imminent."

Ellen Kate was shocked. "You—can't trust us with the information?" she asked in disbelief. The Daughter could see she was deeply hurt.

"Of course I trust you—all of you—it's the authorities We cannot trust."

"The authorities? I—don't understand."

"The one of whom I speak is a fugitive before the law. Indeed it is I who must ask for your trust in this matter."

"You said 'his' arrival is imminent. Then—how will 'he' manage to get in here—past all the security we have?"

"The one of whom I speak is nothing if not resourceful. I am confident he will find a way."

* * *

The next morning Richard Quinn, First among Her Holy Acolytes, departed for Rome. He was clean-shaven—his jewelry and many tattoos now gone. His hair was tastefully styled, his suit and shoes conservative. All bore testament to his recent transformation. He even carried a small portfolio containing his formal Letter of Accreditation, bearing the Seal of the Divine Daughter Herself.

Richie Quinn had never felt so—so friggin' good!

He just hoped he wouldn't forget his lines when he met the Pope.

* * *

That same morning, Finella Bright phoned Zooti Abydos, not realizing he was no longer in Cuba. She delivered her bi-daily report, having had no word from her Prince, or even an inkling herself, that something major was afoot.

But all Zooti had wanted to know was precisely when "Miss High and Mighty" would be departing for China. And exactly how She'd be traveling. Finella had told him she'd try to find out and get back to him.

Her 'Prince' turned out to be oddly uncommunicative. All he'd confirm was that the Daughter had requested that HOLY BIRD ONE be held in readiness the night of the twenty-third.

It was all Zooti wanted to know.

* * *

The Holy Daughter and Karyn were playing with Zoe on the great balcony when Ellen Kate approached.

"Excuse me for interrupting, Holy Daughter, but Sigma just told me something troubling." The Daughter left Karyn to Zoe's devices and turned to face Ellen Kate.

374

"He said that 'Many Mentors are engaged in emergency watch-care,' but he wouldn't elaborate, and that in itself is unusual. Blessed Daughter, what's he talking about?"

"There is to be an attack on CELESTIA. The Mentors are merely keeping their eyes and ears on everything."

"An attack on CELESTIA?" Ellen Kate burst out, giving Karyn a moment of horror. "My God, can this be true?"

"Beloved One, I don't say things which are untrue. The threat comes from one who believes strongly that We have no right to be here. He regards US as thieves."

"Then—you have to be talking about the Abydoses."

"The younger. But speak not of this to Mr. Silvagio. The threat posed is beyond the ken of him and his ushers. Fear not: Our journey to China will not be put at risk nor even delayed. Trust Me."

Ellen Kate missed it; the Holy Daughter had just delivered a small cosmic zinger. Then, all of a sudden, she got it—and almost high-fived a Deity.

Then, in the very next moment, she put two and two together "Oh-my-God; Zooti Abydos is the final member of The Seven?"

"No, My Heart—someone even more ignominious—and far more dangerous."

"Now you're really scaring me—"

"Be at peace. Can you imagine I would invite one who is unworthy? You must remember—I can see into the heart of any man. Hearken: Even the greatest heart is susceptible to being misled. The wayward heart is like a boomerang the farther away it goes, the stronger does it return."

"May we—know the name of this 'wayward heart'?" The Daughter gave the request a moment's reflection before electing to reply.

"He is the one who carried out the attack on Foot Knox and the one who authored the attack on the Panama Canal. He is known as 'Fa Haad'—and he is soon to become your Beloved Brother."

Ellen Kate considered it briefly. "I hate him already."

"I'm—not exactly a huge fan either," offered Karyn.

"Another Thomasina—you doubt Me also?" She picked Zoe up and got a wet kiss for Her trouble. "There, you see? Zoe has faith in Me!"

*   *   *

Fa Haad was deeply conflicted. By one hand, he knew that CELESTIA must be destroyed. By the other, the Daughter was mostly guilty of association. Should She die as well? For that matter, could She even be killed? And, what if She were an actual God? If so, what were the implications of that for his afterlife of virginal bliss—?

He too had accepted the reality of spirit beings and of celestial activity, so forcefully demonstrated were they at ABYTOR. Yet, if that is a reality—could it be a false reality? Or is a reality by definition? He hated philosophy; it only got in the way.

It was the first time Fa Haad had entertained spiritual doubts of any kind—and this fact alarmed him. He dropped to his knees and prayed to Allah for guidance. Prayed as never before.

The concept Fa Haad was trying very hard to not think about was: Is it possible that The One True God—different for each human religion—is in fact One and the Same God? Meaning that every Faith is equally valid?

And, could the Daughter of the Creative Spirit be a Perfect Reflection of that One True God?

This was heresy and it was dangerous, now of all times—on the brink of his greatest sacrifice for Allah!

It scared Fa Haad to be thinking such thoughts—for the first time in all his earthly life.

ORDINATION

Gazing down at an ocean that reminded him of rolling grey macadam, Karl Brasher thought about his soul-buddy and fellow Acolyte, Tony Scorcone.

They'd first met while being initiated into the Blown Heads motorcycle gang. The rap on the Heads was, they were at once cunning and pointedly cruel—and well known to police from Seattle to San Francisco, and to the DEA. (The first Canadian grower who tried to short them had seen his manhood affixed to a doorjamb with a nail-gun, the gang's disciplinary weapon of choice. The story spread, and thereafter the Heads could count on a little something extra with every buy.)

Karl and Tony had been present the night the Daughter of the Creative Spirit descended on their gathering in a dazzling white helicopter. Upon first beholding Her, both felt a powerful draw for reasons they couldn't begin to comprehend.

Since their teens each had felt like a loser, compensating for this with displays of hubris. Neither enjoyed watching the Heads maim or hospitalize some rival, and secretly yearned for different lives. And when the Holy Daughter appeared, Karl and Tony were more than receptive. Ten days later they rode to CELESTIA and sold their bikes, their gang days over.

* * *

Obscured by thick clouds, the sun set somewhere behind the 747. Quickly swallowed in darkness, it inched its way across the sea, and Karl's mind drifted back to CELESTIA—

Their schooling as Acolytes had been intense, yet ever uplifting. Told that they were soon to become Ambassadors of Creative Light and sent forth to address "the desperate needs of this planet"—they began each day with an invocation for a worldwide quickening of the Creative Intellect.

Karl had loved CELESTIA from Day One, struck by its air of high purpose. Their initial training centered on the creative process itself: i.e., the techniques for stimulating the ideational resources of the mind—and then focusing and optimizing the ideas generated into effective solutions.

The second half of training was custom-tailored as each Acolyte learned the particulars and cultural history of the area of their assignment. And so it was that Karl now found himself winging his way to the Middle East, with Tony headed for Northern Ireland—or Ire Land, as he liked to call it. Their not called the fighting Irish for nothing! Karl wasn't especially creative himself, but the Daughter had taught that Her ministers were not charged with producing ideas themselves—only with fostering creativity in others. Karl wondered just how successful Tony and he would be.

The Acolytes had been startled by their physical transformations. By Divine Fiat, body tattoos had vanished before their eyes, scars disappeared, beards were shorn, and hands were manicured—while personal hygiene was mastered by all.

New wardrobes followed, as each Acolyte was fitted with the attire appropriate to his assigned ministry: Light blue tunics for most, light blue robes for the tropics.

The Daughter had tended to the spiritual needs of Her flock, spending private time with each, touching his soul. Her constant mantra was, "Master the art of self-forgetfulness, that you may be perceived and accepted as truly selfless—wholly devoted to the Loving Service of others."

This concept was so alien to the ears of recent thugs, that at first none grasped its meaning. But the Daughter was taking such pains to impart it, that each felt obliged to take what She was saying to heart. And as they did, one by one, the Light of Understanding broke bright upon each mind.

At this moment, the Holy Daughter had reached out, taken each hand in Hers, and, in an act of sublime condescension, kissed it lightly,—spilling forth a tidal wave of Divine Love to wash over and embrace each heart.

Little did the Acolytes realize this was their actual moment of Ordination—and made a matter of Universe record.

Karl often thought back to that supreme moment. The very idea of a Deity bending to kiss the hand of a mere mortal, his hand, had rocked him to the core. He'd never, ever been so emotionally moved! And now, every time he thought of Her, he'd suddenly experience waves of adoration. Did this mean he actually loved Her? And—dare he think it—did he almost desire her as a woman? And if he did, was that blasphemy?

He gazed at the leading edge of the wing, gleaming in the light of a moon which had only just broken through the clouds, and wondered how hot it would be in Tel Aviv.

*   *   *

The terrorist known as Fa Haad was having second thoughts about targeting this 'Daughter of the Creative Spirit.' If she were in fact a Divine being (he'd seen her on television himself), would it be spiritual suicide to attack her? Fa Haad was nothing if not an arch-survivalist.

At first, he had wanted nothing more than to personally vaporize ABYTOR—celebrated icon of American wealth and power. But now that it had been transformed into CELESTIA, headquarters of this

Daughter of the Creative Spirit, he was no longer sure what to do. Yet, something was telling him that he had to go there! He wondered if there weren't a way to present himself at the portals of CELESTIA—and not just be admitted, but actually welcomed! Well, maybe there was—

For the past eight months he'd lived invisibly in a tiny furnished apartment in Portland, Maine. He rarely ventured outside, but with his new laptop he could travel the world. Still pondering ingress, he logged onto CELESTIA's website, hunting for some pretext by which to pay them a visit. He hated the infidel bitch if that's what she were!

He had to see for himself whether she was a God.

The most promising avenue was CELESTIA's Pan-Theology Exchange Network, where leaders of all faiths were encouraged to share and compare beliefs in a search for common theological foundations on which to build bridges of faith.

Suddenly it hit him: the international terrorist Fa Haad would transform himself into a peace-seeking Shiite pilgrim!

After an hour of reflection, a plan began to emerge. Step One, proclaim a new religious sect: The Islamic Sons of Divine Unity (loosely translated). He liked it, figuring that if a group with a name like that didn't capture the interest of a bunch of theological universalists, nothing would.

* * *

Karyn DeLeo had become closer to the Holy Daughter than any other member of The Seven. They spent more time together, spoke more often in private, laughed more heartily, and shared affection more openly than the Daughter did with anyone else in Her human family.

Karyn alone could suggest to the Daughter that She was possibly overlooking something—or could have perhaps spent a bit more time with someone—or was maybe taking something for granted, as true friends can do. Consequently, whenever one of The Seven was unsure how to approach the Holy Daughter on a given matter, the tendency was to run it by Karyn instead—that she might bring it to the Daughter's attention herself.

Karyn still found it hard to accept the fact that the Daughter of the Creative Spirit had chosen her, above all others, to become Her friend and trusted confidant.

379

Of course the Holy Daughter was fully aware of Karyn's lingering feelings of unworthiness, and attempted to build up her confidence at every opportunity. One way to do this was to tell her of events to come, before anyone else. They had just finished a light supper when She did precisely that:

"I should tell you that the final member of The Seven made contact with us this very day."

Karyn was aghast. "You mean that—terrorist!

Karyn was beyond mollification, that upset was she. For the first time, she'd been hurt by a serious disagreement with her closest and dearest friend, the Holy Daughter. Her voice choking back tears, and presuming on their personal relationship, Karyn deliberately raised her voice a notch: "This is the most sacred place on earth—how could You bring aboard an admitted killer, and — and hand him the helm? How could You do that?" (Far from taking offense, the Holy Daughter was well pleased to see Karyn standing up at long last so strongly for her beliefs.)

"Beloved Karyn—let me try to set your mind at ease. Islam is one of the truly great Faiths of your world—its followers as devout as those of any of your religions. And indeed Islam's most dedicated and spiritual adherent and greatest Faith Son is none other than our Ahmet—who believes in his heart that there is but One True God. So I ask that you give him a little time to win you over, which I am more than confident he will do. Will you do this for Me?"

HOOTERS OF GOD

Looking off toward Mount Washington on the far horizon, Fa Haad acknowledged he must have been watching too much American TV as he indulged himself by trying to picture the Hooters of God, as it amused him to call them. As far as he was concerned, unless, or until, the woman were proven to be Divine, it was not sacrilege to imagine her nude.

And with that, a Voice suddenly spoke within his mind:

Perhaps not—but it's in very bad taste.

Ahmet had never heard voices before, and decided it was just his mind playing tricks on him—and dismissed it.

Meanwhile, two thousand miles away, the Holy Daughter knew exactly what Ahmet was thinking—and had a fitting reception in mind for him.

The reception only Karyn knew about.

*   *   *

Sometimes Finella Bright's Prince of the Night made her cross. And sometimes downright angry. Like tonight.

"Why are you being so damned—pushy?" she demanded.

"Dear One, have I not been unfailingly patient all these years? Reflect carefully—and then permit me some small measure of compensation.

Dangerous events are in transaction at ABYTOR—and the hour draws near for an Intervention. Your long years of preparation will enable you to finally attain your Destiny. Hark! Glory attends your efforts! And great will be your reward!"

"Well—that's more like it," Finella sniffed, faking a lingering peeve. "We'll see—We'll see," she adopted an expression of righteous mollification.

Her Guide permitted her several moments to savor her indignation, then continued—

"We have important work before us, you and I. And you must show your trust in me by doing as I might require when there is not time for explanation. Think of me as someone who knows well the road ahead—and is therefore the best able to do the driving. Can you both acknowledge and accept this?"

"Oh—I suppose so. But could things get—risky?"

"Dear One, know that I would never endanger you—nor ask of you more than you are prepared to give. That is my pledge to you."

She crossed her arms and gave a little purse to her lips. Secretly, she was pleased at being needed.

"And what exactly do you have in mind, My Prince?"

"I want you to telephone Zooti Abydos. Inform him that if he wishes to reclaim ABYTOR, he must act quickly. The Mentors know of another who harbors a desire to destroy the complex and all who are in it. For that reason it might soon be placed under their watch-care."

"And—will that make it more difficult for Zooti to do whatever it is he plans to do?" Finella asked.

"Infinitely—"

FALLEN ONES

The Intercession Oversight Commission convened in emergency session at Mentor Headquarters high above the earth.

The agenda listed but a single item:

Second Imperilment of CELESTIA

The Mentors were not charged with providing personal security for the Daughter of the Creative Spirit while She was in residence on the planet. Responsibility for Her personal safety was assigned first, to the Corps of Surety, an attachment to Provincial Universe Headquarters. Second in line of responsibility for Her security were Her Seraphic Guardians. And third came the Mentors, as Hosts to the Divine One. Though serving in a tertiary role, the members of the Commission considered their responsibility primary as the official Hosts of the Visitation. Twelve in number, every demeanor was grave as the Commission assembled. Following an opening prayer, the chairman spoke.

"The Fallen Ones are gathering to make difficult the way of the Holy Daughter. Their interference comes earlier than anticipated, requiring an appropriate response."

"The Fallen Ones have inveigled the assistance a pliant mortal of the rearm—one who remains unaware of their true purpose. Should they manage to succeed in destroying CELESTIA, the Daughter would be embarrassed and Her Mission compromised."

They discussed briefly the spiritual ramifications of Finella's unwitting fall from grace, and confirmed that she could not be held accountable for an act undertaken out of involuntary ignorance, no matter how damaging it might be

Ahmet was a very different matter. Wholly unaware of his true stature as the Seventh of Seven, he continued to conspire against the Holy Daughter. And since Free Will reigns ever sovereign over every mortal's acts, concern remained.

"It will ease you to realize that this very day Ahmet first heard voice of his Divine Pilot, that sure hand will gently ride the tiller of Ahmet's mind from this day forth. In that, we stand reassured."

Discussion returned to the Fallen Ones. The one hundred Mentors who first appeared at ABYTOR would now return—sanctioned to intervene only in the wake of a Free Will catastrophe.

Other decisions were taken as well:

Finella Bright would experience phone service difficulties, in particular with calls to Cuba;

The Seven would shortly be assigned thirty Mission Continuity Specialists;

The Seven would be urged to restrict invitations to visit CELESTIA to the essential few;

The White House would be formally requested to provide around-the-clock combat air patrols in the skies above CELESTIA;

A company of Supreme Seraphim would be dispatched to augment the Holy Daughter's corporeal security staff;

Zooti Abydos would be delayed by obstacles both material and spiritual on his journey to CELESTIA;

And all Commission decisions would be submitted to the Holy Daughter for Her approval.

WHITE ANGEL

Fa Haad no longer wanted to destroy ABYTOR—because the Daughter of the Creative Spirit had already done it for him! When She assumed residence and re-christened it CELESTIA, its days as Shining Symbol of American Corporate Power were over.

As CELESTIA, it was celebrated the world over and became an even greater symbol—but of what: Goodness and Mercy? Peace on Earth? In God We Trust? Homestead of the Gods?

Whatever it was, Fa Haad somehow knew beyond all doubt that his destiny was to go there—and then make it his own!

Not in his wildest fantasy could Ahmet have imagined that this was exactly what the Universe had in mind!

*   *   *

Art Frayles was troubled. He feared things were getting bogged down in a number of areas and conveyed his concerns to Ellen Kate, putative leader of The Seven—who concluded that these were matters for the whole group to consider.

The Seven were in effect The Four, with the Bryces in Beijing and as yet no seventh Member. With the Holy Daughter sitting in, Frayles spelled out his concerns. The first one dealt with how long it was taking to respond to letters and e-mail. It was quickly decided that more form letter categories were needed. Frayles was asked to set them up, and then generate whatever form letters he deemed appropriate.

The Four moved on to other areas, consuming the better part of an hour, following which the Daughter spoke up—

"The issues and problems set forth today speak to an underlying problem: The Seven function ably, though largely by consensus—compelled to serve in the absence of a leader.

As I have informed you, your final Member is to be the erstwhile terrorist known as Fa Haad.

-Know that he was chosen with great care—his intellect is extraordinary and his moral courage unflagging. He is well-educated, broadly experienced, and a natural leader in every sense."

"Many times has he placed his life at risk for his beliefs—and though his actions have been warped by the tenets of his Faith, his heart remains dedicated to the service of God and his Brothers in Islam.

I bid you welcome Ahmet in My name."

There was no reaction; everyone sat mute.

*   *   *

Finella Bright was having trouble raising Zooti Abydos on his cell phone and was forced to resort to Western Union. The communication was crafted with the help of her Guide:

IMPERATIVE YOU ACT QUICKLY TO REACQUIRE LOST PROPERTY (STOP) COME EARLIEST POSSIBLE (STOP) NECESSARY RESOURCES STAND IN READINESS (STOP) (signed) FINELLA

*   *   *

At the behest of the Mentors, and with the assent of the Holy Daughter, Karyn DeLeo released a statement to the press:
"The Daughter of the Creative Spirit will depart for the People's Republic of China this evening, and return to the United States immediately upon the conclusion of Her visit.

The purpose of the trip, as previously announced, is the launching of a World Brotherhood Movement, which President Wu Sen and the Holy Daughter have agreed to Co-Chair. In addition, the President of China and the President of the United States will meet with the Holy Daughter at CELESTIA in July.

Working in triune partnership, they will assume active responsibility for preventing the further proliferation of nuclear weapons, materials, and technology—and will chart an effective course toward achieving total global nuclear disarmament."

What was not revealed was that it was former President Samuel Bryce, American Ambassador to China and trusted friend of the Chinese, who managed to persuade President Wu to agree to both meetings, as well as their agendas. In the field of foreign affairs, Bryce viewed this as a watershed accomplishment trumping anything he'd achieved as President.

*   *   *

Fa Haad had completed his disguise and was pleased with the result. Peering at himself in the mirror, he beheld a venerable Muslim cleric— complete with Osama-like beard, embroidered silk cap, and thick desert sandals of chew-softened horsehide— while under his flowing white robes, Calvin Klein briefs.

He re-read his invitation to CELESTIA: it was for the second Wednesday in May, and suggested the possibility of being presented to the Holy Daughter Herself. Fa Haad was ecstatic over the success of his ruse.

He thought about his last remaining suitcase nuke—now safely locked away in a storage locker outside Bangor. Its destination had been ABYTOR, but it now awaited reassignment. There would be no need for it in Utah after all.

*   *   *

Karl Brasher's first day in Tel Aviv had been a shocker. Not one-hundred and fifty feet from where he had stood, a teenage Palestinian girl had blown herself up in a crowded market, killing four and injuring thirty-six—five seriously.

Almost before the smoke cleared, he watched people scurry about gathering up bits and pieces of the dead, reciting a prayer over each recovery. He was sure they were unknowingly picking up pieces of the bomber as well—destined to become part of a proper Jewish burial. He was struck by the irony.

He headed back to his hotel, in sudden need of a shower.

*   *   *

Ellen Kate Bryce-Klein was going over the flight plan with the Holy Daughter.

"They've assigned new call signs: WHITE BIRD ONE when You're in the GSA helicopter—AIR FORCE HOLY ONE when aboard the presidential 747—and on the ground, Your code name will be White Angel."

"I'm no angel," She quietly smiled.

"From here, the chopper will fly You to the Salt Lake City airport, where You'll switch to the 747. Then, after a refueling stop in Alaska, it's non-stop to Beijing. By the way, President Onager wants You to feel free to use the 747 as Your personal hotel suite while in China."

"I don't anticipate that it will be necessary to remain there overnight," the Daughter said. "Since your father has so capably prepared the way, We should be able to conclude and sign Our agreements in a matter of hours."

"What have You decided about that Grand Parade that Wu wants to stage in Your honor?"

"I don't want to give offense, but to watch young girls by the hundreds or thousands march by in bright costumes would serve no purpose other than to afford the government an opportunity to show off. That would hardly be in keeping with My Mission. Ergo, I must decline."

Ellen Kate could not argue with this. "Incidentally, you mentioned decrees, signing agreements. Decrees—I'm curious, what name will You use when You sign?"

"Oh—I was thinking that 'Beverly' might be nice."

Ellen Kate howled.

386

*   *   *

The Daughter would be accompanied on Her trip by Karyn, her constant companion—and by Ellen Kate, so she could visit her parents. Art Frayles, Peter Klein, and Zoe would remain at CELESTIA to run things.

Departure was on time, and just as Air Force Holy One took off from Salt Lake, Onager phoned from the White House.

"I just called to wish You every success, and to ask that You convey my very best wishes and personal appreciation to President Wu for his cooperation in Your initiatives."

"I will be most pleased to do so. However, the one who truly deserves your gratitude is Former President Bryce—an inspired choice to be your Ambassador."

"Why, thank You, Holy Daughter—and I must say, in all modesty, I couldn't agree more."

"While We have this opportunity, may I suggest that Our triune conference in July be limited to the three principals. Since I understand Chinese, there will be no need for even a translator. I have found that when leaders confer without their advisors, they tend to be more open and forthcoming."

"I think that's a—a divine idea," he punned lamely, then plowed quickly on. "See what President Wu thinks. If he agrees, I will agree as well."

"Splendid. Let's hope he finds it a divine idea as well," She rejoined, a merry twinkle in her voice.

WU SEN

The first one off the plane in Beijing was the Holy Daughter—with President Wu waiting at the foot of the boarding ramp to greet Her. Just behind him, squinting in the morning sun, stood Ambassador and Mrs. Bryce, all smiles.

There were no military bands to welcome Her, because no one had any notion what kind of music would be appropriate for an arriving Deity. Hymns of various faiths had been rejected for fear of giving offense—classical music had been ruled out as too European—while New Age 'celestial' synthesizers were dismissed as so tacky and decadent as to be beneath consideration.

So all was silent save for the murmurings of greetings the serial clicking of heels and the martial snapping of flags in the wind.

The President of China and the Daughter of the Creative Spirit sat side-by-side in the back seat of Wu's Mercedes limousine, chatting amiably in Mandarin—while outside, throngs of waving, cheering Chinese lined their way. Wu kept pointing out points of historic interest, but the Holy Daughter was far more interested in seeing the people.

"Would it be possible to pause for a few minutes, that I might visit with some of your citizens?" She appealed.

Wu hesitated, then ordered the driver to pull to the curb and stop. Moments later a dozen bodyguards materialized to keep the throng at bay. The moment the Holy Daughter emerged from the limo, a great cheer went up as people jumped about excitedly and reached out to Her.

She immediately walked over and began to speak with them, one-on-one. Presently Her eye fell upon a boy at the back of the crowd hobbled by a badly contorted leg. Calling him by name, She bade him come to Her—and he lurched his way past the others, his pain momentarily eclipsed by joy. The Holy Daughter knelt down and placed Her hands on his leg—suddenly, a golden white light surrounded it—and the crowd let out a collective gasp as they saw the pathetic leg straighten before their eyes!

The Daughter then took the boy by the hand and led him over to meet President Wu, who stammered and sputtered in abject amazement at the miracle he had just beheld. No longer did he question Her Divinity. And back in the limo, when She advised him to have his prostate checked, he got a look of shock on his face—and thanked Her awkwardly.

After a memorable luncheon of sea scallops, gingered scallions, kno wei pea pods, and fresh mountain mushrooms sautéed in cashew oil and rice wine—President Wu rose to toast his guest as "a cosmic ambassador of peace, who brings the gifts of Hope and of Faith to China"—astonishing words for the leader of a Godless nation to utter.

The Holy Daughter rose and responded in Mandarin:

"There remain but two great powers on earth. Verily, a Sino-American Union of Peace is the Hope and the Promise of all Mankind.

I am come on a Mission of Mercy and Peace. I am come bearing the Gift of Divine Love.

I AM LOVE."

With those words, a golden White Light began to radiate brightly about Her—

As a wave of Divine Love poured forth to embrace the whole of the Chinese leadership.

All of a sudden, China no longer felt she was alone—and was forever changed.

This one crowning moment had been the great underlying purpose of the Holy Daughter's journey. All else was secondary: signing the Triune Accords, the joint press conference, the airport closing remarks, the heartfelt farewells.

Then it was wheels up—as the story broke big:

CHINA AND U.S. DEMAND WORLDWIDE NUCLEAR BAN

WU AND ONAGER TO WORK DIRECTLY WITH DAUGHTER

THOSE WHOM GOD HATH JOINED TOGETHER

CHINA S-E-E-S THE LIGHT!

DRAFTING AHMET

Promptly at nine, as his invitation stipulated, Fa Haad presented himself at CELESTIA's base station with all the solemnity he deemed appropriate. Before allowing him onto a Vista Cube, an usher slowly passed a scanner over this latest visitor to detect any trace of metal—and found nothing.

On the ride up, Fa Haad was surprised to learn that the Holy Daughter Herself awaited him in the Seminarium. Upon alighting from the Vista Cube, he was immediately taken to Her.

As he entered the room, he saw that She was not alone: at Her side was a second woman, and at Her feet a Dalmatian pup.

"My Peace Be Upon You—Brother Ahmet," She greeted.

Shocked at the use of his real name, his face became wild with confusion—to the quiet amusement of Karyn DeLeo—as he suddenly perceived himself as being stark naked.

389

"Come—sit beside Me," the Daughter invited. After a moment's hesitation, he complied. *"You are surprised that I know your true name,"* She continued. *"You forget; Deity is Omniscient. I am also well familiar with your bold exploits as the one calling himself 'Fa Haad.' Tell Me, Ahmet—did you hear Me bid you come hither unto Me?"*

Flabbergasted by this turn of events, it took several seconds for him to respond. "Wha—why did You summon me?"

"Because it is My will that you serve alongside Me—to hold inviolate the sanctity of Celestia—and to assist Me in carrying forward the supernal business We are about."

Ahmet's head was spinning with questions—but none made it to his lips. The Daughter answered them anyway.

"There is a holy band of Servers here in residence known as The Seven. Until today there have been but Six. However, Ahmet, you are to be the seventh Member—and to become leader of The Seven, as ordained by Me."

"What—do these 'Seven' do?" he asked, bewildered.

"The Seven are responsible for the operation of Celestia, My Headquarters during My Sojourn in the flesh. Yet an even greater responsibility lies ahead: preparing the way for the arrival of a contingent of heavenly Pilgrims, already under transport to this world."

This was news to Karyn, whose expression showed it. The Holy Daughter smiled at her.

"I can reveal no more at this time, but know—both of you—that your world will be forever changed by the work of these Pilgrims. Still, that lies well in the future. For the present Our work is that of shining Creative Light on the real problems of this desperate world." She looked at Karyn. *"Ahmet, may I present Sister Karyn—My companion, and a Member of The Seven."* They shook hands awkwardly. *"Karyn will escort you to a suite adjoining My own, which is to be your home while you are at Celestia. There you will find a full wardrobe in readiness—all in your size. Knowing of your lifelong fascination with American cowboys—I have provisioned your closet with boots and jeans. And in your bath, you will discover a razor,"* She said pointedly. *"Following lunch, Karyn will take you on a tour, and introduce you to the other three Members of The Seven here in residence. I know that you have many questions, and I assure you, all will be answered in the fullness of time. You have, however, one concern which I will address now: You are safe—a Presidential pardon has already been issued and signed."*

On the way to his suite, Ahmet's mind was flying. What insanity was happening to him! What was the Holy Daughter up to? Dare he trust

Her, just because She is a God? It was now clear She wanted him to end one life and begin another—

"Do you trust Her—completely?" he asked Karyn.

"With my very life," came the immediate reply. "And so can you." She looked him in the eye. "Believe me, it's nice to know that God actually is on your side!"

*   *   *

Finella Bright was more than a little apprehensive—as she stared at the four crates of high explosives stacked in her basement. She'd ordered them at the insistence of her Guide, who'd assured her they were perfectly safe, and could not explode without detonation cord—which was out in the garage.

The order had been pre-paid, supposedly purchased for a nonexistent Hi-Butte Mining Company, and drop-shipped at her home for later trans-shipment. Frankly, she was amazed the supplier was willing to deliver explosives to a residential neighborhood. She had offered no explanation and concluded they must have simply wanted the sale.

Her Guide assured her that "everything's been arranged" and "not to worry." Still, she was troubled, fearing even possible arrest. But what alarmed her most was the intended use of the explosives: the destruction of CELESTIA!

*   *   *

Ellen Kate was having a silent conversation with Gamma.

"What do the Mentors think about genetic engineering?" she mentally asked.

"We regard it most positively. There are two kinds of genetic defects: those which are inherent, and are no fault of the parents—and those which are caused—such as fetal damage resulting from drug and alcohol use on the part of a pregnant mother."

"Is this something you could possibly help us with?"

"There is an order of biological uplifters known as Evolutionary Expeditors, who normally function apart from human awareness. During an Angelesis, however, there is precedent for these uplifters to work in conscious collaboration with members of our Order and with the biologists of the world of the Visitation to overcome certain genetic deficits peculiar to the mortal races of that world."

"Is it possible that we might receive such assistance?"

"That is a question you would need to bring to the Holy Daughter Herself."

"I—think I may just do that," Ellen Kate decided. "Are there any of these—'Expeditors' around?"

"Indeed there are. They are of permanent assignment to all the evolutionary mortal worlds."

*　　*　　*

Ahmet and the Daughter had lunch on the circumferential balcony, joined by Karyn, Ellen Kate, Peter, and Art Frayles. It was a spectacular sunny day, with a stiff breeze to cool everyone's bisque.

"Ahmet—tell me, why did you drop a suitcase bomb on Fort Knox?" Peter asked, his tone laced with disdain.

"To demonstrate to the world that the United States is incapable of protecting even its own money," he smiled, a touch of pride in his voice.

"But it failed to go off, so you risked your life for nothing."

"Only, I am told, because the Mentors intervened."

"In retrospect, are you glad it didn't detonate?" Frayles wondered.

Ahmet had to think it over before replying. "In some ways, yes. But in others, no."

"Care to explain?" Frayles pressed.

"I have still not—fully accepted my proposed role here, but if I do agree to join you—then I'm glad the Mentors stepped in." He reflected for a few moments and added, "But it would have been very interesting to watch the United States try to deal with a molten pool of radioactive gold."

"This—would have entertained you?" Ellen Kate asked.

"Mmmm, indeed. It's is always entertaining to see one with great power confounded and looking foolish. Yes, that would have amused me." He turned to the Holy Daughter—"I have a question myself, if I may—When was I chosen to become part of The Seven?"

"An excellent question. The answer is long ago.

"And—was a Divine Visitation part of the plan from the outset?" Frayles probed.

"Interventions are never undertaken at the last minute. Your troubled world has long been of Universe concern, and My Incarnation was a settled issue once Earth discovered oil."

"Were we—that predictable?" Frayles asked.

"Do not think that among the millions of inhabited evolutionary worlds, yours is the first to encounter difficulty. Emergency Missions were not invented simply to cope with the current problems of Earth. In truth, they have been undertaken for billions upon billions of your years."

Everyone was stupefied. Peter Klein sought a clarification. "Did I hear You say 'billions upon billions—'?"

"You heard correctly. Your astrophysicists declare the Universe to be less than fifteen billion years old—yet they miss the mark by more than a trillion years! There was no Big Bang. Life does not arise from violence—rather, it takes origin in a quiet act of Love by the Hand of God: The Prime Mover—and Source of All That Is."

The table fell silent. There was indeed much to ponder.

*   *   *

Karl Brasher was holding his first session with his all-volunteer Creative Task Force—comprised of five Israelites, five Palestinians, and one American, himself.

The meeting was taking place in Tel Aviv in the main ballroom of the British-owned and operated Hotel Connaught. The world's press was seated in the balcony, and a first rate sound system made sure everyone could hear everyone.

As designated chairman, Karl gaveled the room to order.

"My name is Karl Brasher," he opened nervously, reading from a prepared text, "I am here as the personal representative of the Daughter of the Creative Spirit. My Mission is simple: I am here to assist you in finding a creative road to peace in the Holy Land."

"Let no one think this will easily come about—after all, that long-sought road has been strewn with failure upon failure for generations. There is however no need to tread these well-worn paths yet one more time—we would be no more successful than those who tried before us. No, we must look afresh at the problem, seek out possibilities never before considered, and then fashion effective solutions, be they simple or complex. Imagination, Logic, and Reason will be the tools of our craft; and we will not tire nor become dispirited—because the Holy Daughter of the Creative Spirit has poured out Her Spirit upon all flesh and we shall not want for fresh ideas."

At about the same hour, Tony Scorcone gave nearly the identical speech in Dublin—and Richie Quinn in Jakarta.

An on-looking Universe had already begun calling it the Age of Imagination.

*   *   *

The resolving of endemic social conflicts was not the only business of the Acolytes, merely the most conspicuous. In addition, creative task forces around the world were being mobilized to address global warming—rain forest preservation—pollution—fossil fuel depletion—disease—over-population—poverty—crime—family-violence—and addiction: i.e., the full panoply of human strife.

*   *   *

Without any outside help, Hardpan Dotson had hit upon an idea himself: Instead of discarding as worthless what he called "Agazite, the true tattletale of gold"—he'd simply bundle up the multicolored crystals and delivered them to a friendly tribe of Shoshones, to be made into bright sparkly necklaces and bracelets for the tourists. He wanted a cut of thirty-three percent, but after prolonged haggling, settled for twenty.

*   *   *

The White House was calling.

"Good Morning, Mr. President," Peter answered, when he learned the call was for him. "How's the political climate back there?"

"Pretty stormy, I'm afraid. Apparently news of the Fa Haad pardon was leaked by someone at Justice. I suspect it was that Hy Depkawitz, because he felt cheated out of a juicy prosecution."

"Assuming he would be able to catch him, that is."

"Correct. How's Fa Haad doing anyway?"

"Still boggled by it all. He hasn't agreed to stay on with us as yet. But then the Daughter can be pretty darn persuasive. He'll come around, I'd venture."

"So, tell me what he's like," Onager asked.

"Well, he's certainly not your run-of-the-mill terrorist. Flawless English—polished manners—widely read."

"Has he explained his motives?"

394

"Apparently they were mostly spiritual—though he does think America sucks."

"He's not alone. How's Ellen Kate doing?"

"Fine—been spending a lot of time with the Mentors. And even more with Josh of course."

"And how's the little tyke taking to Celestia?"

"Oh, adapting better than any of us, I'd say. He's gone absolutely potty over the Daughter's little pup, Zoe. They now have an official playtime each day—the Daughter loves to watch them together."

The President changed the subject. "How did She say She liked Wu? Is he someone we can work with?"

"They got on quite well, I gather. Especially after She told him to have his prostate checked. She got a very warm Thank You e-mail just yesterday—looks like they caught it just in time. What with that, and the Love Tsunami in the Great Hall, he has all the markings of a True Believer!"

"Not to mention the kid in the crowd She healed."

"Yeah, that played a big part, too. You may just find a whole New Wu when you guys meet in July!"

"In that connection, you might ask Ellen Kate whether any Mentors will be in attendance."

"I'll let you know. Remember me to the First Lady."

*　　*　　*

That night Ahmet was having trouble sleeping. He thrashed about, struggling with what the Daughter wanted of him. Suddenly, that same silent type of Voice he'd heard back in Portland again spoke to his mind—

"Stop second guessing yourself. You decided on this course long ago."

"Wh—what?"

"Beloved, fear not—for I AM with you. And it has been thus all your life on this world."

"Who the Hell are you anyway—some Mentor?"

"I AM no Mentor, as you call them. I AM your one true bulwark against adversity—your devoted Friend—your Partner—and your Betrothed."

"My 'betrothed'?"

"You and I will spend the rest of Eternity as One. You, Ahmet the Mortal, can become One with no other—and I can become One with no other. You and I are

395

John VanOrsdell
ordained to become One—the Divine wedded to the human—throughout all
Eternity.
Be of good cheer. Await the day when you yourself become Divine—All-Knowing—
and All-Loving. Do you find this prospect daunting?"

"You—you speak as if you're—Almighty God Himself!"
"I should, Dear One, I've had considerable practice."

Upon hearing these words, all of a sudden, Ahmet knew—knew beyond all doubt—that his life rested in God's hands, and that it had always been thus.

ESCAPE TUNNEL

A crisis was brewing in Kashmir. Fierce fighting had broken out between India's elite First Mountain Regulars and certain renegade units of the Pakistani Armed Forces. Each side was accusing the other of initiating the hostilities, and the Cabinets of both governments suddenly found themselves contemplating the first-use of nuclear weapons.

President Onager placed an urgent call to the Holy Daughter, and they talked for nearly an hour.

At 10:30 a.m. the next morning, CELESTIA announced that the Daughter of the Creative Spirit would leave for New Delhi at noon. Following a round of talks with the Indian Primer Minister, She would then fly, under U.S. Air Force escort, directly to Islamabad to meet with Pakistan's President.

President Onager's back-up 747 was already in Salt Lake City waiting to pick Her up, and carrier wings in the Indian Ocean had been placed on Ready Alert to provide air cover.

For once, the Holy Daughter would travel without Karyn, inviting Peter Klein instead, which alarmed Ellen Kate. But she said nothing, other than to implore Peter to be extremely careful.

* * *

Karl Brasher couldn't believe his ears. Ideas—fresh ideas—quality ideas were flying about the conference room in an outburst of creativity!

Completely on their own, participants had already begun to look 'outside the dots' for ideas and solutions. Karl was utterly amazed.

This Creative Spirit stuff really works! he thought.

*   *   *

Enthralled by secret compartments and passageways all his life, Sandovar Abydos had had a top secret escape tunnel built into ABYTOR when it was first constructed. A ladder ran down from the floor of his inner office to a horizontal tunnel leading to a hidden hatchway in the granite base, from which a primitive trail zigzagged its way down the mountain.

Wanting to give Zooti every possible advantage in his mission to blow CELESTIA to smithereens, he revealed the existence of the escape tunnel to his son for the first time.

Zooti was thrilled, and promised to make good use of it.

*   *   *

Governments on both sides of the war in Kashmir were so taken aback by the Holy Daughter's unexpected intervention, they ordered temporary cease-fires and placed their nuclear delivery systems on HOLD.

A devout Hindu, the Indian prime minister was rattled by the sudden interjection of this Christian 'Daughter of the Creative Spirit' into India's business. Nonetheless, he went to the airport to personally welcome Her—only to find himself invited aboard Air Force Holy One to confer with the Holy Daughter in private.

"I appreciate your coming to greet Me in person. I confess that I took advantage of the opportunity, and invited you to join Me in here.

"Permit Me to introduce Dr. Peter Klein, senior member of President Onager's National Security Council staff, under current assignment as White House Liaison with My Headquarters in Celestia."

The two men shook hands, mumbling their pleasure, and the Daughter continued:

"You are not going to be pleased by that which I am about to say. Nor will your adversary. The inescapable Truth, the one correct Solution, is to free the people of

Kashmir to affiliate with whomsoever they choose. Or, in the alternative, to establish their independence as a sovereign state, in affiliation with neither of their neighbors. Know that to do otherwise is to invite a catastrophe. As you are no doubt aware, it is the announced intention of the United States of America and the People's Republic of China to induce all nations to forsake the possession of nuclear weapons of any kind. The present crisis speaks eloquently to the need for complete nuclear disarmament."

The Daughter was right: the Prime Minister did not like what he heard.

Any more than did the President of Pakistan a few hours later.

Nevertheless the ceasefire held—as both sides quietly stood down.

Because now everything had to be rethought.

*　　*　　*

The rationale for Karl Brasher's creative task force's solution was unassailable: The conflict was over real estate; ergo, the solution lay in finding more real estate.

Can't argue with that, Brasher had to admit.

And then the fun began.

Hey, the Sinai Peninsula is right next door!

It's twice the size of Israel and sparsely populated, With one-hundred and twenty-five miles of coastline on the Mediterranean Sea. A major seaside resort was already there plus, proven reserves of oil for 300 years!

A perfect homeland for the Nation of Palestine.

Okay—now what are the obstacles?

Well, for openers, the Sinai belongs to Egypt.

Okay, what could induce them to part with it?

How about a whole lot of money? Long-term economic security? Lasting peace in the region?

In that case—who might be willing to pony up?

Haven't the Saudis always said that they'd pay any price for peace? They already have a number of capped, un-pumped oil-heads.

Meaning: they could lease Egypt a couple of their oil-heads—along with the means to pump, refine, and ship their newfound oil.

Sinai would become Egypt's economic salvation!

Yet—there was one enormous problem:

The Palestinians would have to give up their ancestral homeland.

And that could be a deal-breaker.

* * *

A now clean-shaven Ahmet had wrestled with his decision all night—Divine Guidance notwithstanding. He requested a breakfast meeting with the other members of The Seven, and they obliged him. After waffles and eggs he addressed them:

"I've decided to accept the Holy Daughter's invitation to join you in Her service. I've always believed that there is but One True God. Whether we worship Him as Allah, or Her as the Daughter—They are One and the Same.

"Of course there remains another question, namely whether or not I am to be your leader. And that matter rests in your hands, exclusively. Not even the Daughter has a vote—only the four of you. Let me say simply that if it is your wish, I would be deeply honored." With that, he rose and left them to their deliberations.

The four looked at one another and shrugged. Despite what Ahmet had said about Her not having a vote, as far as they were concerned, what the Daughter wanted, they wanted.

Ahmet would lead them—for Good or for ill.

* * *

Zooti Abydos decided that traveling by bus was the least conspicuous way to get to ABYTOR, as he still called it.

It was 3:00 a.m. when his Greyhound pulled into the Salt Lake City terminal. He retrieved his bag, walked a few blocks, and hailed a cab. Finella would no doubt be asleep. Too bad.

He had the taxi drop him several blocks from her house and walked the rest of the way. He double-checked the house number, walked up, and rang the bell. It took four more rings before a light finally came on in the hallway. Finella peered through the peephole—recognized who it was after a few moments—and unchained the door.

"This is a helluva time to be ringing anyone's doorbell," she grumbled, showing him in and drawing her robe tightly about her. "You can set your bag down over there," she pointed. "You want me to make you some coffee—or do you just want to go to bed? The guest room's down the hall on the left." He dropped his bag where he was standing.

"Did all four crates arrive safely?" he asked, taking in her bizarre, left-over hippy decor.

"They're in the basement."

"And the detonation cord and timer?"

"In the garage. What about the coffee?"

"I need to check the crates first."

"Be my guest," she said, indicating the basement door.

Ten minutes later he returned. "Got anything to drink?"

"I have some Lotus wine."

"What the Hell is that?" he winced.

"And there's some ale in the fridge," she appended.

He headed for the kitchen. "That's more like it."

She shot him a sour look. "Drink it in your room," she instructed—and went into her bedroom and locked the door—

*   *   *

Hy Depkawitz still hadn't forgiven the Marshals Service for letting Sandovar Abydos escape. The man hadn't even stood trial yet—hadn't been convicted yet—hadn't been sentenced yet. He'd been arraigned, and that was it! Damn! God Damn! Double God Damn!

Adding insult to injury, Depkawitz knew that Abydos, Sr. was at this very moment living high in Havana. Babes galore—money to burn—the purest coke—along with the full protection of the Cuban Government, which had lost no time in granting him political asylum. This had been done partly for dollars—and partly to enrage Washington. On either score, Mr. Castro would have been more than happy—but with both, he was overjoyed.

Face it, as long as Abydos is in Cuba, he's untouchable, Depkawitz reasoned. The trick will be to somehow lure him out—But what to use for bait? Money? Celestia? His own son? Or none of the above?

This was going to take some thought.

*   *   *

No sooner had the Holy Daughter returned from the subcontinent, than She had to turn around and fly to Boston for Her first in-person appearance before a mass audience.

When the Daughter had sought the advice of The Seven as to where She should make Her first major appearance, Art Frayles had been quick to recommended the new stadium which was home to the New England Patriots. It was magnificent, and the people of Boston could be counted on to open their hearts to Her. She said that sounded fine, and it took but one call to Foxboro to nail down a date: June seventeenth. Today.

Bathed in floodlights, White Bird One touched down in the middle of the playing field—and a great roar of welcome went up from the packed stadium. The night was clear and warm, the air sweet with freshness as it blew across the field. The rotors braked to a stop, and for a few moments nothing happened. The crowd fell silent—

Then the hatch dropped open—and the Daughter of the Creative Spirit stepped onto the field. She walked to Her podium and adjusted the microphone. Then She spoke

My Peace Be Upon You—My Love Embrace You.

I have chosen this time and this place to speak to Mankind on matters of the Spirit.

You are, every one, literally, factually, and in Truth: Children of God. As such, you are Holy. Every one of you.

You are Holy Children of God—

And you are, every one, literally, factually, and in Truth: Brother and Sister. As such, you must Love one another. Every one of you.

Yesterday I returned from a region of fear, hatred, and conflict. I told their leaders that which I just told you and in the exact same words.

And I admonished them—as I now admonish you: You Are Holy Children of God. Act Accordingly!"

With Her words hanging in the air, She walked back to the helicopter, boarded, and took off.

The crowd sat stunned—having seen the face of God—and the displeasure on it.

The Holy Daughter had spoken for less than a minute.

Good thing the tickets were free.

*   *   *

The Holy Daughter was angry—or at least as angry as a Deity ever gets.

She gathered Her human family in the Seminarium bright and early the next morning, and began to lay out the issues as She saw them—

401

John VanOrsdell

"I was perhaps too abrupt with the Boston audience last evening—but then the very brevity of My remarks may serve to emphasize them."

"The more I observe the human condition, the more I ache—and the more work I see before us. During the flight back last night, I watched your television—a prime instrument for observing human behavior. I saw men bash each other about in a wrestling ring—and the crowd scream for blood. I watched children, rage blazing in their eyes, shriek with glee whenever a combatant would cry out in pain."

"I watched police dramas about family violence, rape, murder, kidnapping, drug addiction, prostitution, and every crime you can imagine—all as a form of mass entertainment. I saw young people sing and dance to stimulate sexual desire—I observed politicians in the act of lying—I watched news reports of starvation, of war, of religious hatred, of torture by governments. I saw a film celebrate horror and gore—I watched spectators riot at a soccer match—I saw hockey players stop their game to beat upon each other."

"All of this I observed in the span of four hours. These are the Holy Children of God—these are true Brothers and Sisters—acting in the most Unholy of ways. These are first and foremost spiritual matters—those embraced Values which underlie all selfish and savage behavior—toward which the Divine Spirits and I will address Our efforts."

"Meanwhile, My Holy Acolytes will deal creatively with specific conflicts and the spheres of greatest concern. In addition, the arriving Pilgrims will work to uplift certain social institutions and certain forms of governance—all this while we here at Celestia go about ministering to the spiritual needs of the world."

"And we need to begin at once."

PAPAL OLIVE TREE

Sandovar Abydos was far from alone in his hatred of the Mentors, who had been highly critical of the disproportionate accumulation of personal wealth and in so doing made a lot of enemies among the wealthy and the powerful.

Certain of these individuals had already banded together in secret to fight the common enemy, and anointed themselves The Bastion. They met monthly, most often aboard the private yacht of one of their members in some corner of the Mediterranean. They'd already put together a kitty of one-hundred million—with more if needed.

The problem in dealing with Mentors was that they were invisible. (They could, if they so choose, manifest within the spectrum of human vision, but said they'd not do so again.) Consequently, one never knew when there were a Mentor nearby, listening in. Worse, Mentors could eavesdrop on the private thoughts of anyone at any time. In short, they were next to impossible to take on directly; to get at them, one had to go after one of their 'spheres of interest.'

But this presented problems of its own. For instance, everyone knew the Mentors were particularly interested in preserving the world's tropical rain forests.

But how could that translate into a plan of action?

Of course, there was always Ellen Kate Bryce-Klein—in whose wellbeing the Mentors had a paramount interest. But did The Bastion really want to go after her just to get back at the Mentors, and run the risk of offending God directly? Hardly. Besides, Bryce-Klein was extremely well guarded at CELESTIA.

No, they'd have to come up with some other 'interest' if they wanted to take on the Mentors.

*   *   *

Tony Scorcone had no love of the Irish, and was not happy at being sent to Dublin to undertake a creative search for peace. It would be like trying to put a cobra and a mongoose in the same cage.

What was so vexing was that their whole generations-long conflict was over religion. Not territory. Not trade. Not ethnic hatred. Not even differences in faith, but rather mere denominational differences—meaning who was in charge!

Tony didn't know where to begin.

*   *   *

The Pope had very mixed feelings about meeting the Daughter of the Creative Spirit. She had agreed to come to the Vatican—but since

403

She had already traveled to Beijing, She apparently attached no significance to who went to see whom. This was obviously one Mountain willing to come even to Mohammed!

The real question in the Pope's mind was whether or not the Church would acknowledge Her spiritual primacy. No Pope had ever bowed to kiss the ring of anyone. He wondered if She even wore rings. Or a watch. Or make-up. He'd contemplated God many times—but never quite like this.

Popes wear watches, and he checked his; in twenty-one hours he'd be looking Deity in the eye! A sobering thought. He began to grow concerned that, upon meeting Her, might he be overcome with emotion? Has any Pope ever wept with Joy in the presence of others? And—was it Joy he'd be feeling?

He prayed he'd be up to the occasion.

*   *   *

Air Force Holy One was on final approach, the airspace cleared of all aircraft within twenty kilometers in every direction. (Save for the three F-18s flying escort.)

In the Vatican limousine sent to meet Her, the Daughter and Karyn saw thousands of people cheering Her wildly as they drove by.

"I wonder if His Holiness is feeling a bit upstaged?" Karyn asked rhetorically, eyeing the passion of the crowd.

"Unfortunately he is."

"How will You put him at ease then?"

"That, Beloved, is beyond My power. Though I shall do my very best."

Karyn smiled, knowing that nothing was beyond Her power.

The Pope had eschewed the trappings of office and received the Holy Daughter in the secluded Papal Garden—in the shade of an olive tree, a gift from the Holy Land.

"Most Holy One, I bid You a heartfelt Welcome," he greeted in English, a small but sincere smile on his lips.

"Holy Father, My Peace Be Upon You. You have chosen a truly beautiful setting for Our visit, and I am touched."

They sat, and the Pope carefully poured two glasses of fresh lemonade. He was relieved to find that he wasn't being overly emotional

404

as he had feared; mostly he was trying not to let his nervousness show. The Daughter reached over and placed Her hand softly atop his.

"Ease yourself, Antonio, I expect no fealty. Rather, I am here to appeal for your assistance—that together you and I might bring to an end a savage conflict of odious duration. I speak of course of the Irish tragedy."

"My Evening Devotions always include a prayer for peace in that tortured land," the Pope solemnly assured.

"It will require more than prayer, My Son. And this is the principal reason for My visit. I have faith that if you and I were to make a joint appeal for Peace—not to Our Heavenly Father, but directly to the leaders of the conflict themselves—Our efforts might bring forth a final Peace."

"I—would of course be proud to join You in such a noble quest," the Pope replied. "How would You suggest we proceed?"

"In My view, there is but one way: Appear together, unexpectedly, and use our respective authority to command them to make peace—in the Name of God!"

John Peter considered this bold approach to the problem and decided he was not about to take issue with an Omniscient Being. "When—did You have in mind that we should attempt to schedule this—spiritual summit?"

She replied in Latin: "When the hour to strike is at hand, tarry not."

*   *   *

President Onager phoned the British Prime Minister and advised him that the Daughter of the Creative Spirit and Pope John Peter were presently in the air, en route to Dublin in the quest for peace. It was to be an unannounced visit, designed to catch the warring factions off-guard and deny them the opportunity to prepare.

The Prime Minister didn't like last-minute surprises, but he quickly acknowledged that nothing else had worked so far. "It would certainly seem worth a try. Perhaps neither of them will have the nerve to defy Deity. Let's pray they don't."

"You might inform them that they've been invited to join His Holiness and the Holy Daughter aboard Air Force Holy One upon their arrival at Dublin International—in just over two hours from now," Onager said, noting the time.

"I'll—of course do so. I'll phone them personally. This might actually be fun," the PM mused, wishing he could see their expressions when he told them who was coming.

405

Just as the setting sun kissed the western horizon, the tires beneath Air Force Holy One kissed runway five-zero with simultaneous chirps of blue smoke. Fifteen minutes later, the Daughter and the Pope faced the two leaders, Catholic and Protestant.

"My Peace Be Upon You," She blessed.

With those words—a golden aura appeared around both Her and the Pope. With a gasp, the two Irishmen immediately fell to their knees—and the Daughter did not bid them to rise. Instead, She let them remain in a state of humbled awe.

"His Holiness and I have journeyed here in a joint quest for Peace," She began. "We did not, however, come to appeal for your cooperation. Rather, to give you warning that your mortal souls stand at peril if you do not order an immediate end to the spilling of Irish blood." She paused to give Her words time to find purchase in their hearts. "Now arise, My Sons, that We may look into one another's eyes."

They climbed shakily to their feet, neither daring to not do as She asked.

"I say again: Look into My eyes!" It was not an invitation but a command, which they obeyed. And as they did—Her golden aura slowly embraced them both, and for the first time, each felt the sublime Power of Divine Love.

John Peter was suddenly overcome with emotion—knelt down before Her and kissed the hem of Her robe—and sobbed openly.

And to an on-looking Universe, this single transcendent moment marked the true onset of Peace.

Instead of flying to Utah directly, Air Force Holy One returned to Rome to drop off John Peter. En route, the Holy Daughter spoke of the afterlife which awaits all mortals.

"The ascent worlds are not of natural origin, nor are they evolutionary," She revealed. "Rather, they are intelligent creations of consummate beauty, crafted to provide home and hearth for former mortals—as they learn the ways of God's Creation, and the tongue of their Provincial Universe."

By the time Her 747 touched down at Rome, John Peter had been the recipient of an unprecedented outpouring of Divine Revelation—for the Daughter had seen into his heart, and found it pure and unquestioning in its Faith.

* * *

When the Holy Daughter returned to CELESTIA, She found altogether different problems awaiting Her: Zoe had destroyed one of Her slippers—Rusty Steele and Karyn had had a nasty fight over an interview he was planning—and one of Silvagio's ushers had been caught in bed with a chambermaid.

It was good to be home.

KEEPING THINGS SIMPLE

Special Agent Depkawitz came to the reluctant conclusion that there actually was no bait strong enough to lure Sandovar Abydos back onto U.S. soil—leaving him with but three alternatives: One: Come up with something to lure him to a different country; Two: Kidnap him in Cuba, and then smuggle him out; Three: Find some way to induce the Cubans to renege on their agreement to not extradite him—then let them simply arrest him and turn him over to U.S. authorities.

The first option was probably the safest to pull off—but was also the one with the greatest political uncertainties. Besides, he was at a loss to know what to dangle as bait;

The second choice was by far the most dangerous—as well as having a potential for creating an international incident;

This left option number three. The trick here would be to find something the Bureau, or the U.S., could offer Mr. Castro which would persuade him to renege on his deal—and to do so without running afoul of the State Department. He knew that to upset that bunch was to invite early retirement.

He decided it was time to hold a brainstorming session—what with all this creative energy supposedly on the loose!

*   *   *

Rusty Steele didn't give a flying fig what Karyn DeLeo thought, her journalistic experience in Boston notwithstanding. But being a close friend of the Holy Daughter—well, that was something else. So he came to her office; they needed to have another talk. He slumped into a chair.

"Look, the thing people all over the world are busting to know is, What's the Daughter like personally? Meaning when She's not going about conducting Universe business. They've never seen that side of Her, and that's what they crave."

"Rusty, let me say it one last time: It's none of their business!" Her voice became mocking, "'How many time a day does a God brush Her teeth? Does She ever have bad breath? Does She go to the bathroom like everyone else?' Sorry, pal, that stuff's way, way out of the question."

"Dammit, Karyn, that's not what I'm after, and you know it!" he fired back. "People want to know what, if anything, makes Her laugh— what Her favorite foods are—whether or not She Herself prays—what She thinks of our music—what She watches on TV—if it's true She has a puppy—that kinda stuff!"

"The Holy Daughter is entitled to Her privacy just like anyone else," Karyn snapped. "So back off!"

However Rusty had no such intention. "Fine," he snapped back, "then how 'bout I interview you? You're Her best friend—you know Her better than anyone else—so you tell the world what She's like!"

"Don't hold your breath."

"Okay, look—tell Her that people everywhere yearn to know more about Her—and that all I want to do is interview Her as a real person. Will you at least do that much?"

Karyn wondered whether the Daughter actually thought of Herself as a 'real person'—and reluctantly decided she'd relay Rusty's request when an opportunity presented itself.

"Okay," she sagged, "I'll—ask Her."

*   *   *

Zooti Abydos believed in keeping things simple. Less chance of something going wrong that way.

His father had told him about the secret escape tunnel leading down from his inner office, and Zooti figured it was the perfect way for him to get inside CELESTIA, place the explosives, set the timer—and get the Hell out!

What could be simpler?

Finella, however, was becoming a problem. Increasingly nervous about having explosives hidden in her house, she was paranoid about getting arrested—and was thus becoming an unacceptable risk. But then there was that 'spirit prince' of hers to worry about. He'd proven to be a potent ally up to now—but could probably make big trouble if he ever got the idea Finella were in danger. Even worse: Was it possible that he could, the same as a Mentor, read people's minds?

Shit! If that—he could be listening in right now!

Suddenly alarmed, Zooti tried again and again to not think about what he was thinking about—found that to be utterly impossible—and flew into a rage of frustration.

"Sonofabitch!" he cried, delivering a savage punch to the side of his head to punish it.

Meanwhile, Finella was out in her garden, making life miserable for some errant marigolds which had dared to invade her prized geranium bed.

If her Guide did in fact know what Zooti were thinking, he wasn't sharing it with her. So, other than dealing with the naughty marigolds, nothing was going on in her head.

*   *   *

"Our detractors are up to no good, I'm sorry to say" the Daughter shared.

"What do you mean?" Karyn asked.

"There are those who plot against Us—and I speak not of mortals."

"You—you mean, there really are 'evil spirits'?"

"More accurately: spirits capable of doing evil."

"Who—are they anyway?"

"They are apostates—often called 'Fallen Ones'"

They were seated in the Sacred Suite, picking and sucking pomegranate seeds. Zoe wanted to play too, so Karyn gave her a seed. Repelled, she opened her mouth to let it fall out.

"Why—leave these spirits free do evil things?"

"Because, Dear One, as I have often stated, Free Will is inviolate. Not even I can countermand it!

"But—couldn't you find some way to—say, thwart it—without directly countermanding it?"

"You think like a chess player. And the answer is Yes." She placed a fat juicy seed in Zoe's reluctant mouth. "And, that's where Ahmet comes in." To Karyn's astonishment, Zoe not only chewed the seed, but then begged for another!

"Wha—what happened?"

The Holy Daughter winked. "I made it sweet for her."

"Can You—make one sweet for me, too?"

Senior Agent Depkawitz had assembled his team, tasking them to be creative and come up with something Mr. Castro would find irresistible. They began to ponder the problem—

"What, for instance, would make him look Really Good to his people—?" Hal wondered aloud.

"Something Really Big," Franklin smirked.

"I guess what I'm going for is—something that would be what, wildly popular?"

"Like what, blue jeans? HDTVs? Pepsi? Viagra? We'd run smack into the trade embargo if we weren't careful."

"Unless—we deliver the goodies via, say Mexico—"

Hy sensed they were already onto something. "I think you birds may be on the right track there," he encouraged.

*   *   *

Ahmet and Ellen Kate had deliberately avoided getting better acquainted. She still thought of him as a terrorist—and was certain her father would never have pardoned him.

Ahmet sensed her contempt and kept his distance.

But the Holy Daughter had asked Ellen Kate to fix him up with a driver's license and a passport—which meant spending a certain amount of face-time with him. Summoned, he presented himself at her office.

"Come on in," she bid, indicating a chair. "Let's see now—" She flipped a few sheets in his file. "I assume any driver's license you may have is bogus. Correct?"

"I've used this one several times to rent cars, and it's never been challenged." He passed it over to her. The man in the photo was heavily bearded. 'Jerome Pomerantz'?" She made a face. "You gotta be kidding—"

"Bogus, no—Orthodox, yes," he smiled.

A terrorist and a wit, she mused. "Well, an American passport would be impossible—you're not an American."

"I have a validated birth certificate for one Irving Marsh, born September fifth 1955 in Sandusky, Ohio—and long since deceased—would that do?" He handed it to her; she eyed it skeptically. So he decided to play his trump card—

"Don't forget, I've got a friend in High places. Why couldn't She get me the equivalent of a Vatican passport?"

"The Holy Daughter carries a Diplomatic passport—for which you're hardly a candidate," she dismissed. "Though a Utah license should be doable—Mr. Marsh." She placed the birth certificate in her file. "If we use that, they'll make you take out a learner's permit," she smiled.

"I'm a quick study."

"Tell me, where'd you learn colloquial English so well?"

"Right here in the Good Old US of A, M'am. I watch your television whenever I can—and it's an excellent teacher." He squinted at her. "Has your father ever spoken my name?"

She refused to give him the satisfaction. "I doubt it," she replied.

"You just told a lie!" he pounced, triumph in his eyes.

"Yes—I did," she confessed. "I recall one occasion when he called you 'an animal.' Satisfied?"

*　　*　　*

Hardpan Dotson had managed to put away a little money for the first time in his life. His 'Agazite' jewelry had begun to sell, and his Arapaho partners made sure he received his full cut. Having witnessed the healing powers of his sacred blanket, they were taking no chances. They looked upon him as a bona fide Medicine Man (however unlikely that was for a smelly, white, hard-scrabble prospector)—and treated him with considerable respect. Another first for Hardpan.

He sometimes wondered how "that nice nekked lady" was doing, and resolved to pay'er a visit one o' these days. Then, as he was thinking about nekkedness, he had himself a creative idea: People were so awed by the healing powers of his blanket; "I oughta charge for my services!"; he decided.

Big Mistake.

When an Indian boy with a broken arm was brought to him, he announced there'd be a fee of five dollars. He placed the sacred blanket over the arm—and nothing happened!

Just like that, the blanket had lost its powers. And jewelry sales seemed to dry up overnight.

*   *   *

Zooti Abydos spoke with his father by cell phone—and was instructed to execute his plan as soon as he was ready.

*   *   *

The Daughter of the Creative Spirit met with Ahmet in Her office. It would be their first private conversation.

"Ahmet, My Son, please come in and take a seat. Would you like some coffee—or some pastries? I must confess I've taken a liking to jelly doughnuts, of all things."

This made Ahmet smile and he relaxed a bit. "Yes, thank you—that sounds good. Black, if You please."

She poured him a cup and slid the pastries over. She watched as he took a bite—which left a dusting of white around his mouth. This made Her smile Herself.

"I know that you are still a little anxious about your new role here. It must be difficult to suddenly learn that your Destiny lies here with Us—and that this Mission was and is of your own advance choosing."

"Holy One, I have no difficulty accepting Your Divinity. If I have a problem, it's with how I could have chosen to become a terrorist and a killer in this life—and still be true to my origins. How this is possible?"

"Were it not for your fidelity to your origins, you would not think to pose such a question in the first place. In truth, you have not strayed all that far. Consider: Have you not been prioritized all your life by service to God? Have you not been willing to sacrifice your life in the flesh for that very God? Have you not heard My Voice speak unto you? Do you not hunger to be redeemed by serving your God? And do you not at this very moment feel the Truth of My Words reverberating powerfully within?"

She could see that Her Words were indeed ringing inside him like some great celestial clapper. Her tone changed—

"The reason I wanted to meet with you today is to discuss the World Brotherhood Movement, which President Wu of China and I are jointly sponsoring."

412

Over the next hour the Daughter spelled out what She envisioned for the WBM—and ended by appointing Ahmet as its executive director. He was stunned—but willing.

THE BASTION

The Bastion had been founded, funded, and organized in secret by a sixty-two year-old billionaire importer-exporter named Silvio Androtti, a native of Sardinia, who viewed the Mentors as intolerable meddlers capable of wreaking havoc among the world's ultra-rich and powerful.

To recruit others, he had drafted a succinct, blunt, brazen Mission Statement which he believed put it well:

"TERMINATE THE ACTIVITIES OF
THOSE COSMIC ENTITIES KNOWN AS
MENTORS—THROUGH ASSASSINATION,
SABOTAGE, FORCIBLE COERCION, AND
ANY/ALL MEANS NECESSARY—WITHOUT
REGARD FOR RISK, COST, OR THIRD PARTY
INTERESTS, AND DO SO WITHOUT
COMPROMISING OPERATIVES, OR ANY
MEMBER OF THE BASTION.

He was proud of his creation—and never once suspected it was in part the unfortunate, though direct, consequence of global intellectual excitation by the Creative Spirit.

In pursuit of his stated ends, Androtti had recruited secretly, quickly, and without difficulty, twenty-five members from a dozen countries—men whose combined net worth totaled more than a trillion dollars (U.S.).

Unhappily, two of those whom he approached early on had declined to join his clandestine cabal—and shortly thereafter each fell victim to a fatal accident.

The Bastion took no prisoners.

*   *   *

413

The Holy Daughter directed The Seven to empty and secure a large storage area on the lower level of CELESTIA for use in connection with the anticipated arrival of the Pilgrims. She chose not to reveal the purpose of the space, saying only that it would be used by various celestial beings in the performance of their duties.

Her second directive was even more puzzling, if not outright bizarre. She said She required an enormous, circular piece of glass molded, ground and polished to exact specifications: twelve point thirty-seven feet in diameter, twenty-one point seventy-one inches in depth—clear and absolutely flawless.

Moreover, this massive disk had to be ready in four months time—delivered to CELESTIA by flatbed truck—and rigged for hoisting by heavy-lift helicopter to the rooftop helipad.

The only possible source for it was a firm in California which manufactured reflecting mirrors for the largest telescopes. At first the company had balked, explaining that they couldn't completely disrupt their manufacturing schedule just to accommodate one new customer—no matter who it was.

It took three calls from the White House, including one from President Onager himself, to persuade them otherwise.

*   *   *

The Holy Daughter decided to permit Rusty Steele to interview Her, and chose the great circumferential balcony for the occasion. Necklaces of tiny white clouds, assembled as backdrops, majestically adorned the surrounding peaks. He never dreamed they were intentional.

After a pro forma exchange of pleasantries, he got down to cases: "Holy Daughter, the question I hear most often is, What is Your opinion of the people of Earth—and how do we compare with inhabitants of other evolving worlds?"

"I cherish all the people of Earth. But comparisons are difficult."

"How so?"

"Your world differs in significant ways from all others. You have certain life forms which are unique to this planet. In addition, you remain under spiritual quarantine, cut off from contact with nearby worlds—this being the result of your early rejection of Universe authority and the willful embrace of self-determination. Yet despite that,

know that this world lies cradled in the loving embrace of its Creator. You only think you are alone—spinning on through a cold, unfeeling cosmos—without purpose or direction."

Rusty quickly realized that the Daughter had adroitly turned the intended interview about Her, into a spiritual teaching. What the Hell; It's Divine Revelation time! This is even better! he acknowledged.

"You're saying—we're not free to determine our own course and destiny?" he asked. He sounded a trifle indignant, and this amused Her.

"You are always free to make your own choices—all the Universe can do is to try to influence those choices. That is why those whom you call Mentors made their presence known; why a Universe Revelator made a recent appearance on top of this very mountain—indeed, why I come and why others are soon to follow."

Rusty suddenly had so many questions they were tripping over themselves in his mind.

"Uh—can, can we go back for a moment to what You said about Earth being different from all other worlds—I assume there are other differences as well?"

"In ways too numerous to mention. Yet in one aspect your world stands supreme; you are the designated Master Planet of your Provincial Universe—having gained that eminence in consequence of having been chosen as the host world for the Creator's Incarnation—for His life in the flesh."

"I'm—confused. Are You talking now about Jesus?"

She smiled at his deft grasp of the obvious.

"I am. In Truth, your Creator walked this world just over two thousand years ago. The One named Joshua ben Joseph was—and is—your Sovereign. Despite His ordeal on the cross, He promised to one day return—and His Word was sacred."

*   *   *

Ahmet had been informed by the Holy Daughter that there existed a genuine threat against CELESTIA—and that attack was imminent. She directed him to draw upon his expertise in the destructive arts of terrorists, and use it to foil the attack.

Set a thief to catch a thief, he mused.

Challenged by the assignment, he began by poring over the original blueprints for ABYTOR, looking for ways a determined attacker might employ to gain access. After an hour or so of research, he discovered that, not far from the granite core of the mountain itself, there appeared to be an unexplained void in the same location on each level below the administrative offices. It made no sense; he decided to investigate.

Beginning on the level directly below the offices, he went to the mysterious spot and came upon—a blank wall.

Taking measurements in several directions—he confirmed that there was an area about three feet square that couldn't be accounted for.

He went to the next lower level and repeated the process: same results. He mulled it over, and decided he'd best drill a small hole and take a look-see.

Using a device resembling a sigmoid-ascope, he inserted it in the drill hole, switched on its light, peered inside,and beheld a ladder affixed to the wall of some kind of shaft!

He went back to the prints and discovered that the shaft ran directly down from the office presently occupied by Tony Silvagio, CELESTIA's Director of Security.

Interesting.

He went to Silvagio's office and found him seated at his desk. When Ahmet appeared he looked up, surprised.

"I need to take a peek under your carpet," he announced. The room had wall-to-wall carpeting, so some cutting would be required. Silvagio wanted to know what the Hell was going on and Ahmet told him he'd have to ask the Daughter.

He made the call, and was simply instructed to cooperate. He hung up and told Ahmet he could proceed. After taking a few measurements, Ahmet asked Silvagio to help him move the desk. Begrudgingly, he obliged. Ahmet then produced a small knife—and made a long slit. Two more slits, and he was able to peel back a flap—exposing a thick layer of felt under-pad. Three more slits—and a steel hatch suddenly appeared, set flush in the floor like a manhole cover.

Ahmet knew what was under it, so he let Silvagio open the hatch— and watched him stare open-mouthed down a long shaft which had been directly beneath his desk the whole time. He noticed a light switch to one side and flipped it on; they could now see all the way to the bottom.

"Feel like taking a short journey of discovery?" Ahmet invited.

Five minutes later the two men stood in a portal at the end of a tunnel, gazing down the interior mountain path.

"Well now—ain't this cute—"Silvagio breathed.

*   *   *

The Holy Daughter and Karyn were in the Sacred Suite, watching Josh and Zoe play a riotous game of Slobber Face.

Repeated shrill shrieks of joy and horror, accompanied by salvos of ecstatic yipping, had rendered both women weak from laughter. Finally Karyn found the breath to speak.

"Do You—ever get to laugh like that back—'Home'?"

"Truly, I can't remember laughing so heartily in—a very long time." She paused. "I was about to say 'Ages' but didn't want to be that specific."

Karyn caught the gleam in Her voice. "That was—You being facetious again, wasn't it?"

"You are getting to know Me," She beamed. "So I think it's time you called Me 'Beverly'."

Karyn gave a Yeah, Right snort—and in the next instant realized the Daughter wasn't being facetious this time.

"In that case, Bev—you really do need to do somethin' with Your hair, ya know—?" she ventured tentatively. "I'm not going to go straight to Hell now, am I?"

By way of reply, the Holy Daughter leaned over and hugged Karyn tightly. Just about then, Josh and Zoe collapsed with exhaustion, and curled up together for a time-out quick-nap.

"Bev—I really can call You that? Only in private though, right?" The Daughter grinned. "Then, can You tell me what's with all the hush-hush business down in the storage area? I heard You said it had to do with the Pilgrims—"

"I will speak to you, and only to you, of these matters. The area being sequestered is for the conjoint use of the Life Enablers—the Genetic Custodians—and the Coherence Directors. I know these terms mean little, so let Me simply say that these High Beings are expert in their disciplines, and will reconstitute the Pilgrims following their arrival."

"Say What?"

"Let Me take you back in time. All that has come to pass on this troubled world of yours was foreseen long, long ago. The Overseers of the Provincial Universe anticipated the need for Teachers of Truth to travel here to portray realities as they exist on other, slightly more advanced, evolving worlds. I say 'slightly' because anything beyond that—would be too much beyond—and mankind would be unable to appreciate it."

John VanOrsdell

"What kind of beings are these—'Pilgrims' anyway?"

"Human beings. Very much like yourselves, from a nearby world in many ways similar to your own. In truth, these mortals are so like you biologically, that interbreeding might be possible. However, as material beings, it was necessary to transmute them temporarily into spirit form for travel at the speeds necessary for such a long journey."

"And when they get here—they'll be turned back into flesh and blood?"

"Precisely. In the sequestered area below."

"You're saying—a person can be converted into spirit form—and then back into flesh and blood again?"

"Only in the most extreme of circumstances. That it is taking place at all is Epochal. Only thrice before in your Universe's four-hundred billion year history has this taken place."

"But—why now—and why us?"

"Now, because the emergency is now—and here, because this is the Bestowal World of your Creator's choosing."

"Meaning—"

"For God so loved the world'—Karyn, He saw the strife to come—the consequences arising from the willful embrace of self-determinism. He saw the isolation and the spiritual retardation. He also foresaw the scientific flowering to come—and knew how it would eventuate:

Such a state of technological achievement is not unlike one in which a child is handed a loaded pistol; sooner or later the child will discover the trigger—and pull on it."

"And yours is a world rife with triggers" She added.

"Can we go back for a minute to the Jesus business? Was He—is He—the One True God?"

"He was—and is—the Creator of this, Your Provincial Universe. Through the experiential wisdom gained by living an actual life among those whom He created, He attained full and eternal sovereignty over this Universe of His creation."

"You seem to imply that He is not alone in this regard."

"Indeed. Your Creator Son is but One of many thousands."

TRIGGERS

418

The method whereby a material being is transmuted into a spirit being—and a spirit being back into a material being—is unknowable, as this is a spiritual not a physical transaction, and has but a single purpose: to enable high-speed, long-distance travel through space for material beings such as mortals.

Any transmutation of material beings into spirits is an exceedingly rare occurrence, and is undertaken only in obedience to a Plenary Universe Mandate issuing forth from Universe Headquarters.

The only modality for passenger conveyance across the vast inter-galactic reaches is a unique Order of highly specialized angels, known as the Seraphim of Transit.

A single Seraph can carry but a single passenger, safely enshrouded within the protective cover of her wings and flying at many times the speed of light. Prior to departing their native world, spiritized sojourners enter a state of suspended consciousness, to be awakened upon completion of the bio-procedure to reassemble their material bodies, a process requiring up to twenty-eight Earth days. Such reconsciousized travelers awake fully refreshed, fully aware, and fully energized.

In a process known as reintracorporatization, exactly three hundred Seraphim of Transit were presently en route to the world calling itself Earth. Half of the Seraphim bear males.

*   *   *

Zooti Abydos was fast growing impatient. He was ready; the explosives were ready; his father had given the go-ahead; and CELESTIA lay waiting. All he lacked was a vehicle to carry out the mission; he had thought he had one lined up.

But Finella was suddenly balking.

He'd even offered to buy her car outright. But she would have none of it.

"Just suppose someone notices a car parked off the road and jots down my plate number—this shortly after there's a huge explosion on top of the mountain! What then—?"

"I plan to cover the plates with mud," Zooti reassured. "Don't worry, no one would ever make the connection."

Finella wondered how someone so stupid could be entrusted with such a critical mission. She queried her Prince, but all he'd say was "worry not," pledging all would go smoothly. She was frightened, and felt betrayed. As she saw it, she could already be charged with Conspiracy. And in a matter of days, it could be Accomplice to Murder!

She wanted Out.

That night, as she slept, she got her wish.

*   *   *

Depkawitz's creative task force had the germ of a plan.

Their premise: The thing most Cubans covet above all else is a new car. Something economical to buy and operate—but with enough power to snap heads back. The Cuban people had lived under conditions of automotive drought for half a century, and their '50s era Detroit-made jalopies were now virtually beyond repair.

Perhaps vehicles manufactured in China—by an American subsidiary—Only one problem: overcoming the trade embargo would require an Act of Congress.

"But suppose there were absolutely no American involvement—direct or indirect, what then?" Hal argued.

"If we're behind the deal, that's involvement," Hy said.

"Maybe China would deliver the cars—" offered a member of the FBI's creative task force.

"That won't happen," Depkawitz dismissed, "not with Beijing and Washington starting to hold exploratory talks on certain sensitive issues, such as Taiwan. They're not about to risk this by mucking about in some CIA Black Op, which might backfire." Depkawitz clearly had not heard of the Cardinal Rule of Creativity: Never, Ever Blow-Off a Fresh Idea until you've torn it apart, looking for that Seed of Gold. And its corollary: A Good Idea Doesn't Care Who Has It.

BACK DOOR

After dispatching Finella, Zooti loaded the crates of C-4, Timers, Detonators, Det-Cord and Batteries into the trunk of her Oldsmobile—and headed for ABYTOR, by way of a dirt service road, abandoned once construction was completed. He checked his watch: 1:38 a.m.

*   *   *

(Ahmet and Silvagio had lost no time installing half a dozen super sensitive sonic sensors the full length of the secret escape tunnel which Abydos had built under his office.)

In revealing to his son there was a secret entrance he could use to sneak in the explosives, Abydos forgot all about one tiny detail: there was a 79 cent dead-bolt, mounted on the inside of the steel portal—which had naturally been left in the locked position. And then completely forgotten.

Having already exhausted himself struggling up the mountain with 130 pounds of high explosives—only to find his way hopelessly blocked by a stupid dead-bolt, and he flew into a rage. He wasn't about to wrestle the goddamn crates back down the mountain, crates with his prints all over them.

There had to be a solution. He sat down to think (an activity for which he generally seemed to have fallen on hard times). Looking up at the underside of the Great Balcony, his gaze became fixated on the heavy diagonal support beams beneath it. And began to think. Sort of.

By the time most people realize they have to find a worthy solution to a serious problem, they're often already in desperate straits, without sufficient time to fashion a decent creative solution. Such was the case with Zooti Abydos, who suddenly saw that it was up to him, and him alone to improvise a whole new way to put CELESTIA permanently out of business. Thanks to a single dead-bolt, he was forced to destroy the place by working strictly from outside, using a mere 130 pounds of C-4. And then make a clean get-away. Time was short. It would be getting light in just under three-hours—by when it was his intention to be far, far away.

421

Gazing up, the balcony diagonal struts mesmerized Zooti—blow enough of them, he reasoned, and the whole damn thing would come crashing down the mountain! His father, he grinned, was going to be so proud.

Unable to see the diagonal struts on the far side, Zooti estimated there were 14 or 15 in all. Four were within easy reach, two more if he stretched. It took him just over an hour to wrap and wire together all six, with about 20 pounds of C-4 packed around the base of each. Gathering up the empty crates and anything else with his fingerprints, he headed back to Finella's car, stopping in it just once to heave the incriminating evidence off a high bridge. 40 minutes later he was in the air, headed for Mexico in a rented Cessna.

There was however a fatal flaw in his plan: The diagonal struts supported nothing at all! CELESTIA rested securely on a heavy steel ring, which seated the entire structure on the hand-chiseled peak of the mountain itself—like a perfectly fitting tight collar.

The diagonal struts were purely for psychological comfort.

*　　*　　*

In the dark of the night, a series of loud explosions awoke everyone at CELESTIA—all except the Holy Daughter, who'd been watching the inept little drama unfolding below.

She also took notice of the profound disappointment being experienced by the Fallen Ones, who were at odds over assigning blame for placing reliance on a mortal who had clearly fallen on intellectual hard times.

*　　*　　*

Later that day Ellen Kate and Gamma had a heated exchange.

"I guess I'm just feeling a little left-out. A major attack on CELESTIA was being planned—and I'm kept out of the loop! Or was this merely a small Mentor oversight?"

"To have 'looped' you, would have caused needless anxiety. Since nothing was being asked of you, it was deemed unnecessary. If the decision gives offense, that is most regrettable."

"That's—both condescending and insulting! Spare me your concern in the future."

"Dear One, while we can appreciate your resentment, it is misplaced. The decision was that of the Holy Daughter—and your dispute lies with Her."

This stunned Ellen Kate. Her first impulse was to go and confront the Daughter, but brief reflection made her realize there was no winning of an argument with God. So she dropped it, though not altogether un-miffed.

*   *   *

Ahmet was furious. He'd utterly failed to prevent the attack, by seriously overestimating the professionalism and skill of the attacker(s). Meanwhile, Tony Silvagio was no less displeased with himself.

The two men sat in Ahmet's office, conducting a brutal post-mortem. Each felt unforgivably stupid.

"I'm wondering if I oughtta resign," Silvagio sagged.

Ahmet thought it over. "No point. Where would they ever find as good a dummy like you?"

Offense flashed across Silvagio's face—then crumbled into a grin. "Yeah," he said. "No friggin' point."

At that moment the Holy Daughter walked in.

"Are we perhaps feeling a little foolish today?" She greeted, causing both men to spring to their feet. "The one mounting this morning's assault has already fled to another country. Yet Celestia Stands! Know that he is the one who failed—and not either of you. Know further that you both continue to enjoy My fullest confidence." She turned to Ahmet. "My Son, I would speak with you of other matters. Are you free to join Me for a stroll on the balcony?"

"Of course, Holy One," he said, following Her out.

Until they reached the balcony, the Daughter did not speak. Instead She went to the railing above the location of the blasts, and leaned out for a peek. Ahmet did the same.

"Perhaps We should remove the remaining braces rather than replace them—" She said, almost to Herself.

"Why is that, Holy Daughter?"

"To make Our perch appear all the more precarious—that appeals to Me," She responded, another gleam in Her eye. She then took on a serious mien and began to walk.

"You were born and reared in Iran, were you not?"

"That is correct," Ahmet answered, a little off balance by the question.

Iran is a nation dominated by religious intolerance-which would, if it had them, employ nuclear weapons against 'the Infidels.' With such hatred in so many hearts, I may need to journey to Tehran in the name of Peace. Since there are many in that region who would do Me harm, I need you as an advisor to anticipate the reactions I may expect, both public and private. Would you be comfortable in this role?"

"It's—been many years since I left Iran. I no longer feel Iranian, Holy One."

"Does not an Iranian heart still beat within you?"

From the look in his eyes, he didn't need to reply.

*　　*　　*

Franklin was taken with Hal's idea of manufacturing cars in Cuba, over-reaching though it was. Still, he felt some scaled-down version of the concept was worth exploring.

"How 'bout simply a Ferrari or two for good old Fidel? Or a Ferrari and a Rolls—whatever blows his skirt up."

"In exchange for looking the other way—while we snatch Abydos!" Hal exclaimed, slapping the desk in triumph.

"I say it's worth exploring—but strictly back-channel. Cuban regard for Abydos surely has its limits," Hy reasoned. "Okay, I'll take it to the Director himself—and see if he's willing to run it by the A. G."

"What about State?" Franklin asked.

"They'd probably crap their pants," Hal replied.

"Hell, that alone makes it worth doing!" laughed Hy.

*　　*　　*

PEACE PACT AT LAST!

COMES IN WAKE OF SURPRISE VISIT BY
DAUGHTER OF CREATIVE SPIRIT AND
POPE JOHN PETER.

I. R. A. LAYS DOWN ARMS,

CREDITS PEACE MISSION BY HOLY PAIR

424

PEACE COMES TO IRELAND THANK GOD!

The Holy Daughter was pleased by the world's headlines. She Herself had received word of the settlement just hours before the announcement. She finished Her coffee and phoned to congratulate John Peter—who was beset with gratitude, and stammered about trying to find fitting words.

The Daughter made it easier for him—

"My Beloved Son, this day word peals forth to a waiting universe of your supernal service on behalf of Peace. Your Faith and Sunlight become a beacon of hope for a dark and tortured world. Rest secure in the knowledge that your work serves to inspire Brotherhood among all mankind."

In further consequence, an Acolyte named Scorcone was recruited into the Mortal Corps of Reconciliation, a post of Honor for Divine Service.

This transacted quietly, without any awareness thereof on the part of the mortal honoree.

*   *   *

Art Frayles was having lunch with Rusty Steele and Karyn DeLeo on the great balcony, where a stiff breeze tried to snatch away unwary napkins. It was another magnificent day, with the majesty of high peaks running off as far as the eye could see. The food was trumped at nearly every meal.

"Hope the weather holds for next week's Summit," Art commented.

"Who's scheduled to arrive first, Wu or Onager?" Rusty asked.

"Onager, by a couple of hours, being the host country."

"They still planning on three days?"

"Presumably—assuming all goes well."

"Let us pray—"

Is it still going to be only the three of them in the room?" Karyn asked.

"What are my chances of doing some interviews?" Rusty asked hopefully, turning to Karyn.

"I can ask Her. No promises."

"Tell 'em they get a lollipop with every interview."

"Oooh, that should do it—I hear Wu's a real lollipop kinda guy!" Karyn dismissed.

425

Along about then the salads arrived, and everyone dug in.

A DAZZLING GOLD

The weekend before the Summit, the Holy Daughter made an unannounced trip to San Francisco's Mission District to spend time among the homeless. The Secret Service was not pleased.

She had dressed in ordinary street clothes, not wanting the news-media to spot Her. Looking around, She found a small group of black men in an alleyway off Catherine Street passing around a bottle of red wine. Her bodyguards, visibly apprehensive, took up station at both ends of the alley.

"Yo, pretty momma—what up?" one greeted.

"Hey, baby—" another chimed in, scrutinizing Her closely, "ain't I seen you somewheres?"

"Very possibly. I'm the Daughter of the Creative Spirit, and you may have seen My picture."

"Yeah—!" he said. "Damn! Ain't You supposed to be some kinda God er sumpin'—?"

In response, She began to softly radiate Her golden aura.

"Holy Shit!" one yelped, as they all reared back.

"My Sons: Never think that you have been forgotten by your Creator. His Love for you is Eternal, and I have come to bring His Spirit unto you—and to hear of your dreams." She reached out and took the bottle of wine from the last one to drink from it—and instantly, its contents turned a dazzling gold! "Drink of this—whatever your ills, they will be healed," She promised, passing the bottle back.

After some hesitation, he took it, his hand trembling.

"Yeah, Bro—take a good hit!" one dared.

"Jes leave some for us," another goaded.

"One small sip," the Daughter said quietly, "will more than suffice."

He stoked his courage—and did as She asked.

Instantly, he felt a powerful energy pulsing within:

The curvature in his spine straightened

An abscessed tooth ceased hurting

A deep facial scar vanished
His lungs were cleansed
And a cataract dissolved.

He nearly exploded with joy. The others all gaped.

"Gimme some of that shit!" one suddenly demanded, snatching away the bottle and downing a gulp—and in moments, this man knew he no longer craved crack cocaine.

The others quickly took sips of their own—and one after the other turned to the Daughter, awe in their eyes.

"Now—speak to Me of your dreams," She said quietly, taking a seat on the steps. Silently, the men gathered about Her feet—conspicuously meek and respectful.

Watching closely from half a block away, the Secret Service agents couldn't believe their eyes.

*   *   *

At precisely 10:00 a.m., Marine One touched down on CELESTIA's rooftop helipad, and President Onager alighted alone. Met by Arthur Frayles, he was led below to greet the others. Then they all went to the Seminarium, where the Daughter awaited.

"David, My Son—" She welcomed warmly, reaching out to shake his hand. "I trust your journey was agreeable?"

"Oh—a few bumps over the mountains, otherwise most pleasant," he smiled.

"Perhaps I should smooth the air for President Wu," She smiled back.

"Oh, I wouldn't go that far," he laughed.

"Then I shan't. Let your discomfort be his as well."

"I've always found the weather to be the great equalizer. Incidentally, I'm told he's running about an hour late."

"Fashionably Late," Ellen Kate offered.

"No doubt, no doubt," Onager chuckled.

Everyone took a seat, and the Daughter turned to the President. "Tell Me, My Son—in seeking global nuclear accords, do your advisors favor the carrot or the stick?"

"A little of both. They say the key will be to help Wu see China not only as Sponsor, but Enforcer as well. They suggest we let him wave his stick at recalcitrant nations, while we work on coming up with the carrots—as usual."

"Good cop-Bad cop," Frayles interjected.

"What carrots did you have in mind?" the Daughter asked.

"That all depends. Having already granted China Most Favored Nation trading status, and with investment dollars pouring in every day, there's not a lot left economically that we can do for them. Which leaves technology. And of course—the military," the President summarized.

"'Military'—?" Ellen Kate wondered aloud, trying to recall her father's views on the subject.

"Sure, Katie—we already sell 'em an old destroyer now and then— maybe even a few antique helicopters," Onager explained. "But we could easily sweeten the pot: a submarine or two—a few jets that can go super-sonic—You get the picture. Or, as I said before, technology: nuclear propulsion—over-the-horizon radar—that sort of thing."

"It is My impression the Chinese have something more in mind," the Daughter said "They might seek to forge new and stronger military alliances."

"With whom?" Onager asked, leaning forward.

"With the United States, for one," She replied. "And another, by capitalizing on a new relationship with Taiwan."

"Are You speculating here—or drawing on Your, Your omniscience?" the President pressed.

"I never speculate."

HERESY

President Wu arrived just in time for lunch. Wu, Onager, and the Holy Daughter dined in private, the Daughter translating whenever Wu's English wasn't up to the task. More social than business, conversation revolved mostly around CELESTIA, the majesty of the mountains, the air, and the food—all of which were conducive to harmony.

"I must compliment You on Your choice of a site to serve as Your earthly home," Wu praised grandly, glancing about.

"Please consider it your home as well for as long as you are with Us," She urged— and then switched to the business at hand. "I have an offer for each of you. If you wish, it is within My powers to know your very thoughts, fears, and desires. We can

use this to assist in both communication and comprehension. Would that not be of great benefit?"

Wu and Onager looked at each other with surprised alarm. What would it mean to refuse? What would it mean to accept? Each realized his advisors would be horrified by the utter heresy of the idea—and was quietly amused.

"Fear not, I would reveal no secrets of state—only your true beliefs concerning the matters under discussion. Are either of you wary of hearing nothing but truth?"

"It's an invasion of one's person—for their thoughts and feelings to be stripped bare," Onager opined, noting that Wu's expression said he agreed.

"You may be surprised upon discovering that that is the reality on the higher worlds. You may regard this as mental nudity—but it is in no sense exhibitionistic. It is the way everyone wants it. You can imagine the effect this would have on impure thoughts," She added, with a splash of wry.

*   *   *

At noon a neighbor reported a nasty smell coming from next door, and shortly thereafter, the Salt Lake City police found Finella Bright's body. She lay in her bed, her throat slashed.

An obvious homicide, the entire property quickly became a crime scene, with scores of fingerprints found and lifted.

Her garage was discovered to be empty, and an APB was broadcast for her car. Within hours it was located, parked at a small airfield in Utah's Uinta Mountains.

The Secret Service had designated the attack on CELESTIA an attempted assassination—and by late afternoon Finella's Buick was in their custody.

*   *   *

It was perhaps the first publicly announced Summit with absolutely no press coverage, and Rusty Steele was allowed no interviews. Every major news service had a correspondent camped out at CELESTIA's base station, but they might as well have stayed home. There would be no announcements and no press conference—the world would simply have to wait.

Against this relaxed backdrop, Onager and Wu were able to meet and chat informally whenever they wished, a refreshing change for both. The Holy Daughter joined them from time to time, with President Wu becoming increasingly comfortable in Her presence.

By the second day of the Summit, agreement was reached on a three-pronged approach to the pursuit of global nuclear disarmament:

ONE: DIPLOMATIC PRESSURE VIA THE
UNITED NATIONS;

TWO: TRADE—AND THE THREAT OF
TRADE EMBARGOES;

THREE: ECONOMIC ASSISTANCE
THROUGH THE WORLD BANK.

The bilateral Summit concluded its work by day three and ended on schedule with several announcements, one stunning. It was the final day of the Summit that would capture headlines the world over; The United States and the People's Republic of China agreed to allow one military base apiece to be built and operated on each other's soil. The Americans would construct an airbase on the outskirts of Nanjing, and the Chinese would build a naval base on the coast of Oregon. All this had been at the Holy Daughter's suggestion, and was not altogether unprecedented—after all, the United States had successfully maintained a naval base on hostile soil in Guantanamo, Cuba for decades.

However, the military significance of the accord would take a backseat to the diplomatic: A brand new Sino-American partnership had been formed. Although falling short of an actual alliance, it nevertheless rang up the curtain on a promising new era. One could only wonder how Russia and Japan, in particular, would react to the new relationship between the two behemoths.

*　　*　　*

On July sixteenth Zooti Abydos was indicted for first-degree murder, and a fugitive warrant was issued for his arrest. Hy Depkawitz had learned that Zooti had fled to Cuba—and figured that, to get their hands on Junior now, they might have to toss in an extra Maserati or Bentley for Castro.

*　　*　　*

Ahmet lay on his bed staring at the ceiling—thinking about the suitcase nuke he'd left in storage back in Bangor, Maine. As he saw it, he had three options: One: Retrieve it (and then do what with it?) —Two: Sell it—to some other terrorist (but, who?) —or Three: Leave it where it was—pay no further rent, and sit back and wait for it to be discovered (something guaranteed to drive the Pentagon and the White House totally bonkers!). On that level, he found the third option by far the most appealing. Yet in the end, he picked number two as his best choice. The only problem he could see was the Holy Daughter—what if She already k-n-e-w what he was planning? And, if She did, what would She do—if anything? He remembered well what She had said about the Universe never interfering with the exercise of free will.

But was it a gamble he was willing to take?

He tossed and turned most of the night—and wondered how much he could get for his nuke. Ahmet would never admit it, even to himself, but he loved money—and was just as materialistic as any greedy capitalist on earth.

*　　*　　*

The Holy Daughter phoned Karl Brasher in Israel to check progress on their proposal to turn much of the Sinai Peninsula over to the Palestinians.

"Is the Sinai concept still the first choice of the task force?" She inquired.

"It is, Holy Daughter. But then no one's talked to the Saudis or the Egyptians yet. And they could easily refuse. You failed to mention the Palestinians themselves—does everyone believe they'd be willing to forsake their ancestral homeland?"

"Perhaps it's time to approach the Saudis," She suggested. "But the approach would have to be by the White House, I would think. While the President was here last week, I told him what your team had come up with, and he was highly skeptical. However, I can certainly urge him to at least broach the subject with the Saudis. I'll make the call, and let you know what he says."

*　　*　　*

The Seven had been cooped up together for months and were starting to get on one another's nerves. At their regular Monday morning staff meeting, Peter was the first to show the strain. The Holy Daughter was not present.

"Richie Quinn reports that Jakarta is pretty much a creative dry hole," he stated with a tone of asperity.

"He's only just begun. They probably need more time," Karyn offered.

"Time to dig more dry holes?" Peter snapped.

"Hey, give 'em a chance," Ellen Kate fired back. "We're not peddling a 'Miracle-Quick-Cure', you know."

"Sometimes I think this creativity business is more hype than substance," her husband pressed, his irritation evident.

"What is this—are you attacking the Daughter now?"

Art Frayles had heard enough. "Look, we've just finished holding a watershed Summit, suddenly peace has broken out in Ireland. The Sinai proposal may yet bear fruit. I say give Her a chance, for God's sake!"

Ahmet had sat back watching. He always enjoyed a little heat, and decided to stoke the fire. "Maybe Peter's right. We can't expect miracles every time—but neither can we tolerate failure."

"Oh, piss off!" Ellen Kate attacked. "God never fails, and She damn sure won't this time! Jakarta will come through sooner or later. And as long as we're taking potshots, how are you coming with your World Brotherhood Movement?"

Ahmet looked annoyed. The Movement meant little to him, and he wished the Daughter'd given it to one of the others. "Don't try to change the subject, Ellen Kate. Here we sit, wholly dependent on the Holy Daughter—only to find She Herself is relying on people to succeed!"

Peter was beginning to regret what he had started, and held out an olive branch: "Let's not forget, we're all on board here out of choice. And maybe we all need to be a bit more patient, especially me."

"It's not a matter of patience, Peter," his wife countered, "it's a matter of Faith."

"When all else fails, there's always Faith to fall back on," he grumbled. The others fell silent; this was turning nasty. To Ahmet's private amusement.

Just then the Holy Daughter walked in. Suddenly, everyone felt very uncomfortable and turned their eyes away.

"Good Morning, My Children. It is apparent that you toil in My vineyards with some discord. Oh Ye of Little Faith! Remember, not every striving can bear fruit as long as free will holds sway. That is the lesson the Mentors bore. Our task is to inspire, motivate, encourage, and uplift. Not to judge, criticize, inhibit, and impede.

I am exceeding proud of you all, My human family. My Faith in you is unshakable. Abide in Me."

THE PILGRIMS

The special area set aside for use by the biologic reconstitution team of celestial engineers, along with the large glass disk on the roof, had been sealed off from everyone at CELESTIA. Not even a member of The Seven was permitted to enter. The Daughter of the Creative Spirit alone knew what was transacting behind the locked doors. And something was definitely underway.

The Holy Daughter met with The Seven in the Seminarium to answer some of their questions.

"How can anyone tell anything at all's going on inside?" Peter led off. "There's nothing but silence coming out of that entire area. Not even any electricity is being used."

"The activities in progress require no form of earthly energy, including electricity," She responded. *"But there is indeed enormous activity, as you will soon discover."*

"How soon?" Ellen Kate asked.

"In less than eighty hours the Pilgrims will emerge. When they do, We anticipate they will have a powerful hunger—not only for food, but to see and experience their new home."

"Will they be able to eat—human food?" Karyn wanted to know.

"Most decidedly; otherwise they would starve. They have brought with them no food from their home world."

"What do You suppose they'll want to eat?"

"On their own planet they grew food not unlike that to be found here. Their grains in particular are quite similar."

"Do they eat meat—or fish?"

433

"They do—but their livestock are altogether different. They raise large eating birds somewhat akin to your ostriches—but red meat will be completely new to them."

"Do they have oceans like ours—full of fish and other critters of the sea?" Art Frayles inquired.

"Yes. However, I suspect they will be reluctant to eat a lobster. There's nothing on their world to compare with your crustaceans. And an octopus would likely disgust them."

"Do they have snakes?" Karyn wondered.

"Many, many varieties. Snakes are among the most common life forms on the evolutionary worlds. You are incidentally host to some of the more deadly varieties," She smiled.

"Figures," muttered Frayles.

"What about the people themselves—how much like us are they?" Ellen Kate asked.

"Their world is nearly one point five times as large as Earth. Consequently, the pull of gravity is considerably greater. And you will find that they are somewhat shorter than you—and somewhat stronger as well. Once on Earth, however, their musculature is sure to weaken and shrink."

"Like us, do they come in various colors?" Peter asked.

"They do, but those chosen to migrate to your world are of the red-violet race, the superior strain on most worlds."

"Racial superiority?" Ahmet was suddenly interested.

"Not in the sense you mean. The red-violet race is the product of an evolutionary race which has been enhanced by superior biologic beings. Ones introduced for that purpose."

"Whoa—" Frayles cut in, "this is extraordinarily sensitive ground You're treading on, Holy Daughter."

"By 'superior biologic beings,' I meant precisely that: beings less susceptible to disease, infirmity, and genetic defect. I was not referring to intellectual or spiritual capacity. The choice of the red-violet race was necessary to afford the Pilgrims the greatest resistance to those earthly diseases against which they have no immune system defenses."

Frayles was mollified; Ahmet was disappointed; Ellen Kate, Karyn, and Peter were content to drop it.

*　　　*　　　*

As promised, the Holy Daughter phoned President Onager to appeal for diplomatic overtures to the Saudis, offering the Sinai Solution as the best way to achieve Mideast Peace.

When the President had first heard the notion of giving most of Sinai to the Palestinians as their new homeland, he was taken aback by what he considered the sheer naiveté of the idea. He was certain Egypt wasn't about to give up the Sinai no matter how fat the bribe.

Yet here was the Daughter of the Creative Spirit Herself on the phone, asking him to buy into the concept.

"Please understand that this comes at a particularly sensitive time in Saudi-American relations. And I must confess, Holy Daughter,. I find this whole Sinai proposal a bit hare-brained. But since it's You who's asking, I'll run it by the Secretary of State. If he finds it meritorious on any level, I'll direct him to approach the Saudis as You request. But if the Kingdom has no interest whatever, I see no point in even raising the subject with the Egyptians."

"In all candor," he continued, "the Royal Family is more than a little angry over our ongoing investigations of their links to terrorism. Bear in mind, they too are the targets of rabid hatred—largely because of their ties to us! The whole situation is so convoluted I wouldn't get Your hopes up." He paused. "Have You thought about going to Riyadh Yourself and speaking directly with the Crown Prince?"

"My Mission is in part to help foster Peace, to be sure. But insofar as the elements of the proposed Sinai Solution are fundamentally economic and geographic—and not social or spiritual—success would ultimately depend on negotiation. And I do not negotiate."

"Perhaps You could merely open the door to negotiation by others—"

"Unless the proposed solution makes fundamental sense to all parties involved—and that is very much in question—no amount of Divine Intervention would help. I recognize that, due to the workings of free will, there is a significant risk of failure here. And you need to appreciate that I cannot be seen as having initiated a conspicuous failure."

The President mulled this over for a few moments before replying. "Since You put it that way, Holy Daughter, I have to concur. This leaves the ball in my court, looks like." He paused briefly. "I'll speak with the Secretary."

* * *

The Reconstitution Chamber, as it had been designated by the Holy Daughter, remained sealed until all three-hundred Pilgrims had been fully and successfully re-materialized into their former physical bodies.

It was the night of the August full moon—with the Daughter of the Creative Spirit Herself in temporary occupancy of flesh, a stunning concept for the Pilgrims.

She entered the chamber, accompanied by Her beloved Zoe. And so it was that the first creature of earthly origin which the Pilgrims beheld was a seven-month-old Dalmatian puppy—that immediately bounded up to one of the Pilgrims and licked his hand. When the Daughter spoke, it was in English, the newly acquired tongue of all the Pilgrims.

"I bid you welcome. As does my companion, Zoe.

I see that you have all arrived in good health—no doubt anxious to behold your new home world. It is a sacrifice of supernal majesty which each of you has made—forsaking forever the world of your nativity, to serve another.

The Universe hails your gift, and pledges that those whom you have left behind will be provided for in every regard. Exalted for their own great sacrifice, they are become the cherished wards of the Creator Himself.

You each have been told of the grave problems confronting this troubled world—and you have seen exotic portrayals of its many wonders and beauties. Yet, it greatest beauty lies with its people.

You will discover they are resourceful inventors, talented artists, willing workers, loving, loyal, compassionate, self-sacrificing, idealistic, and widely religious—keen of mind and vast in humor.

But you will also find deceit—hatred—cruelty—greed—vanity—laziness—and ignorance.

It is a colorful, exciting place to live and work—and I commend you to the adventure before you!

You will spend a season here with us at CELESTIA before taking up residence in the capital cities of its nation-states. You will find that staffs await you who are both fluent in the English language, and superior communicators in their native tongues.

Once among the people of Earth, you will be persons of great interest, and very likely of great influence—as is My intent.

The moment you depart this Chamber, you will meet your first humans of this world—and important mutual first impressions will be formed. Know that they fully share your own nervous anticipation. Let Me remind you of your parameters—As proud citizens of another world, at all times you are to reflect only its highest standards and values.

As teachers you have come—as teachers shall you serve. Above all, become not discouraged.

Be among the people—build friendships—make and keep commitments. You are enjoyed, however, forbidden to have physical liaison with any members of this human race except under a declared and recognized marriage. To those among you who are female, I say, conceive not offspring—except under the supervision of physicians schooled at Celestia.

Only under these Terms of Authorization may you serve. Violate any—and you shame the Universe.

You will be compensated as consultants to the host governments, and you may spend and invest as you see fit. Should unavoidable wealth come your way, I bid you find worthy charities and be generous.

You have been given attractive attire, and I note that you have opted to retain your hair styled as before. I find this both appropriate and pleasing.

Come, Zoe—it is time to introduce Our guests."

With these words, the Daughter of the Creative Spirit flung wide the portals of the Chamber—and led forth the citizens of one world to meet the citizens of another.

The interface between the natives of different worlds was fascinating. At first they eyed one another closely, and made attempts at friendliness by smiling nervously. They ventured awkward questions in an effort at conversation, and then began to pair off into small mixed groups as the new arrivals were taken on a tour of CELESTIA. As they walked, the Pilgrims seemed to delight in how much lighter their bodies felt.

By the time the tour ended, the ice had been broken and everyone had relaxed a bit. Almost immediately, interest focused on lunch; the Pilgrims were famished. The Holy Daughter had personally planned the menu for their unearthly guests, taking into account the kinds of food and drink they had enjoyed on their home world.

The appetizers were fresh fruit—melons, peaches, mangos, tangerines, grapes, and raspberries. But the first thing the Pilgrims reached for was water—clear, cold, sweet spring water. They remarked at how similar Earth's water was to that to which they were accustomed. The Daughter explained that the combination of two hydrogen and one oxygen atoms in liquid form was a Universe constant.

The main course consisted of roast chicken, turkey, and duck—plus fresh green salads, rice pilaf, and hot pop-overs. Strangely, none of the visitors seemed to know what purpose butter served, and demurred when it was offered. They did, however, avail themselves of salt, soy sauce, and garlic powder. Their hosts seemed especially enchanted over their apparent love of chocolate milk—in contrast to the faces they made upon first tasting coffee.

When it came time for dessert, they were repelled by ice cream and sherbet. They just couldn't get past the melting, seeing it as decomposition before their very eyes. However, the dark, shiny, chocolate layer cakes were eagerly devoured.

One difference stood out: The Pilgrims were instantly alarmed by laughter—thinking it to be a kind of choking. Human laughter would take some getting used to.

There were gender differences as well. Female Pilgrims were fascinated by the variety of hairstyles and colors of their female hosts, asking permission to stroke each and feel its texture. All Pilgrims, male or female, wore their hair in a swept-up, back-flowing fashion—not unlike the wings on Mercury's feet. And everyone's hair was the same color, a very pale shade of blue.

The Pilgrims stood on average a head shorter than their earthly counterparts, although appearing to weigh slightly more. Their skin was noticeably darker than that of a Caucasian, but considerably lighter than that of the average African. Their eyes were universally blue-green, while their facial features were quite similar to those found on earth—even down to eyebrows and lashes, teeth, mouths, and ear shapes.

Ahmet was quick to note that Pilgrim breasts rode high and bouncy—while Karyn observed that the men all had nice rear ends. Art Frayles was oblivious to both, and the Kleins were pretending not to notice.

Of immediate interest to all the Pilgrims was Josh, who the women seemed eager to hold. Ellen Kate offered him to one, who handled him like delicate crystal. But Josh quickly tired of the attention, and squirmed down to play with Zoe.

After lunch the Pilgrims were shown to their rooms, and given time to bathe, try on more new clothes, perhaps watch a little television—and rest.

* * *

The world had no idea what had transpired at CELESTIA. The only persons informed of the Pilgrims' successful reconstitution were President Onager in Washington and members of The Seven plus Ambassador and Mrs. Bryce in Beijing.

On the third day following the Pilgrims' arrival, an official announcement was made, explaining who the Pilgrims were—why they had journeyed to Earth—where they were to be assigned—how they would spend the remainder of their lives among us—plus advice on how they should be received.

On the seventh day, a video of the Pilgrims at CELESTIA was released—and an anxious world got its first glimpse of living beings from another planet.

The media, however, experienced a major disappointment: absolutely no access to the Pilgrims would be granted. Only after their individual arrivals at their countries of assignment could interviews be arranged through host governments.

* * *

Silvio Androtti and The Bastion were aghast over the sudden appearance of the Pilgrims.

In all likelihood, they were in league with the despised Mentors, and their presence could augur nothing but trouble.

On the other hand, there was one redeeming aspect: Unlike Mentors, Pilgrims were mortal.

John VanOrsdell

"FERVENT COITUS"

The Holy Daughter, the Pilgrims, and The Seven, along with Rusty Steele, Tony Silvagio and his ushers, all met in the main dining room the morning of the twelfth day following Reconstitution. The purpose of the meeting was to have a freewheeling exchange between the humans of Earth and those of Marinor, the Pilgrims' home world.

Everyone had questions. "What is the one thing that most surprised you about us?" Rusty led off.

The Pilgrim leader, a woman named Karshia, rose to respond, She seemed a bit bemused. "As you may surmise, most of us have watched your television rather extensively. It furnishes us with many insights—and often affords us both amusement and amazement." Her English was perfect, with no discernible accent and delivered with a clipped precision of word. "To answer directly, we Marinorians have been most surprised by observing how over-occupied you appear to be with the act of reproduction. Do we conclude correctly?"

Everyone began to smile. The host humans looked self-consciously at one another, shrugging and waiting for someone to reply. Karyn finally opted to answer the question with a question.

"We call it simply 'having sex'—and I can see how we may appear 'over-occupied' with it. But this is relative. How often do the people of Marinor—indulge themselves?"

A chuckle passed through the Pilgrims before Karshia replied. "We view the mating act as being primarily for the purpose of reproduction—enjoyable though it may be. In answer to your query: less than a score of times each year."

"And, exactly how long is your year?" Art Frayles asked.

"Three point two times longer than that of Earth, as we orbit considerably farther from our sun, which is just under five times the size of your own." Everyone did the math—and winced: Marinorians have sex less than six times per earth year.

"Was there ever a time when your world was similarly 'over-occupied' with sex?" Frayles followed up.

"Our historical record reveals that this was once so. Less than a century ago, we too went through a period of fervent and frequent coitus—a time when our own planetary overseers gazed down upon millions of busy buttocks rising and falling everywhere!" Picturing it from this perspective, everyone couldn't help but laugh.

"But, why is this no longer so?" Ellen Kate asked. "Did Marinor's libidos take early retirement?" More chuckles.

"Simply put, we outgrew our carnal appetites, seeing them a primitive over indulgence. And since sexual coupling is now by law a procreative privilege, Marinorians never couple once they exceed child-bearing age. Such activity would be distasteful to us, and regarded as incompatible with enlightenment."

The earthlings found this mildly insulting, but rather than debate the issue they turned to less sensitive topics.

"Is there a crime problem on Marinor?" Rusty asked.

"We have developed highly effective methods for curtailing criminal behavior. But still it does occur."

"What kind of methods?" he pressed.

"Whenever we find individuals who exhibit a propensity for criminal acts, they are placed in preventive detention—that we may counsel them and treat their disorders."

"I'm afraid we would find that to be an unconscionable violation of human rights," Frayles said.

"And far from 'enlightened,'" Karyn added pointedly.

At this, the Holy Daughter elected to step in.

"It is indeed enlightened for any society to take appropriate measures to protect itself from crime, insanity, and the acts of moral degenerates.

Once identified as risks to society, such persons are placed in special agricultural colonies, from which they may be one day paroled. Prisoners are treated with respect and compassion, being regarded as the products of their genetic inheritance, their rearing, and the impact of their surroundings. As such, they are adjudged blameless—and afforded every state resource to restore them to society.

The consequence of having such laws has been the curtailment of crime on Marinor by more than eighty percent. And few today would argue for their repeal."

The room fell silent. Arthur Frayles worried that these new 'teachers' could engender real hostility by giving voice to such beliefs—which could in turn compromise everything else they sought to impart.

"It might be wise if you didn't discuss how Marinorians cope with crime," he advised." But feel free to share your views on sex, however unlikely it is that anyone will agree."

"Before we leave the subject, I have a question," one of the ushers pursued. "Do you have capital punishment?"

"We have many offenses other than homicide which require someone to be executed. Betrayal of public trust is the most serious fiduciary crime, and as such is a capital offense."

This astonished everyone, especially Peter Klein. "If that were the case here," he said, "our Death Rows would be over-flowing with politicians. I figure you all must have a fairly narrow definition of 'public trust.'"

"As is the case on a great many mortal worlds," the Daughter resumed, "elected officials are held to far higher standards of conduct. Since governance is held to be the supreme position of trust which a citizen can be given, its deliberate betrayal is a crime beyond forgiveness."

"I thought nothing was beyond forgiveness," Ellen Kate countered.

"You are correct if you speak of Divine Forgiveness," She replied. "In stark contrast, forgiveness by one's fellow citizens is often unavailable."

And so it went. For the next two hours, questions were posed and questions were answered. The information gained by the hosts was wide-ranging:

There were twenty-five married couples among the Pilgrims—all without children;

On Marinor diseases are kept under effective control—cancer is curable—sleep cycles are much the same as on Earth—and lifespans are approximately twenty percent longer;

A comprehensive education is mandatory for all citizens. Advanced schooling is a requirement for all those possessing superior intellects and who have demonstrated the requisite work ethic, regardless of age;

Wealth is shared equitably, with no economic classes permitted at either extreme. Marital infidelity is highly uncommon—divorce is allowed—and religion is taught and practiced primarily in the home;

Philosophers out-number athletes—artists out-number scientists—the elderly out-number children—music is beloved—domestic pets are commonplace; Men snore—women dance—and children misbehave.

Weather patterns are earth-like, electrical storms being the most deadly, and some snowstorms are able to bury homes.

Lastly, most nations maintain active land, sea, and air forces. Wars, however, are uncommon—and under international law, are settled through compulsory arbitration—backed by the military might of all signatories.

Among the many pleasant surprises awaiting the Pilgrims, there were a few unfortunate ones as well. Judging by what they'd observed on television, the Marinorians concluded that Earthers eat too much, and too often—will go to extreme even fatal, lengths to experience excitement—expect to be deceived, laugh at bodily functions, and at their leaders—gladly gamble their money away—lust conspicuously after the human body—make wealthy the athletic high-achievers—and thrill to music that claws at the eardrums.

All of which was confirmed by The Seven.

To the delight of the Daughter, when sociology took a break for lunch She could see a new camaraderie taking hold. New connections were being made, and genuine friendships were beginning to bloom.

*   *   *

Rusty Steele had set a goal for himself: he wanted to be the first person on earth to have sex with a Marinor. And he already had his eye on one, an ever-smiling young woman with a handsome figure, named Ithia. She was scheduled to be sent to Holland by Halloween, so he had little time to lose.

He began his courtship by sending an arrangement of roses to her quarters. Little did he know that on Marinor cutting flowers in bloom was considered vandalism. And his note only compounded the blunder—

> For Ithia—May these blossoms of red add color to your today. Tomorrow they'll be yellow, the following day white.
>
> Rusty Steele

She gasped at the sheer horror of killing flowers in the name of pleasing her. She suddenly became suffused with guilt. She tried to place his face—and then remembered this "Fachoot"—Marinor for 'creep.'

She'd make sure no more flowers were sacrificed for her—and returned them to the sender with a note of her own:

> A Child slays a flower out of innocent ignorance.
>
> A Man knows to keep beauty alive.
>
> Ithia

So instead of being the first man to bed a Marinor, Rusty Steele became the first man to be rejected by one.

*   *   *

The government of Cuba drew a sharp distinction between political asylum and criminal asylum—whenever it became convenient to do so. And there was nothing so convenient as a half-million dollars worth of luxury automobiles.

Sandovar and Zooti Abydos were dining at their favorite restaurant in the town of Hermosia, outside Havana. Their mood was festive despite their recent failure to destroy ABYTOR. The house specialty was a distant cousin of Jambalaya, and they were on their third helpings when their world came to an abrupt end.

"Senors, you will please come with us," the Major said, pulling them to their feet and placing them in handcuffs. They were escorted to a dilapidated prison van waiting at the curb and thrown roughly inside.

The arrest was all over in less than three minutes.

*   *   *

Peter had asked his wife on several occasions whether he might be allowed to speak directly with one of the Mentors. She finally put the question to Gamma, and to her surprise, he agreed immediately, saying it would both please and honor him. So the following evening Ellen Kate brought the two together, acting purely as a conduit for Peter and Gamma.

GITMO

By the middle of September every delegation to the United Nations had received a package of documents from CELESTIA. Contained therein were detailed descriptions of each Pilgrim, of their home planet of Marinor, and of their purpose in coming to Earth. Included was a specialized manual for each government setting forth the mission and operational needs of the Pilgrims it had been assigned—including housing, transportation, funding, and staffing, and leadership access.

Shortly thereafter, the first groups of Pilgrims were ready to be dispatched to the capitals and major cities of member nations. It was left to each country to announce the Pilgrims' arrivals in the manner they felt most appropriate.

Their missions varied greatly from country to country based on the organization and levels of sophistication, effectiveness, fairness, and operational proficiency their institutions of government had attained.

Representative governments (democracies) would receive very different guidance than would monarchies, aristocracies, oligarchies, pseudo-democracies, plutocracies, totalitarian regimes, and outright dictatorships.

Counseling authentic democracies would be at once the easiest (since they were already the highest evolved form of government)—and the most difficult (also being the most complex, interest-driven, and economically dependent).

Structuring the offices and agencies of a democracy's Executive Branch would involve expanding, refining, fine-tuning, and optimizing the delivery of federal services—as well as fostering wise foreign policies and robust trade.

Legislative Branches would be counseled on the charters, statutes, regulations, and parliamentary rules under which they function. Their body of laws governing property, commerce, labor, taxation, health care, and the elective process itself would be examined and reviewed in detail. The Pilgrims would also be advising bicameral legislatures on the advantages of creating a third legislative house: a Council of Elders.

The Judicial Branches of democracies would likely require the least enhancing of all, save for the manner in which the judiciary is chosen, empowered, and safeguarded.

There were also the nominal democracies—nations which go through the motions of holding free elections, but where all candidates are pre-chosen to perpetuate the status quo.

Such countries, though feigning receptivity, would resist all change, and would be largely uncooperative.

Certain other states—those ruled by monarchs, aristocrats, or oligarchs, and which make no pretense of holding free elections—would be well entrenched, and could be expected openly to resist the Pilgrims' efforts.

On the other hand, former colonies, impoverished third-world countries, and loose tribal confederations—often with many problems and few resources—would be the most receptive, and grateful for any help from the Pilgrims.

By contrast, the purely totalitarian states—warlord-ruled fiefdoms, dictatorships, and authoritarian theocracies—would resist change by all means necessary. Considered far too dangerous, no Pilgrims would be assigned to them.

All in all, the Marinor would face huge challenges.

At a farewell ceremony prior to departing CELESTIA, the Daughter of the Creative Spirit bid the Pilgrims Godspeed—and reminded them that their missions were purely civic and social, with the spiritual left to others. She told them they were to be seen as non-religious and nonsectarian.

"As you venture forth upon your great extra-planetary adventure—forget not the epochal nature of your undertakings, and be not distracted from the accomplishment of your Mission.

Know that the Universe has empowered you as few mortals before you—and that the Heavenly Hosts stand ever-ready should you find yourselves compelled to call out to them for salvation.

GO YE NOW UNTO THE WORLD—AND BE ABOUT THE BUSINESS OF CREATION!"

*   *   *

Sandovar and Zooti Abydos had spent a miserable two weeks in captivity, denied access to a lawyer, and fed spoiled food and foul smelling water. They had been kept in a windowless cell where temperatures reached well into the 90s every day.

446

Then one day they were taken in shackles from their "Hell cell" and thrown roughly into a prison van. For the next eleven hours they bounced along poorly paved country roads.

Given only warm water to drink and nothing to eat, they arrived at their apparent destination in the dead of night. They had no idea where they were—until they heard voices that sounded American. Then it hit them: they were at the Guantanamo Naval Base on the eastern tip of Cuba.

The van pulled into a parking area and turned off the engine. Presently an American lieutenant commander opened the rear door and looked in at the prisoners, comparing them with photos in his hand. Apparently satisfied, the van door was slammed shut again, and everything became quiet save for the cacophony of countless tree frogs.

An hour later the van started up and pulled up to the Main Gate, where it stopped and again turned off the engine. Seconds later, the door slid open and five Shore Police appeared. The Abydoses were led to another windowless van, this one standard naval grey and considerably newer.

As they were being placed inside, they caught a glimpse of several brand new automobiles being driven out the gate: an Audi S8 sedan—a Mercedes SLK convertible—and a Bentley Arnage RL—total value nearly five-hundred thousand dollars.

Fidel and Raul Castro would be going places in style.

*   *   *

The major terrorist organizations around the world had developed a sophisticated, surprisingly simple method for acquiring virtually any kind of weapon, from shoulder-fired surface-to-air heat-seeking missiles—all the way to ready-to-use nuclear devices.

Disguised as obscure, non-existent marine engine parts, weapons were elaborately coded and listed on E-bay—where bids would come in at one-thousandth of the actual offer (in U.S. Dollars). If an acceptable bid showed up, the seller would post a request for an e-mail contact address so buyer and seller could deal directly. Once a deal was consummated, the item would be quietly withdrawn from sale on E-bay.

And thus it was that the erstwhile terrorist known as Fa Haad was able to locate a buyer for his Soviet-era suitcase atom bomb, still in storage in Bangor.

Ahmet never knew who the actual buyer was, but based on its intended destination, it was some well-subsidized Islamic group in Indonesia. The bid was for two-point six million dollars, to be wired to a numbered bank account he kept in Geneva.

Now all he'd have to do was come up with some plausible excuse to be away from CELESTIA for a few days.

After pondering the situation a bit, Ahmet figured his nuke might wind up being used for demonstration purposes only—in a daring attempt to overthrow the regime in Jakarta.

In his mind it was good that the nuke was heading for another country. First, because it could be shipped safely out of the U.S.; only incoming cargo is scrutinized. And second, because he'd frankly hate to see it go off under the Pan Am Building in New York. He'd already spent enough time at CELESTIA to gain a cosmic perspective, and didn't relish sabotaging his afterlife.

But then two point six million dollars was downright irresistible.

The Daughter of the Creative Spirit of course knew everything that was going on in Ahmet's mind—and decided to call him in for a talk.

When he arrived at her office—She simply pointed to a chair, where he promptly sat. For nearly a minute She merely stared at him. Finally She spoke,

"Ahmet, you disappoint me greatly. That which you plan to do with your 'suitcase' is an affront to all mankind." He started to say something, but She put up a hand to stop him, and he kept silent. *"But unwittingly, you have given Us an opportunity to prevent great turmoil and human tragedy—and by so doing, lend powerful stature to Our efforts."*

His mind was spinning, seeing his two point six million vanishing before he even got his hands on it—and fearful that he might have already blown his chances in the afterlife.

"You need not fret over the money," She continued, *"it would never have been yours in the first place—and your standing in the afterlife has yet to be determined."* Ahmet slumped down in his chair, suddenly realizing that he could think or do nothing that She did not know about.

"Richie Quinn is in Jakarta, as you know," She resumed, *"and his Mission will be crowned with success if he is able to expose the insurgents' odious scheme. And you will enable him to do exactly that."* Her tone was grave.

"You will fly to Bangor and ship your 'suitcase' as planned. You will, however, disable it prior to shipment. You will then fly to Jakarta and brief Richie."

And that quickly, Ahmet's scheme for making money was aborted and his reputation as a terrorist left in shambles.

SPIT

Hardpan Dotson had been recognized with a "jeezley tin plaque" by the American Society of Paleo-Anthropologists for his astounding discovery of fossil remains of early man apparently astride a large bird. Dubbed the Flying Horse by the press, it was hailed by some as man's first means of controlled flight.

In addition, the archeological site had been officially designated the Dotson Dig in his honor, and he'd appeared several times on national television.

None of which amounted to "spit," according to Hardpan. To his abject horror, the fossils had been placed on permanent display in a "jeezley museum," producing none of the riches the Daughter of the Creative Spirit had promised. To Hardpan, riches you couldn't spend were nothing more than "piss in the wind." In consequence, he no longer referred to Her as "that nice nekked lady."

But still, he was determined to somehow make money off the Holy Daughter's sudden appearance in his life.

Having drawn upon the new creative resources of his mind, he'd enjoyed short-lived income from his "agazite" jewelry—using two-hundred dollars of the proceeds to purchase a decrepit Corvair delivery van which had driven its last mile. The seller had towed and parked it alongside the now-famous El Rio de Dias, where Hardpan had converted it into an ersatz domicile.

Gazing upon the river one autumn. evening, Hardpan began to ponder his impecunious predicament. And before long, the creative muse visited him once again: He could bottle and sell water from the river—claiming it had Healing Powers!

All he needed were some bottles.

*   *   *

The American Secretary of State and the Chinese Foreign Minister flew to Moscow to meet with their Russian counterpart. As the nation with the most nuclear weapons (after the United States), Russia's cooperation in the quest for global nuclear disarmament was deemed absolutely essential.

But the Russians were cool to the idea, arguing that only if all other nations with such weapons agreed to scrap them, would Russia be willing to consider doing the same.

It was not a promising beginning.

"I'm afraid that's not good enough," said the Secretary. "Were every nuclear power to take that position, nothing at all would change. We need to have you agree in principle. Surely you can appreciate that."

"And what do you propose we do with all our ballistic submarines? They have but one purpose and represent an enormous investment."

"We face exactly the same problem. But if there were an agreement, you would have no further need for them. And as to the investment they represent, well—perhaps something could be worked out."

"And, if there were an agreement, how could we be certain every country were being truthful? Are you both prepared to accept Pakistan's word for it? All it would take is for one nation to lie—and hide a few of their biggest devices!"

For the first time, Beijing's Foreign Minister spoke up. "We share the same concerns. What does the Holy Daughter suggest in terms of enforcement?"

This was of course the central question. President Onager had asked Her the same thing.

"I am told that we will have Mentor assistance," answered the Secretary. "Should anyone try to cheat, the Mentors will immediately inform us. How's that for state-of-the-art, 'Eye in the Sky' intelligence gathering! The Holy Daughter has told us She's prepared to charge the Mentors with being, in effect, Compliance Overseers. With no on-site inspections necessary."

The room fell silent, as implications were contemplated.

"How can any of us be secure in the knowledge that these same Mentors won't reveal other state secrets as well?" China wanted to know.

The Secretary had anticipated this question as well. "We'd have the Word of God! I trust that would be enough."

The Russian Minister was far from reassured. "Would you inform the other governments of this—that there can be no cheating whatsoever—because the Gods will be watching? You realize of course that Her Word would have no meaning whatever for the nonbelievers— Iran for example."

"I take your point. However, for the time being, I think we can assume that the Holy Daughter will know how to deal with the Iranians. But before any of this can happen, we three—as the only nuclear superpowers—must reach an understanding. A trilateral accord, if you will."

"And, how are we to know that the Mentors are always on watch?" inquired the Chinese Minister.

"Take a piece of paper—write on it any ten-digit combination of numbers and letters you wish—fold it and put it in your pocket," the Secretary directed. He did.

Several moments passed—and then the Secretary's cell phone rang. He listened briefly—and jotted down a series of numbers and letters— ten in all. He hung up and turned the slip of paper around so the others could see it.

The Chinese Minister took out the paper he had written on and laid it on the table next to the Secretary's.

The ten digits matched exactly.

*   *   *

Instead of returning directly to Washington, the American Secretary of State flew to Riyadh to meet with the Saudi Crown Prince. He figured he was on a fool's errand, but the President had insisted he make the effort—and find out whether the Saudis had any interest at all in helping the Palestinians acquire the Sinai as their new homeland.

When he laid out the essentials of the concept, he was shocked by the reaction. Far from dismissing it out of hand, the Crown Prince actually exhibited a degree of guarded interest. After an hour's discussion, it became apparent that there was possibly a quid pro quo lurking behind the dunes; the Saudis might be receptive if the United States would cease its efforts to tie the Kingdom to support for terrorism. The Secretary finally realized the Saudis were more interested in buying their own way out of trouble than in buying peace for the entire Middle East. Now why should that surprise me? he asked himself.

Given the Crown Prince's unexpected openness to the Sinai proposal, the Secretary concluded that he had to have gotten wind of it in advance, in time to have discussed it with the rest of the Royal Family. Now who in the Hell could have leaked it? he wondered.

It never crossed his mind that the Daughter of the Creative Spirit had taken a hand in it.

The Secretary briefly considered flying directly to Cairo, but decided against it; he needed time to prepare.

The Egyptians can be real ball-busters, he remembered.

*   *   *

The Crown Prince had always fancied himself a visionary, considering dreams a valid instrument of prophecy—never suspecting they could on occasion be of Divine instigation.

One night his indwelling Deity partner had indeed portrayed within his sleeping mind the Palestinian people living on the Sinai Peninsula. He had awoken with the images still resonating bright and vivid—and quickly seized upon his dream as proof that he truly was a visionary!

Thus, when the American Secretary of State arrived barely a week later, and advanced virtually the identical proposal he'd dreamt about—he was momentarily flabbergasted until it occurred to him in a burst of insight that the lady Deity visiting in America might somehow be involved.

Could the Sinai Peninsula as the new Palestinian Homeland be a reflection of the Divine Will itself? he asked himself—awed by the implications.

USS PLOWSHARES

The Holy Daughter assembled her human family for an important announcement. She waited until everyone was settled in their seats.

"During Mr. Onager's visit back in July," She began, *"I asked him whether there were perhaps some vessel which could be leased to Us for use as a sea-going Spiritual*

Conference Center—aboard which I could commune with world religious leaders. And he found a powerful vessel: an aging Aegis-Class U.S. Navy destroyer! It will finally enable Me to begin My true Ministry."

"But—a warship?" Ellen Kate blurted.

"Indeed. Though one whose weapons have been removed."

"That is one very sophisticated ship, Holy Daughter," Peter pointed out. "Where could You ever find a crew qualified to operate it?"

"The Secretary of the Navy has assembled a full ship's complement of recently retired officers and sailors—ones already proficient in the operation of just such a vessel."

"But—it's still a man-o-war—" Art Frayles worried.

"Not anymore," the Daughter smiled. "It has been repainted a dazzling white, using a high gloss enamel, and rechristened the USS PLOWSHARES. She is presently en route to Okinawa, where I plan to join her. And Karyn—I would very much like to have you and Zoe sail with Me."

"Where—where would we go from there, Holy Daughter?"

"We would sail west—stopping at major ports-of-call in South Asia, and then passing into the Mediterranean and on to Europe. I might mention that the interior of the ship has been remodeled to provide a number of finely appointed staterooms, along with a spacious Convocation Chamber."

"I'd like to come along as well, if I may," Rusty Steele volunteered, shooting a quick glance at Karyn.

"Oh, I'm afraid not, Rusty," the Daughter replied—to Karyn's relief. She knew he still lusted after her.

"The discussions of the Spirit which We undertake will be private, and thus inappropriate for recording." She then turned to Ahmet. "Ahmet, following your work in Indonesia, I bid you join Me aboard PLOWSHARES when she arrives."

The Seven sat speechless. No one had foreseen anything like this. They looked at one another, helpless to prevent the departure of their beloved leader—and wondering what life at CELESTIA would be like without Her.

Their shock would have been even greater, had they known that once the Holy Daughter departed CELESTIA, She was never to return.

* * *

Special Agent Hy Depkawitz wanted to look Sandovar Abydos in the eye. This was the man who had plotted to destroy the Mentors' spaceship in orbit—along with an American shuttle in the process. He couldn't imagine what kind of person was capable of such obscene treachery. He had to see for himself—and managed to hitch a ride on a Navy Orion P-3 headed for Guantanamo Bay. It was just before noon when their wheels touched down—and the moment he alighted a wet-hot blast of tropic air slapped him across the face.

Depkawitz had little interest in Zooti Abydos, who was nothing more than a common murderer. It was the father he wanted to eyeball, and as quickly as possible.

The Abydoses were housed in separate cages, isolated from each other as well as from the more than six-hundred Afghan prisoners still confined on the eastern tip of Cuba.

The senior Abydos was escorted to a small, windowless room in the Administration Building, and armed MPs were posted just outside the door. Shackled waist and ankle, Abydos was clean-shaven and dressed in a white tee-shirt, khaki slacks, and black shoes. They faced each other across a metal table; it was more than a minute before either spoke.

"Who the Hell are you?" Abydos finally asked.

"I'm the one who brought you here."

"When do I get to talk to a lawyer?"

"You don't."

"What the Hell do you mean? I'm an American citizen, and I have Constitutional rights."

"Wrong You're a worthless piece of garbage—and here you have no rights. In fact, outside of a handful of Cubans, no one even knows you're here. And that's the way it stays."

Abydos was shocked, and it took a few moments for him to collect himself.

"You—you can't do that," he snarled.

"Hey, you plotted to assassinate six American astronauts! Do you expect us to overlook that?"

"I—have rights—"

"You have a right to die—which you'll do right here."

"What—what about my son?"

"Same fate. Blame yourself, Abydos."

And with that, Hy Depkawitz got to his feet up and left. An hour later he was winging his way back to Washington.

He'd seen enough.

REFLEX

Ahmet's patience was starting to wear thin. He'd been at his friendly best, but the Seven were still pointedly cool to him, even in front of the Daughter—who felt it would just take a little time.

Karyn had been disappointed when the Daughter asked her to remain at CELESTIA, while She kept a promise to deliver the keynote speech to several thousand avowed pacifests at Madison Square Garden. It would be a quick turn-around flight, and She should be back by midnight.

However the evening would prove anything but uneventful. Just as She was wheels-up for the return flight to Utah, there was a serious mechanical malfunction at CELESTIA: one of the two Vista-Cubes had jammed half-way up the mountain. Fortunately it was empty—or so everyone thought. Zoe had discovered how much fun Vista-Cube rides were, and had taken to sneaking aboard one, as often as an opportunity presented itself—such as when her Mistress was away somewhere.

In velvet tones, a soft feminine voice announced that Cube 2 would be "Out-Of-Service for a short time." Knowing how rare it was for anything to go other than as planned, several of the Seven followed Tony Silvagio—down the Emergency Stairway, built inside a clear Plexiglas tube—which ran alongside the open-air Vista Cubes, each suspended from a heavy overhead cable—and pulled up the mountain by its own powerful motor.

Zoe had felt a mild anxiety when her Cube stopped so suddenly—and relief when some of the Seven appeared, Karyn in particular. But upon discovering that Zoe was trapped aboard the Cube their expressions betrayed real concern, so she did the one thing she could do: BARK LIKE CRAZY!

Instantly, Zoe's sudden alarm and genuine fear flashed directly to the Daughter over Her private personal Emergency Alert circuit enabling Her to draw upon her Divine Powers to come to the aid of someone essential to the ultimate success of Her Mission or, someone who had become emotionally dear to Her. At present, there were only two names on each list: Mission Success—Art Frayles and Ahmet; Personal Devotion—Karyn Deleo and Zoe.

But there arise from time to time certain situations where even Deity can find itself powerless. It was in just such a situation where the Holy Daughter suddenly discovered Herself. Looking down at the Vista-Cube mini-crisis, She realized there were simply no appropriate or even acceptable options. De-materialization is an Incarnation-ending, one-way street—by which She could be a Zoe's side in a matter of seconds, albeit invisibly. But picturing the headlines made her shudder: "Holy Daughter Aborts Mission to Comfort Her Dog."

She ran a few other option possibilities briefly through her mind: She could hire a local alpine rescue team—which would likely terrify Zoe even more. Or She could order up a mighty tailwind; which would likely terrify the pilot.

But in the end, She was left with only Her own ingenuity. She performed some quick Divine Optionization Analysis. She fired off Her most potent Divine Love Bundle to Zoe who felt it at once; and found something oddly familiar and comforting about it and stopped barking.

Tony Silvagio and Ahmet considered the problem, with Zoe's nose pressed hopefully against the wall of the Vista-Cube, her tail wagging like crazy, replacing the bark. Tony figured it would take a contractor, "several hours after the sun comes up" to free the dog. But Ahmet wasn't prepared to wait that long. Zoe had touched his heart, "I'm gonna get Zoe," he said.

As was ever the case, winds of fourty to fifty mph continuously lashed at CELESTIA. Every eighty feet along the emergency stairway, was a hatchway to the outside, for the routine external maintenance and cleaning of the Vista-Cubes. Not surprisingly, since CELESTIA had been built, not a single person had ever ventured after sunset down into the dimly-lit, howling winds, dark realm of the Vista-Cubes. Not that is, until Ahmet, with his stout Iranian heart, and a Love Pup named Zoe came along.

Ahmet estimated the closest hatchway to Zoe was a dozen or so meters uphill. He walked over to Karyn, who was standing as close to Zoe as possible, keeping up a steady stream of emotion-choked reassurances, mostly invoking the Daughters reliable Love.

"Karyn," he said softly, "I need to borrow your jacket, to put on Zoe. I'm going to need both hands just to hold on."

She quickly slipped it off and handed it to him. "See how it fits," he tried it on. "A bit snug, but it's safer that way."

She suddenly threw her arms around him and begged him to be careful. Then, on implulse, she planted a kiss firmly on his cheek.

The instant Silvagio opened the hatchway, a hurricane blew in, uninvited, but not unexpected. After filling every void up and down the stairway, it quickly lost interest and settled down—a portion returning to the night outside, to Whup Ass, if any could be found.

Meanwhile, making his way carefully along the narrow walkway just above the V-Cubes, and holding on by his fingernails, it seemed—Ahmet finally found himself looking down at Zoe, who was doing her straight up and down Rapture Bounce, whimpering at the prospect of imminent salvation. Ahmet found the rescue door, opened it, dropped down, and scooped Zoe up in his arms—and getting a loud, sustained cheer from all those who'd watched the rescue unfold.

Ahmet had to squeeze to get Zoe inside Karyn's jacket; she was a growing dog. But the jacket smelled strongly of Karyn, and Zoe's spirit was awash with joy. Ahmet decided to play it safe for the downhill trip to the still-open hatch and opted to crawl the entire way on his hands and knees with Zoe's head sticking out beside Ahmet's, so she could cover it with non-stop kisses.

*   *   *

Zoe was waiting at the foot of the narrow stairway leading up to the helipad, her whole body quivering with unbridled excitement—when the Holy Daughter suddenly appeared, dropped to Her knees, and buried Her face in Zoe's soft underbelly. Presently She looked up, and saw Karyn beaming down at Her. She rose to Her feet and looked around, "Where's Ahmet?"

"In his suite, I imagine—."

"Bid him come to my quarters, but give me a few minutes to change, if you will."

Fifteen minutes later, Ahmet tapped softly at Her door. She opened it at once, and smiled broadly at him, as he stepped inside. The Daughter was clutching Zoe tightly, allowing only seconds to pass between Divine kisses and soft murmurings of Divine adoration. Amhet was quietly touched, and felt privileged at being invited to witness such intimacy.

The Daughter had slipped into Her favorite jeans, brushed Her teeth, and swept Her hair back in a ponytail. Zoe squirmed mightily, and stretched as far as she could—to reach Amhet's chin, in order a World-

Class Kiss of Gratitude, her tail windmilling at top speed. To ease her struggles, Ahmet leaned in just a bit closer, and duly received a wet reward. The Daughter laughed merrily, kissing Zoe again.

"You put your own life at risk to save that of another," She began softly, "and for that I profoundly honor you. In addition, as you know, the life you saved is one inexpressively precious to Me personally. And for that I thank you with all My heart."

She put Zoe down, reached up, and gently cupped Amhet's face with both Her hands.

"Ahmet—thank you," she whispered ever so lightly, landing a butterfly kiss on each corner of his mouth. "I thank you so much," she breathed, and started to repeat the process. Utterly shocked, and with no time to think, Ahmet fell back on instinct and parted his lips to match Hers, and momentarily touched the tip of Her tongue with his own.

It was as if both had stepped onto a live wire!

Pulling back instantly, Ahmet stammered, "Oh—Holy One…I…I don't know what came over me." He began to shake from head to toe. Reaching up, She placed a reassuring hand gently against his cheek, and the shaking stopped. "You did nothing wrong—it was pure Reflex," She comforted. "Simply know that you've given Me a Moment of Material Beauty that I shall carry with Me forever, and Treasure, when I think of you."

*　　　*　　　*

Karyn, Ellen Kate and Art Frayles were enjoying their morning coffee, and reviewing the details of Zoe's dramatic rescue, and of Ahmet's extraordinary bravery.

"Perhaps we've all been a little harsh on him," Ellen Kate allowed, giving voice to what everyone was thinking

"It's Second Chance time," Art Frayles decreed.

FOUR FEWER ADULT
TEETH

In light of the massive social upheavals, the on-going corruption, and the widespread government mismanagement which followed in the wake of the 2003 Iraq War, the Holy Daughter lost no time in dispatching the first of Her Pilgrim teachers to Baghdad—with the blessing of David Onager, who viewed the Iraq War as an act of personal spite, gone haywire.

The new Iraqi government had designated ten academics to confer with the Pilgrims on a regular basis, in hopes of learning new ways by which the fledgling republic might be able to design itself a superior form of governance. Heading the all-male Iraqi contingent was an English-speaking third cousin of the new president named Afrham Triziz. Nearly half the Pilgrim delegation was female, with their leader being an elderly chap named Kirilia Monfir who'd been a member of the House of Elders back on Marinor.

The two groups convened in secret at one of the former dictator's palaces on the outskirts of Baghdad. There were still car bombers around, and they were taking no chances. Following introductions, they mingled informally the rest of the day, getting acquainted and answering myriad questions. By dusk everyone began to feel at ease, and by the next day they were all anxious to get down to business.

Monfir led off that following morning with a capsulized recitation of the Pilgrims' mission:

"My colleagues and I first wish to express our deep appreciation for the warmth of our reception, and for the many kind expressions of welcome.

As you are aware, we of Marinor have developed certain means and methods of governing which may find useful applications here on Earth. Our purpose in coming to Baghdad is to share what we have learned, in hopes that you may find our experiences and discoveries to be of value in fashioning a new democracy for your citizens.

Perhaps I should begin by reporting how very similar to Marinor the Earth is—in terms of natural resources, world population, and even weather. Our atmosphere is so like yours; we are able breathe your air directly. Even your food is familiar and pleasing to our tongues. There are, however, certain anatomical differences—such as the fact that our brains happen to have evolved with three hemispheres, instead of the two that all of you possess. Another difference: our gestation periods are on average seventeen days shorter than are yours. And we have four fewer adult teeth than you have.

Perhaps the single greatest way in which we differ is in our visual capabilities: our eyes are able to see heat radiating in the dark—much as many of your own native predatory animals. Apart from these few differentiations, we perspire just as you— pass gas—suffer headaches—tend to become overweight—and sometimes forget where we left our spectacles. In other words, our races are far more alike than unalike.

I might mention that we have been pleased to submit to physiological analysis and testing by physicians and scientists at the Mayo Clinic in the United States. We are told they have particular interest in our immune systems; Marinor have great resistance to disease, which is why we have no concern over being infected, or of your viruses. The only malady of yours which we can contract is the one you call 'chicken pox,' and against which we have been recently inoculated."

He took a break to answer a round of questions dealing with the racial differences between the people of Earth and Marinor, then returned to his subject.

"Like most representative governments, we too have three divisions: the Executive, Legislative, and Judicial.

Our Executive, for instance, operates under a federal chief administrative executive— who is limited to serving a single term in office. He—or she—is advised by a super-cabinet comprised of all living former chief executives.

Unlike the American republic, our Legislative division is composed of three houses: an Upper House, elected by workers—industrial, agricultural, and professional; a Lower House, elected by various organizations of society—social, political, and philosophical; and the third, a House of Elders—comprised of one-hundred distinguished men and women, nominated by the chief executive, and elected for life by the elder statesmen themselves.

Lastly, the Judiciary—composed of two principal court systems: the Law Courts, which adjudicate cases much as do your own, including the appellate review process; and the Socioeconomic Courts, which are in turn are subdivided into Parental Courts, Educational Courts, and Industrial Courts.

It would be no exaggeration to say that we have much, very much, to discuss over the weeks and months which lie before us."

With that, he opened the floor for questions, of which there were a great many. Kirilia Monfir had a busy morning.

*　　*　　*

The Daughter of the Creative Spirit hosted Her final supper at CELESTIA with Her human family—knowing, but not sharing, the fact that it was to be the last time they would all dine together.

She finally gave up trying to brighten the mood, everyone being so visibly depressed over the prospect of Her departure in the morning for Okinawa. Even Karyn, who'd not be saying Goodbye to the Daughter as would the others, nevertheless shared their gloom and sensed the underlying solemnity of the occasion. Even Zoe lay at the Daughter's feet, oddly quiet and subdued.

"You all remember the smelly old prospector—the first human I saw upon My emergence in the cave?—My Goodness, I'm sorry to report he's sold his erstwhile healing blanket for a—'grubstake.' It is most sad that he tried to profit financially from a Divine Gift—placing self-interest above the health of others."

"That's the good old profit motive at work, Holy Daughter—what this country is all about," Art Frayles replied.

"I know. And that's part of the problem."

"What problem?" Ellen Kate asked.

The Holy Daughter was about to deliver a Teaching, as the set of Her jaw signaled. And when She spoke, Her words came cloaked in scholarly garb.

"Profit-motivated economies are ultimately doomed—unless and until self-interest is supplanted by devotion to the service of others. Ruthless competition for security, unbridled selfishness, is altogether in the end destructive of all that it seeks to maintain—and wholly unworthy of any advanced, enlightened society. Yet the profit motive, for all its injustices, cannot be summarily excised from an economy or a society before its citizens, wholeheartedly embrace the highest human and social values. Misguided altruism can eventuate in disaster."

The Holy Daughter expanded on Her economic theme for the better part of an hour, considering it to be that important, and allowing Rusty to record it. But She could see on the faces of her family that what they needed most was to cleave unto Her emotionally, not intellectually, on this their final evening together.

She filled a goblet with apple juice, stood, and raised it high, pausing for all of the others to fill their own goblets and join Her.

"Wheresoever thou goest—let this golden nectar pour full your heart with My Spirit. Know that I AM with you in that moment—and will be thus every step along the

path to Eternity. My Love for each of you is Absolute, and it is Infinite. Drink now—that you may experience My Love—"

Each took a small sip, almost hesitantly—not knowing what was about to transpire.

What all felt next transcended every intense pleasurable sensation they had ever experienced—combined. Shortly after, Ellen Kate described it as "an orgasm of the heart!" In a flight of hyperbole, Art Frayles called it "a massive, pyroclastic Love-Flow." And Karyn failed to find words.

Rusty babbled deliriously about a "Glory Gusher," while Peter, radiating pure Joy, didn't even try to express what he was feeling. Ahmet, for his part, dropped to his knees, placed his head between them, and rocked from side to side speed-murmuring from the Koran. Meanwhile, Little Josh was caught up in all the ecstasy about him and squealed with glee—and even Zoe came alive, bouncing straight up and down, wagging her tail as fast as she could.

The Holy Daughter alone was joyless, knowing that tonight was to be their last together.

*   *   *

The transformation was stunning.

By Executive Order of the Commander-in-Chief, full ownership of the Aegis-class destroyer HAWTHORNE had been transferred from the Department of Defense to the General Services Administration. The warship was to become a peaceship.

The contract was awarded to Bath Iron Works in Maine, the shipyard which had built and launched the vessel some twenty years earlier. And by working twenty-four hours seven, days a week, the yard finished the transformation in under three months.

Gone were all weapons systems designed to protect her from attack by air, surface, or beneath the waves. Radar domes were replaced by satellite dishes, and a new helipad graced the fantail.

But the greatest changes were within. The Combat Information Center gave way to a television studio. Whole departments disappeared, replaced by conference rooms, a comfortable library, a theater, and a large auditorium. Living quarters were completely rebuilt and decorated.

Officers and Enlisted messes became formal dining rooms with soft music. There were cozy lounges, a game room, a racquet ball court, a sauna and health spa, and a state-of-the-art media room.

But most transformed of all were the private living quarters of the Holy Daughter. She had a bright, spacious salon with a robust garden of orchids, and a merry fountain above a reflecting pool. Her bed chamber was exquisite, Her bath immense, and there was even a private chapel.

Below in Engineering, the engines had been completely overhauled. The entire ship was now air conditioned, with soft lighting throughout. The bridge had been upholstered in pale leather. There was warm, cherry rosewood paneling, silk wallpaper, oriental tapestries, and hand-woven Persian rugs—even large picture windows with elegant pastel drapes.

Yet most striking change was the exterior—repainted with pure white enamel which set the entire ship ablaze in full sunlight.

Finally, the crew: all men and women in their forties and fifties who'd come out of early retirement to serve aboard the RE-CHRISTENED.

And when the erstwhile warship sailed down the Kennebec River precisely on schedule, cheering crowds and TV cameras lined the banks.

*   *   *

PLOWSHARES—now fully staffed, fueled and provisioned—plowed east-southeast one-hundred and thirty nautical miles off Cape Hatteras, on station and ready to receive a Holy passenger—one who'd essentially take strategic command. It was much like having a flag officer piped aboard. All was in readiness, and the excitement was palpable.

Suddenly someone shouted, "There she is!" and everyone let out a collective gasp—Spinning up from the western horizon was a helicopter, as gleaming white in the setting sun as its own mother ship.

In less than a minute it was hovering above the fantail, the Holy Daughter clearly visible at one window, looking as excited as anyone waiting below.

The craft touched down as lightly as an angel's kiss, its turbine whispering softly to a stop.

Captain Goosek stepped forward to greet and welcome aboard a most extraordinary passenger. The sliding door eased itself open and a God emerged, smiling radiantly and passing Her hand above the assembled throng. Suddenly, as if with one voice, a cheer of exultation filled the air.

"Thank you—thank you all for such a heartfelt greeting. It gives me great joy to at last be among you." She took the Captain's hand and clasped it firmly with both of Hers. *"May we all be Ambassadors of Peace—and the purest of Love."*

Moments later Karyn emerged carrying Zoe, squirming mightily to be set down. The pup took one look at the ship's crew and barked a happy greeting of her own. The Daughter took her from Karyn, and they all moved forward.

The Captain escorted the Daughter to Her quarters, and She seemed well pleased. "When you're rested and refreshed, we hope you'll join us for dinner. We had soft-shell lobsters flown in from Maine, less than an hour out of the sea. We understand they're a favorite of Yours."

"Indeed they are—We can't get them in Heaven."

There was a sudden silence, until everyone realized they'd just been treated to an example of Divine Humor. A good laugh ensued—just that quickly and deftly, the Daughter had put everyone at ease.

*   *   *

"What made You change Your mind?" Karyn asked.

"Several factors. First, the Acolytes and the Pilgrims are making greater progress than anticipated—and faster as well. So I asked that this ship be turned east, instead of making for Indonesia, it headed for Africa. While the amelioration of strife is ever a priority, there is none greater than the easing of suffering—when it is My children who suffer."

"What's Your plan, if I may ask?"

"To make miracles—many thousands of miracles. It is to be a great Benison."

IVORY COAST

As PLOWSHARES made her way east across the Atlantic, she was far from alone. Just over the horizon, her escort followed: a light carrier with a wing of F-18s, three destroyer escorts, a tanker, two supply ships, and, silently submerged, a nuclear attack submarine, fully armed and ready.

David Onager was taking no chances.

* * *

After dark the Daughter slipped out on deck unnoticed to behold the heavens. She found a quiet space aft of the bridge were She would be sheltered from the wind blowing over the bow, but could still drink in the bracing scent of salt air. She knew that once She was back in pure spirit form, the things She'd miss most were the sensory sensations of the flesh. And Her beloved pup—She'd given brief thought to transmuting Zoe into spirit form when She departed, but knew that could be looked upon as an indulgence. And the Gods never indulge.

She'd come out on deck to gaze upon the firmament. She knew She was experiencing what mortals called homesickness. An odd feeling. Brushing it aside, She opened a dialogue with Her attendant staff and felt much better. What she wanted was to speak with her Father, which She also did. Returning to Her suite fully refreshed, She recommitted to the successful prosecution of Her Mission—leaving her Father well pleased.

* * *

Twenty-four hours before PLOWSHARES arrived off the Ivory Coast, the Holy Daughter personally placed a call to General Ferdinand Ozali, longtime head-of-state, informing him that Her arrival was imminent, and inviting him to meet with Her aboard the ship, offering Her helicopter for his use. Without hesitation, he accepted both invitation and offer.

The next day Chairman Ozali was formally piped aboard, escorted to the elegant Convocation Chamber, and presented to the Holy Daughter. *"Thank you for coming," She greeted in his native tongue. A steward served him a goblet of an unfamiliar golden juice, which he sipped—and was astonished by its sweet delicacy. He quickly drained his goblet.*

"I am come on a mission of Mercy," the Daughter stated. "Many, many of your people are malnourished, and afflicted with curable diseases. It is My wish that you gather together as many as possible tomorrow at noon—that I may walk among them." She smiled and then quietly continued.

"The juice you just swallowed will cure the chronic and life-threatening infection which attacks your intestine and causes you such great pain." He looked at Her in shock. *His physician had dismissed it as "stress-related."*

The General and the Daughter conversed formally for several minutes more. Then he took his leave, promising to do just as She had requested.

*   *   *

At exactly noon the next day, a dazzling white aircraft settled to earth on a rolling field teeming with hopeful upturned faces. The twin rotors whispered to a stop—and the Holy Daughter alighted, surrounded by a brilliant golden aura. She raised an arm above the crowd, and suddenly the air was filled with legions of angelic voices in an anthem of exultation. They built in crescendo, then fell silent.

"My Peace be unto you." Her voice called in the native tongue, speaking softly, but easily heard by all those assembled. She walked forth into the throng, Her aura spreading out and embracing every soul.

Immediately all hunger was banished, as every stomach felt filled. Pain was lifted—every sore healed—and every infirmity cured. The blind were overwhelmed with sight—the lame made to walk—and the collective suffering of the multitudes lifted in an instant.

At the same instant, the Daughter knelt down and took an emaciated child in Her arms, and kissed its forehead. Before the astonished eyes of onlookers, the flesh filled out. The child looked up and met the loving gaze of the Daughter—and the next moment its throat exploded with exuberant laughter, the Daughter joining in. The laughter quickly built to a tsunami of seemingly irrational joy, filling and swelling the hearts of the multitude.

An ABC film crew, on assignment in the Ivory Coast to report on a new outbreak of AIDS, by pure luck caught the Holy Daughter's visit. And, filming Her ministry at work, they themselves became caught up in the eruption of mass hilarity—and even the correspondent giggled on camera.

IVORYCOAST
THRONG

On his yacht riding gently at anchor in Corsican waters, Silvio Androtti watched ABC's report of the Holy Daughter's miracles in the Ivory Coast. It was followed by an announcement that before departing for Her next stop, which would be in Nigeria, She had informed the Minister of Resources exactly where they would discover rich deposits of chromium, zinc, and molybdenum—producing sufficient exports to feed the people for decades to come.

Androtti seethed at the report—there She was again, distributing unearned wealth. And with each African nation She visited, it would only get worse. Things had reached the intolerable. It was time to summon the Bastion and draw final plans for action.

*   *   *

The pure white prow parted the waves with barely a whisper, the escorting armada trailing barely twenty miles aft with Nigeria but hours ahead.

The Daughter felt the time had come to take Karyn into Her confidence. As Her devoted companion and only personal friend among mortals, She owed her nothing less.

"The instruments of My departure are gathering," She said softly. *"You are to give absolutely no hint to anyone of that which I am about to disclose."*

Karyn was instantly filled with dread. Even Zoe sensed the alarm and lay still.

"There are those among your rich and powerful who fear My Good Works—and who plot against Me."

"But You have constant seraphic protection. I don't see—"

"Before embarking on My Mission, I instructed My celestial staff to take no action to contravene the exercise of mortal free will—which is ever inviolate, even unto the abortion of My Mission." She reached out and took Karyn's hand. *"Verily, before the completion of My African Benison—I am to be slain. I will not suffer on a cross; My physical death will be instantaneous and painless. But know this—I shall return—and Zoe, you, and I shall season again together."*

467

*   *   *

Calendars were swept clean, appointments re-scheduled, travel plans cancelled—as all fifteen members of the Bastion answered the call.

Androtti put it succinctly—

"Gentlemen—before we depart this place, we shall devise, draft, and perfect detailed final plans for the elimination of the bitch goddess in Africa!"

BUDEGA ONSWEETH

Budega Onsweeth was as morally corrupt as anyone in darkest Cameroon. All three-hundred and twenty pounds of him lived in a filthy four-hundred square foot trailer, palatial by local standards on the outskirts of the capital city of Yaoundé, where he made a good living selling heroin, small arms, and no-questions-asked personal services to the highest bidder.

There was nothing he would not do if the price was right.

His reputation as a drug dealer and serial debaucher was firmly established, and any policeman counted it his good fortune to catch Onsweeth in some scam or outright crime of violence, knowing the bribe would be both assured and generous.

The day was sweltering, like every other in Equatorial Africa, but the fat man didn't mind a bit. With his laptop DVD player, a favorite child porn flick, a jug of fermented beetle juice, and a mound of chocolate cookies buzzed by clouds of hungry horseflies, he diddled himself with happy abandon.

His sweaty reverie was suddenly broken by the insistent chime of his cell phone. He nearly didn't answer, but later was very glad he had. It was a call from a stranger in Europe—with the fattest proposition he'd ever received. Without knowing what he was being hired to do, he was informed that a bank draft in the amount of ten-thousand euro dollars would arrive for him the next day at the Central Post Station, along with sealed instructions plus the guarantee of another twenty-thousand if he performed satisfactorily.

Shaking with excitement, he gave his tally a final whack and sat back to reflect.

All he'd been told was that it involved 'wet work'—well Hell, for that kind of money he'd snuff the Pope himself!

Little did Onsweeth suspect, he was nearly on the right track.

*   *   *

Four days later PLOWSHARES dropped anchor off the coast of Cameroon.

The Holy Daughter had stayed up late in loving and extended communion with Karyn and Zoe. But when Karyn requested permission to ride along in the helicopter, the Daughter was compelled to utter Her first non-truth: "Perhaps next time."

Already anticipating Her return to spirit-form Divinity, the Daughter lingered in the shower, repeatedly rinsing Her perfect, healthy body. What a waste, She thought.

*   *   *

Well hidden by dense foliage atop a hill overlooking the large clearing where the American Goddess was soon to land, Budega Onsweeth looked nervously at his watch. He knew he'd instantly become a hated, hunted man, and even his carefully arranged escape plan afforded little comfort as he pictured the Flames of Hell licking at his body.

Yet to renege was no option; he'd accepted payment, and he fancied himself a professional.

He looked at the weapon by his feet: a brand new, fresh-from-the-crate, fully checked-out and test-fired, hand-held American Stinger surface-to-air missile—all its launch circuits energized. Armed and ready. all that remained was to point and shoot.

*   *   *

Knowing that the lives of Her helicopter crew would soon be forfeit, the Holy Daughter designated all for honored resurrection on the third day. Thus glorified, high stature would attend each throughout all eternity.

Gleaming white in the sun, the Holy Craft made a slow pass above the large clearing, now choked with jubilant, expectant natives, high government officials, and television film crews from around the world—

Suddenly—the cry "ABORT—ABORT—MISSILE INBOUND!" filled the Captain's headphones. But the warning came too late—as flames burst upon the sky and shards of white debris and torn flesh rained down upon the crowd.

As the anguished cries of Archangels rent the air.

WHY EARTH?

For the first time in the trillion-year History of Record of the Universe of Universes, a second Deity Incarnated in flesh had been put to death by the races of the same evolutionary world.

Anguish and heart-grief spilled forth from the worlds of the Grand Universe Headquarters, all the way out to the youngest mortal sphere on the very fringe of Established Creation.

It was a rarity and a supreme honor for a Divine Son to be born unto a world as a babe, and grow to maturity thereon. However it was an epochal travesty for a Holy Son Incarnate to then have His physical life brought to a judicial conclusion, through the intentional infliction of pain and prolonged suffering.

By the Grace of this Sovereign Son, He approved an Emergency Visitation to this same world by a second Deity, One hailing from the Supreme Headquarters World itself. Yet this Visitation too was to end in horror and tragedy—a repetition utterly without precedent. Just why this obscure, violent, morally primitive world engaged the concern and Personal Ministry of the Gods left all creation puzzling.

FIRST APPEARANCE

PLOWSHARES had already hoisted anchor and turned for home, making thirty knots. Her escorts had done the same, while a pair of F-18s circled pointlessly in the skies over Cameroon, both to intimidate and show the flag. But alas, there was no one there to intimidate.

Karyn lay curled around Zoe in the middle of the Daughter's bed, sobbing and shaking with grief. She'd lain there for hours, yearning for her own death in order to once again be at the side of her only true friend and companion.

Eyes clenched, holding Zoe close while kissing her face repeatedly, Karyn didn't notice the bright golden glow that began to fill the suite. Until she heard a familiar voice—

"Karyn, My Love, do not grieve—for I am here."

Karyn's eyes shot open—and beheld the Holy Daughter bathed in a golden aura, looking almost exactly as she had prior to Her assassination. Instantly recognizing the voice as well, Zoe jumped down, and ran over to sniff her cherished mistress. But—there was no scent to sniff, and she appeared confused.

"Is—is that truly—You?" Karyn stammered.

"As promised. Did you not think I would stand by My word?"

Karyn ran to embrace Her—but found that there was no substance to embrace. She swung her arms helplessly back and forth, slashing through the spirit form of her beloved, cascades of tears pouring down her cheeks.

"You must come to accept Me as I now am—no longer flesh and blood, but still Me, unchanged in every meaningful way."

But Karyn was devastated—needing a hug as never before. Seeing this, the Daughter called upon Her seraphic associates, who on occasion could be empowered to manipulate physical matter, to bestow on Karyn what would feel to her like a Divine Embrace. Receiving it, Karyn was overcome and now wept out of appreciation. Moving to Her former bed, the Daughter sat upon it without making a depression. Seeing this, Karyn immediately scooped up Zoe and joined Her.

For the next four hours all three indulged in pure love-making—and Karyn's earlier anguish was replaced with laughter. In the course of their evening together, the Daughter asked Karyn to "assemble the Seven at CELESTIA next week for one last time"—thereby letting her know that she'd be seeing the Daughter at least one more time.

When the time drew near for the Daughter to depart, She Blessed Karyn and told her, "You will be at my side forever, if that is your wish, and great will be your works."

Then, in parting recognition, the Holy Daughter proclaimed Karyn DeLeo Her "Designated Liaison" with the mortal races of the Earth—the sole channel by which She would maintain contact with Her Acolytes and the Pilgrims from Marinor, on both of whom the Holy Daughter would rely to carry forth Her Emergency Mission.

And then She was gone.

BASTION JUSTICE

All fifteen members of the Bastion were gathered in celebration. The American bitch goddess had been blown to smithereens, and all her supposed divine powers had been unable to save her.

"So much for Omnipotence!" Silvio Androtti crowed—" And redistributing the wealth!" he added, clinking glasses with those nearest.

"And what became of our Operative?" asked the world's wealthiest Bulgarian.

"I'm afraid he had a bad fall—from about fifteen-thousand feet above the Sahara," Androtti snorted. "And that bloated lump of grease is now frying under an African sun!"

They sat down to a festive dinner of roast swan, truffles, and wild rice. But just as they were about to enjoy fresh Papaya Cobbler, a bright golden light began to fill the salon. And moments later the Holy Daughter's vivid presence became a salient reality! She glared pointedly around the table, fixing each person with her gaze. Then, using English, She spoke:

"Are you so naive as to think your craven, reprehensible scheme could be prosecuted without celestial notice?

"Did you imagine yourselves so clever as to be able to carry out your odious assassination without consequence in this life and beyond?

"Did you actually believe you could kill a God?"

The members of the Bastion sat frozen and mute, not daring to move or speak. Not one had entertained the possibility of Universe opprobrium—and all that implied in an afterlife—until this very moment.

"Yes, you do well to reflect on that which you have authored.

Know that those you call Mentors, when authorized, are extraordinarily skillful at thwarting mortal ambitions.

Accordingly, over the next year each of you will watch your fortune turn to dust— your holdings vanish—and your assets seized to pay creditors."

She let this sink in before continuing—

"But all that is temporal. Your true suffering will result from the Universal scorn in which you are held. Being already Forgiven, there will be no formal punishment as such, only a deep residual mistrust, an absence of assigned working responsibility, and an ages-long lack of respect. For just as with everyone, you create your own destiny."

473

THE LAST SUN SPOT

Zoe trembled with excitement as she rode the vista-cube up to CELESTIA. She was home again—the only home she'd ever known. Karyn smiled in anticipation of Zoe beholding her mistress once again—albeit for the last time.

Each of the Seven had been overjoyed upon learning that they were to see the Daughter again, and immediately headed for CELESTIA. Being in Indonesia, Ahmet was required to travel the greatest distance, but President Onager happened to have an executive jet in the area and promptly placed it at his disposal.

No one knew when She would appear, and all were greatly surprised when seven Mentors suddenly arrived. They explained that they too had been summoned, but had no idea what the Holy Daughter had in store for them.

After dinner of the first evening when all were present—they had their answer.

Glowing radiantly, the Daughter was suddenly there. She went around the table and greeted each with Her Love and words of joy at seeing them again. But before getting down to business, She owed Zoe some special attention—and for the next ten minutes pointed at various places around the room, and let Her ecstatic pup chase after the 'sun spots' which She projected from Her finger. It was a touching display of Divine Love, and everyone was utterly charmed.

Then She took a place at the front of the room and formally welcomed the seven Mentors.

"It fills Me with joy to once again be among you. My time on earth grows short, and I am saddened that this will be the last time we are all gathered together.

"As you see, I have invited seven Mentors, each of whom as of this moment is permanently assigned to serve with one of you. Through them you will be able to access the full range of Mentor capabilities and resources. Know that such liaising is without

precedent on any evolutionary world, but it is within my Emergency Powers to so direct.

"These Mentors will ever be at your sides, and you will not find it necessary to summon them. You may and should often seek their advice, but the final authority for decisions resides in your hands.

"Ellen Kate, as the only past channel for Mentor communication, you will remain so able, and will be the only mortal empowered to contact Mentors or other celestial beings as you see fit.

"Ahmet, you and I will meet with the Acolytes in Zurich as soon as they can be assembled—at which time you will be designated their leader and permanent director, after which you will coordinate and supervise all their creative enterprises.

"President Onager, you and I will meet in Beijing, to join President Wu to bring about a working plan to rid the world of nuclear weapons for all time. Further, it will be your responsibility to persuade President Gusev to join us. Since Russia possesses the second greatest stockpile of such weapons, any accord which did not bind them would be both futile and worthless."

"That may prove easier said than done," David Onager allowed— "I'm told he's still seething over being excluded from the Convenings."

"Perhaps if you were to pick him up in Moscow, fly him to Beijing aboard Air Force One—and ply him with vodka—"

Everyone laughed, knowing the Daughter wasn't serious about the vodka.

"I suppose I could pay him an unexpected visit Myself—"

"How many appearances do You plan?" Ellen Kate inquired.

"Seven in all—tonight marks my third. I've just spoken of two to come—there are to be two others as well."

Following that, the Holy Daughter met privately with each of the Seven in Her Suite, ending with Karyn and Zoe.

And then She was gone.

John VanOrsdell

ADMONISHES OPEC

The OPEC oil ministers were gathered in Geneva for a special meeting resulting from mounting international pressure to increase production to drive down wholesale oil prices, which currently fluctuated near record highs.

Ever since the price had topped one-hundred dollars a barrel back in late 2007, the world economy had taken a slide from which it had still not recovered—never had the pressure been so great on the major oil exporters.

However, resentful of the pressure, the ministers were in no mood to cave in. Their position was, Let the world economize if it's hurting so badly.

The conference was in its third day, with everyone still holding firm. Another vote was taken, and only Kuwait was prepared to marginally increase production. Heels were dug in all around the table.

And it was at this moment of impasse that the Holy Daughter appeared—for the first time flanked by fourteen shimmering seraphim.

But instead of being awed, several of the Muslim ministers were flattered by the recognition. One even smirked. She then addressed them in perfect Farsi:

"I note that your intransigence is exceeded only by your greed."

Her words caught them off-guard. It was not the spiritual greeting they would have expected, or felt they deserved, and several outright resented it—promptly She set them straight.

"I can tell you that your Western ways and crass materialism fill your beloved Prophet with sadness and shame."

This rocked them—for it bore the ring of Truth.

"Know that there are great changes coming. Within the not distant future, the shipment of oil across the Atlantic Ocean will come to an end. Agreement will be reached among the oil producing states of the Western Hemisphere—namely Canada, the United States, Mexico, Venezuela, and Ecuador—to market and refine all their oil in their own hemisphere, buying and selling none elsewhere.

"Between the oil locked in sand in Canada, and locked in shale in the United States, reserves are more than plentiful."

"The agreement reached will be known as the America's Oil or The Americas' Accord-or the AOAA-and members will set their own price for oil independent of the price in the rest of the world."

The ministers sat stunned. Such a development had never occurred to them.

"You would do well to increase production immediately and substantially, in order to ease human suffering throughout the world, and repair your own highly unfavorable image."

"Know that your personal standing in the next world will, in no small part, depend upon it."

And with that She was gone.

GAZA

Word had gone forth from CELESTIA to each Acolyte around the world that the Holy Daughter commanded their immediate presence in Gaza. The city was the southernmost stronghold of the Palestinian state—and the site of repeated suicide bombings and bloody clashes between warring factions, and with Israel itself.

The scars of battle were everywhere, and the city remained one of the most dangerous places on earth. Why the Daughter had chosen such a hostile environment for Her final meeting with the Acolytes was a matter for Divine speculation.

Nonetheless, they dribbled in one by one until all were present. As instructed, they checked in at the Shinbet Hotel, considered the safest place in all of Gaza for Westerners to stay. Little did anyone suspect the hotel was under around-the-clock protection by legions of angelic guardians—each of whom had received special prior authorization to undertake whatever emergency interventionary action they deemed necessary to vouchsafe their mortal charges. But none was taken, since no threat materialized.

Ahmet was the last to arrive, and promptly took charge, summoning the Acolytes early the next morning to the mezzanine conference room—where they were astonished to find the Holy Daughter there to greet them, one at a time. Her aura was subdued, and she appeared so normal several Acolytes foolishly tried to shake hands with Her—and had to be greatly reassured.

After everyone was seated, the Daughter addressed the group—

"I welcome each and every one of you. I know this was a difficult place to which to travel—and I do thank you."

"I chose Gaza so each of you could behold first-hand the fruits of hatred and aggression, for that are to become the primary focus of your future creative efforts— Indeed, it is the very purpose for which the Corps of Acolytes was formed.

"As you have repeatedly heard, those you call Mentors were mandated to intervene on an Emergency basis: that Emergency being the rapid world-wide emergence and rise of terrorism—state-sponsored and individual—rooted in political hatred and religious fanaticism."

"Therefore, your creative education and training has been in preparation for your true work: the global elimination of organized terrorism."

She paused while everyone considered the implications and ramifications of Her words. She could see misgivings and grave concern registered on most faces.

"I can see many of you are daunted by the scope of the challenge. I can fully understand. Transforming and reversing one's core beliefs is nearly impossible."

"However, fundamental faith transcends all else."

"The hammers of hatred cannot dent the anvils of Faith."

Some shifted uneasily in their chairs.

"It is tragic that some marginal power-seekers in the Muslim community are prepared to pervert the Faith of others, to visit death and sorrow upon so-called Infidels in the name of their God.

"They will issue an order which profanes their faith, and think by shouting out 'God is Great!' they make righteous their perfidy.

"It is My plan to reveal and expose their blasphemy."

*   *   *

That evening at sunset the Holy Daughter, unaccompanied by any of Her Acolytes save Ahmet, appeared on a beach—a metallic Mediterranean behind Her, a single CNN camera before Her. She stood attired in a simple, but resplendent, white robe.

A molten sun shown upon Her face rendered pale by Her aura, which radiated its own shimmering, brilliant golden light. After several moments She addressed all mankind in a strong, clear voice, noticeably deeper than at any time previously—

"I AM a Holy Daughter of God."

"I speak to you from Gaza, in the land of the Palestinian people."

"In My Father's house are many Gods—including My younger Brother Michael, Sovereign Son of your Provincial Universe, known to you as Jesus."

"My Father is the Eternal, Infinite. All-Loving Creator, Upholder, and Protector of All That Is. The One True God—whether you all Him God, the Lord, or Allah."

She fixed the camera with Her eye.

"I am come to shine the Light of Truth upon a dark and troubled world. Long have you suffered—long have you resided in confusion. Yet know that your world enjoys great stature—cherished on High. Few Worlds command such ministry."

She paused briefly before continuing.

"Many of you have already come to know and appreciate the recent immigrants from the neighboring evolutionary world of Marinor."

"They have all made a great personal sacrifice by leaving behind forever the families and friends of their Home world, to come to Earth to share their knowledge. This they willingly did in response to a Universe call for Pilgrims to assist one of God's worlds in desperate need. I bid you allow them to fully share their experiences and their wisdoms."

"This is truly a Divine Benison—and bespeaks the lengths to which My Father is prepared to go on behalf of His Holy Children."

She paused once again to shift Her focus.

"In conclusion, I bear a message for members of the Muslim faith—directly from My Father, whom you call Allah.

"And I quote Him directly—

'ANY MORTAL WHO DIRECTS HIS FAITH FOLLOWERS TO ATTACK, INJURE, OR STRIKE DOWN A BROTHER IN MY NAME PROFANES BOTH ME AND THEIR RELIGION— GRAVELY IMPERILING THEIR OWN SURVIVAL OF PHYSICAL DEATH.

'AS YOUR LORD AND GOD DOWN THROUGH ETERNITY—I COMMAND AND ORDER YOU TO IMMEDIATELY AND WHOLLY REJECT ALL SUCH BLASPHEMY AND TREACHERY, NOW AND FOREVERMORE.'"

And with that she was gone!

John VanOrsdell

AIR FORCE ONE

Air Force One was wheels-up just as the sun slipped below the horizon.

President Onager and President Gusev with only a translator present, raised their glasses and toasted the long flight to Beijing which lay before them. Had either known that the Holy Daughter was close by and observing, they'd have been flabbergasted—and far more guarded in everything they thought and said.

Downing a fistful of cocktail nuts, the Russian President belched his approval.

"So tell me—what is this 'goddess' like in person?" he asked, washing down the nuts with another swallow of vodka, putting Onager in mind of Khrushchev.

"Oh, very personable. I quite like Her—and fully expect you will as well."

"And do you think She's actually—one of the 'gods'?"

"Beyond all doubt, my friend. Beyond all doubt."

"So then, do you pray to Her?"

"I haven't—but I would. I'm curious—do you pray?"

Gusev's stomach heaved with laughter, providing the American President with his answer.

*　　*　　*

Both presidents were greeted and officially welcomed by President Wu on the tarmac. There had been extensive protocol discussions as to whether both presidents should ride with President Wu in his limousine from the airport. This however presented something of a problem: one of them would be obliged to ride backwards. So in the end it was decided they'd travel separately in the motorcade, each in a fresh-from-the-showroom Buick. But this of course presented a new protocol problem—the order in which they would travel. It was finally agreed to draw lots; which left Gusev bringing up the rear. But he quickly forgot

480

the matter—when the Holy Daughter suddenly manifested across from him, her aura radiating as brightly as Her smile.

Stunned, he could not speak, so She did—in flawless Russian.

"In the name of Peace, I greet you. Since I am already well known to the others, I concluded it would be helpful if we were to meet and speak privately before we gather formally. I hope you agree."

He recovered enough to nod his assent.

"Then let us begin by affirming that you are not experiencing a hallucination. It is not necessary to acknowledge Me as a Deity—but merely as a presently visible Spirit Being."

Still unable to believe his own eyes, Gusev simply nodded numbly.

*　　*　　*

The three leaders met in an exquisite fifteenth century Tea Pagoda, within a tranquil water garden in the heart of the Forbidden City. At the Holy Daughter's suggestion, the presidents were meeting without benefit of advisors or staff. Only three official translators attended them. Cutting straight to the heart of the core issue, the Daughter was first to speak, randomly switching back and forth between White Russian and Mandarin Chinese—

"I ask you—other than one of you yourselves, what other nation could pose a strategic threat to any of you?

"There being none, what possible role could a ballistic missile submarine play in your national defense?

"It is abundantly clear that the last thing any of you wants is to go to war, for the simple reason that you each have far too much to lose—and it would be insane to put it all at risk.

"Does anyone disagree?"

Each looked at the other, and their silence acknowledged their concurrence.

"Applying the same logic, your strategic bomber forces while technologically state-of-the-art strategic weapons systems, are all totally obsolete—!

"Happily, you've all had the foresight to install elaborate safety measures to assure that no delusional head of state could ever alone launch a nuclear first-strike.

"And so I ask you, in what way do any of your strategic forces truly enhance your national security—whether real or imagined?

"And I further ask you; since these facts are irrefutable, why not simply announce your agreement to divest yourselves of all strategic forces—and do so before the entire

world—in My name, if you like. Truly, it is just that Simple—and just that Profound!

"You have it within your power—and in candor, never will you be presented with a better opportunity.

"The Universe of Universes is watching—awaiting your decision. Make the decision. Announce the decision. And set your feet firmly on the Holy Road to World Peace!"

TRIUNE ACCORD

The sudden announcement of the Beijing Triune Strategic Accord caught the world completely by surprise. But when word was leaked of the Holy Daughter's direct involvement, it was quickly, and gratefully, accepted.

When President Onager alighted from Air Force One in a downpour, he strode quickly to a bank of waiting microphones—and smiled broadly.

"The world can breathe easier." He paused to acknowledge an unusual round of applause from the assembled press, along with favored White House staffers.

"Less than twenty-four hours ago, the Presidents of China, Russia, and the United States set hand and seal to a historic treaty—one which will purge and destroy all strategic weapons systems from our respective arsenals!"

"Ballistic submarine missile platforms will be the first to go. They will end their patrols—come home—be decommissioned—be stripped of their electronics—have their missile warheads off-loaded and disassembled—have their nuclear power plants removed—and then be towed to a facility where they will be cut into scrap."

"Our strategic bombers, satellites, and ground stations will meet the same fate. In effect, each of us will no longer possess the capacity to wage offensive (strategic) war—and will have only defensive (tactical) weapons and systems. And thus the term `First-Strike' will be relegated to the history books!"

And the world did indeed breathe easier.

*   *   *

The United Nations was in session, and abuzz with talk of the Triune Accord, as it was coming to be known. Some delegates were openly elated, others deeply suspicious. Whenever the Big Three began throwing their weight around, some of the smaller nuclear powers got very nervous.

France worried that the British might seize upon the Accord as an excuse to follow suit—scrapping their own subs more to save money than make a statement. Israel of course would remain apart from all talk of nuclear matters, while Pakistan pressed ahead—and North Korea turned darkly inscrutable.

Even some of the non-nuclear powers were alarmed, notably Japan—which strongly suspected both the Chinese and the Russians would cheat, quietly squirreling away a few megatons here and there.

*   *   *

In the General Assembly virtually every delegate was in his or her seat—discussion of the new Accord being the first item on the Agenda.

At the stroke of ten, the Danish Secretary General took the podium and fiddled with her glasses as she waited for the last delegate to fall silent.

"Good morning, everyone. We have an unusually busy day ahead of us, so let's get started, beginning with the first item on our agenda: 'Discussion and Deliberation: 'Trilateral Strategic Arms Elimination Treaty and Accord'—truly a landmark turning point in relations among nations. The so-called Big Three—Russia, with considerably more territory than any other nation—China, with considerably more population—and the United States with considerably more economic power—have come together."

At this moment a brilliant, golden light suffused the chamber—accompanied by the voices of a Great Choir of Angels raised in exultation—as the Holy Daughter of the Creative Spirit made Herself manifest before the eyes of all assembled. And in a clear, powerful voice, She spoke—

"I bring you the Salutations and Good Wishes of a Loving Universe, sustained by its one Loving God.

John VanOrsdell

"Know that your world spinning on at the fringe of all Creation, is yet held close in the personal embrace of its Divine Creator—for nowhere in the Universe is there a World of such bright Promise or such ingrained Hatred."

Only CBS and CSPAN were covering the General Assembly that day, and so it was their cameras alone which would bring this address of epochal importance to an eager and Revelation-hungry World.

Then the Holy Daughter swept the great chamber with Her hand— and instantly there appeared One Hundred Mentors, positioned around the room.

"I come this day to report that the Universe has adjudged you fully ready to take a momentous step in the evolution of your world—that of completely eschewing warfare to settle disputes among nations."

Shocked looks were exchanged, while all the Mentors smiled broadly.

"Let me outline for you that which has worked well on countless other worlds—

Many of the covenants set forth in the United Nations Charter are commendable.

"What remains is to amend it in certain areas concerning national sovereignty.

This, however, will prove to be highly contentious, as no nation-state, especially the wealthy and powerful, will gladly yield up power to an international body."

Many suspected She was about to call for one-world government, and were starting to bristle. But they were wrong.

"Only in the very limited area of international dispute resolution, is agreement required. A world is never well served whenever a nation-state resorts to war. Appeal to a duly constituted High Tribunal of Peace, with absolute power to arbitrate disputes, is the single most effective instrument for the peaceful, compulsory resolution of differences."

She paused to allow the concept to penetrate.

"Just as it would be absurd for the sovereign states of Florida and Georgia to go to war over watermelons, should it be unthinkable for India and Pakistan to wage war over control of Kashmir.

"War is a primitive, brutal, destructive, and shameful means of settling differences— and your world has but recently evolved beyond it. All you need do here, in this your only world forum, is to demonstrate the truth of that fact by acting upon it."

She elevated Herself a few feet to emphasize what She was about to say.

"Once you adopt this course of action, you must be unswerving in your determination to enforce it. Any nation-state declining to become a signatory—or any which signs and then violates its provisions—must be dealt with forcefully and immediately. Not

484

by military means, but through International Quarantine: all commerce in and out must be suspended, meaning shipments by air, sea, rail, and highway, be it passenger or cargo—along with mail service—banking—the trading of stocks and bonds—and any movement of assets. Additionally, any state which violates the Quarantine on behalf of another must itself be quarantined forthwith.

"An agreement not vigorously enforced is worthless, and nothing but so much propaganda."

She softened her tone a bit.

"The Mentors who you see arrayed about you are at your service during the months ahead. Listen to them carefully. And trust them implicitly."

She ran Her eye around the room before continuing.

"It now gives Me great pleasure to announce that the Russian Republics—the Republic of China—and the United States of America have all agreed to become signatories. I ask now that each of their Delegates rises to so signify."

Each did, and was greeted by scattered applause, which quickly grew to a resounding and sustained crescendo. Even the Mentors joined in. When finally it subsided, all eyes turned to the Daughter.

"You have just confirmed the Universe's faith in you.

"My Mission of Peace being now concluded, I return to My Father's House, never to return to this world. But We shall observe, and all meet again on the higher worlds."

"My Blessings and Love be with each of you."

And with that She truly was gone!

In response to a touching appeal from The Seven, the Holy Daughter delayed Her departure long enough to meet with her human family for a few golden minutes aboard the PLOWSHARES, riding gently upon soft swells twelve miles off the coast of Cape Cod.

In gratitude for Her being among them one last time, Karyn had brought along Zoe—who cried out plaintively upon the Daughter's sudden appearance. She moved to leap up into the Divine Embrace—but to everyone's amazement, did not drop helplessly through spirit arms and fall to the deck. Trembling and whimpering ecstatically, she was even able to kiss the Divine face, which she did nonstop.

At the Daughter's request, Captain Goosek and the entire ship's company had assembled on the helipad to receive Her. Still cradling Zoe in Her arms, the Holy Daughter addressed the crew and The Seven:

"I am grateful my beloved associates prevailed on Me to gather with all of you here— my prior presence aboard this beautiful vessel being such a tragic and grievous time.

John VanOrsdell
"I wish to use the occasion to consecrate this ship as the Headquarters of SEA-LESTIA—that she may sail the world and bring together those in conflict, that they might see themselves for whom they truly Are—and to Act Accordingly.
I now bid you all a loving farewell."

Then, Zoe still being held—the two of them vanished in a brilliant burst of pure White Light.

And with that, the Angelesis officially came to an end.

PART FIVE

AFTERGLOW

John VanOrsdell

AFTERGLOW

The day after the Holy Daughter took Her leave, a series of Messages to All Mankind began to appear as cloud formations in the heavens above each land In the language of those below—

You—Are
You Are Created
You Are Created by God
You Are a Child of God
You Are Holy
You Are a Holy Child of God
LIGHT THE WORLD

*   *   *

AFTERGLOW
Upon Her return to Universe Headquarters, the Daughter of the Creative Spirit was welcomed 'home and universally hailed for the triumphant and supernal achievements of Her Emergency Mission of Divine Love. While curled up at Her side in utter Peace and Contentment—lay Zoe the first canine ever to attain Paradise and Life Everlasting.

OF UNIVERSE RECORD:

Over the first Earth year following The Angelesis, it is of Provincial Universe Record that the stated wishes of The Daughter of the Creative Spirit upon Her physical death was expeditiously carried out on Earth under the close, personal, and able supervision of the Members of The Seven.
CELESTIA was incorporated to serve in perpetuity as the spiritual heart, World Headquarters, and Executive Offices—and granted the same status, territorial

sovereignty, and diplomatic recognition as the Vatican—to carry out its Holy Mission under the full protection of the United States Government.

In order to be able to represent, with the title of Ambassador, the interests of the Spiritual Planetary Government without creating the potential for real or perceived Conflicts of Interest, Peter Klein surrendered his American passport—despite strong and outspoken objections of Ellen Kate—and took a sincere and irrevocable Oath of Unconditional Allegiance to the Spirit Citizens of Earth.

CELESTIA also became the Holy Daughter's World Conference Center for dispute resolution— fashioning enduring, creative endings of longstanding hostilities between nations, faiths, races, interest groups, civil insurrection, and spontaneous uprisings.

All this in the Daughter's name.

*   *   *

The Holy Daughter's final triune wish for CELESTIA was the one which touched Her heart:

The Celestia International Children's Center for Reconstructive Surgery to Repair Disfiguring Wounds of the Young Victims of Warfare.

The Surgical Unit will be outfitted with cutting-edge surgical and monitoring technology, state-of-the-art laboratory facilities, and top Anesthesiologists, Specialists, Technicians, Surgical Nurses, Dietitians, Physical Therapists, and Cosmetologists.

Anticipating that many of these youngsters will require multiple operations, and have to spend considerable time at the Center, provision will have to be made to transport, house, feed, and entertain accompanying family member(s).

Any candidate for surgery will need to communicate with doctors and staff—which will present problems finding translators for obscure tongues. The UN and State Department can be of considerable help.

There is yet another area likely to present problems for youngsters so facially deformed; they were universally shunned—and would in all probability now require extensive psychological counseling.

These are but a few of the unique challenges facing the new Center.

*   *   *

It is also a matter of record that, despite powerful international diplomatic and economic pressure brought to bear on the Palestinian leadership to accept the so-called Sinai Solution, it was formally declared "Unacceptable," for failing to preserve an Ancestral Homeland for the people of Palestine.

(III)

John VanOrsdell

*   *   *

Yet similar pressures, applied half a world away to the government of Brazil, ultimately produced a ratified Agreement with the United Nations to ban for all time timber harvesting of vital, irreplaceable rainforests, and at the same time protect fragile habitat.

*   *   *

The pair of Pilgrims assigned to Iran made the mistake of questioning in a magazine interview the wisdom of a theocracy form of government, in which ultimate power resides in the hands of appointed religious leaders.
Seizing upon the interview to brand the Pilgrims official "Trouble—makers," they were summarily expelled, with Celestia and the UN informed that, "Replacements will not be admitted."

*   *   *

Upon Her departure, the ages-long Quarantine of planet Earth was vacated by Order of the Daughter of the Creative Spirit, and so announced. Accordingly, by the First Anniversary of Her departure, as measured in Earth years, construction was well underway in half a dozen countries of enormous digital amphitheaters—built to exacting specifications and detailed technical drawings supplied by the Mentors— which would at long last enable the eagerly awaited, real-time reception of Trans-Cosmos News Broadcasts emanating each day from Provincial Headquarters.
Now aware that there were unseen Mentors ever-watching and listening, every government was more than a little rattled by knowing that no state secret could ever be kept from the Mentors. One positive consequence of such close scrutiny was that no nation was prepared to risk Universe opprobrium by attacking a neighbor, no matter how grave the affront.

*   *   *

In a surprise, complete reversal of past policy, the United States became a Co-Sponsor of a United Nations Resolution Banning private Possession of weapons of war. The Resolution passed Unanimously.

*   *   *

(IV)

The best (and most expensive) law firm in Rome, specializing in Title Work on high-value properties, was Amilio and Vealio.

Known for taking their time and getting it right, they would not be rushed. But when they finally certified a title, it was iron-clad.

Personally recommended by the Pope himself, the Seven hired Io and Io, as they were known in the trade, to do a full title search on a magnificent Grand Chalet high in the Italian Alps, whose last owner happened to be a member of the Bastion who had fallen on Mentor-induced hard times and was finally left with no choice but to sell the Chalet.

The Seven made an offer, and when title was finally certified seven months later, The Celestia Corporation became the new owner of record.

Karyn never suspected it was soon to become her new home.

CHALET

Just prior to the Holy Daughter's final appearance and departure, She had mailed Karyn a handwritten note, advising her that their working relationship was just at a beginning—and for her to expect to meet a new Mentor, designated 'Kappa,' who would serve as their "personal, bi-lateral, direct link from this day forth."

Karyn nearly showed the note to Ellen Kate, but thought better of it. If the Daughter had wanted that, She'd have said so.

Every day she woke up hoping this would be the day she'd meet Kappa. But each day she was destined to be disappointed. Finally, out of pure exhaustion, she decided she needed a vacation, and what she really craved was to bake in the sun for about a week. Consulting the Internet, she found just the place: a small, isolated island in the Bahamas, complete with luxury beach house and servants, which Celestia could rent for two-thousand and eight-hundred dollars per week. Because it would be her only vacation since long before the Holy Daughter's visit, there'd be no balking at the price.

On her third day in the sun, she at long last met Kappa. He suddenly appeared, standing over her beach towel, casting no shadow. Karyn was taken aback by his appearance—quite un-Mentor like—half-physical, half spirit. What's more, he was decidedly BLUE—robes and all. And his voice—it was, well, almost musical, tinged with the far away peal of carillons—immediately put her in mind of the Daughter's own voice.

John VanOrsdell

"Greetings, Karyn. I am Kappa," he chimed.

"I've been looking forward to meeting you," Karyn replied, betraying a hint of nervousness." Are you in—actual communication with the Holy Daughter?"

"Not at the moment, but frequently. Is there something you would wish me to say to Her?" Karyn hesitated, her mind racing. After a few moments, "Just tell Her I miss Her terribly."

She got slowly to her feet and folded the beach towel. "I must say, you don't look like any other Mentor I've seen," she allowed, heading for the beach-house.

"My responsibilities are quite specialized, and my activities limited. Think of me as your personal celestial cell phone. With unlimited minutes." They climbed the steps to the sun-deck, where a staff waitress instantly materialized and totally ignored Kappa.

"She can neither see nor hear me," he explained. "But I do not partake of refreshment anyway."

They sat and gazed in silence at the setting sun setting on fire the gentle rollers lapping ashore. "Are you material or spiritual?" she asked presently.

"Yes."

She smiled, and they fell silent once more. "I find not speaking is a rather effective way to get to know someone," she commented presently. "And often to like them."

"Yes."

Long pause. "Do you and I share a common Mission?"

"Yes. And if you accept yours, you will be taking up permanent residence in Switzerland or the Italian Alps."

"One of the conspirators in the odious assassination scheme owned a magnificent luxury chalet high in the Italian Alps. It is now in Higher Hands, reserved for the Holy Daughter's and your exclusive Use."

"Are you permitted to tell me what that Use might be?"

"I am authorized to answer fully any question you might pose."

"Good. What exactly is our Mission?"

"In the fullness of time, to bring all Faith Sons and Daughters together in common worship."

Karyn gasped. She had no notion of what this might mean. But it just sounded huge.

*   *   *

A week later she was gazing down at a leaden North Atlantic, Kappa in the next seat—an invisible, nonpaying passenger. She wondered whether he'd ever flown this slowly before, and moments later she was listening to his answer in her mind. 'No, never. But then we don't fly the way you mean it.'

(VI)

Less than an hour later, her chartered helicopter was weaving gracefully through the Alps. Then, up ahead she saw it: A massive, dark-timbered chalet clinging to the side of a mountain—a single, private driveway, miles long and freshly plowed. It was the only way in, save by helicopter.

They touched down lightly, and she welcomed the icy April air as it hit her face. Squinting against a blinding sun, Kappa and she followed the welcoming staffer inside.

The Great Room—more of a gallery—was cavernous. A vaulted timber ceiling soared high above—a wide, gracefully curved staircase took its time getting to the upper levels. A half-dozen enormous fireplaces warmed silently; the central one, softly arched and open front and rear, was large enough for an elephant to walk through.

In sharp contrast to the heavy Medieval architecture, the furnishings were delicate, with gracefully turned armrests and legs, and upholstered in soft pastel silks and pricey brocade. Karyn loved it right off—dismissing the vile conspirator who had last possessed it and wanted to see the Daughter dead. The bitter irony and sweet justice of it all were not lost on her.

Kappa helped Karyn settle in, describing the various facilities, technical capabilities, and guest capacities the chalet offered. Their conversation was overheard by several of the staff—who, able to hear only her side of it, concluded that their new boss talked to herself.

One of the things Karyn saw as a missing necessity was a large, spiritual conference table. She already had a design in mind: seven-sided, each angled fifty-one point forty-three degrees, with a three-inch thick top twelve-feet in diameter and made of stained black walnut (to match the chalet chapel), with fourteen matching high-back chairs, all upholstered in supple, pale green, synthetic leather.

To her delight and surprise, it did not take Karyn long to discover that Kappa came with a nuanced appreciation of the subtleties of some mortal humor, the same things making them chuckle. A genuine friendship was beginning to bloom.

Though highly unusual, close bonds between Mentor and Mortal were not without precedent.

*   *   *

Karyn was exhausted from yet another day of complex preparation. Kappa happily shared his knowledge with her—but exactly when various events would take place, he could not say, they being largely rooted in the realm of mortal free will which he'd given up trying to predict.

John VanOrsdell

She'd put a RUSH on delivery of the seven-sided table, but it was being crafted in Portugal, a nation not noted for its punctuality. Her patience was being tried, and she liked it not.

The Swiss, on the other hand, were nothing if not scrupulous in keeping promises. Precisely on schedule, communications technicians arrived to connect the chalet with the world. However, there were instantaneous trans-cosmos Mind Circuits of which they had no inkling. That evening Karyn told Kappa she'd like to speak with the Daughter. It took but a few seconds to establish the link, and then Karyn heard the Daughter's Voice—as clear as if She were in the next room. Karyn nearly wept.

For several minutes they chatted informally, mostly about how Zoe liked her new home. Karyn learned that not only did Zoe now enjoy Life Everlasting—while she would not age physically and would look like a pup forever, she'd mature mentally. Karyn was thrilled and giggled merrily.

They then turned to matters at hand. Karyn was asked to meet with the world's primary religious Heads of Faith—whether one-on-one, in small groups or large, or over the span of days or weeks, it was left up to her. When Karyn set the date for the Convocation, Kappa promptly sent a stunning Semi-Material Summons to each Head of Faith—leaving no doubt the invitations were of Holy Origin.

Karyn was most reluctant to have her conversation with the Daughter come to an end, but was greatly reassured when she was promised, All you need do is ask Kappa to make contact.

"You will always reach me."

*   *   *

The Daughter made a number of suggestions before they ended their first talk, and Karyn was left with a great deal to think about. The Daughter had urged her to make good use of Kappa in all her dealings. Karyn was astonished to learn Kappa had spent most of the last decade preparing for this Spiritual Convocation, largely through studying the most sacred writings of the Earth's great faiths.

Karyn and Kappa repaired to the cozy black walnut chapel off the Great Room to devise plans. She was terribly confused. "But—but—why call upon someone who's never so much as joined a church for so vital an ecumenical role?" Karyn implored of Kappa.

"In part, you've answered your own question. If you were a member of a church, everyone would think it impossible for you to set aside your beliefs and bring no personal bias to the Convocation."

"But that could be said of any number of people," Karyn countered. "I repeat—Why me?"

(VIII)

"Because you are the one the Daughter chose." He let his words sink in before continuing. *"Virtually all the world now accepts the Divinity of the Daughter. People feel very much drawn to Her—and are prepared fully to trust Her guidance."* Kappa looked Karyn hard in the eye. *"Of all mortals, you know Her best. So—why do you now entertain doubts?"*

"My old feelings of under-adequacy, I guess." Then she remembered something private that the Daughter had shared with her aboard the PLOWSHARES—and suddenly broke into a wide smile.

"The Daughter recommends that you include one of the Representatives in your planning—and suggests the Pope, whom She found to be quite open and flexible during their trip to Ireland."

"I welcome Her advice. Please place a call to the Vatican and invite him—"

"What will be your protocol—a single Representative for each faith?" Kappa switched.

"What do you recommend?"

"Suppose we allow but one Representative at the table—with say, a single advisor or deputy seated close behind them?"

"That would likely do the trick—but with only the Representative permitted to speak." She turned to another issue. *"What about translators?"*

"That's easy. Simply stipulate that each Representative is also to be accompanied by a fluent, English-speaking translator."

She nodded absently, her mind now focused elsewhere. *"That should do the trick—but do you realize we haven't so much as picked a name or a theme for the Convocation?"*

"I'd trust your judgment in that regard. Do you think we should announce it beforehand?"

"No—that's the very last thing we want to do. All it would accomplish is to create media pressure, and heighten expectations due to the Daughter's direct involvement. Getting back to the Pope, I'd feel a lot more confident if he were here for the early planning."

"I'll ring him up after lunch. How long do think he should plan on being here?"

"Maybe a week—starting tomorrow if possible. If he balks, reveal that the Holy Daughter Herself asked for his help and guidance by name. A true Divine Calling! That ought to do it."

*   *   *

John VanOrsdell
Karyn and Kappa were astonished when the Vatican helicopter touched down and His Holiness emerged wearing a sport coat and khaki slacks. The aviator sunglasses provided the final touch.

Karyn started to genuflect, but the Pope would have none of it.

"It's such a rare treat for me to wear mufti, I'm not about to let you spoil it for me—" he greeted, his hand outstretched. He was momentarily taken aback at being able to see through Kappa, and was hesitant as to whether he could or should try to shake his hand. Kappa smiled at his dilemma, and put him at ease by reaching out his own hand.

"Think of me as being here to inspire transparency." Karyn couldn't help the amused squeak which escaped her—causing instant laughter by all. The Pope looked down at his hand, having just experienced semi-materiality.

"Transparent—but—perhaps a bit mushy." This time the loudest laugh came from Kappa.

*   *   *

The Pope proved to be a superb planner, distilling common understandings and conclusions within the first few days. Cardinals, bishops, and monsignors alike back in Rome began to wonder whether the Pope had fallen ill, but were quickly assured he was in excellent health. Only three trusted members of the Holy Father's inner circle knew where the Pope was, and they weren't saying. Neither were the two helicopter pilots, now the pampered, incommunicado guests of the chalet.

Along the way, the Pope insisted he be addressed as Antonio—his actual birth name. Karyn and Kappa acquiesced, agreeing that titles would only get in the way.

Within forty-eight hours, the three planners had hammered out several key decisions:

One: The Spiritual Convocation would be called officially, the Holy Daughter's Global Convocation of Heads of Faith;

Two: The stated policy would be to honor and leave intact the religious tenets and practices of the world's great faiths;

Three: To acknowledge the reality of a God-centered Holy Creation;

Four: To establish Spiritual Circuits of Transactional Communication with Universe Headquarters;

Five: To make use of these Circuits to resolve any religious disputes;

Six: To designate one of their leaders authorized to declare a Truce, and to require the early substitution of Negotiation for Conflict;

Seven: And to declare no new martyrs in the name of Religious Purity.

*   *   *

Decked out in their finest ceremonial costumes, delegates to the Daughter's Convocation assembled at the chalet at the appointed hour, ostensibly for solemn purpose—but mostly to experience firsthand the Mentor Kappa, now rendered semi-visible and conversing freely in many tongues.

The Convocation was not without its disputes. Representatives argued passionately, even to the point of hurling insults at one another. But not until the name-calling became abusive did Karyn feel she had to step in. She assembled everyone in the Great Room and spoke:

"We are here gathered to foster greater respect for—and appreciation of—each religion's great strengths.

The Holy Daughter, Kappa, and I all urge you to redirect your focus many broad and vital commonalities—rather than on your narrow differences.

You have witnessed Spirit Life in the service of our cherished world—the proof of that being in the person of Kappa here. And you all listened to the Daughter's own words while She was all too briefly incarnated in living flesh on our world.

Know that organized, detailed religions are strictly the Social creations of Mortals rather than the divine creations of the Gods.

Instinctively, we intuit that there is a Divine Duality to all Creation—as mortal man reaches up to grasp the Hand of God as God reaches down to clasp the up-stretched hands of His Holy Children. What loving Father could do less?"

She thought she was finished.

Just then Kappa walked over and spoke softly to her. She instantly appeared excited—looked out at those gathered—and allowed the suspense to build. Then she spoke.

"My friends, I have just been informed that the Holy Daughter Herself wishes to address you—"

There could be heard a few seconds of electrical interference—followed by a clear, pure silence. Then the Daughter's Voice rang out, filling the Hall with grace notes of faraway musical harmonies:

"I greet each and all of you across the vast reaches of space—mindful and gratified that all of you have excused yourselves from your normal duties in order to be here present.

You each represent the highest councils of your faith, and, by your very presence here, proclaim that your minds and hearts seek Holy Affirmation of your faith from a Higher Power. I AM that affirmation.

As religious leaders, you have each given yourself over to serving your Holy Brothers and Sisters in this life—on this world—and at this critical time.

(XI)

John VanOrsdell

You are all needed—working in sacred harmony to heal your world. Set aside your intolerances, and cleave you, one unto another, in loving brotherhood, to inaugurate a gleaming new spiritual culture for a new Spiritual Age."

The Daughter used Her personal circuit that evening to speak with Karyn and Kappa in private—

"I have decided to invite one representative prelate of each of the primary faiths of Earth to have an official seat on a pantheistic Spiritual Advisory Council, to serve in the capacity of supreme liaison between the Earth and the Headquarters Worlds—on the theory that the most effective way to induce our Holy Children to behave Responsibly is to assign them Authority as well as Responsibility."

"Who will select the member prelates," Karyn asked.

"You and Kappa, if you so agree. Who better? My only advice is to know well the candidates before making your Appointments. You and only you will have that power."

For the better part of an hour, they explored the value and uses of Advisory Councils—the Daughter revealing that such Councils are in service for many evolutionary worlds. She said they've proven both useful and popular. In the end, both Karyn and Kappa willingly agreed.

After concluding their business, the Daughter asked Karyn if she'd like to speak with Zoe. The pup instantly recognized the familiar voice, and excitedly began bouncing about. As, virtually, so did Karyn. Kappa was charmed, and after the conversation Karyn produced a whole album of Zoe photos, which they joyfully shared for nearly an hour.

*   *   *

The Convocation drew to a close with all the representatives feeling reassured and accepted—and, thanks to Kappa, fully persuaded that spirit life was real. They even felt a warm affinity for the Holy Daughter, despite what their own sacred writings asserted.

Not surprisingly, Karyn felt more confidant and absolutely vindicated, and beyond that, Proud. In Kappa she had a powerful new friend and colleague. And happiest of all—Zoe was back in her life!

She sent a detailed report to Celestia, a little saddened in the knowledge that from now on, the chalet would be her home. But her life was now rich and full—all due to having God for a friend: a delightful, funny, loving, resourceful deity. How good can it get? Beverly, I love you.

*   *   *

(XII)

Hardpan Dotson was not doing well at all. His liver was shot—he was nearly blind—and he had advanced esophageal cancer. His life-expectancy was down to a matter of hours. He huddled in the corner of his cabin—alone, hungry, and cold—wrapped in the blanket that the Nice Nekked Lady had given him at the cave. He pictured her in his mind, and for a few moments felt warm.

Suddenly the whole cabin filled with a golden light, his vision cleared, and the pain vanished. He thought he heard angels singing—and a great calm overspread him. He smiled—and was gone.

John VanOrsdell

WHAT IF?

What if—the Author's portrayals of *PHYSICAL REALITY* are exactly the way it is?

What if—*SPIRITUAL VALUES* portrayed herein are exactly the way it is?

What if—*ANGELESIS* is more than an inspired work of Celestial Fiction?

About the Author

John was born in Manhattan, New York in 1933. He earned his Bachelor of Arts in Economics from the University of Pennsylvania in 1955. John proudly served in the United States Navy. During his professional career he worked on Madison Avenue as a Copywriter. He has been married to his beloved wife Alys for over fifty-seven years. He has two children and five grandchildren. He is now retired and living on a beautiful lake in Boothbay, Maine.